THE MYSTERY
OF
WHARTON LODGE

The Mystery of Wharton Lodge

By
FRANK RICHARDS

HOWARD BAKER, LONDON

FRANK RICHARDS
THE MYSTERY OF WHARTON LODGE
& OTHER STORIES

(The *Magnet*, 1933, 1934)

© Copyright, The Amalgamated Press Ltd., 1933, 1934, 1971
Originally published in single issues

Howard Baker (Greyfriars Press) Hard-cover edition, 1971

Greyfriars Press books are published by
Howard Baker Press Limited,
27a Arterberry Road, Wimbledon, London, S.W.20, England
and printed in Great Britain by
C.G. Colour Printers Ltd.

Frank Richards

The phenomenon known to the world as Frank Richards (real name Charles Hamilton) died at his home at Kingsgate, Kent, on Christmas Eve 1961, at the age of eighty-six.

By then it is estimated that he had written the equivalent of one thousand full-length novels.

His work appeared continuously for over 30 years in those famous Fleetway House magazines, the *Magnet* and the *Gem*. Most famous of all was his immortal character, Billy Bunter, the Fat Owl of the Greyfriars Remove; along with those other boyhood heroes, Harry Wharton and Co., whose exploits in the *Magnet* delighted generations of readers from 1908 to 1940.

The war unhappily saw the end of the *Magnet* but though the post-war years witnessed the return of Greyfriars stories in other formats, nothing quite recaptured the evergreen magic of the original *Magnet* — so here, for the first time, are presented faithful facsimiles of those well-loved papers.

The brilliant character studies of boys and masters created by Frank Richards ensured his own immortality. Apart from the boys of Greyfriars there was the unforgettable Mr Quelch, the Remove form-master ('a beast, but a just beast'), the Reverend Dr Locke, venerable Headmaster of the School, William Gosling, the school porter who firmly believed that 'all boys should be drownded at birth', and Sir Hilton Popper, the irascible school governor. All these characters and many more are to be found within the pages of these volumes.

Frank Richards loved writing for the young and affirmed that no writer could do any better work in life. Certainly none did it better than Richards himself.

Grand Christmas Story "THE MYSTERY OF WHARTON LODGE!"
and FREE GIFT PICTURES INSIDE.

The MAGNET 2

No. 1,349. Vol. XLIV.   EVERY SATURDAY.   Week Ending December 23rd, 1933.

THE GREYFRIARS
HOLIDAY
1934 ANNUAL 1934
FOR BOYS AND GIRLS

NOW on Sale 5/-

AN IDEAL XMAS PRESENT

THE MYSTERY OF WHARTON LODGE

BY FRANK RICHARDS

THE FIRST CHAPTER.
Left !

SLAM !

Click !

It was the door of Study No. 12 —Lord Mauleverer's study—that slammed, the lock of that door that clicked, as Billy Bunter rolled into the Remove passage at Greyfriars.

Bunter heard the slam, and he heard the click, and he snorted:

"Beast !"

It looked as if the fellow in Study No. 12 did not want to see Bunter.

That in itself was not surprising. Fascinating fellow as Billy Bunter knew himself to be, often and often fellows did not want to see him. It was not surprising, but it was annoying, for Billy Bunter wanted to see Lord Mauleverer. Very much indeed did the fat Owl of the Remove want to see Mauly.

The December dusk was falling on Greyfriars School. It was break-up day, and most of the fellows were already gone.

Harry Wharton & Co. of the Remove had gone in the first brake. And Harry Wharton, so far from accepting Bunter's kind offer to go home with him for the Christmas holidays, had left him sitting in the snow when the brake rolled away. Other fellows had gone; the school was almost deserted now. Some of them wished Bunter a merry Christmas before they left. None of them seemed to desire to make that Christmas merry by taking him along. Nice as he was, planned by Nature to make any party a success, Bunter seemed to be a drug in the market.

Lord Mauleverer's departure was

THE MAGNET LIBRARY.—No. 1,349.

rather delayed. The schoolboy earl did not go by train like a common mortal. A magnificent car arrived to take Mauly home. No doubt, owing to snow on the roads, the car had arrived rather late. Nearly everybody was gone. Fellows of all Forms had melted away. Of the Remove, only three were still in the school—Lord Mauleverer, waiting for his belated car; Billy Bunter, waiting also for that car; and Fisher T. Fish, the American junior, who, having nowhere to go, was staying at the school over the holidays.

The magnificent car had arrived at last—Bunter had seen it draw up before the House—and he rolled in to tell Mauly, and to mention that he was going in the car also. At least, he hoped that he was. Mauly was kind and good-natured, and hated saying no to any fellow, which Bunter regarded as "soft," and he had no scruple whatever about taking the fullest advantage of that "softness." It was rather irritating to hear Mauly's door slam and lock as he came up the passage.

However, Mauly was cornered, at least. He couldn't get out of the window, that was clear, and Bunter planted himself at the door. He was sure that Mauly was in the study, for he could hear someone moving there. And who, but Mauly, could have locked Mauly's door on the inside?

Bunter rattled the door handle; then he tapped.

"I say, Mauly, your car's come !"

No answer !

"Gosling's putting the baggage on it, Mauly ! I say, come out, old chap ! You're late already, you know, and it's rather a long step to Mauleverer Towers."

There was no reply from within Lord

Mauleverer's study. Bunter gave a grunt of annoyance. If this was what Mauly considered good manners, the Owl of the Remove did not agree with him. But he restrained his desire to tell Mauly what he thought of him.

"I say, Mauly, can't you speak?" hooted Bunter through the keyhole.

Apparently the junior in the study couldn't. At all events, he didn't. Bunter thumped on the door.

"Your baggage is on, Mauly ! Your chauffeur's waiting to start ! What's the good of keeping him waiting?"

There was a sound in the study. Bunter started. It was the sound of munching. The fellow in the study was eating cake !

That was an occupation in which Billy Bunter was always prepared to join any fellow, friend or foe ! He banged on the door.

"I say, Mauly, it's a jolly good idea to have a snack before starting ! I say, I could do with some of that cake !"

Munch, munch, from the locked study !

"Mauly, old chap, I dare say you know that I'm not going home with Wharton, after all !" said Bunter, through the keyhole. "He rather begged of me to go, but I had to tell him it couldn't be done ! Same with Smithy ! 'No,' I said, 'I'm sticking to my old pal, Mauly.' My very words !"

Munch, munch !

The fellow in the study was going strong on the cake. He seemed to be too busy to speak.

"You'd like me for Christmas, Mauly, old fellow ?"

Munch, munch, munch !

"That's settled, then," said Bunter,

This FREE GIFT Issue Contains ANOTHER SET OF COLOURED PICTURES.

apparently taking silence for consent. "We'll have a jolly good time, Mauly! I'll do some of my ventriloquial tricks—what? Make your uncle jump by making a dog growl under his chair, and that sort of thing. Rather fun to see the old fossil jump—what? He, he, he!"

Munch, munch!

Not a word from the study, but the sound of munching jaws was incessant. Which was rather unusual in Mauly's study, for the schoolboy earl was by no means particularly keen on tuck. But the fellow in the study was devouring cake like Bunter himself, or like Fisher T. Fish, when that lean youth got a cake for nothing.

"Greedy beast!" murmured Bunter. "Rotter! Pig!" Aloud he went on: "Mauly, dear old chap, let me in, old fellow! You might let a chap have a whack at that cake!"

Munch, munch!

Bunter breathed wrath. It looked as if the fellow in Study No. 12 was going to keep him locked out till he had finished the cake. And all the time, it seemed, he was not going to waste a word on Bunter.

"I say, Mauly, you're keeping the car waiting!"

Munch, munch!

"It's a long way home, you know."

Munch, munch!

"Pig!" breathed Bunter. Again he was sorely tempted to tell Mauly, through the keyhole, what he thought of him and his manners. But that, obviously, would not have done—if he was going home with Mauly!

The alternative was not attractive. Billy Bunter was never keen on that glorious abode, Bunter Court, at holiday-time. But even the Bunter home was closed to him now.

Mr. Bunter had been having some hard luck on the Stock Exchange. He had been a "bull" when he should have been a "bear"—or else a bear when he should have been a bull. Anyhow, money was tight. Mr. and Mrs. Bunter were spending Christmas with relations. Bunter's young-brother, Sammy, had been landed on an uncle. His sister Bessie had been landed on an aunt. Bunter himself had to share the uncle with Sammy, if there was no other resource. He had not the slightest desire to share that uncle with Sammy.

Mauly was the only other resource. Bunter was prepared to wait outside Study No. 12 if Mauly kept him waiting till midnight. It was neck or nothing! Fortunately Bunter had plenty of "neck."

He waited.

Steadily, without a pause, the sound of munching continued in the locked study. It seemed to be a large cake from the time it took the scoffer thereof to scoff it. Long, long minutes passed. Bunter still waited. There was no chance of his getting any of the cake. But so long as he caught Mauly when he came out it was all right. Mauly was too "soft" to say no, to a fellow's face. Moreover, Bunter was not the fellow to take "no" for an answer. Nothing short of a kick would have unhooked Bunter, and he felt sure that Mauly would not go to that length. He had only to wait.

The December dusk deepened. Bunter began to feel rather uneasy lest Mr. Quelch, or some other master, should spot him and inquire why he was not gone. The Remove passage, generally in a buzz when the fellows were there, was dusky and deserted and dismal. Even Fisher T. Fish was not to be seen—not that Bunter wanted to see him.

Fishy, Bunter knew, had fished for invitations right and left—a thing Bunter despised. But he had got "left," as he would have described it in his own language. But Billy Bunter wasn't interested in Fishy. All his interest was concentrated on the fellow eating the cake in Study No. 12.

The steady sound of munching ceased at last. He heard a grunt of satisfaction from the study. It was quite unlike Mauly to give such audible expression to his satisfaction. But Bunter was glad to hear it. He had been waiting a quarter of an hour or more; and he was glad to learn that the cake was finished, if that meant the opening of the study door.

"I say, Mauly, buck up!" urged Bunter, through the keyhole. "Don't you want to start before dark? I'm waiting for you, old chap!"

There was a chuckle in the study. Footsteps crossed to the door. The key was turned back. Bunter hardly waited for it to turn before he heaved at the door and hurled it open.

"I say, Mauly——"

He broke off, staring blankly into the study through his big spectacles. A bony youth, with a lean, grinning face, was there. It was Fisher Tarleton Fish. There was no sign of Lord Mauleverer.

"What——" gasped Bunter. "Where the——"

He fairly goggled at Fisher T. Fish. Only Fish was there; it had been Fishy eating the cake! Not for a moment had

---

Every mystery has its solution, but the mystery of Wharton Lodge can be solved only by William George Bunter—for he is the mystery!

Bunter doubted that it was Lord Mauleverer. But, only too plainly, it wasn't.

"Where's Mauly?" gasped Bunter.

"I guess," drawled Fisher T. Fish, "that that guy is moseying for home jest as fast as his car will burn the wind! Yep!"

"What?" yelled Bunter.

"I'll say so!" grinned Fish. "Jevver get left?"

"But—but—but what——" Bunter stuttered.

"That guy Mauly sure asked me to stick in his study, and lock the door when you moseyed along!" explained Fisher T. Fish. "I guess I agreed to stay as long as it took me to eat the cake!"

"Oh!" gasped Bunter.

"It surely was a good cake!" said Fisher T. Fish. "I'll say I've enjoyed that cake! Sure!"

"Mauly," gasped Bunter—"gone?"

Fisher T. Fish chortled.

"Yep! I guess he was waiting downstairs, and he sure hit the trail pronto as soon as you hit this hyer passage! Jevver get left?"

"Beast!" roared Bunter.

"Ha, ha, ha!" roared Fisher T. Fish.

"That—that beast has dodged me——"

"Ha, ha, ha!"

"I—I thought he was in the study all the time——"

"He reckoned you would! Ha, ha, ha!" yelled Fishy.

"Beast!"

Billy Bunter gave the yelling Fish a glare that almost cracked his spectacles. Then he rolled away in haste, leaving Fisher T. Fish still yelling. Bunter did

---

the Remove staircase in jumps, the lower passage in bounds. He leaped out of the House doorway into the dusk and the falling flakes—too late!

The car was gone. It had been long gone. Lord Mauleverer evidently was gone, too—long gone. Billy Bunter gazed into the snowy and dusky space, with feelings too deep for words.

A hand touched his shoulder. He blinked round, at the surprised face of Mr. Quelch, the master of the Remove. Quelch, making his own preparations for departure, was surprised to find a member of his Form still lingering about the school.

"Bunter, what are you doing here? Why are you not gone, Bunter?"

Evidently it was time for Bunter to be gone. And—still full of inexpressible feelings—Bunter went!

THE SECOND CHAPTER.

In the Dark!

"COLD?" asked Harry Wharton. Hurree Jamset Ram Singh, the dusky Nabob of Bhanipur, repressed a shiver. The junior from India's coral strand found the British summer none too warm. The British winter he found decidedly "parky."

"N-n-not terrifically!" said the nabob, through his chattering teeth. "But I shall be preposterously glad to get in and derive warmth from a ridiculous fire!"

It was cold—there was no doubt about that. It was a snowy Christmastide. The Surrey hills gleamed white through the December dusk. Another fall of snow had come on rather suddenly, and caught the two juniors a mile from home. Flakes danced on a keen, searching wind, which seemed to the Indian junior to penetrate through his thick overcoat as if it had been paper. Wharton and the nabob, home for the holidays at Wharton Lodge, had gone for a ramble that afternoon, and they were returning by a snowy and rather sticky lane when the snowfall restarted after the interval.

"We'll take a short cut," said Harry. "It's less than half the distance across the park. Hop over this fence!"

"The shorter the esteemed cut the better!" agreed Hurree Jamset Ram Singh; and he clambered after his chum over the park palings.

Within, the old leafless trees, ridged with snow, rose like spectres in the dusk. The ground was like a mantle of white, with no trace of a path. But Harry Wharton knew every inch of the grounds round his home, and he started across the park, winding among the frosty trunks without a pause, the nabob tramping after him. The darkness was deepening, the snow falling more thickly, and it was scarcely possible to see a yard in advance.

"Ripping weather for Christmas!" Wharton remarked.

"Eh? Oh, yes!" gasped the nabob. "The ripfulness is terrific! Perhaps a little too terrific! Oooogh!"

Harry Wharton laughed. He was enjoying the keen, frosty air, and the falling flakes did not bother him. It was rather different with the dusky junior from the sunny Orient.

"We'll be in in ten minutes!" he said.

And they tramped on among the frosty old trees. Through the winter gloom, the lighted windows of Wharton Lodge began to gleam in the distance—

a comforting sight to Hurree Jamset Ram Singh. But the lights in the distance seemed to make the darkness near at hand more intense. Wharton, leading the way, was only a few feet in advance of his chum, but the Nabob of Bhanipur could not see him.

"My esteemed Wharton!" called out the nabob.

"Hallo!" Wharton called back. "This way!"

"Right-ho, my absurd chum! It would be terrifically unpleasant to be lost in this excellent and ridiculous wilderness!" gasped the nabob. "Wait momentarily for me!"

Hurree Jamset Ram Singh groped on round the big trunk of an oak that his chum had passed. His hand came in contact with an overcoat.

"Oh, here you are!" he exclaimed. "I thoughtfully supposed that you were farther on. Why—what—— Whooooop!"

The nabob gave a sudden yell.

The overcoat he had grasped twisted suddenly from his hand. The next moment a sudden, violent push sent him staggering backwards, and he landed on his back in the snow.

"My esteemed hat!" gasped Hurree Jamset Ram Singh. "Oh crumbs! My idiotic chum, is this a time for absurd larking? Ow!"

There was a swift rustle among the frosty trees. Hurree Singh sat up, gasping for breath. That sudden shove had almost winded him.

Wharton's voice called:

"Coming, Inky?"

"Oooogh!" gasped the nabob. "You silly ass——"

"Hallo! What——" Wharton was heard groping back. "Where are you?" He almost stumbled over the sitting nabob. "Why, what the thump are you squatting there for, Inky?" He peered down at his chum blankly. "Taking a rest in the snow?"

"My esteemed and idiotic chum, I could not help adopting a sitful attitude when you pushed me over backfully!" gasped the nabob. "What are you larking for, you ass?"

"Who pushed you over, fathead?"

"You did, you ass!"

"I did!" exclaimed Wharton, in astonishment. He stooped and grasped the gasping nabob by the arm and helped him to his feet. "What the dickens are you talking about, Inky? I was yards away. You must have bumped into a tree——"

"The tree had an overcoat on, then, and it also had a hand that shovefully pushed me backfully!" grunted Hurree Singh.

Wharton stared at him.

"Look here, Inky, don't be an ass! I never pushed you over; I never knew you'd stopped till I nearly fell over you!"

"Then there is somebody else in this esteemed and terrifically cold spot!" said the nabob. "For certainfully I touched an overcoat, and I was pushfully overturned."

"Somebody else here!" repeated Wharton. He smiled. It was unlikely enough that anyone was wandering in Wharton Park after the fall of dusk in the snow and the bitter wind, and still more unlikely that any unknown wanderer should have pushed the nabob over. "You're dreaming, Inky! You must have got a bump from a branch or something."

"Let us proceedfully go on," said the nabob in a very quiet tone.

"This way, old bean!" said Wharton cheerfully.

He led the way again, and the dusky junior followed him. They came out on

the terrace in front of the house; but Wharton did not head for the entrance porch. He had his own way into his "den" at Wharton Lodge—an old stone stair at the side of the house, which led to a balcony on which his windows opened. Once or twice he called to the nabob, who answered only in monosyllables. They reached the stone stair, one side of which was against the wall, the other protected by a balustrade thick with ancient ivy, now mantled with glimmering snow.

Wharton tramped up the steps, the nabob following in silence. They reached the little balcony, which was thick with snow. Through the french window came the ruddy glimmer of a log fire within. Wharton threw open the glass door, and kicked the snow from his boots.

"Trot in, Inky! You'll get warm at last!" he said, with a laugh.

Hurree Jamset Ram Singh entered in silence. Wharton followed him in, switched on the electric light, and stirred the burning logs in the wide old hearth. The wood fire blazed up with a warmth that was grateful and comforting to the Indian junior. He threw off his coat, and bent over the fire; but the usual cheery smile was absent from his dusky countenance. Wharton pulled up a deep armchair for him.

"Sit down, old bean! You look jolly cold!" he said. "You'll soon warm up." He gave the logs another stir. "That better?"

"Thank you, yes."

Wharton gave him a glance. For the first time he noticed that his dusky chum was unusually silent and grave.

"Anything wrong, Inky?" he asked.

"Not at all-fully."

"Look here! You're not shirty about anything, surely!" exclaimed Wharton, in surprise. It was utterly unusual for the good-tempered, amiable nabob to be "shirty." He was patient and good-tempered, even with Billy Bunter at Greyfriars—still more so with his friends. Even Bob Cherry was not more cheery and good-humoured than the Nabob of Bhanipur. But there was no mistaking the grave coldness on his bronze visage. He did not reply, and Wharton stared at him harder.

"Look here, Inky, old chap! What's the row?" he asked, in his direct way. "If there's anything amiss, cough it up."

"It was exceedingly unpleasant to be shoved over backfully in the snow, my esteemed Wharton!" said the nabob quietly. "And whyfully did you state that you had not done so?"

"You howling ass!" exclaimed Wharton. "I told you I never shoved you over! Why should I?"

"It was an idiotic lark, I suppose," said Hurree Singh. "But whyfully not say so?"

"Because I didn't do it!" exclaimed Wharton warmly. "I'm not ass enough, I hope, to play such a silly trick; but if I did I should own up! Can't you take my word for it?"

"The word of my esteemed chum is as good as gold!" said the nabob, his dusky face clearing. "Nevertheless fully, I was knocked over by some person, who shoved me backfully in the dark!"

"Well, it was not I!" said Harry, a little gruffly. "If it really happened, somebody must have been there—goodness knows whom! I think it must have been a branch that caught you."

"It was nothing of the kind, my esteemed Wharton!"

"Well, it's not at all likely that anybody was hanging about there in the dark and the snow," said Harry. "Anyhow, I never touched you, and I hope my word's good enough?"

"Quitefully!" said the nabob.

And the matter dropped, and seemed to have been forgotten, when the chums of Greyfriars went down to tea with Aunt Amy and Colonel Wharton.

THE THIRD CHAPTER.
A Talk on the Telephone!

BUZZZZZZZ!

Colonel Wharton, smoking an after-dinner cigar by the fire in the hall, glanced up as the telephone bell rang. Miss Amy Wharton, his sister, was knitting on the other side of the cheery log fire. Aunt Amy was generally knitting, for the benefit of the local poor.

Harry Wharton and Hurree Jamset Ram Singh sat on either side of a chess table, deep in a game—too deep to notice the ring on the telephone in the cabinet across the hall. Outside the snow was falling steadily, and the wind wailed round the mullioned windows and red roofs of the old house on the Surrey downs.

The colonel laid his half-smoked cigar down, and crossed to the telephone cabinet, stepped in, and took up the receiver. And Wells, the butler, who had appeared silently from nowhere to answer the ring, faded away again as silently.

"That Wharton?" came a voice over the wires, as the colonel placed the receiver to his ear.

"Speaking!" said the colonel. It did not occur to him, naturally, that he was not the Wharton required!

"Oh, good! Got a cold?"

"What? No!"

"Your voice sounds a bit gruff! If you'd got a cold, it would serve you jolly well right, if you come to that!"

"Wha-a-a-at?" ejaculated the colonel. He had supposed that it was some friend or acquaintance ringing him up; but this did not sound very friendly.

"I mean, after the way you've treated me, you beast!"

"Good gad!"

"Not that I bear malice, you know," went on the voice. "After all, you don't know any better, Wharton! You never had good manners. In fact, your manners were always rather rotten! I dare say you got 'em from that old fat-headed fossil of an uncle of yours."

Colonel Wharton stood as if transfixed. The mention of an "uncle" apprised him that this peculiar telephone call must be intended for his nephew! It was somebody who knew Harry who was phoning. Harry was the "Wharton" who was wanted! But the way in which Wharton's uncle was referred to rather took away the breath of the old soldier.

The voice on the telephone rattled on cheerfully:

"Well, never mind that! I'm not the fellow to think of grudges at Christmas-time! I'll tell you how the matter stands, old chap! I've turned down Mauly! I really meant to give him some time this Christmas; but you know what a thumping bore he is! I felt, after all, that I couldn't stand it! I'll tell you what! I'll give you a look-in!"

"Who is speaking?" hooted the colonel.

"Eh? Don't you know my voice, fat-head? Bunter—your old pal, Bunter! My people are rather keen for me to go to the South of France with them this Christmas! Of course, I should have a gorgeous time! But I really prefer to see old friends. As you'll be having Bob and Nugent and Bull with you later, we shall all be together again—just like Greyfriars, what? That will be ripping! What do you think?"

"Bunter——"

"Yes, Bunter! Don't you know my voice, you ass? I say, Wharton, what about it? You said something about your uncle not liking me very much—but that's all right! I can pull the old donkey's leg all right."

"Wha-a-at?" gasped the colonel.

"He's a bit of a savage old bulldog, I know," went on the happy Bunter. "Bit of a wet blanket at a Christmas party, and all that! But, dash it all, I can stand·him! I've got a lot of uncles myself, and I know what they're like. You only have to pull their silly old legs."

"Good gad!"

"Leave the old ass to me! I'll manage him! Personally, of course, you'll be glad to see me, what?"

last time I stayed with Harry, and—and I shall be so glad to see you again! I—I hope you don't think I was calling you names, sir. I was speaking of another old fool—I—I mean——"

The receiver jammed on the hooks with a jam that made the instrument jump. Bunter was suddenly cut off.

Colonel Wharton strode out of the telephone cabinet, with a brow of thunder. Wharton and Hurree Singh had both heard his angry roar, and they looked at him rather curiously, forgetting chess for the moment.

"Harry!" barked the colonel.

"Yes, uncle!" said Wharton, in wonder.

"Have you asked a—a—a young rap-scallion named Bunter here for Christmas?"

"No fear!" answered Harry promptly.

that Billy Bunter's fat ear was within reach of a pull.

Buzzzzz!

It was the telephone again!

Colonel Wharton looked up with a grunt.

"Probably that's Bunter again!" he said. "You had better take the call, Harry."

Harry Wharton went to the telephone with a rather grim expression on his face. A well-known fat voice came through.

"That you, Wharton? I mean, Harry?"

"Yes, you blithering freak!"

"Oh, really, Wharton——"

"What do you want, you image?"

"I seem to have got on to your old donkey of an uncle by mistake, old

"I wonder if that fat idiot Bunter has got home?" said Harry Wharton. "I hate kicking out even that fat foozler at this time of the year." "The missfulness will not be a terrific calamity," said Hurree Singh. On the other side of the bed-room door Billy Bunter heard every word.

"You impudent young scoundrel!"

"Eh?"

"You disrespectful young rascal!"

"What?"

"You unmannerly young cub——"

"I—I say, is that Wharton speaking?" squeaked a startled voice.

"It is Colonel Wharton speaking!" roared the old, military gentleman, in a voice that almost made the telephone rock.

There was a gasp on the wires.

"Oh! Oh crikey!"

"You young rascal——"

"Oh lor'! It's the old fool himself!" came an involuntary exclamation from Bunter at the other end. "Oh jiminy!"

"If I could reach you, sir, I would box your ears!" hooted the incensed colonel.

"Oh! Oh, really, sir! I—I—I didn't mean—that is to say—oh lor'!" gasped Bunter. "I—I—I—how are you, sir? I hope you're well! I—I've always remembered how nice you were, sir, the

"I am glad of that!" The colonel calmed down. "You have, of course, as you know, every liberty to ask any friend you like, my boy. But—that impudent young rascal! Good gad! You are not in the habit, I presume, of discussing your uncle with your friends, as an old donkey, and an old fossil, hay?"

"Certainly not!" said Harry, flushing. "Has that fat chump——"

"Well, if he's not coming here, never mind," said the colonel. "By gad, I'd like to box his ears! Yes, by gad!"

"If I see him before next term at Greyfriars, I'll jolly well kick him," said Harry.

"The kickfulness is perpetually necessary for the esteemed and ridiculous Bunter!" remarked the Nabob of Bhanipur.

Colonel Wharton sat down again and started a fresh cigar. He was still frowning grimly; and doubtless wishing

chap! He seemed annoyed about something—he cut off rather short! I was going to ask him to call you to the phone——"

"Is that the lot?"

"No, old fellow! The fact is, I'm rather thinking of coming along your way to-morrow——"

"Put a 'Holiday Annual' in your bags first."

"Eh, why?"

"Because if I see you, I'm going to kick you all the way back to the railway station!"

"Beast!"

"Good-bye; and remember my tip!"

"I say, old chap, hold on! I never meant your silly old uncle to hear me calling him an old donkey——"

Wharton jammed the receiver back on the hooks as his uncle had done—with an expression on his face very like his uncle's, at that moment! He also was wishing that Bunter's fat ear was within reach. He went back to Hurree Jamset Ram Singh and chess—and there came no further ring on the phone. Bunter had given it up—for the present, at least !

THE FOURTH CHAPTER.
Snowballs for Bunter !

" I SAY, you fellows !"
"Oh, my hat !"
"The esteemed Bunter !"
It was the following day, and a bright wintry sun shone down on snowy hills and hedgerows. Harry Wharton and Hurree Jamset Ram Singh came out of the gates of Wharton Lodge to take the road to Wimford. There was a circus at that little town, which the two juniors were going to honour with a visit. Outside the gates, a fat figure, muffled in coat and scarf, was pacing to and fro in the carpet of snow, every now and then blinking towards the gates impatiently through a pair of spectacles. As the two juniors emerged, that fat figure turned to them with a grunt of relief.

"I say, you fellows, I've been waiting !" said Bunter peevishly. "I fancied you'd be coming out sooner or later, so I thought I'd hang about a bit, see ? Glad to see you, old fellows !"

Bunter spoke with effusive cordiality; indeed, with affection. At the same time, there was a rather uneasy blink behind his big spectacles. Even Bunter's "neck" was hardly equal to his present proceedings.

"The gladfulness is entirely on your side, my esteemed and idiotic Bunter !" remarked Hurree Jamset Ram Singh.

"Oh, really, Inky——"
"Buzz off, you fat fly !" growled Harry Wharton.

"Oh, really, Wharton——"
"The buzzfulness off is the proper caper !" said the nabob.

"You shut up, Inky !" said Bunter. "I'm talking to Wharton—you needn't butt in. Bit thick you sticking on to the chap, I think, the way you do—sticking him for a holiday nearly every vac——"

"Kick him, Inky !" said Harry.
"Not the sort of thing I'd do !" said Bunter, with a wary eye on the nabob, "But there it is—some fellows are particular, and some ain't ! Harry, old fellow——"

"Have you forgotten what I told you on the phone last night ?" asked the captain of the Greyfriars Remove.

"He, he, he ! I can take a joke, old chap ! I say, it was rather unfortunate my getting through to your uncle by mistake ! These old jossers always get offended if they hear what a fellow really thinks of them ! It was really unfortunate !" said Bunter. "That's why I thought I'd speak to you before coming up to the house."

"Oh ! You were coming up to the house, were you ?"

"Well, naturally, old fellow, as I'm going to give you a few days these hols ! I say, is your uncle fearfully waxy ?"

"Frightfully !"
"I say, old chap, you can soothe him a bit, somehow ! I admit it's rather unfortunate ! Think he'd believe it was all a joke, and that I knew he was on the phone, and was just—just joking ——"

"I fancy not ! And that's not the sort of joke he likes ! Any more to say before I kick you ?"

"Beast ! I mean, look here, dear old chap ! Having turned Mauly down, and refused Smithy's invitation—and having written to that chap D'Arcy of St. Jim's that I can't come to him—

I'm rather in a scrape. Of course, Nugent would be glad to have me, but I can't stand his mob of brothers and sisters ! I might give old Bob a turn, but then there's his father—old Major Cherry's even a grumpier beast than your uncle—— Here, keep off !"

Bunter jumped away just in time.
"The buzzfulness-off——" grinned Hurree Jamset Ram Singh.

"Oh, shut up, Inky ! There's Bull—but I can't stand Bull—not at home among all the other Bulls ! Of course, I'll put up with him here, when he comes along, Harry !"

"You won't !" said Harry.
"Well, good, if he's not going to be here——"

"He's going to be here—but you're not ! For goodness' sake, shut up and cut off ! You've got my uncle's rag out, you blithering fathead, or I might have squeezed you in !" said Wharton impatiently.

"Well, that was unfortunate—but, after all, he's an old ass, and you can stuff him somehow ! I'll tell you how the matter stands !" said Bunter. "My people have gone to relations at Southend—I mean, they've gone to the South of France for the winter. Sammy's gone to my Uncle George—and, of course, Uncle George would be delighted to see me, too——"

"No accounting for tastes !"
"But I should hardly care for it ! There's never enough grub at Uncle George's !" said Bunter sadly. "It's not much I eat, as you know ! Still, a fellow expects something decent- at Christmas. What ? Of course, I could go to Aunt Martha with Bessie—she'd be delighted—she never wrote that if Bessie came she'd have to come without either of her brothers——"

"Ha, ha, ha !"
"Blessed if I can see anything to cackle at ! Look here, old chap, I expect you to stand by me, after all I've done for you !" said Bunter warmly. "You can hardly let a fellow down, I think."

"If you'd had sense enough not to insult my uncle, I might have managed it, you blithering owl !" said Harry. "Now it's no go ! So chuck it !"

"Well, look here, I'd come in quietly and you needn't mention it to your uncle at first !" suggested Bunter. "I'll lie low a bit in your rooms, till you've had time to soothe the old fathead ! What about that ?"

"The old what ?"
"The old fathead—— Here, keep off !" yelled Bunter, dodging again. This time he did not dodge quickly enough. There was a bump as the Owl of the Remove rolled over in the snow. "Yarooooh !"

"Have another ?" snapped Wharton.
"Beast !" roared Bunter. "I jolly well won't stay with you now ! See ? Think I could stand your old fossil of an uncle, and your old frump of an aunt ? No fear ! If you think I can stand your mouldy old relations, Wharton, I can jolly well say—— Yarooooh ! Whooop ! Yow-ow-ow !"

Whiz ! Whiz ! Wharton gathered handfuls of snow, and opened fire.

Snowballs pounded on Billy Bunter right and left.

Wharton seemed angry—why, Bunter did not know ! But there was no doubt about the fact !

"Go it, Inky !" panted Wharton. "Give him a few !"

"The fewfulness will be terrific !" grinned the nabob gathering snow.

Whiz ! Whiz ! Crash ! Smash !
Bunter rolled and roared.
"Ow ! Leave off, you beasts ! Yarooh ! Oh crikey ! Oh lor'! Whoop !"

The fat junior scrambled to his feet. Snowballs still whizzed, hard and fast, fairly raining on William George Bunter.

"I say, you fellows——" squeaked Bunter.

Whiz! Smash! Crash!

"Ow! Oh jiminy! Beasts!" shrieked Bunter.

He ran for it. Snowballs whizzed after him, pounding on his podgy back as he fled. Down the road went Billy Bunter at top speed and behind him, for a considerable distance, ran the two juniors, gathering snow and whizzing snowballs as he ran. Loud howls and squeaks came from the Owl of the Remove as he leaped and jumped and bounded.

Wharton and the nabob stopped at last, panting for breath. Billy Bunter, going strong, vanished in the distance. The chum of the Remove turned back and walked in the direction of Wimford—done with Billy Bunter! So they supposed, at least! But, as a matter of fact, they were far from done with Billy Bunter yet!

— — —

THE FIFTH CHAPTER.
The Uninvited Guest!

"BEAST!" groaned Billy Bunter.
It was dismal!
It was chilly!
It was getting dark!
Bunter was not enjoying life!

Harry Wharton and his chum, in the circus tent at Wimford, had probably forgotten his fat existence. If they had thought of him, they would hardly have guessed where he was at the present moment!

Bunter was on the snowy lawn, below the terrace that ran before Wharton Lodge. From there, in the thickening winter dusk, he could see lighted windows and the ruddy glow from the fire in the old hall.

That ruddy glow looked inviting and hospitable. But it had no hospitality for Billy Bunter! Once, as he stood under a leafless tree, he had glimpsed Colonel Wharton at th open door, looking out at the weather. There was nothing encouraging to Bunter in the old, bronzed visage of the colonel.

Even Bunter realise that it was unfortunate that the colonel had taken that call on the phone, and listened to Bunter's genuine opinion of him! But for that, he had no doubt that Wharton would have taken him in.

Wharton was, in Bunter's opinion, soft, though not so soft as Mauly. Soft enough for Bunter's purpose—but for that dashed, grim, old gargoyle of an uncle! That had torn it!

By a tactful process of buttering-up, perhaps, Wharton could have set the matter right somehow. Instead of which he had snowballed Bunter, and walked away to Wimford, evidently glad to be done with him!

Bunter blinked at the lighted windows and groaned.

But for one circumstance, even the Owl of the Remove would have given it up and taken the home-trail.

But Bunter, like Cortes of old, had burned his ships behind him!

Bunter Court—otherwise Bunter Villa—was shut up. The kind aunt who had accommodated Bessie Bunter, declined Billy Bunter at any price! Uncle George was the only resource.

After being so cruelly let down by Mauly, Bunter had tried Uncle George. Sammy Bunter was there, and Billy joined him there. But a couple of days with Mr. George Bunter had fed him up.

Mr. George Bunter, as it happened, was also fed-up!

The feeling, in fact, was mutual!

On the very first day a cake had been missing from the larder. On the second a pudding was missing! Mr. George Bunter was not one of those hospitable uncles who love to see fellows eat! He seemed to fancy that six helpings at meal-times was enough for a fellow! He was quite cross when the cook complained.

That same evening a cold fowl was missing! Upon which, Bunter's Uncle George informed him that it was time that he was missing, too! Bunter's telephone call to Wharton Lodge had followed.

Owing to the unfortunate fact that Colonel Wharton had taken that call, Billy Bunter told Sammy that he would have to put up with the stingy old codger after all!

Unluckily, the "stingy old codger" came into the room in time to hear the remark! That did it! Bunter had to start in the morning!

Going back was not to be thought of! There was a probability of Uncle George's boot entering into the discussion if he did.

Bunter rang up Mauleverer Towers. He was informed, from that palatial establishment, that Lord Mauleverer was away with friends. This was the last straw! It was Wharton Lodge or nothing!

It looked as if it were going to be nothing!

Darkness was falling!

Bunter, like the unhappy gentleman in the poem, was in danger of finding his lodging on the cold, cold ground! What was to be done?

Who was to be done?

Standing under the leafless tree, in the thickening winter gloom, Billy Bunter thought out that problem.

He was even minus a railway fare! Travelling expenses had reduced his cash resources to threepence!

On threepence a fellow could not get anywhere! Neither could he put up at the humblest inn!

It was, indeed, a knotty problem.

There was, in fact, only one answer to the riddle! Billy Bunter got into motion at last. The darkness was thick enough to screen his movements. He crept along the terrace, and passed round the corner of the building. He knew his way about, from many previous visits. He reached the stone steps that led up to the balcony outside Wharton's room.

Up those steps went Bunter!

Wharton's "den" had a door on the balcony, and it was unlikely that the beast had fastened it in the daytime. Bunter reached the balcony, and groped over the french window.

He gave a grunt of satisfaction as it opened to his touch.

He rolled in and shut the french window behind him.

He did not venture to switch on the light.

There was a glimmering of red embers in the hearth, and Bunter stirred them, and added a few logs, making a cheery and ruddy fire.

Then he stretched himself in Wharton's armchair, with his feet on the hearth, finding the warmth grateful and comforting after the bitter cold out of doors. The snow was beginning to fall again at nightfall. The hapless Owl of the Remove had, at least, found a shelter from the weather.

What he was going to do when Wharton came back he had not yet decided. It was a difficult matter to decide.

Only on one point was Bunter decided—he was not getting out! He had got in—and he was not getting out again!

He remembered that there was an unused attic, up a little stair near Wharton's rooms. As a last resource, he could stow himself away in that! Anyhow, he was staying!

That beast, Colonel Wharton, would get over his beastly temper some time! Harry Wharton might remember all that Bunter had done for him, and show a proper feeling of gratitude! Something might turn up, anyhow! At least, he was under a roof! A judicious moment might be selected for revealing his presence. Anyhow, there he was!

Thinking deeply—much more deeply than was his wont—Billy Bunter rested in the deep, comfortable chair, and toasted his toes at the fire—very much on the alert, in case of a surprise.

Any servant who came to the room would naturally be surprised to find him there, and would certainly report his unexpected presence to the master of the house. And Bunter did not want to meet Colonel Wharton! He would as soon have met his own Uncle George!

He pricked up his fat ears at the sound of a footstep at the door on the corridor.

He sat upright in the chair.

He was on the alert—and intended to dodge out of sight if there was any arrival. But the footstep was followed by the immediate opening of the door. It occurred to Bunter—too late—that he ought to have been out of sight already! Really, it was not prudent to sit before the fire, toasting his toes, when his presence in the house was to be kept—for the present—a dead secret.

But it was too late to think of that now!

The door opened and someone stepped in. The high back of the arm-chair concealed Bunter, unless the new-comer came towards the fireplace.

But as the newcomer was most probably someone who had come to mend the fire, Bunter was booked!

For a moment he was utterly dismayed. It looked as if his little game was going to be knocked on the head at the very start.

But Bunter's fat brain, under unaccustomed pressure, worked swiftly. The Greyfriars ventriloquist had his own resources in a tight corner.

Bunter's trick of ventriloquism was weird and wonderful. It was, as Bunter boasted, a gift. That, certainly, was true; for had it required much intelligence, Bunter could hardly have done it.

He could imitate any voice at Greyfriars, from the bark of Mr. Quelch, to the fruity tones of Mr Prout; from Lord Mauleverer's lazy drawl, to the staccato snap of the Bounder. Something unusual in the fat gullet was perhaps the cause—perhaps even the fatness thereof! Great singers, as Bunter sometimes told the Remove fellows, were always fat!

Not that Bunter was a great singer! But there was no doubt that he was a great ventriloquist!

Bunter had little time to think. Whoever had opened the door had switched on the light, and was stepping across the room towards the fireplace. A few moments, and the fat Owl of the Remove would have been revealed.

Snarl!

It was a sudden, savage snarl as if from some particularly ill-disposed dog, and it came or appeared to come, from the direction of the balcony.

The footsteps stopped.

Bunter heard the unseen person who was crossing the room turn in the direction of the window. Evidently he was surprised.

The footsteps re-started, this time crossing to the window behind the high back of Bunter's armchair.

With his fat heart thumping, Bunter peered round the chair, at the back of the newcomer, who was facing the window.

Although he had only a back view he recognised a lad, who was a relative of Wells, the butler, and employed as a page at Wharton Lodge. His name was Thomas, and Bunter had seen him a good many times before, though he did not want to meet him now.

Thomas went to the french window, opened it, and stared out on the dusky, snowy balcony. Apparently he was looking for that snarling dog, which certainly had no business to be there.

"Shoo!" said Thomas. "Shoo! Get out of it! Shoo!"

As there was no further sound from the dog, Thomas was satisfied that he had "shooed" it away, down the steps to the garden. He closed the window again.

"Thomas!"

It was, or seemed to be, the voice of Mr. Wells, the butler, from the corridor.

"Oh, yes, sir!" called back Thomas.

"Go down to the kitchen at once!"

"I came up to mend the fire!"

"Never mind the fire! Do as I tell you!"

"Oh, yes, sir!"

To Bunter's immense relief Thomas crossed to the door, switched off the light, and went out, closing the door after him.

Bunter gasped with relief.

Thomas, no doubt, was surprised not to see Mr. Wells in the corridor; but he was an obedient youth, and he went down to the kitchen at once.

Billy Bunter grinned.

He had saved his fat bacon. Immediately he quitted his comfortable quarters in the armchair. Thomas was fairly certain to come back before long as the fire had to be kept in, against Master Harry's return. Bunter had plenty of time to get out of sight.

A door opposite the window opened into Wharton's bed-room. Bunter promptly got on the other side of it. There he sat on the bed, prepared to dodge underneath the same at a sound. Ten minutes later he heard a sound of logs being placed on the fire in the adjoining room, and there was a glimmer of light under the communicating door. Bunter dived under the bed, and palpitated there till all was silent again.

THE SIXTH CHAPTER.
The Tortures of Tantalus!

"TEA in the study," said Harry Wharton, with a smile.

And Hurree Jamset Ram Singh smiled a dusky smile, and nodded.

The chums of Greyfriars had returned from Wimford in time for tea. Colonel Wharton and Miss Amy were out, and the juniors were left to themselves. On such occasions Wharton liked to "tea" in his den, which was cosy and reminiscent of the study at Greyfriars School.

So, having given due instructions to Wells, Wharton went up to his room with the cheery nabob.

The little incident of the previous day, when Hurree Jamset Ram Singh had been so roughly and mysteriously shoved over in the dark under the trees, was forgotten now. Wharton's belief was that Inky must have bumped into a branch in the dark; while the nabob was satisfied that some person unknown had knocked him over, though why, he had no idea. There had been for a few minutes a faint "shirtiness" on the subject; but that was quite washed out now, and the matter dismissed. Both the juniors were looking very bright and cheery as they came into Wharton's den. They had enjoyed the circus at Winford, and they were looking forward to the coming of Bob Cherry and Frank Nugent, and Johnny Bull and the festivities of Yuletide.

Christmas was only a few days off now, and already Wharton Lodge had a rather festive look. Aunt Amy had been decorating her dear nephew's room, and bright holly gleamed from the walls.

Thomas brought in the tea. Thomas was a chubby youth, generally wearing

a broad grin on his plump countenance. That grin was now absent, and Thomas looked subdued and glum. Noticing that circumstance, Harry inquired the cause.

"What's up, old bean?" he asked cheerily.

Thomas' grin returned at once.

"Nothing, sir," he answered. "Leastways, it's all right. Mr. Wells did call me."

"Wells called you?" repeated Harry blankly.

"And he forgot," said Thomas. "Jest in a few minutes, sir, he forgot. 'Twasn't my fault."

"Oh, Wells called you, and forgot, did he?" said Harry, rather puzzled. "Well, we all forget things at times, Tommy, old sport."

"Jawing a chap," said Thomas.

"Oh!"

"I come 'ere, sir, to mend the fire, which was my duty," said Thomas. "I wouldn't let you, sir, come in out of the snow and find the fire out. Mr. Wells calls me from the passidge. 'Go down to the kitchen,' he says. And I goes down."

Thomas frowned, evidently with a sense of injury.

"I sees Mr. Wells in the 'all," continued Thomas, "and he asks me if I've mended the fire already. 'You told me to go down to the kitchen,' I says. 'I did not,' he says. Just like that, sir."

"Wells doesn't generally forget things," said Harry. "Sure he called you, kid?"

"Plain as I 'ear you now, sir. And he says to me, says he, 'I did not call you,' he says. 'Go and mend Master Harry's fire at once,' he says; 'and don't be lazy!' 'Me lazy, sir!' said Thomas warmly.

"The forgetfulness is a privilege of advanced and venerable years, my esteemed Thomas," said the Nabob of Bhanipur soothingly. "It is the duty of esteemed youth to exercise terrific patience in dealing with venerable johnnies."

Thomas grinned.

"Oh, yes, sir!" he said. "And Mr. Wells is always kind, and very seldom speaks sharp, sir. Only he did call me."

And, having finished laying the tea, Thomas retired, happily unconscious of the fact that a fat youth, listening on the other side of the bed-room door, was grinning from one fat ear to the other. That little misunderstanding between Mr. Wells and Thomas rather amused Billy Bunter.

"Might fancy ourselves in the study at Greyfriars—what?" said Harry Wharton, as he poured out the tea. "Only I wish that Bob and Franky and Johnny were here, old bean."

"The wishfulness of my esteemed self is also great, but the arrivefulness of our ridiculous friends will shortly eventuate," said the nabob.

"I wonder if that fat idiot has got home?" said Harry, remembering the unimportant existence of Billy Bunter. "Bother him!"

"Bother and blow him!" agreed Hurree Jamset Ram Singh.

"I hate kicking out even that fat foozler at this time of the year, but even if I wanted him, I couldn't land him on my uncle, after what the blithering idiot gabbled on the phone. I don't think uncle would stand it, if I did."

"The missfulness of the esteemed Bunter's company will not be a terrific calamity."

"Hardly," said Wharton, laughing.

On the other side of the bed-room door Billy Bunter shook a fat fist.

Listeners, it is said, never hear any good of themselves; and that was often Bunter's fate.

Bunter was hungry. He was always hungry, if it came to that. But now he was specially, fearfully, frightfully hungry.

He could scarcely resist the temptation to open the door, and take the risk of joining the tea-party in the next room.

But the remarks he heard had a discouraging effect. Obviously if a propitious moment for revealing his presence was to come, it had not come yet.

That stuffy old colonel, it seemed, still had his back up. It was a sad fact that he never had liked Bunter. Why, Bunter could not guess; but there it was.

But to remain in hiding, hungry, while tea was going on, only a few yards from him, was sheer torture to Billy Bunter.

Tantalus, of old, was tormented by the sight of food always just out of his reach. Now Bunter could fully understand and appreciate the tortures of Tantalus. Never had he been so tantalised.

Peering through the keyhole, he could discern the two juniors at the tea-table; and the good things on the table. The click of crockery reached his fat ears. There were poached eggs, and a large cake, and a dish of jam-tarts; and the fragrant scent of fried sausages reached him, and made his mouth water. Tantalus' experiences in olden times were a mere joke to this! Both the juniors, hungry after a long walk in the December cold, were doing justice to the spread. Billy Bunter could have groaned aloud—though he took good care not to do so! He had a horrid certainty that discovery meant the order of the boot!

But he had to eat!

This was more than flesh and blood could stand!

Bunter set his fat wits to work.

Necessity is the mother of invention! Somehow, those two frightful beasts had to be got away from the room for a few minutes, at least, while Bunter took the keen edge off his appetite. The scent of sausages spurred Bunter on.

He tiptoed away from the communicating door at last to the bed-room door in the corridor.

He opened that door, and blinked out cautiously through his big spectacles.

No one was in sight, naturally. A light burned in the passage, and Bunter could see a row of doors in one direction and the landing in the other.

He tiptoed out.

His first proceeding was to switch off the corridor light. He felt safer in the dark.

Then, with beating heart, he tapped at the door of Wharton's den. The Greyfriars ventriloquist was ready for action again!

———

THE SEVENTH CHAPTER.
Who?

TAP!

Harry Wharton glanced round to the door.

"Hallo! Come in!" he called out.

The door did not open.

But a voice—which anyone at Wharton Lodge would have sworn was the rather mumbling voice of Thomas, the page—answered:

"Oh, Master Harry! Please come down at once, sir! There's been an accident, sir, and the colonel's a-talkin' on the phone, sir."

"Oh!"

Harry Wharton leaped to his feet. Why Thomas called through the door, instead of opening it, would have puzzled him if he had given it a thought. But the startling news that there had been an accident banished all other thoughts from his mind. Colonel Wharton and his sister were out in the car—and the snowy roads were dangerous enough. Wharton fairly bounded to the door.

He reached it so quickly that Billy Bunter, outside, had barely time to whip back into the next room and shut himself in.

The next moment Wharton's door flew open.

"An accident!" panted Wharton. "Who——" He stared. The corridor was empty. Naturally he had expected to see Thomas there!

But without a pause he dashed away towards the stairs, with Hurree Jamset Ram Singh at his heels. Both the juniors were equally alarmed and anxious. They did the stairs three at a time, and rushed breathlessly into the hall below.

Bunter, in the bed-room, could hardly believe in his good luck!

He lost no time.

Wharton and Inky were still on the stairs, running and leaping down, when Bunter opened the communicating door and whipped into Wharton's den.

Staying only to stuff a sausage into his mouth, the fat Owl of the Remove gathered up his plunder.

There was a rucksack hanging on the wall, used by Wharton in his camping excursions. Bunter grabbed it down, stuffed the cake into it, and followed up the cake with the tarts and a pile of toast. Meanwhile, he munched the sausage. The sausage disappeared in record time. Another followed it, and then Bunter made a clean sweep of what remained of the poached eggs. There were some other things left—but Bunter dared not linger! Probably for the first time on record the Owl of the Remove turned from a tea-table on which there remained things to eat! With his bag of provender in his fat hands he bolted back into the bed-room, closed the door, and dived under the bed with his plunder. Bunter's motions generally resembled those of the tortoise. Now, a flash of lightning had hardly anything on Bunter!

Meanwhile, Harry Wharton and Hurree Jamset Ram Singh had rushed down into the hall, and Harry bounded into the telephone cabinet. To his surprise, the receiver was on the hooks! He grabbed it off.

"Number, please!" It was a voice from the exchange. If Colonel Wharton had been on the phone at all he was cut off.

"Wells!" shouted Wharton.

"Master Harry!" The butler of Wharton Lodge came across the hall, with surprise in his usually expressionless countenance. "What——"

"Did you take the call? What has happened?"

"There has been no call, sir!" said the astonished Wells.

"No call on the phone!" exclaimed Wharton, stupefied.

"No, sir!"

"Has not my uncle rung up——"

"No, sir!"

"But—hasn't there been an accident and——" Wharton fairly gasped in his amazement.

"Not that I am aware of, sir! Certainly there has been no call on the telephone!" said Wells.

"I—I—I—what—what did Thomas mean, then? Has that young idiot been scaring me for nothing?" panted Wharton. Anxiety gave place to anger. It was a relief to find that there had been no telephone call about an accident. But such a heartless trick was intensely exasperating.

"Thomas——" repeated Wells blankly.

"The young rascal! Has the kid taken to playing idiotic practical jokes, or what?" roared Wharton, red with anger. "He came up to my room and called in that there had been an accident and that my uncle was speaking on the phone!"

"Oh, sir!" gasped Wells.

"It is an esteemed and idiotic practical joke!" said the Nabob of Bhanipur, in wonder. "The execrable Thomas must be off his ridiculous rocker!"

Wells frowned portentously.

"Thomas, sir, is a relative of mine," he said with dignity. "I can hardly believe that he has done such a thing, sir! If so, he must be discharged immediately! The boy has been rather queer to-day, I fancied, or said he fancied, that I called him out of your room this afternoon——"

"Where is he?" demanded Harry.

"Robert!" Wells addressed one of his retainers. "Where is Thomas?"

"Upstairs in the master's room, sir, a-cleaning up some snow which blowed in at the winder, which the colonel left it open——"

"Call him at once!" said Wells.

Robert went to fetch Thomas.

There was a glint in Harry Wharton's eyes as he waited. Such a trick, which had alarmed him for the safety of his relatives, was not to be forgiven. Had Thomas been a Greyfriars fellow, like himself, Wharton would certainly have punched his head, hard. As the matter stood, it was the "sack" for Thomas.

Robert came back in a few minutes, followed by Thomas, who had a wondering expression on his chubby face.

"You young sweep!" shouted Wharton. "What do you mean by it?"

Thomas blinked at him.

"Wot 'ave I done, sir?" he asked.

"You know what you've done, you young rascal! Why should you play such a beastly rotten trick on me?" exclaimed Wharton indignantly.

Thomas' eyes seemed to be almost popping out of his chubby face, in his amazement and dismay.

"I ain't done anything!" he exclaimed in bewilderment. "What have I done, sir? I been sweeping up the snow what

THE MAGNET LIBRARY.—No. 1,349.

blowed into the master's room, sir, which the winder was left open——"

"You came to my room and called through the door that my uncle had had an accident——"

"I didn't!" gasped Thomas.

"You didn't?" stuttered Wharton.

"Course I didn't, sir! Why should I?"

"Thomas, how dare you contradict Master Harry, who saw you——" began Wells.

"I didn't see him," said Harry. "He called through the door. But I know his voice."

"The knowfulness is terrific!" declared Hurree Jamset Ram Singh, his dark eyes very keenly on Thomas' dismayed face.

"I didn't!" gasped Thomas. "I never did, sir! I wouldn't! 'Ere's Robert'll say he come to me in the master's room——"

"I found him there, sir!" said Robert.

"He must have gone back there after calling me," said Harry. "But if you say you didn't, Thomas——"

"I didn't, sir!" gasped Thomas. "I'll swear I didn't! As if I'd play such a trick on you, sir!"

There Will Be

ANOTHER SET

of

MAGNIFICENT

Coloured Pictures

FREE

with next week's grand issue
of the

MAGNET

Make sure of adding them to your album, chum, by ordering your copy NOW!

"Well, I certainly thought it was your voice," said Harry. "Didn't you, Inky?"

"The thinkfulness was terrific."

"It wasn't me, sir!" said Thomas almost tearfully. "I wouldn't go for to do such a thing——"

"Who did, then?" demanded Wells. "Someone did!"

"I dunno! I didn't, Mr. Wells!"

Wharton gave the boy a searching look. Someone, it was certain, had played that unfeeling trick. Why, was a mystery. If it was not Thomas, it was someone else. And the voice had certainly sounded like Thomas'. But the almost tearful earnestness in the chubby face disarmed Wharton.

"Well, if you deny it, kid, I'll take your word," he said. "But I'd like to know who played that rotten trick!"

"So would I, sir!" said Thomas. "I'd like to punch his ead, sir!"

"If you are satisfied that it was not Thomas, Master Harry——" said the stately Wells.

"I'm bound to take his word," said Harry.

"Thank you, sir!" said Thomas.

"I shall inquire into the matter, sir, with your leave," said Wells.

Harry Wharton nodded and went up

the staircase again with the nabob, both of them greatly perturbed and perplexed. They left Wells and the others in a buzz below.

"What do you think, Inky?" asked Harry, as the juniors came back into the den. "The kid looked as if he was telling the truth. But——"

"The lookfulness was terrific," agreed the nabob. "But the butfulness is also preposterous."

"Well, thank goodness it was only a false alarm, anyhow! Let's finish our tea," said Harry. "Why, what—— Great pip! Who's been here?"

He stared blankly at the denuded tea-table.

Hardly a thing remained!

"My esteemed hat!" ejaculated the nabob, equally astonished.

"The—the—the young sweep!" gasped Wharton. "That's why he played that rotten trick—to get us out of the room while he bagged our tea! It must have been Thomas, of course! Who else?"

"The who-fulness is terrific. It is like an esteemed grub raid of the execrable Bunter at Greyfriars," said the nabob in astonishment.

Wharton made an angry stride to the door.

But he paused.

He had told Thomas that he would take his word. And, though he had now found out the motive for the wretched trick, he felt that he could not reopen the matter. Possibly, too, the culprit had not been Thomas—though who else it could have been was a mystery. Anyhow, in the circumstances, he felt that Thomas had to be given the benefit of the doubt—and that was that!

THE EIGHTH CHAPTER.
A Lodging for the Night!

BILLY BUNTER scarcely breathed. Huddled under Harry Wharton's bed, the fat Owl of the Remove blinked in the light that had suddenly come on.

He blinked at a pair of feet at the bedside.

They were not Wharton's feet. It was not yet Wharton's usual bed-time—and on holiday he was rather likely to be later than was usual at school. Bunter fancied they were Thomas' feet. Anyhow, they were the feet of someone who had come into the bed-room to get it ready for the night. Standing beside the bed, that someone was only a yard from the fat Owl, stilling his breathing underneath. Bunter heard the rustle of a coverlet, and a hand brushing on a pillow. Then the feet moved away, and Bunter saw more and more of their owner as he crossed the room to the fireplace. There he knelt down to ignite a wood fire, and Bunter could see that it was Thomas.

Thomas ignited the fire and watched it burn up. But Bunter no longer watched Thomas; he huddled right out of sight of that youth under the bed, fearful that a chance glimpse might discover him.

But Thomas, of course, had no idea that anybody was under the bed, and he did not glance in that direction.

Leaving a cheerful fire burning to greet Master Harry's eyes when he came up to bed, Thomas quitted the room and went along to the next to perform a similar service for the Nabob of Bhanipur. He turned out the light as he went, leaving the room illumined only by the glow from the fire.

Billy Bunter was glad to hear the door shut after him.

In other respects Bunter was not feeling glad. He was feeling worried.

If he had not dared to reveal his presence at Wharton Lodge before, much less did he dare to reveal it since the trick he had played on the captain of the Remove.

A grub raid was not likely to make Wharton angry for long, but the false alarm of an accident to his uncle had certainly angered him deeply.

At present he attributed the whole thing to Thomas, or to some person unknown. The discovery of Bunter would, of course, enlighten him. At the thought of it Bunter could almost feel the impact of a boot on his tight trousers.

He had to lie doggo.

Fortunately, he had had something to eat. He had not had enough, of course; but that was nothing new, he never had enough. He had parked enough to last

him for some time. Now he was both tired and sleepy. Going to sleep under a bed was not to be thought of. Besides, the beast might look under his bed before he turned in.

Where was Bunter to sleep?

He thought of the attic over the bedrooms. From previous visits to Wharton Lodge—under different conditions—he remembered that attic. No light and no fire; but nobody ever went there, which was the chief thing. Sleeping on the bare floor without blankets on a night in December was impossible, especially for Bunter. But there were plenty of bed-clothes at hand. It was easy enough to snaffle them.

He heard Thomas come out of Hurree Singh's room and pass the door, going towards the service staircase. Thomas was gone—and the coast was clear.

Nobody now was likely to be rooting about till bed-time

If bedclothes were snaffled they would be missed. That was a difficulty. It might lead to suspicion that some extraneous person was in the house. That meant a search—and the boot for Bunter!

Thomas had been suspected of bagging the juniors' tea. But Thomas could hardly be suspected of bagging the bed-clothes!

Bunter had to think this out. It was irritating and annoying, because he was drowsy and would much rather have gone to sleep. But there was no help for it.

He rolled out from under the bed at last. There was a lurking fat grin on his face.

He had the idea!

(Continued on next page.)

"Linesman's" store of Soccer knowledge is at the disposal of all MAGNET readers. Send along your queries to him, c/o The MAGNET, The Fleetway House, Farringdon Street, London, E.C.4, and then look out for a reply in this weekly feature.

LEARNING SOMETHING IN ADVANCE !

ONE of the strange things about football, when you come to think of it, is that the big clubs should regard Cup-ties as much more important than League games. But they certainly do in one respect. As soon as the Cup-ties appear on the programme we hear of officials of this or that club going specially to watch the opponents against whom their side has been drawn in the knock-out competition.

I have even heard of a whole team being taken to see a replayed Cup-tie so that they could sum up the possibilities of their ultimate opponents in the Cup competition. As I have told you previously, I am a great believer in this idea of knowing your opponents, because to a certain extent if a football team knows what it is up against, then that team knows what they have to do in order to win the match.

What strikes me as strange, however, is that the big clubs, concerned as they are in winning a Cup-tie, and going to such lengths to work out the schemes beforehand, do not apply the same principle to their League games.

After all, if it is accepted that by watching forthcoming opponents a Cup team has a better chance of beating those opponents, then surely by watching forthcoming League opponents they would have a better chance of beating them.

I am very glad to note, in this connection, that the officials of at least one League club think they can learn something in advance. You know that Port Vale have done particularly well this season. They are among the surprises of League football. Nobody expected them to make a big show in the Second Division, but they have done it And I can now let you into a secret. Every Saturday an official of Port Vale has watched a match in which the opponents of Port Vale for the following week have been concerned. That official has then gone back to the players and given them ideas as to what they should

do—the sort of game they should play in order to beat their opponents. I don't say that this is the sole secret of the success of the Port Vale club this season, but it is just one of the little things which tell.

CLUBS AND THEIR COLOURS !

A MAGNET reader who is very much interested in the Everton club, asks me about the colours which are worn by the players. These Everton players wear royal blue shirts and white knickers with a blue stripe down the sides. I can tell you about that strip of blue. Some time ago the players of the Everton club told the officials that they could not always distinguish a friend from foe without looking up. So the blue stripe was introduced to the knickers to rid the players of this necessity.

So now, when an Everton player has the ball at his toe, he does not need to look up to see a colleague to whom he may pass the ball. He merely looks at the knickers, and noticing the blue stripe down the side, is able to find his colleague with the ball. This is another little thing which counts.

Personally, I have never been able to understand why more originality is not shown in choosing the attire which shall be worn by the players of the leading clubs. There are so many whites, blues, and reds that the clubs which use these colours have to change quite frequently, and the change leads to confusion. I sometimes think that it would be much easier if only two colours of shirts were allowed in football—say blue for the men playing on their own ground, and red for the teams playing away from home.

In the old days it used to be a rule that the club oldest in membership of the League should have the prior right to their own colours. Then the rule was altered so that the team playing at home could wear its own colours in League games. In Cup-ties, however, there is now a different rule altogether. When two teams

are drawn together whose colours clash then both teams have to make a change.

EXTRA TIME FOR PENALTY KICKS !

A SOMEWHAT intricate problem has been sent to me from a reader at Manchester. It refers to the extra time which must be allowed for the taking of a penalty kick after the ordinary time has expired. You know, of course, that if, in the last few seconds of a game, the referee considers that a penalty kick should be awarded, the ordinary time must be extended for the purpose of allowing the penalty kick to be taken. Now comes the query as to how much extra time should be allowed.

Just recently, in a match in the Manchester district, so I am informed, the referee stretched the time so that a penalty kick should be taken. The taker of the kick sent the ball against the goalkeeper, who pushed it out. The taker of the kick followed up, and banged the ball into the net. Should a goal have been allowed ?

The answer is in the negative. If the taker of a penalty kick, for which extra time has been allowed, does not score with the first kick, then the time is up automatically, and the game should be declared finished.

Certain complications arise in regard to this question, concerning which the rules are not very clear. The Scottish Football Association, for instance, have asked for a ruling in the case of a goalkeeper partly stopping a ball from such a penalty kick which twists out of his hands and goes onto the net. Is it a goal ? Personally, I think a goal should be allowed, but the fact that the Scottish F.A. have queried this shows that there is a difference of opinion on the point. I think that the question of a goal or not a goal depends on the result of the one kick from the penalty spot.

I have a letter from a player in the Brighton district who thinks he is good enough to make progress in the game, but who is worried as to how his prowess shall be brought to the notice of the leading clubs of the district. I don't think this ought to be very difficult, and I suggest that a note to the manager of the Brighton and Hove Albion club would at least result in the ambitious player getting a trial. After all if we bring fellows from South Africa—as we have been doing—just to have a trial with English clubs, and all expenses paid, surely the home player can get a trial. If my correspondent does not get the trial which he desires I hope he will write to me again.

"LINESMAN."

He blinked through several drawers in a chest till he came to Harry Wharton's handkerchief-box. From that box he extracted a handkerchief which had Wharton's initials in the corner. He crumpled it in his grubby hands to give it the appearance of having been in a pocket.

Then he rolled to the door and blinked cautiously into the passage.

The coast was clear.

He whipped along to Hurree Jamset Ram Singh's room. From hearing Thomas' movements, he had no doubt that it was the next bed-room to Wharton's. As soon as he entered it he knew that it was right; various possessions of the Nabob of Bhanipur were in sight. Thomas had left a nice fire burning, which gave Bunter all the light he wanted.

He dropped Wharton's handkerchief beside the bed.

Then he coolly stripped the nabob's bed, making up sheets and blankets into a bundle, and pillow and bolster and eiderdown quilt into another bundle.

In the course of that labour he discovered a hot-water bottle in the bed, which he gladly appropriated and stuck into one of the bundles.

A cautious blink into the dimly lit corridor showed him that the coast was still clear. Moving at unusual speed, he bore first one and then the other bundle along to the little stair that led steeply up to the attic under the eaves.

The attic door was locked, the key in the outside. Bunter unlocked it by the light of a match and put the key on the inside.

He carried his bundles in.

Then he locked the attic door after him.

He blinked round rather dismally in his new quarters. There was a little dormer window, through which came a pale glimmer of winter starlight and the gleam of snow on the roofs.

It was cold! It was chilly! It was dismal! But it was a case of any port in a storm!

And Bunter had to make the best of it!

After all, he had sheets and blankets and a warm quilt and a hot-water bottle! Matters might have been worse —much worse!

And he was sleepy!

He rolled himself in the bedclothes, rolled the quilt round him, and lay down, with the hot-water bottle at his feet!

Really, it was not so bad!

There was a grin on his fat face as he laid his bullet head on the pillow. Hurree Singh, finding his bed-room in that dismantled state, and Wharton's handkerchief on the floor, could hardly come to any conclusion but that his chum had been japing him!

It might lead to a row between the chums of the Remove! That did not matter, so long as it did not lead to Bunter!

Or Inky might be deeply offended and dignified, and in that frame of mind, disdain to utter a word of complaint! Unassuming as he was, the nabob never forgot that he was a prince in his own country. That, in Bunter's opinion, would be best—it would make him quite safe!

Anyhow, Bunter had a feeling that he had done all he could, and had acted with great astuteness. He had done his best; and no fellow could do more!

With that happy conviction in his fat mind, Billy Bunter went to sleep—fortunately for him, too far from the occupied rooms for his snore to be heard!

THE NINTH CHAPTER.
Exit the Nabob!

"GOOD-NIGHT, old chap!"

"Good-night, my esteemed Wharton!"

It was ten o'clock; later than bedtime at Greyfriars. The two juniors came up together, and Wharton said good-night to his guest at the door of the latter's room, and then went on to his own.

Hurree Jamset Ram Singh entered his room and switched on the light and closed the door.

His first step was towards the fire; welcome to any fellow on a freezing December night; doubly welcome to the youth from the sunny East! Standing by the fire, Hurree Jamset Ram Singh glanced at his bed—and jumped!

"My esteemed hat!" he ejaculated.

He stared at the bed.

Under the combined supervision of Miss Amy Wharton and the excellent Wells, household matters at Wharton Lodge worked as exactly as if they went by machinery.

It was impossible, of course, that a guest's bed had been left in that state by careless hands.

Indeed, the nabob had been in the room once or twice, and then the bed had been in apple-pie order.

Now it was utterly dismantled! All the bedclothes were gone—even to the pillow and bolster.

Who had played this extraordinary trick?

With a slight grimness in his usually

smiling and good-natured dusky face, the nabob picked up the handkerchief that lay beside the bed.

Crumpled and a little grubby, it looked as if it had fallen by accident from a pocket.

The grimness in his dusky face intensified as he glanced at the initials worked in the corner of the handkerchief.

He laid it down, and stood very silent and still.

It was Harry Wharton's handkerchief! Wharton had been there and dropped it; that was the only conclusion to be drawn. He had dropped it beside the dismantled bed.

Hurree Jamset Ram Singh's lips set in a tight line.

This sort of thing, at school, might be a jape! Such japes were quite out of place at home, between host and guest! Wharton, moreover, was the last fellow to play such a trick—merely as a trick! He was no practical joker like Wibley of the Remove—not even a thoughtless fellow like Bob Cherry. He was not in the least the kind of fellow to act unthinkingly.

The dusky face of the nabob hardened and hardened.

If Wharton had done this, he had not done it thoughtlessly! And Wharton, it appeared, had done it! There was his handkerchief, dropped in bundling up the missing bedclothes! No servant in the house would have dared to play such a trick—or could have had any imaginable motive for doing so!

Back into the nabob's mind came the incident in the park! He had been roughly shoved over—knocked over! Wharton had denied having done it—

but even in denying it, had admitted that he did not believe that anyone else had been at hand! Inky had taken his word! But now——

He had been mystified by that incident! He could not be mystified by the present one!

When a fellow treated a guest in this way, it meant only one thing; he did not want him!

The colour glowed in the nabob's dusky cheek!

Almost always he spent the holidays with Wharton. His native land of Bhanipur was far away. Colonel Wharton, who had known his father in India, took it as a matter of course that Wharton Lodge should be his home in England. Never had it crossed the nabob's mind to doubt that he was welcome there!

But now——

He had other friends! Bob Cherry, Frank Nugent, Johnny Bull, would have made him more than welcome. Lord Mauleverer would have welcomed him to Mauleverer Towers.

Standing very silent and still, the nabob thought it out.

Bob Cherry, in his place, would probably have gone along to Wharton's room and asked him what the thump he meant by it.

Hurree Jamset Ram Singh did not think of doing that.

If he had out-worn his welcome in a friend's house, he had only one wish—to withdraw himself as quietly and unostentatiously as possible. A row would serve no purpose; and he did not want a row.

And there was the colonel to be considered, and his kind sister—both hospitality itself, and attached to their Indian guest. Least said soonest mended!

Hurree Jamset Ram Singh did not ring for Wells and more bedclothes. He did not even think of it. To let the matter come to the knowledge of the servants was too mortifying.

Bunter had wondered whether Inky would kick up a row, or take the thing quietly with offended dignity. He had thought the latter the more probable of the two! Obtuse as Bunter was, there was a considerable vein of slyness in him as in many stupid people. He had read the Indian prince's character aright!

Hurree Singh could not, in the circumstances, go to bed! He could not quit the house immediately without a painful explanation with Colonel Wharton!

He turned off the light and sat in an armchair before the fire, after piling it with logs.

He was not going to say a word! He could not do so, in fact, without landing Wharton in trouble with his uncle, who was very meticulous in matters of hospitality to a guest! Certainly he did not desire that. He was deeply, bitterly wounded and offended; but like a true Oriental, the more deeply he felt, the more deeply he was disposed to hide his feelings.

It was long before his eyes closed.

But they closed at last; and did not open again till the pale winter dawn was glimmering in.

The fire had burned out by that time; and the Nabob of Bhanipur shivered as he rose from the chair. It was a cold and snowy morning.

The hour was early; no one else was stirring yet, except the old colonel, who was always an early riser, and perhaps the early housemaids. The nabob lost no time.

He sat down at the table to write a note, which he enclosed in an envelope and sealed. Then he rapidly packed a suitcase.

Colonel Wharton grasped his nephew by the collar with one hand and Hurree Singh with the other. Then, with a powerful wrench, he dragged them apart. "What the thump——" panted Wharton. "Oh! You, uncle!" "How dare you?" rumbled the colonel. "Fighting, by gad!" The two juniors stood crimson and panting, under the stern, angry glare of the colonel.

Stepping quietly, he descended the stairs. An early housemaid in the hall looked at him. Wells—appearing, as usual, silently from nowhere—bade him a respectful good-morning—his eyes dwelling rather curiously on the suitcase in the dusky schoolboy's hand.

"It's early, sir!" said Wells.

"Quitefully so!" agreed the nabob. "Perhapsfully you will have the kindness, my esteemed Wells, to deliver this note to the worthy Wharton when he comes downfully?"

"Certainly, sir!" said Wells.

He took the note, and opened the door for the nabob. Hurree Jamset Ram Singh stepped out into the December dawn, glimmering on a world of white! At that untimely hour, there was no taxi to be had; and he had to walk to the railway station at Wimford, a good distance from Wharton Lodge. He started down the drive, carrying his suitcase.

Wells gazed after him. He was puzzled. Colonel Wharton had gone out for an early walk; but the nabob could hardly be going for a walk, with a heavy suitcase in his hand.

Wells realised that something was amiss.

He glanced at the note in his hand, wondering what it contained. Then he glanced again after the disappearing form of the nabob.

There was only one conclusion to which Wells could come. There had been some "row" between the schoolboy friends, and Hurree Jamset Ram Singh was going. The note left for Wharton, and the suitcase in his hand, were proof that he was going. Wharton, evidently, did not know.

"Dear me!" said Wells. "Dear me!"

Wells considered the matter.

A quarrel and a parting at Christmas-time between two fellows who had been such chums was not at all the thing.

It rather distressed Wells, who was a kind-hearted, portly gentleman.

Hurree Singh had bidden him give Wharton the note when he came down. By that time the nabob would be gone beyond recall. Having considered the matter, Wells decided that it would be judicious not to wait till Master Harry came down, but to take the note to him at once—which was very judicious of Wells, in the circumstances.

Meanwhile, the nabob, suitcase in hand, was tramping up a snowy road, his face to the wintry wind. Billy Bunter, snoring in the attic, was dreaming—of turkey and mince pies. He did not dream how very successful his astute scheme had been. Had he done so, no doubt the fat Owl would have smiled in his sleep.

THE TENTH CHAPTER.
A Shindy!

"H'M! Master Harry!" Harry Wharton awakened at the sound of a voice and an apologetic cough. He sat up in bed and blinked at Wells.

"Hallo! Overslept myself—what?" asked Harry, rubbing his eyes. "Is it getting late?"

"No, sir; it is very early," said Wells. "I have taken the liberty, sir, to awaken you to give you this note from Master Hurree Singh, who has just gone out."

Wharton was still a little sleepy, but those words from Wells made him very wide awake.

"Hurree Singh gone out, and left me a note! What the thump——" exclaimed Wharton, in astonishment.

"He had a suitcase, sir," said Wells, "and, in the circumstances, I thought I had better bring you the note immediately, although Master Hurree Singh requested me to give it to you when you came down, sir."

Wharton took the note and opened it. Wells turned on the bed-light, and the captain of the Greyfriars Remove read the letter from Hurree Jamset Ram Singh, with gathering amazement and dismay in his face. It ran:

"*Dear and esteemed Wharton,—In the ridiculous circumstances, you will probably not be terrifically surprised at my prompt and welcome departure. The regretfulness is preposterous that I have not soonerfully observed that my absurd company was superfluous. Doubtless you will agree that the least said the soonerfully repaired, and perhapsfully you will explain to the estimable colonel and the admirable miss that my sudden french leave was deplorably unavoidable.*

"*H. J. R. S.*"

Harry Wharton gazed at that letter, almost wondering if he was dreaming. He read it, and read it again, in utter wonder, and then blinked at Wells.

"How long has Inky—I mean, Hurree Singh—been gone?"

"Perhaps a quarter of an hour, sir."

"Is my uncle down yet?"

"Yes, sir. The colonel has gone for a walk before breakfast."

"Tell Thomas to get my bike round."

"There is a great deal of snow on the ground, sir."

"Never mind that!"

"Very good, sir!"

Wells retired, and Wharton bounded from his bed. What Hurree Jamset Ram Singh could possibly mean by his remarkable conduct, Wharton could not

(Continued on page 16.)

THE NEW Greyfriar...

No. 64 (New Series).   EDITED BY...

Masked Mummers Impress Temple

"Remove Nowhere in Comparison!"

In the theatrical line it takes a lot to impress Cecil Reginald Temple. Temple, as you may or may not know, is producer and stage manager for the Upper Fourth Dramatic Society, so his critical faculties are on a rather high plane. If a stage show meets with Temple's approval, it's as good as hall-marked and stamped in every link.

Naturally, Remove standards in theatrical production fall very short of the mark where Temple is concerned. All through the last term Temple has been going to great pains to demonstrate to Greyfriars at large that the Remove are hopeless duds at acting. The notion that Wibley is in any way a born theatrical genius particularly gets Temple's goat.

Temple's views, of course, have not found unqualified acceptance in the Remove—in fact several members of the Dramatic Society have gone so far as to say: "If you know a better set of actors of our weight and age, trot 'em out!" To which pointed remark Temple has hitherto made no response.

But now, ye budding Thespians of the Remove, you'll have to prepare for a shock. Something has come along to impress Temple at last!

On the day after he arrived home for the hols, Temple had a visit from a masked band of strolling players. And those masked mummers could act.

"You Remove kids talk about acting!" said Temple scornfully to our representative, after the show had ended and the mummers were being regaled with supper in the kitchen. "Why, these masked players could act you off your feet—and there's not one of them over fifteen years of age, judging by their build!

"As to your much-vaunted Wibley, I don't mind telling you he couldn't hold a candle to the leader of this troupe! This kid, whoever he was, was simply marvellous—an actor to the finger-tips! My hat! You should just have seen him!"

May we confide a little secret to you, Temple, old bean?

The masked mummers who acted in your house were all members of the Remove Dramatic Society.

And the leader was William Wibley!

We're having this copy of the "Herald" delivered to you specially, accompanied by a small bottle of smelling-salts, which we trust will enable you to remain conscious after the shock.

Merry Christmas, old sport!

DIDN'T MINCE HIS WORDS!

Hazeldene's pater bought a prize turkey, which was accidentally swallowed up by a mincing machine and came out as saveloys.

Hazel says he never "sausage" a sad sight in all his life!

SANTA CLAUS ARRIVES

Coker's Christmas Crash

You'd imagine that that "do or die" look that comes into Coker's face about a hundred times a day would fade out round about Christmas-time, wouldn't you?

Well, it doesn't!

When Coker suddenly decided to dress up as Santa Claus and distribute gifts to the deserving poor in the village hall, determination was writ in block capitals all over his physiognomy. A steely expression was in his eyes and his jaw protruded at least half-an-inch more than usual!

To Potter and Greene he said: "I'll jolly well see that everybody in the village has a real good Christmas!"

He said it in the same tones as he might have said "I'll jolly well see that everybody in the village gets a punch on the nose this Christmas!"

When Coker does a thing he does it in style. He ordered enough tuck to supply a regiment of troops for a month and arranged for the big stores from which he obtained it to send it to his home.

Not content with that, he hired a Santa Claus costume and white whiskers and—not without difficulty—a sleigh and a pair of dashing horses!

To say that there was a sensation when Coker turned out would be to make a serious understatement. If he'd flown straight out of the clouds in a chariot drawn by a brace of pheasants, the excitement couldn't have been much more intense!

Santa Claus Coker drove down the village street at a gallop and drew up outside the village hall.

Unhappily, the gallop was so furious that he experienced a slight difficulty in drawing up in time, the result being that the horses charged through the front entrance and jammed the entire outfit in the main doorway! The villagers, rather to Coker's surprise, weren't a bit pleased about it.

When the horses and the cargo had been extricated from the wreck, Coker got to work on the gift distribution. Here again, there was a slight hitch. By some strange means the stores had sent Coker the wrong articles. It looked like real tuck, but it was only imitation tuck, intended apparently for a wholesale practical joker or some kind of a stage scene!

The villagers beamed with great cheerfulness when they were handed massive-looking hams and turkeys and plum puddings. But you should have seen their faces when they found that the hams were made of cardboard, and the turkeys of canvas, and that the plum

puddings bounced susp... like footballs.

It's marvellous to thi... a cheerful concourse, happiness and gratitu... be changed in the spa... few minutes into a mob, thirsting for gore... wouldn't have thought... sible unless it had been... strated to him. But... demonstrated to him... mistakably that he w... glad to be able to m... exit out of one of the w...

If you think that Col... it up after that you'... wrong. Behind the whiskers he still wore... expression was even m... conquerably determine... it had been before.

What he did was to h... to run him into the tow...

There he called at th... obtained the parcel wh... been intended for hi... also purchased a small s... second-hand police trunc...

Having divided th... cheons between hims... the heroic Potter and... he returned to the vill... in triumph and kept b... aggressive villagers, w... explained that he had ju... made up his mind to giv... happy Christmas and gi... a happy Christmas he w...

And after that there... more trouble. Coker... beamed again and San... Coker did his stuff a... to programme.

So far as we know... first time on record... Claus has ever distribu... with one hand while t... ingly flourishing a poli... cheon in the other. Bu... always is breaking... anyway!

A "SOLELESS" T...

Stott asks if anyone... old footwear to give aw...

Bunter invited him to... Court for Christmas an... has worn out all his boo... to find it!

WOULD YOU BELIEVE IT?

Smithy and Skinner had a wager as to who was the fatter—Bunter or his sister, Bessie, of Cliff House School. The result was a tie—there is nothing to choose between them!

William Wibley's impersonations are very popular in the Remove. His burlesque of Mr. Prout ended in a licking, though, when Prouty came up unexpectedly behind him!

Horace Coker called on Wing... the other day to demand a pl... in the First XI. Wingate s... this was the 37th time this te... that he has had to show Co... the door!

Herald

EXTRA GOOD EDITION

WHARTON. December 23rd, 1933.

BROKE DOWN WHILE BREAKING UP

Skinner's Tearful Farewell

It was quite a shock to us to find Skinner of the Remove quietly weeping in a corner of the quad on breaking-up day.

"Skinner, old chap——" we said, gently.

"Don't—don't ! " moaned Skinner. "Words only make it worse ! "

"But what's wrong, old fellow ? " Skinner gulped.

"It's—it's the thought of leaving the dear old school behind," he said huskily. "The grey old pile of buildings—the noble elms—the grassy playing fields. It seems hard to break with them, doesn't it ? Latin, for instance. I can hardly bear the thought that I shall do no more Latin for a time ! "

"Oh crumbs ! " we exclaimed, involuntarily.

"And no more impots, either ! " went on Skinner, with a deep sigh. "Life will scarcely seem worth the living without impots ! No prefects to send us up to bed at nine-thirty ! Can you wonder that I weep ? "

"Oh, my hat ! "

"Worst of all," groaned Skinner, "there'll be no masters to cane us and no Head to dust our pants with the jolly old birch. Won't it be awful ? "

"Look here, you silly ass——"

"Last, but not least, we shan't have the chance of partaking of doorsteps and scrape in Hall for tea. Somehow or other we'll have to put up with mince pies and Christmas cake and pastries ! Oh, I can't bear to think of it ! "

And Skinner burst into a flood of bitter tears.

We picked up a handful of snow and stuffed it down the collar of the weeping Removite.

For a man so broken by emotion, Skinner hit out in a surprisingly effective manner !

CHRISTMAS DUFF REPLACED REBUFF

Loder Welcomes Remove Waits

Bulstrode thought it would be a great idea to serenade Loder with a few Christmas carols.

Bulstrode's home is near Loder's. Brown and Penfold are staying with Bulstrode, and Carne and Walker with Loder. And Bulstrode and Brown and Penfold have a few old scores to settle with Loder and Carne and Walker.

"It'll just serve him right to have to listen to 'em," Bulstrode said, with quite unChristmas vengefulness. "I can play my cornet. I know Loder doesn't like it."

"My hat ! I should think not, either ! " grinned Brown.

"You can bring your tin-whistle, Penfold ; that's

enough to give a blue fit to anyone with a sense of music ! "

"Here, what the thump ! " protested Penfold.

"And Browny can sing," chuckled Bulstrode. "If that doesn't spoil their Christmas dinner for 'em, nothing will ! "

"You silly ass ! " was Brown's indignant comment. But Browny was willing to agree that in combination with Bulstrode's cornet and Penfold's tin-whistle his voice might sound reasonably painful, so he fell in with the wheeze.

Confidently anticipating that Loder and Carne and Walker would greet their musical efforts with a salvo of such missiles as happened to be in the immediate vicinity, Bulstrode & Co. took with them a healthy supply of ripe tomatoes, over-ripe eggs, and paper bags filled with soot, so that they might effectively respond.

But a surprise was in store for the Greyfriars waits.

There was no question whatever about their musical efforts being painful. We are positively assured that after the first two bars Loder's cat had a fit, and the village fire brigade turned out under the impression that an earthquake had happened.

But Loder & Co., far from disliking it, showed every sign of enthusiastic appreciation !

They appeared at the window before the Remove waits had finished the first verse of "Good King Wenceslas," and the Remove waits surreptitiously held their missiles at the "ready." But much to Bulstrode & Co.'s surprise, Loder & Co. didn't hurl abuse and flower-pots. They invited the waits into the house instead !

Bulstrode & Co. accepted the invitation principally for the reason that they were well-armed.

It wouldn't have made the slightest difference, anyway, for they had no occasion to use their armoury.

Loder & Co. were perfect hosts ! Instead of looking, as they usually do look, like demon kings in a pantomime, they wore seraphic smiles and simply oozed peace and goodwill. They dished out ginger wine and Christmas pudding, complimented the "kids" on their musical prowess, and wished them a very merry Christmas before bidding them farewell.

Bulstrode and Penfold and Brown almost tottered away form Loder's dwelling. The unexpectedness of their experience was almost paralysing !

As Bulstrode remarked afterwards, Christmas is liable to affect people like that ; but who on earth would have thought of Loder & Co. becoming infected ?

SNOOP'S FIRST SNOWBALL

Snoop has never been fond of snowballing.

It's not that he has any moral objection to hurling a snowball at another person. It's the prospect of getting a snowball back that deters Snoop !

Recently Stott has been patiently pointing out to Snoop that by barring the hilarious sport of snowballing, he is missing half the fun of the winter season. Snoop has been listening, learning, and inwardly digesting.

By the time Snoop arrived home for the vac he was almost convinced that it was necessary for his salvation that he should throw a snowball at somebody.

On the first day of the holiday, while on a shopping expedition in the town, he found just the target he could have wished for—an elderly gentleman wearing a topper, who was walking twenty yards ahead of him.

Snoop dived into the snow, collected up a fine double-handful and welded it together.

Taking careful aim, he buzzed the snowball at the elderly gent's napper.

Snoop scored a bullseye first time—and for the first time in his life experienced the delicious ecstasy which comes from knocking a shining topper off its wearer's head. It was a truly delightful experience and Snoop simply howled with mirth.

Unfortunately his mirth was of short duration.

You see, the wearer of the topper turned out to be the Head !

GREYFRIARS FACTS WHILE YOU WAIT !

Tozer proudly announced Friardale was entirely free of gangsters. He changed his mind, however, when Dicky Nugent and Co. laid in wait for him with peashooters !

Cherry and Bolsover majo had a real set-to when Bob caught Bolsover bullying a fag. Bolsover was man enough, though, after being licked, to offer Bob his hand, admitting his fault!

At compulsory footer practice Bunter took 25 shots at goal ; 5 of them went over the bar and 19 went wide ! Only one shot hit the goalkeeper — Squiff — who nearly dropped the ball in surprise!

THE MYSTERY OF WHARTON LODGE

(Continued from page 13.)

begin to guess. Evidently there was some sort of a misunderstanding, though he could not imagine the cause. His one thought was to get after the nabob before it was too late and make him explain. With a good start, and being unlikely to lose time on the road, the nabob would reach Wimford and catch the early train before he could be overtaken if Wharton went on foot. It was no weather for cycling, but he had to risk it.

In five minutes Wharton was running downstairs. Thomas, blinking with sleepy eyes, was holding his bike ready for him outside. Wharton took it hurriedly.

"Lot of snow, sir," said Thomas. "Mind you don't get a skid, sir."

Wharton shot away to the gates, ran his machine into the road, and started for Wimford. He could not doubt that that was the direction taken by Hurree Jamset Ram Singh. The village station was nearer, but there were no early trains there.

The bike shot along the snowy road.

It was hard riding. Snow was on the road, hard and frosty, and several times the machine slipped and skidded, and Wharton barely righted it again. But he kept on fast. Somehow he had to catch Hurree Singh before Hurree Singh could catch the early train from Wimford.

But the nabob, though he had a well-packed suitcase to carry, had made the best of his start, and was making good speed. Wharton was a mile from home when he spotted a dark figure on the white road ahead, bag in hand, tramping steadily and swiftly along in the rising wintry sunlight.

He rode on, rapidly overhauling the nabob. As the bike drew nearer Hurree Singh probably heard it, but he did not look back. Harry Wharton shouted:

"Inky! Hold on!"

Then the nabob glanced over his shoulder. His dusky face was expressionless, but his eyes were like steel.

He gave the captain of the Remove one cold glance, and then strode on again, rather faster than before.

"My hat!" breathed Wharton.

He slogged on through the snow. But for his certainty that there was some strange, extraordinary misunderstanding, his own anger would have risen hot at that icy look from the nabob, and he would have stopped and turned back. As it was, he rode on harder than ever, and drew swiftly nearer the tramping junior.

"Inky! Stop! Oh crumbs!" gasped Wharton, as the bike skidded again, and this time he failed to right it.

It shot away right after the nabob, and before Wharton quite knew what was happening, it crashed into Inky's back.

There was a yell from Hurree Singh as he was knocked over headlong, sprawling in the snow, his suitcase flying from his hand.

Wharton landed with a bump in a

THE MAGNET LIBRARY.—No. 1,349.

drift of snow beside the road, and sprawled there, panting for breath.

Hurree Singh was the first on his feet. But Wharton was quick to clamber up out of the drift.

He ran towards Hurree Jamset Ram Singh, who was rubbing the damaged place where the skidding bike had hit him.

"Inky, old chap——" panted Wharton.

Hurree Jamset Ram Singh ceased to rub his bruise and drew himself erect. He stared the captain of the Remove in the face.

"Whyfully have you followed me?" he demanded sharply.

"I want to know what you mean, you silly ass!" exclaimed Wharton warmly. "What the dickens is the matter with you, I'd like to know?"

The nabob shrugged his shoulders.

"Is that all?" he asked.

"Look here, Inky——"

"I am Inky to my friends!" said Hurree Jamset Ram Singh.

"My only hat! And aren't we friends any longer?" exclaimed Wharton, too astonished to be angry. "What do you mean?"

"I mean what I say!" answered the nabob coldly. "If the esteemed Wells has given you my letter——"

"I have it here! That's why I bolted after you."

"I see no reason for boltfully pursuing a departing and unwelcome guest!" said the nabob, with a curl of the lip. "As I have said in my ridiculous letter, I regret terrifically having outstayed my welcome in your absurd residence——"

"Look here, Inky, let's have this plain!" said Harry. "You've got some sort of bee in your bonnet! What's put this into your head?"

"Is it not the esteemed fact?"

"Of course not, fathead! You must be mad," said Harry, in wonder, "cutting off like this, when our friends are coming in a day or two! If we were at Greyfriars, I should think somebody had been pulling your silly leg—some mischief-making worm like Skinner—but there's nobody at home to do such a thing. Have you been dreaming, or what?"

Hurree Jamset Ram Singh fixed his dark eyes keenly on Wharton's rather excited face. He was puzzled.

"The understanding is not great!" he said. "Your absurd words do not coincide with your ridiculous actions!"

"If I've done anything——" said Wharton blankly. "I haven't the faintest idea what! Give it a name, Inky! I don't know what it is."

"The knowfulness is terrific!" said the nabob coolly.

"You don't mean to say that you don't believe me, Inky?"

"Quitefully so!"

Wharton stood still. His anger was rising now. But he kept his temper.

"If you want to clear," he said quietly, "I don't want to stop you. But you're making out that I've done something that makes you think you're unwelcome in my uncle's house. I want to know what it is! You're bound to tell me that!" He gave a start. "You're not thinking of what happened the other day, when you fancied I'd barged you over in the park——"

"It was not fancy!" said Hurree Jamset Ram Singh. "Some ridiculous person barged me over; but I believed what you said. Perhapsfully I was terrifically dense not to take a hint. But what you have done since leaves me no absurd doubt in the matter."

"What have I done, you fathead?"

"It is absurdly useless to discuss that when the knowfulness is great. What is the use of idiotic humbug?"

"Humbug!" repeated Harry.

"Exactfully! I shall make no complaint to the esteemed colonel, if that is what troubles you!" said the nabob, his lip curling again. "You may tell him what you please, and I shall say nothing."

He stepped to his fallen suitcase, picked it up, and swung away up the road towards Wimford.

Harry Wharton stared after him, almost in stupefaction.

"Inky——" he gasped.

The nabob strode on.

Wharton dashed after him, and caught him by the shoulder. He fairly wrenched away the suitcase, and flung it into the snow.

Hurree Jamset Ram Singh spun round at him. His dark eyes were flashing and his hands were clenched.

"Leave me alonefully!" he rapped. "I am going——"

"You're not going till you've explained yourself!" roared Wharton, his eyes flashing, too. "You're treating me rottenly——"

"That is terrifically appropriate for a rotter——"

"You're calling me a rotter?"

"Precisefully!"

"By Jove, if we hadn't always been friends, I'd——"

Hurree Jamset Ram Singh stepped to the suitcase again. Wharton pushed him back from it.

"You've got to explain——"

"Stand asidefully!" shouted the nabob.

"Not till you've explained——"

There was a push, a shove, a punch, and then, equally angry and excited, the chums of the Remove were fighting.

THE ELEVENTH CHAPTER.

Quite Mysterious!

COLONEL WHARTON started. He almost jumped.

The old military gentleman had been enjoying his walk in the keen, frosty morning. Now he was coming back towards Wharton Lodge, with a good appetite for breakfast and a healthy glow in his bronzed cheeks.

He expected to find his nephew and his nephew's schoolboy guest down when he got to the lodge. Certainly he did not expect to find them on the road, a mile from the house—and still less, undoubtedly, did he expect to find them scrapping!

But that was what he saw as he came swinging along the road with his military stride.

He stared blankly at the unexpected and amazing sight. He came to a halt in his astonishment, hardly believing his eyes.

"Good gad!" ejaculated the colonel. And he strode forward with thunder in his brow.

Two excited fellows were punching one another wildly when the colonel arrived on the scene, his approach unobserved in the excitement of the moment.

Colonel Wharton intervened promptly. He grasped Harry by the collar with one hand and Hurree Singh with the other. Then, with a powerful wrench, dragged them apart.

They staggered to right and left of the angry old gentleman.

"What the thump——" panted Wharton. "Oh, you, uncle!"

"Who the—— Oh!" gasped Hurree Jamset Ram Singh. "Esteemed sahib!"

The two juniors stood crimson and panting under the stern, angry glare of the colonel.

"What does this mean?" roared Colonel Wharton. "Fighting, by Jove!

Harry, is that your treatment of a guest under your roof?"

"Oh! I—I'm sorry I—I——" stammered Wharton.

"The sorrowfulness is terrific!" gasped the nabob. "There was momentary and unfortunate loss of esteemed temper."

"Explain yourselves!" hooted the colonel. "What does this mean?"

The juniors were silent. Colonel Wharton glanced at the bike, sprawling in the snow, then at the suitcase. The bike was Wharton's, the suitcase was Hurree Singh's. The colonel stared at the latter, as if it had been the ghost of a suitcase.

"That is your bag, Hurree Singh?"

"Yes, esteemed sir."

"Where were you taking it?"

"To the railway station."

"Does that mean that you were leaving us?"

"Exactfully so."

"Did you follow Hurree Singh on your bicycle, Harry?"

"Yes!" gasped Wharton.

Colonel Wharton looked from one to the other. He was intensely angry, and his old bronzed face was very grim. But he was cool and calm.

"This must be explained," he said. "Have you been quarrelling?"

"Not that I know of," answered Harry.

"Why were you going, Hurree Singh, without a word of leave-taking?"

The nabob flushed deeply.

"I requested your excellent nephew to explain, sahib!" he answered. "I have reason to depart suddenfully."

"What reason?" barked the colonel.

No answer.

"Can you explain this, Harry?"

"No!" answered Wharton. "Inky's got his back up about something, that's all I know! If I've done anything, I'm sorry, but I can't imagine what it is."

"Has my nephew given you offence, Hurree Singh?"

"I have no execrable complaint to make, my esteemed sahib! For reasons of personal nature I desire to depart from your hospitable roof."

"You mean," said Colonel Wharton grimly, "that my nephew has given you offence, but that you do not desire to tell me so."

"Perhaps you can get out of Inky what's the matter, uncle," said Harry, considerably cooler now. "I can't make him out! I'm sorry I got excited, but it was enough to make any fellow wild! Inky, if you won't tell me what's the matter, can't you tell my uncle?"

"I have nothing to say," said Hurree Jamset Ram Singh icily. "Exceptfully that I desire immediate and prompt departure."

"You will certainly not leave us like this!" said Colonel Wharton. "I shall allow nothing of the kind! During the vacation, Hurree Singh, I am responsible for you to your headmaster. If you desire to change your quarters, you must acquaint me with where you are going, and why! You will now pick up that suitcase and walk back to the house with me!"

Hurree Jamset Ram Singh's lips set. There was a long pause.

"I am bound to obey order of esteemed sahib!" said the nabob, at last, and he picked up the suitcase.

"I'm glad you understand that!" grunted the colonel. "Pick up your machine and come along, Harry!"

Wharton picked up the bike and wheeled it on. Not a word was spoken during the return to Wharton Lodge.

Arrived at the Lodge, Colonel Wharton stalked in, still with a deeply corrugated brow.

Wells, in the hall, eyed Hurree Jamset Ram Singh very curiously. From a housemaid, Wells had received an amazing report, which had caused him to visit Hurree Jamset Ram Singh's room almost running! Wells' eyes lingered on the nabob's suitcase!

Judging from the look of affairs, it really seemed that the guest, at Wharton Lodge had walked off with his bedclothes packed in the suitcase—for they were not to be found in his room! Which was amazing!

Wharton went to put up his bike. Hurree Jamset Ram Singh stood by his suitcase, his dusky face set and expressionless. Wells gave a deferential cough, and spoke to his master in a low voice that the nabob could not hear.

"Excuse me, sir!" he murmured. "But something so very extraordinary has happened——"

"What—what?" barked the colonel.

"The bedclothes are missing from Master Hurree Singh's room, sir!"

Colonel Wharton gazed at his butler.

"The—the bedclothes?" he ejaculated.

"Yes, sir!"

"Missing?" gasped the colonel.

"Yes, sir—sheets and blankets and all, and——"

"What on earth do you mean, Wells?"

"It's very extraordinary, sir!" murmured Wells. "But such is the case. Janet called my attention to it only a few minutes ago, sir, and I went at once to the room. All the bedclothes are missing!"

"Good gad!"

Wells coughed again.

"I—I suppose the dark young gentleman is—is quite right in his head, sir?" he murmured.

"Wha-a-at?"

"It is so very extraordinary, sir, for a young gentleman to pack up his bedclothes in a suitcase, and walk off with them——"

"Very extraordinary, if true!" gasped the colonel. "Are you mad, Wells?"

"Well, sir, they are gone—completely gone!"

Snort, from the colonel.

"Nonsense! Absurd! How can they be gone?"

"They are missing, sir, and cannot be found!"

"Nonsense!" hooted the irritated colonel. "Utter nonsense! Why should the boy play such an absurd trick!"

The colonel stalked away to the breakfast-room. Wells, excellently trained butler as he was, gave the slightest shrug of the shoulders.

THE TWELFTH CHAPTER.
The Culprit!

BREAKFAST at Wharton Lodge was rather a silent meal that morning.

Colonel Wharton was in a state of suppressed irritation. Harry Wharton was puzzled and annoyed. Hurree Jamset Ram Singh wished himself anywhere but where he was. Only Miss Amy Wharton, unaware that anything was amiss, was in her usual kind and placid mood; and, having the conversation to herself, she talked gently and sweetly about little preparations she was making for the benefit of the poor in the village that Christmas.

After breakfast, the two juniors were told that the colonel desired to speak to them in the library, and they repaired to that apartment to wait for him.

They waited in silence.

Wharton made one attempt to break through the quiet, impassive reserve of the nabob.

"Look here, Inky!" he said. "We both played the fool when my uncle came on us on the Wimford road this morning. We lost our tempers! I'm sorry, and I dare say you are! My uncle's upset about this! I can't make you out! Can't you tell me what's the matter?"

Hurree Jamset Ram Singh did not seem to hear.

He moved across to the window, and stood looking out at the snow-gleaming trees, with his back to the captain of the Greyfriars Remove.

Wharton bit his lip, and said no more.

It was some little time before the colonel entered. His brow was grim and stern when he came, and he closed the door after him with almost a bang.

He strode across to the fire, stood with his back to it, and faced the two schoolboys, the nabob coming from the window towards him.

"Now," said Colonel Wharton, in a deep voice, "this matter has to be explained. I can hardly believe, Harry, that you have been guilty of any discourtesy towards a guest—one of your own school friends——"

"I hope not," said Harry.

"Hurree Singh must have had a reason for his action! You do not know what it is?"

"I have no idea."

"Very well. Now, Hurree Singh, explain yourself! You are a guest here, but you are also a schoolboy under my charge, for the moment. I command you to tell me why you left my house at an early hour."

"The departfulness seemed to me the proper caper, sahib!" answered the Nabob of Bhanipur.

"Why?"

No answer.

"Inky seems to think that I don't want him here," said Harry. "What's put the idea into his head I can't imagine. So far as I know, I've done nothing. I was simply astounded when Wells gave me his letter——"

"His letter! Give it to me!"

Wharton passed over the nabob's farewell note. His uncle read it through, with frowning brows.

"There is some misunderstanding," he said. "Certainly it appears that Hurree Singh has a false impression. What has given you this impression, Hurree Singh?"

"I desire to say nothing, honoured sahib."

Colonel Wharton looked from one to (*Continued on next page.*)

the other. Wharton's face expressed only perplexity; Hurree Singh's nothing at all. The old, military gentleman was growing more and more mystified, and more and more irritated.

"It is clear to me," he said, "that you fancy that my nephew has done something, and you will not tell me, because it may make me angry with him. That is all very well; but I must know the facts. You have not been playing some schoolboy trick, Harry, which your friend has taken in bad part?"

"No!"

The nabob glanced at Wharton for a second, with a flash of scorn in his eyes. It was but for a second, but it did not escape the colonel's keen observation.

"So that is it!" he said. "That is what you have in your mind, Hurree Singh! What has my nephew done?"

No reply.

"Now," said the colonel, "I have learned from Wells that some inexplicable trickery has been going on. The bedclothes have been removed from Hurree Singh's room. Do you know anything of this, Harry?"

"My hat! No!" said Harry blankly.

"You did not remove them?"

"Of course not!"

"You, Hurree Singh, are not so foolish as to play a silly trick on the servants in this way?"

"Certainfully not!"

"Very well! A trick has been played! Did you find the bedclothes missing when you went to bed last night, Hurree Singh?"

Wharton started, and stared at the nabob.

"Who on earth could have played such a trick?" he exclaimed. "Inky, you ass, if anybody pulled your leg like that, surely you weren't fool enough to think that it was I!"

The nabob compressed his lips, and did not answer.

"We are getting to the truth, I think!" said the colonel sharply. "Hurree Singh, answer me at once. Did you, or did you not, find your bedclothes missing when you went to bed last night?"

"Yes, sahib!"

"Then how did you spend the night?"

"In the excellent armchair by the fire."

"And why," demanded the colonel, "did you not make the matter known at once?"

Hurree Jamset Ram Singh was silent.

"Was it because you believed that my nephew had played that silly trick on you, and you believed that it was meant to signify that he did not desire you to remain as his guest?"

"Inky, you ass——"

"Let Hurree Singh speak!" rapped the colonel. But the nabob did not speak. Colonel Wharton went on: "A handkerchief belonging to you has been found lying in Hurree Singh's room, Harry. Did you drop it there?"

Wharton's hand went to his pocket.

"No; my hanky's here," he said. "Besides, I haven't it in the room."

"You are sure of that?"

"Of course!"

"Did you see my nephew's handkerchief there, Hurree Singh, and did it lead you to believe that he had played that miserable and foolish trick?"

"So that's it!" said Wharton. "You might have had a little more sense, Inky! Why couldn't you come along to my room and speak out?"

The nabob's lip curled.

"You have acted thoughtlessly and inconsiderately, Hurree Singh," said Colonel Wharton. "Pride is all very well, but there is such a thing as common sense. Someone has been THE MAGNET LIBRARY.—No. 1,349.

guilty of rascally trickery. I have no doubt that I can lay my finger on the person concerned."

Hurree Singh gave a start.

"Wells informed me yesterday of a foolish practical joke played by the boy Thomas!" said the colonel. "It appears that he gave my nephew a false alarm, and brought him running down to the telephone in the belief that there had been an accident."

"Thomas!" exclaimed Wharton. "Of course! That young sweep——"

"Thomas!" repeated the nabob blankly. "I did not think——"

"You ought to have thought!" rapped Wharton. "You might have remembered that he'd played a silly trick before."

Hurree Singh's face set again.

"Your handkerchief was there," he said coldly. "If it was Thomas, he could not have dropped your handkerchief."

"That, of course, was a part of the trickery," said Colonel Wharton. "I take my nephew's word on that subject, Hurree Singh, and expect you to do the same. The handkerchief was placed there by the trickster, to give a false impression."

Hurree Singh was silent.

Colonel Wharton touched the bell, and Wells appeared at the door.

"Send Thomas here," said the colonel.

"Very good, sir!"

Thomas appeared in a few moments. His chubby face had a rather alarmed look, and he blinked from one face to another.

"Thomas!" rapped Colonel Wharton. "Yesterday you played a foolish practical joke on my nephew."

"Oh, sir! I never did——"

"Silence! I should have passed over that incident, but now you have repeated your foolish and disrespectful conduct, and caused a misunderstanding between friends. You will leave this house to-morrow! You are discharged, Thomas!"

"Oh, sir!" gasped Thomas.

"You will tell Wells where you have hidden the bedclothes——"

"I ain't touched them, sir! I don't know nothing——"

"Silence!" roared the colonel. "If you have purloined these articles, and removed them from the house, you will be severely dealt with. I warn you to inform Wells at once where you have concealed them! Go!"

"Oh, sir! But——" gasped Thomas, overwhelmed with dismay.

"Go!" roared the colonel.

And Thomas, in a state of utter bewilderment, went.

"Now, my boys," said the colonel, more calmly, "the matter is cleared up. It was a misunderstanding. Let there be no more."

He dismissed the juniors with a gesture, and they left the library together.

THE THIRTEENTH CHAPTER.
Strained Relations !

"MASTER HARRY——"

"You young rascal!"

"Oh, sir!"

"Don't speak to me, you young sweep! You ought to be jolly well ashamed of yourself!" said Wharton indignantly.

Wharton and Hurree Singh had gone out on the frosty terrace after leaving the colonel. To Wharton's mind the mysterious matter was now cleared up. There seemed no doubt about that. But he was feeling considerably sore about it. Hurree Jamset Ram Singh

hardly knew what to think. Keen and astute as he was, the nabob was quite perplexed. The hapless Thomas came creeping out, looking like a fellow whose world had fallen to pieces. The two juniors were worried and troubled, but their feelings were nothing to poor Thomas'.

"I never did it, sir!" said Thomas, almost tearfully. "As if I'd play such a game on a friend of yours, sir! Won't you speak a word for me to the master, sir?"

"You're not denying it?" exclaimed Wharton angrily.

"Course I am, sir, when I never did it! You don't believe that I did it, Master Hurree Singh, sir?" Thomas appealed to the nabob.

Hurree Jamset Ram Singh shook his dusky head.

"The believefulness is not terrific, my esteemed Thomas," he answered.

"You 'ear what your friend says, Master Harry," urged Thomas. "He knows I wouldn't do it, and him always kind to a feller. If you speak a word to the master——"

"Oh, ring off!" snapped Wharton. "You'd better go and tell Wells what you've done with the things, you young sweep! Cut!"

Thomas gave him a beseeching look, but he "cut" without saying anything more.

Wharton faced the nabob with a glitter in his eyes.

"Now let's have this out, Hurree Singh," he said, between his teeth. "There may be some excuse for you thinking I'd played that rotten trick, finding my hanky there. But you've heard me tell my uncle that I knew nothing of it. Can you take my word, or not?"

Hurree Jamset Ram Singh looked at him in silence for a long moment. From the appearance of things, it looked as if Wharton had played that trick on him, as a hint that he was no longer wanted at the Lodge, and had lied about it afterwards to avoid trouble with his uncle. But that was not in the least in accord with what he knew of Wharton's character. It was scarcely possible to suppose that Harry Wharton had lied like a fellow of Billy Bunter's stamp. Yet he was convinced that the hapless Thomas was innocent. He spoke at last.

"I am boundfully compelled to accept your word, my esteemed Wharton," he said slowly.

"Then what did you mean by telling Thomas you believed him?"

"I believe him completefully."

"You believe me, and believe him, too!" snapped Wharton. "That means that you believe that there's a third party in it."

"That is the lookfulness of it."

"Who, then? Who do you fancy snaffled your bedclothes last night? Old Wells?" asked Wharton, with angry sarcasm. "Or one of the maids?"

"That is scarcely possible. But——"

"Well, who then?"

The nabob shook his head.

"The knowfulness is not great," he answered.

"My uncle, perhaps?" There was something very like a sneer in Wharton's tone. "Do you think the colonel has taken to playing schoolboy japes on a guest?"

Hurree Singh smiled faintly.

"You know that young idiot, Thomas, played a potty practical joke on us both yesterday," said Wharton resentfully. "He gave me a rotten scare, and snaffled the cake while we were gone down to the phone. Isn't it

Billy Bunter struck match after match, to get his bearing, as it were. He could not venture to turn on the light. It was not the most comfortable way of taking supper. But the fat Owl cared little for that as he got busy. For a good half-hour there was a steady sound of munching, varied by an occasional grunt!

as clear as daylight that he's done this, too?"

"It looks like it," admitted the nabob; "but——"

"But what?"

"But I think he was speaking with terrific truthfulness. The putfulness of your idiotic hanky in my room was not a practical joke. It was an act of preposterous rascality. The esteemed Thomas is a fool, perhaps, but I do not thinkfully consider him a rascal."

"Well, I should never have thought so," said Harry slowly. "He always seemed a decent kid enough, and I thought he rather liked me. I always rather liked him. But the facts speak for themselves."

"I thinkfully opine that we have not yet ascertained the ridiculous facts. There is a thirdful party in the absurd matter."

"Well, who then?"

Hurree Jamset Ram Singh could only shake his head. Perhaps, at the back of his mind, he was not wholly convinced of his chum's innocence. There was a silence.

"Oh, let it drop, then!" said Harry, at last. "If you're satisfied now that I haven't acted like a pig, as you supposed——"

"If I have wrongfully doubted you, my esteemed Wharton, the apologise is terrific."

"If!" exclaimed Wharton. "Then you're not satisfied yet?"

"Yes," said the nabob, though with an almost visible effort. "The satisfaction is total. I cannot think that you would tell lies. I am terrifically satisfied on that point."

"Thanks for that much!" said Wharton sourly. "That's something, I suppose." He tried to make his tone more friendly. "Coming out?"

"It is terrifically cold!" murmured the nabob.

"The lake's frozen. Let's get our skates."

Hurree Jamset Ram Singh paused.

"If you will excusefully forgive me, I will proceed to my room and write a letter," he said. "I have long delayed a communication with my old esteemed tutor, the moonshee Mook Mookerjee at Bhanipur."

"Just as you like," said Wharton curtly.

He went for his skates, and went out to the frozen lake by himself. It was a bright, clear, frosty morning, and the ice was hard and good; but the captain of the Greyfriars Remove did not enjoy the skating very much.

Hurree Singh went to his room.

It was true that he had a letter to write to Mook Mookerjee, the wise old moonshee of Bhanipur, who taught him the wonderful English he spoke. And he wrote it in the weird Indian characters which Greyfriars fellows, when they saw them, compared to crawling spiders and ants.

But when he had finished that letter he did not join his chum.

He remained in his room, thinking.

It was not easy for a bitter and unpleasant impression to be removed from his mind. He believed, or tried hard to believe, that his chum had not offended, and that he was as welcome as ever at Wharton's home. But he wished that he wa anywhere else. Yet, in the circumstances, he could scarcely leave. It was a disagreeable position all round; but it seemed that there was nothing to be done.

The chums of the Remove did not meet again till lunch. Then they tried to be as friendly and cordial as of old —but not with much success. Miss Amy, fortunately, noticed nothing; but

her brother did, and his brows knitted grimly more than once.

The chums of Greyfriars, for the present, were not enjoying life—but, if they had only known it, still less was the unknown cause of the trouble finding life enjoyable! Billy Bunter was having an awful morning!

THE FOURTEENTH CHAPTER.
The Artful Dodger!

"OH lor'!" said Billy Bunter, for about the hundredth time.

Bunter had slept till about ten o'clock in the morning. That was so much to the good.

But when he awoke he awoke hungry!

Not a crumb remained of the provender he had bagged the previous day. In the peculiar circumstances, the fat Owl of Greyfriars would have done wisely to put himself on rations! But Bunter seldom acted wisely—and he had not even thought of that!

He had slept quite soundly and comfortably. Had anyone gone up the attic stair, certainly the fat junior's hefty snore would have been heard. Luckily for Bunter, no one did.

"Oh lor'!" repeated Bunter.

He wondered a little what Hurree Jamset Ram Singh had done, and what had happened, and whether there had been a row. But he did not think much about it. The fact that he was hungry occupied his thoughts, to the exclusion of lesser matters.

He rather regretted now that he had turned in and slept so soundly. In the darkness of the night he might have hunted provender.

But it was too late to think of that now.

What was he going to do?

He had landed himself at Wharton Lodge. Apparently he would be able to remain there unsuspected

But no fellow could live without food—least of all Billy Bunter! The question of the commissariat was urgent!

He intended of course, sooner or later, to make his presence known—anxious as he was for a burrow, he was not keen on spending Christmas-tide hidden in an attic—even if there was a supply of grub!

But he had to make sure first that the revelation would not be followed by the impact of a boot on his tight trousers, and sudden departure into a cold, unfeeling world!

How was he to make sure of that?

It was rather a problem.

If he could catch that beast, Wharton, in a good temper—an if the beast, being in a good temper, could prevail on the other beast, his uncle, to get good-tempered, too——

It seemed doubtful!

Still, there was no hurry to put it to the test—if he could only obtain supplies to tide him over for a time.

That was the urgent pressing matter! There was the rub! He got up hungry! He grew hungrier every moment! There was no breakfast! The bare idea of missing lunch also was excruciating

He silently unlocked the door, to blink out of his hidden quarters. Either of the juniors might have left chocolates, or something of the kind, in his room.

Again and again Bunter blinked out, but was frightened back by the sound of a footstep or a voice There were servants about. Once he heard the voices of the maids; and once a snatch of conversation came to him, in voices that he recognised as those of Wells and Thomas.

"I never did it, Mr. Wells, sir!" Thomas was saying

"Don't you tell untruths, Thomas! You're discharged, and you deserve it!" said Wells severely.

They were in the passage below the attic stair, and every word came clearly to Bunter, with his door ajar, and his fat ears pricked up to listen.

"But I never did, sir——"

"You pay attention to me, Thomas!" said Wells. "Tell me at once what you've done with the bedclothes from Master Hurree Singh's room."

"I ain't touched them, Mr. Wells."

"What are you giving all this trouble for, Thomas? I can't believe you're thinking of stealing bedclothes. What have you done with them?"

"I tell you, sir——"

"The colonel may charge you with theft, if you don't return them," said Wells. "Think of that, Thomas!"

"I never did——"

"I've looked in your room! Have you taken them out of the house, or what?"

"I ain't never——"

"Oh, go away, you young rascal!" said Wells.

Billy Bunter grinned over that little talk. He realised that Thomas had been found guilty of the raid on Hurree Jamset Ram Singh's bed-clothes!

Bunter was sorry for Thomas! He quite pitied him Still, it was all to the good, he considered; for this suspicion of Thomas made it improbable that anyone would suspect that there was an extraneous person in the house. Later on, of course, Bunter

would clear Thomas of that unjust suspicion. For the present it was all right!

Later in the morning Bunter blinked out again and listened. All was quiet now. No doubt Hurree Singh's bed had been provided with a new outfit. The servants had finished there. The coast was likely to be clear, unless he ran into one of the juniors.

Bunter was so hungry by this time that he felt that he had to risk it. Besides, he had heard the gong downstairs that announced lunch—though not for Bunter! He thought of boldly presenting himself at lunch, and trusting to his cheek to save him. But the thought of the old colonel's grim, knitted brows daunted him. He dared not!

He crept silently down the attic stair.

Nobody was about!

With beating heart, the fat junior crept into Wharton's "den." A fire was burning there, and he warmed himself before it for a few minutes. But he had no time to waste. If anyone came upstairs to that quarter of the house, his retreat to his hiding-place was cut off. He dared not linger.

"Oh, good!" gasped Bunter, as he spotted a box of chocolates lying on Wharton's table.

It was one of Aunt Amy's many gifts to her dear nephew. Wharton, who was not keen on sweetmeats, had not opened it yet. Bunter saved him that trouble. Rapidly he opened the box and stuffed chocolates into his hungry mouth.

There was only a pound of chocolates in the box. Bunter disposed of them very swiftly. He was about to replace the lid on the cardboard box, when it occurred to him that, if Wharton moved it, he would feel by the lightness that it had been emptied

That was easily remedied. Bunter filled the box with wood-ashes from the grate, and then replaced the lid.

The box now weighed as much as before. No discovery would be made till it was opened.

Bunter could not guard against that! Still, as the beast hadn't opened it yet, probably he wouldn't be opening it in a hurry!

The fat Owl proceeded to root about the room for more provender. But there was no more to be found.

He passed into Wharton's bed-room; but that apartment was also drawn blank! He opened the door on the corridor, blinked out and listened, and then crept along to Hurree Singh's room. With the juniors at lunch, he felt fairly safe in rooting about their quarters.

Nothing of an eatable nature was discovered in the nabob's room. Bunter grunted with disgust.

Whenever Bunter was a guest anywhere, there was always something to eat in his room; he took care of that! But other fellows did not seem to think of such considerations, important as they were.

"Oh lor'!" said Bunter.

A pound of chocolates had, at least, taken the keen edge off his appetite. There might be a chance later of another raid, if Wharton tea'd in his den again, as he had done the day before. All that the fat Owl could do now was to creep back to his burrow, and, as there was nothing more to eat, take it out in sleep. Fortunately, he could always sleep!

He was about to creep out of Hurree Singh's room when there was a footstep outside.

Bunter jumped

There was no escape!

He gave a wild blink round. If it was the nabob coming to his room he was fairly caught.

"Oh crikey!" gasped Bunter.

He leaped to the bed and plunged under it! Hardly a moment later the door opened, and Hurree Jamset Ram Singh came in.

Bunter had a view of his feet as he crossed over to the fire and threw a log on it.

Then the nabob sat down, taking a set of pocket-chess, and apparently working out a game from memory.

Bunter palpitated under the bed.

Ten minutes later there came a tap at the door, and it opened.

"Coming out?" asked the voice of Harry Wharton.

"I am terrifically interested in working out an absurd problem," answered the nabob.

"Very well!" said Harry quietly; and the door closed again.

Terrifically interested as he was in the problem, the nabob laid down the chess, rose to his feet, and paced restlessly to and fro.

Bunter, under the bed, had a continuous view of his feet, passing and repassing.

Obviously, even to the obtuse Owl, there were strained relations; the chums of Greyfriars were not on their old familiar footing. Bunter's trickery had had its results! Serve them jolly well right, the beasts, was Bunter's unuttered comment! It was some satisfaction to know that, uncomfortable as he was, he had caused discomfort.

To his great relief, Hurree Jamset Ram Singh went out of the room at last. Probably now that Wharton was gone he was going out on his own! Greatly relieved to be rid of him, Bunter crawled out from under the bed. Ere long he was safe back in his attic, rolled in blankets, and finding comfort in slumber.

THE FIFTEENTH CHAPTER.
An Alarm in the Night!

MIDNIGHT! Billy Bunter was wide awake!

Probably it was the first time on record that the fat Owl of the Remove had remained awake at midnight's witching hour.

But he had slept a good deal during the day; and he was too hungry to sleep now.

Bunter was not only hungry! He was famished! He was ravenous! He had a keen understanding of the feelings of shipwrecked crews in open boats at sea!

Sleep was impossible!

Again and again, Bunter listened with the door of the attic ajar, till all sounds had died away.

At any risk he had to get hold of something to eat! Even if his presence was discovered, and he was booted out into the winter night, he could stand it no longer! Food was the one thing needful!

But he waited till he heard midnight strike from the clock in the hall downstairs! By that time he felt fairly sure all would be safe!

He knew his way about the house! Even as an invited guest on other and happier occasions, Bunter had displayed a keen interest in the larder! More than once he had paid it a surreptitious visit!

True, his depredations were certain to be discovered in the morning. He had to take the risk! They might think

(Continued on page 22.)

Wonderful GIFT BOOKS FOR BOYS

All these gift books are strongly bound in brightly coloured covers and contain features of interest to boys of all ages. They are splendidly illustrated with photographs and drawings, and some contain beautiful coloured plates. Ask your newsagent or bookseller to show you them all.

The World's Greatest Engineering Achievements

Here's a magnificent new Annual, which describes the wonderful romance of the world's greatest feats of engineering. Experts have written the intensely interesting articles which tell the fascinating story of Man's struggle with and conquest of the forces of Nature. This remarkable new book is crowded with hundreds of illustrations, photographs, and drawings, and contains four full-page colour plates.

Modern Boy's BOOK of ENGINEERING 7/6

School and Adventure Tales

This is an up-to-date book for the modern schoolboy. Its pages are alive with thrills, mystery, and adventure. The stories are of hazardous ventures in every corner of the world ; true-to-life yarns of school and sport ; thrilling tales that carry you breathlessly to the last word. Clever illustrations bring the characters to vivid life and help you to visualize the gripping situations. A book for the fireside o' nights, this, and an ideal gift for a chum. But get one for yourself in any case.

CHAMPION ANNUAL 6/-

Exciting Adventure Stories

Boys like nothing better than adventure yarns—exciting tales of school life and mystery. Such are the contents of the BRITISH BOY'S ANNUAL, which is splendidly illustrated with black-and-white drawings and coloured plates. For five shillings only, here is a gift which will delight the heart of any schoolboy from ten to fifteen years of age.

BRITISH BOYS' ANNUAL 5/-

Thrilling Stories of Modern Marvels

THE MODERN BOY'S ANNUAL is crammed with up-to-the-minute chats about aviation, railways, motor-cars, motor-cycles, engineering marvels, films, thrilling adventure stories, etc. What modern boy doesn't revel in reading about these most fascinating subjects? There are hundreds of illustrations, including two plates in colour.

MODERN BOY'S ANNUAL 6/-

Grand Stories of Gripping Adventure

The POPULAR BOOK OF BOYS' STORIES contains a magnificent collection of thrilling adventure stories that's too good to be missed. The 1934 edition of this famous annual has been enlarged to 192 pages and it is packed with big thrill yarns of adventure on land, at sea, and in the air! In fact, every phase of adventure is represented in this grand, all-fiction annual, which is splendidly illustrated.

POPULAR BOOK OF BOYS' STORIES 2/6

On Sale at all Newsagents and Booksellers

that it was Thomas again—poor Thomas! They might think that it was the cat! Whatever they thought Bunter had to eat.

He crept out of the attic at last.

All was dark!

The last door had closed; the last light had been extinguished. Bunter was free to roam the house as he liked. He realised that he had to be careful! If there was an alarm he might be taken for a burglar! He was going to be very careful indeed!

The old stair creaked under Bunter's weight as he crept from the attic. In the daytime it was hardly noticeable, but at midnight it seemed eerily loud.

On tiptoe the fat junior reached the passage and crept away towards the stairs.

Everyone had long been in bed. Billy Bunter felt a thrill of uneasiness as he navigated the silent staircase. Midnight silence and solitude and gloom did not agree with his nervous system.

Still, there was really nothing to be afraid of. Silence and darkness could not hurt anybody.

He crept across the shadowy hall to the service staircase, and crept down.

Two minutes more and he was at the larder.

It was locked; but the key was in the door.

Bunter struck a match.

Then he got busy.

Every now and then he struck a match to get his bearings, as it were. He could not venture to turn on a light.

It was not the most comfortable way of taking supper! But the fat Owl cared little for that! There was plenty —and that was the chief thing! A cold chicken was absolutely delicious to the hungry Owl! A cold pie was a dream of delight! Other foodstuffs followed the fowl and the pie! For a good half-hour there was a steady sound of munching, varied by an occasional grunt!

Then Bunter sighed!

There was still more to eat—but he could eat no more!

Bunter was not a fellow, as a rule, to think of the future! Generally he left it to take care of itself! But on this occasion, mindful of his hungry hours in the attic, the Owl of Greyfriars exercised foresight. He might not have another chance like this! Scratching matches to light him on his pilfering way, Bunter proceeded to stack his pockets with plunder.

All sorts and conditions of eatables were crammed into his pockets till they would hold no more. But that did not satisfy Bunter! There was a basket at hand, and he crammed that, too! Only too well he knew how soon he might be hungry again!

Taking the basket in his hand he crept away to the service staircase and ascended to the hall above.

It was getting towards one o'clock now; and now that Billy Bunter was as full as he could hold, he felt that he would be able to sleep.

His motions were rather slow as he crossed the hall to the stairs. He had rather a lot to carry!

The darkness was deep, but he knew the way well enough. With the well-laden basket in one hand and the other stretched before him to grope the Owl of the Remove crept onward.

Suddenly he gave a gurgle of horror.

His outstretched hand had touched something in the darkness—something that moved!

Something alive!

"Ooooogh!" gurgled Bunter in utter terror.

He heard a startled gasp, and had a THE MAGNET LIBRARY.—No. 1,349.

glimpse of eyes in the darkness that glared! He had run into somebody— obviously not an occupant of the house, creeping about in the dark as Bunter himself was doing!

A hand grasped at him.

Bunter dodged back, quaking with fear.

"Ow!" he gasped. "Oh! Who—— Ow! Help! Oh, help! Burglars! Help! Help! Help!"

In his terror the fat Owl forgot that he had to keep his presence in the house a secret. He forgot everything but his awful terror of that unseen form that was grasping at him. His frightened yell rang through the House from end to end.

A muttered oath came to his fat ears, and he felt the dim figure grasping at him. A hand gripped his fat shoulder.

Without even thinking—he was too terrified to think—Bunter swung up the basket of "grub" and smote.

Crash!

The burglar, undoubtedly he was a burglar, certainly had not expected that! He could not have expected to find anybody up in the dark, at one in

the morning! Least of all could he have expected the person who was up to be carrying a heavy basket in his hand! Probably the whole affair was a puzzle to the burglar!

The basket crashed fairly into his face, sending him spinning backwards. There was a terrific crash as he landed on his back on the oak floor. The back of his head banged on the hard oak with stunning effect. Foodstuffs of all sorts flew right and left from the basket, and the basket itself flew from Bunter's hand.

There was a sound of a door opening in the distance somewhere. A deep voice boomed:

"What is that? Who is calling? What——"

The sound of Colonel Wharton's voice recalled Bunter to himself. He realised that it was a burglar whom he had floored with the basket. He knew, too, that whoever it was he was sprawling on the floor, out of reach. He remembered that he had to make his own escape.

Colonel Wharton's deep voice had, in fact, almost as terrifying an effect on Bunter as the burglar.

Bunter bolted.

Heedless of the basket he had dropped and the scattered provender, Bunter flew up the stairs. In that thrilling moment

Bunter forgot even food—which was a proof how wildly excited he was!

He reached the wide old oak landing and darted into the passage that led to Harry Wharton's quarters.

Hardly had he bounded into the passage, when the light flashed on in another passage and on the landing and in the hall. Colonel Wharton, alarmed by the sudden outcry in the middle of the night, was coming to investigate, flashing on the electric lights as he came.

But Bunter had disappeared—just in time!

He raced along the corridor on which the juniors' rooms opened. He could hear both Wharton and Hurree Singh moving in their rooms, and see the light gleaming under their doors; the outcry had alarmed them also, and they were turning out.

Bunter did the passage to the attic stair at about sixty m.p.h. Discovery threatened—and never had the fat Owl exerted himself so tremendously.

Wharton's door was opening as the fat junior reached the attic stair and bolted up it.

Again he was just in time to escape before Wharton flashed the light on in the corridor.

Breathless, panting, palpitating, Billy Bunter reached the attic, dived in, and shut the door after him.

He turned the key in the lock.

Then he sank down in a gasping, spluttering heap on the bedclothes and gurgled.

"Oooo-er! Oh lor'! Oh crikey! Oooooogh!"

———

THE SIXTEENTH CHAPTER.
Captured !

"BURGLARS!"

Colonel Wharton rapped out the word.

From a switch on the high landing he flashed on the light in the hall below, and, staring over the oaken balustrade, he beheld a startling and remarkable sight.

A man in shabby attire, with a dirty handkerchief tied over the lower part of his face by way of a mask, was sitting up dizzily on the floor of the hall.

He was gasping spasmodically and rubbing the back of his head, which had hit the old oak with a terrific bang.

He was surrounded by a strange assortment of goods—some dropped by Bunter and some by himself as he fell. A silver candlestick, a bronze clock, and several other such articles lay amid two or three loaves, packets of butter and ham and cold meats, several cakes, and other edibles. It was quite an assortment!

Colonel Wharton, in slippers and dressing-gown, stared down at him. He had grabbed up his old Army revolver when he rushed out of his room. With that weapon in his hand he dashed down the stairs to the hall.

The burglar, for the moment, was too deeply absorbed in getting his wind and rubbing his damaged head to heed him.

But as the old military gentleman jumped from the stairs the rascal scrambled to his feet.

"Stand where you are!" roared Colonel Wharton, raising the revolver. "Stand still, you scoundrel, or I'll pull trigger!"

The revolver was not kept loaded. The old colonel, always a stickler for the exact truth, did not say that he would fire. He could scarcely have done so with an unloaded revolver. But he could pull trigger if he liked.

"Ow!" gasped Bunter, quaking with fear. "Help! Burglars!" Without even thinking, Bunter swung up the basket of "grub," and smote. Biff! The basket crashed fairly in the burglar's face, sending him spinning backwards.

"Lumme!" gasped the man in the grubby mask.

Still rubbing his damaged head he blinked at the colonel. who advanced on him with long strides, the revolver up.

"Stand! Stop!" roared the colonel.

The man in the grubby mask turned and bounded away There was a double staircase in the hall of Wharton Lodge. As the colonel came from one stair the midnight marauder bounded for the other.

Had the revolver been loaded the old soldier might have dropped him with a bullet in his leg; as it was he rushed after him in hot pursuit.

The shabby man fairly flew. Colonel Wharton was an active man for his years, but he had no chance in a race with the thief. The latter would certainly have won the race, but just then two figures in pyjamas appeared ahead of him.

Harry Wharton and Hurree Jamset Ram Singh arrived on the landing together just as the man in the shabby attire reached it.

"Back up, Inky!" shouted Wharton.

"The back-upfulness is terrific!" exclaimed the nabob.

They jumped at the man together.

They got him on the edge of the landing. With a startled howl, he went over, rolling on the stairs, and the two juniors, clutching him, rolled with him. All three went rolling down, and Colonel Wharton jumped back just in time to avoid being swept away by the avalanche.

"Oh, my hat! Got him!" panted Wharton. "Hold on!"

"Oh, my esteemed hat!"

"Hold him!" roared the colonel.

Excited voices were heard on all sides now. Wells, the butler, appeared, Robert appeared, Thomas appeared, in various stages of deshabille. In the distance maids were shrieking. The whole house was alarmed.

Three rolling, struggling figures detached themselves in a heap from the staircase and rolled in the hall. As they bumped there, Hurree Singh lost his hold on the shabby jacket. The burglar wrenched himself away from Wharton and leaped to his feet.

The colonel grabbed at him and barely missed as the desperate man dodged. He flew across the hall.

Crash!

Wells was in the way.

He stayed in the way only a split second. He went rolling, with a breathless gasp, and the burglar jumped over him and sprinted on. He would have rushed down a passage the next moment, but Thomas, with great presence of mind, grabbed up a chair and hurled it at his legs.

The missile caught the burglar across the knees, and he made a sudden nosedive.

Bump!

"Urrrggh!" spluttered the midnight marauder.

"Well done!" boomed the colonel. "Good boy!" His grasp was on the sprawling man the next moment.

"Crikey!" gurgled the burglar.

He struggled. But the muzzle of the revolver was pressed to his ear. The colonel's left hand gripped his collar.

"Surrender, you scoundrel!" boomed the colonel.

"Take that thing away, sir!" gasped the wretched man. "S'pose it was to go orf! Crikey! It's a fair cop!"

He surrendered.

"Got him!" panted Harry Wharton. "Who is it—what? A jolly old burglar, of course——"

"An esteemed and execrable burglar!" gasped the Nabob of Bhanipur.

"Collar him!"

Many hands collared the man in the shabby attire. Thomas grasped one arm, Robert grasped the other; Wells, gasping for breath, took hold of his collar. Then the colonel released him. The grubby handkerchief had been torn away in the struggle and the man's face was revealed—a stubbly face, much in want of a shave, and still more seriously in want of a wash.

Evidently he was no professional cracksman in a good way of business; he looked more like a sneak-thief. Probably he had been on tramp, when—at an unlucky time for himself—he had decided to give Wharton Lodge his attention. Certainly he was very shabby, and there was no sign of professional burglarious implements about him.

"It's a fair cop, guv'nor!" said the man in the shabby attire. "'Ere, 'ands off, darkey!" he added, as Hurree Jamset Ram Singh added his grasp. "They got me all right!"

"The make-surefulness is the proper caper, my esteemed and dishonest friend," said the nabob.

The man blinked at him. It seemed that he had heard that remarkable flow of English before.

"Oh, you!" he ejaculated. "You're the bloke what grabbed me in the park the other hevening—wot? I 'eard you a-talking and nearly give myself away larfing!"

The nabob jumped.

"Wha-a-at?" he exclaimed blankly. "You——"

"You!" yelled Wharton.

"What is this?" exclaimed the colonel. "Have you seen this rascal before, Harry?"

"I've not seen, him, uncle," answered Wharton. "But—but the other evening —the day before yesterday—we were coming back through the park after dark, and Inky——"

"It was this esteemed rascal I ran into in the ridiculous dark, and he punchfully knocked me over!" exclaimed the nabob. "At the moment I supposed it was the esteemed Wharton japing me——"

"And I thought that Inky had run into a branch!" said Harry. "And it was this rotter—watching the place, I suppose, before he tried his hand at breaking in——"

"I was shovefully knocked over——"

"Wot was a bloke to do?" demanded the man in the shabby attire. "You run into a bloke and grabbed 'im! 'Course I pushed you hover! And there I was, be'ind a tree, while you was a-jawing——"

"You ridiculous rascal——"

"So you've been watching the place, you scoundrel?" growled the colonel.

"Couple o' days and nights, sir!" answered the midnight marauder. "And this 'ere night I got a winder open, which I thought was luck—though it ain't turned out lucky."

"Wells, take him down to the cellar, and lock him in till morning," said Colonel Wharton.

"Certainly, sir!" said Wells.

"Don't be 'ard on a bloke, guv'nor! I ain't no burglar!" said the man in the shabby attire. "I jest nipped in for a few trifles! Bless your 'eart, sir, I couldn't hopen your safe, not if I knowed where it was! I picks up a candlestick and a clock, and a few other trifles, sir. You'd 'ardly 'ave missed them, and I wouldn't 'ave got morn'n a couple of quids for 'em from a popshop, sir——"

"Take him away!"

With Wells' hand on his collar, and Thomas and Robert holding his arms, the midnight marauder was taken away to a cellar, and locked in for the remainder of the night.

Then the colonel hurried away to reassure Miss Amy, and the juniors went back to their rooms. After which, Wells and his assistants gathered up the scattered plunder in the hall—all of which, naturally, they attributed to the man in the shabby attire, never dreaming that there had been another midnight marauder on the scene.

That unknown marauder, safe in his hidden attic, was listening, with a palpitating fat heart, till all was silent again. Then he rolled himself in blankets and went to sleep.

THE SEVENTEENTH CHAPTER.
Another Mystery!

"EXTRAORDINARY, sir!" said Wells.

They were at breakfast at Wharton Lodge. Colonel Wharton had a grim expression on his face. After breakfast he was going to telephone for a constable from Wimford to take charge of the midnight marauder, locked overnight in the cellar.

Miss Amy Wharton, who had been very much fluttered and flustered by the alarm in the night, had now recovered her usual gentle equanimity; and was, indeed, considering whether the wretched man in the cellar might not be allowed to go free, considering that it was Christmas-tide; and that, to judge by his apparent exploits, he had been fearfully hungry when he got into the house!

Wharton and Hurree Jamset Ram Singh were both looking very thoughtful. The mysterious incident in the park

had been explained now. The nabob knew that it was not his chum who had knocked him over in the dark, and Wharton knew that the nabob had not bumped into a branch and imagined the rest.

Both were feeling rather compunctious. And both were wondering whether the man in the cellar might not have something to do with the other queer happenings in the house. On his own confession, he had been hanging about the place for two days and nights.

The same idea was in Wells' portly mind. After an apologetic cough Wells got it out.

"Extraordinary, sir!" he repeated, over the coffee-urn. "A silver candlestick, a clock, some golf clubs, several books, sir—picked up in various rooms that were not occupied! But the food——"

"The food!" repeated the colonel.

"The state of the larder, sir, is really extraordinary!" said Wells. "Almost everything eatable was taken away! A basket and a considerable quantity of foodstuffs was found in the hall, where the man had dropped them. But a still larger quantity of eatables is missing, and it is clear that he must have stood in the larder eating them! A very unusual appetite, sir—very unusual indeed!"

"He must have been very hungry!" said Miss Wharton.

"Undoubtedly, madam," said Wells. "Very hungry, madam—very hungry indeed! Amazingly so! Crumbs and fragments were scattered all over the place. Chicken bones, and——"

"Who gave the alarm?" asked Harry.

"That is very extraordinary, sir!" said Wells. "It appears that someone shouted for help, and awakened the master. But none of the servants seems to have been up. I have questioned them all, but no one states that he gave the alarm."

"Someone shouted!" grunted the colonel. "Otherwise I should not have been awakened."

"Certainly, sir! It is very odd that whoever did so does not admit it, as it certainly prevented a robbery! Unless, indeed, the man may have run into something in the dark, and shouted, sir, involuntarily, himself, thinking that he was seized——"

"Very improbable!" grunted the colonel. "I suppose one of the servants was up late, and does not care to admit the fact!"

Wells coughed! If some festive footman had been out late without leave, and had let himself in quietly and run into the burglar, it accounted for the circumstances. But Wells was indisposed to admit the possibility of such

things in his well-ordered household. He passed lightly over that topic.

"With regard to Thomas, sir——" he murmured.

"Thomas! What about Thomas? The boy acted very well last night—indeed, his action caused the rascal's capture," said the colonel. "But that is no excuse for the miserable trick he played on my nephew and his guest——"

"It has occurred to me, sir," said Wells, with his deferential cough, "that possibly Thomas was, as he stated, innocent, in view of what has occurred since, sir! The bedclothes from Master Hurree Singh's room have not been found, and Thomas still denies knowing anything about them."

"Oh, my hat!" exclaimed Harry. "Is it possible?"

"The possibility is terrific!"

"What!" exclaimed Colonel Wharton. "You think, Wells——"

"Well, sir, the man admits having hung about the house for the last two or three days and nights. He may have found a door or window open—possibly Master Harry's window on the balcony, sir! Certainly it is very odd that he should steal bedclothes, but, in view of the very strange assortment of plunder taken last night, such as loaves of bread, sir, and butter, and a ham——"

"Good gad!" said the colonel.

"The esteemed Wells has hit the rightful nail on its ridiculous head!" exclaimed Hurree Jamset Ram Singh. "I was surefully positive that the absurd Thomas was innocent."

"That's it!" said Harry, with a nod. "Wells has spotted it! Poor old Thomas!"

"Good gad!" repeated the colonel. "What you suggest is certainly possible, Wells! The boy seems to have played one foolish trick—but he may not have played the other! At all events, we shall extract the truth from the man now in the cellar! I will make him tell me the facts, by Jove!"

Breakfast over, Colonel Wharton descended to the cellars, followed by Wells and the two juniors. All were anxious to hear what the midnight marauder had to say on the subject of the mysterious happenings that had caused so much trouble.

Wells unlocked the cellar door.

He threw it open.

Colonel Wharton stared in—at blank space!

"Wells!" he rapped. "Where is the man?"

"Oh!" gasped Wells.

The man in the shabby attire was gone!

There was a barred window to the cellar. Or rather, there had been! Now the bars were lying on the floor! The window was open! It looked on a snowy space at the back of the house. Evidently the man in the shabby attire had not waited for the morning!

He had vanished!

"Gone!" murmured Wharton.

"Dear me!" said Wells.

Snort from the colonel!

"We may catch him yet!" he growled. "I shall certainly, in the circumstances, give Thomas the benefit of the doubt; and you may tell him, Wells, that he is not to be discharged!"

"Very good, sir!"

"But that scoundrel must be caught if possible. He may not yet be out of the grounds. I am very anxious to hear the truth from him!"

Colonel Wharton strode away, leaving Wells blinking into the empty cellar. Wharton and Hurree Singh followed the old gentleman. They also were keen to get hold of the man in the shabby attire, and hear what he had to

(Continued on page 28.)

WHEN the GREAT APES CAME!

By STUART MARTIN.

HOW THE STORY STARTED.

GERRY LAMBERT and BILLY MURCHIE, two young airmen, are flying over the African jungle, when they are forced down by an army of apes reared to crush civilisation by a renegade called Stein. By the orders of Big Ling, a giant ape-man, the two pilots are imprisoned—together with a white girl named Lola—in an underground cave. Gerry escapes, but Billy and Lola are taken aboard Big Ling's flying armada, which lays waste a Belgian outpost and captures guns and ammunition in plenty. Billy is then forced to pilot a plane and lead an expedition to strike at Europe. On nearing Algiers, Billy informs Big Ling that the French are signalling and asks for orders. "Tell them we're Belgian troops on air manœuvres," says the ape-man.

(Now read on.)

The Fall of Gibraltar !

OBVIOUSLY this was Stein's instruction. But where was Stein? His big plane was not among the fleet. Billy began to tap out a message. He had been testing Ling. The French station had not signalled, and the message Billy tapped out would be received by every station within a thousand miles. It was a short message the young pilot sent out—a hurried warning to Gibraltar to defend itself against foes from the air.

Having sent it, Billy breathed freely. Morocco loomed up, then Tangier. Gibraltar rose mighty and sullen across the straits. The usual cap of white cloud hung above the peak of the Rock.

Ling raised his gun, holding it close to Billy's body.

"Keep low," he ordered, "and pass over that ship ahead !"

He pointed towards a British battleship that was lying beyond the point of the Rock.

Billy looked back, then down swiftly. In those jerky motions he saw the situation at once. Big Ling was fumbling with the trigger apparatus that controlled the bombs slung below the plane. Close behind came the other planes, driven by the giants, trailing the barges of apes, while down below, the anti-aircraft guns of the warship were being elevated.

A sudden turn of the controls made the plane rock as the bomb fell. Simultaneously, the warship's guns belched shrapnel which fell in showers beyond the plane, the explosion of the shells pitching the craft hither and thither. But the bomb, as Billy intended, missed its objective. The only damage it did was to raise a spout of water ahead of the battleship.

A bellow of triumph from Ling rang out as he ordered the plane to circle the Rock. Round Billy piloted the mighty machine, and soon he saw the reason for Ling's exultation.

The machine following them had dropped a bomb on the battleship's deck. The guns were silenced for a while, and by the time they began firing again the planes containing the apes were out of sight in the low-lying clouds.

Still, at Ling's dictation, Billy circled the crest of the pile. The second time round, while the ship's guns were belching shrapnel, he saw the daring of the attack.

The barges had been unloaded on the very crest. Down the cliffs apes were swarming, while the giants in charge of the other machines were dropping bombs into the town and on the shipping. Explosion after explosion rent the air.

Meanwhile, Ling kept Billy's machine high above the havoc, while he himself craned his enormous head out of the plane and noted the attack. One machine went down in flames, another struck the face of the cliff and was dashed to pieces on the rocks below.

Then other planes came from inland —planes that were new to Billy, but all filled with apes, which were dropped when the planes passed over the Rock.

They came down in their harness, with the helium bladders at their necks acting as parachutes. They landed everywhere, taking advantage of every crack, every jutting cliff, and howling like mad things.

The streets of the town were a mass of flames and smoke now, and the fort guns, captured by the apes, were firing shell after shell in the direction of the warship. The vessel was forced to draw away, although its guns still fired again and again.

All through this pandemonium Billy kept his head, sending out messages as fast as his fingers could tap them. He warned London of a possible attack by Zeppelin. He remembered Stein's boasts of the raid he had forecasted, of the plans, so far as he knew them, of these ape-men headed by Stein. But his messages were fragmentary, for he feared that Ling might grasp the situation.

As he eased off sending out these warnings, Ling's voice roared out an order.

"Follow that plane ! It is signalling ! Follow it ! Stein is there !"

Once more the gun was thrust towards Billy. He saw the plane indicated, travelling rapidly northward, a special flag fluttering from its tail.

Ling kept muttering in jubilation.

"We have taken Gibraltar ! We have captured the Rock ! Now for London ! Now for Spain, France, Germany—Europe !"

Over the plains of Andalusia the two planes soared, then into the mountain region of Spain beyond. They were soon far beyond sight of Gibraltar, threading their way among the peaks.

The plane with the flag dropped at last behind a high mountain and landed on a gentle slope. Down came Billy's in its wake. He sat exhausted at the controls, staring at the strange sight before him.

Stein had stepped from his plane, but it was not Stein that Billy stared at, nor Big Ling who crawled out and sent up a howl of triumph What riveted the eyes of the boy was the fact that here, in the midst of Spain, gorillas were everywhere—on the slopes, on the rocks —crowded like sheep. Thousands of them were there, jabbering and fighting among themselves like monkeys in a zoo.

It seemed as if all the apes in the world had gathered there, and among them stalked giants like Ling, every one holding in his hand a whip of hide. Animals were training animals.

As Billy's eyes travelled over that

scene he became aware of another object that fairly made him gasp with astonishment. In a deep valley to the left he saw the enormous bulk of a Zeppelin, anchored and steady, with passenger cars running the entire length of the envelope. He was still staring at this when Stein, who had been talking with Ling, came over slowly

"Ling tells me," said Stein, looking up at Billy from the ground, "that you behaved well That is good. Will you please use the instrument in front of you to send out a message to the world?"

Watching Billy's movements, he began to dictate:

"The stolen Zeppelin, which was removed from the hangar lately in unexplained circumstances, has been sighted heading southwards. It was captured by the forces of Big Ling, the ape-man, who challenges all nations to fight for the world. His armies have just taken Gibraltar from the English after laying waste the communication lines of Northern Africa. Other victories will be broadcast shortly. Big Ling is now in Europe and declares himself king of the world."

Stein watched Billy's every movement carefully to see that the message was sent out correctly

"And now, Murchie," he said, "we intend to strike swiftly. We will rest here and then strike at London before dawn The Zeppelin is ready."

"I cannot take part in that!" cried Billy quickly. "Kill me if you like. I will not do it!"

"Don't excite yourself," returned Stein, misinterpreting the words and tone. "You are needing a rest, like the others, and we have plenty of forces for this expedition, which is but a skirmish to divert attention. We have bigger work for you in store. Manbe will be here shortly to resume his guard over you, to see you do not get into trouble with the apes. They are apt to be short-tempered, you know," he added, with a leer.

As he spoke he raised his eyes upward. The hum of a plane sounded faint and droning, like that of a bee. The machine was but a speck among the clouds high above them as it winged its way over the mountains. But Billy's heart thumped in his breast as he watched and listened. He could have sworn that he knew that engine's hum, that the plane already passing beyond the peaks of the hills was the Golden Clipper!

———

A Daring Deed!

BILLY was not wrong, either. It was indeed the Golden Clipper that was passing overhead, and at the controls was his pal, Gerry.

If Billy had had an anxious time, so, too, had Gerry. Still, although he had been rendered unconscious by his fall from the tree, he had not been trampled underfoot in the jungle, as Stein and Ling had imagined. He had escaped the hoofs of the numberless beasts by a lucky accident. The reeds into which he had fallen were on marshy ground, and were bordered by the prickly hedge that all jungle animals avoid.

He clambered to his feet, and staggered dizzily for some time, trying to collect his thoughts, and gradually the past came back to him. Darkness was falling, and his one hope was to find the

Golden Clipper, and follow Billy's advice.

He located the plane at last, after cautiously walking in widening circles. He saw Stein, too, in the cockpit of the Belgian fighting plane, just taking off.

Gerry waited until Stein got away before he approached the Clipper.

By this time night had fallen.

Realising he could do nothing in the darkness, he crept into the cockpit to take a much-needed rest.

It was long after dawn when he awoke. Vacating the cockpit, he cautiously entered the subterranean cavern, in search of food. All was quiet in the vast underground cave, save for the hissing of the geyser and the movement of the pool. As he walked round the edge of the lake he noticed that another figure had been added to the resin-coated statues. It was the figure of Captain Bergen!

Gerry turned away from the ghastly, yellow, transparent tomb, sickened at the sight, but more than ever resolved to do his part to defeat the perpetrators of such terrible outrages.

He found plenty of bananas and other food in the cave's stores, and, partaking of a substantial meal, went back to the Clipper.

There was not much petrol in the tank, and it took Gerry most part of the day to repair the damage to the struts and undercarriage. Then he had to break away the obstructions to allow for a take-off. If ever he worked hard in his life it was then. Numberless hindrances arose and had to be conquered; but Gerry conquered the task, and, after much manoeuvring, he was able to take off with safety.

There was no sign of anything unusual taking place below him as he sped northward. His intention was to call at a Belgian station for fuel. He knew every station on the route and headed for the Congo.

When he sighted the station he saw the ruin to which it had been reduced. A tortured, dying soldier, breathing his last, whispered the news of the apes' attack as Gerry knelt beside him. The petrol store had been fired, but a quantity kept underground had escaped destruction, and Gerry was able to obtain a load.

Had the Clipper not been fitted with a robot pilot worked by gyroscopes, which enabled him to snatch sleep now and then, the task before the young pilot would have been beyond human endurance. Gerry flew fairly low, hoping to catch a sign of the gorilla fleet, but all he saw was the trail of massacre and pillage in their wake. Outpost after outpost had been destroyed. Railways had been torn up. Lines of communication, thriving villages and towns had been laid waste. A hurricane of death and disaster had swept the valleys and the plains, leaving only smoking ruins and blackened soil.

The first sign of the despoilers came into view when Gibraltar was sighted. The booming of guns could be heard, and at some distance from the Rock a warship was stationed, sending shells at the mighty pile. As he flew high above the Rock, Gerry observed the situation.

Ships had been sunk in the harbour, and the town was a mass of ruins, while on the bare surface of the cliffs Gerry saw gorillas scrambling into caves and crevices. It seemed as if thousands of them were there, and the guns of the warship were trained on these forms, sending shell after shell towards them.

Gerry flew northward, over Spain, and then headed for the Bay and England. He saw Cornwall looming up, but he did not stop. London! Heston! Croydon! The evening was drawing in now. His petrol gave out when he was within sight of Aldershot. He came down in a field not far from a military camp, and lay back in his seat, exhausted and worn out, unable for the moment to climb to the ground.

But his arrival had been seen. A car came rushing along the road, and out of it jumped two men in military uniform. They hurried over to the Clipper, and Gerry saw that they belonged to the Intelligence branch of the Service.

"We have been watching for you," said one. "This is the Golden Clipper, and you——"

"How could you have been watching for me? I've just flown from Africa, and——"

"We know. We have been receiving some unusual messages from young Billy Murchie. Rather cryptic stuff. Fragments of warnings of some sort, but we can't place his position exactly. One message came from Gibraltar, another from Spain or France—you know, of course, what has been happening? There's trouble with some animals at Gibraltar——"

"Trouble!" cried Gerry. "There is war! Big Ling has opened war on the world——"

"We want you to tell us about it. Accounts are very scrappy. It is most astonishing. Gorillas have broken wild over Africa, we hear——"

When Gerry told his story the aspect assumed a much more serious phase than his hearers had been inclined to imagine. They took Gerry up to their mess and gave him food, then a higher officer came in and listened to his story. When Gerry finished, the officer nodded gravely, and then took a slip of paper from his pocket and laid it on the table.

"This is the latest message from your pal," he said quietly. "The War Office was inclined to take it as a joke, but after what you have said—if you are not suffering from some sort of hysteria, we——"

Every eye was on the slip of paper. On it were typed, in telegraphic form, the words:

"Stolen Zep attacking London to-night. Giant apes in command.— BILLY MURCHIE."

"Your friend Murchie," said the officer, "mentioned your name in some of his messages, saying you would explain things. Unfortunately, our battleplanes are all on manoeuvres just now——"

"Listen!"

There was a sound of approaching aircraft and Gerry leaped from his chair and rushed to the door, throwing it open. His eyes searched the sky. The moon was rising, and there in the distance, high above and approaching fast, was a great moving body.

"The Zeppelin!" he cried. "Look!"

The huge craft could be seen against the heavens, and it was travelling fast towards London!

"There isn't a fighting plane in the camp!" cried one of the officers, a young fellow whom Gerry rather liked. "It will be over London before we can do anything!"

"The Golden Clipper!" cried Gerry. "Give me petrol! Some bombs!"

But there were no live bombs available. Several agonising minutes passed while mechanics filled the Golden

Printed and published every Saturday by the Proprietors, The Amalgamated Press, Ltd., The Fleetway House, Farringdon Street, London, E.C.4. Advertisement offices: The Fleetway House, Farringdon Street, London, E.C.4 Registered for transmission by Canadian Magazine Post. Subscription rates: Inland and Abroad, 11s. per annum; 5s. 6d. for six months. Sole Agents for Australia and New Zealand: Messrs. Gordon & Gotch, Ltd., and for South Africa: Central News Agency, Ltd.—Saturday, December 23rd, 1933

Clipper's tank. Gerry was already in the cockpit, and into the companion seat climbed the young officer.

"Huskin is my name," he informed Gerry, as he settled down. "Lieutenant Huskin. The old man gave me permission to go. Contact!"

The Zeppelin was far ahead when they rose, lost in the night haze, the moon having been obscured by clouds.

They flew in the direction of London. Lights twinkled beneath them—Guildford, Woking, Weybridge, Walton. The Thames was a silver thread in the gloom. Hampton Court, Surbiton, Kingston. The Golden Clipper tore on.

"There it is!" cried Huskin, pointing ahead excitedly.

Against the lights of London the mighty bulk of the Zep showed up. Huskin handed a revolver to Gerry grimly. The young pilot took it, but shook his head deprecatingly.

Over Putney the chase continued. They were now less than five hundred yards behind the Zep, which was slowing down. Knightsbridge was barely a thousand feet below.

Gerry swung the Clipper over suddenly, and Huskin shifted uneasily.

"What's up?" he cried. "What are you doing?"

Instead of answering, Gerry pointed towards the Zeppelin, which was making for Buckingham Palace. It swung to the left slightly, and Gerry grasped the intention of the invaders in a sudden flash. Buckingham Palace! At that very moment the King was holding Court. The palace was a glare of lights.

"What are you going to do?" roared Huskin, as Gerry swung the Clipper higher.

"Hold tight!" came the answer. "Hold tight!"

Up zoomed the Clipper above the Zep, and as they tore past the big gasbag Gerry and Huskin could see that the crew in her saloons were composed of apes, and towering above the apes stood Big Ling, his giant form outlined sharply.

The huge ape-man saw the Clipper, and raised his hand in swift signal. A gun cracked and bullets flew through the Clipper's wings.

Up and up went the plane, soaring high above the Zeppelin, then suddenly it turned and nose-dived.

In a dizzy dive it met the huge envelope, and Huskin and Gerry were thrown from the plane as it hit the envelope and tore a huge hole in its side. A terrific explosion followed, as both pilots landed on the Zep and slid down its smooth sides. They would have fallen to death, but for their clutching hands that caught at the steel struts that bore the weight of the saloons.

The dirigible lurched drunkenly, fell away to one side, and then dropped.

The yells of the apes broke out. Many of them clambered from the cars, and Huskin, holding on with one hand, lifted his revolver and took pot shots at them as they appeared.

Meanwhile, Gerry had escaped death by inches. The Clipper disappeared into the night; but a moment later there was an explosion from below and flames shot up towards the Zep.

It seemed as if the airship refused to fall. She hung, drooping in the air, for the gas had not all escaped. Then, from one of the cars came the giant form of Big Ling, revolver in hand.

He saw Gerry, and his face went terrible in fury. Raising his gun, he fired at the young pilot. The bullet caught Gerry in the shoulder, and he would have fallen, had not Huskin gripped him and hauled him back just in time.

The two pilots looked down to what seemed certain death. They were over Hyde Park. They saw the flaming Clipper and the forms of running people. And still the Zep drooped and drooped. She was going down by the stern.

Her end came swiftly. A tongue of flame from the burning plane caught the sagging end and leaped high. Sheet after sheet of flames shot up.

Gerry yelled to Huskin excitedly.

"Jump! Down the rope!"

They seized a trailing rope, one of the anchoring chains that had broken loose, and slid down, but when they reached the end of the rope they were still twenty feet from the ground.

They dropped together and were flung across the grass by an explosion that thundered in their ears. One of the bombs striking the ground had exploded. And that explosion was the end of the airship. No bonfire had ever let up Hyde Park as that one did, and in the midst of it the apes who had remained on board met their deaths.

(Gerry has certainly saved London from destruction, but Big Ling's not beaten yet by any means, as you'll discover when you read next week's exciting chapters of this fine thrill-packed story.)

COME INTO THE OFFICE, BOYS!

Always glad to hear from you, chums, so drop me a line to the following address : The Editor, The "Magnet" Library, The Amalgamated Press, Ltd., The Fleetway House, Farringdon Street, London, E.C.4. A stamped addressed envelope will ensure a reply.

HERE is a query from Tom Walters, of Croydon. He wants to know

HOW BIG IS THE SAHARA DESERT?

It is calculated to cover an area of more than three and a half million square miles. But the Sahara is not entirely a desert, for there are large patches which are covered with vegetation. There are also rivers, which suddenly come to a standstill and never get anywhere. Apart from the shifting sand-dunes, there are also patches of stony or pebbly desert, and granite hills with volcanic cones. The population of the Sahara is estimated at two and a half millions. In some places the temperature at noon may be as high as 112 degrees Fahrenheit, but at night it drops to several degrees of frost. In fact, it is said that an entire caravan of people were once frozen to death in this region !

Have you ever wondered

WHAT ARE "HIGH" EXPLOSIVES?

Jack Carter, of Barnard Castle, asks me. Explosives are roughly divided into "low" and "high" classes. A low explosive is exploded by the application of heat, and burns more or less uniformly and slowly. But it has a wider range of action. A high explosive explodes under a blow and creates a violent disturbance in a more or less limited area. Gunpowder, for instance, is a low explosive, but picric acid and T.N.T. are high explosives.

The same reader asks how gunpowder is made. It is a mixture of 74 to 75 parts of saltpetre, 9 to 14 parts of sulphur, and 12 to 16 parts of charcoal, and, of course, is much used in the manufacture of fireworks.

NOW for a word or two about our splendid free gifts which have taken readers everywhere by storm. There are 13 more superb coloured pictures for your album in this issue of the MAGNET which brings your total up to 60 pictures all told. But there are plenty more of these handsome coloured pictures to come yet, chums. Next week's set really is "the pick of the bunch." Don't spoil your album through failing to order your MAGNET in good time. The wise reader has already arranged with his newsagent to reserve a copy regularly each week.

If *you* have not yet done so, take my tip and do it now !

By the way,

OTHER THINGS WORTH HAVING

are those magnificent Annuals which are now on sale—" The Holiday Annual " and " The Popular Book of Boys' Stories." At 5s. and 2s. 6d. respectively, they provide the finest value of all boys' books.

You will revel in the budget of ripping school yarns and thrilling adventure stories of the " Holiday Annual." Each tale will hold you enthralled. Here you can meet all the jolly schoolboy characters of Greyfriars, St. Jim's, and Rookwood Schools whose many pranks cannot fail to entertain. There are lots of other interesting features, too, and four beautiful colour plates.

Now for our companion Annual—" The Popular Book of Boys' Stories." What a wonderful budget of thrilling adventure stories, eh ?—a book packed full of swift-moving action that will hold you spellbound until the last page. Here you can revel in big-thrill adventure yarns staged on land, at sea, and in the air—in fact, every phase of adventure is represented in this grand all-fiction Annual which is splendidly illustrated.

Ask your newsagent to let you have a peep at these tip-top books, he'll be only too pleased to oblige.

Meanwhile, here is next week's splendid programme :

"THE GHOST OF WHARTON LODGE!"
By Frank Richards,

is the title of the grand long yarn of the chums of Greyfriars. You all know what to expect when Frank Richards gets going, don't you ? So the title is sufficient to tell you that you are in for a rattling fine yarn that will hold your interest to the very end.

There will be more thrills and exciting situations in our grand adventure story : "When the Great Apes Came!" and a full-of-fun issue of the ever-popular "Greyfriars Herald." "Linesman" will be solving more Soccer problems, and to complete a very fine programme there will be another set of stunning coloured pictures to add to your album. You'll feel like kicking yourself if you miss this bumper free gift issue !

Cheerio,

YOUR EDITOR.

THE MAGNET LIBRARY.—No. 1,349.

THE MYSTERY OF WHARTON LODGE!

(Continued from page 24.)

say! The colonel hurried round to the back of the house with the two juniors at his heels.

Hurree Jamset Ram Singh touched his chum on the arm.

"My esteemed Wharton——" he murmured.

Wharton smiled.

"It was that blighter all the time, Inky!" he said.

"It appearfully looks so," agreed the nabob. "You will rememberfully recollect that I suggestively remarked that there must be a third party in the ridiculous affair! That esteemed pincher was the ridiculous third party. I cannot sufficiently express my regretfulness——"

"You were rather an ass!" said Harry.

"The ratherfulness was terrific and preposterous!" said the nabob in distress. "I distrustfully doubted you, my esteemed and absurd chum——"

"All serene!" said Harry. "Wash it all out, old chap! Let's get that blighter and make him own up!"

But it was not easy to get the "blighter!"

A fresh fall of snow had hidden his footprints; and he had vanished without leaving a trace behind.

Colonel Wharton, after vainly scanning the snow round the building, gave an angry snort. He came to a stop, with a frowning brow, while the two juniors went on hunting for traces.

From a high attic window, a fat face, with a pair of large spectacles on the podgy nose, blinked down at them.

Billy Bunter blinked at the three heads far below, and glared through his spectacles with a glare that almost cracked them.

Outside the attic window was a ledge, thickly carpeted with snow. The fat Owl of the Remove would have been glad to knead a snowball and drop it on the heads below. He thought it over. What the three were rooting about in the snow for, Bunter did not know, or care. But he was wondering whether that stuffy, old, unspeakable beast, the colonel, was in a good temper that morning! If he looked good-tempered, Bunter was inclined to risk showing up, and making his presence known.

So—resisting the desire to snowball the trio below—Bunter blinked at the colonel, anxious to catch a sight of his face, and judge by its expression whether the beast was in a good temper or not.

He sighted that face at last, as the colonel stood looking round him—and its expression was far from encouraging.

The brows were knitted in an angry frown, and the eyes glinted like steel. The burglar's escape had made the colonel angry and deeply annoyed, and those feelings were fully expressed in his stern old face!

Bunter's faint hope died away at once. Evidently, from the colonel's look, this was not a propitious time for revealing himself!

"Beast!" murmured Bunter.

The colonel lit a cigar. He did not see the two juniors, who were stooping to scan the snow for possible footmarks.

Bunter's eyes gleamed.

He gathered up a double handful of snow, and rapidly kneaded a snowball. Bunter's aim was not generally good; but it was fairly easy for even the fat Owl to toss a snowball on a head below! And it was pretty certain that Colonel Wharton would think that one of the two juniors had done it, as there was nobody else in sight! Which would

serve them right all round, for keeping a nice fellow like Bunter a dismal prisoner in a dismal attic!

Whiz!

Crash!

Bunter popped back and closed the window the moment he had hurled the snowball.

Colonel Wharton jumped as his hat flew from his head. He staggered, slipped in the snow, and sat down.

"Good gad!" he roared. "What——"

Wharton and Hurree Singh turned round to him at once. The colonel scrambled to his feet and glared at them.

"Which of you threw that snowball?" he roared.

"Snowball!" repeated Wharton blankly. "I certainly did not!"

"Certainfully I did not, esteemed sahib!" gasped Hurree Singh.

Colonel Wharton glared at them. He stared round—no one was in sight! He picked up his hat, jammed it on his head, snorted, and strode away. The two juniors stared after him, and then at one another.

"Who the deuce——" exclaimed Wharton.

"Who the esteemed dickens——"

It was really mysterious! Wharton Lodge seemed to be haunted by mysteries that Christmastide! And the mysteries were not yet at an end—and were not likely to be, so long as Wharton Lodge still sheltered hidden Bunter!

THE END.

(Now look out for the second grand yarn in this new series, entitled: "THE GHOST OF WHARTON LODGE!" which will appear in next week's bumper issue of the MAGNET. *You'll find more handsome coloured pictures in this issue, too, chums!)*

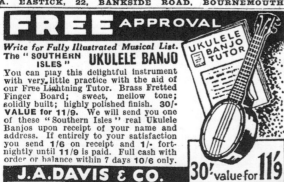

FREE COLOURED PICTURES and a Feast of FUN and FICTION—*Inside!*

The MAGNET 2^D

No. 1,350. Vol. XLIV. **EVERY SATURDAY.** Week Ending December 30th, 1933.

ANOTHER
SHEET OF
SUPERB
COLOURED
PICTURES
**FREE
INSIDE**

Billy Bunter's Xmas Dinner!

The Ghost of Wharton Lodge

By FRANK RICHARDS.

THE FIRST CHAPTER.
Nothing Doing !

"MERRY Christmas, Franky !"

"Oh, my hat ! Bunter !" exclaimed Frank Nugent.

"Glad to see you, old chap !"

"You've got all the gladness on your side !"

"Oh, really, Nugent——"

Frank Nugent had stepped from the train at the little station of Wimford, in Surrey. He was on his way to Wharton Lodge, where the Famous Five of the Greyfriars Remove were to gather for Christmas. He had rather expected Harry Wharton and Hurree Singh to meet him at the station. He had not expected Billy Bunter. But it was the unexpected that happened—in the shape of William George Bunter !

Billy Bunter was on the platform, blinking at the train as it stopped, through his big spectacles. He spotted Nugent at once and rolled up to him. His fat face was irradiated by a friendly grin. Apparently he was glad to see Nugent. Frank Nugent did not seem to share that feeling to any great extent.

"I say, old fellow——"

"Is Wharton here ?" asked Nugent.

"Oh, no ! He couldn't come. Inky couldn't come ,I came instead," said Bunter. "They were coming in the car to pick you up but I fancy something happened to the car. Not that I know anything about it, you know ! I haven't been anywhere near the garage. If anybody poured cinders into the petrol tank it must have been the chauffeur. I never thought much of that chap."

Frank Nugent stared at the fat Owl of the Remove.

THE MAGNET LIBRARY.—No. 1,350.

"Let's take a taxi," went on Bunter briskly. "There's one outside. I'll pay. Leave that to me. You can lend me ten bob. Rather unfortunately, I left my notecase at home with all my banknotes in it when I came over to see Wharton."

"Are you staying at Wharton Lodge ?" demanded the puzzled Nugent.

To his surprise, Bunter grinned at that question as if he regarded it as a joke.

"Yes. No, not exactly," said Bunter. "That is to say, sort of, if you know what I mean."

"I haven't the faintest idea what you mean. If the fellows aren't coming to the station I'd better get off."

Frank Nugent picked up his suitcase and started down the platform to the exit. Bunter rolled after him. Outside the station Frank glanced round him. There was no sign of Harry Wharton or Hurree Jamset Ram Singh, or of the car from Wharton Lodge ; so he started to walk.

Bunter grabbed him by the arm.

"What about the taxi ?" he asked.

"Nothing about the taxi !" answered Nugent. "I can walk a mile, I suppose."

"I've said that I'll pay !" said Bunter, with dignity.

"Well, you take the taxi, and I'll walk."

"Beast ! I mean, all right, old chap ; if you'd rather walk, I'll walk, too. There's a lot of snow on the road, though. A lot more coming down, too, I fancy. Better take the taxi."

"Take it—and be blowed !" answered Frank Nugent, and he shook off the fat hand and swung on his way.

Billy Bunter rolled after him. Bunter had already walked from Wharton Lodge that afternoon, and he did not want to walk back. But, for reasons of his own—good reasons—he did not want to part company with Frank Nugent.

Leaving Wimford behind, they tramped through a carpet of snow down the road that led to Colonel Wharton's house. Nugent walked rather quickly, making little of the weight of his bag, but Billy Bunter puffed and blew as he kept pace with him.

"I say, old chap," gasped Bunter, "not so jolly fast ! After I've taken the trouble to walk to the station to meet you——"

"Oh, all right !" Nugent slowed down. "What the dickens did you come to the station for, Bunter ?"

"I thought you'd like to see me !" said Bunter, with dignified reproach.

"What on earth put that idea into your head ?"

"Beast ! I mean, look here, old chap, let me carry your bag. I mean it ! I want to save you trouble, old fellow."

Nugent could only stare. It was surprising enough for Billy Bunter to take the trouble to walk to the station. It was simply amazing for him to offer to carry a fellow's bag for him.

"Hand it over," said Bunter. "Let's be pally, old scout ! I've been thinking about you ever since we broke up at Greyfriars. We were always pals, weren't we—the best of pals ?"

"Not that I know of."

"Oh, really, Nugent ! I used to be in Study No. 1 with you before that beast Wharton came—I mean, dear old Harry ! Don't you remember how miserable you were when I changed out ?"

"No ; I remember that I was awfully bucked."

"Beast !"

Nugent grinned and tramped on.

Bunter's little fat legs had to trot to keep pace.

"Don't race, you ass!" gasped Bunter. "I've got something to say to you before we get in. I don't want you to get in first."

"Why not?"

"Well, it would be better for us to arrive together," explained Bunter. "The fact is there's been a bit of a misunderstanding. Rotten sort of thing to happen at Christmas-time, you know! Chance for you to act as peacemaker, and all that."

"What the thump are you driving at?"

"Well, you see, it was frightfully awkward, but when I phoned Harry that I was coming for Christmas his uncle took the call, and, not knowing that it was that stuffy old colonel on the phone, I happened to mention that I thought him an old donkey and an old fossil, and——"

"Oh, my hat!"

"He seems to have been offended," said Bunter.

"You don't say so?" said Nugent, with deep sarcasm.

"I do, old chap. You know what these old codgers are like," said Bunter, shaking his head. "It always gets their backs up to hear what a fellow really thinks of them. Well, Wharton makes out that, his uncle being stuffy about it, he can't have me at the Lodge; and when I came along, you'd hardly believe it, Franky, but those beasts snowballed me, instead of giving me the glad hand——"

"Ha, ha, ha!"

"Blessed if I see anything to cackle at! I'd have turned Wharton down at once, only, you see, Bunter Villa—I mean, Bunter Court—is shut up for the holidays, my people being away at Southend—I mean, in the South of France—and there's only Uncle George. And I've had a row with Uncle George, and had to get out. So it leaves a fellow rather stranded, doesn't it, old chap?"

"Then you're not staying with Wharton?" asked the perplexed Nugent.

"Well, I'm going to," said Bunter. "It will be all right with a little tact. I walk in with you——"

"Oh!" ejaculated Nugent. "Do you?"

"You mention to Wharton that you'd like me to be there for Christmas. See?"

"Oh!"

"And he can hardly cut up rusty, you being such a pal of his. As for his uncle, he's bound to be civil, at least, if I come in as your pal. What do you think?"

Nugent gazed at the Owl of the Remove. He did not state what he thought. Bunter seemed to have taken his breath away.

"I fancy it will be all right," said Bunter. "That's why I came to meet your train, old chap. I mean, I came to meet your train because you're my best pal. Lucky I heard those fellows mention the time of your train, wasn't it?"

"Oh, my hat!" gasped Nugent.

"You see how the matter stands," said Bunter. "You're going to act as peacemaker and set it all right. You'll manage it! If you don't you may not have my company this Christmas!"

"What a fearful loss!"

"And Marjorie and Clara will be coming over on Boxing Day, and they'll hardly care for it if I'm not there. Marjorie's rather sweet on me, you know——"

"You fat idiot——"

"Oh, really, Nugent——"

"You blithering bandersnatch!"

"I don't think you ought to be jealous of a fellow, like Wharton and Bob Cherry, Nugent! It's not my fault that I'm a good-looking chap, and that girls run after me! Why, you remember that time I was staying with you, and your sisters were always trying to catch me under the mistletoe—— Oh! Ow! Yaroooooop!"

Why Frank Nugent swung round his suitcase and plumped it on Bunter's podgy chest the Owl of the Remove never knew.

But that was what Nugent did.

Bunter went spinning.

He landed on his back in a bank of snow, with a bump and a fearful yell.

Frank Nugent strode on at an accelerated pace—a pace that Billy Bunter could never have equalled if he had been in a state to try.

But Billy Bunter wasn't!

He sat up in the snow, gurgling for breath, and blinking after Frank Nugent's disappearing form over the spectacles that had slipped down his fat little nose.

"Urrrrggh!" gurgled Bunter. "Beast! Urrrrggh!"

By the time the fat Owl crawled out of the snow, Frank Nugent had vanished

---

THE GHOST THAT WALKED OFF WITH THE CHRISTMAS PUDDING!

---

in the distance. Billy Bunter was left on his own, in a cold and unfeeling world.

THE SECOND CHAPTER.
The Boot for Bunter!

"THERE'S Franky!" exclaimed Harry Wharton.

"As large as lifefulness!" agreed Hurree Jamset Ram Singh.

Harry Wharton and the Nabob of Bhanipur were trudging up the snowy road towards Wimford. Wharton was looking worried and perplexed, and his dusky chum sympathetically serious. Having arranged to pick up Frank Nugent at the station, in the car, they had left it much too late to walk the distance. The colonel's car, they discovered, was mysteriously, but totally, out of action. Instead of having it ready for them, Brown, the chauffeur, was in his shirtsleeves in an oily, grubby, and infuriated state, wrestling with the engine.

Brown, usually a well-mannered chauffeur, had been surly, in fact, savage, plainly intimating his belief that somebody had been deliberately playing tricks with the car, and giving him endless work for nothing! So the two juniors started to walk, expecting to meet Nugent somewhere on the road.

They sighted him in the distance coming along with his suitcase in his hand. And they quickened their pace to meet him.

By that time, having carried his suit-case about a mile, Nugent was finding it rather heavy. So he put it down and sat on it, and waited for his friends to come up. They came up at a trot, and Frank rose and shook hands, with a cheery grin.

"Sorry you had to walk it, old man," said Harry. "But at the last minute it turned out that the car was wonky——"

"The wonkifulness was terrific, my esteemed Franky," said the Nabob of Bhanipur, "and the execrable chauffeur was preposterously infuriated."

"I imagine so!" said Nugent, grinning. "Cinders in the petrol must have given him some trouble."

Harry Wharton stared.

"How the thump did you know?" he stuttered. "That's what Brown said, and I thought he was dreaming! Is this magic?"

Hurree Jamset Ram Singh gazed at Nugent in blank astonishment. Really, it seemed like magic! How Nugent, still half a mile from Wharton Lodge, knew what was the trouble with the car there, was a mystery.

"I've met Bunter!" Nugent explained.

"Bunter!" exclaimed Wharton and the nabob together.

"The one and only!" said Frank. "He met me at the station and offered to stand a taxi! But I can't afford to let Bunter stand me taxis."

"Bunter!" repeated Wharton. "Bunter's not here! I mean, I never knew he was anywhere about! He came along a few days ago and was kicked out. I haven't seen him since. Is he staying in the neighbourhood, then?"

"Must be! He heard you fellows mention the time of my train to-day, so he couldn't have been far off."

"My only hat!"

"The only-hatfulness is terrific."

"But what the thump did he meet you at the station for, even if he had pried out the time of your train?"

Frank Nugent chuckled.

"To walk in with me! I left him a quarter of a mile back, sitting in the snow! His company palled on me slightly."

"But—but has that fat foozler been hanging round the place and playing tricks in the garage?" exclaimed Wharton in amazement. "Did he tell you he'd put cinders in the petrol-tank?"

"No—he told me he hadn't! So I knew he had!"

"Well, I'm dashed!" exclaimed the captain of the Greyfriars Remove. "This beats it! I hadn't the faintest idea he was around. He's done a fearful lot of damage to the car—according to Brown. To keep us away while he met you at the station, I suppose!"

"And to walk in under my wing!" chuckled Nugent. "He seems to have got himself stranded for the hols; and it's a case of any port in a storm. If you want him, I dare say he's still sitting where I left him—he looked as if it would take some time to get his second wind."

Wharton's eyes gleamed.

"The fat villain! Blessed if I know how he could have got into the place without being seen. I've a jolly good mind to go along and kick him all the way to Wimford."

Hurree Jamset Ram Singh gave a chuckle.

"The ridiculous Bunter is in the offing!" he remarked, pointing up the long white road towards Wimford.

Far in the distance, a blot on the white snow, was a fat figure, coming slowly on. A large pair of spectacles flashed back the rays of the wintry sun! Evidently Billy Bunter had got his second wind, and was following Nugent, though at a good distance behind. Perhaps he still hoped to induce Franky to make the attempt to see him

THE MAGNET LIBRARY.—No. 1,350.

through at Wharton Lodge. Hope springs eternal in the human breast.

"Here he comes!" grinned Nugent. "I can do with a rest, if you'd like to wait for him!" And he sat on his suitcase again.

"We'll wait!" said Harry Wharton grimly. "The blithering fat Owl has got to learn that he can't wreck my uncle's car."

And the juniors waited. It was rather a long wait, for the motions of the fat Owl of the Remove rather resembled those of a fatigued snail. Wharton and the nabob stepped out of sight among the leafless trees by the road, before they were within range of Bunter's spectacles. It was probable that Bunter would have halted if he had sighted the captain of the Remove. As it was, he rolled on and arrived panting and puffing at the spot where Nugent sat on his suitcase.

"Waiting for me, old chap!" gasped Bunter. "I say, what did you bump me over for, you silly ass? But it's all right—I can take a joke—he, he, he! I say, old fellow, you're going to see me through at Wharton Lodge, ain't you? That's why you've waited, isn't it?"

"Not quite!" grinned Nugent, as Wharton and Hurree Singh stepped from the trees behind Bunter.

"Oh really, Nugent! I'm relying on you, you know," urged Bunter. "The fact is, that stuffy old ass, Colonel Wharton, has his back up! You know those fossilised old codgers! Wharton has turned me down, like a rotten, ungrateful cad, after all I've done for him. And that rotten nigger, Inky—— Ow! Who's that? What——"

Bunter spun round as Harry Wharton took hold of his collar from behind. His little round eyes almost bulged through his big round spectacles at the unexpected sight of the captain of the Greyfriars Remove.

"Oh!" gasped Bunter. "You!"

"You fat villain!" roared Wharton. "You've been hanging round my uncle's place and playing fool tricks in the garage."

"Oh, really, Wharton! I haven't been near the place! Leggo my collar! Not likely to come near your place after the rotten way you've treated me! As for going to the garage, I don't even know where it is, and the door was open, and I never watched Brown filling up with juice—I wasn't hiding behind the door—— Ow! Stop shaking me, you beast——"

Shake! Shake! Shake!

"Ooooogh!" gurgled Bunter. "S-stop shaking me, I tell you—— Ooogh! If you make my specs fall off—ooogh! —and they get b-b-broken—gurrggh— you'll have to pi-pip-pay for them— wurrrgh!"

Shake! Shake! Shake!

"Wurrrgggh!" gasped Bunter.

Bump!

"Yurrrgggh!"

Billy Bunter sat in the snow and gurgled. Harry Wharton glared down at him.

"Now, you fat rascal——"

"Urrrrggh!"

"I give you one second to get out of reach——"

"Wurrggh!"

"Then I'm going to kick you——"

"Gurrrgh! Beast! Urrrggh!"

"The kickfulness is the proper caper!" agreed Hurree Jamset Ram Singh. "Let us all kick togetherfully."

"Hear, hear!" said Nugent. "Give a fellow room!"

Billy Bunter scrambled up. He made a wild leap to escape. Three boots

THE MAGNET LIBRARY.—No. 1,350.

landed on his podgy person as he leaped.

"Whoop!" roared Bunter.

He rolled.

The chums of the Remove turned and walked away towards Wharton Lodge, leaving him rolling, roaring. When Harry Wharton glanced back, from a distance, Bunter was sitting up in the snow, shaking a fat fist, his very spectacles glittering with wrath. Then he was lost to sight, and the Removites trudged on, nothing doubting that they had seen the last of Billy Bunter till next term at Greyfriars.

But they hadn't!

———

THE THIRD CHAPTER.

The Unbidden Guest!

"THOMAS!"

"Yes, Mr. Wells, sir!"

"Place the table before the fire, Thomas."

Wells, the butler of Wharton Lodge, stood in Harry Wharton's sitting-room, otherwise, his "den." Thomas, the page, was laying the table for tea. Colonel Wharton and his sister, Miss Amy, were dining out that evening, and had already left the Lodge. On such occasions Wharton was accustomed to "tea" in his den, and Thomas was making the arrangements under the lofty supervision of the portly Wells. At the present moment Harry Wharton and Nugent and the nabob were downstairs, chatting by the fire in the hall. Outside, the December darkness was falling, and flakes of snow whirled on a keen wind.

Wharton's room looked very cosy and comfortable, with a log fire blazing in the grate and the electric light gleaming on a well-spread tea-table, and on the red berries of the holly that decorated the walls in honour of the season. Wells thought so, and so did a third party, of whose presence neither Wells nor Thomas had the slightest suspicion. There were french windows to the room, opening on an old stone balcony with steps down to the garden— a way by which Harry frequently came and went. In the windy darkness of the balcony a fat figure crouched, blinking at the window through a pair of large spectacles, and shivering in the wind.

"Beasts!" murmured Billy Bunter, for about the twentieth time, wondering whether Wells and Thomas would ever go

That was Bunter's way in!

Wharton had been astonished to learn that the fat Owl of the Remove was still in the neighbourhood. He would have been still more astonished had he known how very near Bunter's quarters were.

Over Wharton's den was an attic, reached by a steep stair in the passage outside. That attic was never used, and was kept locked.

Nobody at Wharton Lodge even dreamed that that disused attic was no longer disused. but that an unknown and uninvited guest had taken up his quarters there!

With Billy Bunter it was, as Frank Nugent had remarked. a case of any port in a storm

Having had a "row" with the uncle who had taken him in for Christmas, Billy Bunter really could not be very particular.

But this was, perhaps, rather the limit, even for Billy Bunter!

Still, what was a fellow to do?

Sooner or later, Bunter counted on a favourable and propitious moment for revealing his presence. That moment had not arrived

He had hoped that the coming of

Frank Nugent would see him through. It hadn't! If he was staying on, he still had to stay in secret. Somehow or other, his fatuous scheming had made matters worse, instead of better.

A fellow could not, of course, remain imprisoned night and day in an attic! But the secret and unknown guest at Wharton Lodge had to be very, very careful how and when he emerged.

Discovery meant the boot for Bunter, and even the dismal attic was preferable to that.

So far, nobody knew.

The balcony to Wharton's den, and the garden stair, was Bunter's way of ingress and egress; but he had to watch and wait for opportunities.

Now he was on his way back to his lair.

He had cautiously left it till the fall of the winter dusk, when he had been able to creep into the grounds unperceived, and ascend the garden stair to the balcony.

At the usual tea-time at Wharton Lodge he expected to find Wharton's window dark, and his room deserted.

Instead of which, the room was lighted, and Wells and Thomas were there, and the fat Owl had to stay where he was, waiting for them to go.

He only hoped that they would go before the three juniors came up; otherwise, he was booked for a long, long wait on the snowy balcony.

Through the glass he could hear Wells' fruity voice:

"You may go down now, Thomas!"

"Yes, Mr. Wells, sir!" Bunter, blinking in from the darkness outside, saw the lad turn a reproachful eye on the butler. "I 'ope, sir, that that don't mean that you can't trust me, sir."

"I am afraid, Thomas, that I cannot trust you," said Wells, with portly dignity. "I am sorry to say so—but there it is. Being a relation of mine— a distant relation—I got you your present place here, Thomas, speaking for you to the master——"

"And I was thankful to you, Mr. Wells, and I've always done my dooty," said Thomas.

"Up to a few days ago," said Wells coldly, "I had no cause for complaint. But there is some dishonest person in this house, Thomas."

"It ain't me, Mr. Wells!"

"I 'ope, Thomas, that it is not. When Master Hurree Singh's bedclothes were taken away, a few nights ago, it turned out that a vagrant had been about the place, and you were exonerated. When the larder was broken into it was attributed to the same vagrant. Very well! But since then, Thomas, there have been pilferings."

"It wasn't me, Mr. Wells!"

"I hope not. But who was it?" said Wells. "Several times food has been taken from the larder after the whole house was asleep. Candles have been taken—why, I cannot imagine, the value being so small. An electric torch has been missed by Master Harry. A travelling-rug belonging to the master has been missed. Only yesterday the colonel found that there were no biscuits in the box in the dining-room sideboard; yet I had filled that box the day before with my own 'ands. Many comestibles laid in by Miss Wharton for the young people on Boxing Day have been purloined—boxes of chocolates, sweets, candied fruits, and so forth I hope that it was not you, Thomas. But——"

Billy Bunter, with his fat ear to the door, drinking all this in, grinned. The hidden and unbidden guest at Wharton Lodge could have told where the missing eatables had gone!

"So you may go down, Thomas, and

"It's not my fault, Nugent, that the girls run after me," said Bunter. "Why, you remember that time I was staying with you, and your sisters were trying to catch me under the mistletoe—— Oh ! Ow ! Yaroooooooop ! " The Owl of the Remove broke off suddenly as Nugent's suitcase plumped on his chest and sent him spinning.

tell Master Harry that all is ready," said Wells, with stately dignity.

"Very well, Mr. Wells, but——"

"You may go, Thomas !"

Thomas went.

The butler looked after him and shook his head seriously. He had once had a very good opinion of Thomas. But he was very doubtful now. There was somebody at Wharton Lodge who persistently snaffled trifling t h i n g s— especially eatable things ! Who was it ? Suspicion rested on the unlucky Thomas.

Thomas being gone, Wells took a last glance round, to ascertain that all was in order, and then quitted the room himself. He was blissfully unaware that a fat schoolboy on the balcony gasped with relief when the door closed behind him.

Hardly had the door closed when Billy Bunter opened the glass door from the balcony and rolled in. He closed the french window and wiped his feet very carefully on the mat. That was not Bunter's usual custom, but he was very particular now to leave no traces of his entrance and his exits. Then he stood listening.

Any minute the beasts might come up to tea ! It behoved the secret guest to get into his hiding-place without the loss of a moment. But Bunter was hungry—his usual state ! His latest snafflings had long ago been devoured. The good things on the table were irresistible. Listening with both his fat ears, Billy Bunter stood by the table, cramming cake into his capacious mouth with one hand and various articles into his pockets with the other. Seconds were precious; and Bunter did not waste one !

Tea had been laid for three—an ample tea ! In a few moments the supplies

were much less ample. A few minutes would have sufficed for Billy Bunter to clear the festive board from end to end. But he had only moments, not minutes. There was a sound of footsteps and cheery voices in the corridor outside, from the direction of the stairs. Bunter jumped, and nearly choked ! Even then he stayed to grab up a cake before he scudded across to the communicating door of Wharton's bed-room and bolted into the latter apartment.

That door had hardly closed behind him when the door from the corridor opened, and Harry Wharton and his friends came into the "den."

Bunter gasped for breath.

His escape had been narrow.

Indeed, his extraordinary visit to Wharton Lodge had been a series of narrow escapes.

"Here we are, Franky !" He heard Harry Wharton's cheery voice in the adjoining room. "Just like tea in the study—what ?"

"The likefulness is terrific !" remarked Hurree Jamset Ram Singh.

"Yes, rather !" said Nugent. "Topping, old bean !"

Bunter did not stay to hear more.

The bed-room had a door on the corridor, and Bunter headed for that door. He opened it a few inches and peered out.

There was a light burning, and the passage was clear. Bunter tiptoed out, and reached the little stair that led up to the disused attic.

Up that stair he went on tiptoe to the little landing and, taking a key from his pocket, he opened the attic door.

Once inside, he locked the door on the inner side.

Now he was safe !

He lighted a candle—one of the candles that Wells had missed—and sat down on the bedclothes—that had been missed from Hurree Jamset Ram Singh's room. There was little furniture in the attic, and Bunter had had to do some furnishing himself.

"Beasts !" murmured Bunter.

By the glimmering candlelight he turned his plunder out of his pockets, and proceeded to park it in his capacious interior. After which Billy Bunter felt better.

————

THE FOURTH CHAPTER.
Mysterious !

THREE cheery juniors sat down round the tea-table, before the leaping log-fire in Harry Wharton's cosy den.

Frank Nugent was very pleased to be with his friends and his friends were very glad to see him. The next day Bob Cherry and Johnny Bull were coming, when the happy circle of the Famous Five would be complete. Thomas was available to wait on the tea-party, if they had wanted him, but they preferred to wait on themselves, as in the study at Greyfriars School. Harry Wharton took the teapot to make the tea, and sorted out the biscuit-box that was used as a tea-caddy.

"Sosses in the dish, Franky," he said.

Nugent lifted the cover.

He gazed at an empty dish.

"Where are the sosses ?" he asked.

Wharton, busy tea-making, answered over his shoulder.

"In the dish, fathead ! Take off the cover !"

"I've taken it off!"

"Well, then, whack out tne sosses!" Nugent looked across at him.

"Is that a joke, or what?" he asked. "Are you taking to playing practical jokes in your old age?"

"What the dickens do you mean?" asked Wharton. He looked round, tea-pot in hand. "Hallo! Where are the sosses?"

"That's what I want to know."

Wharton stared at the empty dish.

"My hat! Has that young ass Thomas snaffled the sosses?"

"Looks as if somebody has," said Frank. "If there were any. Perhaps they forgot the sosses. Something's been on the dish, though."

Harry Wharton frowned.

"Must have been that kid," he said. "I don't want to get him into a row with Wells, or with my uncle, but really this is too thick. It isn't the first time, either."

"Oh, never mind the sosses," said Frank good naturedly. "Don't get the young ass a ragging from Wells. Lots of stuff."

"Try the ham."

"Where is it?"

"Oh crumbs! Has he snaffled the ham, too?" exclaimed Wharton. He stared over the tea-table. "And where's the cake?"

"Was there a cake?"

"Of course there was! And where are the muffins?"

"Were there muffins?"

"And the jam! Where's the jam?"

"Was there jam?"

Harry Wharton knitted his brows. Not only was the jam gone, but the dish that contained it was gone also. A busy hand had been at work on that tea-table.

"Dash it all, it's too thick!" exclaimed the captain of the Greyfriars Remove. "Too jolly thick!"

"The thickfulness is terrific!" agreed Hurree Jamset Ram Singh.

"I hate to get the kid into a row—especially at Christmas-time; but a fellow can't stand this," said Harry. "I'll get him here." And he rang the bell for Thomas.

Thomas appeared in a few moments, with his usual chubby grin on his chubby face.

"You rang, sir!" said Thomas.

"Yes, you young sweep!" exclaimed Wharton. "What have you been up to here?"

"Ain't it all right, sir?" asked Thomas anxiously. "I did everything what Mr. Wells told me, sir."

"Did Wells tell you to snaffle the cake and the jam and the sosses, you young rascal?" exclaimed Wharton.

Thomas stared.

"No, sir! Cert'nly not, sir! I ain't snaffled nothing!"

"Who has, then?" snapped Wharton. "They're gone." He gave the astonished Thomas a grim look. He was deeply annoyed. "Look here——"

"Well, it wasn't me, sir," said Thomas. "Mr. Wells wouldn't trust me to stay in the room, sir, because there's been pilfering, and he fancies I know something about it which I don't, sir. I went down before Mr. Wells did, sir."

"Oh!" exclaimed Wharton.

"And you can ask Mr. Wells, sir!" said Thomas, with dignity. "Mr. Wells was last in the room, sir. He will tell you so, sir, if you ask him.'

Wharton stared at him, quite nonplussed. It was impossible, of course, to suppose that the stately Wells had snaffled cake and jam from a schoolboys' tea-table. But really it was very mysterious.

"Well, you can see the things are gone," said Harry, at last.

"P'r'aps it was a burglar, sir?" suggested Thomas.

"Oh, don't be a young ass!"

"Well, sir, it turned out that there was a burglar when Master Hurree Singh's bedclothes was took, which the master thought at first that it was me."

"I know that; but that tramp cleared off, after he escaped from the cellar. And he wouldn't come in in the daytime for a pot of jam, even if he was still about. You're talking rot, Thomas!"

"P'r'aps it was the ghost, sir," said Thomas helpfully.

"What!" roared Wharton.

"Oh, my hat!" said Nugent. "Something new in ghosts! I've never heard of a ghost going for a pot of jam and a cake!"

"Well, sir, there's been sounds 'eard at night," said Thomas. "And Robert, who woke up one night and looked out of his room, saw a shadder, sir—a dark shadder."

"You young ass!"

"Yes, sir," said Thomas.

"Did you sneak back through the bedroom after Wells had gone?" demanded Wharton suspiciously.

Thomas started.

"Oh, sir! No, sir! I s'pose I could 'ave, but I didn't, sir. I wouldn't, sir!"

"Well, get some more food, anyhow," said Harry; and Thomas obediently went for a new supply.

The chums of the Remove were able to sit down to tea at last. And Thomas left them to it, with a worried and troubled look on his chubby face.

"That kid looks as if he was telling the truth, Harry," remarked Nugent, as he helped himself to sausages.

"But who the deuce is it, then?" said Harry. "For two or three days now things have been snaffled right and left —such things as food from the larder, and candles, and a torch, and my uncle's rug. It started with Inky's bedclothes, and the silly ass thought I'd played a trick on him, and got his back up."

"The regretfulness was terrific," murmured the Nabob of Bhanipur.

"It's all right, fathead! But it turned out that there was a tramp hanging about the place, and we put it all down to him," went on Wharton. "He was bagged, and locked in the cellar to wait for a bobby, but he got out and cleared. But it's gone on since then. It can't be anybody from outside the house. The place is locked up safely at night. And it's at night that the things go chiefly."

"What about the ghost?" asked Nugent, laughing. "Is there a ghost?"

"There was a ghost once; but it's not been seen in recent times," said Harry, smiling. "There was a jolly old Wharton in the reign of Henry the Sixth. He took the Lancastrian side in the Wars of the Roses, and some enterprising Yorkists surprised him in this very house while he was feasting at Christmas, and there was a terrific scrap, and he was killed, sword in hand. For reasons not stated in the legend he took to haunting the place. It's been rebuilt more than once since then, and perhaps that has discouraged him. He hasn't been seen for a jolly long time. But even when the ghost walked he was never said to snaffle pots of jam or sosses."

"A Bunter family ghost might!" said Frank, with a chuckle. "But a Wharton ghost would be above it. I'll finish

with some of those chocs. Shove the box over!"

There was a box of chocolates on the table; a gift from Aunt Amy to her dear nephew, which Wharton had not opened yet. He pushed the box across to Frank.

Nugent opened it.

Then he blinked. The box was stacked full of dry wood-ashes.

"Funny, I suppose!" he remarked rather dryly.

"Eh—what's funny?" asked Wharton.

"If you're taking up practical jokes, old bean, I'd advise you to chuck it," said Nugent. "You've had rows with Wibley, at Greyfriars, for his fatheaded practical joking."

"What the dickens do you mean? Who's joking?" demanded Wharton. "Don't you like the chocs?"

"Not that kind!" answered Nugent.

"I haven't looked at them," said Harry. "My aunt gave me the box the other day, but I hadn't opened it. They're all right, I suppose?"

He reached across and took the box, and stared into it in amazement. Every chocolate was gone; but the place had been filled with wood-ashes, apparently to make the box weigh as much as before, and defer detection till it was opened.

"My only hat!" gasped Wharton. "Who's done this?"

"Didn't you?" asked Nugent, in the same dry tone.

"Of course not, fathead! Do you think I'd play an idiotic joke like that?" exclaimed Wharton irritably. "Have a little sense!"

He coloured the next moment. As host to his schoolboy chum, in his home, he had to be a little more particular in manners than in Study No. 1 in the Remove passage at Greyfriars.

"Sorry, old fellow!" he said at once. "Of course, some blithering ass has snooped the chocs, and filled up the box from the grate. Thomas, I suppose —it can't have been anybody else. You wouldn't play such a fatheaded trick, Inky?"

"Certainfully not, my esteemed Wharton," said the Nabob of Bhanipur.

Wharton's eyes gleamed.

"Look here, you chaps! It's a rotten thing to happen at Christmas-time, with guests in the house; but there's no doubt that there's some rotter in the place who's snaffling things right and left—generally after everybody has gone to bed! I'm jolly well going to sit up to-night and keep an eye open for him!"

"Good egg!" said Nugent. "I'll stay up, too."

"And my esteemed self also!" said Hurree Jamset Ram Singh. "We will all threefully keep watch with terrific weariness, and if the execrable snaffler takes a walk abroad, the bagfulness will be complete and preposterous."

And so it was arranged. There was likely to be a surprise for the secret guest at Wharton Lodge, if he prowled out of his attic that night!

THE FIFTH CHAPTER.
A Narrow Squeak !

BILLY BUNTER hardly breathed. It was pitch dark in the passage.

Downstairs, all was cheery and bright. The strains of a band on the wireless floated up from below. It was getting towards bed-time for the young people; but it was not yet bed-time. It was, in fact, a propitious time

for the hidden Owl to venture out of his lair and take a little trot.

Bunter was not keen on exercise, or on moving at all, as a rule; but even the lazy, fat Owl felt the effect of being "cabined, cribbed, and confined" within the narrow limits of a garret.

Also, it was cold there, unless he kept snuggled in the bedclothes and Colonel Wharton's rug. And he had eaten all he had to eat, and had a faint hope of snaffling something further. So down from his attic crept Bunter—and his first proceeding was to turn off the light in the passage that ran by the doors of Wharton's rooms and the apartments of his schoolboy guests. It was safer in the dark.

Then he tiptoed along to Wharton's den and slipped in. And then——

He listened at the half-open door, with beating heart. Footsteps came down the passage from one end, up from the other! Two persons were approaching.

Bunter shut the door, but did not venture to latch it. The faintest sound might have been heard. Keeping it about half an inch open, he blinked out, through his big spectacles, as the light flashed on in the passage.

From one direction came Wells, the butler. From the other came Thomas, the page. It was Wells who flashed on

the light. They blinked at one another, and Bunter blinked at both, unseen and unsuspected.

"You, Thomas!" said Wells severely.

"You, Mr. Wells!" said Thomas.

"I think I have caught you this time, Thomas."

"Oh, Mr. Wells!"

"I have been keeping observation," said Wells. "I saw the light turned off, from a distance, Thomas. I came up at once. I find you here. What was your intention, Thomas, in turning off the light?"

"I didn't, Mr. Wells. I thought you had."

"Thomas!" said Wells, in a deep voice.

"I swear, Mr. Wells, that I ain't been anywhere near the switch! Cook being done with me, I thought I'd come up and see if all was right," said Thomas. "Somebody's pinching, I know that."

"Somebody," said Wells, "certainly is! There has been extensive pilfering, Thomas! Almost ever since Master Harry came home for the holidays, it has been going on—night after night! It is my duty, Thomas, to discover the pilferer, and to discharge him—and even if it should be a relation of my own, for whom I obtained a place here——"

"It ain't, Mr. Wells!" said Thomas earnestly. "It ain't!"

"I hope not!" said Wells. "I hope not, Thomas! But it looks suspicious

—very suspicious! To-night, Thomas, I shall call you after everyone has gone to bed, and we shall keep watch together. If the pilfering goes on, while you are under my observation, you will be exonerated, Thomas. If not——"

"I'll 'elp you with pleasure, Mr. Wells," said Thomas eagerly. "I know you don't trust me now, like you did. And the master, he looks at me very odd, sometimes. Even the missus, too! I'll be glad to 'elp!"

"Very well," said Wells. "At eleven o'clock I will tap on your door, and we will remain in the hall, in the dark, on the watch. I hope, for your sake, Thomas, that the pilferer will get on with it again, while you are in my company. Otherwise——"

Wells shook his head portentously, instead of finishing the sentence. Then he went to the staircase.

Bunter grinned.

Many times the hidden Owl, listening with all his fat ears, had picked up information, but never information so useful as this.

That night, most assuredly, he would have walked abroad, like a lion seeking what he might devour but for this timely warning.

Now, it was certain, the fat Owl of the Remove would remain doggo in his attic, so long as Wells and Thomas were on the watch.

Blinking through the narrow aperture of the door, at Thomas, he saw the worried and distressed expression on the chubby countenance of that unfortunate youth.

Bunter was quite sorry for him.

He felt that it was hard lines on Thomas, to be unjustly distrusted like this. Still, as it made things safer for Bunter, it was all to the good!

But the grin faded from Bunter's face as Thomas came towards the door behind which he stood blinking. Thomas was coming into Harry Wharton's den, doubtless to mend the fire.

Bunter scudded across to the bed-room door in time. He shot into the bed-room. But for the fact that the sitting-room and bed-room communicated, he would assuredly have been spotted. That circumstance had saved the artful dodger more than once, when he was rooting through Harry Wharton's rooms. But on this occasion he was barely in time. Thomas, coming in, and switching on the light as he entered, jumped as he saw the communicating door just closing.

He stared at it.

"My eye!" gasped Thomas.

Someone was there! Someone had barely dodged him! It was the secret snaffler or nobody! Thomas' brain was not rapid on the uptake. But he realised that at once.

He tore across to the door and grabbed at the handle! Bunter, on the other side, heard him coming! His fat heart jumped almost into his throat!

A second more, and Thomas would have had that door open! But in the stress of peril Bunter's fat brain worked swiftly. There was a key on the bed-room side of the door. He turned it!

Click!

The key clicked, just as Thomas grabbed the door-handle. Bunter was just in time.

"Oh crikey!" breathed Bunter.

He rushed across the bed-room to the door on the corridor. In Wharton's den, Thomas was doing exactly the same thing!

Bunter stopped.

He knew what Thomas would be doing. He had no time to reach the attic stair. Emerging into the lighted passage was to reveal himself to Thomas.

"Oh lor'!" gasped Bunter.

He heard Thomas in the passage. Thomas was coming to the bed-room door on the corridor. Bunter's escape was cut off!

He thought of dodging under the bed, as he had done before in times of danger. But this time, that was a chicken that would not fight; for Thomas knew that there was someone in the room, and would certainly search it.

Bunter had little time to think.

As he stood there, Thomas' hand touched the door-handle outside. The door opened. Bunter was behind it as it opened.

Thomas switched on the light by the doorpost and stepped in past the door. Bunter was behind him as he stood staring across the room.

Thump! Bunter acted promptly.

It was the only way to escape. His fat fist hit Thomas on the back of the head.

Taken utterly by surprise by that sudden attack in the rear, Thomas pitched over headlong, landing on his face, his nose hitting the floor with a heavy hit!

Before he quite knew what had happened, Bunter had switched off the light, darted into the corridor, and shut the door.

"My eye!" gasped Thomas.

He sat up dizzily, feeling his nose with one hand, and the back of his head with the other.

"Oh crikey!" stuttered Thomas.

He staggered to his feet. He groped in the darkness for the door, and got it open. But the corridor, when he looked out, was vacant. Bunter had not lost a split second. He had vanished as if he had been the ghost of Wharton Lodge. He was already palpitating in his attic —and Thomas, still rubbing his nose and the back of his head in a state of dazed astonishment, went to speak to Mr. Wells, to report this startling and amazing occurrence.

THE SIXTH CHAPTER.
Caught!

MIDNIGHT!

Harry Wharton yawned.

Very seldom did the captain of the Greyfriars Remove hear the chimes at midnight.

And on this occasion there was no doubt that he would have preferred his warm and comfortable bed.

But the three juniors had arranged to stay up, and keep watch that night for the secret snaffler; and that was that!

Lights had been turned out at the usual time. Wharton dozed in the armchair before a dying fire while he waited for twelve, when the vigil was to begin. Now, at last, midnight was chiming.

He yawned, rose from the chair, and rubbed his sleepy eyes. A dim glow from the fire in the bed-room grate faintly illumined the room. There was the faintest of sounds as the door opened and Hurree Jamset Ram Singh and Frank Nugent came in.

"Ready?" asked Nugent, in a whisper.

"Yes! Awfully sleepy," said Harry.

"The sleepifulness is terrific," remarked the Nabob of Bhanipur. "But the wakeful watchfulness is the proper caper."

"Oh, yes, rather!" agreed Wharton. "Got something to swipe him with if we land him? Pillows would show in the

dark. Whoever it is, we'll give him the walloping of his life, if we get hold of him. I've got a cushion!"

"I've stuffed a sock," said Frank.

"And I have a piece of rope with a terrific knot at the end," said Hurree Jamset Ram Singh.

"Good!"

The three juniors crept quietly into the passage. All was dark and silent. They made no sound in their soft slippers.

Groping along silently, they reached the stairs. A wide landing joined the double staircase that led down into the hall. The hall was an abyss of darkness over the balustrade.

For more than an hour Wharton Lodge had been buried in silence and slumber. There was not a gleam of light; no sound save the winter wind whining over the roofs and the old chimneys and rustling the snow-mantled ivy against the windows.

On the landing the three juniors waited, leaning on the dim banisters and listening.

From this central position they were well placed to catch sight or sound of the mysterious marauder of Wharton Lodge, whether he stirred upstairs or downstairs.

Quite cheerfully the chums of the Remove had arranged to keep that midnight watch! But now that they came to keep it, they found that it was anything but cheerful.

It was cold, it was dark, it was dismal —and, above all, it was monotonous. When ten minutes had passed, they felt as if they had been there two or three hours.

They reflected—rather late—that the snaffler might not stir that night. Also, that if he did, he might not stir till nearly dawn!

Undoubtedly it was weary work.

The only consolation was that if they caught the marauder, they were going to give him the full benefit of the cushion, the stuffed sock, and the knotted rope's-end.

By the time they felt as if they had been waiting and watching for the best part of the night they heard the half-hour chime out.

It was only half-past twelve!

Wharton, suppressing a yawn, heard a half-suppressed yawn at his elbow. It came from Nugent. Then, suddenly he heard another sound in the well of darkness below. It was the distinct sound of a movement. Someone was stirring.

With a beating heart, he leaned over the banisters and listened. A quick breath on either side of him told that his comrades had also heard it.

Faintly from the darkness came a whisper. The words were not to be distinguished. But the whisper had a warning note. The juniors realised that there were two persons in the hall below—not one, as they had expected. One, it was clear, had clumsily made a sound—the other had whispered to him to be more careful. Obviously there must have been at least two, or there would have been no whisper.

Wharton's eyes glinted.

He groped for his companions in the dark, and drew them back from the banister. He was going to whisper, and having heard that whisper from below, he was taking care that his own whisper should not be heard from above.

"They're there, you fellows!" he breathed. "Must be two of them!"

"I heard!" breathed Nugent.

"The hearfulness was terrific!" murmured the nabob.

"Don't make a sound! If they hear us, there's a dozen doors they can dodge away by, and leave us no wiser! We

know already it's somebody belonging to the house—no need to watch to find that out! We've got to drop on them and catch them."

"What-ho!"

"Come down after me and don't make a sound."

"Go it!"

Slowly and cautiously, and without a sound, Harry Wharton led the way down the stairs, his comrades creeping stealthily after him.

Noiselessly, they reached the hall below.

It was pitchy dark there.

Standing in the darkness, they listened with straining ears, suppressing their breathing. But there was somebody in the dark hall who was not suppressing his breathing. Faintly, but unmistakably in the silence of the night, they heard a sound of breathing in the middle of the hall.

Harry Wharton listened intently, and calculated carefully the exact position of the breather.

Then, on tiptoe, he stepped towards that spot.

His cushion was held high in the air, ready to smite! Dark as it was, he had a glimpse of a face when he was close to it!

Crash!

The cushion came down, hard and heavy. It landed fairly on the head to which that dim glimmer of a face belonged.

Bump!

"Got him!" panted Wharton.

He had got him! There was no doubt about that. The cushion had smitten the shadowy head, fair and square, and the owner thereof had gone down with a bump, and was sprawling on the floor, gasping and spluttering.

Wharton flung himself on the sprawling form.

His knee was planted on a portly chest.

"Got one of them! Get the other, you men!" he panted.

Another figure was already wriggling in the grasp of Frank Nugent.

"Got him! Turn on the light, Inky!" shouted Nugent.

The nabob's dusky hand switched on the electric light. The hall was suddenly flooded with illumination.

Nugent gave a yell as he recognised the fellow he had grasped.

It was Thomas.

Thomas blinked at him, like an owl in the sudden light.

"Oh! Master Nugent!" he stuttered. "I thought——"

"It's Thomas after all!" gasped Nugent. "We've snaffled him! Who's the other, Harry?"

But Wharton did not reply.

He could not.

Dumb with amazement, he stared down at the portly plump face of the man on whose portly chest he was kneeling. It was Wells, the butler.

THE SEVENTH CHAPTER.
The Ghost Walks!

"URRRRRRGGGH!" gurgled Wells.

Harry Wharton jumped up.

Wells sat up.

He gurgled breathlessly.

"Oh, my hat!" Wharton found his voice at last. "It's Wells! It's the butler! What the thump——"

"The esteemed and ridiculous Wells!" ejaculated Hurree Jamset Ram Singh, "And the fatheaded and absurd Thomas!"

Never had the chums of the Remove been so astonished. The discovery was utterly unexpected. They had had no doubt that when they jumped on the unseen figures in the dark hall, the secret snaffler of Wharton Lodge would be in their hands. Evidently there was a mistake somewhere.

"Look here, Wells, what's this game?" gasped Wharton. "What the dickens are you and Thomas doing out of bed?"

"Ooooogh!" said Wells, gurgling. "Wooooogh!"

"Oh, Master Harry!" gasped Thomas. "We was a-keeping watch, Mr. Wells and me, sir, for that feller what pinches things at night, sir——"

"Oh crumbs!" murmured Nugent. "So were we!"

Harry Wharton burst into a laugh. Evidently there had been two parties of watchers that night; and one party had dropped on the other in the dark.

"Urrrggh!" gasped Wells. "Ugggh! Perhaps you would kindly give me a hand, sir. I am a little—urrrggh!—winded! Wurrrggh!"

Wharton and Nugent helped the portly gentleman up. Wells stood gasping for breath. There was no doubt that he was winded. His breath came and went spasmodically.

"So you were keeping watch, too?" exclaimed Wharton.

"Urrrgh! Yes, sir!"

"I wish you'd told me what you were going to do, Wells—then I shouldn't have got you with the cushion. I hope you're not hurt."

"Gurrrgggh!"

"It is a terrific and lamentable mistake," said the Nabob of Bhanipur, with a grin on his dusky face. "But it is preposterously fortunate that I recognised the esteemed Wells, before beginfully whopping him with this absurd rope's-end."

"Ha, ha, ha!"

"Urrrggh!" said Wells. "Wurrggh! Young gentlemen, you should not have been up. I do not think the master would be pleased if he knew. Gurrrggh!"

"Well, if the jolly old snaffler has heard this row, there's not much chance of catching him to-night," said Frank Nugent. "May as well get to bed, I think."

"The thinkfulness is terrific."

"Urrrggh! Leave it to me, young gentlemen," said Wells. "It is my intention to keep on the watch, that being my duty; but really—urrrggh!—I shall do so with more peace of mind, if you are in bed."

Harry Wharton laughed.

"All serene," he said. "I shall be jolly glad to get to bed, if you're going to keep on the sentry-go, Wells."

"Certainly, sir! Urrrgh!"

"We'll ketch him, sir, if he turns out to-night!" said Thomas.

Wells, undoubtedly, was anxious for the juniors to go to bed. A swipe from a cushion and a bump on the floor had considerably disturbed Wells. Harry Wharton & Co were quite willing to leave the night-watch to the butler. They had made a catch, certainly; but a very unexpected one. And at nearly one in the morning they were frightfully sleepy.

"Well, we'll cut," said Harry. "Good-night, Wells!"

"Good — urrrggh! — night, sir!" gurgled Wells.

The light was turned off again. Wells, still gurgling spasmodically, was left to his vigil, with the faithful Thomas.

The three Greyfriars juniors groped up the staircase, across the landing, and into the passage that led to their rooms.

They passed the little stair in the passage that led up to the disused attic.

Certainly it did not occur to any of them that the attic door above was ajar, and that a fat pair of ears listened there.

Billy Bunter was not asleep that night.

Bunter was too hungry to sleep.

Only his knowledge of the fact that Wells and Thomas were up and watching had kept Bunter in his attic. That was rather fortunate for the hidden Owl, for there was little doubt that he would have run into the juniors had he emerged.

That the juniors also had been keeping watch, Bunter was not aware; but his listening ears had caught a sound from downstairs, and he was wondering what it meant.

"Good-night, you men!" Bunter caught Harry Wharton's voice and gave

CHRISTMAS-TIME
IS
JOKE-TIME!

Read this amusing storyette for which T. M. Cox, of Hewick House, Ormesby Road, North Ormesby, Middlesbrough, has been awarded a TOPPING SHEFFIELD STEEL PEN-KNIFE.

First Navvy: "Why don't old Bill come down off his steam-roller and have his dinner with us?"
Second Navvy: "Oh, he says he ain't takin' no chances with all these car thieves about!"

Have a shot at winning one of these useful prizes RIGHT NOW!

a start. He heard Nugent and the nabob reply, and then there was a faint sound of closing doors.

"Oh lor'!" murmured the fat Owl.

He realised that the juniors had been up at that unearthly hour. He could guess why, and what a narrow escape he had had!

But they had gone back to bed now, that was clear, and the problem that worried Bunter was, whether Wells was still keeping it up.

For a long time after the three Removites were in bed, and fast asleep, Bunter stood at the attic door listening. He heard no sound.

Many times he was tempted to lock the door and turn in. But the inner Bunter kept him awake.

His fat thoughts ran on the Christmas pudding, which was in Wells' pantry, all ready for Christmas.

His mouth watered at the thought of that pudding. He had spent a previous

Christmas at Wharton Lodge, and he knew what the pudding would be like. His fat soul yearned for that pudding.

But if that unspeakable beast, Wells, was on the watch—— The fact that he knew that Wells was on the watch had saved him from discovery by the juniors. He was really having a wonderful run of luck. But what was the use, if he had to go to bed hungry? And there was the following day to be thought of. He had to be fearfully careful about venturing out of his hiding-place in the daytime. He might not have a chance of getting out at all, and, anyhow, in the daytime he could not venture near the grub department. Was Wells still on the watch?

Billy Bunter's fat brain was not accustomed to hard work. But his podgy intellect was spurred on by the danger of famine.

He went back to his bed and groped for a sheet. More than once, during his hidden sojourn in Wharton Lodge, he had heard talk among the servants of the "ghost" that was supposed to walk at Christmastide. That ghost was rather a topic now, for there was no doubt that sounds had been heard at night, and one of the servants had actually seen a "shadow" stirring in the hours of darkness.

Bunter draped his fat figure in the sheet, and fastened it on securely. He placed a white pillow-slip over his head, in the form of a hood, and drew it round his fat face, leaving only his eyes—and spectacles—in view.

In that ghostly guise the fat Owl ventured, at last, out of his hiding-place.

Silently, in a soft pair of bed-room slippers—bagged from Wharton's room several nights ago—the fat junior crept down the attic stair to the passage, and tiptoed along to the landing.

All was dark and silent there.

Groping along the wall by the staircase, he made his way down to the hall below. If watch was being kept, he had no doubt that the fact would be revealed, when a ghostly white figure loomed up in the dark.

He was right.

Mr. Wells was still keeping watch; but he was seated in one of the deep armchairs in the hall, and nodding a little. It was Thomas who beheld the white figure glimmering in the dark.

Thomas stared at it with distended eyes for a moment as it glided down the stairs, and then let out a terrific yell.

"The ghost!" yelled Thomas.

Wells started up from a half-doze.

"Wha-a-t?" he gasped.

"Ow! Look! The ghost!" shrieked Thomas wildly. He stayed only for that shriek. Then he bolted. He headed for the service door on the hall, which he tore open and rushed through, in panic terror. A sound of bumping told that Thomas was doing the service stairs in one.

Wells stood rooted to the oak floor of the hall, gazing at the white figure, frozen with astonishment and alarm.

"Oh!" gasped Wells.

The ghostly figure flitted up the staircase before his staring eyes. It flitted up very swiftly! Billy Bunter knew now that watch was still being kept, and was only anxious to get away.

"The—the—the ghost!" gasped Wells. The ghost vanished!

Wells still stood rooted to the floor, as if petrified. In the servants' hall, Wells was accustomed to pooh-pooh the story of the ghost of Wharton Lodge! Now he had seen it! He stood and gazed, his eyes bulging from his plump face.

THE MAGNET LIBRARY.—No. 1,350.

He did not even think of switching on the light. He stood frozen.

But the light was suddenly switched on from above. Colonel Wharton, in his dressing-gown, stared down over the banisters.

He stared blankly at the horrified Wells.

"Wells!" he barked.

"Oh!" gasped Wells. "Yes, sir?" He blinked up at the frowning face over the balustrade above.

"What are you doing up at this time of night? What was that yelling that awakened me?" barked the colonel testily.

"The—the ghost, sir!" stammered Wells.

"What? What? Nonsense! Have you been drinking, Wells?"

"I—I assure you, sir, I—I—I saw——"

"Nonsense!"

"Thomas saw it also, sir——"

"Rubbish! What are you doing out of bed?"

"We were keeping watch for the pilferer, sir, and—and——"

"And you have been frightened, and awakened me!" snorted the colonel. "Go to bed! Tell Thomas to go to bed! Absurd!"

"But, sir——"

"Nonsense! Go to bed!" hooted the colonel.

"Very well, sir!"

Colonel Wharton went fuming back to his room. At the colonel's age it was not an easy matter to get to sleep again after being awakened in the night. He was distinctly irritated.

The light was turned out; and Wells disappeared after Thomas. As a matter of fact, he was rather glad to obey the colonel's injunction and go to bed. After what he had seen, he was not keen on staying up any longer in the dark.

Billy Bunter, on the attic stair, heard the colonel's deep voice, and grinned! The coast was going to be clear now! But the fat Owl waited nearly half an hour, to make sure, before he descended.

Then the ghost walked again! But this time there were no eyes to behold it! The ghost's walk took the ghost in the direction of the pantry! When the ghost walked back again, the ghost was breathing rather hard—being heavy-laden! It was not till the following morning that the household learned that the ghost had walked off with the Christmas pudding!

THE EIGHTH CHAPTER.
A Perplexing Problem !

COLONEL WHARTON wore a grim frown at breakfast the following morning. Miss Amy Wharton looked worried—quite a contrast to her usual placid benignity. Wells, hovering over the dishes, had a very thoughtful and serious expression on his portly face—not to call it solemn! Thomas, who helped wait at table, was in a jumpy state—looking over his shoulder every now and then, as if half expecting to see a spectral figure even in the daylight. Not that there was a lot of daylight; the December morning was misty and dim. Harry Wharton and Frank Nugent and the nabob were more silent than usual. There was rather an electric atmosphere at Wharton Lodge that morning.

The ghost had been seen!

Two pairs of eyes had seen it, so there could be little further doubt. In the servants' hall there was breathless debate on the subject. Thomas had several bumps and bruises, due to his rather hurried descent of the service stairs. But they did not worry him so much as the ghost did.

THE MAGNET LIBRARY.—No. 1,350.

The ghost did not worry the old colonel at all! But the fact that the Christmas pudding was missing did! Colonel Wharton, assuredly, was not keen on that delightful comestible; he had reached an age when the less Christmas pudding he disposed of, the better he felt!

But it was an outrageous act of pilfering which exasperated him intensely; it was really the climax!

Several times his stern eye turned grimly on Thomas! He was not the man to be severe without proof; but his suspicions of Thomas were strong.

The ghost story only made him snort! But it annoyed him all the same! He did not doubt that Wells had seen a figure in white! Neither did he doubt for one moment that it had been the figure of some person with a misdirected sense of humour, playing ghost to frighten the servants. Altogether, the old military gentleman was in a rather explosive state that wintry morning.

The three juniors were not sorry when breakfast was over. That morning they were going down to Wimford to meet Bob Cherry and Johnny Bull, who were arriving that day. They were sauntering on the snow-powdered terrace when Colonel Wharton came out. The grim look on his old bronzed face was quite unlike his usual hospitable and kindly expression.

"Which of you was it?" he barked, rather to the surprise of the juniors.

"To what does the whichfulness refer, esteemed sahib?" inquired Hurree Jamset Ram Singh.

"Someone played ghost in the house last night!" grunted the colonel. "What you would call a jape, at Greyfriars, I suppose?"

"Oh, my hat!" exclaimed Harry. "Surely, uncle, you don't imagine that it was one of us?"

"I don't imagine anything else!" said Colonel Wharton. "With schoolboys in the house, I think one need not look very far for a young duffer who plays ghosts!"

"Not guilty, sir!" said Frank Nugent, with a smile.

"The not-guiltiness is terrific!" said the Nabob of Bhanipur.

"I certainly know nothing about it!" said Harry.

Colonel Wharton eyed them.

"It was not Thomas!" he barked. "I suspect Thomas of the pilfering. But he was with Wells when the pretended ghost was seen. It was certainly not Thomas that played ghost."

"Couldn't have been," agreed Harry. "But perhaps Wells fancied it, uncle! Might have fancied something in the dark——"

"He saw something!" growled the colonel. "And that something was a young ass playing ghost! I'm bound to take your word, of course! But if it was not one of you, I can't understand it!"

The old soldier stalked away, evidently very much puzzled and annoyed. The mysterious happenings at Wharton Lodge were having a rather deteriorating effect on his temper.

Nugent gave a whistle.

"Uncle's getting his rag out a little!" said Harry. "It's really not surprising. It's pretty thick for a pilfering rogue to bag the Christmas pudding! And if somebody really has played ghost——"

"But who the dickens!" said Nugent. "It's clear that it wasn't Thomas, this time! You haven't been larking with a sheet over your head, I suppose?"

"Of course not, ass!"

"Nor you, Inky?"

"Certainfully not! Nor you, my esteemed Franky?"

"Never opened my eyes after I shut them last night," answered Frank. "I was jolly sleepy after keeping watch. I'd have kept it up later, though, if I'd known the ghost was going to walk!"

"I'd like to catch the silly ass!" growled Wharton.

"The catchfulness of the esteemed ghost is the proper caper," assented Hurree Jamset Ram Singh. "And the whopfulness will be terrific! Now it is time to start for the station if we are to meet our ridiculous friends."

The juniors went in for their coats. Hurree Jamset Ram Singh went up to his room for a muffler, to fortify himself against the winter cold, which he felt more severely than the natives of the climate. He passed the door of Wharton's den on his way; and beheld Thomas standing there tapping, with a puzzled expression on his face. The nabob stopped.

"My esteemed Thomas!" he remarked. "If you want the absurd Wharton, he is downstairs!"

Thomas blinked at him.

"Then who's in his room, sir?" he asked.

"Is there anybody in his ridiculous room?"

"I came up to mend the fire, sir, and jest as I got to the door, the key was turned," said Thomas. "I s'posed it was Master Harry! So I knocked."

The nabob's eyes gleamed.

If there was someone in Harry Wharton's den who had locked the door on the inside at the sound of approaching footsteps, it certainly was not Wharton, who was downstairs with Nugent, waiting for Hurree Singh.

"Perhapsfully it is the esteemed pilferer!" suggested the nabob, and he stepped quickly to Wharton's bed-room door, passed through the bed-room, and entered the den by the communicating door. Thomas followed at his heels.

They looked round the sitting-room.

It was empty!

"My eye!" said Thomas blankly. "There ain't nobody 'ere, Master Hurree Singh! But I 'eard the door locked!"

Hurree Jamset Ram Singh stepped to the corridor door. It was locked on the inside!

"My esteemed hat!" he murmured.

Someone had been there! That seemed certain! Whoever it was, he was gone! Hurree Singh stepped back into Wharton's bed-room, and looked round it. No one was there! Then he crossed the den to the french window on the balcony. That window was closed; but it was only latched, not locked. Possibly the mysterious intruder had gone that way. But the industrious Thomas had swept the snow from the balcony and the steps that morning, and there was no trace of footprints.

Leaving Thomas still staring, the nabob went to his room and fetched his muffler, and descended to join his friends in the hall. Someone, it seemed, had used Wharton's room surreptitiously as a means of egress from the house. Who it was, was quite a mystery! Billy Bunter had had another narrow escape!

THE NINTH CHAPTER.

Bunter Again !

"HALLO, hallo, hallo !" roared Bob Cherry.

Bob's ruddy, cheery face looked from a carriage window, at Wimford Station. He waved a woolly gloved hand to three fellows on the platform, and roared. Then the carriage door was hurled open, and Bob jumped out, followed by Johnny Bull. Wharton, Nugent, and Hurree Singh trotted up the platform to meet them.

"Here we are again !" boomed Bob Cherry, the powerful voice that was wont to wake the echoes of the Remove passage at Greyfriars School now rousing those of the little Surrey station. "Hallo, hallo, hallo ! Enjoying life, old beans ?"

"The enjoyfulness is terrific, now that we once more behold the light of your esteemed and absurd countenance, my idiotic Bob !" declared Hurree Jamset Ram Singh.

Bob Cherry chuckled.

"Same old Inky !" he said. "Same jolly old flow of beautiful English ! Ripping weather, isn't it, you men ? Freezing everywhere !"

"The ripfulness is preposterous !" said Hurree Singh. "The freezefulness is perhapsfully a little too terrific ! But what is the oddfulness, so long as the happiness is complete and execrable ?"

"Ha, ha, ha !"

"Jolly cold in the train," said Johnny Bull. "Here's your bag, Bob ! Chuck out my rug !"

"Here you are !" answered Bob, chucking out the rug, as requested. It landed on Johnny's head, and enveloped him, and he sat down suddenly on the platform.

"Ow !" roared Johnny Bull. "You silly ass !"

"Ha, ha, ha !"

Johnny struggled out of the rug, and folded it again. Bob Cherry chuckled. Bob was evidently in his usual exuberant spirits, only a little more so, under the genial influence of Christmas. Really, it was not quite safe to be too near Bob when he was in high spirits.

"The car's outside," said Harry, laughing. "Got your bags ? Come on !"

The Famous Five walked out of the station. The colonel's car was waiting outside, and Brown, the chauffeur, was standing by it, with a rather peculiar expression on his face.

"Is the other young gentleman going in the car, sir ?" he inquired.

Wharton stared.

"Which other ?" he asked. "There's only us five."

"I mean the stout young gentleman——"

"The which ?"

"Well, sir, he got in the car !"

"Who the dickens——" Harry Wharton stepped to the car. He stared in, at a fat face and a big pair of spectacles.

"Bunter !" he gasped.

"Bunter !" exclaimed Nugent blankly. "The esteemed and r i d i c u l o u s Bunter !"

"Hallo, hallo, hallo ! Jolly old Bunter turned up again like a bad penny !" exclaimed Bob Cherry. "I didn't know Bunter was here !"

"Neither did I !" said Harry Wharton grimly. "You fat, frabjous foozler, what the merry old thump are you doing in that car ?"

"I say, you fellows——"

"Hop out !"

"Oh, really, Wharton——"

"Sharp, fathead !"

Billy Bunter blinked at the Famous Five through his big spectacles. Where he had turned up from nobody knew !

Certainly nobody was likely to guess that he had turned up from Wharton Lodge ! Bob Cherry grinned ! Johnny Bull grunted ! Nugent and Hurree Singh looked blankly surprised ! Harry Wharton was frowning ! He had had enough of Bunter—in fact, a little too much—though he was far from suspecting how much he had had of Bunter since Greyfriars had broken up for the Christmas holidays.

"I say, old chaps——" said Bunter.

"Get out !" roared Wharton.

"Oh, really, you know !"

"Where on earth did you spring from ?" demanded Wharton. "Are you staying in Wimford, you fat foozler ?"

"Eh ? Oh ! Yes ! I'm staying at the George Hotel !" explained Bunter.

"There isn't a George Hotel here, you fat ass !"

"Isn't there ? Well, I forget its name ; but I'm staying there !" said Bunter. "But the fact is, you fellows, I——"

"Jump out !"

"The fact is——"

"Get a move on !"

Billy Bunter did not get a move on. Ensconced in the car, he blinked at the chums of the Remove uneasily.

Bunter was "trying it on" again ! He had not done so badly in his attic, all things considered—especially since he had snaffled the Christmas pudding ! But Bunter, naturally, did not want to spend Christmas in that surreptitious manner, if he could help it. He wanted to spend it as an honoured guest—if he could !

"I say, you fellows, do listen to a chap !" he urged. "Having fixed it up with you for Christmas, Wharton, old fellow, it's rather late to alter arrangements now. You can't let a fellow down !"

"Are you waiting to be slung out on your fat neck ?"

"Beast !"

"My uncle's in Wimford this morning," said Harry. "He came in the car with us. If he spots you he's pretty certain to smack your head."

"The smackfulness will probably be terrific !" grinned Hurree Jamset Ram Singh.

"Is the old beast still huffy about that mistake on the telephone ?" asked Bunter. "Of course, I shouldn't have called him an old donkey if I'd known he was taking the call. Can't you smooth him over somehow, old chap ? Tell him that Christmas will be absolutely rotten if I'm not there ! That ought to do the trick !"

"I can't tell whoppers to that extent !"

"Beast ! Think of Marjorie, when she comes on Boxing Day !" said Bunter. "What will she feel like if I'm not there ?"

"Frightfully bucked, I suppose !"

"The buckfulness will be——"

"Terrific !" chuckled Bob.

"Look here, you fat duffer ! Hook it !" exclaimed Wharton impatiently. "I might have managed it for you, but you've put my uncle's back up, and that's that ! Now get going !"

"Beast !"

A tall figure approached the group by the car. Colonel Wharton had come to Wimford with the juniors, and left them waiting at the station for the new arrivals. Now, spotting the group from a distance, he was coming over to speak a cheery word of greeting to his nephew's school friends. Brown, the chauffeur, saw him coming. But the Famous Five were all looking at Bunter, in the car, and did not observe him. Neither did Bunter, who was blinking at the Famous Five. Colonel Wharton strode up unnoticed.

"Now, look here, W h a r t o n !" squeaked Bunter. "Do the decent thing ! After all I've done for you——"

"You fat idiot !"

"You can pull your silly old uncle's leg somehow ! After all, he's a silly old donkey !" said Bunter. "I wouldn't have told him so on the phone, if I'd known he was taking the call—but facts are facts, ain't they ? All these old military men are silly old codgers, and your uncle is the silliest old codger I've ever struck ! A blithering old fathead, if you ask me ! Well, you can stuff him up somehow ! An old idiot like that is——"

"Like what ?" roared Colonel Wharton.

"Oh, my hat !" exclaimed Bob.

The juniors spun round. They had not been aware of the old colonel's approach till that moment. Now they were aware of it—and aware that he was in a state of towering wrath ! His bronzed face was purple, and his eyes gleaming and glinting at the fat face in the car !

"Oh crikey !" gasped Bunter. "Is—is—is that your uncle, old chap ? Oh lor' ! I—I say, sir, I—I wasn't saying that you were a blithering old fathead, sir ! I—I—I'm much too respectful to say what I think of you, sir ! I—I mean——"

A hand that seemed of iron gripped Bunter's collar, and he was hooked out of the car, like a winkle from a shell.

"You disrespectful young rascal !" roared the colonel.

"Ow ! Leggo !"

"If I had my cane with me I would thrash you—yes, thrash you, sir, by Jove !" roared the colonel.

"Yarooooh !"

"As it is, I will box your ears !"

"Whoooop !"

Smack, smack, smack !

Three smacks were enough for Bunter ! He tore himself away, and fled ! Colonel Wharton glared after him as he went.

"What is that young rascal doing here, Harry ?" he demanded.

"Haven't the foggiest !" answered Harry. "I think he must be staying in Wimford, goodness knows why !"

"The impertinent young jackanapes !" growled the colonel. "By Jove ! If I see him again——"

The old colonel did not finish that sentence. But evidently something of a drastic nature was going to happen to Bunter if the colonel saw him again. Billy Bunter vanished round a corner, going strong.

Even Bunter realised that there was nothing doing, so far as the colonel was concerned ! Evidently it was still the attic for Bunter !

— —

THE TENTH CHAPTER.

Shut Out !

"OH lor' !" murmured Billy Bunter.

It was dark.

It was frightfully cold !

When Billy Bunter stole out of his attic and got out of Wharton Lodge, he had to take the risk of doing so in the day-time—for the excellent reason that he was too lazy to get up before daylight.

But when he returned to his hidden den he was careful to do so after the fall of the December dusk. A fellow in such very peculiar circumstances couldn't be too careful !

So it was after dark that evening when Bunter, having trudged back from Wimford once more, dodged into the grounds of Wharton Lodge, and stealthily sneaked round to the old stone garden-stair under Wharton's balcony.

In the dark he crept up to the balcony, and was relieved to find the window dark.

Having timed his return for the period when the family were at dinner, he naturally expected to find the schoolboys quarters deserted, and hoped to dodge in unseen, as he had done several times before.

But this time there was, so to speak, a lion in the path.

The french windows were locked on the inside!

Generally, the door of Wharton's den on the balcony was left on the latch, as an easy way in and out for Harry and his friends. That had suited Bunter admirably.

Perhaps the incident of the morning had made Thomas take this precaution; or, perhaps, the late mysterious happenings had caused Wells to keep all doors secured; or, perhaps, one of the juniors had locked the french window after going in.

Anyhow, it was locked!

Nobody was in the room—Bunter, with his fat face pressed to the glass, could see that much, by the glimmering, ruddy glow of the log fire.

The coast was clear—if only he could have got in! But he couldn't! Unless he cracked a pane and put a fat paw through to unfasten the door, the Owl of the Remove was shut out.

That, of course, was a very last and desperate resource! It would have furnished rather too palpable a clue to Bunter's surreptitious proceedings. Had suspicion been awakened that there was some extraneous person in the house, a search would soon have unearthed the unbidden guest. That was less desirable than ever since the little scene with Colonel Wharton at the station in Winford.

Bunter shivered in the winter wind, and groaned.

He had to wait and trust to luck!

So far, luck had befriended him in a really wonderful manner! But it seemed to have deserted him now!

Indeed, had Bunter had the railway fare in his pocket he might have been tempted to take his departure, and try his fortune once more with his incensed Uncle George! But he hadn't!

The light came on in the "den" at last! Blinking through the glass, Billy Bunter saw Harry Wharton & Co. come in.

They looked bright and cheerful—a contrast to the fat Owl shivering on the balcony outside.

Wharton stepped across to the french window, and Bunter popped back, huddling under the stone balustrade in deep shadow, in fear of discovery.

But the captain of the Greyfriars Remove did not think of looking out into the darkness. He put his hand to the curtains, and drew them along in front of the french window. Then he turned back to his friends.

Bunter approached the window again. The curtains did not quite meet in the middle, having been carelessly drawn, and there was a slit between them, through which the fat Owl could still blink into the room within.

Harry Wharton had laid a large cardboard box on the table, and was proceeding now to unpack it.

Bunter watched him, and the members of the Co., gathering round the table, watched also.

From the box, Harry turned out a number of fancy costumes. Bunter, who had heard a good deal of talk in the house, remembered that he had heard that there was a be a fancy dress

function on Boxing Night, when a number of young people were to gather to dance and make merry.

"Pick out what you like, you fellows!" Bunter heard the captain of the Remove say, with his fat ear glued to the keyhole. "Plenty here! Costumes or plain dominoes, and masks all round. Unmask at supper on Boxing Night——"

"Jolly good fun!" said Bob Cherry. "I rather fancy this blue domino. There's a couple of them, I see; but two fellows had better not dress alike. Anybody else want it?"

"Stick to it, old chap!"

Bob Cherry picked out a blue silk domino, and draped it on himself. There was a blue mask to match, which he fastened over his ruddy, cheery countenance. Domino and mask completely hid him from sight from head to foot, and no eye could have detected his identity. He surveyed the result in a tall glass, and gave a nod of satisfaction.

"Good egg!" he said. "Topping fun! Nobody could guess who a fellow was! I wonder if Marjorie will spot me?"

"Sure to, if you dance with her!" said Nugent.

"Eh—why?"

"She will know you by your weight when you tread on her foot."

"Ha, ha, ha!"

"You silly ass!" roared Bob.

The juniors, chuckling, proceeded to pick out the costumes that they fancied, with the masks belonging to them. Quite a number were left in the box, to be lent to other guests who might want them. Harry Wharton lifted the box from the table, and placed it in a corner of the room.

Then the juniors went out of the den, each carrying the costume he had selected to his own quarters. Harry Wharton passed into the adjoining bedroom with a cavalier costume on his arm.

The light was turned off; the room was deserted and dark again.

Billy Bunter groaned.

Having finished the matter of the costumes, the chums of the Remove had gone downstairs again, little dreaming of the fat Owl on the balcony, like a podgy Peri at the gate of paradise.

"Beasts!" groaned Bunter.

The sight of the costumes had put an idea into Bunter's fat brain. At a function where all the people were costumed and masked there was a chance for a "gate-crasher."

Bunter had already resolved to get hold of one of those costumes, and join the party on Boxing Night. He would make sure of a supper, at least! The guests were to unmask at the supper, but that was all right—Bunter would be early at supper!

But for the present the fat Owl was shut out! How was he going to get in? He had grumbled at his quarters in the attic, but he would have been very glad of the attic now! At least, it was a shelter from the December wind!

What awful beast had locked that french window? Several times, since his extraordinary visit to Wharton Lodge, Bunter's weird ventriloquism had stood him in good stead. But it could not help him now! It looked as if he was booked for a night out!

He groped over the window. But it was fast—there was no chance! Almost he made up his fat mind to break a pane and get at the key inside! But it was altogether too risky.

But what was a fellow to do?

Apparently, he could only wait and hope! Bunter waited—but he felt less and less hopeful as the long, cold minutes passed!

At last, there was a light again in the room! Bunter blinked through the gap in the curtains. It was the portly Wells who entered.

Judging by the way the butler looked round the room, Bunter guessed that he had slipped up for a few minutes to see whether all was right. Wells was fed-up with keeping watch at night for the mysterious pilferer, but at other times he was very watchful and wary. Now that everybody was downstairs, no doubt it occurred to him that this was a chance for that mysterious snaffler, and he was taking a cautious look round.

Bunter blinked at him.

At the sight of the watchful Wells, his first thought was to seek the darkest and shadiest corner of the balcony, in case the butler looked out.

But second thoughts were best!

This, he realised, was a chance! Bunter was getting desperate at the prospect of a night out; and he had to take chances. Under the stress of his painful position his fat brain worked at an unusual rate.

He tapped at the window!

Wells gave a start, and looked round at the french window, evidently surprised by the tap.

And the Greyfriars ventriloquist, in a voice that anyone at Wharton Lodge would have sworn was that of Hurree Jamset Ram Singh, the dusky Nabob of Bhanipur, called out:

"Please let me infully, my esteemed Wells! The door is lockfully fastened on the inside!"

"Dear me!" ejaculated Wells.

He came towards the window, nothing doubting that Hurree Jamset Ram Singh had gone out of the house and returned by way of Wharton's den, expecting to find the french window on the latch. He pulled the curtains aside.

Bunter popped back into cover of a thick mass of ivy beside the window.

The next moment it opened, and Wells looked out.

"Master Hurree Singh——" Wells stared into the darkness, surprised not to see the nabob standing there. "Dear me! Where are you, sir?"

From the steps of the balcony, at a little distance from the window, came the voice of the Greyfriars ventriloquist!

"Please come and helpfully assist me! I have slipfully fallen on the idiotic snow."

"Good gracious!" exclaimed Wells, and he stepped quickly from the french window and crossed the balcony to the steps.

He stood on the top step, peering down into the darkness.

His portly back was towards Bunter and the window.

With his fat heart beating fast, Bunter moved from the ivy and stepped silently in at the french window.

In a twinkling he shot the window, turned the key, and dragged the curtains across. He closed them more carefully than Harry Wharton had done. He had his reasons. Not a fraction of a gap was left by which Wells could have looked in.

Bunter grinned.

"Bless me!" he heard Wells ejaculate. "Where are you, sir? Please call out! Why—what—who—upon my word!"

Wells tramped back across the balcony to the french window. His portly face wore a frown. He tried the handle and found the door locked, and his frown intensified. He could only conclude that Hurree Jamset Ram Singh had played a practical joke on him, tricking him out on the balcony and shutting him out in the cold. He tapped sharply on the window.

"Please let me in at once, Master

Thomas, the page, stared at the white figure with distended eyes as it glided down the stairs. Then he let out a terrific yell. "The ghost!" Wells, the butler, started up from a half-doze. "Wha-a-at!" he gasped. "Ow! Look! The ghost!" shrieked Thomas.

Hurree Singh!" he called out sharply. "I am bound to say, sir, that I do not like this kind of joke! I beg you to let me in at once."

Billy Bunter gave no heed. Wells could not get in, and could not look in! If he wanted to get back he had to go down the steps, round the house, and in by the door downstairs. That gave the fat Owl of the Remove plenty of time.

Tap, tap, tap! came unheeded at the window! Wells was not anxious to go round the house in the December wind, without even a coat on!

"Master Hurree Singh!" he shouted. "Let me in at once!"

Bunter turned a deaf ear.

He whisked across to the box of costumes and opened it. He picked out the blue domino and mask, exactly like those selected by Bob Cherry! He jammed the mask into his pocket and crammed the domino under his arm, and then whisked to the door. The passage outside was clear; and Bunter lost no time in getting back to his attic!

There he chuckled a fat chuckle!

Wells, on the cold and windy balcony, did not feel like chuckling! He tapped again and again! But as there was no response, he realised that the practical joker did not intend to let him in, and he made up his mind, at last, to descend the steps and go round the house to the door. And when, at last, Wells got in, cold and shivering and deeply exasperated, only his well-trained respect for his master and his master's guests prevented Wells from telling the Nabob of Bhanipur what he thought of him!

THE ELEVENTH CHAPTER.

The Christmas Ghost!

CHRISTMAS DAY was rather a quiet day at Wharton Lodge. The festivities followed.

Quietest of all that Christmas Day was the unbidden and unsuspected guest who had the disused attic all to himself! Several times during the day, certainly, Bunter ventured out when the coast was clear. But he did not venture far; and a footstep or a voice sent him scuttling back to his attic, like a fat rabbit to its burrow.

Bunter had had an idea that on Christmas Day he would show up and take his chance! On that day, of all others, a fellow was least likely to get the "boot."

But for the unfortunate row with the colonel at Wimford, doubtless Bunter would have taken his chance.

But that, so to speak, had put the lid on!

All Bunter's proceedings, in fact, since he had been an unsuspected guest at Wharton Lodge had made matters worse instead of better.

He had, as it were, run up a long account, which had to be paid off if he was discovered there.

All his various snafflings, which had been attributed to some unknown pilferer from below stairs, would be traced to their genuine author as soon as it was known that Bunter had been hidden there all the time.

The identity of the "ghost" would be known at once. Nobody would doubt where the Christmas pudding had gone!

Still, Bunter would have risked it, but for that row with the old colonel! Colonel Wharton had not finished

smacking his head on that occasion when Bunter got away. Bunter did not want him to finish.

He pondered over it dismally in the seclusion of the attic, but he felt that it would not do!

Fortunately, he was not short of provender.

The pudding was still lasting him!

It was, luckily, an enormous pudding! Even Bunter was a long time getting through it! Christmas pudding, delightful as it is, might have palled on any other fellow in the long run. But it did not pall on Bunter! He enjoyed every crumb and every plum.

The pudding, of course, had been replaced downstairs. There was another pudding for the family. Probably they did not enjoy the second pudding so much as the fat Owl of the Remove enjoyed the first one.

But everything comes to an end! The last fragment of that big pudding was gone on Christmas Day.

In the dusk of the evening the fat Owl ventured out of his hiding place again and as far as the landing. The hall below was brightly lighted and gleaming with holly and mistletoe.

Peering through the banisters, Bunter blinked at bright and cheery faces. Miss Amy Wharton with her kind and gentle smile, was pulling a Christmas cracker with Hurree Jamset Ram Singh. Bob Cherry's ruddy face grinned under a tall paper cap. Harry Wharton was trying the wireless, to see what was coming through—ready to turn it on if there was something cheerful and to

(Continued on page 16.)

THE NEW Greyfriars

No. 65 (New Series).

EDITED BY

"MANNERS MAKYTH MAN"

Bunter Laments Lost Chivalry

Having failed to discover Bunter Court, our reporter had a look round the suburbs and found Billy Bunter in front of an enormous fire in the dining-room of a modest villa, munching chocolates. He nodded thoughtfully, when asked for a New Year message to the world.

"That's easy," he said. "My New Year message to the world is: 'Be Better Mannered!'

"'Manners makyth man' is an old saying and a true one; but it's forgotten to-day. Everywhere around us nowadays, we see the decay of good manners, and it simply disgusts a gentleman of the old school like myself. Don't sit there, you silly idiot; you'll be in my way!

"The laws of hospitality seem to have vanished completely. Hosts treat guests as though they were dirt. It seems awful to chaps like me, who treat their guests as honoured and revered friends. Leave those chocs alone, you beast; they're mine!

"The Age of Chivalry is past. Time was when gentlemen regarded the fair sex as a race of superior beings, entitled to worship and veneration. But alas, not many can say with me, that their chivalry towards the fair sex remains unchanged. Mind your eyesight, by the way; here comes that pie-faced sister of mine!

"Well, you'd better buzz off now. Dinner will be served in a jiffy, and if you barge in, there won't be enough left for me!

"Don't forget to tell your readers to Be Better Mannered next year, will you? See yourself out; I'm too jolly tired!"

'LONZY'S LITTLE LETTERS

Dear Editor,—Peradventure your perceptive powers had recently intimated to your intelligence the circumstantial phenomenon of the superimposition on my physiognomy of a discoloration particularly related to one of my visual organs.

May I, in justice to my known views on the pacification of juvenile social animate existence and my preference for pusillanimity over pugnacity, asseverate with the utmost vehemence that the ophthalmic irregularity revealed is not the consequence of a fistical encounter, but the sequel to an inordinately violent causation of contiguity between the anterior portion of my anatomy and the study door?

Earnestly yours,
ALONZO TODD.

(If all this means: "I didn't get my black-eye from a scrap, but from a bash from the study door," then, 'Lonzy, we believe you!—ED.)

MY WORST AND BEST EXPERIENCE

By Bolsover Major

It was in the last week of last Christmas term that I struck my worst experience, and I don't mind broadcasting it as a warning to others.

When I went into Courtfield to buy a few Christmas presents, there was nothing but peace and goodwill in my heart. It's true that on the way I tweaked one fag's nose and twisted another fag's ear, and knocked the heads of two other fags together, but it was done in a purely jovial spirit.

When I got to Courtfield, however, peace and goodwill took a back seat. The shopping crowds were enough to try any man's patience. They jostled me off the pavement, trod on my toes in the shops, and jabbed me in the eyes with their elbows when I sat down to have a cup of tea. By the time I got back to Courtfield Station, well laden with purchases, I don't mind telling you I was not in a very good mood.

The train for Friardale was pretty full. I made a rush for the only vacant seat I could see; but a grinning youth, who wasn't hampered with parcels, calmly stepped in front of me and claimed it.

It was the last straw! Having dumped my parcels on the rack I said: "My seat, I believe!" and yanked him out.

The youth stopped grinning and told me it was his seat. I promptly sat down, and told him he was welcome to the seat if he could get me out of it!

Much to my surprise, he grabbed me by the hair and tried to force me out. Seeing that he was about a stone lighter than myself, I had no hesitation in giving him a biff on the jaw. Naturally, I expected that would end the matter.

But it didn't! Before I had time to say "Jack Dempsey!" an earthquake and a hurricane combined seemed to hit me. An instant later, I found myself lying on the platform, with all my parcels piling on top of me!

It turned out that the grinning youth was Young Slasher, the featherweight champion of Wapshot!

Moral: Before you tackle any grinning youth who weighs a stone less than you weigh yourself, see that his hands are tied behind his back!

I speak as one who knows!

DICKY NUGENT'S WEEKLY WISDOM

When Tubb of the Third went karolling last week, a bulldog tore out the seat of his trowsers.

Tubb has everybody's hartfelt simperthy, and I'm sure we all wish him a HAPPY NEW REAR!

My best experience ... Christmas party last y... for reasons I couldn'... everybody seemed t... violent fancy to ... fellows plied me wit... ments and hung on e... I spoke, while the girl... round me, and almo... for the privilege of ... with me. Even the ... seemed to follow my m... with fascinated eyes... over themselves wit... when I spoke to the...

Could it, I wondere... I had at last got int... where my true me... appreciated? Wha... explanation, it was j... fying to me to be the ... evening, and I enjo... I've enjoyed no oth... before or since.

Afterwards, I lea... reason for all the fu... had been expecting a... named Alfonso Dark... turn up, and I happen... rather like him!

But I didn't learn ... late in the evening, a...

meantime, I'd been b... time of my life!

Temple's theatrical ... village hall was spoile... the audience felt cold ... the failure of the hot w... But there's no need f... to worry.

We feel sure it w... been a complete "fros... case.

WOULD YOU BELIEVE IT?

Harry Wharton is a skilled "figure" skater, and has given some remarkable exhibitions on the Sark. Marjorie Hazeldene is the best of the Cliff House girls.

When W. G. Bunter visited the London Zoo, he took a huge bag of buns—but not for 'he bears! Bunter cruelly "scoffed" the buns, while the bears looked on helplessly!

Captain "Larry" Lascelles young subaltern, won the ... in the Great War, 191... Very few people know ab... however—"Larry" bein... modest and retiring her...

Herald

EXTRA GOOD EDITION

WHARTON.   December 30th, 1933.

COKER ORDERS MORNING DIP

But Guests Laugh Last

On waking up the first morning after their arrival at Coker's house, Potter and Greene were surprised to find their clothes missing and bathing-costumes and bath-wraps lying in their place. Ere they had recovered from the first shock of this discovery, Coker himself came along the landing, whistling cheerfully.

"Show a leg, you wasters!" he greeted boisterously, as Potter and Greene looked out from their respective bed-rooms. "Ready for your morning dip?"

"Our morning WHAT?" howled Potter and Greene in chorus, with a horrified look at the icicles hanging outside the landing window.

"Your morning dip!" repeated Coker, with a hearty laugh at their evident surprise. "I believe in starting the day well with a dip in the river before brekker. No rooting about in a stuffy bed-room for me!"

"But the river's frozen!" shrieked Potter.

"Only to a depth of about two inches; we can soon break through that," smiled Coker. "Somehow, I thought you slackers would jib, so I got the gardener to take your clobber to the other side of the river. Unless you want a mile walk to the nearest bridge, you'll simply have to go across—see? Well, let's go!"

And Coker, who was also attired in bathing-costume and bath-wrap, led the way down the stairs.

To say that Potter and Greene objected would be putting it mildly. Their eyes goggled, and they foamed at the mouth as they followed their leader. But, knowing Coker, they knew that all the objections in the world would make no difference to him; so willy-nilly they tramped with him across the ice-bound fields to the river.

As Coker had anticipated, they had no difficulty whatever in breaking the ice. Coker made sure of their having a real good dip by running ahead of them and jumping through in several places!

Eventually, with a final string of maledictions, Potter and Greene took the plunge, and waded through the ice floes to the other side, where a grinning gardener was waiting with two suit-cases full of clothes and a supply of rough towels.

"Br-r-r! Well, that's that!" remarked Potter, as he started rubbing himself vigorously with a towel. "These my clothes, Smithers?"

"Yessir; an' these here are Master Greene's. Which, I hope, you enjoyed the dip, gentlemen!"

"Br-r-r! S-s-s-simply g-g-glorious!" said Coker enthusiastically. "N-n-now we'll have g-g-good appetites for b-b-breakfast! By the way, w-w-where's my c-c-clobber?"

It was then that Smithers' jaw dropped.

"Well, if that warn't silly of me, Master 'Orace! I remembered the other gents, but I've forgotten you!" he gasped.

"WHAT?" shrieked Coker.

Coker's turn came now to goggle at the eyes and foam at the mouth! Alas! No photographer was present to preserve a record of his expression for posterity, but we are assured by Potter and Greene that for a few minutes Coker would have taken a prize at any freak show.

Potter and Greene, for reasons which Coker still fails to understand, found something humorous in the situation.

Coker didn't wait for them to finish dressing. He beat it for the bridge, and didn't stop running till he got back to his bed-room.

LANGUID LORD'S LUXURIOUS TOBOGGAN

Winter Sports a la Mauly

If you imagine that tobogganing at Mauleverer Towers is just a matter of getting out an old soap-box and sliding down the hill, you've made a big mistake.

Mauly does things in style, believe us. First he tells the Butler that he is going tobogganing. The Butler tells the Head Footman, and the Head Footman tells the

Second Footman. The Second Footman passes the word to the Third Footman, and the Third Footman passes it on to the next three—who pass it on to the Page.

The Page rings up the Winter Sports Garage, and the Head Chauffeur orders one of the Assistant Chauffeurs to get out the toboggan. The Assistant Chauffeur sits in the driver's seat of the toboggan, which is then hauled by a team of Garage Hands to the front of the Towers.

We need hardly say that the toboggan is a handsome, plush-upholstered affair, designed by one of London's most exclusive firms of body-builders, with seats for a driver and three footmen, in addition, of course, to Mauly himself.

As soon as Mauly has donned his fur coat, top-hat, and mittens, and been carried to the cushioned passenger-seat, and the electric foot-warmers have been adjusted to the required heat, the toboggan is hauled to the top of a hill and released.

The run having been accomplished in safety, Mauly is hauled back to the Towers, and carried up to bed for a well-earned rest.

And that is tobogganing at Mauleverer Towers!

If we've slightly exaggerated the facts, we apologise.

The fact is, this is the first time our Winter Sports Representative has visited Mauleverer Towers, and he's so overwhelmed by it that his impressions are apt to get a little distorted!

Our New Year

Resolved—

THAT we're going to make the "Greyfriars Herald" even better and brighter than before.

THAT we'll worthily uphold the fine old traditions of Greyfriars.

THAT those who add to the laurels of the old school in field or Form-room shall receive our unstinted praise.

THAT rogues, bullies, bad sports, and boasters shall be fearlessly exposed in our columns.

THAT we'll anoint the first spring poet who calls on us with a bottle of best blue-black ink.

THAT we'll strew Billy Bunter in little pieces all over the Remove passage every time he burgles the Editor's tea.

THAT we'll buy Dicky Nugent a book on Spelling—if he'll promise not to burn it in the Form-room grate during the next Second Form herring-frying jamboree!

THAT any request from Mr. Quelch to publish the first 1,000,000 words of his "History of Greyfriars" in serial form, shall be gently, but firmly, declined.

THAT we're going to bump Coker every time he offers to become Editor.

THAT even if he stops offering to become Editor, we're going to bump him just the same!

GREYFRIARS FACTS WHILE YOU WAIT!

...cy Bolsover gives lessons in art of self-defence. His clients ...quently leave his study after first lesson with black eyes ...swollen noses—and they don't come back!

Besides boxing and football, Dick Russell goes in for Natural History, and enjoys studying minute organisms under a powerful microscope. He has some weird specimens in stock!

Fisher T. Fish estimates that if all his money-making schemes this term had "come off," he would now be worth roughly £50,000. Unfortunately, however, his schemes have left him 'broke'!

The Ghost of Wharton Lodge

(Continued from page 13.)

turn it off if there was one of those interesting and improving talks! Everybody looked happy, and Bunter, blinking down at them unseen, considered once more whether it would be judicious to "show up." Colonel Wharton, standing before the fire with his hands under his coat-tails, looked unusually amiable. Frank Nugent's voice floated up!

"Heard from Mauly, Wharton?"

"Yes; he's coming over to-morrow," answered Harry.

"Good egg! Is Bunter staying with him?"

"Not that I know of."

"I wonder whom Bunter's staying with?"

There was a laugh.

"Bunter!" It was the colonel's deep voice. "That impertinent young jackanapes! Huh!"

"My dear James!" murmured Aunt Amy.

"Oh, quite so, my dear Amy!" said the colonel. "At Christmas-time one must feel kindly towards everybody. Still, I think I should box that cheeky young rascal's ears if I saw him, all the same. What is there on the wireless, Harry?" he added, evidently to get rid of the disagreeable subject of that impertinent young jackanapes, Bunter!

Billy Bunter glared through the banisters.

He gave up the idea of "showing up" and trusting to luck and the spirit of Yuletide. It looked evidently had not got over it. It was still the attic for Bunter!

Squeals and Morse came from the wireless. Wharton shut it off.

"What about a ghost story?" asked Bob Cherry. "Harry tells us that the jolly old ghost has been seen this Christmas. Lucky bargee to have a family ghost; they forgot to tell the builder to put one in at Cherry Place."

"Ha, ha, ha!"

"Tell us about the ghost, sir," said Johnny Bull.

Colonel Wharton smiled.

"If you would care to hear it——" he said.

"Oh, yes, rather!"

"The ratherfulness is terrific."

There was general attention while the colonel told the story of the ghostly figure that haunted—or did not haunt—Wharton Lodge. At Christmastide, it seemed, when the snow was white on the roofs, and the wild wind wailed round the chimneys, the ghost walked on the scene where he had been slain so many hundred years ago, and announced his presence with deep and dismal groans.

"Of late," the colonel wound up, "the ghost has not been seen or heard——"

Groan!

Colonel Wharton broke off sharply.

Groan!

"What—what—what was that?" ejaculated Miss Amy. Her face became quite pale in the firelight.

"Good gad! What——" The colonel stared round.

Groan!

All the juniors were on their feet.

Every groan seemed to come from a different direction. They were, naturally, unaware that a ventriloquist was at work.

It was startling—eerie—unnerving.

"What the thump——" exclaimed Bob Cherry blankly. "Did you fellows hear that?"

"The hearfulness was terrific."

"Hark! There it is again!"

Groan!

It was a long, horrible, hair-raising groan. This time it seemed to Colonel Wharton that he detected the sound from the oak-balustraded landing over the old hall. He glared up.

"Someone is playing a trick!" he snapped. "Run up the stairs, some of you, and search!"

Billy Bunter was generally like the tortoise in his movements. But as he heard those words he outstripped the hare. He was back in his attic almost in the twinkling of an eye.

Harry Wharton & Co. ran up the stairs.

"Nobody here!" called out Harry.

The groans were heard no more. Billy Bunter, locked in his attic, was groaning dismally over the absence of supper. But in the attic his groans were unheard.

———

THE TWELFTH CHAPTER.

Beastly for Bob!

CHIMING bells sounded in the frosty night, mingling with the wail of the wind.

In the old oak-walled hall of Wharton Lodge there was still a dim glow from the red embers on the ancient hearth. Every now and then came a faint crackle from a log. At long intervals there was a little leaping flame, that died down again and left all black.

The household slept—with some exceptions. Five fellows were very wide awake. It was a lark, Bob Cherry had declared, to celebrate Christmas with a ghost-hunt. Johnny Bull agreed that a ghost gave the festive season the finishing touch. Harry Wharton was very keen to lay hold of the mysterious practical joker who was playing ghost—who had scared Wells and Thomas with a sheet over his head, and startled the whole party by groaning on Christmas evening from some unsuspected nook. The whole Co., in fact, were keen on bagging the ghost, and at the chimes of midnight they turned out for that purpose.

There was no danger this time of bagging Wells by mistake. Colonel Wharton had frowned so severely on the butler's exploit that Wells was not going to repeat it. The Famous Five had the field to themselves. And if the ghost walked they were going to "lay" it.

They were going, in fact, to lay it hard. Each of them had provided himself with a weapon of offence for laying the ghost. If that ghost was caught he was likely to be the soundest thrashed ghost in the whole world of spectres and phantoms.

The chums of the Remove had laid their plans carefully. They posted themselves at various points to watch for the ghost.

Harry Wharton and Frank Nugent tiptoed down into the hall. Johnny Bull posted himself on one wing of the double staircase, Hurree Jamset Ram Singh on the other. Bob Cherry took possession of the long, wide landing that connected the two above.

Thus posted, the five juniors were well placed to bag the ghost if he showed up that Christmas night. They hoped that he would. It was, perhaps, a "lark" to go ghost-hunting; but it was cold, and the fellows grew rather sleepy, and they were not fearfully keen to repeat the performance. So they hoped that they would have good luck this time.

Certainly there was a good chance of it—for the ghost of Wharton Lodge was frightfully hungry.

Another raid on the larder was indicated, and Billy Bunter could only hope that everybody was sleeping soundly on Christmas night.

Anyhow, he had to risk it.

If anybody was up, and he was seen, a ghostly aspect would save him from detection if he got clear. Carefully, by a dim candle-light in his attic, the Owl of the Remove draped himself in a sheet, and put the pillowslip over his bullet-head. It was well after midnight when he made the venture. He blew out the candle, opened the attic door silently, and crept out. For several long minutes he listened.

All was silent and still.

He hesitated, but he made up his fat mind. The thought of cold turkey lured him on.

On tiptoe he crept down the attic stair and crept stealthily along the passage to the stairs.

Faintly from below came a dim red gleam from the dying fire in the hall; otherwise, all was black.

At the end of the passage Bunter listened again.

There was no sound.

He stepped forward to grope his way to the stairs. And as he did so there came a sudden, startled gasp from the darkness on the landing.

"My hat! Hallo, hallo, hallo!"

Bunter stopped dead. He knew Bob Cherry's voice. The beasts, as he had half suspected, were on the watch for the ghost.

"Oh lor'!" breathed Bunter.

"Come on, you men!" shouted Bob.

He was running along the landing in the dark towards Bunter. Bunter popped back into the passage from which he had emerged.

There were calling voices and footsteps on the stairs. The Co. were running up in the dark to join Bob.

Bob did not wait for them.

He rushed after the disappearing ghost.

Bunter turned the corner of the passage. With really wonderful presence of mind, he tore off the sheet and the pillowslip. Bob was only a few yards away; there was no escape by running. In sheer desperation Bunter stopped just round the corner of the passage, backing close to the wall.

Two seconds later Bob Cherry came barging round.

Something white fluttered in the air and descended like a cloud over his head. It was the sheet.

"Oh, my hat!" gasped Bob.

He struggled in the enveloping folds of the sheet on his head. That was Bunter's chance.

He darted up the passage, leaped up the attic stair, and vanished—as swiftly and completely as a real ghost.

Bob grabbed wildly at the sheet that had so suddenly descended on his head and enveloped him. He had been taken quite by surprise by that peculiar manœuvre on the part of the ghost.

There was a rush of footsteps across the landing. Johnny Bull's voice shouted:

"Here he is!" He glimpsed a white, ghostly figure just round the corner in the passage and leaped at it. "Got him!"

Crash!

Bob Cherry, enveloped in the sheet, went with a crash to the floor, with Johnny Bull sprawling over him.

"Back up!" panted Johnny. "Got him!"

"Hurrah!"

"Pile in!" panted Wharton.

"Urrrggh!" came from Bob Cherry, choked and blinded by the sheet and unable to get rid of it in Johnny Bull's hefty clutches. "Yuuurrrggh!"

Wharton was on him the next moment. A second later, Nugent and Hurree Jamset Ram Singh added their grasp.

"Got the rotter!" gasped Nugent.

"The gotfulness is terrific!"

"Where's Bob? Lend a hand here, Bob!"

"Urrrggh!"

"My hat! He's pretty hefty! Hold him! Don't let him get away!" panted Wharton. "Never mind if you damage him."

"What-ho!"

"Urrrggh! Grooogh! Oooooogh!" came in muffled splutterings from the interior of the tangled sheet. "Whurrrggh!"

"Keep hold of him!"

"Get a light, somebody! Switch it on, one of you!" exclaimed Wharton. "I've got the rotter all right!"

Wharton's arm was round the prisoner's neck, half suffocating him. Nugent and Hurree Singh held his arms, tangled in the sheet. Johnny Bull let go, ran along to the switch, and turned on the light. Then he ran back and grasped the prisoner again.

"Where's Bob!" he exclaimed. Only four members of the Co. were holding the capture. "Bob! Back up, Bob!"

"Yurrrggh! Leggo! I'm chook-chook-choking! Yurrrggh!" came in suffocated tones from under the tangled sheet.

"Serve you jolly well right, whoever you are!" grinned Johnny Bull. "You're going to have a jolly good hiding, too! Are you Thomas?"

"Grooogh! Gooogh! Leggo!"

"I seem to know that voice," said Harry. "Hold him tight, while I get the sheet off him. Don't let him get away."

"No fear!"

"Where's that ass, Bob, all this time?" grunted Johnny Bull.

"Gurrrggh!"

"Keep him safe!"

Wharton grasped the sheet to pull it away, while the other three fellows held the prisoner as if in a vice. The captain of the Remove tore away the sheet.

(*Continued on next page.*)

Linesman Calling

"Linesman," who is an expert on Soccer, will be pleased to hear from MAGNET chums who have problems to solve. Write to him, c/o The MAGNET, The Fleetway House, Farringdon Street, London, E.C.4.

AT certain big football gounds, where the space between the goal-lines and touch-lines is some distance from the nearest spectators, it is the custom to employ boys to kick the ball back when it goes out of play. Haven't you sometimes felt a bit jealous when watching the boys who have been given this job? I confess that I have. They have a splendid view of the match.

In this connection, one of my readers sends me an out-of-the-way query this week. He wants to know how those boys get the job at a ground like that of Chelsea, at Stamford Bridge, for instance. This reader friend of mine says he would like such a job. I dare say he would. There are no end of applications from boys for this task.

I am afraid, however, that a merely ordinary application to the Chelsea club—or to any other club which uses these boys—would not be of much use. These nice jobs—like so many other jobs—are mostly obtained by "influence."

At Hampden Park, Glasgow, which is the biggest football arena in the British Isles—bigger than Wembley even—they employ eight lads for all the big matches to kick the ball back to the field of play when it has run over the line. These boys at Hampden Park, where the Scotland v. England matches are usually played, are booked for two years, after which they are then given what might, in a sense, be called an international cap. And they retire with that honour to make way for other boys who have grown big enough.

SURPRISE RESULTS!

EACH season, when the Cup-ties come along, we get a certain number of shocks. Teams which scarcely seem to have a chance, somehow manage to beat their much more fancied competitors. Last season, for instance, Arsenal, then leaders of the First Division, were drawn against Walsall, a club which had done very little out of the ordinary even in the Third Division. But on their own ground, Walsall beat Arsenal by two goals to nil.

How is it that this sort of thing happens in the Cup competition? That is a question which has been put to me. There are different ways in which we can account for these surprise results. For instance, it may well be that a mistake is made in supposing that the clubs in the Third Division, by way of example, are so much inferior to the clubs of the First Division. We have seen teams like Portsmouth climb upwards, fairly rapidly, from the Third Division, through the Second Division, and up to the very top class.

Again, it may happen that occasionally the players connected with a club in the very top class, meeting a team from a lower League, are inclined to treat their opponents with a certain amount of contempt; to say to themselves: "We need not worry much about this game, which we can win as we like." Often the players who adopt that attitude towards a match don't wake up to their mistake until it is too late.

It seems to me, however, that the biggest reason for these surprise Cup-tie results is that the lowly club is in the happy position of having everything to gain and nothing to lose.

They know that everybody expects them to be beaten, and that nobody will be disappointed if that is their fate. Therefore, they settle down to the game in a care-free spirit, and if, by their enthusiasm and energy, they manage to get the lead, they hang on to it with grim determination.

On the other hand, if the players of the highly-placed First Division club do happen to fall behind they begin to worry. They know that the whole football world will laugh at them if they are defeated, and knowing this, they get anxious, and don't play their natural game.

Anyway, whatever the explanation, these surprise results are part and parcel of the Cup competition. This knock-out affair gives all the clubs a second chance. By the time the Cup-tie part of the season comes along it is obvious that some clubs haven't the faintest hope of winning the championship of their League, or even getting near it. So they concentrate on the Cup competition, and thus try to make up for their failure in the League. It is a striking fact that success in League and Cup very seldom go hand in hand. It is thirty-six years since the same team won the First Division championship and the F.A. Cup in the same season.

HALF-TIME!

"WHEN watching a match the other day," writes one of my readers, "I noticed what seemed like an argument going on immediately after the referee had blown the whistle for half-time. It was a dull day, and the referee seemed to be ordering the players to change ends without going off the field so that the match could be finished while the light lasted. Has the referee the right to order the players to change ends at half-time without going off? "

In reply, I have to say that the referee has no such right.

He can, with a view to getting the match finished while the light lasts, ask the players if they would mind changing ends immediately, without going off the field. But according to rule the players, if they feel so disposed, can demand that they have an interval of five minutes' duration.

So when you read—as you often do in the newspapers—that the referee ordered the players not to leave the field at half-time, the statement is wrong.

There is endless romance in the finding of football players who rise to the top of the tree. This season, Tom Mills, the inside-left of Clapton Orient, has played for Wales. Do you know how he was discovered? I'll tell you. When he was growing up he was a waiter at a restaurant. The firm which employed him had a football team, and that team got to the final of a trade Cup competition. At that final tie, Arthur Grimsdell, who was then manager of the Orient, happened to be present, and being struck with the promise of Mills, he gave him a trial. Mills was duly signed on. You never know, my football friends, when somebody of importance may be watching!

"LINESMAN."

THE MAGNET LIBRARY.—No. 1,350.

"Now, who—— Oh, my hat!"

In utter stupefaction the juniors gazed at the red, wrathful, and infuriated face of Bob Cherry!

— — —

THE THIRTEENTH CHAPTER.
Wrathy!

"BOB!"

"Bob Cherry!"

"Oh crikey!"

"Oh, my esteemed hat!"

Bob Cherry gurgled. The other fellows gasped. They gazed at their prisoner as if they could hardly believe their eyes.

"Bob! You silly ass!" gasped Wharton. "You—playing ghost——"

"You unspeakable idiot!" exclaimed Johnny Bull. "Calling out to us to come on—and playing ghost yourself all the time! Call that sense!"

"The senselessness is terrific!"

"Urrrrggh!" gurgled Bob. "Wurrrggh! Oh crikey! I'm nearly suffocated! Urrrrrggh!"

"You silly ass!" exclaimed Nugent indignantly. "Serve you jolly well right! What the thump are you playing this game for?"

"You blithering idiot!" gasped Bob.

"There's a blithering idiot here, that's a cert!" said Johnny Bull. "And his name's Cherry!"

"You howling ass!"

"Look here, Bob, it's really too thick!" exclaimed Harry Wharton. "You've spoiled the whole thing! What on earth put it into your silly head to play ghost?"

"You burbling chump!"

"Oh, chuck it!" growled Johnny Bull. "Of all the unspeakable, howling asses to start playing ghost yourself——"

"I didn't!" shrieked Bob Cherry.

"Oh, don't be an ass! Here you were, with a sheet over your head——"

"That tricky rotter chucked it there, you blithering idiot!" hissed Bob. "I nearly had him when he chucked the sheet over my head and bolted."

"Who did?"

"How should I know, ass? The fellow who was playing the ghost! I ran round this corner after him, and he chucked the sheet over my head!" hooted Bob. "Then you silly idiots rushed me over——"

"Oh, my hat!"

"And while you've been playing the fool he's got away!" snorted Bob. "You silly owls, I've got about a dozen bumps and bruises——"

"Mean to say you weren't playing ghost?" gasped Johnny Bull. "Well, you silly ass, what was a fellow to think, coming up in the dark and finding a blithering idiot with a sheet over his head?"

"I tell you he chucked it over me and scooted!" shrieked Bob.

"Why did you let him do it?"

"You—you—you burbling bandersnatch, how could I help it? Do you think I let him do it for fun?" hissed Bob.

"Well, you shouldn't have let him!" said Johnny Bull, shaking his head. "You've spoiled the whole thing. He's got away now, whoever he is. You ought to have had a bit more gumption, old chap!"

"I tell you——" roared Bob.

"Don't wake the house, old bean," said Johnny. "If Wharton's uncle comes out he won't be in the best of tempers. And he mayn't believe that you weren't playing the ghost when he hears that we found you with a sheet over your head in the dark."

"If you want your nose pulled, Johnny Bull——"

Bob Cherry's usually amicable temper seemed to be failing him.

"Order, old beans!" said Harry Wharton. "No rags! Anyhow, we nearly had the fellow. Better luck next time!"

"Perhaps the betterfulness of the esteemed luck next time will be terrific!" said Hurree Jamset Ram Singh soothingly.

"We've got the sheet, anyhow," said Harry. "The housekeeper may be able to tell which bed it came from, when she sees it to-morrow. That may be a clue to the blighter."

"No sheet missing from your bed, Bob?" asked Johnny Bull.

Johnny still seemed to have his doubts.

Bob Cherry's answer was not in words. He was punched and pommelled, breathless and winded. He was wrathy. It was due, from his point of view, to the headlong haste of his comrades. To be suspected of playing ghostly tricks himself was altogether too much! Instead of answering Johnny's question verbally he jumped at him and got his head into chancery!

Thump! Thump!

"Oh, my hat! Stop that!" gasped Harry Wharton.

"Bob, you ass!" exclaimed Nugent.

"My esteemed and idiotic Bob——"

They grasped Bob Cherry and dragged him back. Johnny Bull, gasping for breath, glared at him.

"You silly ass!" he spluttered. "What the thump—— I've a jolly good mind—— I'll—I'll——"

"Let me go, you fatheads!" howled Bob. "If that howling ass thinks I was playing ghost, I'll jolly well punch a little more sense into his silly head."

"Quiet, fathead! You'll wake the house!"

"I tell you if that blithering ass thinks——"

"I know what it looks like!" said Johnny Bull. "I don't mind your practical jokes, as a rule. But this——"

"Let me get at him!" howled Bob.

"Rats! Shut up, Johnny, we can all take Bob's word," said Harry. "Look here, the game's up for to-night. Let's get back to bed. We've lost enough sleep over that rotten trickster."

Wharton and Nugent walked with Bob to his room.

The unfortunate outcome of the ghost-hunt seemed likely to end in fisticuffs, in Bob's present excited and wrathy state—which, of course, would never have done.

Johnny Bull shrugged his shoulders as he went to his room. He did not exactly doubt Bob's word on the subject, but, as he had said, he knew what it looked like! Nobody had seen the "ghost" except Bob; and Bob had been caught with the ghostly sheet over his head. Perhaps the other fellows had a lingering doubt, too. Bob was well known to have a rather exuberant sense of fun, which might have led him over the limit, for once.

"Good-night, old chap!" said Wharton and Nugent amicably at Bob's door.

"Good-night, you silly fatheads!" grunted Bob.

And they smiled, and went to their own quarters.

Lights were turned out; all was dark. One o'clock chimed. Two! Three! At that unearthly hour there was no eye open, no ear alert, to see or to hear a figure that glided and crept by dark passages and staircases.

It was a very late hour when the unsuspected guest at Wharton Lodge ate his supper of cold turkey by candlelight in the attic.

But the turkey was good! And it was better late than never!

THE FOURTEENTH CHAPTER.
The Blue Domino!

STRAINS of merry music floated through Wharton Lodge.

The gramophone was grinding out dance music.

Outside, snowflakes were falling and dashing against the windows on the winter wind.

Within, all was merry and bright.

The old oak-walled hall was glistening with evergreens and red berries. Everything had been cleared out of the way to make room for the dancing. Already some couples were gliding over the polished floor.

Colonel Wharton was telling the story of the ghost that haunted Wharton Lodge when there came the sound of a long, horrible, hair-raising groan. "What—what—what was that?" ejaculated Miss Wharton, her face turning quite pale. The party, naturally, was unaware that Bunter, the ventriloquist, was at work on the landing above!

Guests had been arriving during Boxing Day.

Lord Mauleverer had turned up in the biggest car ever. Hazeldene of the Remove had come, with his sister Marjorie, and with Marjorie came Miss Clara and several other Cliff House girls. Fisher T. Fish, the American junior of Greyfriars, was there. Fishy, whose home was in New York, stayed at Greyfriars over the holidays. Nobody was keen on Fishy's company; the fellows would almost have preferred Bunter of the two. But Harry Wharton had a kind thought for the fellow who was left at school on his lonely own, and he had rung up Greyfriars and asked him for Boxing Day.

Fishy had a mental struggle before he accepted the invitation, welcome as it was to a fellow who was passing his holidays in the far from enlivening company of Gosling, the porter, and Mrs. Kebble, the House dame.

But, after a rapid mental calculation, he decided that what he would get to eat at Wharton Lodge would be nearly worth the railway fare.

So Fishy came, still a little worried by the unavoidable expenditure of cash, but prepared to make the best of it.

Other Greyfriars fellows turned up, too, among them the Bounder and Tom Redwing, the two of them coming over in Smithy's pater's car—or, rather, in one of Mr. Vernon-Smith's many cars. Some fellows brought sisters or cousins. So there was quite a numerous company; on all of whom Miss Amy Wharton smiled her kind and hospitable smile, and the colonel grinned his most amiable grin. Wharton was happy in an uncle and an aunt who did not mind if the house was turned upside-down on occasion, so long as their dear nephew enjoyed himself. And there was no doubt that the house was considerably turned upside-down.

There was dancing in the wide old hall to the merry strains of the gramophone, in charge of which stood Thomas, with his widest grin on his chubby face. The dining-room was the supper-room, arranged in a way that would have made Billy Bunter's mouth water had he seen it—as he was going to, if all went well. The colonel's study, opening off the hall, was turned into a cosy corner, with chintzes and holly decorations.

Fisher T. Fish ascertained that supper started whenever a fellow liked, and that a fellow could have all the suppers he liked, one after another. Fishy was early in beginning. He only wished that he had had an appetite like Billy Bunter's. In that case, he could have been absolutely certain of indemnifying himself for the cost of his railway fare. Anyhow, he was going to do his best, and he calculated and reckoned and guessed that, on the whole, he would not be much of a loser.

Wharton's den swarmed with fellows, selecting costumes from the ample box, and most of them talking at once. Some of them had brought their fancy dress, some hadn't; but there was an ample supply in the box.

Cheery voices floated up the attic stair and reached the fat ears of a fat junior who was lying doggo there. Fellows swarmed in the rooms and in the passage of the quarter of the house assigned to Wharton and his friends. Some of them even sat on the attic stair while they talked, little dreaming whose fat ears heard them from farther up.

"Seen anything of Bunter these hols?"

Vernon-Smith's voice floated up to Bunter, as he sat on the attic stair putting on his dancing shoes. Apparently, he was addressing Lord Mauleverer, for it was Mauly's lazy voice that answered.

"No. Splendid luck—what?"

"Beast!" breathed Billy Bunter, in the darkness above.

"Better luck than ours, Mauly!" said Bob Cherry, with a chuckle. "We've seen the fat foozler! He was in Wimford a day or two before Christmas."

"What was he doin' there?"

"You mean, whom was he doin'?" chuckled the Bounder.

"Ha, ha, ha!"

"I rather like this jolly old blue domino," remarked Bob Cherry, who was in costume. "The blessed hood makes a fellow's napper rather warm!"

"Better put on the mask, too!" said the Bounder.

"I'm going to. But why?"

"You'll be better-lookin' in it!"

"Fathead!"

"Your sister's asking for you, Hazel," said Redwing, from the stairs.

"Is she?" said Hazeldene. "I'm not ready yet. Here, don't shove a fellow over, Bob Cherry, you ass! What's the hurry?"

The junior in the blue domino did not answer that question. Hazel stared after him as he raced for the stairs. Hazel was not in a particular hurry to join Marjorie in the hall—he saw no occasion for haste. Apparently, Bob Cherry did.

Billy Bunter, in his attic, waited for the coast to clear.

By candlelight he had fitted himself up in the blue domino and hood and mask that he had borrowed from the box in Wharton's room.

The hood made him look rather taller than was natural to the fat junior, and THE MAGNET LIBRARY.—No. 1,350.

the loose folds of the domino, which reached to his fat ankles, completely concealed the rotundity of his ample figure.

Bunter had no doubt of passing undetected in the crowd.

Except that he was shorter, he looked exactly like Bob Cherry, whose costume was similar, and the hood over his bullet head lessened the difference.

Bunter grinned under the mask.

A fellow in domino, hood, and mask might be anybody in the merry company, and, unless they were seen together, anyone would take him for Bob. That added to his sense of security. But he had to wait till the coast was clear before he descended from the attic.

Bunter peered cautiously out through his big spectacles and the eye-holes of his mask.

All the other fellows had gone down, so far as he could see.

The fat Owl rolled down the attic stair to the passage.

"Oh gad!" came a startled exclamation.

Bunter jumped and stared round.

Lord Mauleverer, in evening clothes—his lordship was too lazy to change into fancy dress—was leaning on the wall, just making up his lazy mind to negotiate the staircase.

He stared at the apparition in the blue domino. He had seen Bob Cherry put on a blue domino exactly like this one, but he had also seen Bob rush down the stairs early.

"Where did you spring from, old bean?" asked Mauleverer. "I thought you were down in the jolly old hall, trippin' the light fantastic toe and treadin' on Marjorie's feet."

The fat Owl grinned under his mask.

Instead of answering, he stepped towards Lord Mauleverer. This was the fellow who had left him behind when Greyfriars broke up for Christmas, instead of carrying him off to Mauleverer Towers! It was due to this beast that Bunter was passing his Christmas in such a very remarkable manner. Stepping quickly towards his unsuspecting lordship, Bunter disentangled a fat paw from his domino, and delivered a sudden and unexpected punch, which landed on Mauly's noble nose, taking him quite by surprise.

Bump!

Lord Mauleverer sat down suddenly.

"Oh gad!" he gasped, in bewilderment. "Oh, great gad! Mad, or what? By Jove! Ow!"

Bunter fled.

He had vanished before the astounded Mauleverer clambered to his feet again. Mauly dabbed his nose with his handkerchief. There was a trickle of red.

"Oh gad! Is the fellow mad, or what?" gasped Mauly. "Punchin' a fellow's nose like that! Oh crumbs! I'll jolly well have somethin' to say to Bob when I see him again, by Jove!"

Not till he had abolished the last speck of crimson from his nose did Lord Mauleverer descend the staircase into the hall. The gramophone was roaring, and a dance was going on.

Lord Mauleverer spotted a blue domino—the only one to be seen. Bob Cherry had had one dance with Marjorie, and now he was standing by a window, watching her as she glided round with the Bounder.

As there were rather more boys than girls, Bob was not in demand; and, indeed, it was only kind friendship that could have induced Marjorie to dance with Bob, who was a great man on the football field, but rather like a rhinoceros in the dancing line. If he

did not tear a yard off a dress, or tread on a foot, Bob considered that he got through pretty well; keeping time to the music was an art he had not yet acquired. He was looking on contentedly and cheerfully, when Lord Mauleverer touched him on the arm, and he glanced round.

"Hallo, hallo, hallo! Why aren't you dancing, Mauly?" he asked. "You're the man they want, you know."

"Have you gone off your rocker?" asked Mauly.

"Eh?"

"Look at my nose!"

"Knocked it hard against something?" asked Bob in wonder. "It looks as if you have, old chap. Hard luck!"

"I can't very well punch you here——"

"Wh-a-at?"

"But remind me next term at Greyfriars, if I forget——"

"What the jolly old thump do you want to punch me for, Mauly, you howling ass?" demanded Bob.

"Because you punched me, you obstreperous idiot! If you're not off your rocker, what did you do it for?"

"I did?" gasped Bob.

"Yaas!"

"You're dreaming!"

"Oh rats!" grunted Mauleverer, and he moved away, leaving Bob Cherry staring after him in blank amazement.

In the supper-room, out of sight, there was another fellow in a blue domino. Mauly did not see him. Neither was he likely to see him for some time. Bunter was going to distinguish himself in the dancing, which he did as elegantly and gracefully as an elephant. But supper came first! Bunter had several lost suppers to make up for! Now he was making up for them. Also, he would not be able to join the supper-table when the unmasking came on. So he had to fill up in advance! Which he was proceeding to do—with a steady determination that left Fisher T. Fish far in the rear.

THE FIFTEENTH CHAPTER.
Extraordinary!

"MY esteemed Bob——"

"Hallo, hallo, hallo, Inky!"

"Do you knowfully recognise me?"

Bob Cherry grinned.

"You've changed your domino," he said. "But I sort of fancy I know your jolly old variety of my native language, Inky."

Bob was standing by a big tub of palms, waiting for the moment when he could claim Marjorie Hazeldene for another dance. A blue domino joined him there. He had seen Hurree Jamset Ram Singh putting on a pink domino, so he concluded that the nabob had changed. For there was no mistaking the variety of English that was spoken from behind the mask. As Bob did not know that Billy Bunter was anywhere within a dozen miles, and had, in fact, quite forgotten his fat existence, he was not likely to suspect that the speaker was that fat and fatuous youth, skilfully imitating the nabob's beautiful flow of English.

"Been at supper already, Inky?"

"Eh?"

"There's some jam on your domino," grinned Bob, "and your mask looks a bit sticky! Hallo, hallo, hallo! I've got to cut off——"

"Hold on an absurd moment——"

"Can't! Let go my arm, Inky, you ass—can't keep Marjorie waiting, you fathead!"

"You are desirefully wanted on the esteemed telephone. The absurd colonel asked me to find you and tell you."

"Oh, what rot!"

"It is a call from Cherry Place, and I fearfully think that something is wrongful——"

"Oh, my hat!" A telephone call from home, on Boxing Night, could hardly mean anything, except that something was amiss. "I say, thanks, Inky, old man—— I say, this is my dance—Marjorie, you know—— I say, will you explain to her, old chap? She's yonder. Smithy's just taken her to that seat by the holly."

"The explainfulness will be terrific."

Bob Cherry hurried away. Even a dance with Marjorie counted for nothing if something untoward had happened at home. And what else could a trunk call from Dorsetshire mean?

Billy Bunter grinned under his mask.

Bob had not the faintest suspicion. He passed a pink domino as he hurried away, but never suspected that Hurree Jamset Ram Singh was inside it. He fancied that he had just been speaking to Hurree Jamset Ram Singh in a blue domino like his own.

Bunter rolled over to Marjorie.

Smithy, who was the man in possession, so to speak, was rather reluctant to quit; but Bob's name was down on Marjorie's programme and that was that! Neither the Bounder nor Miss Hazeldene had any suspicion that the fellow in the blue domino was not Bob. Certainly, he was not to be recognised; but the Bounder had seen him putting on a blue domino, and Marjorie had danced and talked with him. It was as easy as pie for Bunter, now that he had got the genuine article out of the way.

Marjorie gave him a sweet smile; all the sweeter because she rather dreaded dancing with Bob. She liked Bob immensely; but she feared his feet.

The gramophone was roaring again. Many couples were tripping the light fantastic toe, and Bunter and Marjorie glided into action. At all events, Marjorie glided and Bunter rolled.

"Here, look out!" gasped a handsome cavalier, in the voice of Harry Wharton, as the blue domino barged into him.

"Clumsy ass!" said Bunter.

"Dash it all, don't knock a fellow over!" came Nugent's voice, as the fat Owl hurtled into a Spanish matador.

"If you can't dance, why not get off the floor!" said the blue domino.

He barged on.

"Bob!" murmured Marjorie softly.

She was surprised to hear Bob talk to his friends in that style. She was also surprised by the clumsiness of his movements. Bob was a bad dancer, there was no mistake about that; but he had never seemed quite so clumsy as this before.

"Silly lot of asses, what?" said the blue domino. "They can't dance, old thing! Barging into a fellow!"

"Oh!" murmured Marjorie.

"Rotten floor, what?' said Bunter.

"I thought it quite good."

"Not what I'm used to! Pokey little place for a dance; but, after all, these people ain't well off," said Bunter, "what?"

Marjorie did not answer that. She was too utterly astonished at hearing such remarks from a fellow whom she believed to be Bob Cherry.

"Keep off my feet!" came a hissing voice recognisable as Hazeldene's. "You bargee! Keep off a fellow's feet!"

"Don't spread your silly feet all over the floor, you ass!" answered the blue domino as he barged on.

"I—I think I should like to sit this one out, Bob!" gasped Marjorie.

"Oh, rot!"

"Wha-a-at?"

"Let's show them some real dancing! Tired?" asked Bunter. "I dare say that clumsy ass Bob—I—I mean, Smithy—tired you out. But you've got a good partner now. I say, did you see that old ass of a colonel at it? Bit of a goat, at his age, what?"

Marjorie was dumb.

"Crummy lot!" went on Bunter agreeably. "Hardly my style, a show of this sort! Beastly floor—I jolly nearly tripped then! Rotten dancing—see how they barge into a fellow! Oh crikey!"

Blue domino shouldered a pink domino and slipped! Billy Bunter clutched wildly at Marjorie to save himself; but the girl, fortunately, escaped his wild clutch. The fat junior went skating.

"Oh, my hat!"

"Look out! Who's that?"

"That's Cherry—— Ha, ha!"

Crash! Bump!

Billy Bunter, staggering and skidding wildly, clutched a cavalier with one hand, and a Spanish matador with the other. He dragged them both down in his fall. It was quite a mix-up. The Bounder slipped in, bagged Marjorie, and steered her away from the disaster. Really, she was not sorry to get to a safe distance from the blue domino.

"Oh, my hat!" gasped Harry Wharton. "Let go, Bob, you ass!"

"Leggo, you fathead!" spluttered Nugent.

"Ow! Oh! Oh crikey!" gurgled Bunter.

Wharton and Nugent wrested themselves loose, and jumped up. The blue domino lay gasping, amid a ripple of merry laughter.

"Bob, you ass——" gasped Wharton. He grabbed the blue domino by the arm and helped him up.

Thump!

"Oh crumbs!" howled Wharton, as the blue domino rewarded him with a thump on the chest, and he sat down suddenly.

"Bob!" howled Nugent.

"My esteemed Bob!" gasped the pink domino.

"Well, that's the jolly old limit!" chuckled the Bounder. "Punching a fellow at a dance. What's the matter with Bob to-night?"

"I can't understand him!" said Marjorie blankly. "I—I suppose that is Bob! He seems very different from usual."

The blue domino—the cynosure of all eyes now—rolled away. Wharton got on his feet, too astounded even to be angry. Almost everyone had seen that amazing incident. Unless Bob Cherry had gone out of his senses, it was not to be accounted for.

"Is Bob mad?" gasped Nugent.

"The madfulness must be terrific," murmured the Nabob of Bhanipur. "But the leastfulness said, the soonerfully mended."

The dance went on. Blue domino disappeared into the supper-room. Even Billy Bunter could not consider that he had scored a howling success as a dancer. But there was comfort in supper. That, after all, was the chief thing. It was an hour since Bunter had had his first supper, so he was ready for another! He tucked in again and was comforted.

THE SIXTEENTH CHAPTER.

Two of Them!

BOB CHERRY, his blue eyes glinting through the eyeholes of his mask, came back into the hall.

He was looking for a blue domino. There was none to be seen, save his own; but he spotted a pink domino, strode over to it, and tapped it on the shoulder. Hurree Jamset Ram Singh, who was standing by a tub of palms, speaking to Miss Clara, who was sitting there, turned his head.

"My esteemed Bob——" he murmured.

"So it's you!" said Bob, in a tone of concentrated anger. "You've changed your domino again."

"Eh?"

"You silly, burbling idiot, what do you mean by it?"

"By what, my esteemed and idiotic Bob?" asked the astonished nabob.

"Your silly fool trick, you dummy, making me believe that there was something wrong at home!" hissed Bob. "Are you mad, or what?"

Hurree Jamset Ram Singh gazed at

him. Miss Clara gazed at both of them; but just then Harry Wharton came up to take her away, and the two juniors were left to themselves.

"If we weren't here, I'd punch your silly head!" said Bob, in a low, savage voice. "I wasn't wanted on the phone! I've got through to home, and they tell me they never rang up. What do you mean by it?"

"The understandfulness is not terrific!" murmured the astounded Nabob of Bhanipur.

"You pulled my leg, telling me I was wanted on the phone from home——"

"You are dreaming, my esteemed Bob!" said Hurree Jamset Ram Singh. "I certainfully did nothing of the kind."

"What's the good of telling lies, you ass?" snapped Bob. "Did you do it to bag my dance with Marjorie, you rotter?"

"Y-your dance with Marjorie!" stuttered the nabob.

"Yes—I've missed it, all through you. By gum, if we were in a quiet place, I'd jolly well punch you!"

Hurree Jamset Ram Singh looked at him in real concern. The weird proceedings of the blue domino that evening had made some of the fellows wonder whether Bob had gone off his "rocker." Hurree Singh could hardly doubt it, as he listened to this—having, as he supposed, seen Bob in that dance with Marjorie, and the disaster that had occurred.

"Did you dance with Marjorie?" demanded Bob.

"Certainfully not! You did!" gasped the nabob.

"What do you mean, you idiot?"

"The meanfulness is the same as the sayfulness, my esteemed Bob! Keep calmful, my absurd chum!" murmured the nabob. "This is not a place for esteemed excitefulness and execrable ragfulness."

He slipped his arm through Bob's, and gently drew him away towards the supper-room. In this extraordinary state of affairs, his one idea was to get Bob out of the general view. A fellow in a state of high excitement, who fancied that he had been telephoning, when the nabob had actually seen him dancing and tumbling over, evidently required to be led to a quiet spot and reasoned with.

Bob jerked savagely at his arm. But the nabob held on to it, gently but firmly.

"Come onfully," he whispered. "The explainfulness is better in private, far from the madding crowd, as the poet remarkably observes."

"Oh, all right!" grunted Bob. And he went. He was more anxious, at that moment, to punch his chum's dusky head, than anything else; and if a sufficiently quiet and secluded spot could be reached, there was no doubt that he was going to do so. So he went.

There was only one fellow in the supper-room at the moment; in a blue domino, with his mask pushed up to give free play to his active jaws. The two juniors did not observe him; he was partly screened by floral decorations on the table. But, as he saw them come in, that fellow ceased operations on the wing of a chicken, and hastily pulled down his mask to cover his fat countenance entirely.

"Now, Inky, you silly, cheeky ass!" breathed Bob.

"The calmfulness is the proper caper, my esteemed Bob!" murmured Hurree Jamset Ram Singh. "The excitefulness is too terrific. Perhapsfully you had better go up to your room——"

"What do you mean, you cheeky ass?

I'm not going up to my room, unless you like to come up there to have your cheeky nose punched."

"The punchfulness has already been too preposterous, my absurd Bob. You have alreadyfully created ludicrous amazement——"

"Eh? What have I done, I'd like to know?" demanded Bob. "I've been bothering over the telephone the last half-hour——"

"You have punched the esteemed Wharton——"

"Are you mad?"

"I think you must be, my absurd and ridiculous Bob! Pleasefully keep calm!" urged the nabob. "If you are ill——"

"Who's ill, you idiot?"

"Then what is the matterfulness?"

"I've told you what's the matter! You pulled my leg with a rotten trick, and made me miss my dance with Marjorie——"

"But you did not miss the esteemed dance," said the bewildered nabob. "Do you not rememberfully recollect that you tumbled over, and when the esteemed Wharton helped you up, you thumped him——"

"You're mad! I've been on the telephone! If anybody did it, it was somebody else——"

"You are the only fellow, I think, in a blue domino——"

"What do you mean? You had on a blue domino yourself, when you pulled my leg about the telephone call?" snorted Bob. "I see you've changed back into your pink one now."

"Oh, my esteemed hat! I have not changed at all, my absurd Bob!" Light suddenly dawned on the nabob. "Great pipfulness! Is there another fellow here in a blue domino? I remember that there was a second one in the esteemed Wharton's box——"

"Oh!" gasped Bob. "But—but I knew your voice when you spoke to me —at least, I knew your fatheaded lingo! Look here, do you mean to say that a fellow in a blue domino has been dancing with Marjorie, while I was away at the phone?"

"Certainfully! You have been taken infully! Some terrific blighter pulled your esteemed leg, to bag your dance. The seefulness is preposterous now! It was not you who punched the absurd Wharton——"

"Did you think it was, you blithering idiot? I suppose that's it—some japing ass has bagged that other blue domino—— By gum! I'll smash him! I'll—I'll—— But where is he? I didn't see him in the hall."

"He must be about somewherefully— why — what—— Look!" exclaimed Hurree Jamset Ram Singh as, glancing round, he spotted a half-hidden blue domino on the other side of a table.

Bob Cherry jumped.

So did the blue domino!

Bunter leaped to his feet.

"That's the rotter!" hissed Bob, and he started round the table, followed by the Nabob of Bhanipur.

"Oh lor'!" gasped Billy Bunter.

He blinked through his big spectacles, from the eyeholes of his mask, in deep alarm. Discovery was imminent. Bob, evidently, meant to know who it was who had played that extraordinary trick on him—though certainly he had not the remotest suspicion that it was Billy Bunter. But if the mask was jerked off the fat face, Billy Bunter would be revealed—and the game would be up!

In that awful emergency the fat Owl's podgy brain worked swiftly. Bob had almost reached him, when Billy Bunter grabbed a soda siphon from the table.

Squizzzzz! Squish! Fizzzz!

"Urrrrggh!" spluttered Bob, staggering back from the sudden torrent that splashed on his mask.

Squizzz! Whizzz! Fizzz!

"Yurrrggh!" gurgled the Nabob of Bhanipur, as Bunter's defensive weapon was turned on him.

Smothered and blinded for the moment, the two juniors staggered back helplessly. That moment was enough for Bunter.

He dropped the siphon and fled.

Wells, who presided over the supper-room, beheld that amazing scene in astonishment and consternation. He made a step into Bunter's path as he fled for the door on the hall.

Crash!

Bump!

"Wurrrggh!" gurgled Wells.

He went over as if a cannon-shot had struck him. A charge from Billy Bunter was not unlike that of a battering-ram.

Bunter, desperate, leaped over him and bounded on.

He bounded out into the hall where the gramophone was grinding out a merry melody, and nearly everybody was dancing. Bunter did not heed the dancers. He had no time to think of them. He was thinking only of escape. He barged wildly through, and there were startled cries and exclamations on all sides.

"Bob, you potty ass!" yelled Wharton, as he reeled to the right.

"Bob, you dummy!" roared Johnny Bull, as he staggered to the left.

"Oh gad!" gasped Lord Mauleverer, going over with a crash.

"That man Cherry's mad!" panted the Bounder.

"What on earth——"

"What the thump——"

The blue domino vanished up the staircase. Nobody could have guessed that it was Billy Bunter, from the speed he put on. He fairly flashed. The blue domino vanished above, leaving amazement and consternation below.

Fortunately for the fat Owl the upper part of the house was deserted. He whipped into the passage, tore off the blue domino and mask, hurled them into the open doorway of Wharton's room, and dashed up the attic stair. A moment more and he was palpitating breathlessly behind a locked door.

THE SEVENTEENTH CHAPTER.
The Ghost's Last Walk!

"WHAT the thump——"

"Good lord!"

"Bob's mad!"

"Mad as a hatter!"

"Why, what—— Look! Who—what is——"

Another blue domino hurtled out of the supper-room into the hall. There was a buzz of amazement at the sight of it.

"Who's that?"

"Two of them——"

"What——"

"Where is he?" roared Bob Cherry.

Colonel Wharton strode up to him, and grasped him by the arm in a grip of iron. His eyes glinted under his grey brows.

"What does this mean, boy? What are——" hooted the colonel.

"That rotter!" panted Bob. "Who was it? Where is he gone? He's been making out that he's me—I mean, I'm Bob Cherry, and he——"

Bob pushed up his drenched mask. He, at all events, could be recognised now. The identity of the other fellow in a blue domino was still a mystery.

Billy Bunter, staggering and skidding wildly, clutched a cavalier with one hand and a Spanish matador with the other, and dragged them both down in his fall. Vernon-Smith slipped in, bagged Marjorie Hazeldene, and steered her away from the disaster !

"Where is he gone?" gasped Bob.

"H-he ran upstairs!" stuttered Nugent. "Who was it? What's the row?"

"Explain yourself, Cherry!" snapped the colonel.

"Bob, you ass——"

"But who the dickens was it?" exclaimed Wharton blankly. "I thought it was you, Bob——"

"It's some japing ass!" gasped Bob. "He's been making out that he's me in a domino like mine, and he bagged my dance with Marjorie, and——"

"Oh!" exclaimed Marjorie.

"Oh, my hat!" ejaculated the Bounder. "What a game!"

"Ha, ha, ha!"

"But who was it?"

"Well, well," said the colonel testily. "It was a foolish joke; but this excitement is out of place, Cherry."

Bob Cherry crimsoned. He realised that himself.

"Sorry!" he stammered. "Only—only the brute pulled my leg, making out that I was wanted on the phone. And —and well, never mind. Sorry! He's drenched me with soda water, too. I shall have to go and change."

"Poor old Bob!"

"But who the dickens was it?"

"Ha, ha, ha!"

Bob Cherry scudded up the stairs. It was true that he wanted to change; but still more he wanted to ascertain whether there was a chance of getting hold of that blue domino.

The domino itself met his eyes, lying inside the doorway of Wharton's room. But it was unoccupied now, and the identity of the wearer still remained a mystery.

Evidently the wearer had discarded it in haste, left it lying there, and cleared. Bob looked along the passage, but there was nobody to be seen. Either the fellow had got away by another staircase, or he was lying doggo in some room; and Bob had to give it up.

Certainly, he would not have given it up had he been aware that there was an unknown and unsuspected person in Wharton Lodge, palpitating at that moment in the locked attic!

But that, of course, never crossed his mind. He could only conclude that one of the fellows had been japing him; but which one it was, among the many fellows there, he could not guess. He could only make up his mind that, if he discovered that fellow later, he would find a quiet spot and a quiet moment for altering his features for him.

When Bob came down at last, Lord Mauleverer tapped him on the arm, with a cheery grin.

"Sorry, old bean," said Mauly. "I know now that it wasn't you who tapped my boko—it was the other idiot—I mean the other chap! He seems to have made it a point to make himself jolly unpleasant all round. Who was it?"

"Goodness knows!" said Bob. "I'd like to find out. Must have been one of the fellows—goodness knows which!"

Bob was still considerably wrathy; till he secured another dance with Marjorie. Then oil was poured on the troubled waters.

"I ought really to have guessed that it wasn't you, Bob," said Miss Hazeldene.

"Well, he was got up just like me— you couldn't really——" said Bob.

"I mean, because he danced so badly!" said Marjorie sweetly.

And all was calm and bright!

It had been a rather exciting and somewhat perturbing episode! But it was forgotten; and all went merrily— for everyone except the fat junior in the attic.

Billy Bunter listened to merry music and merry voices from below, but he did not think of venturing again to mingle in the throng of the happy and the gay! Fortunately, he had parked an ample supper; and that, after all, was what really mattered! And later, he was going to make that beast Cherry sit up —Bunter knew how!

.   .   .   .   .   .

Bob Cherry awoke suddenly.

Groan!

It was late.

Long ago the last door had closed, the last light had been turned out. Harry Wharton & Co. were sleeping the sleep of healthy youth—Bob as soundly as any. But he awoke and stared into the deep darkness, a cold shiver running down his back.

Groan!

It was a hair-raising groan in the darkness and silence of his room. Bob sat up in bed.

Groan!

From the darkness near the door came a glimmer of white. Bob felt his heart thumping.

Just within the doorway a dim, white, ghostly figure stood. Bob's startled eyes fixed on it.

The ghost of Wharton Lodge was walking again.

Groan!

Eerily the ghastly sound came through the gloom.

For a moment or two, Bob, sitting up in bed, gazed at the phantom figure as if spellbound.

Then, silently, he groped for a missile. His hand encountered a heavy book—the Greyfriars Holiday Annual—which was lying on the little table within arm's reach.

Bob did not move from the bed. He suspected that if he did, the ghost would

(Continued on page 28.)

WHEN the GREAT APES CAME!

By STUART MARTIN.

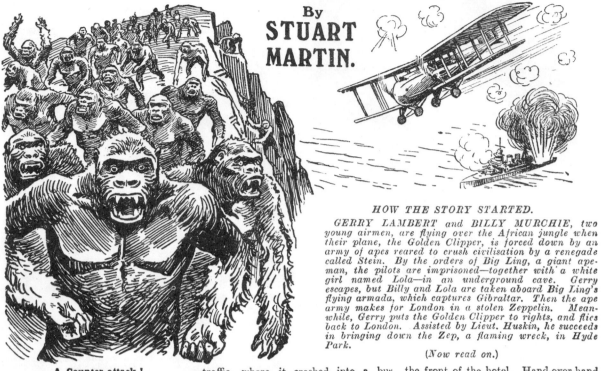

HOW THE STORY STARTED.

GERRY LAMBERT and BILLY MURCHIE, two young airmen, are flying over the African jungle when their plane, the Golden Clipper, is forced down by an army of apes reared to crush civilisation by a renegade called Stein. By the orders of Big Ling, a giant ape-man, the pilots are imprisoned—together with a white girl named Lola—in an underground cave. Gerry escapes, but Billy and Lola are taken aboard Big Ling's flying armada, which captures Gibraltar. Then the ape army makes for London in a stolen Zeppelin. Meanwhile, Gerry puts the Golden Clipper to rights, and flies back to London. Assisted by Lieut. Huskin, he succeeds in bringing down the Zep, a flaming wreck, in Hyde Park.

(Now read on.)

A Counter-attack !

AS Gerry and Huskin stood there watching the blaze, two mounted policemen came towards them.

"What are you two doing here, and where did you come from?" asked one of them.

"Take us somewhere we can have a bath, officer," said Huskin dizzily, giving his name and rank. "This boy has saved London from destruction. Big Ling's army has lost this trick, anyhow."

Gerry was not listening. He was looking at a great form that bounded into the darkness among the tall trees and disappeared from sight! It was the form of Big Ling!

The crowds gathered in Park Lane from Hyde Park Corner to Marble Arch knew that something mysterious, something terrible, had happened. There was a smouldering airship in the Park, its dying fire lighting up the sward with a baleful glare. Dozens of policemen were arriving in vans, and armed soldiers were marching out of Wellington Barracks.

All sorts of rumours were being whispered, some even saying that another European war had broken out. Then something suddenly emerged from the shadow of the trees near Park Lane that sent the crowds scurrying pell-mell in all directions. It was the monster ape-man, Big Ling.

Blood was dripping from a wound in his breast, and for a moment he stood there, dwarfing everything around him. The traffic was blocking the road, but Big Ling, in one stride, cleared the thoroughfare.

A taxicab coming out of a side street struck his leg before the driver could pull up. Ling stooped, lifted the cab bodily, and then hurled it among the

THE MAGNET LIBRARY.—No. 1,350.

traffic, where it crashed into a bus, throwing passengers into paroxysms of terror.

The crowd lost its nerve at the sight of the monster and ran hither and thither, filled with panic and impeding the movements of the bands of police, who still strove to handle the situation. Then, from the direction of Hyde Park Corner, came the sound of marching men. The soldiers had arrived, and the first battalion entered the Park at the double, an officer at their head. The latter was somewhat hazy as to the actual situation; his orders had been that an enemy airship had been brought down in the Park by Lieut. Huskin, of the R.A.F. and a flying ace. He halted his troops, and ran forward to a group of officials.

"Is Lieutenant Huskin here?" he inquired.

"That's my name, sir," said Huskin, stepping forward. "And this is Gerry——"

"The airship is burning itself out, sir !" interrupted a police-inspector. "But look over there !"

Out of the tangle of traffic in Park Lane the monstrous figure of the ape-man towered beside the flood-lit entrance to one of the newest hotels. Seizing the hotel doorkeeper, he hurled him high into the air, to fall and lay still almost at the officer's feet.

Wheeling round sharply, the officer ordered his men to charge. As the troops raised their rifles, Big Ling's great hands tore at the glass canopy, lifting the frame entirely from its socket in the wall. Another heave, and he raised it above his head and threw it as the soldiers took aim.

The missile broke in fragments as the rifles crashed out, and bullets whizzed perilously near the giant ape-man. Clutching at one window-sill after another, Big Ling hauled himself up

the front of the hotel. Hand-over-hand he went, turning a corner of the building for cover, and was within reach of the roof before a second volley could be discharged. Then, lying there on the tiles of the immense hotel, he tore at the roof and flung broken rafters and chimney-pots at the soldiers below.

This fusillade did not last for long, however, for the troops scattered at an order, and, pushing their way through the disorganised traffic and the mob, endeavoured to surround the hotel, and thus cut off Big Ling's retreat. Some were ordered to enter the hotel, while others were sent to position themselves on the top floors of neighbouring houses.

Gerry and Lieut. Huskin were among those who entered the hotel. Guests were panic-stricken, crouching in every corner, and the staff was helpless to preserve order. Up the stairs ran Gerry and Huskin with the officer, followed by a company of soldiers.

They reached the top floor, where, by means of an emergency ladder, they were able to climb up on to the flat roof. There was no sign of Ling, save the holes he had torn in the roof and the broken chimneys he had smashed in his rage.

"There he goes !" cried Gerry suddenly, pointing northward; and all eyes turned in that direction.

Several buildings away, the figure of Ling could be seen as he leaped across the roofs, some of which gave way under his weight and impeded his progress. He fell more than once, and now the troops on the roof of the hotel had a good sight of him as he was outlined against the glare of the lights of Oxford Street.

The soldiers fired, but whether the ape-man was hit it was impossible to say; for, big though the target was, Ling was dodging and twisting with all the agility of a gorilla.

The ape-man succeeded in reaching Oxford Street at last, dropped to the ground, and then sped away up one of the side streets.

People who were in the vicinity saw the monster striding ahead, heedless of the terror his appearance occasioned. As Big Ling passed on his way, he snatched at the food which was exposed in small shops that were still open.

A fruiterer's window was raided, and its contents strewn across the road as Ling grabbed at the trays that were displayed. A butcher near Marylebone Road, who was closing for the night, was lifted by an immense paw and thrown into the street, while Ling thrust his other hand into the shop and tore the carcass of an ox from a hook. He flung the carcass over his shoulder and marched off, eating his stolen food as he did so.

His passage was swift and terrible, like the passing of a frightful dream. In two strides he was across Marylebone Road. Before those who saw him could believe their eyes, he was in the gloom of Regent's Park, where all trace of him disappeared.

The alarm had been telephoned to every district police station. Armoured cars had been summoned, and more troops had been rushed to Park Lane; but it was impossible to trail the monster with accuracy. By the time the news of his appearance in Marylebone had been sent to the authorities, he had vanished again.

Inquiries, however, showed that if he had entered Regent's Park, there were a dozen ways by which he could emerge.

Quickly a cordon of troops were thrown round the place. Machine-guns were hurriedly brought up. Searchlights were trained, and poured their beams into every likely corner, along every yard of the ground, and into the branches of every tree. All this took time, and while it was being carried out, scouts were scouring the outlying districts on swift motor-cycles and in cars in the hope of picking up a clue.

Little did the pursuers know that Big Ling was actually sitting within reach of their guns and within earshot of their massing.

For Ling had made for the Zoo within the park, and was at that very moment preparing for a counter-attack such as his pursuers did not dream.

While the searchlights were throwing their floods of light across the greensward and into the clumps of trees, Big Ling sat on the ground near the Zoo pavilion. Around him roamed the lions he had let loose by tearing the bars of their cages asunder. Elephants which had borne children on their backs were standing behind him. Wolves were sneaking here and there, while bears crouched on the grass. Every animal was present at that strange meeting.

The peculiar sense which animals have when they meet their master had penetrated the blood of the inmates of the Zoo.

There were two among these dwellers of the jungle, however, who were rebels.

Alone of all that multitude of beasts, the tigers were unknown to the taming hand of Ling; and, although the massive brutes had, like the others, crawled from their cages at his command, the two natives of the Indian forests had not yet developed the slave-like attitude of the other creatures.

Ling had massed the animals where he might imbue them with his savage desire for revenge. He had spoken to them in the jungle growling, the forest method of communication that is the language of the beasts; but all the time

he knew that the tigers were suspicious. They were natives of a land he had never visited, and the sight of this ape-man had aroused in them the ferocity exhibited to their own keepers.

One of them, a great striped beast, kept up a continuous low growl, first raising its head and glaring at Ling, then snarling and clawing the ground menacingly. The carcass of the ox which Ling had stolen from the butcher's shop during his travels had been devoured by the lions and the beasts that fed on flesh. The bones lay around, and this tiger, having scented blood and having eaten flesh, kept eyeing Ling.

The huge ape-man rose to his feet and sent out a loud cry, the howl that had brought the beasts to him in the forests of Africa. It was the war-cry of the jungle. Then he made for the direction of the main gateway with the beasts at his heels.

As he did so, however, the tiger made a bound and landed on Ling's broad shoulders, slashing at him with claws and teeth.

Down went Ling, rolling over and over, his great hands seeking the hold he knew in such a fight. In a matter of moments his great fingers spread like a steel band round the tiger's throat.

Then, heaving himself to his knees, Big Ling raised the tiger in his powerful arms, heedless of its wild clawing, and sent it crashing to the ground, to take no further part in the fight.

Sending forth another howl, the huge ape-man moved towards the gate. One heave, and the sidepost was drawn from its socket, and the gate crashed to the ground, and away across the park streamed the freed pack of savage creatures, let loose on London!

For a moment Ling listened to the riot of sound. The machine-guns broke out in a rattle of death. The searchlights flashed up and down, then steadied. Ling leaned on the broken gate and watched.

He saw the troops pouring a hail of bullets into the maddened animals. Some of them broke the cordon and escaped. For long time the ape-man watched the battle; then, with a savage grin on his face, he turned and tottered towards the Mappin terrace. Into one of the caves in that terrace he dragged his limbs, and lay down to rest, listening eagerly.

He had killed in plenty that night. Two night-watchmen of the Zoo had been slain by him, besides the people

he had killed when he escaped from Hyde Park. The lust for killing was strong within him. His Mongolian face had assumed the aspect of a gorilla. His wounds gave him no thought. They would heal as other wounds had healed. He lay, listening and watching.

After a long time his quick ears heard a stealthy footstep on the gravel outside. Someone was moving by the terrace.

A moment later a voice whispered his name:

"Ling, are you there?"

The ape-man crawled out of the cave in which he had stowed his bulk.

"Is that you, Stein?"

"Yes. Come!"

Big Ling stood up, and saw the other on the steps beside the polar bears' pool.

Together they slipped through the deserted grounds.

"I arrived just in time, Ling," said Stein. "They'll be searching soon. Everything is ready."

He piloted Ling under the bridge towards the canal. They entered the water and waded under the bridge, climbing the bank some distance down. Then they clambered over the railings, close to where a large pantechnicon was drawn up. The doors of the pantechnicon were open, and Big Ling slipped inside.

Stein closed the doors, mounted the driver's seat, and drove off, passing through the police cordon and the crowds that were gathered in the street.

Billy to the Rescue!

THE telephone-bell in the brightly lit room in the War Office rang furiously, and the Chief lifted the receiver, with a sigh.

It was after one o'clock in the morning, and he had been receiving and answering calls incessantly for some hours. Mostly they were calls giving him details of the chase of Big Ling and the outbreak at the Zoo.

So far as the latter was concerned, the late calls had been reassuring. Most of the wild animals had already been accounted for, while many of them had been slain by the machine-guns. But of Big Ling there had been no sign. It was expected that he would be discovered when daylight came, however.

But this call made the Chief sit up rigid in his chair.

"This is Billy Murchie speaking!" came a voice over the wires, tense and anxious.

"Billy Murchie?" cried the Chief. "You mean you are the person who has been sending us the mysterious messages of warning?"

"Yes, that's me. I'm in London—in a house somewhere; I don't know the district. I was brought here to-night with Stein, the madman who is behind Big Ling!"

"What is your number?"

"I don't know. Listen to what I have to say. I've only got a moment to speak. There are bargeloads of apes in the Thames now! They are going to attack London——"

The voice died away, as if the speaker had been forced from the instrument. The Chief listened eagerly.

"Hallo, hallo!" he shouted several times.

But there was no response.

A knock sounded on the Chief's door.

"Come in!"

Into the room marched Gerry and Lieutenant Huskin. Both were weary and tired after the night's events, and the Chief turned to them swiftly.

THE MAGNET LIBRARY.—No. 1,350.

"You are Gerry, the boy I have heard so much about? Tell me your story right away. I have just had a telephone call from your friend, Billy Murchie."

"From Billy?" cried Gerry quickly. "Is he in London?"

"Evidently. He tells me that there are bargeloads of apes in the Thames. I want you to tell me in a few words how you came into touch with these apes. Hurry!"

"We were made prisoners by them when we were on a flying record-breaking trip to the Cape. I escaped, and Billy was taken prisoner with a girl named Lola. They are led by Big Ling, who has been taught by a renegade called Stein."

"That's all right. I have reports here that tell me something of this. I sent for you two to be brought here after this Big Ling was chased across the roofs in Park Lane. Lieutenant Huskin, you will write out a report of how you came into this affair, but in the meantime tell me a few details."

"I was sent up in the plane with this boy, sir, to pursue the airship. We brought it down in Hyde Park——"

"And we have other planes up now searching for any further raiders," interrupted the chief, as if speaking to himself.

Then he turned towards Gerry.

"Now I want to hear the whole story, boy, so far as you know it, of the organisation behind this fantastic affair. Do you know any of the plans of these apes? What is their object?"

Details, details, details were what the chief wanted, for the events of the evening had crowded so closely that everything seemed a jumble. The official mind wanted to meet an attack in the usual leisurely manner of officialdom, and Gerry was on his feet, about to give what information he could, when a noise outside broke in on the room.

The Chief rushed to the window that overlooked Whitehall. From the wide thoroughfare came the strangest rumbling, then howls broke out. The telephone bell rang again and again.

Gerry grabbed the receiver.

"Is that you, Billy?" he yelled.

But it was not Billy. It was a voice asking for the Chief, who snatched the receiver quickly.

In a moment he dropped it like a stone, and began to press buttons summoning assistants from different parts of the building.

"It is true," he said, his face white and set. "Apes have been brought up the Thames in barges. They are disembarking at Westminster. That was Scotland Yard—— What's the matter?"

His query ended in a gasp of terror, for the door of the room had been flung open, and a gigantic figure, that filled them with terror, entered the room. It was Big Ling!

He stood viewing them, gloating over the impression his appearance had created, his shoulders bowed and touching the ceiling, his gigantic head thrust forward.

His eyes, filled with malice and grim hate, were on Gerry.

"I've come in time!" he said growlingly. "Your friend tried to speak our plans over what you call a telephone. We got him in time. You must not be allowed to tell what you know."

He stepped forward, brushing the table and the chairs aside with his leg,

and laid a hand on Gerry's shoulder. With the other hand he tore the telephone-receiver from its position, ripped the cord from the wall, and flung it into a corner.

"I am Big Ling, King of the World!" he cried, in a voice that thundered through the room. "My troops are in your streets!"

He waved his arm in a magnificent gesture, and gave vent to a howl that was answered from the street. In vain Gerry fought against that clutch. He might as well have tried to escape from the claws of a steel trap. Ling held him by the collar and dragged him towards the door.

As he did so, Gerry saw Ling's mighty arm raised towards the chandelier that hung from the ceiling.

One tug, and the lights were extinguished, and half the ceiling came down in a smother of plaster and mortar.

Along the corridor and down the wide stairs strode the giant. Reaching the door, he raised his hand in salute to his apes, who were massed in front of the War Office.

An ape-man stepped forward, seized Gerry in his arms, and ran round the corner. A large saloon car stood there, its engine throbbing.

Into the car Gerry was bundled, and the ape-man followed, still clutching the boy in a grip that almost strangled him.

Next moment the car gathered pace, swept out into Whitehall, through into Trafalgar Square and then up Charing Cross Road, to disappear into the night.

Half an hour or so passed before the car drew up in front of a tall building in a terrace of large houses. Here Gerry was dragged out and carried up a flight of stone steps. The door was opened, and he was bundled into the hall, and then pushed into a room, the door of which was afterwards closed on him.

It was a perfectly bare room in which Gerry found himself. Over the window a massive sheet of heavy material had been hung, and the only light in the place was a tall candle that was stuck on the mantelpiece. The faint glimmer of the light added a weird condition to the atmosphere of the place. There was a curious smell, too, everywhere; it was the odour of gorilla.

But Gerry's eyes had been busy as he was dragged up the stone steps. He had observed that the house was one of several which had "To Let" boards in front of them. He heard mutterings beyond the door of the huge apartment.

The door opened after a while, and in stepped Stein, followed by a squad of the young giants who were the lieutenants of the ape armies.

They squatted on the floor, forming a semicircle on both sides of Stein, muscular half-men, all of them, gorillas from the waist downwards. Mongolian from the waist upward.

"Stand over there!" commanded Stein sternly; and Gerry took up a position facing his captors.

"You are going to be tried for your life," went on Stein. "This is the court and these are your judges. The charge against you is that you are an enemy of Ling's army, that you were instrumental in destroying the Zeppelin and its crew. Have you anything to say in your defence?"

"Yes," said Gerry, between his teeth. "And I'd do it again if I had the chance!"

Stein turned to the ape-men surrounding him.

"You hear that?" he cried fiercely. "The prisoner has admitted his guilt and defies us."

A murmur of anger arose from the ape-men as they glared at Gerry.

"Listen to me," said Stein venomously, turning to Gerry. "The verdict of this company is that you have merited death. Is that not so, men of the forest?"

Without exception, the ape-men raised their hands to their heads and bowed.

"Death!" they cried in deep tones that sent a shudder through the boy.

"Death it will be," said Stein, "but the manner of it will be left for the final decision of Ling. He will be here before long. For the present he is busy disorganising London."

Stein then gave orders for Gerry to be tied up, and a dozen hands were laid on the boy, and he was roped securely and thrown in a corner.

Meanwhile, Stein took from his pocket a large map, which he laid on the floor. Then, taking the candle from the mantelpiece, he placed it beside the map. Next he bent down and carefully marked off several points on the map.

"Our work must be done in the darkness," he said, addressing his ape-men, "for it can then be done with the best results. I have here marked the various points which we shall attack before dawn to-morrow. The racing car is at the door. I will do the driving. Each one of you will come when I call for you. The first is you——"

He pointed to a young ape-man who stood up and squared his shoulders.

"We shall carry bombs. It will be your duty to throw them where and when I say. First, we shall wreck the force that drives this city—we are going to the electrical works. We shall break into them by swiftness. One bomb will wreck the machines that make electricity. Are you ready?"

"I am ready."

"And you others remain here. I shall be back soon."

Stein was in the act of rising to his feet, when a voice rang out:

"Sit still, all of you! One move of a finger, and I'll blow you all to pieces!"

Gerry twisted his head round and uttered a cry of surprised delight, for Billie Murchie was standing on the threshold, holding a Mills bomb threateningly above his head

Billy's face was white and drawn, but his set expression told the group of ape-men that he was in deadly earnest.

"Crawl this way, Gerry!" he said. "Can you make it?"

"You watch me, old son!"

Across the floor Gerry managed to wriggle until he lay beside the door.

"Now out into the corridor, Gerry," said Billy anxiously. "I'll fix this bunch."

Gerry obeyed, while his chum held the bomb menacingly.

The ape-men had not stirred a muscle. Stein was about to leap to his feet, but Billy raised his arm to throw, and Stein slid back to the floor.

"Lola!"

A girl's form came out of the darkness at the end of the passage. She knew the cue, and in a trice had cut Gerry's bonds, pushed a revolver into his hand, and urged him towards the door.

"I won't go without Billy!" said Gerry.

Printed and published every Saturday by the Proprietors, The Amalgamated Press Ltd., The Fleetway House, Farringdon Street, London, E.C.4. Advertisement offices. The Fleetway House, Farringdon Street, London, E.C.4 Registered for transmission by Canadian Magazine Post. Subscription rates: Inland and Abroad, 11s. per annum; 5s. 6d. for six months. Sole Agents for Australia and New Zealand: Messrs. Gordon & Gotch, Ltd., and for South Africa: Central News Agency. Ltd.—Saturday, December 30th, 1933.

"I'm coming, Gerry!"

Out of the room Billy leaped, slamming the door behind him and locking it He withdrew the pin from the bomb, laid it on the floor, and then raced away with Gerry and Lola.

Stein's car was by the pavement. Into it the three scrambled, Billy taking the wheel. A moment later they were speeding down the street.

They had gone some distance, when the girl, who was in the back seat of the car, uttered a scream.

"What is it, Lola?"

"Someone—something is climbing up the back of the car!"

As Gerry turned, the windows of the car suddenly darkened, and there came the sound of scratching above their heads.

The girl screamed again.

"It is one of them!" she cried. "He is climbing on the roof!"

At that moment a hairy arm appeared at the window beside Gerry. A bright brass bracelet was on the wrist, and the fingers were fumbling for the door-handle.

"It is Manbe—the one who was our gaoler!" cried the girl.

Gerry drew his revolver and fired. A grunt of pain was heard, and the arm was withdrawn.

(*Continued on next page.*)

COME INTO THE OFFICE, BOYS!

Always glad to hear from you, chums, so drop me a line to the following address; The Editor, The " Magnet " Library, The Amalgamated Press, Ltd., The Fleetway House, Farringdon Street, London, E.C.4. A stamped, addressed envelope will ensure a reply.

WELL, chums, for many years now—twenty-six years to be precise—I have picked up my pen at this festive season of the year to wish you all the old, old wish of

A VERY MERRY CHRISTMAS AND A HAPPY AND PROSPEROUS NEW YEAR!

And, I need hardly tell you, that I hope I'll go on wishing you this same wish for many, many years to come! Every day now Christmas cards are coming in by the hundreds from readers who are scattered all over the earth, and I can tell you I appreciate them! Many of these readers are "old boys," and there is a bond of affection between them and their old paper which seems to be strengthened as the years roll on. I feel that all of us, new readers, old readers, and, of course, my staff, form a happy family bound together by the traditions of the MAGNET, and you may take it from me that those traditions are going to be worthily carried on.

And now, here is a greeting to you all from the man who has won a place in your estimation for his wonderful school stories. As toastmasters say at big banquets: "Pray silence, gentlemen, for Mr. Frank Richards!"

Here is his Christmas greeting to you all:

"All you wish yourselves, chums, is the heartfelt wish of one who likes to think that he can number you all amongst his sincerest friends. May you all live long and be happy, and may our friendship be ever strengthened in the years to come.

"FRANK RICHARDS."

By the way, how do you like this week's set of free coloured pictures? Aren't they really top-notchers? How glad you must feel that you're a reader of the MAGNET and able to come into possession of so wonderful a collection of pictures, the like of which has never before been presented free by any other boy's paper. Don't forget that next Saturday's bumper number of the MAGNET will contain another set of coloured pictures to stick in your album. Don't miss them, whatever you do!

THE much-discussed Indian rope trick has bobbed up again, and I've had a letter from a Halifax reader who claims that

HE KNOWS HOW TO DO IT!

You all know the trick, of course. An Indian magician suddenly takes a rope and throws it into the air. The rope stiffens and stays upright in the air, while a small boy actually climbs up it. There have been so many arguments about how it is done—and even about whether it ever has been done—that perhaps this latest solution of the mystery may interest you.

According to this reader, the rope has a rubber tube inside it. When it is thrown into the air a hidden pump forces a tremendous pressure of water into the tube. There are also three invisible silver wires attached to the rope like the guys of a tent, and these are held by unseen helpers in the crowd. They hold the rope steady enough for a very light, small, and agile boy to climb.

That reminds me of a yarn I heard of a conjurer who was travelling in China. He gave a performance before a mighty mandarin out there, and the mandarin was greatly impressed. When the conjurer left, after a stay of several days, he told the mandarin he would do

AN EVEN MORE MARVELLOUS PIECE OF MAGIC!

He said that if the mandarin climbed to the topmost tower of his palace on a certain day, several months later, he would find his name written on the opposite hillside in letters of blood-red.

The conjurer confesses that he never went back to see if this actually happened, but it should have done! For, during his stay, he had been on that hillside every day and he had sown the seeds of a quick-growing and blood-red flower, forming them into the characters of the mandarin's name. The day he had told the mandarin to look from the tower was the day the conjurer reckoned the flowers would be in bloom!

I HAVE been looking up a few more

THINGS YOU'D HARDLY BELIEVE

in response to many requests from readers. Here they are:

Feathered Huntsmen.—Golden eagles have been trained by a tribe in Central Asia to hunt for game. In China cormorants are used to catch fish. A collar round the bird's neck prevents it from swallowing the fish, which it takes back to its master.

The Steeplejack Cow.—A man found a cow on the roof of his house in North Calcutta. He had been in the habit of giving it food, but, as he was away from home, the cow entered the house. Not finding him on the ground floor, it climbed up the stairs from floor to floor until it reached the roof! The local fire brigade rescued it!

Crows Like Golf Balls.—Golfers in Australia are perturbed by the number of crows which prey on the golf courses and steal the balls. Rewards have been offered for dead crows, but the crows are too wily. Local boys are earning extra pocket-money by acting as crow-scarers.

Is He the Oldest Swimmer?—A man in Colorado swims regularly, although he is a hundred and one years old. He claims to be able to beat most local swimmers for speed.

SOME of you fellows are certainly adventurous — and ambitious. Here is a letter from Tom Gibbons, of Helensburg, who wants to go

PROSPECTING FOR GOLD!

Is there much to be done nowadays, he asks? Certainly there is, so long as the would-be gold-finder confines himself to "placer" mining, which does not require much knowledge of geology and minerals. "Placer" mining means washing deposits of sand, gravel, and debris to discover whether it contains gold. The beginner must learn to "pan"—that is, to wash out lighter material from a pan while retaining the heavier substance. If Tom wants to practise he can mix some iron and lead filings with sand and light gravel in a pan, then let water drip in the pan, and wash it round until he separates the filings from the other matter.

Prospectors in certain parts of the United states and Canada are finding "pay dirt" along streams where former placer deposits have been worked out, because even when a deposit has been worked out, a certain amount of gold has been left behind, and in time this has become concentrated in new deposits.

Needless to say there is not a fortune to be made in placer mining nowadays, or the big commercial gold-mining companies would set to work. But there is still enough gold to be found to make things pay for a solitary prospector who does not mind the loneliness and monotony of washing tons of dirt in order to obtain ounces of gold.

There's a first-rate "New Year" yarn for you next week, entitled:

"BUNTER, THE CRASHER!"
By Frank Richards,

in which all your favourite characters play a prominent part. Mr. Richards has put his very best into the yarn, which for excitement and enjoyment has all other school stories "licked to a frazzle."

Stuart Martin is going very strong, too, with "When the Great Apes Came." I have received letters galore congratulating me on selecting this magnificent yarn, which will add to the long list of MAGNET successes. Don't miss next week's full-of-thrills chapters.

You'll find chuckles galore in the "Greyfriars Herald," while "Linesman" will be answering more Soccer queries.

Most important of all—don't forget that there will be another set of superb coloured pictures FREE with this issue.

YOUR EDITOR.

THE MAGNET LIBRARY.—No. 1,350.

"The roof, Gerry—fire through the roof!" called Billy, at the same time pressing his foot on the accelerator and manipulating the steering-wheel in an effort to throw the unwanted passenger off.

Crack, crack! went Gerry's revolver, as he aimed directly above his head.

Crack, crack!

Something slid past the window at the back, and the car seemed to leap forward.

Lola looked back, and p e e r e d cautiously through the rear window.

"He is gone!" she cried excitedly. "It is Manbe! He lies still!"

The car's headlights picked out a figure standing in the middle of the road. It was a policeman, and the man in blue was flashing his lamp as a signal for them to stop.

Billy put his foot on the brakes.

"Now, then, what's all this?"

The policeman blew his whistle for assistance, and then flashed his lamp into the car, revealing the girl in her jungle attire, and the two boys.

"What are you doing with that gun?" was the policeman's next question.

In a few words Gerry explained the situation. Other policemen arrived, followed by an inspector.

The latter scrutinised the trio closely, listening to the jerky explanations.

Suddenly he became alert.

"All right," he said. "I've heard of you two at the Yard. So you're Billy Murchie, then? All right, we'll have the house you describe surrounded right away, and get hold of this Stein and his ape-men. This has been a night. What with the animals at the Zoo breaking loose, a monster in Park Lane, and trouble in Whitehall——"

He turned and issued some orders to the policemen, who ran off, blowing their whistles as they ran.

"Where are you going in this car?" asked the inspector.

"I was thinking of making for the War Office," replied Billy. "I can give them information about the gorilla attack——"

"There's a police-box down the road. Drive there, and I'll come with you. I want reinforcements to surround that house—and machine-guns, too!"

"Be careful with the ammunition, inspector," said Billy quickly. "The cellars of that house are stored with bombs and stuff. Here's the police-box!"

They drew up, and the inspector and Billy dashed to the box, its bright light burning above, twinkling like a star to attract attention.

The inspector lifted the receiver and made his call.

Impatiently he waited, urging the operator to hasten. While he waited he was questioning Billy, who outlined the position swiftly.

"Stein came over with me, having arranged to meet Ling at the Zoo at a certain hour. The Zoo business was only a kick-off, so to speak. One of their armies commandeered some barges in the Thames. Their only hope is to make sudden raids until they have consolidated their positions——"

"How many armies have they got?"

"I don't know, but they have several, all under the leadership of ape-men like the one Gerry shot dead a minute ago on top of the car——"

The inspector broke off suddenly, and darted from the box into the street.

A terrible explosion had rent the air, and some distance off a fierce glare lit up the sky. Flames and smoke rose in a pillar into the heavens.

"It's the house you've escaped from!" he cried. "They have blown it up!"

He dashed back to the police-box, lifted up the receiver, and began shouting into the mouthpiece. Presently a puzzled expression came over his face.

"They can't get any connection with the Yard or with the War Office!" he said, in a strange voice. "I wonder if——"

He lifted the receiver again and tried other connections—local police stations, reserve corps.

He put the receiver down at last, and wiped his brow.

"The Chief is taking command," he said. "I'm to take you to Whitehall at——"

"But if the gorillas are there——"

"There are no gorillas in Whitehall now," replied the inspector. "I'm told that all is quiet there. The Chief, however, can't get in touch with the Yard. I'm to go down direct and make my report. Come on!"

The car sped along, and it was a good thing that the inspector was with the party, for they were held up time and again by officers hurrying to the scene of the explosion.

"There are short cuts we can take," the inspector told Billy. "Don't worry about speed limits."

They whirled through the main thoroughfares, reached Oxford Street, and then sped down Regent Street into Piccadilly Circus. Here a cordon of soldiers barred the way, and they had to cut through a side street, only to be confronted by more cordons of police and soldiers.

"Seen any gorillas, inspector?" asked an officer, as the car drew up before an inquiring official.

"I was about to ask you that. What's happened to the mob that got into Whitehall?"

"Don't know. We are only just on the scene. But the gorillas have gone. They raided Covent Garden—cleared the stalls and the shops of everything eatable, I hear. As for Whitehall—I don't know."

(Billy & Co. are booked for the biggest surprise ever when they reach the War Office! Don't miss next week's full-of-thrills chapters, whatever you do!)

THE GHOST OF WHARTON LODGE!

(Continued from page 23.)

(Continued from page 23.)

hear him, and vanish before he could get to close quarters.

He gripped the Holiday Annual silently and took careful and accurate aim.

Whiz!

Crash!

"Yooooooooop!" roared the ghost.

The Annual flew—and so did the ghost! The bulky volume landed on a fat nose, and the ghost flew backwards into the passage, and sat down with a heavy bump!

"Urrrrggh!" came a wild and breathless splutter. "Wurrggh! Urrrgh! Ow! Wow! Urrrggh!"

"Got him!" gasped Bob.

He leaped from the bed, and rushed to the door. At the sound of his movements, the ghostly figure leaped up. There was a pattering of rapid footsteps! Bob rushed down the passage in pursuit. Something white tangled in his feet and he stumbled. It was the sheet thrown down by the ghost as he fled.

"Oh!" gasped Bob as he stumbled over.

Bump!

The pattering footsteps died away. Bob Cherry scrambled up, groped along the passage for the switch, and turned on the light.

But the passage was empty, except for himself! The ghost had vanished!

Bob Cherry looked up and down the passage. He even glanced up the attic stair. But there was nothing to be seen—and he turned off the light at last, picked up his Holiday Annual, and went back to bed. For some little time he stayed awake, rather hoping that the ghost would put in another appearance. But he fell asleep at last!

He had, in fact, laid the ghost!

In the attic, Billy Bunter was tenderly caressing his fat little nose, which felt considerably damaged from the impact of the Holiday Annual. Bunter had not expected that whizzing book. As so often occurs, it was the unexpected that had happened. Billy Bunter was fed-up with playing ghost. It was getting too exciting!

How his extraordinary visit to Wharton Lodge was going to end, Billy Bunter did not yet know! But the ghost of Wharton Lodge had walked for the last time.

THE END.

(Now look out for next week's grand New Year and Free Gift Number of the MAGNET, which will contain another rollicking fine yarn of Harry Wharton & Co., entitled: "BUNTER, THE CRASHER!" It's full of fun and exciting situations, chums. Be sure to order your copy EARLY!)

The MAGNET

TEN MORE SUPERB COLOURED PICTURES FREE INSIDE

NO. 1,351. Vol. XLV. EVERY SATURDAY. **2D**

Week Ending January 6th, 1934.

Billy Bunter on the Ice!

BUNTER, THE CRASHER!

BY FRANK RICHARDS.

THE FIRST CHAPTER.

Unexpected !

"INKY!"

Hurree Jamset Ram Singh fairly jumped.

The dusky junior of Greyfriars was startled.

It was a fat whisper that fell suddenly on his dusky ears—the fat whisper of Billy Bunter of the Greyfriars Remove.

And as Hurree Jamset Ram Singh had no idea that Billy Bunter was within a dozen miles, he was naturally startled.

It was a sharp winter's morning. The new year was beginning bright and cold and clear. It was freezing hard, and the lake in the grounds of Wharton Lodge was a sheet of glistening ice. Four Remove fellows were skating—Harry Wharton and Frank Nugent, Bob Cherry and Johnny Bull. With cheery, ruddy faces, and scarves flying in the wind, they whizzed over the ice, evidently enjoying life.

Hurree Jamset Ram Singh had walked down from the house with his friends. But the freezefulness, as he would have expressed it in his wonderful English, was rather too terrific! The dusky nabob preferred the shelter of the hut on the bank, from the keen and searching wind, which seemed to the junior from the warm and sunny East to penetrate through his overcoat to the marrow of his bones.

From the shelter of the hut he watched his comrades disporting themselves on the ice, with a cheery smile on his dusky face. And then, from behind him, came that fat whisper which made him jump almost clear of the floor in his surprise, and spin round in amazement.

THE MAGNET LIBRARY.—No. 1,351.

He had supposed that nobody was in the hut when he entered it. Least of all had he supposed that Billy Bunter was there! Now that he looked round, however, there was Bunter! In the farthest corner of the hut a fat figure was visible, and a big pair of spectacles glimmered.

"The esteemed and idiotic Bunter!" ejaculated Hurree Jamset Ram Singh.

"Don't yell!" gasped Bunter.

"What the preposterous thump——"

"Don't shout! Can't you see that the old hunks is coming? And if he spots me here——"

The Nabob of Bhanipur stared blankly at Billy Bunter, and then glanced out of the hut. Harry Wharton's uncle, the colonel, was coming along the bank. Apparently Colonel Wharton, like Inky, preferred the shelter of the hut to the bitter winter wind, for he was heading for it, though he paused every now and then to glance at the skaters, with an amiable smile on his bronzed face.

"I say, Inky, bar that old donkey off!" whispered Billy Bunter, in deep anxiety. "He's got his back up with me, you know! If he spots me here, what do you think he will do?"

Hurree Singh grinned.

"The kickfulness will probably be terrific!" he answered. "What are you doing here at all-fully, my esteemed fat-headed Bunter?"

"Well, I dodged in here out of sight when I saw the fellows coming," said Bunter. "I was just taking a—a—a walk, you know. I—I happened to—to come this way just by—by chance. I say, keep that old beast away, Inky! He smacked my head when he saw me in Wimford the other day, just because he heard me call him an old fool——"

"Probably there will be some more

smackfulness," chuckled Hurree Jamset Ram Singh. "When you call an esteemed old johnny an old fool, my idiotic Bunter, it would be safer to keep clear of his ridiculous residence."

"Well, I didn't know he could hear me, you ass! Besides, he is an old fool!" argued Bunter. "They talk about it being up to a fellow to tell the truth, and all that—but when an old donkey hears you telling the truth, he just gets his back up——"

"Ha, ha, ha!"

"Oh, don't cackle!" exclaimed Bunter irritably. "Just keep that old fossil away before he spots me! He's coming here! Stand by a pal, Inky, old chap, after all I've done for you! Cut off and tell him——"

"What shall I tell him, my esteemed Bunter?"

"Tell him the house is on fire——"

"Wha-a-at?"

"Or that old Miss Wharton has fallen downstairs——"

"Eh?"

"Anything you like, so long as you bar him off!" whispered Bunter hurriedly. "I don't mind what you tell him, old chap, so long as you keep him away!"

Hurree Singh chuckled.

"But I mind what I tell him, my idiotic Bunter," he answered. "I have some regard for absurd veracity."

"Beast!"

Billy Bunter blinked anxiously out of the hut through his big spectacles. Colonel Wharton was coming along slowly—but he was coming! Hurree Singh had not observed the fat junior crouching in the shadowy corner, when he stepped into the hut. But it was probable the colonel would do so. Bunter, at all events, did not want to run the risk. He was uneasy—and he had cause for uneasiness.

Whether it was the truth or not, there was no doubt that Colonel Wharton had been fearfully wrathy when he heard Billy Bunter's genuine opinion of him!

He had smacked Bunter's head, and would have gone on smacking it had not the fat Owl of the Remove got away.

Now, if he spotted Bunter, it was fairly certain that the smacking would restart after the interval, so to speak.

It was an alarming and distressing position for the Owl of Greyfriars.

Hurree Singh, on the other hand, seemed to find it amusing. A cheery grin wreathed his dusky features.

"Oh lor'!" gasped Bunter. "He—ho's coming, Inky! I say, old chap, stand just in front of me, will you, and—and hide me!"

"Ha, ha, ha!" yelled the nabob.

The idea of the slim Indian junior hiding the fat Owl of the Remove by standing in front of him, was enough to make a fellow yell. Bunter's ample form would have been visible on both sides of Hurree Jamset Ram Singh.

"Blessed if I see anything to cackle at!" hissed Bunter. "I say, Inky, old chap, stand here and screen me——"

"But you forget that you are double-width, my esteemed Bunter!" chuckled the nabob.

"Beast!"

"Ha, ha, ha!"

Colonel Wharton was quite near the hut now. The sound of the Indian junior's merriment reached his ears, and he glanced at Hurree Singh, and came on, with a smile.

"You seem very merry, my boy," he remarked. "What—why—who—— By Jove!"

Billy Bunter backed into the farthest corner. But it was in vain! The old colonel, as he looked in, spotted him, and stared at him in surprise and gathering wrath. He was as surprised as Hurree Jamset Ram Singh had been to see the fat Owl there. But he was not amused, like the nabob! He looked anything but amused.

"By Jove! Is that that impertinent young jackanapes?" hooted the old military gentleman. "What?"

"Ow! No!" gasped Bunter. "I—I'm not here! I—I mean——"

"Bunter, hay?" roared Colonel Wharton. "What are you doing here, what? Cheeky young rascal! What?"

"Oh lor'! I—I say, sir, I—I—I wasn't speaking of you, sir, when I called you an old fool!" gasped Bunter. "I—I was speaking of another old fool, sir——"

"What?" roared Colonel Wharton.

"I—I assure you, sir—I—I—you're not the only old fool in the world, sir, and I—I assure you——"

If Bunter hoped that that explanation would placate Colonel Wharton, his hope was unfounded. Rather it seemed to add to the old military gentleman's wrath. He strode past Hurree Jamset Ram Singh into the hut, and made a grab at Bunter's collar.

Only too clearly the smacking was about to recommence.

Colonel Wharton had a heavy hand! Bunter had had some, and he did not want any more! Very much indeed he did not want any more! Escape was cut off—the colonel was between him and the doorway. Bunter was desperate. As the colonel's hand was outstretched to grasp him by the collar, the fat Owl lowered his bullet head, and butted.

Possibly, had he stopped to think, Bunter would not have done it. But

there was no time to think. And thinking was not much in Billy Bunter's line, anyway.

Crash!

Bump!

"Oh gad! Ooooough!" spluttered Colonel Wharton, as Bunter's bullet head landed where he had packed his breakfast. "Urrrrrgh!"

The colonel sat down, quite suddenly, with a bump that shook the hut.

"Oh, my esteemed hat!" gasped Hurree Jamset Ram Singh.

"Urrrgh! Seize that young scoundrel! Hold him! Urrrrggh!" gurgled Colonel Wharton.

Bunter made a bound for the doorway. Hurree Singh's foot shot out as he bounded. It landed on the tightest trousers in the United Kingdom, and Bunter roared and rolled. Colonel Wharton scrambled up, red with wrath, gurgling for breath.

"By gad! I—I—I will—— Urrrgh! Bunter, you young rascal—— Urrrgh!"

Bunter bounded up and fled. Behind him came the heavy footsteps of the

---

Who wants Bunter? Nobody! At least, nobody from Greyfriars, for the juniors see enough of him at school without being burdened with him over the holidays! But somebody's *got* to have Bunter. Read how he "crashes" in on Harry Wharton & Co.!

---

enraged colonel, and Bunter, in sheer desperation, shot out on the ice and slid for his fat life!

THE SECOND CHAPTER.
Slippery!

"HALLO, hallo, hallo!" yelled Bob Cherry.

"Bunter!" exclaimed Harry Wharton, in amazement.

"That fat owl!" exclaimed Johnny Bull.

"Yaroooop!" roared Frank Nugent, who did not see Bunter so soon as the other fellows.

But though he did not, for the moment, see Bunter, he became aware of his presence. For Bunter, as he shot on the ice, slipped and slid, and travelled a good deal like a bullet from a rifle—straight at Frank Nugent and Harry Wharton! He collided with the two Removites, clutching them round the neck and sending them spinning.

Nugent spun, and his skates flew in the air. Wharton crashed the next moment. Bunter swerved from the shock, but, wonderful to relate, did not roll over. He shot away at a tangent, and before Johnny Bull knew that he was coming in his direction, Bunter had come!

Crash!

"Yawp!" gurgled Johnny, as he sat.

"Oh crikey!" gasped Bunter.

He sprawled over Johnny Bull. He clutched at Johnny to save himself, and got Johnny's nose with one hand, his ear with the other. The yells that emanated from Johnny Bull, as he was dragged over on the ice by his nose and his ear, were absolutely fearful.

"What's that blithering idiot doing here?" gasped Bob Cherry. "He keeps on turning up like a bad penny!"

"Seize him!" roared Colonel Wharton. "Stop that boy! Seize him! I am going to thrash him! Seize him!"

"Oh, my hat!" gasped Harry Wharton.

"Yoooop!" roared Bunter, as Johnny Bull succeeded in getting in a punch. Bunter released a nose and an ear, and rolled over on the ice. "I say, you fellows—— Yarooooh! I say—— Help! Whoooooop!"

Colonel Wharton had halted for a moment on the margin of the lake. But the desire to get within smacking distance of Bunter was too strong for him. He had an ache where Bunter's bullet head had butted His breakfast had been seriously disturbed. He stepped out on the smooth ice, and headed for the sprawling Owl of the Remove.

Bunter saw him coming and scrambled up. He scrambled frantically As fast as he landed one foot, it slipped away before he could land the other. He looked as if he was going through an extraordinary series of physical jerks. The ice was as smooth as glass, or smoother. Colonel Wharton strode at him grimly. But that military stride, suitable to the parade ground, was disastrous on slippery ice. The old colonel's feet suddenly flew, and he sat down, and shot towards Bunter in a sitting position.

"Oh, my esteemed hat!" gasped Hurree Jamset Ram Singh, from the bank.

"Oh jiminy!" ejaculated Bob Cherry.

"Great gad!" gasped the colonel. "What—what—what——"

He crashed into Bunter, and the fat junior rolled.

"Yaroooh!" spluttered Billy Bunter.

The old colonel was sprawling on the ice. Bunter grabbed at him, to get righted. He simply could not get up on the slippery ice—his feet played him false. But, with a hold on the colonel, he managed it. Grabbing a collar and a white moustache in his fat hands, Bunter planted a knee on a heaving chest, and heaved himself up from the ice.

"What—what——" gurgled Colonel Wharton, hardly knowing what was happening. "Great gad what——"

The skaters closed in to the rescue. With the unintentional assistance of the colonel, Bunter was up. He slid away across the lake, leaving Colonel Wharton sprawling on his back, gasping for breath, and dizzily wondering whether he was on his head or his heels.

"Uncle!" exclaimed Harry. "Here, lend a hand, you men!"

The juniors grasped the gasping old military gentleman, and got him on his feet. Colonel Wharton spluttered for breath.

"Where is he?" he gasped.

"Bunter? Oh, he—he's gone!"

"The young scoundrel!" Colonel Wharton glared round, evidently unappeased. "I will thrash him! I—I—There he is!"

He spotted Bunter. The fat junior had slid across the lake, and bumped over in the frozen rushes on the opposite side. Picking himself up there, the Owl of the Remove staggered onward, heading into the snowy, leafless park.

Colonel Wharton started after him. This time he did not proceed with a swinging military stride. He walked very carefully. Smooth ice was not to be trifled with.

THE MAGNET LIBRARY.—No. 1,351.

Bunter blinked back from his side of the lane, his little round eyes popping behind his big, round spectacles.

"Oh lor'!" he gasped, as he saw the tall form of the master of Wharton Lodge in pursuit astern.

He bolted among the trees.

"Stop!" roared the colonel, as he reached the edge of the ice and tramped through the rushes. "Stop! I am going to thrash you! By gad, I'm going to thrash you within an inch of your life! Stop!"

If Colonel Wharton supposed that such an inducement would make Bunter stop, he was mistaken. Bunter did not stop. He flew!

After him went the colonel, his long legs whisking almost as rapidly as Bunter's short, fat ones. Harry Wharton & Co. stared after them blankly till they vanished among the frosty trunks of the park.

"Oh crikey!" spluttered Bunter.

He blinked back over a fat shoulder. At a distance behind, but coming on fast, was the exasperated colonel.

Bunter panted onward, running his hardest. How and why he was within the walls of Wharton Lodge, only Bunter knew; but there was no doubt that at this moment he was extremely anxious to get outside those walls. A path, carpeted with snow, led through the park towards a fence at a distance, and Bunter went along that path at top speed, only hoping that he would reach the fence before the colonel reached him!

Naturally, Billy Bunter did not expect to meet anyone on a snowy path among the frosty trunks in the wind-swept park. But it was the unexpected that happened. As he came round a curve of the path like a runaway steamroller, he crashed into a man who was coming towards him with a terrific crash.

"Oooooh!" gasped Bunter, reeling from the shock, and sitting down with a bump in the snow.

"Oh!" spluttered the man he had run into, staggering back against a tree.

The shock fairly winded Bunter. He could only sit and gurgle and blink at the gasping man in front of him. He was a rather powerful man, in soft hat and shabby clothes, with a clean-shaven face and hard features. He did not look a good-tempered or amiable man, and at the present moment he seemed frightfully bad-tempered. He glared at Bunter almost like a tiger. He had narrow, steely eyes, and they glittered savagely at the fat junior.

"You young fool!" he snarled.

"What—— By James, I'll kick your fat carcass across the park!"

He made an angry stride at Bunter.

"Ow! Keep off!" yelled the alarmed Owl. This was worse than Colonel Wharton. "I say, I didn't see you! Yarooh! Keep off! Beast! Whoop!"

Tramp, tramp, tramp! came Colonel Wharton's footsteps on the path behind Bunter. And Bunter was actually glad to hear him coming. The steely eyed man was kicking him in sheer savage temper, and it was painful—worse than a box on his fat ears from the colonel. But the sound of the new arrival caused the man to turn his attention from Bunter. He stared along the winding path.

"Yarooh! Help!" roared Bunter.

Colonel Wharton came tramping round the curve in the path. The steely eyed man gave a start at the sight of him, and his teeth came together with a sharp click. Bunter, blinking at him, could see that the stranger knew Colonel Wharton, and his look indicated clearly enough that he knew him as an enemy.

Billy Bunter, unheeded by the man who had been kicking him only a minute before, squirmed away.

"By James! It's the colonel!"

Bunter heard the exclamation, or rather the snarl, from the steely eyed man.

"Great gad! Corkran, you scoundrel! What are you doing here?" roared Colonel Wharton, as he came face to face with the man "You—— Why—— Hands off, you scoundrel!"

"Oh crikey!" gasped Bunter, his eyes almost bulging through his spectacles at the startling sight as the man leaped on the colonel with the spring of a tiger, and bore him backwards to the earth.

Colonel Wharton went down with a crash, the man he had called Corkran upon him. Billy Bunter gave them one astonished blink, and scuttled on. If there was going to be a scrap between the colonel and the stranger in the park, Bunter did not want to linger to watch it. It gave him the chance he needed of making his escape.

He heard sounds of a struggle behind him as he scuttled on. But he did not pause or look back. Gasping for breath, he reached the park palings and clambered over, and dropped into the lane on the other side.

"Oh lor'!" gurgled Bunter.

He was safe now.

That was all that mattered. What might be happening to the old colonel was a matter of very small moment in comparison.

THE THIRD CHAPTER.

The Man from India!

"THAT ass!"

"That fat chump!"

"That blithering fathead!"

"That footling frump!"

"That preposterous porpoise!"

The Famous Five of the Greyfriars Remove were, of course, referring to Billy Bunter. They stood staring in the direction in which Bunter had vanished among the trees, and the colonel had vanished after him.

The apparition of Billy Bunter, within the walls of Wharton Lodge, was surprising. Several times during the Christmas holidays they had seen Billy Bunter, but generally at a distance from the Lodge.

Bunter, so far as they could make out, was staying somewhere in the neighbourhood, though exactly where they had no idea.

Certainly it never crossed their minds to imagine how near—how very near—the Owl of the Remove had been during the hols.

Now he had turned up again. How and why they did not know. They were aware that he was at a loose end for the holidays. His people were away; Bunter Villa was shut up, and his Uncle George, upon whom Bunter had been

landed, had cut up rusty, which was not astonishing, with so very peculiar a guest as Billy Bunter.

After a row with his Uncle George, Bunter had decided to favour Harry Wharton with his company for Christmas. And no doubt Wharton would have suffered the infliction, as he had suffered it before, but for the fact that the fatuous Owl had put the colonel's back up.

That, so to speak, tore it!

Where the fat Owl was hanging up, and what he was up to, the chums of the Remove did not know, or care very much. In fact, they rather forgot Billy Bunter's fat existence, except when he turned up like a bad penny.

"The fat, foozling, footling frowster!" said Harry Wharton, kicking off his skates. "What the thump is he doing here? He ought to be jolly well kicked!"

"The kickfulness is the proper caper," agreed Hurree Jamset Ram Singh. "Probably the esteemed and absurd colonel will bestow the necessary and ridiculous kickfulness."

Harry Wharton laughed.

"I—I think I'd better get after them," he said. "Uncle's got his rag out with the fat duffer, and no wonder, but——"

"But he may lay it on a little too thick," chuckled Bob Cherry. "Let's go and pick up what he's left of Bunter —if he's left anything."

"Let's!" agreed Nugent.

And, leaving their skates on the bank, the chums of the Remove followed the path into the trees. Billy Bunter was undoubtedly a most exasperating ass, and deserved to be kicked; but in his present mood it was quite probable that the colonel might lay it on too hard. And Wharton hoped that his arrival might have a pacifying effect on the old military gentleman.

As they hurried up the path, winding through the frosty wood, the juniors fully expected to hear sounds of loud howls from the Owl of the Remove.

But they heard nothing from Bunter.

A voice came suddenly to their ears through the frosty thickets, but it was the voice of Colonel Wharton, in panting tones:

"You scoundrel! Release me! By gad! You villain!"

"What the thump——" gasped Bob Cherry.

It sounded as if Bunter had turned on his pursuer, and got the better of him, which was wildly impossible.

But another voice followed—a sharp, sneering, disagreeable voice—a man's voice, strange to their ears.

"Likely! You hound! I've been looking for this chance! I told you I'd remember, Colonel Wharton, and, by James, I haven't forgotten! As soon as I came back from India——"

"Corkran, you scoundrel——"

"You laid a stick about me—years ago! You remember?"

"By gad, I'll lay a stick about you again for your impudence in coming on my land, you rascal! Release me, or——"

"I'm handling the stick this time!" came the sneering, snarling voice. "You won't be in a state to lay a finger on me when I've done with you! You thrashed me like a dog once—now it's my turn! I've got you where I want you! And, by James, you're going through it!"

Harry Wharton heard the words as he raced up the path, his comrades at his heels. For a second or two the captain of the Greyfriars Remove had been utterly amazed. But he realised very quickly that, startling as it was, his uncle was in the grasp of an enemy, out of sight beyond the trees, in his own park. And the colonel's nephew ran as he had never run on the football field as he realised that.

He came speeding round the curve in the path.

His eyes blazed at what he saw.

Colonel Wharton was on his back in the snow, and a powerfully built man was kneeling on him. The old colonel was savagely but vainly struggling to rise. He was pinned down, and his assailant, in his uplifted right hand, held a short, thick stick. That weapon would have crashed down on the colonel's defenceless head, but for the arrival of Harry Wharton. He put on

him, running hard, when he reached the park palings, leaped up and caught the top, and swung himself over. A sound of running feet died away outside as the juniors came panting up to the fence.

The rascal was gone.

"Rotten luck!" grunted Johnny Bull.

And the juniors, panting for breath after the rapid run, walked to where they had left Harry Wharton and his uncle.

The old colonel was leaning on a frosty trunk, gasping.

"Has he got away?" he panted.

"Sorry, sir; but he was too quick for us," said Bob. "He ran like a jolly old hare."

"The rascal! He will not get away

What had happened had quite driven the fat Owl of Greyfriars from his mind.

But Harry Wharton & Co. did not go back to the skating.

"I'm going to look for that scoundrel Corkran," said Harry. "You fellows coming?"

"Yes, rather!"

"The ratherfulness is terrific."

And the Famous Five followed the way the man from India had gone, clambered over the palings, and dropped into the road. For a long time they hunted up and down the lanes and field-paths, very keen to get hold of the rascal and march him off to Wimford police station. But they saw nothing of him; it was clear that he had lost no time in getting away from the vicinity.

" Look here, don't you start a shindy here ! " said the waiter warmly. " You'll pay your bill at the desk——" " Shan't ! " came a deep growl very like Johnny Bull's. " The cakes were rotten ! " " Johnny——" gasped Wharton. " Eh, —what ! " stuttered Johnny Bull. " I never spoke. Who the dickens said that ? " Billy Bunter, the ventriloquist, looked quite unconcerned.

a desperate spurt, and reached the steely eyed man, even as the blow was descending.

Wharton crashed into the man, hurling him backwards with his weight, and sending him rolling off the colonel. He rolled over himself from the shock.

Corkran spat out an oath, and he rolled in the snow. His hard-featured face was convulsed with rage. He scrambled up swiftly, glaring round. And then as he saw the crowd of juniors coming charging up the path he jumped back.

For an instant he stood glaring at them; and then, suddenly turning, took to his heels.

"After him!" roared Bob Cherry.

Harry Wharton sprang up and ran to his uncle to help him to rise. The other four fellows rushed on in pursuit of Corkran.

But the steely eyed man ran like a deer. They were still panting behind

from the police; and they will soon be looking for him!" gasped the colonel. "I'll charge him with assault, by Jove, and he will be taken care of for six months. Lurking in my own park, watching for me, by Jove!"

The colonel calmed down. The juniors were exchanging wondering looks. The incident was surprising enough to them.

"A man I knew in India!" grunted the colonel, as if feeling that some explanation was needed. "A swindling rascal in Calcutta! I thrashed him, by Jove, and I'm glad to remember that I laid it on hard! I'm not too old to thrash him again, by Jove, only he took me by surprise! Get back to your skating, my boys! I will walk back to the house."

Still breathing hard, obviously much disturbed by the startling episode, Colonel Wharton walked back through the trees, forgetful of Billy Bunter.

Neither did they see anything of Billy Bunter. But that fat and fatuous youth was not, if they had only known it, very far away.

———

THE FOURTH CHAPTER.
Mysterious !

"WELLS!"

"Sir!" said the butler of Wharton Lodge.

"It's getting too jolly thick!" exclaimed Harry Wharton warmly.

"The thicktfulness," remarked Hurree Jamset Ram Singh, "is truly a little terrific."

"But what, sir—" asked Wells.

"That dashed pincher has been at it again!" exclaimed Wharton.

"Oh, sir!" said Wells.

It was afternoon. The winter dusk

was falling. Harry Wharton was in his "den"—a very pleasant room, with a balcony outside the french windows, and old stone steps leading down to the garden at the side of the house. The Nabob of Bhanipur was with him; the other fellows in their rooms, getting ready for a walk.

The Famous Five were going down to the pictures at Wimford, and they were going to "tea" in the tea lounge attached to the picture-house But the captain of the Greyfriars Remove was not, for the moment, thinking of the intended excursion. He had rung for Wells, and now he was pointing to the bookshelf beside the fireplace. A number of handsome gilt volumes had been placed there—Christmas gifts from various relatives to Harry—and he had just noticed that they were no longer in their place. And he was wrathy.

"Half a dozen books," said Harry. "I've looked round the room; they're not here anywhere. Look here, Wells, it's up to you !"

Wells stood distressed.

All through the Christmas holidays it had gone on. There was some unknown pilferer lurking within the walls somewhere. Certainly it was up to Wells, as chief of the household staff, to put a stop to it. But Wells seemed quite helpless in the matter.

"Thomas !" he called out.

Thomas, the page, came in from the passage He had heard Wharton's words, and his chubby face was as distressed as Wells'.

"Thomas," said Wells, "a number of books are missing. Do you know anything about it ?"

"No, Mr. Wells !" said Thomas. "I noticed they were gone when I dusted the room this morning, sir. I thought p'r'aps some of the young gents had them to read.   They was there last night, sir."

"They have been taken during the night, then," said Wells, with a very doubtful look at Thomas. Suspicion, as far as suspicion existed, rested on that unfortunate youth

"It's too jolly thick !" said Harry. "It's been going on almost ever since I came back from school. All sorts of things—bedclothes and rugs and socks and shirts—and now books !"

"It has been going on still more below stairs, sir," said Wells. "Food from the larder, sir, has continually disappeared. Everything is now kept locked up at night, since the Christmas pudding and the cold turkey went.   It is a very strange mystery, sir."

Bob Cherry came in

"One of you borrowed my 'Holiday-Annual'?" he asked.

"Oh, my hat !" exclaimed Wharton, in great exasperation.   "Is that gone, too ?"

"Well, it isn't in my room," said Bob. "I thought one of you fellows——"

"That dashed pilferer has been at it again, Bob ! I'm awfully sorry !" said Wharton, colouring with vexation. The loss of his own property was irritating enough, but pilfering from a guest under his roof was much more mortifying.

"Oh, it's all right, old bean !" said Bob.

"It isn't all right !" growled the captain of the Remove.   "There's some rotter in the house pinching things ! It's never happened before ! It's got to be stopped. Wells !"

"Certainly, sir, but——"

Johnny Bull stepped in at the door.

"If one of you chaps has borrowed my 'Modern Boy's Annual'——" he began.

"Oh crumbs ! Is that gone ?"

"I thought I'd mention it, as it's not in my room——"

"The jolly old pincher seems to have made rather a clearance," said Bob, with a faint grin.   "Must be a cove with literary tastes, to borrow so many books all at once."

"They've been taken to be sold, of course," said Harry. "The brute can't want them !   It's too awfully thick !"

Nugent came in.   All eyes turned on him at once.

"You missed anything ?" asked Harry.

"Eh ? No ! Anything up ?"

"More pinching !" said Harry. His face was crimson.   "It's fearfully rotten for it to happen while you fellows are here ! Look here, Wells, something will have to be done about it ! It can't go on !"

"Certainly, sir," said the worried Wells. "But——" Wells was evidently at a loss.

Wharton's face was clouded when he went down with his friends and started to walk to Wimford. The peculiar depredations that were going on at Wharton Lodge worried him deeply.

Nothing of any great value had been taken; that was the most curious circumstance.   Schoolboys are careless; and plenty of times one or another member of the Co. had left money in his room, in pockets of clothes, or even on a dressing-table. It had never been touched. Such things as watches and pins might have been snaffled by the mysterious snaffler—but they never had been.

Food seemed to be his chief object—though that had been stopped since Wells had taken to locking up everything very carefully before going to bed. Next he seemed keen on articles of clothing, as if he was a fellow in need of a change—as perhaps he was ! Now he seemed to have concentrated on books: it was hardly likely he wanted so many at once to read, so no doubt he had taken them to sell for what they would fetch second hand.

It was odd enough that a fellow who would not touch money would bag property—but that, after all, was not uncommon. The stupidest fellow, if he took money or valuables, could not delude himself into the belief that he was not a thief. So long as he only "snaffled" trifles of little value, perhaps he succeeded in persuading himself that he was not exactly dishonest. Certainly there existed plenty of fellows with obtuse intellects like that. Billy Bunter of the Greyfriars Remove was one of them !

No fellow's cakes or tarts at Greyfriars were safe from Bunter. He would "borrow" a fellow's socks or shirts surreptitiously and unscrupulously.   He had even been known to "borrow" a fellow's school books and sell them to Fisher T. Fish, the business man of the Remove ! But Bunter would have been very shocked and indignant had anybody accused him of dishonesty.   He had wonderful ways of working out that whatever he did was somehow right—or right if fellows would only look at it properly.

But nobody, of course, thought of Billy Bunter in connection with the mysterious happenings at Wharton Lodge. So far as anyone knew, Bunter was some distance away.

Wharton's face cleared, however, under the influence of a walk in the keen, fresh air, and by the time the chums of the Remove arrived at Wimford he had dismissed the disagreeable incidents from his mind.

Quite a good picture was on show at the cinema—one of the good British

films which are slowly but surely ousting American crook stuff from the screen. The Famous Five saw it through, and then adjourned to the tea lounge for tea. There were several people at the little tables in the tea lounge, and among them was a fat youth in spectacles, who caught the eyes of the juniors at once.

"Hallo, hallo, hallo!" ejaculated Bob Cherry, with a grin. "Is that a porpoise escaped from the Zoo, or jolly old Bunter?"

"Bunter again!" grinned Nugent. "The fat foozler must be staying in Wimford, as he told us he was. I thought he wasn't, as he said he was."

"Bother him!" grunted Harry Wharton. He was not pleased by the sight of William George Bunter. Fascinating fellow as Bunter was, it often happened that people were not pleased to see him.

"Somebody's been handing him a Christmas tip!" grinned Bob, with a glance at Bunter's table.

The fat Owl was certainly "doing himself" very well! He was happy and shiny and sticky and jammy—his usual state when he was in funds. He blinked across at the Famous Five and grinned a fat and sticky grin.

"I say, you fellows," he squeaked, "come over here—lots of room for you. My treat, old chaps."

The Famous Five did not accept that kind invitation. They sat down at another table to tea. A treat from Bunter generally meant that the fellow he treated would be landed with the bill, at the end of the treat. They knew their Bunter!

Giving the fat Owl the "marble" eye, they proceeded with tea. Billy Bunter sniffed, and devoted his fat attention to the foodstuffs. He had been at it some time, to judge by his sticky aspect; but he was not the fellow to leave off so long as there remained anything to eat. Several times it might have been observed that Billy Bunter paused and made a little mental calculation, as if he realised that he was in danger of going beyond the limit of his financial resources—a danger that Bunter constantly incurred. Apparently Bunter reached the limit of his cash before he reached the limit of his unearthly appetite—for he rose from his table, casting a longing, lingering look at a pile of cakes that remained there. Having blinked at the cakes, he blinked across at the Famous Five.

"I say, you fellows——"
No reply.
"I say——"
Same result!
"Deaf?" hooted Bunter.
Stony silence.
"I say, can you lend me a few bob?"

Ten deaf ears were turned to that request! Billy Bunter snorted, sniffed, sorted out his cash, and paid his bill. His calculations, evidently, had been correct; for the bill amounted to exactly the amount of his cash. There was nothing left over for the waiter, who had been kept rather busy for some time and who gave the fat junior a rather expressive look. But expressive looks had no effect on the Owl of the Remove.

He rolled across to the juniors' table.
"I say, you fellows——"
"Hook it!" said Harry Wharton briefly.
"I've had my tea!" said Bunter, with dignity. "I'm not going to stick you for a tea, Wharton."
"You're not!" agreed Wharton. "Take your face away, old fat bean! We have to stand it in the term at Greyfriars; but it's not fair to spoil the landscape with it in the hols."
"Beast!"

Billy Bunter blinked round for a chair. Spotting one, he drew it up to the table. Freezing stares from the Famous Five had no more effect on Billy Bunter than the expressive look of the waiter.

"Make room for a chap, Franky—is that your foot I trod on, Bob?—you shouldn't have such big feet. He, he, he!" And Billy Bunter sat down and grinned agreeably at the chums of the Remove.

THE FIFTH CHAPTER.
A Little Ventriloquism!

BILLY BUNTER blinked over the tea-table. The chums of the Remove had nearly finished tea, and little remained. On the cake-dish was one sticky cake, to which the Owl of the Remove helped himself. It did not last long.

"Shall I call the waiter, old beans?" he asked.

"Certainly—if you want him!" answered Harry. "We don't!"

"You haven't had much of a tea——"

"Enough's as good as a feast!"

"Well, look here, I haven't seen much of you these hols—have some more at my expense," said Bunter.

"Can't afford having anything at your expense, old fat bean," said Bob Cherry, shaking his head. "Comes too expensive."

"Oh, really, Cherry——"

"Time we were getting a move on," remarked Harry Wharton.

"Don't walk away while a fellow's talking to you, Wharton! Dash it all, there's such a thing as manners!" said Bunter warmly. "Not that I expect much from you in that line. He, he, he! I say, has the old hunks got over it yet?"

"The who?"

"Your duffy old uncle—he seemed excited this morning," grinned Bunter. "Did that chap in the park damage him? I'd have stopped and lent him a hand, but he really couldn't expect it, in the circumstances, what? Barging after a chap like a wild Indian! I hope that fellow gave him a jolly good hiding. He, he, he!"

Harry Wharton looked fixedly at the Owl of the Remove. In the tea lounge of Wimford Picture Palace he could not very well take Bunter by the scruff of his fat neck and bang his head on the table. So he had to be contented with looking at him—expressively. Which did not bother William George Bunter in the very least.

"What the thump were you doing there at all, you fat ass?" asked Bob Cherry. "If you wanted a walk you needn't have walked on Colonel Wharton's estate? Plenty of other places to walk in."

"He, he, he!"

"What are you cackling at, fathead?"

"Your face!" answered Bunter agreeably. "Your features rather have that effect on a fellow, you know."

Bob Cherry breathed hard. Like Wharton, he regretted that it was out of the question to bang Bunter's head in the tea lounge of the Wimford Picture Palace.

"The fact is, I've been looking for a chance to speak to you, Harry, old chap," said Bunter, blinking at the captain of the Remove. "As you know, I kept the hols open for you—it was understood that I was staying with you——"

"Not by me!"

"Beast! I mean, oh, really, old fellow! Having turned down a crowd of invitations on your account, I was rather stranded when you turned me down," said Bunter. "I admit it's not wholly your fault—that stuffy old ass of an uncle of yours got his back up——"

"Do you want me to pull your nose, Bunter?"

"Eh? No!"

"Then you'd better speak of my uncle a bit more respectfully."

"Oh, really, Wharton! You know as well as I do that he's a stuffy old ass! But never mind that. Look here—don't get up, old chap, I haven't finished yet! What I meant to say is, can you fix it with him? I'm willing to apologise, if that will be any use. I don't mind pulling an old goat's leg. He, he, he! If you can fix it, I can give you a week! Not more—as I've so many friends anxious to see me these hols. What about it?"

Harry Wharton rose from the table.

"Let's get going, you men," he said.

"I say, Harry, old chap——"

"Go and eat coke!"

"I was going to say that I decline to stay with you, Wharton, if you ask me on your bended knees——"

"The bendfulness will probably not be terrific!" grinned the Nabob of Bhanipur.

"But look here!" said Bunter. "Hold on a minute—I'm in rather a scrape. I'm short of money."

"Not really?" asked Johnny Bull, with deep sarcasm.

"Yes, really, old chap, and it's rather rotten! You see, I'm not used to it, like you fellows."

"Oh, my only hat!"

"To tell you the truth——" went on Bunter.

"You couldn't!" said Bob, shaking his head.

"Beast! Look here, to tell you the truth, I've just blowed my last bobs on tea here," said Bunter. "I got only seven-and-six for the lot——"

"Eh?"

"I mean, I had seven-and-six, and lunch was five bob," said Bunter. "That left only half-a-crown! That's all I've had for tea."

"We've managed on a bob apiece," remarked Nugent.

"Well, that's all right for you fellows," said Bunter. "You're poor! But I'm rather accustomed to the decencies of life, and all that. I suppose you can lend me a quid. It's only four bob each, if you whack it out."

"The whackfulness will not be preposterous!"

"Well, look here, make it ten bob if you're hard up," said Bunter. "I can tell you I've been going jolly short lately. The fact is, I'm getting fed-up with the whole thing, and I've a jolly good mind to go back to my Uncle George! Still, he's rather a beast—mean with the food, too! Your place is better than that, on the whole, Wharton."

"Better or worse, you'll get the boot if you get within kicking distance there!" growled Wharton.

"He, he, he!"

"What is the fat blitherer cackling at?" asked Bob. "Is there some joke on, Bunter?"

"He, he, he! Oh, no! Not at all! He, he, he! Look here, what about that ten bob? To tell you the truth—"

"Great pip! Is he going to tell the truth twice in one day?" ejaculated Bob Cherry.

"Ha, ha, ha!"

"To tell you the truth," hooted Bunter, "I'm stony! I've been disappointed about a postal order!"

"Good-bye, Bunter!"

Five juniors turned away from the table.

"I say, you fellows——"

No answer.

Billy Bunter's eyes gleamed behind his spectacles. He gave a fat little cough—the usual preliminary of the Greyfriars ventriloquist when he was about to begin operations.

"Waiter!" came a voice, which Bob Cherry's nearest and dearest relative might have taken for Bob's. "Here, waiter——"

"Yessir?"

"What do you mean by bringing us those rotten cakes? We're jolly well not going to pay for them!"

The waiter, coming up probably in expectation of a tip, stared blankly at Bob Cherry. So did his comrades.

"The cakes were all right," said Harry.

"Who said they weren't?"

"Eh? You did!"

"I did?" gasped Bob.

"What was the matter with the cakes, sir?" demanded the waiter, rather aggressively. "You've eaten them all, at any rate, and they're on your bill!"

"Nothing the matter with the cakes that I know of!" gasped Bob in bewilderment. "What——"

"You silly idiot, shut up!" came a voice that was either Johnny Bull's, or a twin to it.

Bob stared round at him.

"What? Who's a silly idiot?" he demanded. "Look here, Johnny Bull, if you can't be civil, keep your head shut, see?"

"What the dickens do you mean? I——"

"For goodness' sake don't rag, you men!" exclaimed Harry Wharton. "Everybody's staring already! Let's get out——"

"You preposterous ass, stop your idiotic jawfulness and give us a rest!" came from the Greyfriars ventriloquist; and Harry Wharton spun round at Hurree Jamset Ram Singh, crimson with anger.

"Inky, you cheeky ass——"

"My esteemed chum, I did not speak!" gasped the Nabob of Bhanipur. "I assure you terrifically——"

"Look here, young gentlemen, don't start a shindy here," said the waiter warmly. "You'll pay your bill at the desk——"

"Shan't!" came a deep growl, very much like Johnny Bull's. "You're a rotten swindler. The cakes were rotten!"

"Johnny——" gasped Wharton.

"Eh? What? I never spoke! Who the dickens said that?" gasped Johnny Bull.

"You did——"

"I didn't——"

"Look here——"

"Oh, shut up, Wharton! You talk too much! You're too jolly conceited," came the twin to Bob Cherry's voice.

"My hat! You cheeky, silly ass——"

"Pay your bill at the desk and leave the place, please!" barked the waiter. "You can't kick up a row here!"

Harry Wharton, with a set face, went to the desk and paid the bill. Then he walked down the stairs and out, followed by his friends—all of them frowning. Billy Bunter, left on his own, grinned a fat grin. The Greyfriars ventriloquist considered that he had got his own back, and a little over!

THE SIXTH CHAPTER.
Giving Bunter Beans!

FIVE fellows, with frowning faces, walked down the old High Street of Wimford. Dusk was falling, and with dusk came a fall of snow, and the street was glistening white. They tramped in silence under the falling flakes.

It had been quite a happy party till the Greyfriars ventriloquist weighed in! Now it was far from a happy one!

But suddenly, from Hurree Jamset Ram Singh, there came an exclamation. He halted.

"My esteemed chums!" he exclaimed.

"Well, what?" asked Frank Nugent.

"We have been diddlefully done! My esteemed and absurd Wharton, pray lend me your ridiculous ears——"

Wharton had not stopped. Bob Cherry caught him by the arm.

"Hold on, old bean!" he said.

Wharton shook his hand off. Bob stared at him.

"What the thump's the matter with you?" he demanded.

"Oh, nothing!" said Wharton sarcastically. "Only I talk too much, and I'm too jolly conceited! Frightfully polite to tell me so!"

"I never said anything of the kind!"

"What's the good of rotting? You know you did!"

"I did not!" bawled Bob Cherry.

"Oh, rats!"

"My esteemed and ridiculous chums, please lend me your absurd ears," urged the Nabob of Bhanipur. "We have been donefully diddled by the absurd and execrable Bunter——"

"Bunter?" repeated Wharton.

"You have forgotten that the esteemed and execrable Bunter is a ridiculous ventriloquist—and he has been pulling our absurd legs, as he has done at Greyfriars——"

"Oh!" exclaimed Bob Cherry.

"Bunter!" gasped Wharton. "That fat villain! We might have known—he's always playing some fool game like that at Greyfriars—we've kicked him up and down the Remove passage for it——"

All was clear at once! Frowning faces divested themselves of their frowns! As soon as the keen-witted nabob tumbled to the trick that had been played, the chums of the Remove knew that the ventriloquist of Greyfriars had been at work.

"The podgy villain!" breathed Bob Cherry. "Here, let's go back and wait for the fat scoundrel to come out! He's spent all his money, so he won't be long!"

"Yes, rather!"

The Famous Five walked back towards the picture-house. A fat figure was rolling out as they reached the entrance. Billy Bunter was grinning. Evidently he was enjoying the discomfiture of the chums of the Remove. But the fat grin vanished from his podgy features at the sight of five wrathful faces. He blinked at them in alarm.

"I—I—I say, you fellows——" stammered Bunter.

"You fat scoundrel——"

"Oh, really, Cherry——"

"It was you!" roared Johnny Bull.

"Not at all, old chap! If you mean that little bit of ventriloquism, it was only a lark, and I never did it, neither! The fact is, I can't ventriloquise at all! As for imitating a fellow's voice, I couldn't do it to save my life! I say—Yaroooooop! Grooooogh! Oooogh!" spluttered Bunter, as a snowball, plopping on his capacious mouth, cut short his remarks.

"Urrrrrrgggh!"

"Give him beans!"

"Give him jip!"

"Give him terrific and preposterous jip!"

Whiz, whiz, whiz! Crash! Smash, smash! There was plenty of snow, and Billy Bunter had the benefit of it. Five fellows pelted him with snowballs with accuracy and wonderful rapidity. It seemed to Billy Bunter that the air was full of snowballs. They landed on him right and left.

"Yooogh! Urrgh! I say, you fellows—wurrggh—it wasn't me—urrggh—and it jolly well served you right—gurrggh—oh crikey! Oh lor'!"

Billy Bunter fled for his fat life. Through the falling flakes, the Famous Five followed him, gathering up snow as they went, and hurling snowballs. Bunter felt as if he had collected tons of snow by the time he dodged round a corner and escaped.

After which, the Famous Five, chuckling, took their way back to Wharton Lodge, tramping cheerily through the snow, with harmony once more restored in their happy circle.

Billy Bunter was not feeling happy!

It was a breathless and winded and gasping Bunter that tramped out of Wimford some time after the chums of the Remove.

He tramped in the same direction, gurgling as he went.

The winter darkness was falling thickly, and had Harry Wharton & Co. looked back, they would not have perceived the fat figure that was rolling on behind them.

By the time they arrived at Wharton Lodge they had almost forgotten Bunter.

Certainly they never suspected that Billy Bunter was still tramping in the same direction, with the same destination!

But he was!

Bunter's proceedings, those holidays, had puzzled them a good deal, especially his extraordinary way of popping up like a jack-in-the-box on unexpected occasions. They had concluded that he must be passing the holidays at some place not far away. They little dreamed how near that place was!

The fat junior reached Wharton Lodge an hour after the chums of the Remove had gone in. He did not approach the gates. He clambered over a fence into the park, and—blinking cautiously round him through his big spectacles—crept stealthily through the shadows till he passed through the shrubbery at the side of the house. There he blinked up at the french windows of Wharton's "den."

There was no light in the room. Reassured on that point, Bunter crept up the stone stairs to the balcony. He tried the french window! Once he had found that window locked on the inside. Luckily, it was not locked now! The Owl of the Remove opened it, stepped in, and closed it again. He stole on tiptoe across the room to the door on the corridor. There he blinked cautiously out, before he emerged. The coast was clear! Bunter whipped out and down the passage to the little steep stair that led to the attic over Harry Wharton's rooms. He gasped with relief when he had negotiated that stair and was safe in the attic.

Billy Bunter was home again!

THE SEVENTH CHAPTER.

Cornered !

COLONEL WHARTON started. It was past midnight.

At that hour all should have been silent and still at Wharton Lodge. All was, in fact, silent and still; but through the silence and the stillness there came the sound of a thud, as if someone, moving in the dark, had bumped into some article of furniture.

The colonel's eyes gleamed under his grey, knitted brows.

The old military gentleman was in his study, a room that opened off the hall next to the dining-room. It was far from his habit to keep late hours. But he had been rather disturbed that day by the unexpected meeting with the man from India, and his nervous system was still rather feeling the effects of the struggle with Corkran.

He had gone to bed at the usual time; but found himself unable to sleep, and at last he had turned out, donned dressing-gown and slippers, and descended to his study, with the intention of reading himself to a sleepy state. He threw a few logs on the embers of the fire, and settled down in an armchair with a volume of Darwin's "Origin of Species" in his hand—a volume specially selected for its soporific effects. And he had not been perusing that great work for more than a quarter of an hour when the faint thud from the direction of the adjoining room came to his ears through the silence and stillness.

He laid Darwin in the armchair and stepped quietly to the door. Someone was astir in the sleeping house—moving about in the dark! It could scarcely be anyone but the secret pilferer whose mysterious purloinings had caused so much perturbation during the Christmas holidays. The old colonel picked up a golf club from a bag in the corner, opened the door, and looked into the dark hall grimly.

The door of the dining-room was close at hand, and it was open!

Someone was there!

Darker and grimmer grew the brow of the old colonel. His grip closed hard on the golf club.

He stepped out into the hall and switched on the light there. Then he stepped towards the open doorway of the dining-room.

The secret snaffler was fairly cornered in that room. When the colonel got to close quarters with the golf club there was no doubt that that mysterious individual would wish that he had made a New Year's resolution to give up snaffling!

Why he was there the colonel had no

doubt. In the provender department everything was now safely locked up at night, and Wells inspected the process. There was no chance of the secret snaffler getting at the pantry or the larder again. And it was food that he chiefly snaffled! But in the dining-room there was a sideboard, and in the sideboard there were biscuits. That, the colonel did not doubt, was what the pilferer was after. Once before the biscuits had vanished from the box in the sideboard. Now they were going to vanish again—or, rather, they would have vanished, if the colonel had not happened to be wakeful that night! Grimly gripping the golf club, Colonel Wharton stepped towards the dining-room.

There was a startled gasp in the darkness of that room.

The sudden flashing on of the light in the hall had, of course, alarmed the unseen person there.

A fat figure that was groping at the

RAISE A LAUGH
and
BAG A POCKET KNIFE !

The following rib-tickler was sent in by Ronald Dane, of Wentworth, Woad Lane, Great Coates, Lincs. He's proud of his penknife, too !

Doctor: "You're far too fat. Don't you ever take any exercise ?"
Patient: "Oh, yes, doctor: I'm rolling my own cigarettes now ! "

sideboard—and had already knocked over a chair in the dark—leaped up!

"Oh lor'!" gasped Billy Bunter.

Terror rooted him, for a moment, to the floor.

But only for a moment! It was necessary to act swiftly! Bunter had a glimpse of a tall figure in sweeping dressing-gown, then he leaped to the dining-room door and slammed it.

Swiftly he turned the key in the lock. The next moment Colonel Wharton's hand was on the door-handle.

"Good gad!" hooted the colonel. "Locked! By Jove! Open this door at once, you scoundrel!"

"Oh crikey!" breathed Bunter.

He was not likely to open the door! He was only too glad that he had succeeded in locking it before the colonel spotted him.

What Colonel Wharton would have done, had he discovered that the Owl of Greyfriars was a secret and unsuspected resident in his house, Bunter did not quite know! But he had no doubt that it would have been something drastic—very drastic indeed!

The door-handle rattled.

"Is that you, Thomas?" hooted the colonel. Many circumstances had fixed suspicion on poor Thomas.

Bunter grinned breathlessly.

He did not care whom the colonel supposed that it was so long as he did not guess that it was William George Bunter.

"Open this door at once."

"Beast!" murmured Bunter.

Thump! Bang! Rattle! The colonel was angry and impatient. He did not know who the secret snaffler was, but he knew that he had cornered him. And he was very anxious to put in some work with the golf club.

Bunter, on the other hand, had no desire whatever to establish contact with that golf club! Nothing would have induced him to unlock the door.

But what was he going to do? Too late, he repented that he had stolen out of his lair to snaffle the biscuits in the dining-room. But he had been hungry—too hungry to sleep. The sale of certain books at a second-hand shop in Wimford had provided him with funds for lunch and tea. But he had had no supper! It was the biscuits or nothing—and Bunter naturally preferred biscuits to nothing! Now, however, he would have given the whole output of Huntley & Palmer to be safe back in his attic!

"Beast!" breathed Bunter.

He was fairly cornered! For the moment he was safe! But there was no escape for him, except by the window. That meant a night out.

Since the fat and fatuous Owl had ensconced himself, secretly, in the house, he had been accustomed to use the french windows of Wharton's "den " as a mode of egress and ingress. But at night those windows were locked. If he got out, there was no getting in again—till the following day! On a winter's night that was not an attractive prospect.

Bang! Thump!

"Open this door, you rascal!" came the colonel's voice in tones like those of a Royal Bengal tiger in a particularly ferocious frame of mind.

"Oh lor' !" groaned Bunter.

He heard another voice from the hall, the portly, fruity voice of Wells, the butler. The thumping on the door had awakened Wells and brought him forth.

"Is anything amiss, sir?" asked Wells, with a cough.

"Amiss!" hooted the colonel. "Yes, by gad! That rascally pilferer is in the dining-room, Wells, and has locked the door."

"Dear me !" said Wells.

"We shall now ascertain who the scoundrel is," said the colonel. "I will thrash him, by Jove, thrash him soundly, and then kick him out."

"Beast!" hissed Bunter, under his breath.

"I will call Thomas, sir——"

"Huh! Probably it is Thomas in the dining-room at this moment. I do not see who else it can be——"

"Oh, sir," said another voice, "I ain't in the dining-room, sir—I'm 'ere, sir !"

"Good gad !"

"I think, sir, that it cannot be Thomas '" said Wells respectfully. "As Thomas is here, sir, I think——"

"Huh !"

"I was about to suggest, sir, that I should call Thomas, because he would be able, being a small person, to get into the dining-room by the serving-hatch," said Wells. "As he is here——"

"Good! At once !" barked the colonel.

"Oh crumbs !" breathed Bunter.

He scudded across to the dining-room window. There was no help for it now, and no time to lose! Bunter had that window open in a few seconds. Heedless of cold wind and falling flakes he rolled out. He bumped into snow, picked himself up, and fled.

A minute later the active Thomas was in the dining-room, and he had the door open for the colonel and Wells.

Colonel Wharton strode in and switched on the light, and fixed his eyes on the open window, through which the snowflakes were blowing in on the January night-wind.

"By gad! He is gone—by the window!" roared the colonel.

"Dear me!" said Wells.

"'Ooked it!" said Thomas.

Colonel Wharton glared at the open window. He strode across to it, glared out into the snow and darkness, and then closed and fastened it. Then he turned to Wells.

"Wells, the scoundrel is out of the house now! Ascertain at once if any of the servants are out of their rooms!"

"Very good, sir!"

Wells glided away. He came back in ten minutes—which the colonel spent in snorting and fuming.

"None of the servants, sir, is out of the house," said Wells.

"Good gad! Are you sure?"

"I have ascertained the fact, sir!" said Wells, with dignity.

Colonel Wharton stood silent. It had been taken for granted that the secret snaffler was a member of the household staff. This discovery, however, obviously cleared them—much to the satisfaction of Wells, but to the great puzzlement and perplexity of the colonel. Thomas brightly weighed in with a suggestion:

"P'r'aps it was one of the young gents, sir, a-larking!"

"Don't talk nonsense, Thomas!" barked the colonel testily.

"Oh! Yes, sir!" said Thomas.

But he looked at Wells, and Wells looked at him. Colonel Wharton refused to entertain for a moment the idea that his nephew, or his nephew's school friends, might have been "larking" at that hour of the night, and in such a way! But to the butler and the page it seemed rather probable. Indeed, they did not see what else there was to believe!

"Some intruder must have obtained admission to the house," said the colonel, at last. "We must examine doors and windows——"

Quite a considerable time was spent in examining doors and windows. But they were found safely secured on the inside. The matter had to be given up at last, and it remained a mystery—one more of the mysteries of Wharton Lodge!

THE EIGHTH CHAPTER.
The Man at the Window!

"OH lor'!" murmured Billy Bunter.

It was wild and windy that night in early January. Snow fell lightly, but persistently. Billy Bunter stood under a tree: but that afforded little shelter and no warmth at all! Bunter was cold. His teeth chattered! He had not even got away with the biscuits; but he was so cold that he almost forgot that he was hungry.

"Beasts!" groaned Bunter.

Had it been practicable, the fat Owl of the Remove would have "chucked" his secret sojourn at Wharton Lodge, and returned at once to the inhospitable roof of his Uncle George.

But it was not practicable!

Even had Bunter possessed a railway-fare, there were no trains at that time of night!

Bunter was fairly "for" it!

On the whole, he had not done so badly during his secret and surreptitious stay at Harry Wharton's home. He had snaffled sufficient bedclothes and rugs to keep himself warm and comfortable in his attic. Supplies had been rather irregular, but he had done fairly well.

His comings and goings had had to be very cautious and stealthy, but he had escaped discovery. All the time, he had hoped that a propitious moment might arrive when it would be safe to reveal himself; but in that he had been disappointed. Still, on the whole, he had found it rather better than Uncle George!

But now——

Now it was awful!

It was windy! It was cold! He was shut out! It was long hours before morning! It was awful!

"Oh lor'!" groaned Bunter.

If that brute of an old colonel had only got over his temper it would have been all right! He could have managed Harry Wharton somehow! But all Bunter's proceedings seemed to have made the old colonel's temper worse, instead of better!

One thing was certain. He had to get in somehow! A night out in the wind and the snow was out of the question.

And at last the fat Owl made up his mind to it.

He left his shelter under the tree and tramped away through the falling snow and frosty shrubberies, to the old stone steps that led up to the balcony of Harry Wharton's den.

To break a pane and put a fat paw through and unlock the door was the only resource!

It was a desperate resource, for it could scarcely fail to warn the occupants of the house that someone had entered from the outside during the night.

But it was a case of "needs must." The Owl of the Remove had to get out of the cold and the snow. Risk or no risk, discovery or no discovery, that was essential.

He reached the stone steps at the side of the building, thickly carpeted with snow. He trod up them in the deep darkness.

Click!

Bunter jumped.

It was the click of a lock that he heard. Someone was opening the french window of Wharton's den.

It was past one o'clock in the morning! It seemed impossible that anyone could be up, opening the window from the inside.

Bunter's fat heart jumped.

If the window was not being opened from the inside, it was being opened from the outside!

That meant that Billy Bunter was not the only surreptitious intruder seeking an entrance into Wharton Lodge in the small hours.

He hardly breathed for a moment or two!

If it was a burglar——

He blinked with terrified eyes through his big spectacles, across the dark balcony, not daring to move.

Dark as it was, he made out a dark figure close to the french window! It was the figure of a man in an overcoat, muffled up against the wind.

One wing of the french window had been pushed open. Evidently the man had picked the lock from the outside, and opened it.

Now he was standing with his head bent, listening cautiously before he entered. Billy Bunter gave him one scared blink, and turned to grope his way down again. The snowy ivy rustled as he moved; and the figure at the french window spun round instantly towards him at the sound.

Bunter had a glimpse of gleaming, steely eyes—of a hard mouth and a hawkish nose; and, even in the gloom, he knew that it was the man who had attacked Colonel Wharton in the park that morning.

He had only time for that one glimpse. The man had heard him, and instantly taken the alarm.

He came across the balcony towards Bunter at a bound.

There was no time for the fat Owl to retreat. That rapid bound brought Corkran fairly upon him.

Scarcely knowing what he did in his terror, the Owl of the Remove lashed out with both fists, his only idea—so far as he had any idea in his frightened, fat mind at all—being to keep the rascal off.

There was a sudden, startled gasp, as his lashing fists hit the man in the shabby clothes. The figure disappeared.

Bunter blinked in wonder.

Bump, bump, bump!

As he heard that bumping sound from the darkness he understood. The sudden punch in the darkness had caused the man from India to slip on the edge of the balcony steps, and he had gone down the stone steps headlong.

Bump, bump, bump!

There was a crash in the snow at the foot of the stone stair, and a sound of gasping and groaning. Apparently the man was damaged by his fall.

"Oh crikey!" panted Bunter.

Like a hunted hare, the fat junior darted across the balcony, and into the open french window. In a twinkling he had shut the window and turned the key in the lock. The man from India had evidently turned that key back from the outside with some burglarious implement, and so unlocked the window. Now it was locked again.

Bunter stood panting within. But only for a moment or two! Whether the man from India was too damaged to renew his attempt, whether he had taken the alarm and fled as was very probable, Bunter did not know—and did not even think! Bunter's fat thoughts, as usual, were concentrated wholly on his fat self.

Having recovered his breath, he scudded across the room, got out of it, and groped up to his attic!

Bunter was safe. Bunter was all right! That was all that mattered! When Bunter was all right, everything was all right!

THE NINTH CHAPTER.
Something Like Strategy!

HURREE JAMSET RAM SINGH came out of his room, in coat and muffler clad as if for an Arctic expedition.

There had been no snow since dawn, but the day was bitterly cold—indeed, the Nabob of Bhanipur declared that the cold-fulness was terrific. Harry Wharton & Co. were in the passage, waiting for him—also warmly clad, though not to the same extent as the Indian junior. They grinned cheerfully as he joined them.

"Got 'em all on?" asked Bob Cherry. "The cold-fulness is——"

"Terrific and preposterous!" agreed Bob, with a chuckle. "Well, if you've stacked on all your coats and mufflers and things, we may as well get going. The jolly old colonel is ready, I believe. Jolly decent of him to run us across to see the 'Spurs play."

And the Famous Five went down the staircase in great spirits.

The cold weather did not worry four of them, at all events; and the fifth had wrapped himself up remarkably well.

There was a League match that afternoon, ten miles away, and Colonel Wharton was taking the schoolboys over in the car to see it, so it was going to be an agreeable afternoon.

Five cheery juniors packed themselves in the car and glided away, little dreaming that their cheery talk, before they started, had been overheard by a fat youth in spectacles, lurking at the half-open door of the little attic over Wharton's rooms.

Five minutes after they had gone Billy Bunter crept out, blinked down the attic stair, and descended on tip-toe.

Reaching the passage on which the juniors' rooms opened, Bunter, like Moses of old, looked this way and that way; and, like Moses again, saw no man!

And he rolled across into Wharton's den. In that apartment, on several occasions, the hidden guest at Wharton Lodge had been able to "snoop" such articles as chocolates, or toffee, or candied fruits. And as Bunter had had no breakfast or lunch that day, so far, he was desperately anxious to get hold of something to eat.

His experience the previous night had rather fed Bunter up with his peculiar visit to Wharton Lodge! He had almost made up his fat mind to quit.

But, on reflection he decided to stick it out.

His parents were staying with relatives, who not only did not want Billy in addition, but had made that fact abundantly clear. His sister Bessie was staying with an aunt, who had received her for the holiday on the express condition that she came without her brothers. His brother Sammy was staying with Uncle George—and Bunter had "rowed" with Uncle George, which made it exceedingly difficult and unpleasant to return to that avuncular abode. On the whole, Billy Bunter decided that he would try it on a little longer at Wharton Lodge.

His present idea was to snaffle any eatables that might be in Wharton's den, and then borrow a few more books, for disposal at the second-hand shop in Wimford!

Later on, when he received several postal orders that he had been expecting for quite a considerable time, he would redeem those books! Bunter hoped that he was honest! In the meantime, however there seemed to be no other resource.

"Beast!" murmured Bunter, as he blinked round the "den."

There was nothing of an edible nature to be seen! So much pilfering had perhaps caused unusual care to be taken.

Not even a packet of toffee rewarded Bunter's quest. There was not so much as an apple or an orange.

Bunter could not venture downstairs in quest of supplies in the daytime. Colonel Wharton and the juniors had gone out, but the servants were about! Indeed, he was not safe where he was, for Wharton's fire was kept in during his absence, and somebody had to come up to see to it.

Billy Bunter was about to make a selection of books from the bookshelf, when he heard footsteps—and, guessing at once that it was Thomas coming to see to the fire, he darted across to the communicating door of Wharton's bed-room, and promptly closed that door after him.

It was not the first time, my many a one, that Bunter had had such narrow escapes. Indeed, ever since he had taken up his extraordinary residence at the Lodge, his life had been a succession of hairbreadth escapes!

Quietly he locked the communicating door. On the other side, he could hear Thomas poking at the log fire. The bed-room had a door on the passage also, and Bunter stepped to that and locked it, too. An idea was working in Billy Bunter's fat brain!

Ideas did not, as a rule evolve very easily in the depths of that podgy intellect! But, if anything could make Bunter think, and think hard, it was the need of "grub."

Spurred on by that dire need, Bunter was capable of really brilliant strategy. There was going to be a little ventriloquism.

Now that both doors of Wharton's bed-room were locked, the fat Owl of Greyfriars was safe from observation. That was an essential preliminary, before he got to work with his ventriloquism.

He gave his fat little cough and approached the communicating door again. He could hear someone putting logs on the fire in the den.

"Thomas!" It was Harry Wharton's voice, tone for tone, that proceeded from the fat ventriloquist of Greyfriars. "Is that you, Thomas?"

"Yessir! Is that Master Harry?" exclaimed Thomas, turning from the fire in astonishment.

He had seen Master Harry start in the car with his uncle and his friends, so it was naturally astonishing to hear his voice proceeding from his bed-room.

"Yes. Who did you think it was, you young ass?"

"I thought you'd gone out, sir!" said the amazed Thomas.

"I came back, Thomas."

"Yessir, I suppose you did," said Thomas "Ain't you going, sir?"

"No—my uncle thinks I'm catching a cold, and I'd better stay in," said the voice through the door.

"Oh, sir! I'm sorry, sir!" said Thomas.

"I shall have tea in my room, Thomas—tell Wells."

"Yessir," said Thomas staring blankly at the bed-room door.

It was no business of his, of course; but it really was odd that Master Harry should speak to him through a closed door, instead of opening it.

"Tell Wells at once, Thomas."

"Oh, yessir! Tea at the usual time, sir?"

"No. I'm going to feed my cold, Thomas—you have to feed a cold and starve a fever you know. I'll have tea at once."

"Oh!" gasped Thomas.

As it was only about an hour since lunch, this was very surprising indeed.

"I want a really good tea," went on

the voice. "Tell Wells! Plenty of everything—ham and eggs and sosses, and cake and jam and scones."

"Oh, yes, sir!" gasped Thomas.

"Tell Wells to send it up to my den at once! I'll stay here till it's ready—I'm putting on some warmer things."

"Yessir."

Thomas, in a very surprised state, departed. Billy Bunter grinned; but it was a rather uneasy grin. Thomas, evidently, was completely taken in; but the thing was risky. Bunter realised that. Still, there are times when a fellow has to take risks; and this was one of them. Even discovery, and the order of the boot, was better than going without grub!

Bunter waited. In a few minutes there were footsteps in the den. A tap came at the communicating door.

"Are you there, Master Harry?"

It was Wells' fruity voice.

"Eh! Yes!"

"I was not aware that you had returned, sir——"

"Well, you're aware now!" snapped Bunter, still in the voice of Colonel Wharton's nephew. "Hasn't Thomas told you——"

"Oh, yes, sir, but it is so very unusual, sir, I thought I would ask you and make sure, sir——"

"Don't be an ass, Wells!"

"Wha-a-at, Master Harry?" ejaculated Wells.

"I'm catching a cold! My uncle has advised me to eat! I—I haven't much of an appetite, but I shall do exactly as he says!"

"Oh, yes, sir, certainly!"

"Mind you send up a good tea, and plenty of it! A dozen sausages——"

"A—a—a dozen, sir?" gasped Wells.

"Yes—and a dozen poached eggs——"

"A—a—a dozen poached eggs——"

"And plenty of buttered toast, and a pot of jam, and a cake—mind, a big cake—and some scones—say a dozen—and a couple of pounds of ham——"

"Dear me!"

"And buck up, Wells! You're wasting time!"

"Oh! Yes, Master Harry!" gasped Wells dazedly.

"Call me when it's ready!"

"Certainly, Master Harry!"

Wells almost tottered away. If Master Harry was catching a cold, and was going to feed it, it was clear that he was going to feed it on a very generous scale! Still, it was not for Wells to argue! He went down to give the necessary directions in the kitchen—where those directions caused much surprise and great activity.

Bunter waited anxiously.

Before long, there was a sound of footsteps, and of trays being laid on a table! Thomas, as a rule, brought up anything that was required in the den. But unusual quantities were now required, and Wells was lending his own assistance. There was a tap at the communicating door at last.

"Master Harry!" Wells called through the door. "Your tea is ready, sir!"

"Thank you, Wells! You can go down!"

"Very good, sir!"

"Thomas can go down, too! I—I don't want to risk giving anybody my—my cold! Both of you go."

"Very good, sir! Come, Thomas!" said Wells.

Billy Bunter waited, and listened, anxiously, till he heard the door of the den close. Then he opened the communicating door, and blinked in. An ample—not to say gargantuan—tea was laid, and Wells and Thomas were gone!

THE MAGNET LIBRARY.—No. 1,351.

Bunter cut across to the door by which they had left, and turned the key in the lock! He whipped across to the french windows, locked them, and drew the curtains across, to guard against the bare possibility of somebody coming up the steps to the balcony. He was safe on all sides now!

Then he stepped to the well-spread table.

For one ecstatic moment he gazed at it, at the magnificent supply of good things that he owed to his weird gift of ventriloquism!

Then he sat down and started.

His fat face beamed, as his active jaws worked. This was happiness! This was life! This was something like! Glad now was the Owl of the Remove, from the bottom of his fat heart, that he had not shaken the dust of Wharton Lodge from his feet, as he had thought of doing! Wharton Lodge was all right. It was as right as rain!

Gobble, gobble, gobble!

Billy Bunter's fat face grew red and shiny! His breath came short and spasmodic! But he kept on manfully!

Gobble, gobble, gobble!

Harry Wharton & Co. were enjoying their afternoon. But Billy Bunter was more than enjoying his! Billy Bunter was in the seventh heaven!

THE TENTH CHAPTER.
A Fat Young Gent of the Name of Bunter !

COLONEL WHARTON drove up to the garage, handed the car over to Brown, and walked to the house.

He had landed the juniors at their destination in good time for the League match, and left them to enjoy tremselves watching the exploits of the famous 'Spurs. Wells came to take his hat and coat, and the old, military gentleman rubbed his hands before the fire in the hall.

"My nephew and his friends will be back rather late for tea, Wells," he said. "You had better have tea laid for them in Master Harry's own quarters."

Wells jumped.

It was quite unlike Wells to jump. He was the most sedate of butlers. But he could not help it! He jumped, and almost dropped the colonel's hat!

"What—what did you say, sir?" he ejaculated.

Colonel Wharton glanced round at him. He was astonished by the butler's astonishment.

"I said that my nephew——"

"Master Harry, sir?" gasped Wells.

"What do you mean, Wells?" snapped the old colonel. "I have no other nephew! Of course I mean Master Harry!"

"But—but I don't understand, sir!" stuttered Wells. "Master Harry is back already——"

"What?"

"He came back soon after you started in the car, sir——"

"Have you been drinking, Wells?"

"Sir!"

"If you have not been drinking, what do you mean?" snorted Colonel Wharton. "My nephew is ten miles away, with his friends, watching a football match. What do you mean by saying that he came back?"

Wells almost staggered.

"Sir! Colonel Wharton! Master Harry with his friends!" he stuttered.

"Certainly he is!"

"Tut-tut-ten miles away!" gurgled Wells. "You—you—you left him there, sir?"

"Of course I did! What do you mean?"

"But—but—but he came back, sir—he's in his room now!" gasped Wells. "I—I assure you, sir, that he came b-b-back, and—and ordered tea in his room, and—and is having his tea there now, sir!"

Colonel Wharton gazed severely at his butler.

"Wells, I am surprised at you! I am astonished and shocked! This is the first time you have shown signs of intoxication——"

"Thomas!" howled Wells.

"Yes, Mr. Wells, sir!" Thomas appeared from the service stairs.

"Is Master Harry in his room, or is he not?"

"Yes, sir!" answered T h o m a s. "Having his tea, sir!"

Colonel Wharton transferred his gaze to Thomas.

"Is the boy mad?" he snorted. "Are you mad, Wells? I tell you that my nephew is at this very moment watching a football match with his friends. He is ten miles from this house!"

"Then who," gasped Wells, "is in his room?"

"Is anyone in his room?"

"Master Harry, sir—at least, it was Master Harry's voice spoke through the bed-room door, sir—I did not see him!" gasped Wells. "Did you see him, Thomas?"

"No, Mr. Wells; he spoke to me through the door, sir——"

"Do you mean to say," roared the colonel, "that someone is in my nephew's room, and that you supposed it to be my nephew?"

"Yes, sir, certainly sir, it was certainly Master Harry's voice, and he said he was catching a cold, and you had sent him back——"

"Great gad!"

Colonel Wharton strode to the stairs, with a brow of thunder. Wells and Thomas, in a dazed condition of amazement, followed him up. The colonel reached the door of his nephew's den, and turned the handle. The door did not open. A heavy fist banged on it.

"Who is there?" roared Colonel Wharton. "Who is in this room? I can hear someone! Who is it?"

"Oh lor'!" came a startled ejaculation from within. The formidable roar of the angry colonel startled Billy Bunter so much that he quite forgot his ventriloquism.

"That is not my nephew's voice!" snorted the colonel. "It seems familiar, but it is nothing like Master Harry's voice. How you could possibly have been deceived, Wells, I cannot imagine. Open this door! Do you hear? Whoever you are, open this door at once!"

Billy Bunter jumped up from the table. He blinked in alarm at the door, deeply thankful that he had taken the precaution of locking it.

"Who is there?" roared the colonel. "It is not my nephew! I have just left my nephew ten miles away! Who is it?"

"Oh crikey!" breathed Bunter.

He shook a fat fist at the door.

Bunter had not foreseen this. Colonel Wharton having driven off in the car with the juniors, Bunter had taken it for granted that he was safe off the scene, as well as Harry Wharton & Co. Really, he might have foreseen that the colonel would probably drive home after taking the schoolboys to their destination. But Bunter never foresaw anything.

Ventriloquism was of no use now. Colonel Wharton was not likely to believe that his nephew was there when he knew that he was elsewhere.

Bang! came at the door.

"Who are you? What are you doing there? Who is it?" shouted the colonel.

"Wells, go through the bed-room! There is another door——"

"The bed-room door is locked, sir!" said Wells, a moment later.

"Good gad! The rascal has locked himself in, then! But who can he be? Some pilfering thief——"

"Oh crikey!"

"He deluded me, sir, into supposing that he was Master Harry, and he ordered tea—a very substantial tea——"

"Extraordinary! Some unscrupulous rascal! But how did he gain admittance to the house?"

"No doubt by Master Harry's door on the balcony, sir."

"Yes; no doubt—no doubt! Then it must be someone who knows the place! But I will soon discover! Will you open this door, you rascal, whoever you are?"

Bang! Thump!

The door did not open. Bunter was not very bright, but he was far too bright to open that door!

Colonel Wharton stepped back, fuming. This was his experience of the night over again, and he suspected that it was the same rascal concerned.

Thomas stooped and applied an eye to the keyhole.

"I see him!" gasped Thomas.

"You see him?" exclaimed the colonel.

"Yes, sir; a fat cove——"

"A what?"

"A fat feller, sir, in specs. I've seen him before, sir," said Thomas, in great excitement. "A fat young gent of the name of Bunter, sir!"

"WHAT!" roared Colonel Wharton.

"Oh jiminy!" gasped Bunter. "I—I say, sir, I'm not here! It—it isn't me, sir! It—it's quite another party, sir!"

"Good gad! I know his voice now! That impertinent and disrespectful young rascal, Bunter! Thomas, fetch my riding-whip!"

"Oh crikey!"

"Wells, remain here to see that he does not escape through the house! I will go round to the door on the balcony! Be quick with that riding-whip, Thomas!"

The colonel's heavy tread rang down the staircase.

Billy Bunter stood transfixed with terror.

Once more he was cornered.

The door on the balcony was locked, certainly; but it was not likely to stop the angry old military gentleman long. It was fairly certain that he would knock in a pane of the french window with the butt of the riding-whip and open the door. And then—

Bunter had not yet finished with that substantial tea. But he was not thinking of finishing it now. He was not thinking of it at all. He was thinking only of his fat skin!

For a moment he stood transfixed. Then he bounded to the french window, dragged aside the curtain, unlocked it, and tore it open.

His first thought was to bolt before the colonel got round the house, but he stopped. Bunter's fat brain was working at double pressure now.

Leaving the door wide open, to give an impression that he had bolted that way, he tiptoed across to the communicating door of the bed-room, passed through, and silently shut it after him.

Then he crept under Harry Wharton's bed.

When the colonel arrived and found the french window open, surely he would suppose that the fat Owl had

Billy Bunter's fat form established sudden contact with Wells' equator, and the butler went backwards as if he had been shot. "Why—what—— Oh gad!" roared Colonel Wharton, as Wells hurtled down the balcony steps and crashed into him, sending him spinning.

bolted! If he did, Bunter was safe. If he didn't—— But Bunter preferred not to think of that. It was really too awful to contemplate!

THE ELEVENTH CHAPTER.
Hunted Bunter!

TRAMP, tramp! came heavy footsteps up the balcony steps.

Colonel Wharton had lost no time.

He had waited only for Thomas to get him his riding-whip. With that article in his hand, he strode round the house, and ascended the balcony steps to his nephew's window.

He was prepared to knock in a pane if he found the french window locked. But he found it standing wide open.

He strode in, with a brow of thunder, swishing the riding-whip. He glared round.

"Good gad! Gone!" roared the colonel.

"I heard him unlock the window, sir!" came Wells' voice, from outside the passage door. "I was afraid he would be gone, sir."

"The young rascal! He knew what to expect!" fumed the colonel. "By gad, I would have given him the thrashing of his life! I would have taken the skin off his back, by Jove! Thomas!"

"Yessir!"

"Go at once and look for that young rascal! If you find him in my grounds, kick him—kick him out! Do you hear, Thomas? Kick him as hard as you can!"

"Certainly, sir!"

Thomas cut away to hunt for the fat young gent of the name of Bunter, gleefully ready to carry out the colonel's

instructions if he found him in the grounds.

The colonel strode across the room and unlocked the door where Wells stood. Wells glanced at the tea-table. Bunter had not had time to finish, but he had made remarkable progress. Where he had packed it all was a mystery. Two-thirds of that ample supply of provender had vanished.

"It is extraordinary, Wells, that you should have been deceived by that young scoundrel!" snorted the colonel.

"The voice was so like Master Harry's, sir——"

"Nonsense!"

"H'm! I assure you, sir——"

"That balcony door had better be kept locked! You may tell my nephew so. The young scoundrel may venture to repeat his impudent trick. By Jove, I have no doubt that it was he in the dining-room last night! Let me catch him! Let me catch him playing tricks here, by Jove! Huh!"

The colonel strode away, fuming. He was deeply disappointed that the riding-whip had not established contact with the fat young gent of the name of Bunter. But he still hoped that Thomas had run him down in the grounds and carried out his instructions.

Thomas did his best. But as the fat young gent was still within the house, Thomas really hadn't even a sporting chance of finding him outside. After a long hunt, Thomas could only report failure.

Meanwhile, Billy Bunter remained palpitating under the bed.

Luck had befriended him again. The open french window had given the desired impression, and it was taken for granted that he had bolted. That was

all right, so far as it went. But the fat Owl was very anxious to be safe back in his attic.

There was no chance of that at present, however. He dared not venture out till he was sure that the coast was clear.

When at last he put his head out from under the bed, like a fat tortoise from its shell, it was to hear sounds in the adjoining room. No doubt Thomas was there, clearing away the wreck of Bunter's feast, and making preparations for the return of Master Harry and his friends. Bunter suppressed a groan and popped back.

He palpitated, and listened.

When all at last was silent, the fat junior crawled out from under the bed. He crawled out in fear and trembling. The bare thought of the old colonel and his riding-whip made Bunter shudder. He had kept on hoping that, sooner or later, the old gentleman would get over his "tantrums," but it was clear that the tantrums were getting worse instead of better. Discovery at an earlier date meant the order of the boot; now it meant a thrashing before the boot was applied. It was borne in on Billy Bunter's fat mind at long last that his extraordinary sojourn at Wharton Lodge had better come to an end, and that it could not come to an end too quickly.

The game was, in fact, up!

With the balcony door kept locked, as the colonel had instructed Wells, there would be no more surreptitious comings and goings. With all the food carefully locked up at night, there could be no more secret grub raids in

(Continued on page 16.)

THE NEW Greyfria

No. 66 (New Series).

EDITED BY

MYSTERY OF MASKED MARAUDER

Armed Man at Bedside

There's a mystery about the armed burglar who appeared at the bedside of a guest in the Bounder's house one night last week.

The guest in question was a fearful old bore called Sir Frederick Frump. Mr. Vernon-Smith, who knew him in the City, had invited him down for Christmas; but he decided to stay much longer and did his utmost to spoil everybody's holiday by monopolising the conversation with stories of his amazing bravery in the face of danger in many parts of the world.

As yarns, they wouldn't have been bad, had they been true. But it was so obvious that Sir Frederick was drawing largely on his imagination that nobody derived the slightest pleasure from them.

On the night of the burglary, by a strange coincidence, Sir Frederick had been talking of burglars. Apparently, he had encountered any number of armed burglars and treated them all in the same way—with a smashing left that had knocked them into the middle of the following week!

Well, on this particular night, he met one more.

He awoke to find a masked man standing at his bedside, prodding him in the ribs with a revolver

Did he arise in his wrath and send the man staggering with a smashing left-hander? HE DID NOT!

What he did was rather strange for a man of his exceptional courage. He slid out of bed, fell on his knees, and begged the intruder in quavering accents to take all his wealth and shoot the rest of the household—so long as he spared Sir Frederick Frump!

Peculiarly enough, however, the burglar took nothing. He told Sir Frederick that he had only come to have a look over the place and that he'd call for the swag on another occasion—and that it would pay Sir Frederick to keep out of his way in the future!

The masked marauder then quitted Sir Frederick's room and went along to the Bounder's

room. Nothing more was seen of him.

Sir Frederick went back to London the following day, only too pleased to shake the dust of the Bounder's home from his feet. The rest of the guests were glad, too.

Sir Frederick didn't breathe a word about the burglar.

How do we know about him, then? Why, the Bounder told us!

How the Bounder came to know everything is nobody's business!

Big Bungle at Blundell's Beano

Coker Brings the House Down

If you've never seen Horace Coker play Blind Man's Buff, you've never lived! In the words of Mabel, one of the waitresses at Blundell's New Year party: "Of all the screams——!" That gives you only a faint idea of how funny Coker can be!

It was obvious when Coker suggested Blind Man's Buff that he had something up his sleeve. It was taken for granted, when he wanted to be the first Blind Man, that his shrieks of merriment would soon make the welkin ring. One look at the merry twinkle in his eye gave the game away!

And Coker didn't disappoint the party. He certainly WAS funny. Funnier than he had expected to be, as a matter of fact!

His idea, you see, was to stagger round the room laying hands on all kinds of impossible objects and pretending they were people we all knew. He touched the Christmas-tree and said: "This is Mr. Blundell; I can tell him by his whiskers!" Then caressed a coconut and said: "Own up, Potter, old man; I'd know you anywhere by your head!" And so on.

It was when he leaned against the Lucky Dip Barrel in the centre of the room that Coker achieved his piece de resistance. Hugging it affectionately, he cried: "What an unexpected pleasure! I didn't know you were here, Mr. Prout!"

And just as he said it, Mr. Prout himself unexpectedly arrived!

Coker brought the house down, we can assure you!

A minute later, when he pulled off his bandage and saw Mr. Prout standing in front of him, Coker almost brought himself down, too!

Did they go red? Well, they're both rather ruddy at any time and on this occasion their faces were the colour of ripe tomatoes!

There was still a very peculiar look in Mr. Prout's eye when he left the party later in the evening, and we can't help thinking that Coker may hear quite a lot more about his humorous proclivities next Term.

But it really was a yell while it lasted. If you want to make your party a howling success, ask Coker round and get him to play Blind Man's Buff—but don't ask Mr. Prout!

First, may I say joyfulness I feel requestfully asked bute to this este ludicrous paper is weekly request fro the sameful lines, m editor, would be caper; and a regu article from my typewriter would, bring happiness your august reade for my contributic learned and prepos cussion!

My worstful exp curred in the ju native Bhanipur. dodgefully eluded and, while taking care to keep with distance of them, s hoping to secure wi camera some wi pictures which wou stagger the world.

I stood as st esteemed statue an film whatever sh To my sorrowful r ever, there seemed animal life in evide placeful situation, almost turning to party, when I hear rustling sound beh

Turning round, python of immens ness advancing or one lookful glance fearsome snake co that he was going

I must confessf

DICKY NUGENT'S WEEKLY WISDOM

They say Horris Coker's unpopular because he's too fond of interfering; but I don't believe myself that he's disliked simply because he has a finger in everybody's pie.

The real trubble is that he usually mannidges to put his foot in it, too!

See the Point, Fishy?

Fisher T. Fish has lost his horn-rimmed specs.

But you're quite mistaken, dear reader, if you imagine that this is the first time he's been 'acking in vision!

WOULD YOU BELIEVE IT?

Cecil Reginald Temple, the Upper Fourth captain, had his photograph taken prior to a match with the Remove. Temple looked very "natty" before the game started—but when it ended, he looked a freak! Remove won.

Sammy Bunter has a great weakness for mincemeat, and even raided the Remove studies in search of it! Bolsover major speedily dispatched Sammy back to the fag quarters—minus the mincemeat!

It is rumoured among the that Gosling, the schoo has attained his hundredth Gosling denies this strenu claiming 60 odd years produces no birth certi however!

Herald

EXTRA
GOOD
EDITION

WHARTON.   January 6th, 1934.

MY WORST AND BEST EXPERIENCE

By Hurree Singh

that I was paralysed with horror for a few moments. I could only eyefully stare at the monster, hoping that it would turn away; but instead of doing that, it attacked me with fierceful ferociousness! When I at last found my voice, it seemed too late, for the python was already curling round my body, preparefully getting ready to crush me deathfully!

You may guessfully imagine my joy when, in the time nickfully, a shot rang out and the bullet, after whistling past my ear, buried itself in the snake's head! By sheer good luckfulness, one of my party, who fortunefully happened to be an excellent and ludicrous shot, had seen my dilemma and fired!

Neverthelessfully, it remains the worstful experience I can mindfully remember!

My bestful experience was when a professor of English who was callfully paying a visit to Greyfriars requested me to talkfully discourse to him in the esteemed and preposterous English language. As is generally known, I take a great and absurd pride in speaking good and correctful English, as taught me by learned moonshees in Bhanipur. But the number of people who laugh at it is simply terrific and great is my sadfulness thereat.

The esteemed and ludicrous professor, however, listened to my speechful discourse with serious gravefulness, and became intriguefully interested in my correctful and

Bulstrode tells us a strange story.

He'd fixed up to go to London with Bolsover to see a boxing match.

It was going to be a frightfully gory encounter between two bloodthirsty heavy-weights—"Tiger" Lyons and Kong King.

So Bulstrode quite expected to find Bolsover waiting at his front door with his hat and coat on and the wild light of anticipation in his eyes.

But Bolsover wasn't at the front door; and he didn't even show up when a maid showed Bulstrode into the lounge and went off to report his arrival.

Bulstrode wondered where he was. He also wondered what on earth was the cause of the strange discord that floated in from an adjoining room.

Bolsover's absence and the discord's presence were simultaneously explained when Bulstrode looked into the adjoining room. There was Bolsover, calmly strumming away on a ukulele and making strange noises with his mouth, just as though

idiotic way of expressing myself, and I soon found myself warmfully glowing with pride to think that this expert in the great and preposterous English language should be so much impressed.

But my joyful happiness at that thought was nothing compared with my feelings at the end of our talkful interview. For when he shook hands with me before departfully going, he said: "Your English is simply preposterous; I have never heard anything like it in my life!"

The recollection of that praiseful admiration is still my most happyful memory!

(Dicky Nugent will make a characteristic contribution to this series next week, chums! —Ed.)

"MUSIC HATH CHARMS—"

Bolsy's Uke's So Soothing

"Tiger" Lyons and Kong King had never been brought to his notice!

Bolsy had a dreamy look in his eye, too. And when Bulstrode asked what train he intended catching to get to the boxing match Bolsy shook his head.

"Sorry, old chap," he said. "'Fraid I shan't be able to come along after all!"

"You won't be able to come along, eh?" remarked Bulstrode, in measured tones. "May I ask why?"

Bolsy struck a chord on his musical instrument and smiled.

"Yes; I'll tell you," he said. Somebody gave me this ukulele for Christmas and I've been practising on it. The result is that I've discovered I'm a born musician and I've decided to go in seriously for crooning!"

"And that's the reason you're not coming to the big fight?" Bulstrode asked in an icy voice.

Bolsover nodded cheerfully and, having thus dismissed the matter apparently to his entire satisfaction, returned to his practice.

Bulstrode watched him for a full minute.

At the end of that period, he grabbed a handy flower bowl nicely filled with water and inverted it over Bolsover's head.

Bulstrode tells us that the crooning that came from Bolsy during the few seconds that followed beat anything ever dreamed of!

This Week's Bright Remark

Dicky Nugent and young Paget both want to be wireless operators aboard ship when they grow up, and their conversation is full of unintentional wireless allusions as per example herewith, collected one day last week:

"I don't care a DASH for you, young Nugent!"

"If you say that young Paget, I'll give you a DOT on the eye!"

Note that their mutual interest in radio topics doesn't make them any more peaceable—MORSE the pity!

'LONZY'S LITTLE LETTERS

Dear Editor,—My behaviour is ordinarily, I apprehend, exempt from any suspicion of irascibility; but I find it difficult, nay, wellnigh impossible to preserve my characteristic restraint in referring to the hostility which I have unwittingly aroused by the execution of an act of altruism, conducive, I maintain, to nothing but social amelioration.

You are cognisant, dear Editor, of the fact that the purity of the atmosphere has been recently vitiated through its suffusion by fogs which have obliterated the normal solar illumination and plunged the neighbourhood into Stygian obscurity. With the intention of assisting in the dissipation of this insalubrious and fuliginous atmospheric adumbration, I have been visiting junior studies during the absence of the occupants and effecting the extinction of such coal fires as I discovered therein. To my inexpressible dismay, this supererogatory performance has resulted not in congratulation, but in vociferous abuse.

I confess that such obscurantism among my juvenile acquaintances is to me incomprehensible.

Yours for atmospheric lucidity,
ALONZO TODD.

(He thought he'd dispel the fog by putting out study fires—and he wonders why fellows object! 'Lonzy, old bean, we're afraid something was "mist" when your brain was made up!—Ed.)

GREYFRIARS FACTS WHILE YOU WAIT!

Prout is very particular about cigars he smokes, and insists a special Havana brand. He not pleased when he tried to a chocolate one substituted a mischievous fag the other day!

Tom Redwing is familiar with the old smugglers' caves in Pegg Bay, and once guided the Famous Five on a treasure hunting expedition. They found nothing but rusty iron bands which might at one time have bound a treasure chest!

Frank Nugent keeps the accounts of the Remove football and cricket elevens, being secretary and treasurer combined. It says much for Frank's integrity that the accounts are always in perfect order!

MOST SUITABLE!

After upsetting a bottle of ink over himself, Snoop can find nothing that will remove the traces from his head.

May we suggest sand-paper?

BUNTER, THE CRASHER!

(Continued from page 13.)

the small hours. The game, evidently, was up!

Bunter could get out—as soon as the coast was clear—but he would not be able to get in again! But the angry roar of the colonel, and the sound of the riding-whip swishing, made Bunter feel more anxious to get out than to get in!

He had thought it out while he lay palpitating under the bed.

Once safe back in his attic, he would wait for the fall of the winter dusk. His hat and coat were in the attic, and he could scarcely go without them. And it was impossible to go empty-handed. The difficulty of a railway fare stood like a lion in the path. Borrowing a few more of Wharton's books would see him through.

Then he would shake the dust of Wharton Lodge from his feet, with the scorn that such an inhospitable place deserved.

Later, when he was in funds—Bunter always hoped and expected to be in funds at some undefined future date—he would redeem all those books, and send them back to their owner with a curt note expressive of the scorn and contempt he felt.

That, he hoped, would make that beast Wharton jolly well ashamed of himself.

His plans were now settled, cut and dried. But he was not back in his attic yet. He crept to the bed-room door on the passage, silently unlocked it, and opened it half an inch to listen. A fruity voice came to his ears.

"I am sorry, Thomas, that I distrusted you. I have little doubt—I may say that I have no doubt—that that very unpleasant and disagreeable young person Bunter was at the bottom of it all the time."

"Thank you, Mr. Wells!"

Bunter's eyes glittered behind his spectacles. Wells and Thomas were in the passage, talking. Of course, the beasts had to talk there—just when Bunter wanted to dodge across that passage.

"That unpleasant boy," resumed Wells, little dreaming that his remarks fell on the fat ears of the unpleasant boy himself, "has stayed with Master Harry on previous occasions, Thomas, and, of course, knew his way about the house. That accounts for it."

"It do, Mr. Wells," assented Thomas.

"Obviously," said Wells, "knowing about Master Harry's balcony door, and knowing the interior of the mansion, Thomas, that unscrupulous boy Bunter has continually let himself into the 'ouse."

"It looks like it, sir."

"Why he has pilfered such things as clothes and rugs and candles I cannot imagine, unless he is a kleptomaniac, Thomas."

"Wot's a kleptomaniac, Mr. Wells?"

"A kleptomaniac, Thomas," said Wells, "is a person who steals from

some natural kink in the character, and cannot help it."

"Good lor', Mr. Wells!"

"I am very sorry," said Wells, "that the master did not catch him, and thrash him with the riding-whip."

"Same 'ere, sir!"

"I have seldom seen the master so angry. I could almost pity the young rascal if the master did catch him," said Wells. "It is a most extraordinary affair altogether, Thomas. But I cannot doubt that that unpleasant boy of the name of Bunter has been at the bottom of the pilferings. However, we shall, I think, see no more of him."

"If Master Harry's door is kept locked, sir——"

"Exactly!"

"And if I should see him about, sir, I s'pose it 'olds good what the master said about kicking him, sir?"

"Certainly!" said Wells. "Most decidedly! If you see him, Thomas, carry out the master's instructions to the very letter, and kick him as hard as you can. I shall do the same. I shall also mention to Robert that the boy is to be kicked, if seen. I hope, Thomas, that it may do him good. And, indeed, I should be so glad to kick him, Thomas, that I am sorry he is gone."

Behind a door a fat fist was shaken, and Billy Bunter's eyes gleamed with wrath through his spectacles. This was the way these dashed menials talked of Bunter. Actually thinking of kicking him if they saw him! The cheek of it. And the worst of it was that they meant it. It was very clear that they meant it. More than ever the fat Owl of Greyfriars realised that it behoved him to keep carefully out of sight till he could make his escape from that inhospitable abode.

There was one consolation, however. Evidently it was not suspected that he was still in the house, or had been staying secretly in the house. That suspicion had occurred to nobody as yet.

It was not, in fact, a thing that anyone was likely to suspect. Only Billy Bunter was capable of such weird proceedings, which were quite outside the experience of ordinary mortals.

Voices and footsteps receded at last. There was silence, and Bunter ventured to blink out.

The passage was deserted.

In deep relief the Owl of the Remove tiptoed out, and crossed to the little steep stair that led up to the attic.

He fairly flew up that stair when he reached it.

At the top was a narrow landing on which the attic door opened. As the attic had long been disused and kept locked up that spot was seldom or never visited save by an occasional maid with a broom.

It was Bunter's custom when he left his lair to lock the door after him, and put the key in his pocket.

Breathing hard and deep on the little landing, Bunter felt in his pocket for the attic key. So long as it was daylight he was visible there if anyone passed along the passage below, and happened to glance up. He was in a hurry to get out of sight.

But his fat hand came out of his pocket with nothing in it! The key was not there!

Hastily the fat junior ran his hands through his other pockets.

The key was not there, either.

"Oh, lor'!" breathed Bunter.

The attic door was locked! **And he had lost the key!**

THE TWELFTH CHAPTER.

No Exit!

BILLY BUNTER groaned. He could not help it. At the risk of being overheard he groaned aloud.

It was a crushing blow.

Once more in feverish haste he ran his fat hands through his pockets. He knew that he had put the key in one of them.

But it was in vain that he searched for it. It was not there. Evidently he had dropped it somewhere—either in Wharton's den, where he had feasted, or in Wharton's bed-room, where he had hidden from the angry colonel. Most likely it had dropped from his pocket when he dodged under the bed—that was most probable.

He could not get into his hiding-place without it. He could not remain where he was. He could not even take his chance of dodging out while it was still daylight, for his hat and coat were in the locked attic. To start on his travels on a bitter January day, hatless and without a coat, was hardly to be thought of. He had to go back and hunt for that key.

He groaned.

But groaning did not improve matters. He listened intently, and heard no sound from the passage, and at last tiptoed down again. The passage was still deserted, and he cut across into Wharton's bed-room once more.

He closed the door and stood panting. The winter dusk was beginning to fall. There was plenty of light still out of doors, but indoors it was growing very dusky.

Bunter stooped and peered under the bed in the hope of spotting the lost key. Under the bed was very dark indeed, and a keen eye might have failed to spot a small key lying there. Bunter's eyes were far from keen. Indeed, even with the aid of his big spectacles, his vision was limited. He blinked in vain.

He had to grope for it. And perhaps all the time he had dropped it somewhere else. And any minute——

Once more Billy Bunter's fat brain worked at double pressure.

He might be a long time finding that key. He might not find it at all. And those beasts would be back from the football match before long. And a servant might come up any minute.

After all, if he was going, it was certain that he could not go without a coat and a hat. But there was no need to go in his own coat and hat. Such things were available nearer at hand. In the circumstances, Bunter felt that he would be justified in borrowing them. He did not, as a matter of fact, worry a whole lot about the justification. At a pinch, indeed, he could have done without it.

As soon as the idea came into his fat mind he abandoned on the spot the thought of hunting for the lost attic key, and turned to Harry Wharton's wardrobe.

Wharton, of course, had a coat on that afternoon. Fortunately he had several coats. Bunter had only to make his choice. In the big wardrobe there were coats hanging up, and several caps.

He selected a handsome, natty, grey coat. It was a new coat, and Wharton had worn it only once or twice over Christmas. It was, in fact, going to be his best coat, for the new term at Greyfriars. Being the best coat in the collection, it was naturally selected by Billy Bunter. Bunter did not believe in helping himself to the second best in anything.

He found a grey tweed cap to match. He had seen Wharton in that grey coat and cap, in which the captain of the Remove looked very well-dressed and good-looking. Bunter had no doubt that he did the clothes more credit. Having put them on, he surveyed the result in the glass of the wardrobe door, and gave a smirk of satisfaction. This was all right! No need to get his own rather shabby and rumpled coat from the attic now! So long as he could keep out of sight till dark it was all right! All he had to do now was to make a further selection from Wharton's bookshelf, for the purpose of raising the wind at the second-hand shop in Wimford! Bunter was feeling quite relieved.

He opened the communicating door into Wharton's den and went in. The glowing log-fire on the hearth dispelled the gathering winter gloom there.

"Beasts!" murmured Bunter, as he saw that the table was laid for tea for five.

Apparently the chums of the Remove were going to have tea in Harry Wharton's den, as they sometimes did. The foodstuffs were not yet on the table, however, as Bunter ascertained with a very rapid glance. Had they been there, they would not have remained to greet the Famous Five. Billy Bunter had taken on board a generous cargo that afternoon. But he always had room for a little more.

But the fact that the tea-table was laid in the den warned him that he had no time to waste. The beasts, evidently, would come up there when they came back from the football match. Thomas might come up any minute with something for tea.

Bunter hurriedly scanned the bookshelf. Even Bunter felt a slight inward doubt as to whether he was quite, quite justified in taking these measures to raise the wind! Still, as he was going to set the matter right later, when he received some postal orders that he had long been expecting, surely only a very captious critic could find fault

(*Continued on next page.*)

If you're in doubt over any Soccer query, "Linesman" will be only too pleased to help you out. Write to him, c/o The MAGNET, The Fleetway House, Farringdon Street, London, E.C.4.

THE BEST SIDE OF THE SEASON!

KING SOLOMON was supposed to be very wise. He gave such finely balanced judgments that everybody was satisfied, apparently. I sometimes wonder if that old-time king would have gained the same sort of reputation if he had been called upon to give judgment on football topics. I can tell you this: that I oft-times sigh for the wisdom of Solomon to enable me to settle football arguments to the satisfaction of everybody.

Take a question which is raised by a MAGNET reader this week. While the members of his team were dressing after a recent match an argument arose. It centred round the question of whether the football team which won the F.A. Cup or the team which won the First Division championship could lay claim to being the best side of the season.

Some thought that the Cup winners took the primary honours of the season, while others held that the First Division champions earned the title of the best side. Finally it was agreed to send the question along to me for settlement. Thanks very much.

I am prepared to give my judgment, however, and hope that my argumentative friends will agree.

My view, definitely, is that the team which wins the First Division championship has the right to the title of the best side of that season.

The team thus successful must have staying power over a long period: they must pick up points consistently on all the varying types of pitches which are met with during the course of the season. The reserves of the side must be good, too. Indeed, I would say that the side which wins the championship plays more Cup-ties, really, than the team which wins the Cup.

Every match in which the top team of a League is concerned has something of the Cup-tie spirit about it. Every set of opponents put forth special efforts to bring the top-notchers down a peg. The team which pulls through must go on picking up points, roughly, at the average rate of three points from each couple of games. It often requires sixty points to win the championship.

Having given the judgment that the best team of the season is the one which wins the First Division championship, I must now add that there is much merit in Cup-winning. Different clubs have to be met—clubs that is, from different sections of the League, and consequently with different styles. The Cup winners must be able to play their own game against those various types of opponents.

There is this to be said about Cup-winning, however. The element of luck enters into it to greater extent than in a League tournament. There is the luck of the draw, for instance. Teams have been known to win the Cup without playing a match on their opponents' ground. Everton only played one Cup-tie away from home prior to the semi-final last season.

A team which runs into form in the second half of the season can win the Cup, too, concentrating on that competition, and keeping their very best for the knock-out games. So, on the whole, don't you agree that the team which wins the First Division championship can be labelled the best of the season?

THE INDIVIDUAL SIDE OF FOOTBALL!

A SCHOOLMASTER friend who is very anxious that the boys under his care should develop as all-round footballers asks me if I can give him a hint on how to frame what he calls an individual championship. He wants to award a prize to the best all-round footballer.

By way of reply I cannot do better than refer this schoolmaster to a system in vogue in France which has for its object the cultivation of players of all-round merit. I once had the pleasure of being present at a French boys' Soccer competition. Seventy-eight lads took part in it. Each of the boys occupied the field for a few minutes, and points were awarded for dribbling, passing, shooting, heading, kicking with a dead ball, and volleying. The boy who got the biggest total of points from his prowess at these various phases of the game was awarded the championship prize.

While I must say that I am not very keen on stressing the individual side of football, remembering that it is essentially a team game, I think it is wise to spur young footballers on in the all-round sense, and a little healthy competition on these lines can do no harm. It certainly encourages the young players to practise.

JUST BAD LUCK!

NOW for another argument to be settled by me. A Ryde reader was playing in a boys' match on the ground of a man's club. The original goal-posts had been left in place, and the original crossbar as well. But for this particular match a new crossbar had been placed about a foot below the other one to constitute the "goal" for that particular game.

During the match a shot was sent in which struck the top crossbar. The ball came back into play, and the inside-left, gaining possession, took another shot, and this time sent the ball below the lower crossbar. The referee awarded a goal and my friend was surprised. I don't blame him. I should have been surprised, too.

It seems to me that when the ball struck the top bar the referee should have given a goal-kick.

This, of course, is one of those cases which are not provided for in the rules, but I give it as my view that common sense dictated the award of a goal-kick immediately the ball struck the top bar. For the purposes of that game the height of the crossbar was not eight feet, but seven, and a shot which would have gone over the lower bar should have been treated as if it had gone over. Doubtless the referee concerned would be able to give what, from his point of view, were good reasons for the other decision. While dealing with this question another can be answered in which a referee was concerned. He happened to be standing near the goal during a scrimmage following a corner-kick. A shot was sent in. The ball struck the referee, and then went into the net. Should it have been a goal?

The answer is yes, even though the ball might not have gone into the net if it had not struck the referee.

There was a similar instance in a Stoke v. Everton match a few weeks back. A shot which was going into the net struck the referee, and was deflected outside the post. But the man with the whistle could not award a goal. It was just bad luck.

"LINESMAN."

with his proceedings! And Bunter had never been a captious critic of his own actions!

He selected the volumes with care. He had received only seven-and-six for the last lot, and he hoped to do better this time. People gave hardly anything for second-hand books, even when they were nearly new! Volume after volume was selected, and Bunter was making a little pile of them on the shelf when there was a footstep in the passage.

Bunter's fat ears were on the strain. He detected that footstep before it was near the door. He stepped quickly away from the bookshelf, and behind a screen that stood across a corner. He had spotted that convenient hiding-place, and kept it in mind.

The door opened, and Thomas entered with a basket of logs. He switched on the light when he came in, and crossed to the fireplace.

Behind the screen Bunter made no sound.

Thomas stirred the fire, placed logs on it, and disposed the other logs in their place. He was quite leisurely in his movements, being, of course, totally unaware that a fat Owl behind the screen was feverishly impatient for him to be gone.

When he went at last, he left the door open, and the light on. Apparently he was coming back again.

"Beast!" hissed Bunter, under his breath

Thomas came back with a kettle, which he placed in the fender. When Harry Wharton & Co. "tea-ed" in the den they liked to make the tea and look after themselves generally, as in the study at Greyfriars. So the kettle was needed.

Again Thomas departed, but again he left the light on and the door open. It was some time before he reappeared, and this time he brought a tray, which he laid on the table Then he proceeded to set out the contents of the tray.

There was a rent in the screen—in fact, there were several small rents. Through one of them Billy Bunter watched Thomas with a malevolent eye.

He was getting tea ready for Master Harry and his friends, who were expected back very soon now, Brown having gone to fetch them in the car. Outside, the January dusk was thickening to darkness. If that unutterable beast Thomas would only have cleared, Billy Bunter had only to grab his pile of books and let himself out by the french window. Thomas, however, did not seem to be clearing!

Having finished, at last, with the tea-table, Thomas went across to the french window. He felt the window to ascertain that it was locked, and then drew the curtains across, with a swish of rings. Then, to Billy Bunter's intense exasperation, he sat down in an armchair before the fire! That, of course, Thomas had no right to do, and certainly would not have done had Mr. Wells' eye been upon him. But the only eye upon him was the hidden eye of William George Bunter, so Thomas allowed himself the luxury of taking it easy for a while.

Could looks have slain, Thomas might have reached a sudden termination of his career in that comfortable armchair. For the look that Billy Bunter gave him, through the rent in the screen, was absolutely homicidal.

But that look, deadly as it was, produced no effect whatever on Thomas! Perhaps Thomas was tired. He had many little duties to perform, and, as he sometimes confided to the cook, he was up and down stairs all day. Safe from the butler's severe eye, and unlikely to be disturbed till Master Harry came back to tea, Thomas stretched himself luxuriously in Master Harry's armchair, toasted his toes, and grinned with satisfaction.

Bunter waited!

Minute after minute passed—and minutes were precious now! It really seemed as if the surreptitious guest at Wharton Lodge was going to have more difficulty in getting out than in getting in! Any minute now those beasts might come crowding in——

In that desperate extremity the Owl of the Remove bethought himself once more of his ventriloquism. It was that or nothing. Suddenly, and apparently

from the passage, came a barking voice, marvellously like that of the old colonel in a cross mood.

"Thomas! Where is that boy, Thomas?"

"Oh, my eye!" gasped Thomas in alarm. He bounded up from Master Harry's armchair as if the seat of that armchair had become suddenly red-hot! "'Ere, sir! Coming, sir!"

Thomas fairly scudded to the door.

"'Ere, sir! You called me, sir!"

He stared into the passage. Colonel Wharton was not to be seen there. Thomas hurried out of the room in the direction of the stairs.

Billy Bunter gasped with relief. He had got rid of the brute at last!

He whipped out from behind the screen! As he did so he heard the sound of many footsteps, and a cheery voice that roared:

"Hallo, hallo, hallo! Tea ready, what? We're all as hungry as jolly old hunters!"

"Yes, Master Cherry, sir, tea's ready, sir——"

"Oh lor'!" groaned Billy Bunter.

He popped back behind the screen. He was only just in time, as Harry Wharton & Co., cheery and ruddy from the frosty air, tramped into the room.

———

THE THIRTEENTH CHAPTER.
Exciting!

COLONEL WHARTON glanced into his nephew's den, and his grim, bronzed face relaxed into a smile.

It was a very cheery scene that met his eyes. Five ruddy faces were gathered round the tea-table, five fellows were doing ample justice to an excellent spread, and five voices were talking all at once. The juniors jumped up, however, as the colonel looked in, rather as if they had been in the study at Greyfriars and Mr. Quelch had dropped in.

"Don't mind me, my boys," said the old colonel genially as he came in. "I dare say you are hungry. Did you see a good game?"

"Topping, sir—'Spurs in great form!" said Bob Cherry. The juniors resumed tea.

"You have seen nothing of that extraordinary and disagreeable boy Bunter, I suppose?"

"Bunter!" repeated Harry. "We saw him yesterday in Wimford."

"He has been here!" grunted the colonel, and his brow resumed its frown. "The boy's impudence and audacity seem unbounded. He actually came into the house, by this window apparently, and somehow deceived Wells into believing that it was you who had returned, Harry—apparently he has some rascally trick of imitating voices——"

"Oh, my hat!"

"He carried his impudence to the length of ordering a meal here, and, unluckily, escaped before I could get at him with my riding-whip," said Colonel Wharton. "On reflection I have no doubt that he has played such tricks here before, many times, in fact. I find that Wells thinks so, also—and indeed there can be little doubt of it. He has, I believe, used this french window for getting in and out of the house."

"Phew!" murmured Nugent.

"That would account for many strange occurrences that have puzzled us during the holidays," said the colonel.

"By Jove! It would!" exclaimed Harry Wharton. "But—but would even that fat foozler have the nerve——"

19

" Hold him fast, my boys—I will deal with him ! " said Colonel Wharton. The Greyfriars juniors dragged the man's hands together and tied them. Then, for security, the end of the rope was knotted to the end of the banisters.

"The esteemed Bunter's nervefulness is terrific!" remarked Hurree Jamset Ram Singh.

"This french window had better be kept locked," said the colonel. "But that is not all. I should like you boys to keep a very sharp eye open for this young rascal Bunter, and if you discover him within the grounds, bring him to me. I desire very much to see him !"

"Certainly," said Harry; and the other fellows nodded assent.

Colonel Wharton left the Famous Five to themselves. They had been discussing the League match before—now they discussed Bunter! Certainly it did not occur to them that a pair of fat ears behind the screen in the corner were drinking in every word.

"If your uncle's right, that accounts for a lot of things," remarked Frank Nugent. "But if Bunter has been doing all the pilfering, he must have been hanging about a jolly long time."

"Well, we've spotted him again and again," said Harry thoughtfully. "But it certainly never occurred to me that he had been dodging into the house. Still, it was easy enough for him, knowing his way about here as he does. It was that frabjous ass that snaffled the books, of course—he's played that game at Greyfriars, you know. 'Member how he sold your 'Holiday Annual' to Fishy once, Bob?"

"Yes, rather !"

Bob Cherry chuckled.

"Fancy the fat villain having the nerve to barge in here and pull Wells' leg with his blessed ventriloquism. Well, if we catch him and take him to the jolly old colonel, I fancy he will wish he had steered clear."

"I suppose he dodges in after dark—easy enough, as it gets dark so early now," said Harry. "And it's all been put down to poor old Thomas ! By

Jove, he ought to be jolly well thrashed, and——"

"The thrashfulness will be terrific, if the esteemed and absurd colonel catches him hopfully !" grinned Hurree Jamset Ram Singh.

"Not much doubt about that, judging by the look in the colonel's eye," chuckled Johnny Bull. He glanced towards the curtained window. "If that's the fat villain's way in and out, he may be there now, watching for a chance to barge in——"

"Oh, my hat !"

Harry Wharton stepped to the french window and pulled the curtains back. Only the ivy could be seen in the darkness of the balcony outside.

"Look here, if he's playing that game, the sooner he's snaffled the better." said the captain of the Remove. "We'll go out and scout for him after tea. Ten to one we shall bag him if he's around !"

"Good egg!"

Behind the screen, Billy Bunter grinned. In the circumstances, he was not likely to be caught Once the juniors were gone, and the way of escape was open, it was Billy Bunter's intention to go also! Things were getting much too hot for the secret guest at Wharton Lodge!

While they finished their tea, the Famous Five discussed that little scheme for bagging Bunter. Then they left the den, to go along to their rooms for their coats.

Bunter blinked out from behind the screen.

Now was his chance! The coast was clear! The door had been left wide open, so the interior of the room was visible from the passage. The communicating door with Wharton's bedroom was half open, and he could hear Wharton moving there. But he had to take the risk !

He tiptoed from his hiding-place to

the bookshelf. He was not going without his plunder if he could help it! He had at least a few minutes!

He had—so far as the juniors were concerned! But there was a tread in the passage, and Wells looked in.

"If you have finished tea. Master Harry, I will tell Thomas to clear away !" said Wells, glancing across at the figure in the grey overcoat and cap that stood at the bookshelf, its back to Wells.

Bunter's fat heart missed a beat !

He stood petrified !

For an awful instant he saw himself discovered !

Then he realised—indeed, Wells' words left no room for a mistake in the matter—that the butler, seeing him from the back in Wharton's coat and cap, had taken him for Master Harry ! Wells knew that handsome grey coat—he had held it more than once for Master Harry to get into !

Bunter did not stop for the books now ! He did not stop for anything ! Keeping his back carefully to Wells, he moved to the french window and opened it ! If only he could get away before Wells discovered that he was not Master Harry——

Wells gazed at his back.

He concluded that Master Harry had not heard him speak.

Bunter had the window open in a twinkling!

He stepped out on the dark balcony. Wells came into the room.

Bunter crossed the balcony with a bound !

He had only to scuttle down the stone steps and vanish into the winter darkness !

But at the top of the steps he stopped suddenly.

In the darkness below there was a

stirring shadow, and the red glow of a cigar-end!

"Oh lor'!" breathed Bunter.

He knew that it was Colonel Wharton, walking on the shrubbery path there—perhaps keeping an eye open for Bunter!

Bunter stood quite still.

Escape was cut off!

A lion in his path would hardly have terrified him so much as the irascible colonel.

To his horror, the glowing cigar-end came to a halt at the foot of the stone steps! The colonel was looking up. He had seen the window open! Bunter shrank back into the frosty ivy.

"Is that you, Harry?" called up the colonel. "Who is there?"

Bunter, crouching in the ivy, made no sound—though he almost expected the colonel to hear the thumping of his fat heart!

He was between the devil and the deep sea! Wells was in the room; and the colonel at the foot of the steps! Only the darkness and the ivy saved Bunter for the moment!

"Who is that?" rapped the colonel, irritated at receiving no answer. "I've said that that window is to be kept closed!"

Wells looked out of the french window.

"Is that the master? Did you call, sir?" asked Wells, blinking out into the darkness.

"Wells, I have given instructions for that french window to be kept secured in case that young scoundrel Bunter tries——"

THE FOURTEENTH CHAPTER.

Who Did It?

"HALLO, hallo, hallo!" ejaculated Bob Cherry.

Bob was the first to come back to the den with his coat and cap on, ready for the excursion. Bunter, again in his hiding-place behind the screen in the corner, strove to suppress his breathing. What was going to happen now Bunter did not know, and could not guess. But he knew that he was going to remain out of sight till the latest possible moment, at all events!

Bob was staring at the open french window. From outside, strange sounds reached him.

"Urrrrggh!"

"Oh gad! What—— Wurrrggh!"

"Oh, sir! Gurrrggh!"

Bob ran across the room, and ran out on the balcony. It sounded as if something had happened!

Below was darkness, and a garden carpeted with snow. Two dim figures were staggering up from the snow. One was the colonel: the other was Wells. Both were breathless.

"Hallo, hallo, hallo!" gasped Bob, staring over the balustrade. "Has—has anything happened?"

"Urrrggh! Oh gad! Urrrggh!"

"Wurrggggh!"

"Wells, are you mad? What do you mean by falling down the steps on me?" spluttered the colonel.

"It was not my—gurrgh—fault, sir!"

to get a little excited, after being hurled headlong down a flight of steps! Wells forgot, for the moment that he was a butler at all, and only remembered that he was a man—a damaged man, and a very angry one!

"Are you calling my nephew a rascal?" roared the colonel.

"I am, sir!" bawled Wells. "A ruffianly young rascal, sir! A most inconsiderate and rascally young ruffian, sir!"

"You dare——" gasped the colonel.

"I tell you, sir, that your nephew hurled me headlong down those steps, sir, and I demand that his punishment——"

"It is impossible!" gasped Colonel Wharton. "Harry—where is Harry?"

"Wells must be dreaming!" exclaimed Bob Cherry. "Wharton couldn't have done such a potty thing! Wharton, come here, old bean! Where are you?"

"Here," answered Harry Wharton, coming across the den to the french window. "Keeping you waiting——"

"Wells is saying——"

"Harry!" roared the colonel.

"Yes, uncle! Here!" Wharton joined the astonished juniors on the balcony. "What's the trouble?"

"Wells says that you pushed him down the steps off the balcony——"

"What?" howled Wharton.

"If you did——"

"I did not! Is Wells mad or what?" gasped the captain of the Remove. "I've been in my room, getting a coat——"

"You hear that Wells——"

"It is all right, sir! Master Harry is here," answered Wells. "He opened the window a moment ago and came out. Did he not come down, sir?"

"Eh? What? No! I've not seen him!"

Wells stepped across the balcony to the steps and peered down. Dimly he made out the figure of the old military gentleman staring up.

"But Master Harry came out a moment ago, sir!" said the bewildered Wells. "I saw him go out of the room, sir!"

Wells turned round. The junior in the grey overcoat and cap had certainly gone out on the balcony under Wells' eyes. Wells looked round for him.

"Master Harry——" He glimpsed a grey overcoat in the shadows and stepped towards it. Why Master Harry was crouching back in the frosty ivy was a mystery to Wells.

Another moment and Bunter would have been discovered! Wells did not see his face. He saw the top of the grey tweed cap! And he saw that only for a fleeting second—a split second! It established sudden contact with Wells' equator! Wells went backwards as if he had been shot.

"Why—what—— Oh gad!" roared Colonel Wharton as something heavy came hurtling down the balcony steps and crashed into him.

The colonel went spinning. Wells dropped at his feet! The colonel roared! Wells gurgled! And Billy Bunter, gasping with terror, darted in at the french window again, and bolted behind the screen in the corner. Just then, that seemed the safest place for Bunter!

gurgled Wells. "I have been assaulted, sir, by your—gurrrrgggh!"

"What?"

"I was knocked over, sir, by—wurrrgghh!" Wells struggled madly for breath. "I was struck, sir, by—gurrggh!"

"What's the row, Bob?"

Frank Nugent joined Bob on the balcony.

"The rowfulness seems to be terrific!" remarked Hurree Jamset Ram Singh, coming out after Frank.

"What do you mean, Wells?" roared the exasperated colonel. "You fell on me, sir, and knocked me over—urrggh! My cigar, sir, went into my—urrggh—mouth! I am burnt, sir! What do you mean by it? What?"

"Master Harry, sir, pushed me off the balcony!" spluttered Wells. "I was taken quite by surprise, sir—gurrgh! I am considerably upset. I am breathless—wurrggh! Such an assault——"

"Are you mad, Wells? My nephew did nothing of the sort! He is incapable of such a foolish trick!"

"Sir, I have been assaulted—I am hurt—I am bruised and breathless! Sir, this is not the treatment that a butler has a right to expect in a gentleman's house! I have a right, sir, to demand that that young rascal——"

"Who?" roared the colonel.

"Your nephew, sir!" roared back Wells.

The impassive expressionlessness of Wells was quite gone now. Even the most excellently trained butler is liable

"I am not surprised, sir, that a young ruffian who committed such an assault should deny it afterwards, sir!" bawled Wells. "I have always, sir, had a very great respect for Master Harry, and I have, I trust, treated him with the respect due to my master's nephew, sir. But now, sir, I tell you he is a young ruffian, and——"

"Wells!" gasped Wharton.

"And unless that boy, sir, is adequately punished for this act of ruffianly brutality, sir, I resign my position in your household, sir!" hooted Wells. "I leave in the morning, sir!"

"You may leave in the morning, or you may leave in the middle of the night, if you choose!" roared Colonel Wharton. "How dare you cast doubt on my nephew's word!"

"I saw him, sir—and I can believe my eyes!" roared Wells. "I will not remain under your roof, sir, to be treated with ruffianly brutality, sir! I am no longer your butler, sir!"

"Certainly you are not! You are discharged! Pack your things and leave as early as possible in the morning! By gad! My belief is that you have been drinking!"

"I repudiate the suggestion, sir—I repudiate it with scorn!" gasped Wells. "I am a strict teetotaller sir, as you are well aware. For twenty years, sir, I have been entrusted with the key of the wine-cellar, and I defy you, sir—I defy you to assert that a single bottle——"

"Enough! If you are not drunk, you are mad! Go!"

"Wells!" howled Harry Wharton from the balcony. "You're mistaken,

Wells! I never touched you—I wasn't here—I give you my word——"

"Pah!"

"You must have slipped and fancied——"

"Pah!"

Having "pahed" twice, to express his utter scorn, Wells limped away, still gurgling painfully for breath. The colonel glared after him as he disappeared, as angry as Wells, or angrier.

"Harry, there is not one word of truth in Wells' statement——"

"Not a word uncle! He must have slipped—there's some ice here, and——"

"No doubt, no doubt! It is extraordinary, amazing that he should fancy that you pushed him over—unless he has been drinking! By gad! In that case, the sooner he goes, the better! I have been deceived in him!"

"I can't understand——"

"Drink!" snorted the colonel. "It must be drink—that is the only explanation!" Colonel Wharton calmed down a little. "If you are going out, Harry, lock that french window, and take the key in your pocket. It must be kept locked!"

"Very well, uncle."

Colonel Wharton strode away in the gloom, still fuming. When, a little later, the Famous Five went out to scout for a possible Bunter, the french window was locked and the key reposed in Wharton's pocket. And a fat junior in a grey overcoat, behind the screen in the corner of the den groaned! There was no escape for Bunter now!

THE FIFTEENTH CHAPTER.

In the Dead of Night!

CLICK!

Billy Bunter started.

He thrilled!

It was past midnight; but Billy Bunter was not asleep. That, in itself, was rather a record.

Sleep was impossible!

The fat junior was sprawling in Harry Wharton's armchair, before the almost dead embers of the fire. He was huddled in the grey overcoat. But he was cold! He was hungry! He was fed-up to his fat chin! He was longing to be away from Wharton Lodge, even if he had no alternative but the inhospitable roof of Uncle George.

But he was still there. The french window had been locked, to keep Bunter out if he essayed to get in! Nobody dreamed that it would keep Bunter in when he wanted to get out!

When the juniors came back from their ramble they came in downstairs. The key of the french window was still in Wharton's pocket. As only he and his friends used that french window, there was no need to replace the key till he came upstairs.

Bunter heard the wireless on below without deriving any entertainment whatsoever from it. Then he heard the gramophone, which lasted till supper. It was not till after supper that Harry Wharton & Co came up, to chat in the den before going to bed.

Bunter, squatted behind the screen in the corner, was still as a fat mouse. Through the rent in the screen he saw Harry Wharton replace the key in the french window. That was that!

A little later the chums of the Remove bade one another good-night, and went to their rooms. Lights were turned off. All was quiet in that part of the house. And now that the key was on the inside of the french window again Billy Bunter was free to go if he liked.

But he did not like—at that hour! It

was past ten o'clock. Snow was coming down, and a bitter wind howled round the old roofs and chimneys. Bunter did not want a night out. There was no shelter for his weary head. He could not raise the wind for a railway fare —by the sale of a selection of Wharton's books—now that all the shops had long been closed. Walking about all night was a prospect that did not appeal to him in the least.

There was only one thing for Bunter to do—remain where he was, and escape early in the morning. As he really had no choice in the matter, it was easy to decide.

But it was rotten!

He was safe from discovery, so far as that went! But there was no supper— nothing to eat! It was cold—and he dared not even build up the fire, lest it should lead to discovery.

Wharton was in the next room. The communicating door was closed; but he was not a heavy sleeper. When Bunter moved, he moved on tiptoe. The crackling of logs might have caught his ear —the gleam of firelight under the door might have caught his eye! Bunter dared not risk it!

He settled down in the armchair

before the fire, and tried to sleep. But sleep would not come!

He dozed a little every now and then, but only to start into wakefulness and remember that he was cold and hungry. When he heard twelve strike he wondered if that endless night would ever end. He thought of his attic with longing. But the attic was locked—the key probably somewhere under the bed in which Wharton had turned in. Bunter had to make the best of it. And then—

Suddenly through the silence came that click from the window, and the fat junior sat bolt upright in the chair, thrilling with alarm.

He blinked round in the gloom with terrified eyes behind his big spectacles.

Back into his fat mind came the incident of the previous night!

Bunter had quite forgotten that incident. In the stress and distress of his own peculiar circumstances he had had no time to think about that, or any other trifling matter.

But he remembered it now, as he heard the lock of the french window click—as it was opened from the outside.

He could see nothing!

But he knew, just as plainly as if he could have seen, that the man he had surprised on that balcony the previous night had come back to make another attempt. The opening of the lock could mean nothing else.

Bunter hardly breathed.

He felt a cold draught of bitter wind across the room. The french window was open.

Then his straining fat ears caught a sound—a soft sound of the window closing. Blinking through the gloom, he made out a dim figure against the glass panes.

His fat heart almost died within him. It was the man from India—the man Corkran, who had attacked Colonel Wharton in the park! Bunter could make out only dim outlines, but he knew it. What did the man want?

He was no ordinary housebreaker or burglar, that was certain. His attack on the old colonel had been inspired by revenge. Had he "got away" with that attack he would have gone. It was clear enough that he was in the house not for such a purpose as robbery —Bunter could not doubt what his purpose was! He was seeking the man he regarded as his enemy—for revenge! Bunter remembered the hard, cold face, the cruel, steely eyes, and repressed a shudder of fear. What would happen to him if the ruffian found him there?

There was a tiny gleam in the darkness.

It was the glimmer of a torch. Bunter crouched deep in the roomy chair. The tiny beam of light glittered round the room, but evidently the man from India had no suspicion that there was anyone in the apartment—he had only turned on the light to ascertain his bearing. It was shut off again, and Bunter heard him cross stealthily to the door on the passage.

That door opened quietly. It was left open—no doubt as a ready retreat for the rascal in case of alarm.

Faint stealthy footsteps died away.

Bunter dragged himself out of the chair and blinked through the open doorway. A faint twinkle of light caught his eyes for a moment. There was no sound—and the light twinkled only for a second. The man was "after" the old colonel, that was certain; but it dawned on Bunter that he could not know which was Colonel Wharton's room. Possibly, watching the house, he might have seen the old soldier at his window, but finding the room from the inside was not an easy task. Billy Bunter knew that the man from India was searching for that room now.

"Oh crikey!" breathed Bunter.

The fat Owl of the Remove was scared to the marrow of his bones! He dared not make a sound or a movement that would have drawn the revengeful rascal's attention to himself. But he had to do something! The old colonel was a "beast"—he was going to thrash Bunter if he saw him—it was only because of his tantrums that Bunter had had such an extraordinary and exciting sojourn under his roof! Still, Bunter evidently could not leave him to it. The man from India meant mischief— a cruel and brutal attack upon an unwary man! Bunter had to do something!

He crept to the communicating door of Harry Wharton's bed-room and opened it with almost agonised caution. He rolled into the bed-room.

Dimly he made out the bed and groped to it. There was a startled gasp from Harry Wharton, as he awoke

suddenly with a fat paw groping over his face.

"Who—what——" gasped Harry.

"Quiet!" hissed Bunter.

"What——"

"Do be quiet! He'll hear you— Oh lor'!"

"Bunter!" gasped Wharton in utter amazement.

"Quiet! He's in the house——"

"Eh? Who is?"

"That man!" gasped Bunter. "I saw him! The man who tackled your uncle in the park! Corkran! He—he's going to his room——"

"Wha-a-at?"

Harry Wharton switched on his bed light. He sat up, staring blankly at the fat, terrified face of the Owl of the Remove.

Bunter's presence was utterly amazing to him. But for the moment he gave that no thought. One look at Bunter's fat face, white as chalk, quivering with terror, showed that he was in earnest.

Wharton leaped from the bed.

"That man—Corkran—is in the house?" he breathed.

"He got in at the french window."

"You saw him?"

"Oh lor'! Yes! Oh crikey! Oh dear!" gasped Bunter. "I—I say——"

But Harry Wharton did not wait to hear what Bunter had to say. If the man who had attacked his uncle was in the house, after midnight, there was no doubting what he intended, and there was not a moment to lose. Wharton leaped across to the door, tore it open, and ran out. He ran down the passage to the landing, and along it to the passage that led to his uncle's room. There was a sudden crash in the dark, a muttered gasping oath, and then hands in the darkness grasped Harry Wharton, and he found himself fighting fiercely with an enemy he could not see.

THE SIXTEENTH CHAPTER.
Because of Bunter !

"I SAY, you fellows!" yelled Billy Bunter.

From the darkness of the long landing above the hall Billy Bunter could hear the sounds of a struggle, of scuffling and panting breath. He knew that Wharton, hurrying to his uncle's room, must have run into the man from India in the dark.

And he yelled!

"I say, you fellows! Help! Murder! Fire! Help! Whooop! I say, you fellows! Oh crikey! Help!" yelled Bunter in a voice that not only awakened the juniors in the rooms along the passage, but might have awakened Rip Van Winkle and the Seven Sleepers of Ephesus.

"Hallo, hallo, hallo!"

"What the thump——"

"That's Bunter!"

"The esteemed and idiotic Bunter!"

Doors opened and lights flashed on. Bob Cherry and Johnny Bull, Frank Nugent and Hurree Jamset Ram Singh ran out in their pyjamas. They stared blankly at the fat figure in Wharton's doorway, in Wharton's grey overcoat and cap! Bunter, blinking in the electric light as it flashed on, roared and yelled!

"I say, you fellows! After him! Oh crikey!"

"What's the matter?" roared Bob Cherry.

"Help!" came a shout from the landing—a gasping, breathless shout in the voice of Harry Wharton. "Oh, help!"

"Come on!" roared Bob Cherry.

He ran up the passage, switched on the landing light as he turned the corner. His comrades were at his heels, alarmed and amazed. Bunter, behind them, still yelled and roared.

"Harry!" shouted Nugent, as the light flashed on.

Harry Wharton was struggling desperately in the grasp of the man from India. He had no chance against such an adversary, and it would have gone hard with him had not help been at hand.

The juniors fairly raced to the spot. Four pairs of hands clutched at the midnight intruder at the same moment and dragged him down.

"Back up!" roared Bob Cherry.

Wharton panted.

"Hold him! It's the man Corkran! He's after my uncle——"

"We've got the brute!"

The man from India was still struggling, though it was only of escape that he was thinking now. But there was no escape for him. In five pairs of hands he had not the ghost of a chance.

And plenty of help was coming! Lights flashed on in the hall and the passages. From one direction came Wells and Thomas and Robert. From another came Colonel Wharton, whisking in a voluminous dressing-gown, in a towering state of irritation at the midnight disturbance.

"Harry! What——" roared the colonel.

"We've got him, sir!" panted Bob Cherry.

"Who—what——"

"The gotfulness is preposterous!" gasped the Nabob of Bhanipur. "Sit on his esteemed head, my absurd Bob!"

"Oooooogh!" came in a gurgling gasp from the man underneath.

"Great gad! Corkran!" roared the colonel. "You rascal! You scoundrel! In my house at midnight! By Jove! Hold him securely! Wells!" In the excitement of the moment the colonel forgot that Wells was sacked. "Get a rope, tie his hands, secure him. No, you get a rope, Thomas. Wells, go and telephone this instant to the police station!"

"Yes, sir!" gasped Wells.

"Yes, sir!" gasped Thomas.

"Hold him fast, my boys—I will help you!"

The colonel took a grip on the wriggling man's collar.

Thomas was not long getting a box-rope. Wharton and Bob dragged the man's hands together, and Thomas tied them. Then, for additional security, the

" Bunter !   Where are you ? " roared Colonel Wharton, entering the room and switching on the light.   " Why—what——"
A fat foot was sticking out from underneath the bed, and the colonel grasped at it and pulled.   " Yarooh ! " yelled Bunter,
from his hiding-place.   " I'm not here ! "

end of the rope was knotted to the banisters.

Then Corkran was allowed to rise. He leaned on the banisters, gasping for breath. On the floor lay a short, thick stick, which the ruffian had dropped when Wharton ran into him in the dark. It was, perhaps, fortunate for Wharton that he had dropped it. Thomas picked it up.

"Keep that!" rapped the colonel. "The police will want that! By Jove! You rascal! What have you to say—hay?"

The man from India had nothing to say! He had no breath to say anything with. He gasped and gurgled. Wells came up the stairs.

"A constable is coming from Wimford, sir——"

"Very good! I am thankful, my boys, that you discovered this scoundrel, and seized him!" said Colonel Wharton. "There is no doubt what he intended to do with that stick. in revenge for a well-deserved thrashing I gave him in India years ago—a swindling rascal, by Jove! But how——"

"It was Wharton spotted him, sir," said Bob. "We came along to help——"

"Harry, my boy! But how——"

"Bunter woke me up——"

"Bunter!"

"Yes." Wharton gave a breathless laugh. "Bunter—he's here—goodness knows how! He woke me up and told me the man was in the house, and I came to wake you, and ran into him in the dark, and then——"

"Bunter woke us all up!" grinned Nugent. "He was yelling fit to raise the roof! Lucky he did!"

"The luckfulness was terrific!"

"Bunter!" repeated the colonel dazedly. "That young rascal here! How came he to be here? Where is he?"

"I left him in my room."

"Take care of that scoundrel, Thomas! Watch him! Bunter here—great gad!"

Colonel Wharton strode away along the landing and headed for his nephew's room, the juniors following him, and Wells following the juniors. Now that they had time to think about it, all were utterly astonished by the amazing presence of the Owl of the Remove.

A fat figure in a grey overcoat was gasping in Wharton's doorway. At the sight of the colonel it squeaked and vanished into the room. There was a bump, and a sound of scuffling, which indicated that somebody was hurriedly taking cover under a bed.

"Bunter! Where are you?" roared the colonel, striding in and switching on the light.

"Bunter, you ass!" gasped Harry. A grey cap lay beside the bed, and a foot was sticking out from underneath. "You blithering idiot, come out from under the bed!"

"Yaroooh! I'm not here! Keep that old brute off!" roared Bunter. "I say, you fellows—— Whoooop!"

Colonel Wharton stooped, grasped a fat ankle, and tugged. There was a howl, and Billy Bunter came out from under the bed, like a winkle from a shell.

"Yaroooh!" roared Bunter.

"Ha, ha, ha!"

"Bunter!" roared Colonel Wharton.

————

THE SEVENTEENTH CHAPTER.
All Right for Bunter !

BILLY BUNTER had the spotlight!

Bunter was the cynosure of all eyes.

Billy Bunter filled the scene !

He was the goods!

Colonel Wharton stared at him blankly. The Famous Five stared at him and grinned. Wells stared at him from the doorway and frowned. Everybody stared at Bunter, frowning or smiling !

"How did you get here?" gasped the colonel, at last.

"I—I'm not here! I mean I didn't get here—that is I haven't been here! I mean——"

"It was he, sir!" gasped Wells.

"What? What do you mean, Wells?"

"That coat, sir!" gasped Wells.

"Coat! What coat? Bunter's coat?"

"Master Harry's coat, sir!" gasped Wells. "He is wearing Master Harry's grey overcoat!"

"My hat! So he is!" ejaculated Wharton. "I thought I knew that coat!"

"You young rascal!" growled the colonel. "Pilfering a coat——"

"Oh, really, sir! I suppose I can borrow a coat when my own coat's locked up in the attic!" exclaimed Bunter warmly. "I suppose you don't think I was going to keep this coat! I don't suppose I should even have sold it !"

"Sold it! Good gad!"

"Not if I could have raised enough on the books—I mean——"

"The books——"

"I mean, I haven't touched any books——"

"The—the coat, sir!" stammered Wells. "It was the coat I saw, sir, on the balcony this evening — Master Harry's grey overcoat, sir, which I knew very well, and that led me to believe——"

"Oh!" exclaimed Harry. "That fat
(Continued on page 28.)

WHEN the GREAT APES CAME!

By STUART MARTIN.

HOW THE STORY STARTED.

GERRY LAMBERT and BILLY MURCHIE are flying over the African jungle when they are brought down by an army of apes —led by Big Ling, a giant ape-man—reared to crush civilisation by a renegade called Stein. Gerry escapes, but Billy is taken prisoner with a white girl named Lola. Billy and Lola are forced to accompany Big Ling's army, which, after laying waste villages and towns, makes for London, headed by a stolen Zeppelin. Flying back to London, Gerry, assisted by Lieut. Huskin, succeeds in bringing down the Zep in Hyde Park. As a counter-attack, Big Ling makes for London. Gerry, Billy, and the girl are eventually reunited, and, in company with a police-inspector, make all speed in a car for the War Office.

(*Now read on.*)

A Plan that Failed!

THROUGH Trafalgar Square the car swung, and then into Whitehall, to eventually draw up in front of the War Office, where policemen were grouped. The inspector and Billy dismounted, Gerry and the girl at their heels.

In the hall were officers and officials. A strange silence pervaded the place.

The inspector stated his business, and explained the presence of Billy, Gerry, and the girl.

An officer looked curiously at the party.

"Come upstairs," he said. "I want a word with you, please."

The trio mounted the stairs. On the landing Billy spoke.

"If I could see the Chief of the War Office——" he began.

The officer shook his head.

"You may see him, but you can't
THE MAGNET LIBRARY.—No. 1,351.

explain anything to him. Look here!" He opened a door, and pointed.

On the carpet of the big room lay several bodies, one of which Gerry quickly recognised.

"Lieutenant Huskin!" he exclaimed. "Dead!"

"Strangled," said the officer quietly. "Every man in the building was strangled by gorillas, who overran the place. It all happened quickly, before we could get here. Every telephone line was broken, every room wrecked. For ten minutes, I'm told, it was pandemonium. And then they cleared off."

"But where have they gone?"

"We don't know. Many of them were killed. The troops got lots of them during the raid on Covent Garden; but the main body scattered. Most of them went into Pall Mall and the Green Park, and then down to Westminster that way. It wasn't a fight, it was a raid."

"And where did they go after leaving Westminster?"

"We don't know. The barges in which they came have disappeared. We are waiting for news. We have scouts all along the Thames. There isn't a live gorilla in Whitehall or in the West End now. As for Scotland Yard——"

"Well?" cried the inspector.

"It was raided, too. They've captured some of the animals and put them in the cells. We don't know where the remainder will break out next."

"I can tell you!" cried Billy.

"Where, youngster? You are the person we want most in this affair."

"There will be nothing doing during the day," said Billy. "Ling's plan is to attack during the night. It was Stein's

idea to wreck the electricity works, and then to tear up the railway lines around London, so as to isolate the city. While parties are doing this, Big Ling will be leading shock troops to-night to collect stores and ammunition."

He drew from his pocket a chart, and spread it before his listeners.

Where were the gorillas and their leaders? That was the question that puzzled Whitehall.

That an army of beasts could raid London, keep their plan of campaign a secret, and hide themselves without leaving a trace, was the puzzling situation that faced the authorities.

Yet there was Billy Murchie's chart which he had shown to the officers in the War Office, marked with strategic points which the invaders intended to attack.

All that day there was no sign of Big Ling, the monster ape-man, and his forces. London life went on as usual, following the scare of the previous night. Billy and Gerry had earned a sleep which they were enjoying in a hotel close to Whitehall. The girl Lola had been taken in charge by officials who were getting into touch with her family in Belgium to whom they intended to send her.

Every precaution had been taken to guard the electrical works, and the various other sources and channels of the city's life; but, in spite of the seeming calm, there was an undercurrent of foreboding.

Army planes swept the sky, droning like bees as they kept up their vigil, and messages were flashed out at regular intervals.

"No news of enemy. No sight of enemy."

A slight mist began to descend over London in the early evening when Billy and Gerry awoke after their rest. They were due at the War Office where Billy had left the chart he had marked of Big Ling's intentions. And, having dressed and had a meal, they emerged from the hotel into the Strand.

It seemed strange to think that the hurrying crowds did not dream of the danger that was overshadowing the city; but the authorities had determined not to cause undue alarm by issuing bulletins. Everybody thought that Ling's attack had been a raid, not an advance thrust of war.

Half a dozen paces from the hotel door, Gerry seized Billy's arm and suddenly dragged him aside. At the same moment a pedestrian who was about to pass them staggered and fell. A second man dropped beside the first. Then a third went down. The boys were standing in a shop door, sheltered by the jutting wall.

"Stein!"

Gerry whispered the name excitedly. He pointed to a hurrying figure that was racing across the Strand, dodging the traffic as he went.

In a moment the crowds began to gather round the fallen men. A cry went up. The men had been shot; two were dead, the third was wounded by a shot that had caught him full in the chest.

"Those shots were meant for us," exclaimed Gerry. "I saw Stein coming towards us, his hand in his pocket. He must have used a gun with a silencer."

They followed the dodging figure across the street. But the traffic gave Stein cover, and by the time the boys reached the other side there was no sign of him. Whether he had gone down a side turning towards the Embankment, or dashed to right or left, could not be ascertained. As they stood for a second looking up and down the street, however, a bullet hit the pavement by their feet, ricochetted through a shop window, and left a starred, broken mark that startled everybody in the neighbourhood.

Smash-and-grab raiders was the thought in everyone's mind. By this time Billy had caught a glimpse of a car that had glided past them in the stream of traffic. And at the wheel was Stein! Another face peered through the window of the car—the Mongolian face of one of Ling's lieutenants!

In a flying leap Billy was on the running board of the car, clinging to the door handle. Gerry, too, had followed Billy's lead, and was at his chum's elbow.

The window of the car dropped, and a hairy hand made a grab at Billy, who dodged. Stein lifted his right hand, still holding the wheel with his left, and fired at the boys. But a bus touched his rear mudguard at the moment, and the shot went wide. There was no report—just a faint plop!

Then the car swung jerkily into the thick traffic.

Stein jerked his head round and shouted an order, and the door of the car to which Billy and Gerry clung, swung open.

They hung to the handle desperately, but the open door was in the path of an oncoming vehicle. It was Stein's plan to "rub them off" the running-board, and he was prepared to sacrifice the door in the crash that seemed inevitable. His front wheel just missed the vehicle—a bus—by inches; but Billy and Gerry leaped clear just in time.

They landed safely in the road together, and there was a screech of brakes, followed by yells from drivers. The boys paid no attention to the noise and the shouting. An empty taxicab was moving slowly in the thick of the stream. The boys hailed it, and ordered the driver to follow Stein's car, which could be seen threading its way ahead, and forcing other vehicles to draw up and swerve dangerously.

Widespread Destruction!

THE driver of the taxi did his best. Through the window the boys saw Stein's car dash up past Charing Cross Hospital. There was no obeying the road rules or signals. Policemen on point duty at St. Martin-in-the-Fields raised their hands, but Stein heeded them not. A sharp turn and the car was going down towards Trafalgar Square.

Through the square they flashed, pursuer and pursued. In Northumberland Avenue, however, the taxi driver's nerve gave way, and he drew up in obedience to a policeman who came rushing out of a side street.

Stein's car was then barely twenty yards ahead, held up by some oncoming traffic. But the policeman never reached either vehicle.

Out of Stein's car there tumbled the most strange cargo—first Stein, then a monster ape-man, fifteen feet high, squeezing himself out of the doorway, and after him three gorillas. Then something flew from Stein's hand, and

a blinding flash tore the street into red flame just as Billy and Gerry jumped from their taxi. They were thrown to the ground, blinded by smoke and debris, deafened by the roar of the bomb

Scrambling to their feet the boys saw the wreckage the explosion had caused. Their taxi was but a heap of smoking ruins. Of the policeman and the taxi-driver there was no sign. They had been blown to pieces.

Gerry saw Stein and his apes dash along the pavement. Pedestrians fled at their approach. Howling and snarling the three gorillas raced on all fours beside Stein and the huge ape-man. Once more Stein turned and threw a bomb.

The boys dropped in their tracks, burying their faces in their arms to protect themselves from the explosion.

By the time the boys rose to their feet again Stein and his apes had disappeared, and the crowds were surging from the Embankment towards the Underground Station. Voices were shouting on every side. It was with difficulty that Gerry and Billy managed to force their way through the press of people that had gathered. There was only one way that Stein could have gone, apparently, and that was into the Underground Station. People were crowding round the entrance, pointing to the hall, where the apes had caused consternation by their appearance.

A ticket-collector at the barrier was explaining, in bewilderment, how he had been thrown aside by a gorilla, and as Gerry and Billy reached the barrier there came from below a muffled roar that made the ground heave under their feet.

The thunder of that subterranean explosion was followed by another, and then a third. Smoke came drifting up the staircase.

From outside the station there came other sounds—a strange echo of hissing water, an occasional splashing, and then a riot of sound burst out. The Embankment had been heaved up by the explosion below the ground. Tramcars swayed and fell on their sides, a part of the Embankment wall fell into the Thames, and the water flooded over and swept across the roadway, several inches deep.

Billy and Gerry forced their way out of the station, and saw a figure clawing its way through the panic-stricken crowd.

It was Stein, making his way towards the river wall.

After him went the boys, knowing that in the state of affairs around them it was impossible to raise a shout, useless to try to explain who Stein was, or why he should be caught. They kept to their objective, and that was the cap-

ture of this arch-criminal, who was spreading death and disaster wherever he went.

"There he goes!" cried Gerry, pointing to a small, dark motor-boat that shot out from the steps of the Needle.

Stein was seated at the rudder, as he swung his craft downstream.

The only other craft on the river was a tug in midstream labouring against the down-flowing tide with a string of barges behind her. The river was still pouring through the gap in the wall.

"Westminster Pier!" cried Billy. "The police boat!"

The boys turned and ran towards Westminster. They had not gone half the distance, however, when suddenly the street lights were extinguished. Darkness fell on the Embankment like a pall that had been dropped suddenly from above. Darkness also fell on the lighted buildings on both sides of the river—the Houses of Parliament, Scotland Yard—on every hand darkness. The tug's lights were tiny specks moving on the river. That was all, save for an occasional light on the other side of the river.

"That puts the kybosh on our pursuit of Stein for the time being," remarked Gerry "We'd better see what the Yard has to say."

"We'll need the Yard's sanction for a boat, anyway," said Billy.

The boys eventually found their way to Scotland Yard, where here and there policemen were flashing lamps. Giving their names they were shown into the office of the chiefs, who, in the light of flickering candles, were discussing the terrible situation.

Telephone messages were coming through from various quarters. There had been explosions at intervals along the various Underground electric lines. In every case the officials were able to give similar information. A small band of apes had burst through the barriers and had descended to the tunnels. Bombs had burst, and the roofs of the tunnels had collapsed. The rails were buried in debris.

Trains were caught between the explosions. The heavy loads of passengers were buried underground, with no hope of escape.

And the lights, how had they been extinguished? It was impossible to say There had been explosions in the electrical works—fuses had been blown out, had been repaired at once, and had blown out again and again. Dynamos had been wrecked. Yet there had not been any sign of Big Ling or his gorillas. The works had been under the guard of soldiers.

London streets were crammed with people groping in various directions. Shops were being closed hurriedly, and fears of gangsters were abroad.

Then, while Billy and Gerry were listening to the information that was pouring into the Yard, there came other news that added to the crisis.

A shipload of gorillas had descended on Southampton, and were spreading devastation in the town. From Liverpool it was reported that the authorities were battling with apes who had descended from the sky. The animals at the Edinburgh Zoo had broken loose, and were clambering over Calton Hill and destroying Prince's Street, the fashionable thoroughfare And from Reading: an army of apes was marching up the Great West road on the way to London!

The Chief dropped the telephone receiver with trembling hands.

"If only I could lay my hands on this Stein!" he cried, in despair.

"Chief," said Gerry, "my pal and I

came to ask for the use of a boat—a police boat—to track him. He is down the river somewhere, he and Big Ling. Give us passes, with full authority, and we will go where an ordinary policeman could not."

Tracked Down!

THE Chief gave the necessary permission, and ten minutes later the boys emerged into the dark street with firm determination to find Ling, and every authority to back them in their search.

"Who's that?" came a voice; and a boat rubbed the side of the boys' fast craft some distance below Tower Bridge.

A police boat had crept up to them in the darkness, and a light was flashed into their faces. One look at the boys' passes, however, changed the challenge into a greeting.

"We were told you might be about," said the inspector, who was muffled in a greatcoat, and had two assistants beside him. "Any news of anything?"

"Not yet, inspector," answered Billy.

"They've found out what put the lights of London out," went on the inspector. "Somebody has been interfering with the electric cables in various parts of London, which resulted in the blowing of main fuses at the stations. They're getting light now, though."

He waved his hand towards the upper reaches of the river, where lights were beginning to show again.

"And, another thing," he went on, "the cars this madman Stein used were all stolen. He must have selected his cars from the various parking places."

"Inspector," said Billy, "have you any report of abandoned barges on the river within the last twenty-four hours?"

"Abandoned barges? Well, there were some that broke from their moorings, but they were found below the Pool yesterday——"

"Below the Pool?"

"Yes. And there was another thing. A shipkeeper of one of these cargo steamers has disappeared——"

"Which cargo steamers?"

"There are several about here, lying in the stream waiting for discharge."

The inspector pointed upward towards the dark hulls of ships at anchor.

"What kind of cargo did they hold?" asked Gerry.

"Produce and fruit mostly, and one had a cargo of frozen meat. They can't be handled now, as they can't get out below the Tower, since we have troops on the bridge, and orders are that the bridge is not to be raised——"

"Not to be raised!" said Billy, aghast. "But look!"

He pointed to the gaunt framework in the distance. From the bridge came sounds of commotion. Against the sky it could be seen opening its gigantic leaves.

The inspector made a grab at the tiller of his boat, and was off up-stream at once, while Billy and Gerry remained where they were, sheltered beside a large ship moored in midstream.

Up went the big leaves gradually. The figures of the troops on the roadway could be seen hurrying towards the ends of the moving platforms; and then the crack of rifles broke out.

At first the reports came singly, then they were as one volley. A few splashes came to the boys' ears. They started their engine and moved upward.

"Look, Gerry!" cried Billy.

Across the water under the bridge a small boat shot out and disappeared in the shadow of the shipping. The commotion on the bridge increased, and the firing continued. The two sections of the roadway across the bridge were nearly half-way raised, and hanging to the edges strange figures could be seen. They were the figures of apes.

From the ends of the bridge the troops were firing rapidly. One figure after another dropped. The bridge began to close again, trembled, and rose once more. More firing, and more apes appeared. Some were running along the top, some were swinging on the trellised ironwork of the bridge. A large steamship moved through the opened bridge, going seaward, followed by a second ship.

As their boat swept under the tall structure the boys saw the gorillas running hither and thither. One dropped, shot through the chest, into the water close to them. A large paw made a grab at the gunwale of their boat, and next moment a hideous face of an ape-man appeared.

His weight bore the boat down until the gunwale touched the water. He was clambering in, when Gerry pulled out a Service gun with which they had been supplied and aimed at the terrible face.

"Don't shoot!"

It was the ape-man who spoke breathlessly, in agitation, and with intense earnestness.

Blood was streaming from his wound. He made no attempt to board the craft, for he was terribly wounded and almost exhausted. His face, ghastly in the faint light, seemed to become more human than usual.

"I am no friend of Big Ling," he breathed. "I hate him. The master sent me to death!"

"Who is the master?" asked Billy, watching the ape-man closely, as he hung there, while the boat drifted with the tide.

"Him you call Stein. My name is Tree Climber."

"Why do you hate Ling?"

"He promised us to be rulers. But I die!"

"Where is Ling?" cried Billy. "Where is the master?"

"Over there."

The ape-man stabbed his finger across the river. His strength was ebbing fast, but he still clung to the boat.

"Save me!" he said in a rumbling tone. "I am afraid of your people. The master tied explosives to our shoulders. We did not know that the bombs would kill us in the tunnels!"

His huge head sank, his hand lost its grip on the boat, and, with a terrible sigh, he dropped into the water and slid out of sight.

"What do you make of that, Billy?" asked Gerry.

"I understand now how the underground explosions took place, Gerry. Stein sacrificed his men and apes to make the explosions. I'll bet that was Stein's boat we saw shoot across the river. Where could it have gone?"

They scanned the opposite bank, heedless of the fight that was still taking place on Tower Bridge.

Up against the sky rose the mass of the Tower of London, its turrets silhouetted against the heavens and the racing clouds.

Billy and Gerry steered the boat over to the wall that rose as a buttress against the river, but there was no sign of Stein's boat.

"What was that?" cried Billy suddenly, as a flickering light appeared ahead.

It was extinguished at once, but it had shown for an instant.

Then the truth burst on the two boys at the same moment.

They were opposite the Traitors' Gate, that passage leading to the Tower which in the past has seen so many tragic passengers.

The portcullis was up; the water flowed into the passage without hindrance.

Billy steered the boat straight for the dark opening, and then shut the engine off. They passed the entrance, and as they did so the ancient portcullis dropped into place.

Were they trapped?

The boat rubbed against the dripping walls. They drew their revolvers and waited. Not a sound.

Feeling their way against the wet stones, they pushed the boat forward until its prow touched an obstacle. It was the ancient steps into which they had bumped, and beside their boat they discovered another craft—Stein's boat.

Still not a sound; but from somewhere came the odour they had learned to detest—the odour of gorilla.

A grunt made them start. A pair of eyes gleamed in the darkness, rising from Stein's boat.

Crash!

Gerry's gun descended on the ape's head, and it slumped to the bottom of the boat without a cry. Then from above came a voice shouting in a strange tongue. It was the voice of Stein.

The boys crouched low, waiting for the attack they believed would follow. It did not come, however; but again that flicker of light appeared above. It wavered at the top of the flight of old steps, then disappeared.

In the darkness Billy leaned over and whispered into Gerry's ear.

"We've got to go up," he said. "Are you ready?"

"Yes."

They stepped out of the boat into water, found a foothold, and climbed up the steps. A small door stood open. They edged through and found themselves in a wide cellar, one of the dungeons. Another passage of stairs, and they were faced with another door, which also was open. Beyond it another dungeon; and then the light appeared again. A footstep sounded on the flag-stones.

The light threw a sudden flicker into the apartment. There were several deep recesses in the stone walls, and into one of these the boys dodged.

Hardly had they done so when Stein appeared.

He was holding a candle above his head. He did not look round, but continued on his way. Clearly he was wondering why his ape had not followed him.

The moment he had passed, the boys slipped into the passage through which Stein had come. More stairs, winding and narrow. The smell of gorilla grew stronger. They reached another room, and in here they saw a group of animals, crouched on the floor beside wooden cases which had been broken open, jabbering and growling as they fed. A candle stuck on a stone ledge was the only illumination.

"The produce stolen from the ships," whispered Billy, pointing to the contents of the cases.

Printed and published every Saturday by the Proprietors, the Amalgamated Press Ltd., The Fleetway House, Farringdon Street, London E.C.4. Advertisement offices: The Fleetway House, Farringdon Street, London, E C 4. Registered for transmission by Canadian Magazine Post. Subscription rates: Inland and Abroad, 11s. per annum; 5s. 6d. for six months. Sole Agents for Australia and New Zealand: Messrs. Gordon & Gotch, Ltd., and for South Africa: Central News Agency, Ltd.—Saturday, January 6th, 1934.

The floor was a litter of the remains of fruit and cold storage provisions.

The gorillas took no notice of the boys beyond a swift glance.

At the sound of approaching footsteps, however, Billy and Gerry dashed into the gloom of a passage and round a corner, where they pressed their forms into what had in the old days been a cell. Peering out, they saw Stein enter the chamber where the apes were feeding and then pass through another doorway, holding his candle high above his head.

Billy and Gerry tiptoed in his wake. They dared not get too close to him lest he heard them. Suddenly Stein's candlelight ceased to glimmer as he

entered a doorway on the right of the passage.

Reaching the spot, the two investigators found themselves faced with a heavy curtain. Pulling it aside cautiously, they saw a strange sight. They were looking into the ancient chapel. There sat the enormous figure of Big Ling; but not the Big Ling they had expected to see. Around the huge ape-man lay the Tower jewels, while on his head he wore, balanced in an odd fashion, the crown.

Big Ling was garbed in a bright-coloured robe. In his right hand he held a spear, its gleaming sharp point towering above him.

At Big Ling's side was a machine-gun, its belt of cartridges hanging loose

ready for its deadly work, while astride the gun itself sat Stein, an eyeglass in his eye, dressed in a light grey suit which looked new.

Ranged along each side of the chamber were other ape-men, and behind them gorillas only slightly less in stature, but each armed with a weapon.

It was like a court of ancient days, savage and frightful. The armoury of the Tower had been stripped of its weapons to provide these monsters with death-dealing implements.

(*Look out for further thrilling chapters of this popular adventure story in next week's FREE GIFT NUMBER of the* MAGNET.)

COME INTO THE OFFICE, BOYS!

Always glad to hear from you, chums, so drop me a line to the following address ; The Editor, The " Magnet " Library, The Amalgamated Press, Ltd., The Fleetway House, Farringdon Street, London, E.C.4. A stamped, addressed envelope will ensure a reply.

WELL, chums, 1933 has come and gone and still the MAGNET reigns supreme as the best boys' paper on the market. Well done, everybody ! Last year, if you remember, I said that the Old Paper was out to break all records—and it certainly has done so ! Cheers ! Frank Richards has triumphed all along the line with his magnificent Greyfriars yarns, our serials have all been top-notchers, and our shorter features have gained full marks ! Isn't the MAGNET the ideal boys' paper ? I'll tell the world it is ! And I'll say this, that 1934 is going to see the MAGNET rise to even more dizzier heights ! For days now I have been working at tip-top pressure on

ANOTHER GREAT FREE GIFT OFFER

which will follow immediately after our present series of free gifts come to a close. But more about these coming Free Gifts next week ; I'm only just whetting your appetites now !

TEN more stunning coloured pictures for your album this week, chums. Your collection must be looking well worth while now ! You should have 76 pictures all told, and there are still two more marvellous sheets of pictures to come, bringing the total up to 100 coloured pictures all told. Whatever you do, don't miss any of these grand free pictures, or your album will be spoiled !

Having told you fellows to fire away as much as you like at me, I suppose I've got myself to blame when you put up a real poser to me. Jimmy Cameron, of Belfast, Ulster, gave me a task this week. Jimmy has been having an argument with a friend named " Stewart," who said that his name was originally French. Jimmy argued that it was Scottish, so now I've got to settle the business.

FRENCH OR SCOTTISH ?

is the question—and here is the answer : The ancestor of the Stewarts was a Breton noble named Alan, a cadet of the ancient Counts of Dol and Oman, in Brittany. He crossed to England, was appointed Sheriff of Shropshire, and through his third son, Walter Fitz-Allen, became the founder of the House of

Stewart. Walter crossed the border, and was made Great Steward of Scotland by King David I.

I dare say I have a number of readers who bear the same name, so they will be interested in the above reply. And having settled that argument, here is where the name " Cameron " came from. Jimmy wants to know that, too.

The Camerons got their name from the Cam-shron, or " wry nose " of some early chief. The first assured Chief of the Clan was Donald Dhu, who flourished in the year 1411. Make a note of it, you Cameron lads.

MOST of my letters this week can be dealt with by means of my

RAPID-FIRE REPLIES.

The first comes from " A Glasgow Reader," who asks :

How Did Scotland Yard Receive its Name ? Quite simple ! What we generally term " Scotland Yard " is the headquarters of the Criminal Investigation Department of the Metropolitan Police, and it gets its name because it is built in New Scotland Yard—just in the same manner as we sometimes talk about " Whitehall," when we mean certain Government departments. The police station attached to " Scotland Yard " is officially known as Canning Street, W., Police Station. But the public prefer to dub the C.I.D. " Scotland Yard," after the name of the site on which it is built.

How to Kill and Mount Butterflies. (" Scientist," of Birmingham.) Butterflies and moths are killed by being put into a " killing bottle "—an ordinary well-stoppered bottle which contains ammonia, or some other powerful " killing " liquid. The ammonia is protected, of course, to prevent the insects dropping into it. The fumes kill them, or—in other words—they are " gassed."

The best way to mount them is to pin them upon tiny circles of cork, which are, in turn, glued down to strong cardboard in whatever design the collector prefers.

If this reader applies to his local library, he will most certainly be able to obtain a book on the subject which will give him much more information than I have space to print.

Incidentally, I am bearing in mind the interesting suggestion he makes, and will see what I can do in a future issue of the MAGNET.

From Which Country do we Obtain Radium ? (Robert Niblock of Mile End, London.) Small deposits of radium are found in various parts of the world. By far the greatest amount, however, comes from the Belgian Congo, and a Belgian company owns the radium mines. Radium is very scarce, which accounts for its terrifically high price.

Getting Rid of Freckles. (" Constant Reader," of Port Elizabeth, South Africa.) Don't worry about them. A weak solution of diluted peroxide of hydrogen will help you to get rid of them, and will not harm you.

HERE comes a query from Tom Mathers, of Croydon. He asks :

ARE THERE SEALS ROUND THE ENGLISH COAST ?

Yes ! Any amount of them ! Seals breed extensively on certain islands round our coasts, notably the Farne Islands, off Northumberland. In the season the rocks are sometimes swarming with young seals, and they are so tame that they pay practically no attention to visitors or the fishermen who work just off the islands. But that is because visitors are scarce in the breeding season, and no one lives on the islands except three lighthouse-keepers. Needless to say, you won't find many seals in the more crowded holiday resorts round our coasts, although an isolated one is sometimes seen.

Many thanks to all the readers who have sent me so many congratulatory letters on the subject of our stories. You may be sure that I will always see to it that the standard of MAGNET stories remains as it is at present—and that means the finest schoolboy fiction published.

You'll find evidence of this when you read :

" BILLY BUNTER'S DIAMOND ! "
By Frank Richards,

which appears in our next issue. As usual, Mr. Frank Richards gives you a yarn that starts off " bang " with a real interest-holding opening—and the interest is held continuously until the very last line. This yarn will make you wish it were twice as long, so the best thing I can do is to repeat my oft-given advice—" order your copy in advance, and don't run the risk of the MAGNET being sold out " !

There are thrills in store for you in next week's chapters of our thrilling " apo " story, and two pages full of chuckles and laughs in the " Greyfriars Herald " supplement, not to mention " Linesman's " interesting Soccer talk.

And fire in your queries, chums ! The more there are, the better I like it !

YOUR EDITOR.

BUNTER, THE CRASHER!

(Continued from page 23.)

villain was there in my coat, and you saw him, and thought——"

"I did not see his face in the dark, sir!" gasped Wells.

"Oh gad!" exclaimed the colonel. "I understand now! Then you really were pushed off the balcony, Wells?"

"Yes, sir; though I am now aware that it was not Master Harry who pushed me off, but that unscrupulous boy who has pilfered his overcoat——"

"That's all right, Wells," said Harry. "You could hardly think anything else when a fellow in my overcoat pushed you over in the dark."

"And it was that young rascal!" boomed the colonel. "Wells, your mistake was a natural one. I shall forget what you said, and you will remain. The whole thing was a mistake, due to that pernicious young rascal!"

"Thank you, sir! I shall be very happy——"

"As for Bunter——"

"It wasn't me!" roared Bunter, watching the colonel warily across Wharton's bed. "I never pushed the old ass over! Never touched him! Besides, what was a fellow to do? I only wanted to get away, and he would have collared me in another tick!"

"Ha, ha, ha!"

"Blessed if I see anything to cackle at! You're practically doubting my word! Pretty thick, I call it!"

"Why did you put on my nephew's coat?" roared the colonel.

"What was a fellow to do when his coat was locked up in the attic! It would have been all right if I hadn't lost the attic key! It was your fault, making a fellow hide under a bed——"

"Ha, ha, ha!"

"Not that I've been in the attic!" added Bunter. "You needn't fancy that I've been here for days and days sleeping in the attic! As for getting in and out of the house by Wharton's french window, I never did—in fact, I didn't know there was a french window. If there is, I don't know anything about it! I never camped in the attic, and never went round at night looking for grub; and if anybody's missed Christmas puddings, and turkeys, and such things, it's no good asking me! I don't know anything at all about them! You'll be making out next that it was me played ghost at Christmas!"

"Oh, my hat!" exclaimed Wharton.

"Bunter all the time!" gasped Bob Cherry.

The Famous Five were beginning to understand now quite a lot of things that had puzzled and mystified them.

"Upon my word!" gasped Colonel Wharton.

"You keep off!" said Bunter. "I haven't been here through the holidays, and I haven't touched a thing all the while I've been here. And——" The colonel made a movement, and Bunter broke off, with a yell of alarm. "I say, you fellows, keep him off!"

"You ridiculous boy!" exclaimed the colonel. "You have acted like an impudent and unscrupulous young rascal, but——"

"I haven't! Perhaps you're thinking of Wharton, sir, or Bob Cherry——"

"Oh crumbs!"

"But," hooted the colonel, "it seems that you awakened my nephew to-night, when that rascal Corkran got into the house, and gave the alarm. But for that, I might have received injury at the rascal's hands. In view of this, cannot you understand, you absurd boy, that your ridiculous and rascally proceedings will be forgiven——"

"Oh!" gasped Bunter.

"It was fortunate, as it turns out, that you were here, and I shall certainly not give you the thrashing you deserve——"

"Oh!" repeated Bunter.

"Wells, if you will oblige me by overlooking the act of this absurd and harebrained boy——"

"Certainly, sir!" said Wells.

"Oh!" said Bunter again.

It dawned on his fat mind that he had, in fact, made his peace quite unexpectedly. All the while he had been a hidden guest at Wharton Lodge he had hoped that something might turn up to placate the old colonel and get him over his tantrums. He realised now that something had.

In fact, all was calm and bright.

As Bunter realised that, a fat grin overspread his face. He was not to be kicked; he was not to be thrashed. The riding-whip was a thing of the past.

"Wells, will you see that a bed is prepared for this boy?" said the colonel.

"Very good, sir!"

"Oh!" gasped Bunter. "Good! What about supper?"

"Eh?"

"I'm hungry——"

"Perhaps, Wells, you may be able to——" gasped the colonel.

"Oh, certainly, sir!" said Wells.

"Nothing much, you know," said Bunter. "A cold chicken—say, a couple —a pudding or so—and a pie or two— anything you've got handy——"

"Ha, ha, ha!"

Bunter was led away to supper.

. . . .

Harry Wharton looked into Bunter's room at eleven o'clock the next morning. Bunter was snoring. Wharton shook him.

"Urrggh!" grunted Bunter. "Beast! Wharrer you waking me up for?"

"I thought you might be catching a train——"

"Well, I'm not!"

Bunter blinked at him.

"If that's what you call gratitude, Wharton, after I came here specially, at the risk of my life, to save your uncle from being knocked on the head——"

"Oh crikey!"

"Has the old brute——"

"What?"

"I mean, the dear old gentleman— has the dear old gentleman got over his tantrums? I suppose he has, after my risking my life for him—what? Well, I've not been treated well here; but I never was the fellow to bear grudges. I forgive you all round."

"Oh, my hat!"

"I mean it," said Bunter. "I always was a forgiving chap—kindest friend and noblest foe, and all that! It's all right, old fellow! I'm not going! I'm staying with you till the end of the hols."

"Oh!"

"Tell them to send up my brekker at twelve; then I'll turn out for lunch! Don't disturb me again till then! I'm sleepy!"

"I say——"

Snore!

Harry Wharton gazed for a long moment at the snoring Owl. Then he left him to it, and Billy Bunter snored on!

THE END.

(Next week's grand long yarn of the chums of Greyfriars is entitled: "BILLY BUNTER'S DIAMOND!" and it's full of amusing and amazing situations. You'll vote it great, chums, same as you will the sheet of topping coloured pictures which will be given FREE with our next issue.)

The MAGNET

No. 1,352. Vol. XLV. Week Ending January 13th, 1934.

EVERY SATURDAY.

2ᴰ

A startling incident from " **BILLY BUNTER'S DIAMOND !** "—this week's grand school yarn.

Billy Bunter's Diamond

BY FRANK RICHARDS

THE FIRST CHAPTER.
Bunter's Baggage!

"WALK!" ejaculated Billy Bunter.

He blinked at Harry Wharton through his big spectacles.

"Did you say walk?" he exclaimed.

"Yes; walk!"

"Well, my hat!"

Bunter seemed as surprised as if Harry Wharton had suggested that he should fly.

"Walk?" he repeated. "Well, I like that! Walk?"

"Well, if you like it, all right!" remarked Bob Cherry. "Let's get going."

Snort, from Billy Bunter.

Evidently his statement that he "liked" it, had been in sarcastic vein. His meaning was that he didn't like it! Not a little bit!

Walking, in fact, was not much in Billy Bunter's line. He had such a lot to carry along with him. Bunter was not one of those active, strenuous fellows, always on the go. Both his circumference and his diameter were against it.

"Walk!" said Bunter, with a snort of scorn.

"The walkfulness," remarked Hurree Jamset Ram Singh, "is an excellent and execrable form of ridiculous exercise. And a little absurd exercise may help to bring downfully your terrific fatfulness, my esteemed Bunter."

"You shut up, Inky! Now, look here, Wharton!" said the Owl of Greyfriars. "I can't walk to Wimford! That's that!"

"Only a mile and a half!" said Frank Nugent.

THE MAGNET LIBRARY.—No. 1,352.

"And we're all coming with you to see you off!" said Bob Cherry.

"A real pleasure to see you off, Bunter!" remarked Johnny Bull.

"The pleasure will be terrific!"

Snort!

This little discussion was taking place in Harry Wharton's "den," at his home, Wharton Lodge, in Surrey.

The captain of the Greyfriars Remove was home for the holidays, and his friends were with him. So was Billy Bunter!

Now the Famous Five were going on to Johnny Bull's place for the rest of the "hols." Bunter had no objection to going. But Johnny Bull had! And Johnny had stated his objection so emphatically and unmistakably, that there was no getting away from it.

So Billy Bunter was catching his train on the home-trail that afternoon. He was not in the best of tempers. And the suggestion that he should walk to the station put the lid on, so to speak.

"When I have a guest at Bunter Court," said the fat Owl, with a scornful blink at Wharton, "I send him to the station in the car. I mean, in one of the cars. I know you've got only one car here—a Ford, isn't it?—but——"

"You fat, frabjous ass——"

"If that's how you talk to a guest, Wharton——"

"I—I—I mean, don't be a goat, Bunter! The road's too thick with frozen snow for a car. I've asked my uncle, and he says 'No.'"

"Just like him!" said Bunter. "Your uncle's manners are the limit, Wharton. Blessed if I know how I've stood him all this time. I suppose you can phone to the station for a taxi?"

"They won't come, owing to the state of the roads."

Snort!

"Like me to wheel you, in a wheel-barrow?" suggested Bob Cherry.

Snort!

"Or shall we up-end you, and roll you along like a barrel?" asked Johnny Bull. "That's not a bad idea."

Snort!

Harry Wharton glanced at his watch. Speeding the parting guest was not an exactly agreeable occupation. But Bunter really had to catch his train. And there was no doubt that it would be a pleasure to see him off. It was always a pleasure to see the last of William George Bunter.

"Well," said Billy Bunter, in a tone of finality, "I'm not going to walk a mile and a half! That's that!"

Wharton picked up a time-table.

"There's a train from the village station," he said. "That's only half a mile. But it goes only as far as Woodgate—you'd have to change there."

Wharton did not add that it was a slow local train, and that there would be a long wait at Woodgate. He did not want to discourage Bunter.

"Well, that's better!" grunted the Owl of the Remove. "If your stuffy old uncle won't let the car go out, and if you're too jolly mean to get me a taxi, I——"

"Ready?"

"But somebody will have to carry my bag!" said Bunter. "If you think I'm going to fag along through snow and ice carrying a heavy suitcase, you're jolly well mistaken, see?"

"Your bag!" repeated Harry blankly.

"My bag!" said Bunter firmly.

The Famous Five gazed at the Owl of the Remove. Bunter had arrived at

Wharton Lodge not only without a bag, but without any baggage at all. That was rather his custom, when paying visits. Like the freebooters of olden times, he lived on the country he invaded.

"Whose bag?" snorted Johnny Bull.

"Oh, really, Bull——"

"If it's mine——" began Johnny, in a voice like that of the Great Huge Bear.

"I shouldn't care to borrow your shabby old bag, Bull, when I'm going to a place like Mauleverer Towers," said Bunter. "I've borrowed one of your bags, Wharton, to carry my things. I suppose you don't want me to walk out of the place carrying shirts and pyjamas under my arm?"

"Whose shirts?" asked Frank Nugent.

"Whose pyjamas?" inquired Bob Cherry.

"The whosefulness is terrific!" grinned Hurree Jamset Ram Singh.

"I say, you fellows, if this talk is going to turn into a sordid discussion about a few things I've borrowed during my stay here, it had better cease," said Bunter, with dignity. "As I'm going to give old Mauly a look-in, I've no time to go home for my own things. I don't want to arrive at Mauleverer Towers without even a suitcase. They rather keep up style there! A bit different from your show here, Wharton!"

"Oh!"

There was a tap at the door of the den, and Thomas, the page, looked in.

"I've strapped your bag, Master Bunter, sir," he said. "Shall I carry it down, sir?"

"Yes!" grunted Bunter.

"No!" hooted Johnny Bull.

"Look here, Bull, you beast——" roared Bunter.

"Bring that bag in here, Thomas!" said Johnny Bull determinedly. "Shove it over this way! You can cut—that's all right!"

Johnny Bull took the suitcase, pushed he surprised Thomas out, and closed the door on him. Then he started unstrapping the bag.

"Johnny, old bean——" murmured Wharton.

"You can lend him your bag, if you like," said Johnny Bull. "But I want to know how many of my shirts are in it before Bunter clears!"

"Beast!" roared Bunter. "If you're going to make a fuss about a few shirts, I——"

"I jolly well am!"

"They're not yours, either! They're Nugent's!"

"Oh, my hat!" ejaculated Nugent.

"As for the pyjamas," said Bunter scornfully, "they may be yours—I didn't notice when I put them in. And the socks——"

The suitcase—quite a large one—was well filled.

The chums of the Remove stared at the overflowing contents. Apparently Bunter had made rather considerable preparations for his stay with Lord Mauleverer, at Mauleverer Towers. He had been rather a long time packing that morning, while Harry Wharton & Co. were out skating. He had packed not wisely, but too well!

Johnny Bull, breathing hard, jerked a couple of suits of pyjamas from the bag, and laid them aside. Frank Nugent picked out three very nice shirts. Hurree Jamset Ram Singh, after staring blankly into the extensive assortment of apparel, selected socks, ties, and a number of other things.

Harry Wharton, with a quite peculiar expression on his face, lifted out his best evening suit. Bob Cherry selected a jacket and a waistcoat and a cap. Then

there was quite a scramble for boots and shoes.

"I say, you fellows!" protested Bunter.

But Bunter was not heeded.

Each member of the famous Co. appropriated the articles that belonged to him. The result was that the suitcase was left empty. Billy Bunter blinked at the Famous Five.

"Look here, you beasts——"

Four members of the Co. walked out of the den heavy laden. Harry Wharton was left alone with his peculiar guest.

"If you want to borrow the bag, Bunter——" murmured Wharton.

Bunter did not want to borrow the bag. He did not want to start on his travels with an empty suitcase.

"Well, look here, come on. We've got to walk to the village, you know."

Four members of the Co. had disappeared, and they stayed disappeared. They seemed to have had enough of Bunter; which, perhaps, was not surprising. Harry Wharton had the pleasure—or otherwise—wholly to himself of walking to the village station with his guest.

The biggest bargain Billy Bunter ever drove was when he bought a hundred pound diamond tiepin for one shilling! But Bunter, in his ignorance, thought it was only an imitation diamond!

THE SECOND CHAPTER.
Bunter's Farewell!

"HOLD my arm!" grunted Bunter.

Harry Wharton held his arm.

The road was thick with frozen snow, practically impassable to traffic, and not easy for walking. Except for that drawback it was a delightful day for a walk — clear, bright, keen, frosty January weather. Frost was hard on trees and hedges; the ice like iron in the ditches. No vehicle of any kind was to be seen, except that, to his surprise, Wharton spotted a cyclist coming from the direction of the town of Wimford. He was a keen cyclist himself, but he certainly would not have liked to take his machine out on the glassy roads that freezing afternoon. Looking towards the distant rider, he expected to see him skid and shoot into the hedges any second. But he was not given leisure to take much heed of the man coming from Wimford. Bunter claimed his attention.

Bunter slipped and nearly fell. After which Harry Wharton held on to a fat arm to help him navigate the slippery road.

"Beastly weather!" growled Bunter.

"Jolly healthy!" remarked Wharton.

"Silly idiot!"

Harry Wharton smiled. Bunter had been under his roof as a guest of sorts, and he was, therefore, extremely unwilling to kick him. He had made a resolve—a sort of New Year's resolution —not to kick Bunter before he left, if he could possibly help it. Patience was wearing rather thin, but he was manfully resolved to hold out till the happy

moment when he saw Bunter off in his train.

From the Wimford road they turned into the lane that led to the village and the local station. Bunter grunted and groused at every step. It was undoubtedly rather an exertion to get through frozen snow. Bunter had never liked exertion. Elmdale—the village where there was a railway station—was only a half-mile from Wharton Lodge, but the fat Owl of the Remove was puffing and blowing before he had done a tenth of that distance. He threw a great deal of weight on Wharton's arm, which the captain of the Remove bore with manly fortitude.

A sound of swishing in the snow behind caused Wharton to glance round. The cyclist he had seen coming from Wimford had turned into the lane and was coming on after them. Now that he was close at hand Harry looked at him rather curiously. Difficult as it was to ride on such a road, he was putting on some speed, evidently exerting himself to the uttermost. And he was not an athletic fellow to look at. He was short and slightly built, with a thin, narrow face and pale red eyebrows and eyelashes. His exertions were telling on him, judging by the beads of perspiration that ran down his sallow cheeks in spite of the bitter cold.

He buzzed his bell impatiently as he drew near the two schoolboys, who were walking in the middle of the narrow lane. Wharton jerked at Billy Bunter's fat arm.

"Stoppit!" hooted Bunter. "Beast! You nearly made me slip! Wharrer you dragging at a fellow for, you beast?"

"Get aside, old fat bean!"

"Shan't!"

"There's a bike behind!"

"He can go round us, can't he?" snorted Bunter.

"You silly ass, get out of the man's way!" roared Wharton,

"Beast!"

Buzz, buzz, buzz! came angrily on the bell behind. The cyclist was close now, and Wharton had already noted that the man was, for some reason of his own, in hot haste.

The lane was narrow, and going round the fellows walking in the middle of it meant going among deep cartruts ridged with frozen snow, at the imminent peril of a crash.

"Hi!" yelled the man with the ginger eyebrows. "Hi! Get out of the way! Hi! Have you bought this road? Hi!"

"Bunter, you ass——"

"Beast!"

Harry Wharton tugged at a fat arm. Bunter was dragged out of the way by main force. With a snort of wrath, the Owl of the Remove wrenched his arm from Wharton's grasp. He staggered as he got it loose, slipped on icy snow, and spun.

"Yarooooh!" roared Bunter, as he went.

He rolled over, fairly in the way of the oncoming bicycle. The rider had just time to twist aside and avoid him, or certainly he and his machine would have been heaped on the sprawling Owl.

But that sudden twist of the bike on a slippery road did the trick. The wheels ceased to grip, the machine shot away in a skid, and the next moment it was crashing into a hedge.

Crash! Smash! Bump!

"Oh, my hat!" gasped Wharton.

"Yaroop!" roared Bunter, struggling in snow. "Whooop! Help me gerrup! Oh crikey! Oh lor'! Beast! Help!"

THE MAGNET LIBRARY.—No. 1,352.

But Wharton did not heed him. He ran across to the overturned cyclist, who was much more in need of help.

The bicycle was jammed in the hedge, and looked as if it was tied in a sailor's knot. Obviously that jigger was badly damaged. Its rider was damaged, too, apparently. He sat up in the snow, clasping an ankle with both hands, and gasping and spluttering. Harry Wharton reached him swiftly.

"Hurt?" he panted.

"Hang you! Yes, I'm hurt!" howled the man with the ginger eyebrows. "You cheeky young scoundrel, why couldn't you clear the road?"

"Not my fault! I——"

"Hang you!"

Harry Wharton stepped back, his eyes glinting. He was wholly blameless in the matter. Bunter was rather to blame, but the fact that the sandy man had been riding fast on a frozen road was the chief cause of the accident.

The man staggered to his feet.

He did not give Wharton another look. He glanced back quickly in the direction of the Wimford road. Then he gave a look at the wrecked bike, muttered something between his teeth, and started to walk.

Wharton stared after him.

"Leaving your jigger there?" he called out.

"Mind your own business!"

"Oh, all right! Go and eat coke!" retorted Wharton, sorry that he had wasted any time or trouble on the unmannerly fellow.

The man hurried on. He was limping with his left leg; it was clear that his ankle had had a hard knock, and that he was hurt. But he covered the ground pretty quickly all the same. Evidently he was sorely pressed for time, as he had abandoned his machine where it had fallen and was going on as fast as he could move in spite of a damaged leg. And Wharton, who had noticed his quick, backward glance towards the Wimford road, glanced back also, wondering whether the man had some cause for hurry that he would not have cared to explain. But if he was pursued, there was no sign of a pursuer on the road.

Billy Bunter had succeeded in righting himself now. He was perpendicular once more, gasping and gurgling for breath. Harry Wharton rejoined him.

"Beast!" gasped Bunter. "Wharrer you push me over for?"

"You blithering owl!" snapped Wharton. "Look what you've done to that chap's bike!"

"Blow his bike!"

"He's gone trotting on with a game leg!"

"Blow his leg!"

"Oh, come on!" said Harry, and once more he took the fat arm and navigated Billy Bunter onwards.

He was feeling that if he did not say good-bye to Bunter soon his resolution would fail, and he would kick him before they parted. And he was still trying hard to get through without that.

Bunter rolled and plunged and skidded and slid and grunted and groused for the remainder of the half-mile. But Elmdale was reached at last, and the railway station there. They learned that the local train for Woodgate was in the station, and had been in the station for some time. Matters moved on easy and leisurely lines at Elmdale. Harry Wharton bought Bunter's ticket—an indispensable preliminary to the journey—and walked him on to the platform.

The train was there; but hardly a person was to be seen on the platform.

THE MAGNET LIBRARY.—No. 1,352.

Puffing vapour from the engine announced that it was getting ready to go. Harry Wharton opened the door of a carriage.

"Here you are, old fat bean!"

Bunter clambered in.

"All right now!" said Harry, glad that he had, after all, got through without kicking Bunter.

"No, rotten!" answered Bunter. "You might have lent me a rug! And a hot-water bottle! But, of course, you were too jolly slack to carry them!"

"Good-bye, Bunter!"

"Hold on—the train's not going yet. What about my fare from Woodgate? You'd better lend me a pound or two!"

"Oh!"

"I shall have to get a snack at Woodgate, too, before I go on. I can manage on a couple of pounds——"

"Not on less?" asked Wharton, with deep sarcasm.

"You needn't be afraid I shan't square!" sneered Bunter. "I told you, last term at school, that I was expecting some postal orders——"

"Oh, my hat!"

"They never came to Greyfriars——"

"Go hon!"

"So I expect they've accumulated over the holidays. I shall be in funds. I'll send you back the two pounds as soon as I get my money."

"Ten bob wouldn't be any use?"

"None at all!"

"Then I won't offer it to you. Good-bye!"

"Hold on!" yelled Bunter, as Wharton was turning away from the carriage. "I dare say I could manage on ten bob. I'll try."

The captain of the Remove turned back. Two half-crowns, four shillings, and two sixpences were transferred to Bunter's fat paw. He slipped the coins carelessly into his pocket, as if ten shillings wasn't much to him. No doubt it wasn't—it was more to the fellow who parted with it! But that did not worry Bunter.

"Hold on, Wharton——"

"Train's going," said Harry, and he shut the door.

"Hold on a minute," said Bunter, leaning from the window.

"Oh, all right!"

"Just a word before I go," said the Owl of the Remove.

"Buck up, then," said Harry, wondering what was coming. Some departing guests might have expressed something

in the way of thanks or acknowledgments; but that was hardly to be expected from William George Bunter. However, Wharton, still glad that he had succeeded in resisting the temptation to kick Bunter, was more than willing to part with him on as amicable terms as possible. So he remained at the carriage door.

Bunter blinked down at him through his big spectacles.

"I've had a rotten time at your place, Wharton," he said. "I might have expected it, knowing you as I do! I dare say it's my own fault letting pushing fellows rush me into staying at their miserable places. Your stuffy old uncle is the limit! Your frumpy old aunt is a corker! Your pals are a set of hooligans, and you're the worst of the lot. Yah!"

Harry Wharton gasped.

There was a shriek from the engine; just in time to save Bunter from the kicking he had, several times, narrowly escaped. Wharton, grasping the door handle, let it go again.

Bunter reached out with a fat paw from the window, snatched Wharton's cap, and threw it along the platform.

"You fat rotter! Why, I'll burst you!" roared Wharton.

"He, he, he!" gurgled Bunter.

The train was moving. Harry Wharton rushed after his cap, retrieved it, and glared after the gliding carriage, his feelings too deep for words. The fat face of the Owl of the Remove, safe out of danger, grinned back at him.

"He, he, he!" floated back from the train.

And Billy Bunter was gone!

Harry Wharton banged the dust out of his cap, and replaced it on his head. Then he walked out of the station, to return to Wharton Lodge and his friends—deeply regretting, after all, that he hadn't kicked Billy Bunter while there was still time!

THE THIRD CHAPTER.
Snatched!

"HALLO, hallo, hallo! That jolly old sportsman looks excited!"

"The excitefulness seems terrific!"

"Had a tumble in the snow, perhaps!" remarked Frank Nugent.

The Co. had strolled down the drive to the gates of Wharton Lodge, after the departure of Harry Wharton and Bunter. Being quite fed-up with Billy Bunter, they had left it to his host to see him off at the station; but they thought of walking out and meeting Harry on his way back from Elmdale. As they came out on the Wimford road, their attention was drawn to a stout gentleman coming from the direction of the town. They really could not help giving him a second glance, and then a third.

He was a rather short, plump gentleman, and looked all the plumper in an immense fur-collared coat. It was a very expensive coat, and still more striking than expensive. A shining silk hat on his head reflected the rays of the winter sun. His face was fat, of a rather dark complexion, and adorned by a prominent nose rather like an eagle's beak. Something, it was plain, had occurred to annoy the fur-coated gentleman. His fat face was crimson with wrath, his black eyes glittered, and he gripped a gold-headed umbrella as if with the desire to use it as a weapon of offence. And as he came rolling along the snowy road he stared, or rather, glared, to right and left as if in search of someone. He looked as if he might prove quite dangerous if he spotted that someone; but there was nobody to be seen on the road, except the four schoolboys who had just come out.

Spotting them, the fur-collared gentleman accelerated, and shouted to them as he drew nearer.

"Have you seen him?"

"Whom, sir?" asked Bob Cherry politely.

"That scoundrel!" roared the fur-collared gentleman.

"Eh?"

"That rascal!"

"He can't mean Bunter, I suppose!" remarked Johnny Bull. "And we haven't seen any other scoundrel or rascal."

"That thief!" roared the stout gentleman. "He was on a bicycle."

"Sorry, sir, we haven't seen anybody," is the place. You can telephone to the police from here, and very likely they'll bag him before he can get clear. A man won't get far on a bike on roads like this."

"Goot! Yeth, yeth!" said the stout gentleman, who seemed to be slightly afflicted with a lisp. "It is not ten minutes since he ropped me. He cannot be far away—he must have passed here—he came in this direction. So thith is Wharton Lodge, what, what?"

"Yes, sir—straight up to the house—Colonel Wharton is at home——"

The stout gentleman hurried in at the gateway and trotted up to the house, panting. The four juniors went on their way towards Elmdale.

"Might keep an eye open for that pickpocket," remarked Johnny Bull. "He must have turned into this lane, I think——"

"In which case, my dear Watson," said Bob, in playful imitation of the celebrated Sherlock Holmes, "I deduce that he will hoof it for the nearest railway station."

"Bound to," said Johnny Bull.

"And that's Elmdale," said Bob. "And here's the jolly old tracks in the snow leading right on."

The chums of the Remove were all Scouts, and the "sign" was plain enough for any Scout to read. The footprints left by Wharton and Bunter were clear. At this spot a third set of footprints started from where the fallen bike lay—evidently those of the cyclist who had abandoned his wrecked jigger. The track went on towards Elmdale, and Bob, whose eyes were very keen, even noted that the track of one foot was lighter than the other, which looked as if the man had been hurt by

"Yaroooh!" Billy Bunter slipped on the icy snow and rolled over, fairly in the way of the oncoming cyclist. The rider tried to avoid a collision, but in so doing, his bike skidded and went crashing into the hedge. Crash! Smash! Bump! "Oh, my hat!" gasped Wharton.

said Bob. "Only just come down from the house."

"A shrimp of a man with a sandy complexion! He was on a bicycle! He snatched my tiepin and jumped on his machine and got away! By Chove, he has got away with a diamond worth a hundred pounds."

"Oh, my hat!"

The juniors suppressed their desire to smile. The stout gentleman, with his magnificent fur collar, looked as if he might have had a diamond tiepin worth a hundred pounds. Probably his fur-trimmed gloves concealed rings of even greater value.

"The rascal! The villain!" spluttered the stout gentleman. "I stopped him to ask the way to Wharton Lodge, by Chove! And he got off his machine to point out the way, by Chove—at least, I thought so—and then he snatched my tiepin—the rascal—the scoundrel——" He gurgled with wrath. "You are sure you have not theen him?"

"Sorry, sir, no," said Bob. "But if you're looking for Wharton Lodge, this

"Hallo, hallo, hallo! Look!"

Bob Cherry pointed to a wrecked bicycle, jammed in the hedge. The juniors stopped and stared at it. Someone, evidently, had come to grief there, and bikes were few and far between on the frozen roads. Anyone riding fast on that frozen surface was likely to come to grief; and a pickpocket getting away with a diamond pin worth a hundred pounds was likely to have put on all the speed he could. In fact, there could scarcely be a doubt that this bike was the thief's machine. It was not a valuable bike—a second-hand dealer might have hesitated to give a pound for it. Still, it was extremely unusual for a cyclist to desert his machine and leave it abandoned by the roadside, unless he had very pressing reasons for haste.

"Ten to one that's the sportsman's jigger!" said Bob. "He came a cropper here—what?"

"A hundred to one!" said Nugent. "In fact, it's pretty certain. The man's on foot now."

his fall, and was limping as he went. The juniors stared up the road.

"Might catch the blighter, if we raced for it," said Bob. "From what that old johnny said, we can't be more than twenty minutes behind him."

"Better get back and tell the old bean," said Frank. "He can tip the police station on the phone."

"Yes; let's."

The juniors ran back, and up the drive to Wharton Lodge. The big door stood open, and the fur-collared gentleman was in the hall. Colonel Wharton was there, also. And Wells, the butler, had taken the fur-collared coat, and Thomas had taken the shining, silk topper.

"My dear Mr. Isaacs," the colonel was saying, "what—what——" The fur-collared man had only just got in.

"Ropped!" he panted. "Ropped of my diamond pin! A scoundrel on a bicycle! Where is the telephone? What is the numper of the police station —what?"

THE MAGNET LIBRARY.—No. 1,352.

"This way!" said the colonel.

"Hold on, sir!" exclaimed Bob Cherry breathlessly. "We've got something for you to tell the police."

The stout man spun round at him. There was a flash of precious stones on his fat fingers, now that his gloves were off. Evidently he was a very expensive gentleman in the jewellery line.

"What?" he exclaimed. "You have theen the rascal?"

"No, sir; but I'm pretty sure we've spotted his bike," said Bob; and he hurriedly explained.

"Good!" exclaimed Mr. Isaacs, when Bob had finished. "Very good, my boy! A very observant lad, by Chove! If the rascal makes for a railway station, he will be caught with the diamond on him, by Chove! If I may use your telephone, sir——"

"This way!" said Colonel Wharton; and he led the stout gentleman to the telephone cabinet.

A minute more and Inspector Stacey, at Wimford Police Station, knew all about it, and had promised to take instant and adequate measures.

Meanwhile, Bob Cherry and his friends restarted to walk down to Elmdale. The deserted bike still lay in the hedge when they passed the spot again. They followed the track of the limping man in the thick snow. It led directly onward, and there was little, or rather no doubt, that he had gone on to the village on foot after deserting his machine. Having lost his machine he had little choice but to take to the railway to get away from the vicinity with his plunder. He could hardly have hoped to escape on foot—especially if he had a "game" leg. Probably he had caught the same train as Billy Bunter at Elmdale.

Half-way to the village they sighted Harry Wharton, and hurried on to join him, curious to know whether he had seen anything of the man who had got away with a hundred pound diamond belonging to his uncle's visitor.

THE FOURTH CHAPTER.
The Man Under the Seat !

BILLY BUNTER grinned as he sat down.

He was feeling rather bucked. It was some satisfaction to have told that beast Wharton what he thought of him, of his relatives, and of his friends. It was a still greater satisfaction to have snatched off Wharton's cap, and thrown it along the platform, and got away safely after that performance. And Bunter had still more solid causes of satisfaction—in the shape of various refreshments that he now proceeded to turn out of his overcoat pockets. He had a nice packet of sandwiches prepared by Miss Amy Wharton herself, in blissful ignorance of the fact that Billy Bunter regarded her as an old frump and a "corker." He had a box of chocolates that he had picked up in Wharton's den; a packet of toffee that he had found in Bob Cherry's room; a bag of bullseyes that Johnny Bull had missed; some toffee-apples that Frank Nugent had bought in Wimford, and two or three other rather nice things which their legitimate owners were never likely to see again.

And though Bunter had been so heartlessly and unfeelingly deprived of his baggage, he had on Johnny Bull's warmest pair of socks, Hurree Singh's warm, wool muffler, and a collar and tie for which Harry Wharton was likely to hunt in vain. And Bob Cherry's pullover under his coat kept him nice and warm. And as the handkerchief that stuck out of his pocket was clean, it was obviously not Bunter's own.

Altogether Bunter had not done so badly over the Christmas holidays. And if he succeeded in "sticking" Lord Mauleverer for the rest of the vacation, he felt that it would be all right. As a last resource there was home. His people had now returned from their Christmas visit to relations, and home, sweet home was once more available. But Bunter was not frightfully keen on home, sweet home. He preferred to roam from Dan to Beersheba.

If Mauly failed him—and Mauly, like nearly everybody else, except Bunter, was a beast—there was Smithy; he might give Herbert Vernon-Smith a look in, with a wary eye open, of course, for Smithy's boot.

He sat and grinned over his farewell to Wharton, and finished the sandwiches, and then chewed chocolates with great satisfaction. The train was slow; but he had plenty to occupy him till he reached Woodgate. He had not started on the toffee, or the toffee-apples yet. There was no stop till Woodgate, which was the terminus of the little local line, so Bunter had the carriage to himself. At least, he naturally supposed that he had, as he was the only passenger sitting in it. But there was a surprise in store for Bunter.

A toffee-apple slipped from his fat fingers, and rolled on the floor. He stooped to pick it up.

Then he gave a startled squeak.

"Ow! Oh crikey!"

He remained stooping, transfixed with astonishment and alarm, his little, round eyes almost popping through his big, round spectacles, at a face that stared at him from under the carriage seat.

He was not alone in the carriage. A slim, slightly built man with sandy eyebrows was stretched under the seat, and would probably have remained there undiscovered, had not Bunter dropped that toffee-apple.

His narrow eyes glittered at Bunter. Evidently he was not pleased at being discovered.

"Oh lor'!" gasped Bunter. "Wha-a-at are you doing there?"

The man crawled out from under the seat.

Although it was clear that he had desired to remain there undiscovered, it was a relief to him to stretch his cramped limbs in freedom now that his presence was known.

Bunter blinked at him, recognising the man now.

It was the man who had tumbled over on the snowy road when the bike skidded. Evidently he had headed for Elmdale Railway Station, and had caught the same train as Bunter. Billy Bunter gave him a very severe blink. He fancied that he could guess why the fellow had been hidden under the seat.

Bunter had travelled under the seat of a railway carriage himself more than once when he was minus a ticket.

On the present occasion, however, Bunter was travelling like an honest citizen, with a ticket, bought and paid for, in his pocket.

So he was very contemptuous of "bilks."

He sat down in his corner again. The sandy man gave a quick glance from the window. Only a snowy landscape and leafless trees met his eyes; the train was

nowhere near Woodgate yet. He sat down opposite Bunter.

Bunter regarded him with scornful indifference, and chewed toffee-apples. The man watched his fat face intently as he chewed. No doubt he recognised Bunter as the fat fellow who had helped to cause that spill on his bike. But if he was feeling resentment, he did not show it. His face was deeply clouded with thought.

"How long before we get to Woodgate, sir?" he asked, breaking the silence and speaking very civilly.

Bunter thawed. The man addressed him as "sir," and was very civil, indeed, respectful. That pleased Bunter.

"'Nother ten minutes," he answered with his mouth full. "You'd better jolly well look out when we get there, too!"

The man gave a start.

"What do you mean?" he exclaimed sharply. "Have you seen——" He broke off. "What do you mean?"

Bunter gave him a fat wink.

"They collect tickets there," he said. "It's the terminus."

"Tickets!" repeated the sandy man blankly.

"Think I don't know why you were travelling under the seat?" grinned Bunter. "I've been there myself—I mean, I jolly well know that you're bilking the company."

"Oh! I—I see!" The sandy man smiled. "Exactly! You are a very keen young gentleman, sir."

Bunter smiled.

"I know my way about," he remarked complacently.

Any fellow less obtuse than Bunter might have guessed, from the man's look and tone, that whatever might have been his reason for travelling under the seat, it was not because he was bilking the railway company. But the Owl of the Remove had no doubt.

"I believe they're rather sharp on this line," added Bunter, with an amiable desire to make his fellow-passenger feel uneasy. "They'll nail you at Woodgate all right."

"Think so, sir?"

"Sure of it!" said Bunter cheerfully.

The man sat silent again, his brows wrinkled with thought. The train crawled and rattled on its slow way. The sandy man spoke again.

"Trade's pretty bad, sir, and a man may be short of money."

Bunter blinked at him sternly. If this fellow was thinking of "touching" Bunter for the price of his railway ticket, he had to think again! Bunter's worldly wealth amounted to exactly ten shillings; and he was not going to part with any of it if he knew it.

"I think I've seen you before, sir!" went on the sandy man, eyeing Bunter keenly and furtively. "Your name's Montague, I think, sir?"

"No, it isn't; it's Bunter."

It did not even occur to Bunter's mind that the man was "pumping" him, and had some reason for wanting to know his name.

"Going back to school, sir?"

"Eh! Not till the end of the hols," answered Bunter. "We don't go back to Greyfriars for a couple of weeks yet."

"Greyfriars!" repeated the sandy man.

"That's my school!" said Bunter loftily.

The sandy man nodded and smiled. He knew now Bunter's name, and where he was to be found again, if that was what he wanted to know. He was silent again, thinking hard, though the mental problem he was wrestling with had nothing to do with a railway ticket, as Bunter supposed.

"Look here, sir," he went on, after a pause. "I'm hard up, as you've guessed. If you'd like——"

"I never lend anything!" said Bunter. Which was true. Borrowing was Bunter's long suit.

"I didn't mean that, sir! If you like to buy something——" The man slid his hand into an inner pocket. "To tell you the truth, sir, I'm a dealer in artificial jewellery, and I've got a diamond pin——"

"Catch me wearing paste jewellery!" said Bunter, with a sniff. "Not our style at Greyfriars, I can assure you."

"It's rather decent, sir, and even an expert could hardly tell it from the genuine article," said the sandy man. "Anybody looking at it would think it was a real diamond worth a hundred pounds. I'll let you have it for—for enough to pay for my railway ticket."

"That's only a bob from Elmdale," said Bunter. "But I'm not buying any rubbish, thanks!"

"Well, just look at it, sir!" said the sandy man, and he drew his hand from his pocket.

Billy Bunter looked, and fairly jumped at the sight of the gleaming, glittering diamond that lay in the man's palm.

———

THE FIFTH CHAPTER.
A Bargain for Bunter!

"PHEW!" gasped Bunter.

He blinked at the diamond tiepin.

Bunter knew little or nothing about precious stones and their value. But even Bunter could see that this was a magnificent stone. If it was an imitation, even Bunter could see that it was a wonderful imitation of the genuine article.

"Not bad, sir, for an imitation diamond!" remarked the sandy man, with furtive eyes on Bunter's fat face.

"Jolly good!" said Bunter. "Blessed if I shouldn't have thought it was real."

"Wonderful things they make nowadays, sir," said the sandy man. "I usually get ten shillings for these, sir," —he coughed—"but in the present circumstances, sir, if you'd make it a bob——"

Bunter blinked at the glittering diamond.

"Well, of course, I can see it's not real," he remarked, on second thoughts, as it were. Bunter was not going to admit that he could possibly be taken in. "I can see that all right."

"Can you really, sir?" asked the sandy man, with quite a peculiar intonation in his voice.

"Oh, yes!" said Bunter carelessly. "You see, I've a good many diamond pins and things at home. I'm rather used to expensive things. Still, it's a jolly good imitation—I don't mind saying that."

"Just the price of my railway ticket, sir!" murmured the sandy man.

Bunter's eyes gleamed behind his big spectacles.

At Greyfriars, it was true, fellows did not sport diamond pins; such adornments were considered bad form. But the Bounder had one or two, which he sometimes wore, and other "dressy" fellows had such things, which they put on, on occasion. Billy Bunter, certainly, would have been very pleased indeed to display an expensive pin like the Bounder's.

Obvious paste even Bunter would not have worn. But this imitation diamond looked wonderfully real. It looked as real as Smithy's, that was certain. Bunter undoubtedly would have taken it for a real one. Indeed, he would have

believed now that it was real, but for the fact that the sandy man offered it to him for a shilling!

With that gleaming diamond in his tie, Billy Bunter saw himself making quite a sensation in the Rag at Greyfriars!

Nobody would dream that he had bought it for a shilling! It looked absolutely the genuine article.

Little did the fat and fatuous junior guess that it was, in fact, the genuine article, and that he was getting landed with stolen goods!

Neither did it occur to him that his ownership of the diamond pin was intended to be merely temporary.

Had the sandy man got away on his bicycle, Mr. Isaacs' big diamond would have gone with him, and he would never have been seen again till it reached a receiver of stolen goods.

But the spill in the snow had put the stopper on that. The sandy man had got to Elmdale with his "game" leg, and got into the train—carefully ensconcing himself under the seat to avoid the public eye! But he was well aware that the telephone would be at work before him. The man he had robbed was not likely to lose time.

On his bike he might have put a safe distance between himself and the scene of the snatching. But he had had to take to the railway. And at every railway station there was a telephone.

The police, no doubt, would be looking for a man on a bike! But they would hardly overlook the fact that he might dodge into a train, especially as the roads were in an almost impassable state.

It seemed only too probable to the sandy man that some obnoxious official at Wimford Police Station had already phoned through to all the railway stations in the district, and that some disagreeable man in a blue uniform might be watching at Woodgate, and elsewhere, for a sandy man of his description.

In which case, the sandy man did not want to have Mr. Isaacs' diamond in his pocket when he was tapped on the shoulder.

Neither did he want to pitch it out of the train window, after all his trouble and risk.

Since Bunter had discovered him in the carriage, the sandy man had been putting in some hard thinking—though not, as Bunter supposed, on the subject of the lack of a railway ticket.

Bunter, in fact, had turned up quite luckily for him—if only he was obtuse enough to believe that that gleaming diamond was a sham, and to take it off the snatcher's hands temporarily.

After which, the sandy man would be able to step out at Woodgate easy in his mind.

If he was tapped on the shoulder there, the diamond was out of his hands; and even if he went to the "stone jug," there would be a prospect of recovering it later from Master Bunter, of Greyfriars School.

On the other hand, if he was not stopped at Woodgate, the recovery of that diamond would not be long postponed. He had only to follow Bunter, and do another "snatching" trick! That was easy enough.

Little dreaming of what was in the rascal's mind, Billy Bunter blinked at the diamond, and felt in his pocket for one of Wharton's shillings!

He had no doubt that the diamond was a sham! But even as a sham it was a bargain at a "bob." Bunter had seen sham diamonds before—but never one that looked so real as this!

He extracted a shilling from his

pocket, and passed it across to the man, and received the diamond pin in exchange.

He stood up and adjusted it in his tie in the little glass over the carriage seat.

"Looks real now I've got it on!" he remarked, with satisfaction. "What?"

"Quite, sir!" said the sandy man.

"Most fellows don't know so much about diamonds as I do," remarked Bunter. "I fancy it will pass all right."

The sandy man smiled.

Bunter sat down again. The train, slow as it was, was very near Woodgate now.

The sandy man eyed the gleaming diamond in Bunter's tie rather uneasily. He would have preferred the fat Owl to put it in his pocket. Still, it was not likely that suspicious eyes would be turned on a fat schoolboy. If a man in blue was waiting for that train at Woodgate, he was watching for a small, thin, weedy, sandy-coloured man, not for a fat schoolboy with cheeks like ripe apples.

"Here's the station," grinned Bunter at last. "You'll be able to pay your fare now—what?"

"Yes, sir, thanks to your kindness!" said the sandy man.

"Oh, not at all!" said Bunter benevolently.

The sandy man, keeping his cap low over his eyes, peered from the window anxiously as the train ran into Woodgate station. His thin lips came hard together at the sight of a portly police-constable on the platform, in talk with a man who was plainly the station-master. Two or three porters loitered about, with unusually keen eyes on the incoming train.

The sandy man knew what it meant. From the bottom of his rascally heart he was glad that he had landed Mr. Isaacs' pin on Bunter! Its recovery later was probable; but that was not of so much importance as getting rid of it at the present moment.

As the train stopped, the sandy man opened the carriage door and jumped out. He walked quickly down the platform before the train had quite stopped.

He was a dozen yards from the window where Bunter was when the stationmaster, the police-constable, and a couple of porters gathered round him.

He was politely requested to accompany the constable to the stationmaster's office; and as it was clear that the man in blue would take no denial, the sandy man did so with the best grace possible in the distressing circumstances.

Of that little scene Billy Bunter saw nothing.

He was busy packing into his overcoat pockets the remnants of tuck that he had not guzzled on the journey.

When he stepped out of the carriage the sandy man was already gone from the platform, and Billy Bunter did not give him a thought.

He rolled away to the bridge over the lines, where he had to change trains; and five minutes later he was seated in an express, finishing what remained of the tuck, and absolutely forgetful of the sandy man.

THE SIXTH CHAPTER.
Where?

"HALLO, hallo, hallo! Seen him?" asked Bob Cherry.

Harry Wharton laughed.

"Whom?" he asked. "I've seen several people since I left you. Best of all, I've seen the last of Bunter. The fat scoundrel snatched off my cap and threw it along the platform at the last minute——"

"Ha, ha, ha!"

"I'll jolly well kick him first day of the new term!" said Harry.

"The kickfulness is the proper caper," agreed Hurree Jamset Ram Singh. "But have you seen the esteemed and disgusting pickpocket?"

"Eh, what?" Wharton stared. "Not many pickpockets in these parts, old black bean! Somebody lifted your watch?"

"Sandy man, small build, recently spilled off a bike!" said Bob Cherry. "He's pinched a jolly old diamond from a gent of the name of Isaacs, who's visiting your nunky."

Wharton gave a start.

"My hat! That must be the blighter who was pitched off his bike when that fat idiot Bunter got in his way! I wondered at the time if there was somebody after him," he said. "He seemed in a frightful hurry. But how did you know, Bob?"

Bob winked at his comrades.

"Deduction, my dear Watson," he said, again in playful imitation of Sherlock Holmes. "We found the bike lying in the hedge, looking as if it had been under a lorry, and deduced that there had been an accident."

"Not a fearfully difficult deduction," said Harry, laughing. "But how do you know about the man on it?"

"From the brand of the tyres, my dear Watson, I deduce that the rider had a sandy complexion——"

"Wha-at?"

"And, from the make of the mudguards, I deduce that he was a small size in sportsmen—in fact, a shrimp of a man."

Harry Wharton stared blankly at his chum. Certainly, Bob had described the cyclist accurately. But he was not likely to believe that Bob had made those "deductions" in the well-known manner of Sherlock Holmes.

"And how did you know he had pinched a diamond?" he asked.

"From the size of his boots, traced by his footprints in the snow," said Bob gravely. "To the trained eye of a detective, my dear Watson——"

"And how the thump did you know that a man named Isaacs was coming to see my uncle to-day?"

"I deduced that, my dear Watson, from the fact that I heard Colonel Wharton address him as Mr. Isaacs."

"Ha, ha, ha!"

"Oh, you've seen the man, then?" exclaimed Harry.

Bob Cherry chuckled.

"Yes, old bean! I dare say Sherlock Holmes could have deduced his name, age, form, and starting price from the bicycle-tracks or the pickpocket's sandy complexion——"

"Ha, ha, ha!"

"But the fact is we ran into him when we started after you, and he told us that a small-sized blighter on a bike, with a sandy chivvy, had snatched

his jolly old diamond tiepin," said Bob, laughing. "Quite simple when I explain it, my dear Watson—what?"

"That was the man, then," said Harry. "He damaged his leg tumbling off the bike, but he went on pretty quickly, and I lost sight of him. I suppose he went to Elmdale."

"You didn't see him there, at the station?"

"No; I only walked as fast as Bunter—which is about as fast as a snail on its last legs. He had lots of time to catch the train if he wanted to. Poor old Isaacs!" said Harry. "He's lost his diamond, then."

"Well, he seems to have lots," said Bob. "Never saw such a decorated merchant; he will hardly miss one. But he seemed fearfully excited about it, all the same. Who is the sportsman?"

"Uncle mentioned him to me this morning—a City man coming down to see him about mining shares, or something," said Harry. "The car would have been sent for him if it had been possible. Look here, ten to one that thief got a train at Elmdale, and if they telephone——"

"That's done already," said Nugent. "We left Mr. Isaacs doing a solo on the phone when we came out. So it was Bunter that upset Mr. Sandyman?"

"Yes, there was only one bike on the road, and Bunter had to get in the way of it. Rather lucky, as it turns out, if the man was a thief!"

The Famous Five walked back to Wharton Lodge. When they arrived there Mr. Isaacs was shut up in the library with the colonel; doubtless having dismissed the affair of the "snatcher" from his mind, for the time, and reverted to the business on which he had come to Wharton Lodge. The chums of the Remove had their packing to do, and they proceeded to get it done, as they were leaving after tea, to take the train from Wimford for Johnny Bull's home.

At tea, however, they had the pleasure of seeing Mr. Isaacs. He proved to be quite a genial and pleasant gentleman, though his taste in jewellery was on the expansive side. Whenever he moved there was a glitter and a sparkle from some part of his person. He seemed to have recovered from the excitement and wrath caused by the loss of his big diamond pin, and the juniors rather liked him, dazzling as he was.

Just as tea was over Wells brought in the news that Mr. Isaacs was wanted on the telephone. When he came out of the telephone cabinet he was smiling and rubbing his hands.

"Good news. I hope, sir?" said Colonel Wharton, with a smile.

"I think so," said Mr. Isaacs. "A man answering the description I gave the police has been detained at Woodgate. He arrived by the train from the village close by here. His name, it seems, is Sniggerson, and he has a doubtful reputation. I have no doubt he is the man. I shall have to go over and identify him."

Harry Wharton & Co. had to leave for their train soon afterwards, so they did not learn the result of Mr. Isaacs' visit to Woodgate.

That visit, in point of fact, was rather a disappointment to Mr. Isaacs.

Certainly, he identified the sandy man who had snatched his tiepin, and Mr. Sniggerson, who had hitherto been detained on suspicion, was now detained to go before the magistrates.

But a search of Mr. Sniggerson failed to reveal the diamond pin.

That he had snatched it and got away with it was assured; but that it was no longer in his possession was equally certain.

As the train began to move, Bunter thrust a fat paw out of the window, snatched Wharton's cap, and threw it along the platform. "You fat rotter!" yelled Wharton. "Why, I'll burst you!" "He, he, he!" floated back from the train.

What he had done with it, Mr. Sniggerson declined to state; indeed, he maintained stolidly that it was a case of mistaken identity, and that he had never seen Mr. Isaacs before.

That he had passed it on to some confederate seemed possible.

But that he had passed it on to a fat and fatuous youth named Billy Bunter, who was going to take it back to school with him for purposes of "swank," no one was likely to guess!

Mr. Sniggerson was not likely to mention that.

Whether he would escape "chokey," as the stolen goods had not been found on him, or whether he would get the three months' "hard" that he richly deserved, Mr. Sniggerson did not yet know.

But he knew that, sooner or later, he was going to interview the fat schoolboy named Bunter, at the school called Greyfriars, and get that diamond pin away from him again.

That prospect was a consolation to the sandy man in his present time of trouble.

THE SEVENTH CHAPTER.
A Happy Meeting!

"MAULY!" yelled Billy Bunter. It was real luck!

"The shades of night were falling fast," as a poet has already remarked.

Billy Bunter had alighted at the station for Mauleverer Towers, in Hampshire, many a long mile from Wharton Lodge.

Mauleverer Towers was his destination now.

Having expended the whole of Wharton's ten shillings on the purchase of a diamond pin, railway tickets, and a little refreshment, Billy Bunter was minus the necessary sum to hire a taxi to Mauly's stately abode.

It was rather a long walk, and Bunter was not keen on walking.

During the afternoon the sun had come out very brightly, and there had been a thaw. The roads were fearfully sloppy, and, apart from his rooted objection to exertion, Bunter did not want to tramp through melted snow and sloppy mire and arrive at Mauleverer Towers in a mud-bespattered state.

He was by no means certain of what kind of welcome he would receive there, anyhow, as Mauly did not know that he was coming, and could not—by the widest stretch of imagination—be supposed to want him there.

Still, now that Wharton Lodge had, as it were, dried up, Bunter had to land himself somewhere, and he was going to land himself on Mauly if he could.

At such a place as Mauleverer Towers, Bunter would have preferred to arrive in decent style. But the unfeeling selfishness of the Famous Five had prevented him from arriving there with a well-packed suitcase. Still, he could avoid arriving in a muddy and spattered state by taking a taxi—if only he could be sure that Mauly would pay for the taxi! Even Bunter realised that it was a little "thick" for an uninvited guest to land himself on a disconcerted host and ask, first of all, for that host to pay his taxi-fare! On the other hand, the roads, though dreadfully sloppy, were now safe for wheels, and there were taxis to be had at the station.

Bunter was debating that knotty point in his fat mind when a big car glided along, and, in surprise and satisfaction, he recognised a rather slim and well-dressed youth who was sitting in it.

It was something like luck!

He did not want a taxi now! He fairly bounded into the road, waved a fat hand, and roared:

"Mauly!"

The liveried chauffeur who drove Lord Mauleverer's handsome car stared at him. So did Lord Mauleverer.

"Oh gad!" ejaculated the schoolboy earl; and even Billy Bunter could not imagine that he looked delighted.

"Stop, old chap!" yelled Bunter.

Mauly signed to the chauffeur to halt. He would have preferred to tell him to stamp on the gas. But the schoolboy earl of Greyfriars was always good-natured and easy-going.

Bunter hooked open the door.

"Fancy meeting you, old chap!" he beamed.

"Yaas."

"Going home?"

"Yaas."

"Give me a lift."

"Where?"

Bunter coughed.

"Well, the fact is, Mauly, I—I've got to put up for the night somewhere—just for the night, you know. The fact is, I'm going to stay with Smithy—he's been so pressing that I haven't felt able to refuse. But just for to-night, I dare say you could give a fellow a bed?"

Lord Mauleverer gazed at him.

He knew his Bunter!

If William George Bunter was landed at Mauleverer Towers for the night, nothing short of a boot, applied vigorously to his tight trousers, would get him out of Mauleverer Towers again.

Mauly seemed rather at a loss.

Perhaps his aristocratic brain did not work swiftly. Bunter's, however, did! While Mauly gazed at him, Bunter clambered into the car.

"You can drive on!" he said to the chauffeur.

"Oh gad!" said Lord Mauleverer.

"Jolly to meet like this—what, old chap?" said Bunter affably. "Sheer chance, you know. Hadn't an idea I was within miles of you."

"Oh!"

"Your chauffeur seems deaf. Tell him to get a move on! To tell you the truth, old chap, I'm rather hungry!"

Lord Mauleverer still gazed at him. He seemed to be thinking something out. Finally he spoke.

"Did you say you were hungry, Bunter?"

"Yes, old chap! Frightfully!"

"There's a pastry-cook's next to the station——"

"I noticed that!" said Bunter. The Owl of the Remove had an eye for such establishments.

"What about gettin' a cake?" asked Lord Mauleverer.

Bunter beamed.

"Dear old chap!" he said affectionately. "If those rotters at Wharton Lodge were more like you, I wouldn't have turned them down! But I had to, you know! I simply had to! 'No, old fellow,' I said to Wharton; 'I can stand you, and even your dashed old uncle, but I'm not coming on to Bull's place with you! You can't expect it!' My very words. Bull was rather cut up, but——"

"Well, hop out and get that cake!"

"Like a bird!" said Bunter. "By the way, though, I lent Wharton my last banknote——"

"Oh gad!"

"The fact is, I'm absolutely stony! You'd hardly believe it, but——"

"Yaas, I can sort of believe it," said Lord Mauleverer. "Any objection to me lendin' you half-a-crown?"

"None at all, old fellow! I never borrow, as a rule; but from a pal like you——"

Bunter stepped out of the car, with the half-crown in his fat hand, and scudded into the pastry-cook's. He was gone three minutes. During those three minutes Lord Mauleverer talked to his chauffeur.

A faint grin dawned for a moment on the chauffeur's face as Lord Mauleverer talked.

"You understand, Robinson?" asked Mauly.

"Yes, my lord! Quite!"

Lord Mauleverer sank back in his seat as Billy Bunter came scudding back to the car with a cake under his arm. The fat Owl of the Remove clambered in. The door banged and the car moved on.

Bunter unwrapped the cake.

"Have some, Mauly?"

"'Hem! No, thanks! Pile in, old fat man!"

"It's a jolly good cake," said Bunter with his mouth full. "Happy thought of yours, Mauly!" He blinked out of the car. "I say, your man isn't going on to the Towers—he's taking another road——"

"I'm going for a drive," said Lord Mauleverer.

"I thought you said you were going home?"

"So I was."

"Changed your mind?" asked Bunter, puzzled.

"Sort of feel I'd like to have a long drive now you're in the car, Bunter!" answered Lord Mauleverer blandly.

"My dear chap, all right!" Bunter beamed. "I say, though, the roads are filthy for a long drive. Couldn't get a car out at all early this afternoon, or I should be in the pater's Rolls now. Still, if you want a drive, old fellow, I'm

agreeable. Sure you won't have some of this cake?"

"Quite, thanks!"

"Then I'll finish it!" said Bunter. And he did, without undue delay.

THE EIGHTH CHAPTER.
Home, Sweet Home!

LORD MAULEVERER leaned back in the cushioned seat in the soft, shaded light in the car.

Darkness had fallen now, and the big Rolls was going at a good speed through deep gloom and shadows. The roads, as Bunter had declared, were filthy; thawed snow and mud splashed from the revolving wheels. A light drizzle was falling, too. But inside the car all was comfortable and cosy; and Billy Bunter's fat face expressed satisfaction. Mauly's expressed nothing. It seemed that Mauly had taken a fancy to a rather long drive, for mile after mile ran under the wheels. Bunter did not mind, so long as he arrived at the Towers by the time he was hungry again after the cake. A half-crown cake formed a fairly good "snack," even for Bunter; and for the moment he was not hungry.

But he was a little puzzled. Lord Mauleverer, he gathered, had run out in the car after tea, and had been going back to his home when Bunter had spotted him by the railway station. Now, because Bunter was in the car, he had decided on a long—a very long—drive! If this was because Bunter's company in the car was so very pleasant, it was rather flattering. But was it?

The weather was not really agreeable for motoring. Darkness, road lamps, glimmering village lights, floated by the car; drizzle wetted the panes. And still the car ran on and on and on.

Billy Bunter leaned back, closed his eyes behind his spectacles, and dozed! He was tired after his travels.

He was soon snoring!

A deep snore mingled with the hum of the car. Lord Mauleverer glanced at him once or twice.

Mauly was not exactly an observant fellow. He never noticed what anybody wore! But he could not help catching the glitter of Bunter's magnificent diamond pin.

The fat junior started into wakefulness at last. Inward premonitions warned him that it was time for another meal.

He rubbed his eyes, blinked, set his spectacles on his fat little nose again, and looked round. The car was still eating up the miles through the January dark and drizzle.

"I say, Mauly——"

"Yaas?"

"What time do you dine at the Towers?"

"Eight!"

"Isn't it eight yet?"

"Yaas!"

"Then you'll be late for dinner?"

"Yaas!"

"I say, old chap, you shouldn't be late for meals," said Bunter anxiously. "I'm not thinking about myself—I never do, you know——"

"Eh?"

"But you have to consider your health, old fellow! It's frightfully bad for the health to be late for meals. Better tell your man to buck up." Bunter blinked from the window into the winter gloom. "Are we far from the Towers now?"

"Yaas!"

"Well, you're rather an ass, old chap!"

"Yaas!"

Billy Bunter suppressed his irritation. But it was not easy! He was getting

hungry—seriously hungry! What was the use of rushing about in a car after dark, in a dismal drizzle of wet, when a fellow might be sitting down to a solid, substantial meal? Bunter thought it simply idiotic!

But Lord Mauleverer gave no sign; and the car sped on.

"Shall we be long getting in now, Mauly?" asked Bunter at length.

"Yaas! I mean, no!"

"Well, the sooner, the better!" grunted Bunter.

"Yaas!"

"Like my diamond pin, Mauly?" asked Bunter, remembering that adornment. "Rather neat, what?"

"Yaas."

"It's an heirloom, really," said Bunter. "Been in the family hundreds of years. But I had rather a fancy for having it made up into a tiepin, you know! What are you grinning at, Mauly?"

"W-w-was I grinnin', dear boy?"

"Rather a decent stone, what?" said Bunter, fingering the pin. "I don't mind telling you that it cost a cool couple of hundred, Mauly!"

"Oh gad!" said Mauly.

"Two-fifty, to be exact!" said Bunter airily, and apparently forgetful of his statement that it had been in the family hundreds of years. "Rather extravagant, do you think? Still, when a fellow has tons of money, why not spend it, what?"

"Oh! Yaas!"

"Hallo, your man's stopping!" said Bunter, blinking round. "We're not at the Towers, are we?"

"No!"

"What's he getting down for, then?"

"Askin' the way, perhaps!"

"Doesn't he know the way?" yapped Bunter, who was getting very impatient. "If one of our chauffeurs couldn't find his way, Mauly, we should sack him!"

"Yaas."

"The fact is, I'm hungry!" said Bunter.

"Yaas."

The car was at a standstill by the roadside, the engine still running. The chauffeur seemed to have disappeared in the gloom. Bunter blinked round with growing impatience and annoyance. He really failed to understand all this! It was odd, to say the least, that Mauleverer had suddenly decided on a very long drive as soon as Bunter was in the car. And the drive was not only very long, but very long indeed! After all this time they were apparently so far from home that the chauffeur had to inquire his way! It was all very puzzling and irritating to a fellow who wanted a solid meal.

But the man came back at last, remounted into the driving-seat, and ran the car on. Another mile glided under the wheels.

Then there was another halt.

The chauffeur dismounted and opened the door. Bunter, with a grunt of relief, rose to his feet. It seemed, after all, that they had not been far from their destination. All was dense darkness, with a drizzle of rain and a blurring of mist. But there was a faint glimmer of light from some window at a distance.

Bunter stepped from the car and blinked round him.

"Step straight on, sir!" said the chauffeur.

"Come on, Mauly!" said Bunter over a fat shoulder.

He stepped on, anxious to get out of the dark and drizzle. He was not bothering much about Mauly.

There was a buzz of the car behind him. It was in motion again, and Bunter supposed that it was going round to the garage.

But he blinked about him in annoyed

puzzlement. There was a gate in front of him, dim in the dark, but there was no sign of the lofty portals of Mauleverer Towers. Why the thump had the car stopped there instead of driving up to the mansion?

"I say, Mauly!"

Bunter blinked round.

There was no answer.

"Mauly!" roared Bunter.

No reply.

Either Mauly had lost himself in the darkness, or he had remained in the car.. And the car was gone!

"Mauly!" yelled Bunter.

But only echo replied from the rain. More and more puzzled, more and more irritated, Bunter stamped on to the gate and opened it. If this was one of the entrances to Mauleverer Towers, it was utterly unlike any that he had seen on a previous visit to that palatial abode. But what else could it be? The chauffeur could hardly have stopped at the wrong house!

Bunter tramped up a weedy, gravel path. Before him loomed a double-fronted villa, which even in the gloom had a familiar aspect somehow. But it was nothing whatever like Mauleverer Towers. Blinds were drawn at the windows; lights glimmered dimly through. Where was he?

Was it possible—barely possible—that Mauly had been pulling his leg? Had he arrived at Mauleverer Towers at all? If not, where had he arrived? More and more the aspect of the place seemed familiar.

He groped to the door and rang the bell. That was the only way of discovering where he was.

A small maid opened the door.

Bunter blinked at her.

"Sarah!" he ejaculated.

A fat face with a large pair of spectacles, remarkably like Billy Bunter's own visage, looked out of a door on the hall. It was the face of Sammy Bunter—William George's young brother.

Billy Bunter blinked at him.

"Sa-a—Sammy!" he stuttered.

Sammy grinned.

"Hallo, Billy! Home again, fatty? Couldn't they stand you any longer?"

"Home!" said Bunter faintly.

He staggered in.

The dreadful truth rushed on his mind now.

He knew why Mauly had suddenly decided on that long, long drive. He knew why the car had shot away with Mauly in it after landing him. He was nowhere near Mauleverer Towers; he was a hundred miles from Mauleverer Towers He was home again!

And Billy Bunter's feelings could not have been expressed in any known language as he tottered into Bunter Villa!

THE NINTH CHAPTER.

Unexpected !

HERBERT VERNON-SMITH, the Bounder of Greyfriars, scowled. Smithy did not seem in a good temper that morning.

He had come down late. He had had an interview with his father, Mr. Samuel Vernon-Smith. To judge by his looks, he had not enjoyed the interview.

He had had no breakfast, late as it was. But he did not want any breakfast. Larkin, the butler in Mr. Samuel Vernon-Smith's mansion, in Courtman Square, London, brought him coffee and biscuits, receiving a grunt and a scowl by way of acknowledgment.

Smithy drank the coffee and munched half a dry biscuit. He was feeling rotten. His face was pasty in colour;

there were dark shadows under his eyes. He had what he would have described as a "next-dayish" feeling, and wished that he had not stayed quite so late last night at that delightful resort, the Pink Pelican night-club. He rather wished, too, that he had devoted less attention to that absorbing game, chemin-de-fer. He had left his last "bean" at the Pink Pelican.

"Oh, you!" grunted Smithy, as the door opened and Tom Redwing came in.

Redwing's bright and healthy face was a startling contrast to Smithy's. He had been in bed at ten, and up at seven.

Tom Redwing was staying with his chum for a week in the holidays. But it was on rather odd lines.

His tastes and Smithy's were so utterly different that hardly any fellow at Greyfriars could understand why they had ever become friends at all.

Still, they were friends—great friends. They liked to be together. Yet Redwing saw very little of his host and chum while he stayed at Courtman Square. Certainly Redwing never accompanied Smithy to the Pink Pelican, or any such place. Neither did Smithy want him to. Tom would have been the heaviest of wet blankets at such a place.

While he stayed with Smithy, Tom was thrown very much on his own resources. He did not mind. A walk in the park, a ride on or of a bus, or a visit to the British Museum, seemed enjoyable to the sailorman's son. He thoroughly enjoyed every "show" to which Mr. Vernon-Smith took the two juniors. But the millionaire financier had little time to give them He left his son to look after his guest, and his son left his guest to look after himself.

Redwing's bright face clouded a little

as he glanced at the Bounder's tired, pasty, scowling visage.

"Been out?" grunted Smithy.

"Yes, old chap. It's a beautiful morning," said Tom. "I called you, but you didn't hear, so I thought I'd let you sleep. I suppose you were in rather late."

"Two o'clock."

"That's rather thick, isn't it, Smithy?" said Tom gravely.

"The pater thinks so. He's taken away my latchkey."

"Well, it's about time he did, I think, Smithy," said Redwing. "You're not looking very fit, old fellow."

"I'm not feelin' very fit. Of course, you're feelin' as fit as a fiddle, as usual!" sneered the Bounder.

Tom made no answer to that. Smithy was the fellow to "row" even with a guest when his temper was bad. And Redwing did not want to row. He walked across to the window and stood looking out into the square

Herbert Vernon-Smith scowled at his back.

"I've had rather a row with the pater," he remarked, after a long silence.

"I'm sorry, Smithy."

"I don't see that it's my fault," argued the Bounder. "I've always been indulged. And who's indulged me, I'd like to know? But the pater had a shock when I was turfed out of Greyfriars last term. He fixed it up all right, and the Head 'et me go back. But it gave him a shock."

"No wonder!" said Redwing. "He couldn't fix it up again, Smithy. If you get the boot again it will be for good. I can understand your father feeling anxious."

Grunt—from the Bounder.

"Well, I'm going to be careful next term at Greyfriars," he said. "I'm not going to give Quelch or the Beak any chance at me. But I don't see why a fellow shouldn't cut loose a bit in the hols. The pater's never kicked up a row about it before."

"He's anxious about you now."

"I'm in a hole! I'm stony broke, and haven't a bean: and the pater's absolutely refused to let me have sixpence. Last hols I had only to ask him for a tenner, or a pony, if I wanted it. It's rather a change"

Again Redwing made no reply. He could not help thinking that it was high time that that change had occurred, and that it was for Smithy's good But it was no use saying so to the Bounder.

"What am I goin' to do the rest of the hols?" grunted Vernon-Smith. "Like me to come to some dashed museum with you, or go to see them changing the guard! My hat!"

Redwing smiled.

"Or shall we go to a concert?" asked the Bounder, with bitter sarcasm.

"There's some jolly good concerts in——"

"Oh, chuck it!"

There was silence while the Bounder crumbled a biscuit.

"Can't you say anything?" inquired Vernon-Smith at last

"Like me to make a suggestion?" asked Tom, with a smile.

"Yes—bother you!"

"Right-ho! You've been playing the goat, Smithy: you're a silly ass! Now, you've got to chuck it if the money's run out. I've been with you a week. Now come and stay with me a week at Hawkscliff."

"Wha-a-at?"

"My father's away at sea," said Redwing "We shall have the cottage to ourselves. We can do our own cooking, make our own beds, sail the old boat on fine days, and clamber over the cliffs."

"Oh gad!"

"And it will pull you round, and make you clean and wholesome again after your foolerics——"

"You cheeky ass!"

Redwing laughed. The Bounder stared at him blankly. But slowly his expression changed, and he smiled.

As a matter of fact, the blackguardism in Smithy's nature was largely superficial; there was good stuff underneath. The change from the millionaire's mansion in Courtman Square to the humble cottage perched over the chalk cliffs at Hawkscliff was rather a startling one. Yet at the bottom of his heart the Bounder despised a fellow who needed servants to wait on him hand and foot, and had all a healthy boy's pleasure in fending for himself. Redwing had made his suggestion in jest, but the Bounder took it in earnest.

"Reddy," he said slowly, "you're a blithering idiot, old chap, but you talk sense sometimes. We'll go."

"My dear chap, think first!" said Tom, laughing. "It will be like caravanning; there isn't a servant of any sort within miles of Hawkscliff——"

"Do you think I have to have my hair combed for me, like that ass Mauleverer?" grunted the Bounder.

"There isn't a French cook——"

"Don't be an ass!"

"You'd have to clean your own shoes, Smithy!"

"Think I can't?"

"If you mean it, Smithy." Redwing's face brightened. "I say, old chap, we could really have some good times in the boat—risky in this weather, but you'd like it all the better for that."

"It's a go! The pater will be pleased, too," added Smithy, with a half-sneer. "He was down on you when I first palled with you, because you're not up to your neck in money; but he's frightfully keen on you now—thinks you're a good influence for me."

"Oh, my hat!" exclaimed Redwing suddenly, staring from the window at a fat figure that was mounting the steps.

"What——"

"Bunter! Have you asked him here, Smithy?"

"Not that I know of." Vernon-Smith rose and joined his chum at the window. He stared out blankly at a fat face adorned by a big pair of spectacles. "Great pip! Has that cheeky porpoise really got the nerve to barge in here? I thought he was sticking Wharton for the hols. Wharton's the kind of silly ass to let him."

Billy Bunter rang the bell.

"Well, my hat!" said the Bounder. "Let him come in; he will go out again so fast that it will make his head swim!"

Then the Bounder burst into a laugh. A new idea had come into his mind—an idea that appealed to his sardonic nature.

"Ha, ha, ha!" he roared. "What a lark!"

"I don't see——"

"You will!" grinned the Bounder. "Don't you say anything; leave it to me. Hallo, what is it, Larkin?"

"A young gentleman of the name of Bunter, sir," said the butler.

"Show him in here," said the Bounder.

And Billy Bunter rolled in, with his most ingratiating grin on his fat face, but an extremely wary look in his little round eyes behind his big, round spectacles.

THE TENTH CHAPTER.

Bamboozling Bunter !

"I SAY, you fellows——"

"It's dear old Bunter!" said the Bounder cordially.

Bunter blinked; Redwing stared. Bunter had hoped, but hardly expected, to hear such a greeting from the Bounder.

"Fancy seein' you here!" went on the Bounder. "Whom are you doin' in London? I mean, of course, what are you doin', old fat bean?"

"The—the fact is——"

"Makin' a round of the West End, callin' on your titled friends and relations, after the rush of the house-parties at Bunter Court?" asked Vernon-Smith, with owl-like gravity.

"Eh? Oh, yes! Exactly!" stammered Bunter.

"And you've found time to give me a look-in!" continued Vernon-Smith. "I take that very kindly, Bunter! It's decent of you."

Billy Bunter blinked at him, as if he could hardly believe his fat ears. In his most hopeful moments he had hardly hoped for this. But Bunter was the fellow to rise, like a fat gudgeon, to any bait. The Bounder's face was serious, and he seemed to be speaking seriously. So the fat and fatuous Owl of the Remove rose to it guilelessly.

"Well, I had a few minutes, Smithy," he said affably. "I remembered your address by sheer chance. Most of the

---

---

addresses I call at are rather farther West. He, he, he!"

That was Bunter all over! Immediately he found that he was not to be kicked out, he started to swell.

Redwing glanced rather curiously at his chum. Courtman Square was West End; but not awfully West End, as it were. But the Bounder took that remark from Bunter without turning a hair.

"Too bad, that you've got only a few minutes, Bunter," he remarked.

"Well, old chap, I could stretch it a bit," said Bunter. "I could manage to stay to lunch. In fact——"

"Couldn't give us a few days?" asked Smithy.

Bunter again could scarcely believe his fat ears. This was rather better than that beast Wharton, or that other beast Mauly!

"Well, look here, Smithy, if you'll let me use your phone, I'll put some people off and fix it," he said. "Look here, I'll make it a few days——"

"What about a week?" asked the Bounder.

"Well, dash it all, I might manage a week! Yes, I'll manage a week, somehow. I've half promised that chap D'Arcy, of St. Jim's; and there's Mauly, you know, keeps on reminding me that I haven't seen him for a long time; but look here, Smithy, I'll cut them both off. Say a week, old chap."

"Done!" said the Bounder. "If you're free to-day——"

"Oh, quite! I mean, I shall have to wash out one or two engagements in the West End. But that's all right; rely on me."

"Well, this couldn't have happened better, could it, Reddy?" said the Bounder heartily. "Just when we're going to start, Bunter blows in like this, and can come with us!"

"Oh!" ejaculated Redwing, and he suppressed a laugh. He was beginning to see the Bounder's drift now.

"Going away?" asked Bunter, his fat face falling a little. Bunter preferred the millionaire's mansion, and a round of gaieties in the West End, if he could contrive it.

"Off in an hour," said the Bounder. "Just time to pack, in fact. Only just settled it, you see! Of course, where we're going is hardly what you're used to, Bunter, at Bunter Court. I understand that you have dukes by the dozen and princes by the peck. But in our humbler way we're going to have rather a good time, ain't we, Reddy?"

"I hope so," said Tom, smiling.

"Well, I'll come," said Bunter. "But look here, would you be able to lend me a few things, Smithy? My baggage got left behind at Wharton Lodge the other day, and you know Wharton—he's never taken the trouble to send it on. And——"

"Leave that to me!" said Vernon-Smith. "Come in what you stand up in, old bean! It's you we want, not your baggage."

Bunter beamed.

"Just squat down and wait a tick while we pack," said the Bounder. "The pater's in the city; he'll be frightfully disappointed at not seeing you, but we're not waiting for him. Come on, Reddy!"

"I—I say," began Redwing.

"Come on, I tell you."

"Oh, all right!"

Redwing followed the Bounder from the room. Billy Bunter sat down to wait for them. His fat face was wreathed in smiles.

Never had he dreamed of a welcome like this from a hard nut like Herbert Vernon-Smith! But there it was; there was no doubt about it. Where the Bounder was going for the rest of the vac, Bunter did not know; but he knew that Smithy generally did everything in great style and a most expensive fashion, and he had no doubt that his destination was one of Vernon-Smith's country residences, or something equally attractive. Anyhow, a holiday with a millionaire's son, who spent money so recklessly and lavishly as the Bounder, was exactly what Bunter wanted. Bunter did not care much where he went, so long as it was comfortable, and there was plenty to eat, and some other fellow footed all the bills.

Smithy and Redwing came back under half an hour. Each of them had a packed bag in his hand.

"Come on, Bunter!" said the Bounder.

Bunter blinked at the bags. At the millionaire's mansion he would have expected to see liveried menials carry much larger bags to a magnificent car. Instead of which, the two juniors walked out, bag in hand, and there was no sign of a car.

Vernon-Smith left a message with Larkin for his father, and walked down the steps. Quite another side of the Bounder's character seemed to be uppermost now. His face was bright and cheerful, and he was evidently looking forward to the trip to Hawkscliff. Bunter, looking forward to something very different, rolled after him.

"Where's the car?" asked Bunter, rather pointedly.

"Catch it at the corner!" said Smithy. "This way!"

The car they caught at the corner was a motor-bus. Bunter clambered on it, puzzled and not pleased. Staying with

Bob Cherry released the handle of the carriage door and reached through the open window.   Before Vernon-Smith knew what was happening, his rather prominent nose was gripped between a finger and thumb, and tweaked.   "Gurrrrggh!" gasped the Bounder.   "Urrrgh! Led do! Wurrgh!"

a millionaire's son did not mean travelling on buses, according to Bunter's idea. However, a bus it was, and it landed them at Charing Cross.

Tom Redwing took the tickets, and Bunter was further puzzled and further displeased to find himself landed in a third-class carriage.

"Are we travelling third?" he asked.

"Looks like it," said Smithy.

"But why?"

"Because there isn't any fourth," explained Smithy.

"Oh!" gasped Bunter.

Still more perplexed was Bunter when they got out of the train at Courtfield, a couple of miles from Greyfriars School. Smithy, certainly, couldn't be going to Greyfriars in holiday-time; but Bunter began to wonder where the dickens he was going.

"Here's a taxi, Smithy!" he called out.

"This way!" answered Smithy.

He walked down the High Street, with Redwing, and Bunter followed.

"You do the shopping, Reddy!" said the Bounder. "You can do it better than I can—besides you've got all the tin!"

Redwing laughed, and went into a shop. He went into two or three more shops, Smithy and Bunter waiting outside.

Finally, he had a shopping-bag packed fairly full when the three walked out of Courtfield. More and more puzzled, Bunter rolled on with them. On the Redclyffe road they caught a motor-bus, which carried them miles on their way. But no bus or any other conveyance went within a couple of miles of Hawkscliff; and the last two miles had to be walked.

In the clear, frosty air Smithy and Redwing enjoyed the walk—the keen sea-winds blew away the dismal reminiscences of the Pink Pelican from Smithy's mind. But Bunter did not enjoy the walk. He was not only puzzled and perplexed, but he was growing extremely irritable. He did not understand this at all.

"I say, you fellows, I'm tired!" he gasped.

"Oh, put it on!" said Smithy. "Come on, Reddy!"

"Look here, where are we going?" demanded Bunter.

"Another mile, and you'll see."

"But, I say——"

"If you don't want this holiday with us, old fat man you can turn back. Lots of time to catch any train you like at Courtfield."

"My dear chap, I'm not really tired —that's all right! Don't mind me!" gasped Bunter. "Don't worry about me, old fellow!"

Vernon-Smith did not need telling that. He was not worrying about Bunter in the least.

"Look here, Smithy, hadn't you better tell him——" murmured Redwing.

"Shut up, Reddy!"

They tramped on and up into the rugged, irregular street of the little village of Hawkscliff, perched on the chalk cliffs over the sea. Billy Bunter blinked round.

"I say, you fellows, isn't this Hawkscliff, where Redwing used to live before he came to Greyfriars?" he exclaimed.

"Just that!"

"Then—where are we going?" gasped Bunter. "There ain't any hotels in this place—not even an inn—or a house— only cottages!"

"Here we are!" said the Bounder, stopping at the neat little cottage that belonged to John Redwing, now away at sea. "Got the key, I hope, Reddy?"

"Yes, rather."

Redwing unlocked the door. The Bounder went in with him. Billy Bunter stood in the doorway, blinking at them, as they opened doors and windows to air the cottage. The Bounder glanced round at him.

"Get your coat off, Bunter! Bring in some firewood—there's a stack in the shed at the back!"

"Wha-a-t?"

"Make yourself useful old bean! No servants here, you know—none of the pampered flunkeys of Bunter Court! You don't keep a butler here, do you, Reddy?"

"Hardly!" said Redwing laughing.

"We—we—we're going to—to—to stay here?" gurgled Bunter.

"That's the big idea!"

"But——" gasped Bunter.

"Buck up with that firewood. We're roughing it here, you know—every man's got to lend a hand! You're not going to slack round doing nothing, as you did when you were hiking with Wharton's crowd in the summer! Get some wood chopped—sharp!"

"Beast!" roared Bunter.

"Eh! Anything the matter?"

"You—you—you——" gurgled Bunter. "Think I'm going to rough it in a blinking fisherman's cottage chopping wood and lighting fires?"

"It's quite good fun——"

(Continued on page 16.)

THE MAGNET LIBRARY.—No. 1,352.

THE NEW Greyfriars

No. 67 (New Series).

EDITED BY

MY WORST AND BEST EXPERIENCE

By DICKY NUGENT

My very worst eggsperience, deer readers, happened one tea-time, in the study of the Skool's most notorious booly and tirant—Loder, of the Sixth !

Smarting under a thowsand injustisses, I had made up my mind to have a terribul revenge on this feendish fag-torcherer. So when Loder ordered me to prepare tea for 4, I prepared one or 2 serprizes for him at the same time. I put Plaster of Paris in the kreem buns, mustard in the aprikot jam, soot in the sardines, and salt and pepper in the tea. I couldn't help larfing hartily when I looked at the teatable. Judging by appearances, there was a jolly good feed in store for Loder and his guests. But appearances were deceptive : the grub I had given them to DIGEST would be almost enuff to make them " die jest " as soon as they'd touched it. (Joak !)

Ere the echo of my harty larf had died away, Loder walked in, followed by Carne and Walker.

"Ah ! This looks jolly good to me !" he eggsclaimed.

Then Walker said something that made me jump.

"I should think it will give the Head quite an appetite !" was his remark.

"D—d—did you say anything about the—the Head ?" I cride, in dismay.

"Yes ; I should have told you to make this tea extra-special, as the Head is with us in his presence," said Loder carelessly. "However, you haven't done badly ; stand by in case we need you !"

Deer reeders, I tried to tell them of my garstly mistake. But, somehow, my tung clave to the roof of my mouth, and I couldn't !

Let me draw a vale over the paneful seen that followed after the Head came in ! I can only say that after he had tried sandwiches, sardines, aprikot jam, kreem buns and my speshal tea, his fizz was more feroshus

than my wildest dreems of my famus fiktional creation, Dr. Alfred Birchemall !

And when Loder suddenly realized that I was the kulprit—but no ; there are some things in life too garstly to kommit to cold print ! This was one of them !

My best eggsperience was quite a recent affair. To be precise, it happened at the Braking-up Concert. For some time there had been roomers of a Serprize Item which was being rehersed by the Remove, and I must say I didn't feel very eggsited about it. It didn't okkur to me for a moment that my major and the rest of the old fogeys in that Form were capable of doing justiss to a theatrical show—not, as we in the Second can do it, anyway !

When the nite of the show came along, however, I must admit that the Serprize Item gave me the serprize of my life !

The reason being that the seen of the play was St Sam's Collidge, and the cheef carrickter, Dr. Birchemall ! The Remove Dramattick Society had paid me the kompliment of bringing my imajinery carricketers to life !

As a crittick, I must konfess that the acting was not eggsactly up to West End perfessional standard.

As a litterary man, I was forced to admit that the play itself was by no means a brilliant masterpeece.

But as a member of the Second Form at Greyfriars, I was overwhelmed by the honner which the old fogeys had bestowed upon me and I've hardly got my breth back yet !

ANSWER TO CORRESPONDENT

"REGRETFUL REMOVITE."— "I tattooed myself during the vac. and it won't come off. Do you think I should tell my pater about it ?"

We advise you to get it off your chest without any delay, old bean !

Porpoise in Pilot-Teste

Bunter's Hair-raising Awakening

Billy Bunter called on Smithy, the other day.

Smithy was out. Bunter said he'd wait and asked to be provided with a light snack.

After a series of light snacks, sufficient tuck to keep a fair-sized menagerie for about a fortnight, Bunter looked around for a comfy chair where he could have a nice, quiet snooze.

He found what seemed to be just what he wanted in the Bounder's miniature private gymnasium. It was a queer-looking chair, suspended in the middle of a complicated framework of steel ; but it was nicely sprung and it was tilted at just that angle Bunter needed to send him right off to sleep !

How long Bunter slept, he never knew. It didn't matter, anyway. The only thing that did matter was that he awoke to such a horrid experience that it was a long time before he could realise it was anything else but a ghastly nightmare.

He seemed to be strapped to a chair which had become possessed of an evil spirit, and started performing the most extraordinary convolutions imaginable !

First it would whirl round like a spinning-top about a hundred times. Then it would stop dead and whirl around in the opposite direction. Then it would turn a dozen or so high-speed somer-

saults ; and after start pitching and like a ship in a stormy

For two or three m Bunter was just spe with terror. Then gained his voice su and emitted one long cry that continued un chair unexpectedly ca a standstill and he foun self staring dizzily grinning faces of V Smith and Tom Redw

"Hallo, Bunter !" S said coolly. "What o made you sit in that testing seat ?"

"Mmmmmmmmm ! ooogh ! This—ooch !— shrieked the ghastly Porpoise.

"Pilot-testing seat course ! Didn't you what it was ?" the B asked genially. "It's a apparatus for intendin plane pilots, made them accustomed to movements in midair v giddiness following !"

"Fancy Bunter sitt it without knowing w was !" grinned Tom Re "Hope you're still all right, Bunter !"

Bunter's reply, repr to the best of our ability

"Ooooo — oooo — o Mmmmmmmmm ! Gro

DICKY NUGENT'S WEEKLY WISDOM

When the Second axxepted a challenge to run a relay race against a prep skool last term, we all took it as a joak till our Formmaster told us Eesop's fable about the hare and the tortuss. But, after that, we went into strikt training and just won the race.

Serprizing, but true—a worth-while lesson was taught us by a tortuss !

THAT'S HOW IT TASTES

We hear that a contractor in Friardale is offering a penny a gallon for muddy rainwater.

Presumably he hopes to make a profit by selling it to the School authorities for next term's tea in Hall !

WOULD YOU BELIEVE IT ?

Mr. Prout and Mr. Quelch became involved in a heated argument when Mr. Quelch referred inadvertently to Mr. Prout's double chin. Mr. Prout fondly imagines that he is just well-developed— not fat !

When W. G. Bunter appeared resplendent in the quad, he was found to be wearing Mauly's topper, Smithy's suit, and Johnny Bull's shoes ! The owners swiftly claimed their belongings— and left Bunter a wreck !

Masquerading as a " ghost " suit of armour taken from school library, Harold Skinne headlong down the staircase the Hall ! Skinner had to released—bent, battered, repentant !

Herald

EXTRA GOOD EDITION

WHARTON. January 13th, 1934.

PETER TODD PREFERS COLD

After Hot Night

You all know what a lean weak Peter Todd is. Well, knowing that, it won't surprise you to learn that Peter always finds it hard to get warm in bed.

But he thought he'd solved the difficulty, this vac.

When he stayed with Tom Dutton for a few days, he found that Dutton's mater had provided electric blankets to the beds in her house.

Peter went to bed with the juice turned full on, happy in the knowledge that he'd be warm all through the night.

But he didn't realise how warm he'd get before the night was through. In his innocence, Peter imagined he had to leave the juice turned on all the time, instead of switch-off before going to sleep !

What awakened him at about 2 a.m. was the clouds of choking smoke and leaping lines of flame around his body ! The bed was alight !

Peter gave one yell and did a jump that carried him clean out of bed. In another instant he was rushing to the bath-room for water.

We're glad to be able to report that the fire was quickly extinguished without doing much damage.

But Peter Todd's attitude to cold beds has changed.

Before this vac he was never heard to complain of excessive heat in bed. But now, he gently but firmly declines all offers of electric blankets. He's had enough !

BROWN'S ECONOMICAL CAR

"Cheaper Than Fretwork"

"Motoring nowadays is within the reach of all," remarked Tom Brown to a "Greyfriars Herald" representative last Wednesday.

Brown was just setting out for Pegg to fetch a second-hand car he had arranged to purchase. Bulstrode and Hazeldene and about a dozen other Remove chaps were going with him.

"Take this bus I'm buying to-day, for instance," Brown went on, as we all tramped along the frostbound highway. "I'm paying thirty shillings for it. Why, it's cheaper than fretwork !"

"What's the petrol consumption ?" the "Greyfriars Herald" man asked.

"A mere nothing," was Brown's reply. "It does a hundred miles to the gallon, provided it's running downhill."

"What about uphill work?"

"Oh, you have to push it uphill ; that's why I'm taking these fellows along with me."

"Then it doesn't go at all, really ?" our representative grinned.

"Exactly !" nodded Brown. "That's what makes running costs so low, you see ; no licence or insurance is needed. All it costs me is thirty shillings—plus, of course, one or two minor incidental expenses."

Of course, the incidental expenses have to be considered.

Brown found that on the way home.

Pushing the car up the first hill turned out to be such thirst-provoking work that he felt morally obliged to stop at a wayside tea hut and buy ginger-pop all round.

And even that wasn't so expensive as what happened afterwards.

It happened at the bottom of the slope leading down to Friardale Lane. The car worked up quite a good speed on the way down, and Brown felt doubts arise within him as to what was going to happen when he reached the bottom.

Those doubts were only too well-founded ! It so happened that a man was standing at the top of a ladder doing something to the street lamp that stands at the crossroads. And the foot of the ladder had to be right in the way of Brown's car !

Brown's car won ! The foot of the ladder shot up in the air and the top of the ladder shot downwards, carrying its human burden with it !

Fortunately, the man wasn't seriously hurt. He says that a mere five-pound note by way of compensation will satisfy him. But a five-pound note is a five-pound note, when you're considering incidental expenses, isn't it ?

Brown says he's willing now to sell his car for what he paid for it.

Our own idea is that he'll have to pay that amount to get anyone to take it from him !

"NO MORE WAR!"

Coker Advocates Peace

There was a full attendance of Removites in the Fifth Form-room to hear Coker lecture on "No More War." This was probably accounted for by the fact that things had been so quiet for a couple of days. The only occurrence of note in that period had been a sale of cast-iron wrist-watches in Fish's study, and the fellows had consequently found time hanging rather heavily on their hands.

Coker woke things up with a vengeance ! In a voice vibrant with passion, he declared that this grand old country of ours stood, as she always had stood, for peace.

"Why ?" asked Coker, "should we plunge the youth of this land into the horrors of war ? Nobody wants war. I don't want war myself and I'm quite prepared to give a sock on the jaw to anyone who does want war !"

Coker admitted that he was a pacifist. He added that he was proud to be a pacifist, and he was quite prepared to give a punch on the nose to anyone who disagreed with him over it.

It wasn't right—it wasn't sportsmanlike —it wasn't English—to want to fight our brothers across the seas. In defence of peace, he was quite prepared to fight anyone who wanted to break the peace.

"I stand here as an unqualified supporter of peace," said Coker. "And I'll jolly well mop up the floor with anyone who doesn't support my plea for peace. Who wants war ?"

"WE DO !" yelled forty members of the Remove Form.

That yell was all that Coker needed ! Tearing off his jacket, he jumped off the rostrum and plunged into the fray.

The last impression we got of the apostle of peace was a whirling windmill of arms and legs, as he fought furiously under a crowd of Removites.

Unquestionably, the cause of peace had found a great fighting ally !

"SOLELY" HIS OWN FAULT !

Treluce admits that he made a shocking mess of it when he tried to mend his own footer boots last week.

Yet he strongly resented it when somebody accused him of being an awful snob.

FOR TO-NIGHT'S SUPPER—

We strongly advise you to go along to the Upper Fourth Debating Society. The speakers will supply you with enough "tripe" to last you for the rest of the month !

Wot I Says Is This 'Ere—

Thank'ee kindly, one an' all, for your inquiries re my 'oliday illness. Which it was caused by a gent pouring me out a glass of lemonade—after he'd ask' me to 'ave a DRINK ! Which it was a very severe shock to my nervous cistern. But wot I says is this 'ere, it's wonderful 'ow a man can pull through, an' I 'ope to be my old self by the New Term !

(Signed) WM. GOSLING,
School Porter.

GREYFRIARS FACTS WHILE YOU WAIT !

Leon Dupont, the French boy, says that ski-ing is the thrilling sport. He hopes to do the famous Cresta Run one day, and his practice during holidays has already made him an adept on skis !

Hurree Singh, who feels the English winter intensely, wears an extra heavy overcoat, with fur-lined collar. He smilingly ignores Bob Cherry's suggestion that he should wear two coats, one over the other !

Old Mimble, the Head's gardener, won first prize at the Courtfield Show last summer with a giant marrow Dicky Nugent says Mimble sat up all night with it more than once—believe it or not !

Billy Bunter's Diamond

(*Continued from page 13.*)

"Beast!"

"Don't waste time, old fat man! You've got to get your bedclothes out, and aired——"

"Beast!"

"And then fill the lamps—there's no electric light here, you know, not even gas——"

"Rotter!" roared Bunter.

"Bunter seems dissatisfied about something, Reddy!" said the Bounder. "Do you know what's the matter with him?"

"Oh, you rotter!" gasped Bunter. "Pulling my leg——"

"He seemed quite keen on coming with us," said the Bounder. "He washed out a lot of engagements in the West End, and all that, to come. Now he seems dissatisfied. What's the matter, Bunter?"

"Beast!"

"Look here, buck up with that firewood——"

"Shan't!" howled Bunter.

"And fill this kettle at the pump! If the pump's frozen——"

Billy Bunter gave the Bounder a glare that nearly cracked his spectacles. Then he turned on his heel and stalked away.

"It's too bad, Smithy!" said Redwing, laughing

The Bounder stepped to the door.

"Bunter!" he roared.

"Beast!" floated over Bunter's fat shoulder.

"Where are you going?"

"Yah!"

"Aren't you staying with us a week here?"

Billy Bunter did not trouble to answer that question. He rolled away, only anxious to reach the road, where it was possible to pick up a motor-bus for the station!

Chopping wood, making fires, wrestling with frozen pumps was not Bunter's idea of a holiday—not in the least! Bunter Court was better than that! And William George Bunter lost no time in getting back to Bunter Court, otherwise Bunter Villa; and Smithy and Redwing were left at Hawkscliff without his fascinating society! Which, probably, they did not miss very much!

THE ELEVENTH CHAPTER.
Pon is Playful!

CECIL PONSONBY, of the Fourth Form at Highcliffe School, stared.

Then he shaded his eyes with his hand, as if dazzled.

His friends, Gadsby and Monson, grinned.

There was a crowd on the platform of Lantham Junction

It was the first day of the new term; and as both Greyfriars and Highcliffe started the term on the same day, there were plenty of both Greyfriars fellows and Highcliffians about.

Pon & Co. were walking along the crowded platform, with their noses in the air, and their usual supercilious looks when they sighted Billy Bunter.

Bunter was blinking round him through his big spectacles, apparently looking for somebody, and did not observe Pon & Co.

But Pon & Co observed him.

They observed, too, the dazzling glitter of a diamond in Billy Bunter's tie. It was a big diamond—quite a big diamond—and it caught the wintry sunshine and flashed and glittered in great style.

Hence Pon's playful action. He shaded his eyes as if Bunter's big diamond dazzled him like the sun at noonday.

Not, of course, that Pon fancied for a moment that it was a real diamond. If it was real, it was worth a good hundred pounds. A hundred pence was nearer Bunter's mark.

"Jevver see anything like that, you men?" asked Pon.

"Hardly ever!" grinned Gadsby. "Must have bought it by the ounce."

"By the pound!" said Monson.

"Ha, ha, ha!"

Bunter blinked round at the sound of laughter. He blinked at the grinning Highcliffians.

"I say, you fellows, seen Wharton?" he asked. "I spotted him a minute ago, but he seems to have got lost in the crowd."

"Can't see anybody or anythin'," answered Ponsonby shaking his head.

"Eh! Why can't you?" asked Bunter.

"Too dazzled!" explained Ponsonby.

"Ha, ha, ha!" chortled Gadsby and Monson.

"Oh, really, Ponsonby——"

"Do you buy your diamonds by the pound?" asked Pon "If you gave a penny a pound for that one, it must have cost you a lot."

"Ha, ha, ha!"

"Yah!" retorted Bunter, and he turned his back on the dandy of Highcliffe, and blinked round through his spectacles for Harry Wharton who had—perhaps—accidentally disappeared in the crowd.

Pon winked at his friends.

"Watch me!" he murmured.

He tiptoed behind Bunter. The Highcliffe fellow was taller than the fat Owl of Greyfriars. Bunter was tall sideways! Pon, watched by his grinning friends, reached over Bunter's podgy shoulder and coolly jerked the pin from his tie.

Had Pon believed, for a moment, that it was a real diamond, certainly he would not have played foolish tricks with it. But it never occurred to him for a moment that it was a genuine stone. He had no doubt whatever that Bunter had picked it up for sixpence or a shilling and that it was a particularly glaring sham.

Holding the glittering diamond aloft, the playful Pon jumped back. There was a startled yell from Bunter.

He spun round like a fat humming-top!

"Beast! Gimme my tiepin!" he roared.

Ponsonby held it up out of reach. Billy Bunter grabbed up at it in vain! He could not get anywhere near it. Gadsby and Monson roared, and a dozen Highcliffe fellows gathered round, laughing, too. Billy Bunter was the centre of a merry circle

"Gentlemen what offers for this gorgeous diamond?" sang out Pon. "A specimen of the famous Bunter collection——"

"Ha, ha, ha!"

"Warranted of the purest water, and worth——"

"Ha, ha, ha!"

"Gimme my pin!" shrieked Bunter, clutching wildly. "You beast, that stone's worth twenty pounds."

"Not twenty thousand?" roared Gadsby.

"Ha, ha, ha!"

"If you lose it, I'll make you pay for it!" howled Bunter. "Give it to me, you beast! My diamond pin——"

"Some diamond!" chortled Monson.

"What offers?" called out Ponsonby. "Going—going—going—what offers for this magnificent Bunter diamond, best paste——"

"Twopence!" said Gadsby.

"Threepence!" said Monson.

"Going at threepence!" shouted Ponsonby, in the style of an auctioneer. "Going—going—this gorgeous diamond is going at threepence! What offers over threepence for this magnificent gem? No gem equal to this can be got for less than sixpence at the bazaar——"

"Ha, ha, ha!"

"You beast, I gave thirty pounds for that diamond pin!" roared Bunter.

"Then you were done out of twenty-nine pounds nineteen-and-six!" said Gadsby.

"Ha, ha, ha!"

"Beast! Rotter! Gimme my diamond!" shrieked Bunter. Since that diamond had come into his possession Bunter had swanked with it considerably, and had stated so often that it was real, that he had almost come to believe so himself.

"Hallo, hallo, hallo! What's the jolly old row?" asked the cheery voice of Bob Cherry as he came along with Johnny Bull and Frank Nugent.

"I say, you fellows——"

"Dear old Bunter! Fat as ever!" said Bob. "Hallo, hallo, hallo, what's Pon waving his diamonds about for?" Bob stared at the flashing, glittering gem in Pon's uplifted hand.

"It's mine!" yelled Bunter.

"Eh? Yours! Rats!" said Bob.

"I tell you it's mine—a Christmas present from my Uncle George!" yelled Bunter. "My diamond tiepin! Make him hand it back to me, Bob! You can lick that Highcliffe cad."

Bob Cherry chuckled.

"If it's yours, old bean, it can't be worth a lot," remarked Bob. "Let him have it for the tanner it cost."

"Ha, ha, ha!"

"I tell you it's real," roared Bunter. "It's the best New Year's gift I've had from my Uncle William——"

"Ha, ha, ha!"

"Any advance on threepence?" chortled Ponsonby. "This gorgeous Bunter diamond going at threepence—worth sixpence of any man's money——"

"Look here, if it's Bunter's, hand it over, Pon!" said Bob Cherry. "I suppose it's only paste, but a fellow's property is his property."

"Mind your own bizney!" retorted Ponsonby. "Who's asked you to barge in?"

"Well, Bunter has!" said Bob good-temperedly. "A joke's a joke; but let him have it back."

"Rats! Gentlemen, what offers——"

"Gimme my diamond, you beast, or I'll hack your shins!" yelled Billy Bunter, in great wrath and excitement.

"There'll be a burst porpoise lying about soon afterwards, if you do," grinned Ponsonby "I—why—what—yaroooh—— Whoop!" roared Pon, as Bunter suited the action to the word and hacked.

Pon's hand, clenching the diamond pin in it, descended on Bunter, and there was a roar from the Owl of the Remove. Bunter sat down suddenly on Lantham platform.

"Oh crikey! Wow!" roared Bunter.

"There's your rubbish, you fat fool!" snarled Ponsonby, and he flung the diamond pin at Bunter, and it missed him and rolled on the planks.

"Ow! Beast! Wow!"

Frank Nugent picked up the pin. Pon, who had a pain where Bunter had hacked, reached out with his foot to give the fat Owl a lunge in the ribs as he sat gasping.

Bob Cherry pushed him back.

"Chuck that, Pon!" he said quietly.

"Stand back, you Greyfriars cad!" yelled Pon.

"Rats to you, you Highcliffe cad!" retorted Bob.

"Take that, then!"

Smack!

"Oh, my hat!" gasped Bob as he staggered back from that sudden smack, which landed with all Pon's force on his ruddy face. "Ow!"

"Here, let's get out of this!" muttered Gadsby uneasily, and Pon & Co. pushed hastily through the crowd and ran for the train.

THE TWELFTH CHAPTER.

Smithy Asks For It !

HERBERT VERNON-SMITH, standing at the open doorway of a carriage, waved a hand to three fellows who came hastily along the train. Tom Redwing, who was looking out of the window, touched him on the arm.

"Keep the places for Greyfriars men, Smithy," he said. "We don't want those Highcliffe outsiders in here."

"I do!" said the Bounder coolly.

"Well, why?" demanded Tom rather sharply.

(Continued on next page.)

Post your Soccer queries to "Linesman," c/o The MAGNET, The Fleetway House, Farringdon Street, London, E.C.4. It's his job and his pleasure to answer knotty problems from readers.

PREPARING FOR THE BIG BATTLE !

THIS is the period of the football season when we hear a lot about special training ; of the members of this or that football side being taken away to the seaside, or to some inland resort, to make extra preparations for a Cup-tie. This special training business is, really, nothing of the sort. If you visualise, by the words "special training," intensive preparation ; more running exercises, more skipping, more ball practice, then I have to say that you are all wrong.

The sole objective of taking players away to the seaside in preparation for an important Cup-tie is that the men .shall have a rest and a change of air.

I'll tell you a story connected with the so-called special training of Huddersfield Town for the Cup Final of 1922. The members of the team went off to Blackpool to "get ready." I pictured them out and about working schemes for the downfall of their opponents in the Cup Final. You know the sort of thing—deep-laid plans of attack and defence being practised. Actually, I got a shock. One day I w..nt to the special training quarters of the Huddersfield Town team and asked the manager if I could take a few pictures of the players in action, passing the ball to each other, and that sort of thing. The manager was very polite, and willing to help. But he couldn't do much to assist because, as he told me, "If you want to take photographs of our footballers playing with a football, you will have to buy them a football. They haven't brought one with them." It seems strange to imagine a football team preparing for a big football Cup Final without a football, but that was an actual fact so far as the Huddersfield Town team of that year was concerned.

When I remember these days, I wonder what I shall say to the correspondent who asks me what is the most common form of training for efficiency at football. The trouble is that there is no accepted system. My Oldham reader will find that he really does not need a lot of training provided that he is ordinarily fit. A few laps round some ground one or two evenings a week, a little ball practice and some exercise in the gymnasium.

The simple fact of this training matter is, of course, that once a player is thoroughly fit he does not need a lot of training. Indeed, too much training is as bad as too little.

More teams have lost the championship, and lost the Cup, because of too much training rather than because of too little. Too much training results in stale footballers—players who are not eager for the fray. So my advice to my Oldham friend is to get fit, and then the minimum training will keep you going.

A STRANGE COINCIDENCE !

A CORRESPONDENT signing himself "Footballer" is clearly interested in the doings of the Manchester City club past and present, and I think the answers to his questions may be sufficiently interesting to be given here. For instance, he wants to know how many times Manchester City have won the Cup. The reply to that question is that Manchester City have only won the Cup once, according to the records. That was in 1904.

I guarantee, however, that I could introduce my correspondent to people who would tell him that Manchester City have never really won the Cup.

On the one occasion on which Manchester City were returned victorious there was a big to-do. The goal which won the match was scored by Billy Meredith, the fellow who played in fifty international matches for Wales. The players of Bolton Wanderers, the opponents of Manchester City on that day, contended that when Meredith scored the goal which counted he was in an offside position. Whether Meredith was offside or not doesn't matter now, of course. The referee said he was not offside, and he is the fellow with the deciding "vote." But I shall never forget travelling back to Lancashire after that 1904 final with the players and officials of the Bolton Wanderers team. From the appearance of the railway compartment in which we travelled you would have imagined that we had been holding a paper chase. The compartment was full of bits of paper on which the travellers had sketched their ideas of the position of Meredith when he scored the winning goal.

Since then, Manchester City have been in two Cup Finals. In 1926 they were beaten by Bolton Wanderers, who thus got revenge for that 1904 affair, and last season Manchester City were beaten by Everton at Wembley. Isn't it a strange coincidence, by the way, that on the three occasions on which Manchester City have been in the Cup Final they have met opponents from Lancashire.

One man who tried desperately hard to prevent Manchester City being beaten in their last Cup Final was Eric Brook, the outside-left. He has since played regularly for England, and before joining Manchester City was associated first with Mexborough and then with Barnsley. This will answer another question from my Manchester friend.

THE ONLY ALTERNATIVE !

AN interesting story may be told concerning the transfer of Brook from Barnsley to Manchester. The officials of the two teams had agreed on the terms, but Brook was nowhere to be found. Eventually information came to the officials of the clubs that he was in a local cinema, so a notice was put on the screen at the cinema asking for Brook to come outside. This winger duly came outside, agreed to the transfer from Barnsley to Manchester City, and then went back to see the finish of the film.

It frequently happens that the goalkeeper of a football team falls on the ball, and there is then a scramble in the hope of getting it from him. What should the referee do in these circumstances ? That is a question which is put to me.

In reply I have to say that the goalkeeper, like other footballers, can only be charged legitimately. If he is charged other than by the shoulder, then the punishment is a free-kick.

Now it is obviously difficult to charge a man who is lying on the ground with the ball beneath his body. What usually happens in these cases is that the referee decides that somebody has fouled the goalkeeper, and a free kick is given. If the goalkeeper does not rise with the ball and is not fouled, then the only thing the referee can do is to blow the whistle and drop the ball.

A Marlborough reader is disturbed because a free kick was recently given against him when the ball struck his hand. If this is so, then the referee made a mistake. The rule distinctly says that a free kick must only be given for intentional hands. Therefore, if a player who is running with his hand by his side finds the ball kicked against his hand his side should not be penalised.

Rugby football is not my strong point, but even on this head I am able to reply to a correspondent, and say that Salford won the Rugby League Cup in 1914 and 1933, and that Risman plays for Salford.

"LINESMAN."

THE MAGNET LIBRARY.—No. 1,352.

"It's nearly half an hour's run to Courtfield—it will be a bit more lively with Pon & Co.——"

"You're not friends with them."

"That makes no difference! This way, Pon!" shouted the Bounder.

Redwing rose from his seat. That week at the cottage up at Hawkscliff had been quite a success It had certainly done the Bounder good. But after it was over he had gone back to London, and Tom had not seen him again until to-day, when they met at Lantham. And even in a few minutes he had already observed that his wayward chum was in one of his reckless and wilful moods.

"If they're coming in here, Smithy——" said Redwing.

"They are!"

"That means cards, I suppose——"

"You can shut your eyes!" grinned the Bounder.

"I'd rather get out."

"Nobody's stoppin' you."

Redwing, compressing his lips, stepped out and walked along the train. Ponsonby and Gadsby and Monson came up to the carriage door a moment later, rather breathless. After smacking Bob Cherry's face, Pon was rather anxious to get on the train, out of reach.

"Hop in!" said the Bounder amicably.

And the three Highcliffians hopped in. Drury and Vavasour, also of the Highcliffe Fourth, followed them in, and then the Bounder shut the door. They eyed Smithy rather curiously. The Bounder of Greyfriars was sometimes on friendly terms with the black sheep of Highcliffe—sometimes the reverse. Now, apparently, he was willing to be friendly, and Pon had no objection. He was more than ready for a little game while the train ran on to Courtfield, and hoped to extract profit therefrom, if Smithy was, as usual, in funds.

"Had good hols. old bean?" asked Pon, quite affably.

"Oh, rippin'," said the Bounder. He grasped the doorhandle as it was grasped from without. "No room!" he said through the window, with a grin at Bob Cherry's flushed and wrathful face.

"Pon's in there!" panted Bob. "I saw him get in."

"What about it?"

"He smacked my face!" roared Bob. "I'm going to knock his features through the back of his head. Let go the door, Smithy."

"Keep that hooligan out, Smithy," said Ponsonby. "What a blighter he is for kickin' up rows!"

"Absolutely!" said Vavasour.

Bob wrenched the doorhandle. The Bounder, with a mocking grin, held it fast on the inside.

"Hook it, old bean," he said. "Pon's travellin' with me! Run away and play."

"Let go that door, you rotter!" roared Bob.

"Bow-wow!"

"Smithy, you cad, let me in! Are you standing up for that Highcliffe rotter? I tell you I'm going to whop him!" roared Bob Cherry. "Will you let go that handle?"

"My dear man——"

"Let go!" bellowed Bob.

The Bounder grinned from the window. He seemed to find Bob's crimson and wildly excited face amusing. Pon & Co. laughed. They found it amusing also—so long as Bob could not get to close quarters. And he couldn't so long as the Bounder held the door.

Johnny Bull and Frank Nugent joined Bob. Nugent caught his arm.

"Time to get in, old man. Wharton's got a carriage farther on."

"Pon's in here, and I'm going to wallop him!" hooted Bob. "I'm not having my face smacked by a Highcliffe cad!"

"Well, the train will be starting——" said Johnny Bull.

"Blow the train!" Bob did not seem disposed to listen to reason.

From a door along the train Harry Wharton was waving his hand, and Hurree Jamset Ram Singh's dusky face looked out.

"This way, you men!" shouted Wharton. "I've got your seats!"

"Buck upfully, my esteemed and absurd fatheads!" yelled the Nabob of Bhanipur. "Otherwise the losefulness of the train will be a sine qua non!"

"Come on, Bob!" urged Nugent.

"Rats!"

"Pon can wait——"

"Rubbish!"

"Look here——" growled Johnny Bull.

"Let go this door, Smithy!" roared Bob, in almost frenzied tones. "You cheeky rotter, I'll punch your head for this!"

The Bounder laughed. It was chiefly from sheer mischief that he was opposing Bob's entry into the carriage. Though, as he had decided to travel with Pon, it was true that he did not want a shindy in the carriage between a Greyfriars man and the dandy of Highcliffe. Anyhow, he was not going to give way. Having taken his line, for whatever reason, the Bounder was not the fellow to back down. With both hands gripped on the door-handle, he kept the door shut, and Bob raged in vain.

Doors were slamming now along the train. There was no more time to lose, if Bob was not to be left behind at Lantham.

"Will you let go?" he panted.

"No!" answered the Bounder coolly. "I won't!"

"Come on, Bob!" urged Nugent.

Bob released the outside handle. He reached through the open window, and grabbed at the Bounder's nose.

Smithy's grinning face was within reach, and that sudden change of tactics took him by surprise.

Before Smithy knew what was happening, his rather prominent nose was gripped between a finger and thumb, and tweaked.

"Gurrrrrggh!" gasped the Bounder.

"Oh, my hat!" gasped Ponsonby.

"Urrrgh! Led do—— Wurrggh!"

Bob let go, and let his friends rush him away along the train. They bundled into Harry Wharton's carriage barely in time.

The Bounder clasped his crimson nose, which had a distinct pain in it, panting with rage.

"By gad!" he gasped. "I—I—I—I'll——" He tore open the door he had lately been holding shut.

"Hold on!" exclaimed Ponsonby. "You'll lose your train!"

"It's just startin'!" exclaimed Gadsby.

The Bounder did not heed. He was as keen to get at Bob, as Bob had been to get at Pon. He leaped from the carriage, stared round for Bob Cherry, and ran along the train. The door was slammed the next moment by a porter, and the train was moving.

Vernon-Smith ran along, glaring at window after window. He grabbed the handle of the door that had closed on Bob and his friends. But the train was in motion, and a Lantham porter grabbed him by the shoulder and jerked him back.

"Too late, sir!"

"You fool, let go!" howled the Bounder.

"Stand back!"

"You meddlin' idiot——"

"Get back there!"

And the porter, who perhaps did not like being addressed as a fool and a meddling idiot, gave the Bounder a push, which caused him to "get back" so suddenly that he sat down on the platform.

Panting with rage, the Bounder sat and saw the train glide by. From one carriage window, Pon & Co. smiled at him—apparently amused. From another, Bob Cherry grinned cheerily, and Hurree Jamset Ram Singh waved a dusky hand. From another, the fat face of Billy Bunter grinned, and he squeaked:

With a sudden movement, Billy Bunter twisted out of the jacket. "Come !" boomed Prout, jerking at the collar, and unconsciously helping the fat junior off with his jacket. "Why—what—Bunter—what—impertinent young rascal— good gad—what——" He broke off suddenly as the fat junior scudded wildly away.

"He, he, he !"

Then the train was gone, and the Bounder was left behind at Lantham to wait for the next.

THE THIRTEENTH CHAPTER.
The Wild Adventures of W. G. Bunter !

"I SAY, you fellows !"

"Just the man I want to see !" said Harry Wharton.

"Oh, good !" said Bunter. "Is it a study supper ?"

"Not at all !"

"Then what ?"

"You grabbed my cap and threw it along the platform when I saw you off at Elmdale in the hols——"

Bunter jumped back.

"Oh, really, Wharton——"

"One good turn deserves another !" said the captain of the Remove. "Keep your head steady !"

Bunter made another backward jump. The Co. chuckled.

They did not, perhaps, want to be bothered by William George Bunter on the first day of term. And certainly Wharton had to pay Bunter back for snatching off his chap. So it seemed quite a good idea to pay that debt.

To Bunter, however, it did not seem a good idea at all. Perhaps he did not believe in paying debts. Certainly he seldom paid any. He backed away, blinking warily through his big spectacles.

"I say, you fellows, no larks ! I say, have you heard the news? I was going to say—— Keep off, you beast !"

Bunter backed away again, and Harry Wharton followed him up, and the grinning Co. followed Wharton.

"Quelch——" said Bunter.

"Oh, Quelch !" said Bob Cherry. "I

haven't seen the old bean yet ! What about Quelch ?"

"He's not back !" said Bunter. "I hear that he's not coming back yet— may not be back this term at all—got a cold in the hols, or something—and, I say—keep off !"

Another backward jump.

The juniors had already discovered that their Form-master, Mr. Quelch, was not in evidence, and wondered what had become of him.

"I say, you fellows, if he's got a cold, it may turn to pneumonia, or something, and he may not come back at all !" said Bunter brightly.

"Oh, my hat ! You fat villain——"

"Oh, really, Cherry ! If we get another beak, he could hardly be worse than Quelch !" argued Bunter. "He had a bad cold last term, you know, and it was rather ripping while he was in sanny ! Think of getting shut of him for a whole term ! I say—keep off, Wharton, you beast !"

Harry Wharton reached out towards Bunter's cap. The Owl of the Remove made another rapid backward jump.

Then there was a sudden yelp.

Bunter, naturally, had no eyes in the back of his head ! Jumping back, he could not see what was behind him.

It was rather unfortunate that Mr. Prout, the master of the Fifth, was bustling by.

Bunter landed on one of Mr. Prout's feet, and, still more unfortunately, on a favourite corn that adorned that foot.

Mr. Prout's sudden yelp was full of anguish.

"Oh crikey !" gasped Bunter, spinning round. "Who—what——"

"Oooogh !" spluttered the Fifth Form master, hopping on one leg. "Ow ! Ooooh ! Woooogh ! Upon my—grooogh —word ! Whooooh !"

Harry Wharton & Co. faded away

across the misty quad. Billy Bunter would gladly have done the same. But a finger and thumb closed like a vice on Bunter's fat ear.

"You young rascal !" roared Prout.

"Ow ! Leggo ! lt wasn't me !" gasped Bunter. "I mean—I didn't see you— ow !"

"How dare you jump on my foot ! Ow ! How dare you ! I shall take you to your — ow ! — Form-master — wow ! Come with me !"

"I—I—I say, sir——" gasped Bunter.

"Come !" boomed Prout.

Keeping hold of Bunter's fat ear, Prout led him to the House. Had he let go that fat ear Bunter would have vanished as suddenly and swiftly as a Hunter of the Snark on beholding a Boojum. Prout's finger and thumb held on like a steel vice. Bunter was led to Masters' Passage, and with his free hand Prout tapped on the door of Mr. Quelch's study, and opened it.

"Quelch !" he barked.

The master of the Remove was not there. The study was unlighted. There was not even a fire. Prout blinked round.

"I—I say, sir !" gasped Bunter. "Quelch ain't back, sir !"

"What ?" boomed Prout.

"Mr. Quelch hasn't come back, sir !"

"Oh !" said Prout.

He released Bunter's ear, but he stood between him and the doorway. Bunter blinked longingly at the doorway, past Prout's portly form.

"If your Form-master is not here, Bunter, I cannot report you to him !" boomed Prout.

"I—I don't mind, sir !" gasped Bunter.

"What ?"

"I—I really don't mind, sir—not in

THE MAGNET LIBRARY.—No. 1,352.

the least. I—I—I'd prefer to—to let the matter drop," stammered Bunter.

"As I cannot report you to Mr. Quelch for punishment, Bunter, I have no resource but to take the matter into my own hands."

"Oh lor'!"

"I do not see a cane here."

Mr. Prout stared round the deserted study. Bunter was rather glad that he could not see a cane there.

But it booted not, as a poet would say.

"You will come to my study, Bunter."

"I—I say, sir, I—I've got to see the Head," gasped Bunter. "I—I haven't seen him yet, sir, and he told me to come to his study at once."

"What? If you have not yet seen Dr. Locke, how could he have told you to come to his study at once?" boomed Prout.

"I—I mean——"

"Come with me!"

Prout took hold of Bunter's collar this time. He led him from Quelch's study, and along the passage to his own. There was a cane there. Prout, with fearful shooting pains in his corn, was anxious to get hold of that cane. He was keen to put in some work with that cane.

But all the keenness was on Prout's side. Billy Bunter had no desire whatever to establish contact with that cane.

Prout's grip was on his jacket collar. It was quite a firm grip; but the jacket, if not the grip, was detachable.

When that grip had been on Bunter's ear the case was hopeless. Bunter could not part with his ear, leaving it in Prout's grip. The thing was impossible.

But he could part with his jacket, leaving it in Prout's grip—and he did. With a sudden movement Bunter twisted out of the jacket, and darted down the passage in his shirtsleeves.

It was rather a desperate proceeding; but then the case was desperate.

"Come!" boomed Prout, jerking at the collar, and unconsciously helping Bunter off with the jacket. "Why, what—Bunter—what an impertinent young rascal! Good gad! What——"

Prout stared at the unoccupied jacket in his hand. He stared at a fat figure in shirtsleeves that scudded wildly away.

"Bunter!" he roared.

He rushed in fierce pursuit.

Bunter turned the corner.

Crash!

It was one of the many gifts of Horace Coker of the Fifth Form at Greyfriars that he was always in the wrong place at the wrong moment. If there was, at any given moment, any place where it was better for Coker not to be, Coker of the Fifth was sure to be there.

Thus it was at the present moment.

Coker of the Fifth was coming along with his hands in his trousers pockets, when Bunter came round the corner.

What happened next Coker hardly knew.

Something that might have been a battering-ram, or a runaway rhinoceros, smote Coker of the Fifth where he had lately parked his tea.

Coker rolled.

With his hands in his pockets he could not even clutch at Bunter, or at the wall to save himself. He just rolled.

"Oh crikey!" gasped Bunter.

He staggered from the shock; but he flew on. He did not stop to ask Coker whether he was hurt. It was indeed unnecessary—he knew that he was. Bunter, going strong, vanished into space.

THE MAGNET LIBRARY.—No. 1,352.

Coker sprawled and rolled and roared.

And Prout, in fierce pursuit of Bunter, came round the corner like another runaway rhinoceros.

What happened next was regrettable, but inevitable.

When a stout gentleman, going at full speed, ran into a fellow sprawling at full length on the floor, he was bound to come a purler.

Prout came a fearful purler.

His feet caught in Coker, and Coker, wildly clutching, captured Prout's knees. Prout rolled over Coker.

"Oooooogh!" gasped Coker, as the wind was driven out of him. "Urrggh! Wurrrggh!"

"Oh! Ah! Ow! What?" gurgled Prout.

He sat up dazedly.

For the moment he was unaware that he was sitting on Coker. It seemed to Prout that an earthquake was going on—that the floor heaved and rocked under him. But it was not the floor—it was Coker!

"What—what—where—who—which—what!" stuttered Prout.

"Urrggh! Gerroff!"

"Bless my soul! Who—what——" Prout got off, and stared down at the breathless, gasping Coker.

Bunter's jacket was still in his hand. He hurled it aside, and concentrated on Coker. He flamed with wrath.

"Is—is—is it you, Coker?" stuttered Prout. "You—you—you incredibly stupid boy! You—you idiot!"

"Yurrrggh!"

"Lying down in the passage to trip up people. I have never heard of such amazing stupidity! What do you mean by it?"

"Wurrrggh!"

"Take five hundred lines, Coker!" roared Prout.

"Urrgh! I say—— Gurrggh!"

"Pah!"

Prout stalked away. He was too bumped and shaken to give any further thought to the vanished Owl. He tottered back to his study, gasping and spluttering, and sank, gurgling, into an armchair. Coker, in a dazed and dizzy state, limped off the scene.

Ten minutes later a fat junior in shirtsleeves peered cautiously along the passage, through a pair of big spectacles, whipped up a jacket, and vanished again. Once more fully clad, Billy Bunter put on his cap and rolled out into the quad in search of the Famous Five, to learn whether there would be a study supper going. He found them, but he did not learn anything about a study supper.

His bullet head was tapped hard against the school wall instead, and the five juniors walked on, chuckling.

THE FOURTEENTH CHAPTER.

Just Like Smithy!

"SMITHY'S keeping it up," remarked Skinner, after last roll-call in Hall.

On the first day of term, fellows coming from the four quarters of the kingdom arrived by widely different trains, and at widely different times. But there was a calling-over at nine o'clock, by which time the last and latest Greyfriars man was expected to have put in an appearance, barring accidents. Herbert Vernon-Smith, of the Remove, was the only junior who hadn't.

Great men of the Sixth Form might come in later. Such tremendous big guns as prefects of the Sixth did what was right in their own eyes.

It was different with the small fry. Loder and Carne of the Sixth, as a matter of fact, had not turned up yet, and fellows who knew them well wondered whether they had stopped on the way to renew old acquaintances at the Cross Keys. But Loder and Carne were prefects. Vernon-Smith was a Remove junior, and when the Head marked him absent at roll, the Head was observed to frown.

It was like the reckless Bounder to begin the new term, after all his trouble in the old term, with a cool disregard of authority. Skinner was rather amused; Tom Redwing was rather anxious.

Bed-time for the Remove was half-past nine, and the juniors speculated with keen interest whether the Bounder would "keep it up" till dorm. He was reckless enough to keep it up still later.

"He lost the train at Lantham," said Bob Cherry. "But there's been six or seven trains since then."

"I wish I knew where he was," muttered Redwing.

"You can use Quelch's phone," suggested Skinner. "Give him a ring!" Redwing stared.

"How can I get him on the phone, fathead?" he asked.

"Easy enough. The Three Fishers number will be in the book!"

"Ha, ha, ha!"

There was a chortle from the Removites; but Tom Redwing turned away with a frowning and troubled brow. He knew that it was only too likely that the Bounder had dropped in at the Three Fishers instead of coming on to the school—it was a forbidden resort for Greyfriars fellows, and therefore a favourite one for Smithy when his blackguardly mood was uppermost.

And Redwing was well aware that his chum could not afford to take chances this term. He had had the narrowest possible escape from expulsion once, and the eye of suspicion was upon him.

But that was not the worst. His father had been alarmed and angered by that narrow escape, and it was not only the Head's anger but his father's that Smithy had to fear if he came another cropper.

The commonest of common sense should have led the Bounder to be careful, for a time at least. But this was how he was beginning.

It was twenty minutes past nine, and first night's supper in Hall was finishing when Billy Bunter's squeak was heard:

"I say, you fellows, here's Smithy!"

Many eyes were turned on the Bounder as he strolled in.

He was quite cool and unconcerned. He nodded to fellows at the Remove table cheerfully, only bestowing a scowl on Bob Cherry, doubtless from a recollection of the nose-pulling episode at Lantham.

"Oh, here you are, Smithy!" said Redwing, in great relief.

The Bounder had not kept it up till dorm, at all events.

"Yes, here I am," yawned Smithy. "Make room for a fellow."

"Seen the Head?"

"Not yet."

"Hadn't you better?"

"Oh, lots of time! Has Quelch been inquiring after me?"

"Quelch hasn't come back," said Peter Todd "They say he got a cold in the holidays and won't be back yet."

"What splendid luck!" drawled the Bounder. "I'm not sure that Quelch would have believed that I walked from Lantham and lost my way——"

"Oh, my hat!"

"But it's good enough for the Head!"

"Not so jolly sure of that!" grinned Skinner. "The old bean's got a wary eye on you, Smithy."

"Lost your way, old chap?" said Lord Mauleverer sympathetically. "Was it foggy round by Lantham? I didn't notice it in the train."

"Ha, ha, ha!"

"Oh, fearfully foggy," said the Bounder gravely. "That's how it was. I've walked about for hours and hours——"

"Hard cheese, old bean," said his unsuspicious lordship.

"Yes, wasn't it?"

"Are you going to tell the Beak that?" gasped Bob Cherry.

"Why not?"

"Oh, lots of reasons why not, though I don't suppose you would understand any of them," said Bob, with a grunt.

"He, he, he!" chortled Billy Bunter. "Fancy Smithy walking about in this weather for hours and hours, without even making his boots muddy!"

"Ha, ha, ha!"

"By Jove!" said Lord Mauleverer. "That's quite queer, Smithy. How did you keep your boots so jolly clean in those muddy lanes? Oh gad!" A light broke on Mauly's noble mind. "You never lost your way at all!"

"Go hon!" said the Bounder. "Are you gettin' suspicious in your old age, Mauly? I hope the Head won't catch it from you."

"Vernon-Smith!" came Wingate's deep voice from the high table where the prefects sat.

"Yes, Wingate."

"You're to go to the Head at once."

"Mayn't I have a bite of supper first, Wingate?" asked the Bounder meekly. "I'm fearfully hungry after a long, long walk——"

"You may do exactly as you're told, if you don't want to start the term with a whopping!" growled the Greyfriars captain.

"Oh, all right!"

The Bounder lounged carelessly out of the Hall, followed by a good many glances—amused, concerned, some of them admiring. Fellows who approved least of the Bounder's wild ways could not help admiring his nerve.

He was not seen again till dorm.

He joined the Remove on their way to the dormitory, and his look showed that he had not found trouble in the Head's study.

No doubt it was fortunate for the Bounder that Mr. Quelch was not there to call him to account. Quelch certainly would not have been likely to believe that the Bounder, having lost his train at Lantham, had walked, and got lost in foggy lanes.

Perhaps Dr. Locke did not quite believe it, but was willing to give the scapegrace of Greyfriars the benefit of such doubt as there was.

Anyhow, Vernon-Smith had escaped scot-free, and he was grinning as he came into the Remove dormitory.

"Not licked?" asked Skinner.

"Do I look licked?" drawled the Bounder.

"Well, you jolly well ought to be, Smithy," said Lord Mauleverer.

"We don't all get what we ought to get, old bean," said the Bounder. "F'rinstance, you ought to get a ticket of admission to a home for idiots. But you're still outside."

"I jolly well think——" growled Johnny Bull.

"Gammon!" said the Bounder. "You've nothing to do it with."

"I say, Smithy!" squeaked Billy Bunter. "Was Pon with you at the Three Fishers?"

"Shut up, you fat owl!" hissed Bob Cherry, as Wingate of the Sixth looked in at the doorway.

"Oh, really, Cherry! I was only saying—— Yarooooh! Stop stamping on my foot, you beast! Yooooop!"

"Now, then, turn in—lights out, you know!" said Wingate; and the Bounder, with all his nerve, was glad that Wingate appeared to take no note of Bunter's words, which he had certainly heard. The captain of Greyfriars gave Smithy one keen, expressive look, but that was all, and the lights were turned out, and the Remove left to themselves.

THE FIFTEENTH CHAPTER.

Unsold !

"YOU let me down, Mauly!"

"Yaas."

"It was a rotten trick!"

"Yaas."

"Not the sort of thing I'd do!"

"Yaas."

"But I've forgiven you, old chap——"

"Oh, don't!" said Lord Mauleverer anxiously. "I'd rather you didn't, if you don't mind, Bunter! I'd rather you cut me."

It was a day or two after the opening of the new term, and Billy Bunter had cornered Lord Mauleverer in the quad. During that day or two the fat Owl of the Remove had treated his lordship to distant, withering, and scornful looks. Mauly, Bunter felt, deserved it after the rotten way he had let Bunter down in the hols.

But the more distant, withering and scornful Bunter was, the better Mauly liked it. He seemed to like it much less when Billy Bunter cornered him, and was no longer distant, withering, or scornful. The fact was that in Billy Bunter's case distance lent enchantment to the view. Absence undoubtedly made the heart grow fonder.

"Oh, really, Mauly," said the fat Owl, blinking at him through his big spectacles, "I mean it! And look here—I'm going to do you a good turn. You've noticed my diamond?"

Lord Mauleverer grinned.

Nearly all Greyfriars had noticed

Billy Bunter's diamond by that time. Nobody, of course, supposed that it was a real one. But they could not help noticing it. It flashed and it glittered —it almost glared—and a blind man could hardly have escaped noticing it.

"Well, would you like it?" asked Bunter.

"Eh!" ejaculated Mauleverer in astonishment.

"The fact is I'm not really a dressy chap," explained Bunter. "I don't care for jewellery, really! I'll let you have it, Mauly. You've got pearl studs and things, and a diamond will go well with them. See?"

"My dear man, I really couldn't accept such a gift," said Lord Mauleverer, shaking his head.

He did not want to be ungrateful, but, really, Mauly would not have been found dead with a diamond that size! But he had slightly misapprehended Bunter's meaning.

"Eh? Who's talking about a gift?" asked Bunter. "I mean I'll let you have it for twenty-five pounds. See?"

"Oh!" gasped Mauleverer.

"A diamond this size is worth a hundred pounds," said Bunter.

"Yaas—a diamond!" assented Mauly.

"If you think this isn't a genuine stone, Mauly——"

"If!" gasped Mauly. "Oh gad!"

"My Uncle Robert would hardly be likely to give me a dud stone for a Christmas present, Mauly," said the Owl of the Remove, with dignity. "I don't know how much he gave for it——"

"Ninepence?" suggested Mauly.

"Beast! I mean, look here, old chap, what about a tenner?"

"Nothin' about a tenner, old fat bean."

"Dash it all, I'll take a fiver from a pal!" said Bunter, in a burst of generosity. "There!"

"Will you, really?" asked Lord Mauleverer.

"Yes, old chap! I mean it!"

"Then my advice is, go and look for a pal, and make him the offer!" said Lord Mauleverer, and he dodged Bunter and walked away.

"Beast!" roared Bunter.

Lord Mauleverer disappeared in the distance.

Billy Bunter snorted.

Bunter, thus early in the term, was in the state he had often, often known before—the state of the seed in the parable, which fell in a stony place! A number of postal orders that he had been expecting had not arrived.

It was natural that Bunter, desiring to raise the wind, should think of his diamond tiepin. To do the fat Owl justice, he had asserted so often, by this time, that it was a real, genuine diamond, that he had almost come to believe so. Every fellow who saw it agreed that it was the best imitation he had ever seen—indeed, it looked so real that only the fact that it belonged to Bunter made them believe that it was an imitation at all!

Bunter, at the bottom of his heart, could hardly believe that it was a genuine stone when he had bought it for a shilling from a shabby man in a railway train. But Bunter had a wonderful way of believing, or at least believing that he believed, just what he wanted to.

If a wealthy fellow, like Mauly or the Bounder, sported a diamond like that it would certainly be accepted as genuine. That was near enough for Bunter.

But Mauly, it seemed, was not taking any! So Billy Bunter looked round for the Bounder.

He rolled up to the Remove passage. A sound of voices from Study No. 4 told that Smithy and Redwing were at home. The voices were rather raised, as if a warm argument was going on.

That did not bother Bunter. He pushed the door open and blinked in. Redwing's face was flushed, and Smithy's scowling.

"You've had rows enough with Pon & Co.!" Redwing was saying. "Why can't you leave that crew alone?"

"I shall do exactly as I jolly well please!" retorted the Bounder.

"I know that; and it's no credit to you!" snapped Redwing. He stared round at the opening door. "Oh, get out, Bunter!"

"You shut up, Redwing! I want to speak to Smithy! I say, Smithy, old chap——"

"Get out, you fat fool!"

"It's rather important!" said Bunter. "Look here, I want to sell my diamond——"

"Fathead! Ask a pedlar to give you a penny for it, then."

"It cost my Uncle Philip twenty pounds——"

"Shut the door after you!"

"I'm going to let you have it cheap!" urged Bunter. "You've got lots of money, but you're stingy with it——"

"What?"

"So I'll let you have it at a bargain. It will suit you," urged Bunter. "You like sporting jewellery, and showing off——"

The Bounder gazed at him.

"Mauly thinks it's a bit too prominent for him to wear, you know; but you wouldn't mind that! Otherwise, Mauly would have jumped at it. But you like sticking on jewellery to show fellows what tons of money you've got, don't you, Smithy? That's why I've come to you!"

"For goodness' sake, Bunter, buzz off!" exclaimed Redwing, quite alarmed for the fat Owl.

"You shut up while I'm talking to Smithy! I say, Smithy, I'm letting this splendid diamond tiepin go for a fiver! What about it?"

Vernon-Smith rose and stepped towards Billy Bunter. Bunter blinked at him hopefully, and took the tiepin from his tie. He held it out to the Bounder.

"Take it, old chap, and look at it!" Vernon-Smith took it.

But he did not look at it! Taking the tiepin in his right hand, he took Bunter's collar in his left.

With a swift jerk he slewed Bunter round.

Then he jabbed with the pin.

The gold pin was quite sharp! Nobody in the Remove believed that that pin was genuine gold. But, gold or not, it was undoubtedly sharp at the end.

Bunter found it so!

A fearful yell rang the length of the Remove passage.

"Yoooooooop!"

Bunter made a bound for the doorway. Smithy followed him up, jabbing again with the pin.

"Yaroooocoh!"

Bunter leaped desperately into the passage. Two jabs with that sharp pin were enough for Bunter—he did not want a third.

Vernon-Smith flung the tiepin after him, went back into Study No. 4, and slammed the door.

"Ow, ow! Wow!" roared Bunter, clasping the places where the pin had jabbed with both fat hands. "Wow! Ow! Wow! Beast! Wow!"

"Hallo, hallo, hallo!" Bob Cherry came along the passage. "What——"

"Look out—don't tread on my tiepin!" howled Bunter. "If you tread on

it, you'll have to pay its value, you ass!"

"Oh scissors! That will take my last twopence!" said Bob.

"Beast!"

Billy Bunter fielded his diamond pin, stuck it in his tie again, and rolled disconsolately away. He headed for Study No. 14, where Fisher T. Fish, the business man of the Remove, had his den. Fishy, who was busy at accounts—Fishy always had accounts on hand—waved an impatient pen at him.

"Absquatulate!" he snapped.

"I'm going to sell my diamond pin——" said Bunter.

"Found a jay?" asked Fisher T. Fish.

"I'm going to sell it to you, old chap——"

"Guess again!"

"It's worth pounds and pounds," said Bunter. "My Uncle Herbert gave at least twenty pounds for it——"

"He didn't get it for fourpence from a rag-and-bone dealer?" asked Fisher T. Fish.

"No!" roared Bunter. "He didn't! Look at it, Fishy—you can take my word for it that it's a diamond of the purest water, about thirty or forty carats——"

"Oh, Jerusalem crickets!"

"I'm letting it go for a pound, Fishy!"

"Not in this study!" grinned Fisher T. Fish.

"What about ten bob?" asked Bunter desperately.

"Nunk!"

"Five bob——"

"Nix!"

"Look here, you mean skinflint, what will you give me for it?" yelled Bunter.

"Threepence!"

"Why, you—you—you beast, I gave a shilling for it myself!" howled Bunter.

"Ha, ha, ha!" roared Fisher T. Fish.

"Yah!"

Bunter rolled away. He was hard up; but he was not going to part with his diamond pin for threepence! Fisher T. Fish chortled, little guessing, reckoning, or calculating that he had refused to give five shillings for a diamond of which the market value, in point of fact, was a hundred pounds!

THE SIXTEENTH CHAPTER.

Bunter's Diamond Has a Narrow Escape!

"SHADE your eyes!" said Bob Cherry.

"Eh—why?"

"Here comes Bunter's diamond!"

"Ha, ha, ha!"

There was a flash and a sparkle in the wintry sunshine. It announced Bunter and his tiepin.

It was the first half-holiday of the term, and the Famous Five had turned out for a ramble. Bob Cherry was rather in hopes of falling in with Ponsonby, of Highcliffe—having a smack in store for Pon's aristocratic features when they met. The chums of the Remove had stopped to sit on a stile, and dispose of the contents of a packet of toffee, when that gorgeous tiepin glittered on their sight.

Billy Bunter was rolling up the road, easily recognisable at a distance, not only by his unusual circumference, but by the flash of his diamond, which he wore as prominently as it was possible to wear a diamond. Genuine or not, Bunter liked it to be seen.

Harry Wharton & Co. regarded him with smiling faces as he approached. Bunter was still at a little distance when a small, slim, slight man stepped

Billy Bunter did not stop to see whether Coker was hurt, but fled down the passage like a hare. Mr Prout, unaware of the "obstacle" round the corner, came panting on, in fierce pursuit of Bunter !

out of the hedge and stood looking at him. The man was about half-way between Bunter and the Famous Five, but he was looking towards the fat junior, and evidently had not observed the juniors sitting on the stile.

They saw his profile for a few moments, and then his back was turned to them as he stood watching Bunter rolling up.

Harry Wharton stared hard at the man.

There was something familiar in the meagre, bony figure, in the narrow, rat-like eyes and sandy eyebrows, he had glimpsed. He had seen that fellow before somewhere.

"My hat !" he ejaculated suddenly.

He remembered !

"See that sportsman ?" he exclaimed. "I've seen him before—at home in the hols. That's the man on the bike."

"The which ?" asked Bob. He had forgotten about Mr. Isaacs and his adventure with the man on the bike.

"You remember—the sandy fellow who robbed that City johnny who came down to see my uncle !" exclaimed Wharton. "The Woodgate police got him, and Mr. Isaacs went over to identify him."

"Oh, I remember !" Bob nodded.

"I heard afterwards that he'd got off for want of evidence or something after being remanded," said Harry. "But there isn't any doubt that he snatched Mr. Isaacs' tiepin. I don't know whether it was ever got back again. The man's a pickpocket, and—— Look at him !"

"Ha, ha, ha !" yelled Bob. "He's got an eye on Bunter's pin. He doesn't know it's a dud ! What a sell for him if he got it and found that it had cost a bob !"

"Ha, ha, ha !"

"That's its jolly old value !" chuckled

Nugent. "He let out to Fishy that he bought it for a bob."

The chums of the Remove chortled. The sandy man—whose name, they remembered, was Sniggerson—was watching Bunter like a cat as he came up the road. They could hardly doubt that the glitter of the diamond had caught his eye, and that the rascally pickpocket was thinking of repeating his performance on Mr. Isaacs. Certainly it was not likely to occur to them that it was the same diamond pin, entrusted to the fatuous Owl to keep it safe from the police, and that Mr. Sniggerson had been hanging about Greyfriars for days watching for a chance to get at Bunter.

Harry Wharton slipped from the stile.

"Look here, Bunter's spoof diamond isn't worth anything, but we're not going to see him robbed," he said.

"No fear !" agreed Nugent.

"The no-fearfulness is terrific !" said Hurree Jamset Ram Singh. "But we can hardfully collar the esteemed and disgusting scoundrel on suspicion, my absurd chum."

"No ; but if he grabs Bunter's paste diamond, we'll jolly well grab him before he gets clear with it !" said the captain of the Remove. "Keep behind these trees, and keep an eye on the rotter !"

"Right as rain !" agreed Bob.

The Famous Five watched curiously. Billy Bunter had almost reached the spot where the sandy man stood. Mr. Sniggerson was lighting a cigarette, or affecting to light one, with his head bent and his hands up before his face ; so the fat Owl would not have recognised him, even if he had looked at him, which he did not. Bunter was thinking of a very important matter—whether he would catch Lord Mauleverer at the bunshop at Courtfield. With that important matter on his fat mind, he was not likely to bestow any attention

on a shabby man lighting a cigarette by the wayside.

But the Famous Five, at a little distance, were bestowing very keen attention on Mr. Sniggerson ! They had no right to touch him so long as he had not done anything. But if he touched Bunter's diamond pin, they were going to touch him—promptly

When it happened, it happened swiftly. The sandy man dropped his cigarette, made a spring, and then bolted up the road. The tiepin, neatly and swiftly snatched, was concealed in his palm as he ran.

Bunter staggered.

"Ow !" he gasped. "Why—what—— Oh crikey !" His fat hand went over his tie, no longer adorned by a glittering diamond "Oh lor' ! Stop thief !"

Bunter yelled.

"Beast ! Stop thief ! Oh lor' !"

The sandy man ran like the wind. Undoubtedly he would have got clear with his prize had he had only Bunter to deal with. But as he ran he passed the clump of trees by the stile where the Famous Five stood, and like one man they rushed out to him.

"Collar him !" bawled Bob Cherry.

"Bag him !" roared Johnny Bull.

The sandy man, panting, stopped, swerved, dodged, and leaped, crashing through a frosty hedge, with the outstretched fingers of the Removites almost touching him. He was taken by surprise as they came whooping at him, but no doubt his peculiar line of business caused him to be quick on the uptake. Certainly he acted with great promptness.

Bursting through the hedge, he scudded away at desperate speed across a snowy field.

"I say, you fellows "—Billy Bunter
(Continued on page 28.)

WHEN the GREAT APES CAME!
By STUART MARTIN.

HOW THE STORY STARTED.

GERRY LAMBERT and BILLY MURCHIE, two young airmen, are brought down in the African jungle by an army of apes—led by Big Ling, a giant ape-man—reared to crush civilisation by a renegade called Stein. Gerry escapes, but Billy is taken prisoner and forced to accompany Big Ling's army, which, after laying waste villages and towns, makes for London headed by a stolen Zeppelin. Flying back to London, Gerry, assisted by Lieut. Huskin, succeeds in bringing down the Zep in Hyde Park. As a counter-attack, Big Ling lets loose the animals at the Zoo, while his armies spread devastation in all directions. Re-united once more, Gerry and Billy eventually track the enemy down in the Tower of London. Peering through a heavy curtain into the ancient Tower chapel, the boys see Big Ling and Stein surrounded by ape-men armed with weapons raided from the armoury.

(Now read on.)

A Narrow Escape.

AS the boys peered through the curtains they saw Big Ling rise from his chair and raise a hand in which he held a spear. Then he gave vent to his roar of triumph which had so often echoed through the forests of Africa. From the throats of his "court" an answering roar issued that made the apartment ring.

"I am king!"

"You are king!"

Billy raised his revolver, which had been fitted with a silencer, and took careful aim. Gerry did likewise. Both guns spoke at once with the faint "plop" peculiar to silenced firearms.

Both bullets struck Big Ling squarely in the chest.

The boys saw him stagger under the double blow. But he did not fall. It THE MAGNET LIBRARY.—No. 1,352.

was the bullets that fell. They dropped to the floor at his feet as if they had been hailstones.

Big Ling's hand clutched at his chest and pulled open the robe he had slung about him, to reveal a coat of mail tied around his body, covering his heart.

Up went the revolvers of both boys like one. This time they aimed at Big Ling's head; but Stein's quick eye had seen the movement of the curtain. His hands jerked up the machine-gun, and a stream of lead poured forth.

Billy and Gerry jerked themselves back just in time, and the bullets beat a tattoo on the opposite wall. Then a shower of spears came through the doorway, tearing down the curtain.

"This way, Gerry!"

Billy had been in the Tower often enough to know the lay-out of the premises. Along the passage the boys dashed, and down the staircase, where they were faced with an ape-man on guard. Their guns spoke their message, and the ape-man fell, writhing. Then out into the courtyard they sped.

Apes big and small prowled about the grounds, squatting on the grass and crouching in groups in corners. On the lawn here was a heap of what looked like stores covered with a tarpaulin, but in the darkness it was difficult to see it clearly. A faint light glowed in the keeper's house; but at the door stood another ape-man.

He heard the tumult, and advanced in giant strides; but the boys were too quick for him. As he launched his spear they dodged, and Billy's gun plopped.

The ape-man coughed, went down on his knees; but was up again in a moment.

He caught at Gerry as the two reached the door of the house.

Billy fired again and again at the monster, but the latter paid no heed. He had one of them, and he staggered towards the parapet, holding Gerry high above his head. One heave, and he would have thrown the boy into the moat to death; but Billy snatched up the fallen spear and drove it with all his strength into the ape-man's side.

A groan, and the giant sank down, his hand plucking at the haft of the weapon in nervous spasms.

But the fight had occupied precious time, and now the other ape-men were swarming through the doorway into the courtyard. The shelter of the keeper's house—if shelter was there—had been cut off. The boys lay under the shadow of the parapet, gaining their breath.

In a moment or so they must be found and killed, for Stein's voice was ringing out with orders and commands in a dialect that only the apes understood. And towering amid the dark forms was Big Ling, immense and frightful.

"We'd better slide over, Billy."

Cautiously they reared themselves, and dropped over between the raised portions of the parapet, hanging on to the stone and digging their feet into the old wall for support.

Again Stein's voice spoke quite near to them, and the gigantic form of Ling stood within a yard of their precarious perch.

"Who was it, Ling?" asked Stein. "Did you see?"

"No. It could not be the prisoners. They are still behind that door. It must have been the mutineer—Tree Climber. I suspected him of mutiny."

"Could it not have been those boys of England?"

Ling's reply could not be heard; but presently Stein spoke again.

"We have changed our plans once because of these boys. We cannot wait here until dawn, or we will be hemmed in. Our army is marching on the Great West Road towards London. They need us. Our ships have escaped from the soldiers on the bridge. We must go."

"Very well. I am king!"

Orders cracked out sharp and swift. Already the streaks of dawn were showing in the east, the roofs of the city were becoming blurred in the misty rising of the new day.

Hanging to the wall, Billy and Gerry saw, as they peered over, ape-men throw the cover off the heap in the centre of the lawn. Then the apes were assembled and driven, by whips and shouts, across the courtyard, and could be heard swarming down the passage towards Traitor's Gate. When all had gone except for a few ape-men and Stein and Ling, the group gathered round the stores and began to work feverishly.

A moment later the meaning of these stores became clear. They were harnesses fitted with the helium gas for lifting the invaders.

Up into the air went one ape-man after another, the bladders slung between their shoulders. Then up went Big Ling, followed by Stein. And as they rose into the dimness of the early morning fog, Billy and Gerry climbed back to safety and stood beside the parapet, gaining their breath.

From above them, although they could not see it, they heard the drone of a plane that became loud and roaring; its great shadow seemed to sweep over the Tower. It passed, and again came another drone, another roar as a second plane rushed overhead. And then a softer whirring sound—a plane cruising, sailing with engine subdued.

Another sound then burst on the boys' ears, and a minor explosion shook the dwelling-houses of the courtyard. From a window came the glare of flames, the rush of smoke. These spread until the whole square seemed alive with flame.

The Tower of London was on fire, and the boys were hemmed in by a circle of death!

It was not the thought of death, however, that made them both leap towards the tarpaulin that lay on the ground in front of them. The same thought had struck both boys at the same moment. They tore the tarpaulin aside, to reveal two sets of harness, two envelopes of helium gas, and two folded parachutes. They were the gear intended for the ape-men whom they had slain.

In a moment Billy and Gerry had buckled on the harness, unfastening the straps that bound it to an iron ring in the ground.

Up above the rising mist they might yet chase Stein and Big Ling.

"Ready?" asked Billy.

"You bet!" said Gerry.

Up they went, drawn like toy balloons, the earth dropping from their feet, up into the mist side by side, and in the hands of each boy was a spear lifted from the litter on the ground.

Bad Luck for Billy!

IN a matter of minutes Billy and Gerry were floating gently five hundred feet or so above the Thames.

They would have separated in the gentle current of air that was moving the topmost layer of fog had they not been hand-in-hand; and as they cast their eyes around they saw clearly for a considerable distance.

They could feel the heat of the fire that was blazing in the Tower below them. It had a queer look, that fire—a red, leaping furnace dimmed by a veil of mist.

The sound of a Moth plane approaching from the other side of the river caused the boys to look southward.

"Look down there, Billy!" cried Gerry, pointing to the river over which they were floating.

A large ship was passing under Tower Bridge. Billy, staring down, saw what had attracted the attention of his pal.

The ship was churning her way downstream. On her bridge stood an officer, his hand on the telegraph. Beside the officer stood a huge figure pressing something that glinted against the man's side.

There was no mistaking this huge figure. It was one of Big Ling's ape-men, and he was compelling the officer, at the point of a gun, to take the ship out.

The next moment the attention of the boys was drawn to the Moth plane that was circling the turrets of the bridge. It was fitted with floats as well as wheels for landing. But the pilot made no attempt to land, nor was he taking note of the ship. He was signalling to the boys, flagging in quick gestures, his arm moving up and down spasmodically.

He was flagging them to drop.

Manipulating the cords of the harness, the boys descended slowly towards the river. The ship was now some distance down-stream. As they came down, the Moth's engine ceased to throb, and the

plane descended in a long dive and settled on the surface of the water.

The boys reached the water almost at the same instant, and the plane taxied forward and came to rest on its floats.

"Come aboard, lads!" hailed the pilot. "We haven't got any time to waste!"

The boys scrambled aboard and were soon tucked into the seating accommodation, which was barely enough to give them room. The engine was started again, and the plane was soon moving ahead.

"Commander Walsh," grinned the pilot. "That's my name. I'm doing scout duty—been at it all night. I was after the enemy when I saw you two bob up from the fire, so I came back."

"Where has Stein gone?" asked Billy. "And Ling?"

"They separated forces," replied the pilot. "I came on the scene by chance when they were having their air-barges dragged off. They've got two of the finest planes in existence. Stolen, I hear. Absolutely the latest. Autogyro."

He thrust his head forward and began to speak into the wireless instrument in answer to signals from headquarters.

"Hallo, hallo! Walsh speaking. I'm over South London, pursuing enemy plane with barge. Another has gone due west. A ship has gone down the Thames from Tower Bridge, and I have suspicions it is in enemy hands. Very good!"

He turned to Billy and Gerry.

"That was headquarters calling. They'll be keeping up a conversation now. I've already reported the fire at the Tower, and I've told them I have you two on board."

He peered forward, and then, pulling back the joystick, sent the plane up to a great height. Having done this, he handed a pair of field-glasses to Billy.

The later focused the glasses ahead and made out a speck to the right.

"I don't think we can catch it," cried Walsh, "but we'll hang on to its tail! Have you any idea where it is making for? My petrol-tank isn't full, by any means."

"I can guess," said Billy. "There is an army of apes doing damage at Southampton—or were last night——"

"That's the place. I had a message through not long ago that an army of apes had left the town. Here's another message."

The instrument in front of him gurgled, then a voice came distinctly:

"Hallo, hallo! Commander Walsh? Thank you! One-three-one speaking. Your report received. O.K.! Orders are that you are not to make for Southampton. Gorillas have left the town and are moving south-west. Search and report movement. Repeat."

Walsh repeated. The voice went on:

"Troops being sent from Salisbury and other depots. Have you used any bombs? O.K.!"

Billy, looking on the floor of the carriage, saw the apparatus for releasing bombs, and counted three deadly missiles ready for emergencies.

The Moth flew straight on, keeping the fugitive plane in view and gaining ground gradually.

"It's a huge plane," said Walsh. "I was on my way back to go off duty when I spotted it. Where's he heading for now?"

The big plane suddenly turned, and in a moment was enveloped in a black cloud.

"They've seen us chasing them, and turned into the raincloud instead of rising above it!" cried Gerry. "Look out; we're in it, too!"

They were in it without a doubt. Blackness closed upon the machine, and for some time they were flying blind in what seemed to be a cavern of wetness.

Commander Walsh suddenly banked and dived, and the movement came with such unexpectedness that Billy and Gerry were dashed to the floor of the cockpit. As they lay there their ears were deafened by the mighty roar of a passing engine. The enemy machine had missed them by inches, and the whirl of its wash sent the Moth staggering like a stricken thing.

Walsh brought the plane up to a level keel with supreme effort, and swung round in the enemy's wake.

"They tried to wreck us!" he roared, in the gale. "Did you see the bomb they dropped?"

Through the cloud they charged, dripping and smoking. But there was no sign of the enemy plane—not even a sound of her propellers. The cloud stretched for miles, deep and black.

"Look below!" yelled Gerry suddenly. "What's that?"

Billy and the pilot looked in the direction indicated, and saw the great plane swimming gracefully towards an anchorage, slanting like an arrow as it glided forward to a green patch. Behind it trailed a barge, with its covering of gasbag billowing out in the breeze.

For miles on either side of the green patch lay the waving tops of trees, intersected by what appeared to be long, white ribbons of moving objects.

"The New Forest!" cried Gerry. "Military lorries on the roads!"

"Get ready to release a bomb!" cried Walsh. "I'm diving!"

Down went the Moth in a wide sweep, and when it was in the required position Walsh roared again:

"Now!"

Billy pulled the lever and released a bomb. As he did so, however, the enemy plane rose again like an enormous gull, skimmed the trees, and launched itself northward. The bomb fell on the green patch, sending up a shower of earth, and bringing down trees like ninepins.

Up rose the Moth again, keeping up the pursuit until the enemy came to rest at a crossroads. The Moth swooped down again, and another bomb was released. But the giant plane missed the missile by the same manoeuvre. The bomb, however, fell on its tracks and lifted the crossroads in a cloud of earth.

There was only one bomb left now, and this time there must be no mistake, if such it could be called. The enemy did not rise high this time, but swung round, heading for a track of glimmering roadway. Along the track it ran, hovering, then came to rest, with its wings cracking and smashing against the trees on either side.

Down came the Moth for the third time. The boys saw the occupants of the big plane scrambling out. Among them was Big Ling. His arms were waving directions when Gerry pulled the lever for the release of the last missile.

There was no mistake this time. Looking back, the occupants of the Moth saw the enemy plane distinctly for a second, and then it was lost in a cloud of smoke and dust.

Half a mile or so farther on the Moth landed on the road, and Walsh and the two boys leaped out. The petrol tank was empty.

Not a sound in the forest. A strange quietness was in the air. The giant plane was burning out on the road.

"Whoever piloted that plane had brains!" exclaimed Walsh. "He has caught us nicely! The troops are cut off!"

It was true. The manœuvres of the enemy plane had been deliberate ruses to get the Moth to drop her bombs at certain spots, and these spots were strategic ones. The broken roads had stopped the military from advancing.

Armed with guns, as well as the spears Billy and Gerry carried, the trio ran into the forest for cover. As they did so the silence was broken by a din that sent their blood leaping through their veins.

First came the howl of Big Ling, then the deep roaring of gorillas.

There was no time to climb the trees: there was death in the branches had they climbed. Dark forms could be seen swinging from limb to limb, swarms of apes, while the tall forms of ape-men could be seen breaking their way through the shrubbery.

Led by Big Ling, the army of beasts were coming towards the Moth.

Diving into the thick shrubbery, the three crawled under cover, pulling trailers and leaves over them. Holding their weapons ready, they waited.

The ground shook with the stamping beasts. Wave after wave of gorillas swept past, some on all-fours, some erect, beating their breasts, snarling, and howling. And above the racket the voice of Ling sounded, curt and sharp.

The huge ape-man stopped suddenly, and they heard him sniffing like a hound. His great hand fell on the covering above them, shaking it gently. Then he passed on.

From the distance came the rattle of machine-guns. The troops had opened fire. The Battle of the New Forest had begun. Shells burst among the trees, uprooting and smashing in every direction.

For half an hour the barrage continued, pouring high explosive and shrapnel into the forest. It ceased as suddenly as it began, and the three crawled out of their cover.

Devastation lay around them. The bodies of several wild ponies were stretched on the ground, while others stood trembling beside fallen trees. In the distance men's voices were cheering. The advance had started.

There was not a sign of gorillas to be seen, and Billy, Gerry, and the pilot pressed forward until they found themselves on the edge of the woods. In front was a deep valley, one of the many in the New Forest, sheltered by thick shrubbery and bushes several feet high. The spires of the village of Ringwood rose in the distance.

Towards the end of this valley moving men could be seen. They were the advancing troops thrusting their way onward, rifles held high above their heads.

"They're driving the apes into the valley!" cried Walsh. "Look down there!"

Sure enough, the lurking, stealthy forms of gorillas were to be seen hastening into the depths.

"There's Ling!" cried Billy, as he pointed across the slope.

The tall figure of Ling had risen from the shrubbery, and stood like a statue watching the movements of the troops. Bullets whistled in his direction, but he never moved. He seemed to be intent on something else. He raised his hand to his mouth, and a long whistle shrilled in the air.

"It's a trap! Look—look!"

Gerry had mounted a tree, and waved to his companions to climb up. In a

moment they were by his side, and what they saw took their breath away.

The advancing soldiers were walking right into a snare set by that monster criminal.

The gorillas in the valley, seemingly retreating, were all small animals; but, circling in a wide sweep, so as to take the troops in the rear, were others, the main force. They were invisible to the soldiers and the officers who led them, but from their position in the high tree the three boys could see clearly.

As the soldiers advanced, throwing bombs at intervals, so the massive brutes circled behind them. Ape-men were guiding them, and Big Ling was directing the entire manœuvre.

"We must get word through to them!" cried Billy, as he dropped from the tree. "Listen, you two! I'm going to carry word to the battery on the road!"

"How?"

"This way!"

He pointed to where a sturdy wild pony was standing on the edge of the wood, apparently the leader of a small group of smaller animals.

As Billy advanced, the animal started, but before he could make a getaway Billy had seized his mane and leaped on his back, driving his knees into the pony's sides.

With a bound he was away, and the other animals scattered.

Bending over the pony's neck, Billy urged it towards the roadway. The thought of the massacre that would occur if the troops fell into the trap made him shudder.

Leaping and dodging the swaying branches and broken trees and torn ground, he gained the roadway, forced the pony on to the stretch, and raced as he had never raced before.

It was a main road, and the pony's hoofs hardly touched it in its wild career. There were no obstacles except a pit some distance ahead, beyond which the troops had drawn up with their guns and trucks.

Billy had not gone far, however, when he encountered a new danger. Stones were being thrown at him and his mount from the forest edge. He glanced round and saw the faces of gorillas, ape-men, and monkeys. They were following him side by side, racing as fast as his pony, hurling rocks, sticks, anything they could pick up.

Some distance ahead a tree crashed down across the road. The pony cleared it in a bound, slid on the hard, concrete surface, regained its feet again, and clattered on. A stone struck Billy, and another struck the pony; then a gorilla leaped from the forest edge.

The impact of its body sent the pony slithering, but the gorilla was thrown off.

Crack, crack! went Billy's revolver. Two more apes went down. But more stones were being thrown. More apes were taking up the chase. A massive brute could be seen twenty yards in front, balancing itself on the branch of a tree stretched across the road, ready for a spring.

Up went Billy's weapon again, and he took a flying shot. The bullet struck the gorilla, but it did not stop his spring. His weight fell on the pony's neck, and Billy was pitched to the hard road, where he lay still.

Through a dark mist he saw an ape-man bending over him, and heard a guttural voice say:

"Take him to Big Ling. Throw the pony to the beasts!"

Big Ling's Headquarters!

LATE that afternoon Big Ling strode through the forest with head erect, flushed with victory. His plan had been carried out. Deep in the valley lay the bodies of several hundred British soldiers, killed by the apes.

There had been casualties on the beasts' side, too. The shrubbery was strewn with dead apes, shattered by hand grenades, shot by rifles, or stabbed by bayonets. But the guns had been silenced, and those who had escaped that massacre of the New Forest had gone to carry the news to amazed commanders.

Ling strode among his battered forces with the air of a conqueror. Perched on his head was the crown he had stolen from the Tower of London. He still wore the chain armour, and carried his club. He was under no misapprehension as to what would follow. More troops would come, heavier guns would belch their messages of death. But he had his plans for meeting them, and for the moment dismissed the thought from his mind.

The battle had been fought in surroundings which suited him and his forces. The forest was their natural home, and trees were their natural cover and protection. Civilised soldiers were hampered by that confusion of nature, while the apes revelled in it; and Ling had the further advantage that his beasts went to their deaths without thought. To them fighting was nature.

There was much of the beast in Ling himself, and although he was tired, the lust of killing had whetted his appetite for more. The day was not far advanced; the story of his victory in the New Forest must not stay his hand. He had learned from Stein, the Master, that to strike was but a reason for striking again. To conquer he must spread dismay and fear. It was the law of the jungle, and he was a child of the jungle.

Big Ling gathered together his remaining forces and led them, growling and savage, their lips tinged with the blood of their victims, to his headquarters in the forest. Here were a number of uprooted trees, so placed as to form a gigantic wigwam.

He strode into the peculiar abode, flushed with victory, ready for more conquests. His lieutenants were gathered about the enclosure, armed with spears and rifles taken from the soldiers who lay dead in the shrubbery of the valley.

He saw the form of Billy Murchie lying on the ground, roped hand and foot.

"You did well to bring him," he said sharply. "After to-day's work he will be handed over to the beasts. We will make a sacrifice of him. Find his companions."

Taking a chart from his shirt of mail, Big Ling sat down on the ground and began to study it, while he ate food that was placed before him. He seemed to have forgotten everything but his ambition. The ape-men waited in silence.

"Is there any news of the Master?" asked Big Ling, addressing one of his lieutenants.

"No, king!"

"Marshal the beasts, then! We are marching now!"

"Yes, king!"

"Have you secured the lorries of the enemy?"

"Yes, king!"

Printed and published every Saturday by the Proprietors, The Amalgamated Press, Ltd., The Fleetway House, Farringdon Street, London, E.C.4. Advertisement offices, The Fleetway House, Farringdon Street, London, E.C.4. Registered for transmission by Canadian Magazine Post. Subscription rates: Inland and Abroad, 11s. per annum; 5s. 6d. for six months. Sole Agents for Australia and New Zealand: Messrs. Gordon & Gotch, Ltd., and for South Africa: Central News Agency, Ltd.—Saturday, January 13th, 1934.

"Good! Then you will drive them. I travel in the first. You lead the army. Bombs. Ammunition. Forward!"

He rose and marched out of the wigwam and gave his howl of command. The forest echoed with the answering roar.

Swinging round, Ling selected another ape-man.

"You take a party in that direction." He pointed south, towards Southampton. "Wreck! Spread death! Lead the enemy that way."

The ape-man stiffened, and his head bowed.

"Why me, king? Have I not led enough such parties and yet returned?"

Ling's eyes snapped at his subordinate. The ape-man was fifteen feet high, but he seemed small compared with Ling.

Up went Ling's club in a great stroke.

It descended on the ape-man's head with a crash, and the subordinate fell like a tree before the axe of the lumberman.

Billy Murchie felt the ground shiver under that fall. He guessed why the ape-man had protested. Ling was conducting his campaign with all the cunning of an animal brain linked to a human one. He had sent out batches of his beasts to mislead the British troops while he himself struck at other points.

He had done it in every attack he had made; and by consigning these scare-raising parties to certain death, he had gained the vulnerable points. What was a sacrifice of a handful of gorillas and an ape-man to this self-constituted king?

"You!" he roared, lifting a finger and pointing to another ape-man.

The monster indicated stepped forward and raised his spear in salute.

"I go, king!"

A sign from Ling, and the gathering broke up. Then Ling stood looking down on Billy with a sneer on his brutish face.

"There were three of you," he said in his deep, broken English. "I saw you from across the valley. It was I who tempted your plane to bomb mine. But for the Master's wish to torture you in his own way, I would stamp the life out of you now!"

He raised his foot as if tempted to crush Billy under it. His face was the picture of frightful savagery.

(Look out for further thrilling chapters of this popular adventure story in next week's free gift number of the MAGNET.)

COME INTO THE OFFICE, BOYS!

Always glad to hear from you, chums, so drop me a line to the following address : The Editor, The "Magnet" Library, The Amalgamated Press, Ltd., The Fleetway House, Farringdon Street, London, E.C.4. A stamped, addressed envelope will ensure a reply.

HALLO, chums, are you pleased with this week's set of topping coloured pictures? I thought you would be! Next week's MAGNET will contain the tenth and last set of coloured pictures, so don't spoil your album through failing to get hold of next Saturday's MAGNET.

Now for some more news of the next batch of

GREAT FREE GIFTS,

about which I made a brief mention last week. These take the novel form of delicious toffee, and the first "give away" will be made with the MAGNET in a fortnight's time—that is, immediately after our present series of free gifts pictures come to a close. How's that for a big surprise? Are you cheering? I'll say you are! Now listen in closely : For four weeks—commencing, remember, with our issue dated January 27th—every reader of the MAGNET will receive

A BAR OF WALTERS' DELICIOUS "PALM" TOFFEE !

This toffee is the real goods, boys! I've had some and, like the celebrated Oliver Twist, I asked for more! Each of the four bars to be presented with MAGNET is of a different flavour ; and each bar is calculated to "tickle the palate" of any average boy.

Don't forget, chums, the first of these delightful Free Gifts will be found in the MAGNET in a fortnight's time, so be sure and give your newsagent an order for the MAGNET without delay. That done, please do me the favour of passing on the good news to your pals. I feel only too sure that they will want to share in this stupendous treat.

ONE of my readers asks me this question :

DOES THE SEA-SERPENT ACTUALLY EXIST ?

I think there have been more arguments caused in scientific circles by that question than by any other! Most people "pooh-pooh" the suggestion of there being vast marine monsters, but on the other hand the number of people who claim to have seen what they call "the sea-serpent" is considerable.

Certain scientists claim that it is quite possible that entirely unknown monsters may lurk in the depths of the sea in places where it has been impossible to obtain any data regarding what is to be found on the floor of the ocean. Even in the last few years certain forms of life have been discovered in the ocean of which, until their discovery, everyone was ignorant. This is held to be proof that we know nothing about what may be in the lower depths of the sea, and therefore we should keep an open mind as to whether sea-serpents exist or not.

In fact, some people go so far as to say that great prehistoric animals of the kind which have been "faked" in films may possibly still roam the earth in places where, even to-day, explorers have never penetrated!

Talking about real life beating the films, here's a case of

A REAL-LIFE HOUDINI

who puts the exploits of stage and screen "prison-breakers" well in the shade. Up to the present he has escaped from prison fifteen times. After his fifth escape they decided to put him in the "Chain Gang," where, with shackles riveted on his legs, they thought he would be safe. A few days later he had vanished! The next time he fell into the hands of the law they not only shackled his legs, but made him sleep in an iron cage in the middle of a camp, with bloodhounds sleeping just outside the cage, and a guard calling on him at intervals during the night. But, believe it or not, he got out of that cage and made a "getaway" without disturbing either the dogs or the guard!

Once, when it seemed likely that a pardon would be granted to him, this amazing prisoner broke out of gaol once more, and turned up amongst his friends, who persuaded him to go back at once. Dawn found him at the prison gates, asking the guards if he could go back to his cell !

At the present time, with his accumulated sentences, this "prison-breaker" has to serve no less than 110 years! But the prison guards are getting a bit "fed up" with him, and there is a movement on foot to get him a pardon, in the hope that he may go straight.

HOW often have some of you fellows wanted to be cowboys? It sounds a pretty good life, doesn't it, but, believe me,

TRAINING FOR A COWBOY

is a most arduous job! I've just been reading about the "pleasant" little tricks the old hands play on youngsters new to the ranch. An old cowboy has just been telling about his earliest experiences on a ranch.

The crowd had camped for the night in a spot where they were surrounded by coyotes. The boy was told to go to a nearby creek for water, and when he said he felt ill, the old hands reckoned he was scared of coyotes. Taking him out of camp, they tied his hands and feet to a stake, built a bonfire to attract all the coyotes for miles around, and left him there until the morning !

Next night the new hand went for the water ! Coyotes were howling all around him, and he whistled to keep up his spirits. When he got back the old hands told him to go once more, and threatened to stake him out again if he whistled ! The new hand didn't whistle the next time ! After that he thought no more of coyotes than of tame kittens ! So you fellows know what to expect if you want to become a cowboy.

I HAVEN'T much space left, chums, so I'd better let you know what there is in store for you next week. Topping the bill is :

"THE PROFITEER OF THE REMOVE !" By Frank Richards.

The title of this long complete yarn of the chums of Greyfriars suggests that Fisher T. Fish is playing a star role, and that is sufficient to let you know that you are in for a feast of fun and thrills. When Frank Richards gets going on yarns of this description there isn't another boys' author to touch him. So look out, chums, and don't run the risk of being told that your favourite paper is "sold out."

Next time you write to me let me know what you think of our thrilling adventure yarn : "When the Great Apes Came !" There will, of course, be another quick-fire, full-of-thrills instalment in next week's issue, and when you have finished it, you can turn to our "Greyfriars Herald" supplement, and loosen your waistcoat buttons, because you're in for a good laugh. If there's any truth in the saying, "laugh and grow fat," you'd better watch out, or you'll be turning into Billy Bunters! Of course, I must not forget "Linesman's" interesting Soccer replies, and our final set of stunning free coloured pictures.

And roll, bowl, or pitch your queries in to me, chums! I'm here to be shot at !

YOUR EDITOR.

BILLY BUNTER'S DIAMOND!

(Continued from page 23.)

spotted the Famous Five—"I say, I've been robbed! I say, get hold of that pickpocket! I say——"

But Harry Wharton & Co. did not stop to listen to Bunter. They crashed through the hedge after the sandy man.

He was running hard; but all the five were good at sprinting. They put it on vigorously.

"After him!" panted Harry Wharton.

"We'll get him all right!" chuckled Bob Cherry breathlessly. "Put it on, my infants! Tally-ho!"

The sandy man glanced back over his shoulder. Five juniors, in a row, were coming on hard and fast. All of them were keeping pace, and Bob Cherry and Harry Wharton were drawing ahead. Mr. Sniggerson panted, and tore on, bounding over a fence, and getting to the open common. After him, leaping the fence in their turn, went the Famous Five, and the chase was taken up across the wide expanse of Courtfield Common.

Billy Bunter was left far behind. He was anxious about his diamond—but he could not have put up a race like that for all the diamonds that ever came out of South Africa.

Mr. Sniggerson put on a desperate burst of speed. Harder and harder he ran, his feet seeming scarcely to touch the ground.

But Bob Cherry and Harry Wharton did not lose an inch, though their comrades were dropping a little behind.

"We've got him!" breathed Bob, his ruddy face crimson with exertion. "He doesn't seem to know this country—he's heading straight for the pond—he will have to lose ground going round when he spots it——"

"Good!" gasped Wharton.

It was some minutes later that the running pickpocket spotted the gleam of water through the leafless trees ahead of him. He paused, swerved, and cut off to the left to avoid the pond that lay in his way.

"Stop, you rotter!" bawled Bob Cherry. "We've jolly well got you! Chuck it!"

But the sandy man ran desperately on. Slowly and surely the juniors were gaining now, and they were close on him. Breathless, panting, he stumbled, and as he rose again, Bob Cherry's grasp landed on his back.

The sandy man spun round, panting with rage, and struck. Bob gave a roar as a set of bony knuckles crashed on his nose and he went over.

The next moment Harry Wharton's fist crashed on the sandy man's jaw, and he rolled over beside Bob.

Before he could attempt to struggle up, the captain of the Remove leaped on him and pinned him down.

"Got him!" panted Wharton. "Bear a hand, Bob!"

"What-ho!" Bob struggled up breathlessly and bore a hand. The sandy man was struggling; but he gave in as soon as two pairs of hands were on him. The two juniors held him fast while Nugent and Johnny Bull and Hurree Jamset Ram Singh came panting up.

"Now for Bunter's jolly old diamond!" grinned Bob, and he grasped the man's wrist and forced open his clenched hand.

The sandy man gritted his teeth with rage, spitting like a cat.

"Hang you!" he panted. "I——"

"That's enough from you!" said Bob cheerfully. "My hat! Wouldn't anybody believe that was a real diamond?" he added, as the clenched hand was forced open, glittered and flashed in the sun.

"The rotten pickpocket thinks so!" grinned Nugent.

"Ha, ha, ha!"

The juniors laughed breathlessly. Bob Cherry took the diamond pin and slipped it into his pocket, the sandy man's rat-like eyes following it hungrily and greedily.

---

14 MORE SUPERB COLOURED PICTURES to complete your Album.

Watch Out For Them in NEXT WEEK'S MAGNET

Boys, you'll have a treasure of a collection when you've completed your Album!

"You young 'ounds——" he muttered between his teeth.

"You rascally thief!" said Harry Wharton contemptuously. "You're the man who robbed Mr. Isaacs weeks ago in Surrey, though you seem to have got off!"

"I never——" he began.

"Oh, chuck it! I know you!" said the captain of the Remove. "You ought to be jolly well handed over to the police for this, though this time you've only bagged a dud diamond worth about a bob——"

"You fool!"

"It's you that's the fool, old bean!" chuckled Bob Cherry. "That jolly old diamond you snatched is a dud."

"But a thief's a thief!" said Harry Wharton. "You fancied that it was a real diamond when you snatched it from Bunter. We're not taking the

trouble to march you down to the police station for pinching a worthless diamond; but you're going to have a lesson, all the same! Chuck him into the pond, you fellows!"

"Hear, hear!"

"Look here!" gasped the sandy man, beginning to struggle again. "I—— Oh—ah—yah—gurrrrggh!"

Splash!

"Ha, ha, ha!"

The sandy man sprawled in shallow water and mud. He emerged gasping and gurgling, streaming mud from head to foot.

"That's a tip to keep your hands from picking and stealing, old bean!" chuckled Bob Cherry. "You're lucky not to be run in! Have another?"

Evidently the sandy man did not want another! He shook a muddy and furious fist at the Greyfriars fellows and started at a run across the common. In a few moments he had vanished.

"Now we'd better find Bunter and hand over the glittering bob's worth!" remarked Bob Cherry.

The Famous Five walked back to the road. They spotted Billy Bunter in the distance and bore down on him.

"I say, you fellows!" gasped Bunter, as they came up with smiling faces. "I say, somebody's robbed me—a man on the road—you saw him—he got away with my diamond pin—did you get hold of him?"

"We did!"

"The didfulness was terrific, my esteemed Bunter!"

"Oh, good!" gasped Bunter. "Did you get the diamond from him?"

"He hadn't any diamond on him!" said Bob Cherry, shaking his head. "All we got from him was this!"

He drew the tiepin from his pocket and held it up.

"Ha, ha, ha!"

"You—you silly ass!" gasped Bunter. "That's my diamond, ain't it? Gimme my diamond!" Bunter grabbed it. "I say, you fellows! As you've got my diamond back for me I'll let you have it if you like—what about a pound?"

"Ha, ha, ha!"

"Blessed if I see anything to cackle at! Just to show you that I'm grateful for the trouble you've taken, I'll let you have that diamond for a pound—look here, say ten shillings—I say, you fellows, don't walk away while a fellow's talking to you!" roared Bunter.

But the Famous Five did walk away, chuckling as they went. Billy Bunter snorted and rolled on to Courtfield, with his precious diamond sticking in his tie—still unsold!

THE END.

(Now look out for next week's MAGNET *and another rollicking fine yarn of Greyfriars, entitled: "THE PROFITEER OF THE REMOVE!" And don't forget that this issue will contain our tenth and final set of free coloured pictures. Be sure to add them to your collection!)*

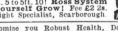

The MAGNET 2ᴰ

No. 1,353. Vol. XLV.   EVERY SATURDAY.   Week Ending January 20th, 1934.

THE PROFITEER OF THE REMOVE!

BY FRANK RICHARDS.

THE FIRST CHAPTER.

Called Over the Coals!

"BUNTER!"

Billy Bunter jumped.

"It—it wasn't me, sir !" he gasped.

"What ?"

"I—I don't know anything about it, sir !"

Dr. Locke, the headmaster of Greyfriars, gazed at Billy Bunter. The Remove fellows looked round at him, grinning.

It was second lesson at Greyfriars, and the Head was taking the Remove. That was very unusual. Seldom indeed did the Lower Fourth Form of Greyfriars enjoy the distinguished honour of being "taken" by their headmaster.

It was an honour they would willingly have dispensed with. The Head was rather a terrifying personage to Lower Fourth juniors.

But the Remove had started the new term without a Form-master. Their own "beak," Mr. Quelch, had not come back after the Christmas holidays, being laid up with a severe cold. So matters were rather at sixes and sevens until he came.

The Remove were on their best behaviour with the Head. Bob Cherry tried hard not to shuffle his feet. Skinner carefully refrained from projecting ink-balls at other fellows' necks. Lord Mauleverer suppressed his inclination to yawn. Even the Bounder was quiet and respectful; and Billy Bunter had not brought anything eatable into the Form-room. Really, it was quite a model Form that morning, every fellow anxious not to catch the Head's eye.

THE MAGNET LIBRARY.—No. 1,353.

But that eye fixed on Billy Bunter ! Bunter was alarmed.

There were many sins, of omission and commission, on Billy Bunter's fat conscience, and, as Dr. Locke rapped out his name, the Owl of the Remove could only wonder which of them had come to the Head's knowledge.

He blinked at Dr. Locke in great alarm through his big spectacles, and promptly denied the accusation, without waiting to hear what it was.

"Bunter !" repeated the Head.

"I assure you, sir, that it wasn't me !" said Bunter, in a great hurry. "I haven't been near the Fifth Form passage this term."

"What ?" ejaculated Dr. Locke.

"If Coker says that his cake is gone, sir, I don't know anything about it. Besides, that was yesterday——"

"You are a very stupid boy, Bunter !" said the Head mildly. "I have heard no complaint from Coker of the Fifth Form."

"Oh !" gasped Bunter.

"But," said the Head in a deep voice, "if you have abstracted a cake from Coker's study, Bunter——"

"Oh, no, sir ! Not at all ! I—I don't think Coker had a cake ! I never heard him mention it to Potter and Greene, nor——"

"Ha, ha, ha !" came from the Remove.

"Bless my soul !" said the Head. "Bunter, I fear that you are a very untruthful boy, as well as a very stupid one—very untruthful indeed !"

"Me, sir ?" exclaimed Bunter. "Oh, no, sir ! Perhaps you're thinking of Wharton, sir, or Nugent——"

"You blithering owl !" murmured Harry Wharton.

"Oh, really, Wharton——"

"Silence !" rapped the Head. "Bunter, stand out before the Form !"

"Oh lor' !"

Billy Bunter rolled out dolorously. Evidently the trouble, whatever it was, was not connected with Coker's cake. Bunter wondered whether the cook or the House dame had been complaining. It would be just like those old cats, Bunter thought, to make a fuss about a pie being mysteriously missing from the regions below stairs.

"Now, Bunter——"

"I never touched it, sir !" said Bunter.

"You never touched it ?" repeated the Head.

"No, sir ! I haven't seen it."

"You have not seen it ?"

"No, sir ! There's a very strict rule about fellows going down into the kitchen, and I'm always very careful about the rules, sir ! If there's a pie gone, it's news to me !"

"Bless my soul !" said the Head.

"The fact is, sir, that I don't care for beefsteak pie !" said Bunter. "It's not a thing I like at all ! And it wasn't a nice pie, either, sir ! You can ask Skinner ! I gave him some !"

Dr. Locke was not so used to the fatuous Bunter as Mr. Quelch was. He seemed to be quite taken by surprise by him. He gazed at him as if Bunter had taken his breath away.

"Bunter," he gasped at last, "I have certainly received a complaint from Mrs. Kebble with reference to a missing pie, but I was not aware that you were the culprit."

"Oh lor' !" gasped Bunter.

"I called to you," said Dr. Locke, "with reference to that extremely conspicuous diamond pin in your tie, Bunter."

"Oh!" stuttered Bunter.

His fat hand went up to his tie, in which gleamed and glittered and flashed a big diamond.

Everybody at Greyfriars had seen Bunter's diamond except the Head—and now the Head saw it!

Nobody, of course, believed that it was a real diamond; even Bunter, who had bought it for a shilling from a shabby man in a railway train, could hardly believe that it was genuine.

But it looked the genuine goods, there was no doubt about that. And Bunter had swanked very extensively with his diamond pin.

According to Bunter, it was a diamond of the purest water, and its value was almost fabulous.

Greyfriars fellows did not sport diamonds; it was considered bad form. But Billy Bunter did not care much about that, so long as he could flash and sparkle and glitter.

It was still early in the term; but Bunter's diamond had become as well known at Greyfriars as the clock-tower or the ivied library wall or the football field. It had become one of the sights of Greyfriars. It was familiar to almost every eye. And—though it did not occur to Bunter's fat mind—it was certain that the Head would want to know about it as soon as he became aware of it.

"No boy in this school, Bunter, is allowed to wear such prominent and expensive jewellery," said the Head. "It is in bad taste, Bunter. But, apart from that, I require to know how you came into possession of such an article? It is far too valuable to belong to a junior schoolboy. Where did you obtain that diamond, Bunter?"

The Remove fellows looked on, with grinning faces.

The Head, apparently, was taking Bunter's diamond as genuine. Certainly it looked it.

But if it was genuine, it was worth a hundred pounds—in which case, a Lower Fourth fellow would have found it very difficult to explain how he had come by it.

Bunter had to own up now.

The fat Owl had told many tales about that diamond. It was an heirloom in the Bunter family which had been made up into a tiepin. It was a Christmas present from his Uncle George. It was a New Year's gift from his Uncle William. Bunter never could remember that a certain class of persons should have good memories! None of these yarns, however, would do for the Head. The Removites listened with keen interest to hear what the hapless Owl would say.

He blinked dismally at the Head. It was a relief to learn that he was not called on in reference to a cake or a pie. But he did not want to own up before all the Form that his famous diamond was paste!

"Answer me, Bunter!" rapped the Head.

"The—the fact is, sir——" stammered Bunter.

"Well?"

"My—my Uncle George——" stuttered the fat Owl.

"Oh, my hat!" murmured Peter Todd blankly. Against all probability, the fat Owl was going to spring his Uncle George on the Head!

"Your uncle?" repeated the Head.

"Yes, sir! He—he—he gave me this —this pin for a Christmas present, sir."

Bunter was risking it. Anything, from Billy Bunter's peculiar point of view, was better than stating the facts before a whole grinning Form.

Dr. Locke's brow grew very stern.

"A most extraordinary thing!" he exclaimed. "Surely, Bunter, your uncle should know that an article of such value should never be placed in the keeping of a junior schoolboy. Give it to me at once——"

"Eh?"

"I will return it to your uncle——"

"Wha-a-a-t?"

"With a letter explaining my reasons. Take that pin from your tie at once, Bunter, and hand it me."

"Oh crikey!" gasped Bunter.

He had not expected that. Really, he might have—but he hadn't. He stood rooted with dismay, blinking at the Head.

"Bunter——"

"Oh lor'! The—the fact is, sir——" gasped Bunter.

"I am waiting——"

"The—the fact is, sir, my—my uncle George never gave it to me, sir—that— that's what I really meant to say, sir!" stuttered Bunter.

And as Dr. Locke stared at him blankly, from the Remove there came a howl:

"Ha, ha, ha!"

THE SECOND CHAPTER.
Bad for Bunter!

"SILENCE!" hooted Dr. Locke. He turned a grim frown on the Remove. For a moment the kind old Head looked as grim as Mr. Quelch had ever looked. The Re-

---

To Fisher T. Fish, parting with money is almost as painful as having his teeth extracted. But even Fishy, the profiteer of the Remove, doesn't mind parting with 50s. for a £100 diamond tiepin—until he learns where the tiepin came from!

---

move men contrived to control their merriment.

"There is nothing," said Dr. Locke, "in this boy's obtuse untruthfulness to cause laughter."

On that point the Remove did not agree with their headmaster. Dr. Locke could take Billy Bunter seriously if he liked. But to the Remove, the fat Owl was a scream—a real shriek.

Silence, however, was restored, and Dr. Locke fixed his eyes again on the hapless Owl. Bunter, standing first on one leg, then on the other, then on the first again, was longing to escape. He fairly wriggled under the Head's stern eye. But there was no escape for Bunter. Dr. Locke evidently meant to know all about that big diamond.

"Bunter! I command you to tell me the truth at once!" snapped the Head. "You have made a statement, and immediately contradicted it. Can you, or can you not explain how you came into possession of that diamond?"

"Oh! Yes, sir!" gasped Bunter.

"The—the fact is, sir——"

"Listen to the facts," murmured Frank Nugent.

"The factfulness will probably not be terrific," murmured Hurree Jamset Ram Singh.

"Speak, Bunter, and at once!" rapped the Head impatiently.

"The—the fact is, sir, that—that diamond is an heirloom in our—our family, sir——"

"Oh, my hat!" ejaculated Bob Cherry, in sheer wonder at the fat Owl's fatuous nerve.

"Silence! Did you say an heirloom, Bunter?" exclaimed the Head.

"Yes, sir; handed down from generation to generation," said Bunter, recovering confidence a little. "It came over with the Conqueror, sir—I mean, with one of my ancestors who came over with the Conqueror——"

"Do not talk nonsense, Bunter!"

"Oh! Yes, sir! I mean, no, sir!"

"If that stone, Bunter, is a family possession, as you say, how comes it to be in your hands?"

"It—it isn't in my hands, sir."

"What?"

"It isn't really, sir!" gasped Bunter. "It's in my tie, sir."

"Ha, ha, ha!"

"Silence! Bless my soul!" gasped the Head. "Is it possible for a boy to be so obtuse as this? I mean, Bunter, how comes that stone to be in your possession if it is an heirloom, as you say?"

"I—I thought I'd have it made into a tiepin, sir, instead of leaving it with the—the other family jewels, sir——"

"Bunter! I shall cane you severely for telling untruths."

"Oh lor'!"

"And I can only conclude, Bunter, that you obtained possession of that large and valuable diamond, in some questionable manner!" thundered the Head. "Obviously it cannot belong to you. Have you purloined that stone, Bunter?"

"Oh crikey!" gasped Bunter.

"If you came by that stone dishonestly, Bunter, confess the truth at once. You will, of course, be expelled from Greyfriars——"

"Ow!"

"But possibly the police——"

"The pip-pip-police!" stuttered Bunter.

"The police may take a lenient view of the matter, when they observe your crass stupidity and impenetrable obtuseness. But you must make a complete confession this instant."

The fat Owl gasped. Obviously, prevarication was not going to save him. So long as the Head believed that the diamond was real, he would not believe that it was Bunter's.

Bunter was driven to tell the truth. It was a last and desperate resource.

"I—I—I say, sir, I—I—I never pinched this diamond, sir!" gasped Bunter. "The—the fact is, sir, it—it ain't real, sir."

"Ha, ha, ha!"

"What?" roared the Head.

"It's only paste, sir!" groaned Bunter. "I—I gave a man a shilling for it, sir, in the holidays—a shabby man—he sold it to me in a railway train for a—a—a bob, sir!"

"Ha, ha, ha!"

"Upon my word!" exclaimed the Head, angrier than ever. "After so many absurd prevarications, Bunter, you confess that you are wearing sham jewellery. How dare you do anything of the kind?"

"I—I—I——"

"The stone certainly appears to me to be genuine, Bunter, and I can hardly credit your statement. Hand it to me."

Billy Bunter unwillingly extracted his famous pin from his tie, and passed it over. It flashed and sparkled, in the wintry sunlight that came in at the windows of the Remove Form Room. If that diamond was imitation, there was no doubt that it was a remarkable imitation, and might have deceived anyone. THE MAGNET LIBRARY.—No. 1,353.

Dr. Locke examined it with great care, the Removites watching him curiously. Everybody knew that Bunter had picked it up for a trifle; and so nobody, of course, supposed for a moment that it was real. So the fellows were surprised by the keen and lengthy attention that Dr. Locke gave it, and the puzzled expression on his face. Dr. Locke, of course, was not an expert in precious stones. But so far as his knowledge of such matters went, this stone certainly impressed him as the genuine article.

He fixed his eyes on Bunter at last.

"Bunter, I can hardly believe your statement that this diamond is not genuine, and that you bought it for a shilling. Once more, I command you to tell me the truth."

"Oh lor'! All the fellows know, sir!" stammered Bunter, in alarm. "I—I've tried to sell it for five bob, sir—I mean five shillings—but nobody will take it off my hands. Fishy offered me threepence; but I wouldn't take that, as I gave a bob for it—"

The Head scanned his fat, alarmed face keenly. Bunter was telling the truth now—terrified at the bare idea of the Head taking that stone for a real diamond, and in consequence supposing that Bunter had "pinched" it. And it was easy for the Head to see that the fat junior was speaking the truth—so far as he knew it, at least. He was as anxious now to prove that the diamond was artificial, as he had previously been to make fellows believe that it was real.

"Does any boy here know anything

about this?" asked the Head, glancing over the grinning Remove.

"We all knew that Bunter had a sham diamond, sir!" said Harry Wharton. "He brought it back to school this term."

"Oh, yaas, sir!" said Lord Mauleverer. "I saw him wearin' it in the hols, sir."

"I guess he offered it to me for five shillings, sir!" said Fisher T. Fish. "I sure said nope; and he let out that he had bought it for a shilling, sir, when I offered him threepence."

"Ha, ha, ha!"

The Head gave an impatient frown. He could not help being impressed by the genuine aspect of that stone. But if Bunter had offered to sell it in the Remove for five shillings, it was clear that Bunter could not believe that it was real; which bore out his story that he had bought it as a sham stone for a trifling sum. Greatly to the fat Owl's relief, Dr. Locke handed it back to him. Sham or not, Bunter wanted it.

"Very well; I must accept your statement, Bunter," said the Head. "But you must not wear such a pin in public; it is in the very worst of taste in a schoolboy, all the more so if the diamond is an imitation. Put it in your pocket."

Bunter was very glad to get it safely into his pocket.

"And now," said the Head, taking up Mr. Quelch's cane from the Form master's desk, "now, Bunter, you will bend over that chair! You have wasted my time with your absurd prevarications, and I shall punish you severely for your untruthfulness. Bend over!"

"Oh, really, sir! I——"

"Bend over!" snapped the Head, in a voice that made Bunter jump.

"Oh lor'!"

Bunter bent over the chair! The cane swished.

Whack, whack, whack!

"Yarooooooh!"

Whack, whack, whack!

"Whooop! Yow-ow-ow! Yooop!" roared Bunter.

"Silence! Go to your place!" rapped the Head, laying down the cane.

"Yow-ow-ow-ow-wooop!"

"Another sound, Bunter, and I will cane you again!"

"Oh crikey!" gasped Bunter. He bolted to his place without another sound.

Then second lesson proceeded! Billy Bunter wriggled painfully on his form, dolorously reflecting that the Head was as beastly a beast as Quelch, and almost wishing that Mr. Quelch was back. But the rest of the Remove were feeling rather bucked. A quarter of an hour of second lesson had slipped by while the Head was dealing with Bunter; which, from the point of view of the Lower Fourth, was all to the good! So all the Remove—excepting Bunter—were rather glad that the fat Owl had been sporting his diamond pin in the Form-room that morning.

THE THIRD CHAPTER.
Smithy Asks For It !

HERBERT VERNON-SMITH, the Bounder of Greyfriars, drew a little packet from his pocket and selected a cigarette therefrom.

It was morning break at Greyfriars, and the Bounder was strolling under the elms in the quad with his chum, Tom Redwing. The latter's face was a little clouded; and it clouded still more as he noted the Bounder's action. It only needed the slightest expression of disapproval to confirm the Bounder in any wilful idea that came into his reckless head. He took out a match-box and struck a match.

"You silly ass, Smithy!" said Redwing in measured tones. "If you must play the fool, haven't you sense enough to keep out of sight? If a prefect catches you smoking in the quad——"

"Bow-wow!"

"There's Wharton looking at you——"

"Let him look! A cat may look at a king!"

And the Bounder, stopping under an elm, deliberately struck a match and lighted the cigarette. Redwing, with an angry grunt, walked away and left him, and the Bounder laughed mockingly.

Harry Wharton came along the path under the leafless trees.

"Is that how you're keeping fit for football, Smithy?" he asked quietly.

"Why not?"

"You'll want all your wind when we play Redclyffe on Wednesday."

"Lots of time to recover from a poor little harmless fag!" drawled the Bounder, and he blew out a cloud of smoke almost in the face of the captain of the Remove.

Wharton's brow darkened.

"You footling fathead!" he said contemptuously. "Haven't you the sense of a bunny rabbit? All last term Quelch had an eye on you——"

"While the cat's away, the mice can play!" grinned the Bounder. "We're safe from Quelch's jolly old gimlet eye this term!"

"I say, you fellows!"

Billy Bunter rolled up. For once there was no glitter of a diamond pin in Bunter's tie. He had taken the Head's warning to heart for the time, at least, and discarded that sparkling adornment.

"I say, having a smoke? I'll have one, Wharton!"

"You blithering fat Boojum," growled the captain of the Remove, much incensed. "Do you think I'm playing the fool like Smithy?"

Sniff from Billy Bunter.

"Oh, you're too jolly goody-goody for anything!" he said scornfully. "Might have known you wouldn't have the nerve! I say, Smithy, got a smoke for a pal? We're sportsmen, ain't we?"

"Oh, go and eat coke!" snapped Vernon-Smith. The Bounder smoked, not because he wanted to, but because it was against the rules, being a rebel by nature. He smoked in the quad, simply to display his nerve; to irritate his

chum Redwing, and to show the captain of the Remove that he did not care two straws for his opinion. But if anything could have made him ashamed of his dingy folly, it would have been Billy Bunter claiming him as a fellow-sportsman!

"Don't be mean, old chap!" urged Bunter. "Dash it all, you might hand round the smokes! Be a sport!"

"I'll hand you a thick ear, if you don't roll off, you obnoxious barrel!" snapped Vernon-Smith.

"Beast!"

"Look here, Smithy——" began Wharton.

"Keep your pi-jaw for your pals!" sneered the Bounder. "I've no use for it."

Wharton breathed hard.

"If you crock up in the Redclyffe match, you've a good chance of being dropped out of Remove footer!" he said.

"I'll take the chance!" jeered Vernon-Smith. Smithy was only too well aware that he was a tower of strength in the Remove eleven; and it was rather like him to presume upon it.

Wharton opened his lips again—but closed them. He did not want to quarrel with the Bounder, who had started that term in his most wilful and arrogant frame of mind. His recent narrow escape from the "sack" seemed to have made Smithy rather more careless than more careful; at all events, his recklessness seemed to be on the increase.

Harry Wharton controlled his annoyance, turned away, and walked up the path under the elms, leaving the Bounder grinning over his cigarette. Wharton swung away angrily round a turn of the path; and stopped suddenly as he almost ran into a tall and stately figure that was coming towards him.

"Oh!" gasped Wharton.

It was the Head, taking a walk in break.

Wharton stopped, utterly dismayed. The Head stopped, too, smiling slightly. He attributed the obvious dismay in the junior's face to the fact that they had nearly collided.

But that was not what Wharton was thinking of. If the Head took a few more paces the way he was going he would sight the Bounder—smoking his cigarette! Any fellow would have been landed in trouble for such a breach of the rules. But in the Bounder's case the matter was much more serious. He was a dog with a bad name, the eye of suspicion was on him! Harry Wharton, personally, was angry with the Bounder, and feeling inclined to kick him for his

sion that suddenly came over Bunter's fat face. Bunter saw the Head coming, and his little round eyes almost popped through his big round spectacles at the sight of him.

"Oh lor'!" gasped Bunter.

"What the thump——"

The Bounder turned round to see what it was that had startled Bunter.

Then his heart gave a jump as he found himself facing his headmaster, the cigarette still in his mouth.

Instantly he clutched it away. But it was too late! And Herbert Vernon-Smith, with all his nerve, felt a cold chill run down his back as Dr. Locke's eyes fixed on him.

"Vernon-Smith!" The Head's voice was very deep. "I find you smoking!"

The Bounder was silent. It was not

The Bounder's teeth came hard together.

"I admit I was smoking, sir! But no fellow at Greyfriars has ever been flogged for that!"

"You are an exceptional case, Vernon-Smith—and you will be dealt with with exceptional severity. Follow me at once!"

The Head rustled away.

THE FOURTH CHAPTER.
Flogged !

"I SAY, you fellows!"

Billy Bunter's fat face was red with excitement. He was bursting with news. He rolled up the passage to the door of the Remove Form

"I say, Smithy, don't be a pig, smoking yourself and not standing a fellow a fag." "You fat frog——" The Bounder broke off, startled by the expression that suddenly came over Bunter's fat face. Bunter saw the Head coming, and his little round eyes almost popped through his big round spectacles at the sight of him. "Oh lor'!" he gasped.

check; but he certainly did not want the headmaster to catch him out. If he could delay the Head for a minute and let the sound of his voice reach the Bounder, the situation was saved. Smithy was quick on the uptake!

But even as that idea flashed into Wharton's mind, he discovered that it was too late! For the fat voice of Billy Bunter floated to his ears—and to those of Dr. Locke also!

"I say, Smithy, don't be a pig, smoking yourself and not standing a fellow a fag!"

Dr. Locke gave a sudden start.

He heard every word as clearly as Wharton did.

Instantly he strode on, passing the dismayed captain of the Remove. In a moment more he had his eyes on the Bounder.

Smithy did not see him coming! He was scowling at Bunter, his back turned.

"You fat frog——" he snapped.

He broke off, startled by the expres-

much use to deny it. Billy Bunter, glad that the Head's eye did not turn on him, backed away among the elms. He was deeply glad that Smithy had not "whacked out" a smoke, after all!

"I find you smoking!" repeated the Head. "In open quad!"

"Yes, sir!" said Vernon-Smith.

"In any other junior boy," said the Head, "I might regard this as an act of thoughtless folly! But in you, Vernon-Smith, I fear it indicates that the leniency with which you have been treated has been misplaced; and that, so far from striving to reform, you are the same wilful, disobedient, disreputable character that I have known you to be!"

The Bounder breathed hard, but he said nothing.

"Any other junior would be caned!" said the Head. "In your case, Vernon-Smith, I shall use greater severity! You will be flogged!"

"Flogged?" repeated the Bounder.

"Follow me to my study!"

Room, where the juniors were gathering for third school after break.

Wingate of the Sixth was going to take the Remove in third lesson that morning. Mr. Quelch was still away, and it seemed that the Head was unwilling to replace that old and trusted colleague with a temporary master if it could be avoided. At all events, the Remove were still without a master of their own; and the time-table was filled up with extra French, extra maths, lessons from some of the prefects, and generally one class a day with the Head. On this occasion it fell to Wingate, the captain of the school, to take the Lower Fourth, but he had not put in an appearance yet, when Billy Bunter rolled up, bursting with news.

"I say, you fellows!" he gasped.

"Hallo, hallo, hallo!" exclaimed Bob Cherry. "He hasn't got his diamond on! Have you sold somebody a pup, Bunter?"

"Ha, ha, ha!"

"Oh, really, Cherry——"

"Anybody been ass enough to give Bunter sixpence for his jolly old heirloom?" asked Johnny Bull.

"Ha, ha, ha!"

"I say, you fellows," yelled Bunter, "Smithy——"

"What about Smithy?" asked Tom Redwing quickly.

"He's copped!" yelled Bunter.

"Smithy copped!" grinned Skinner. "Well, he's always asking for it! Who's copped him, and for what?"

"The Head——"

"Oh, my hat! Must be a footling fathead to give the Beak a chance at him!" said Skinner, with a whistle.

"I say, you fellows, the Head copped him smoking! Smoking like a furnace!" gasped Bunter. "He's taken him to his study for a flogging!"

"Rats!"

"The ratfulness is terrific!"

"I was there!" roared Bunter. "Smithy was smoking, and, of course, I wouldn't have any of his filthy fags——"

"You mean he wouldn't give you any?" asked Skinner.

"Yah! The Head came up and copped him fairly in the act! Smoking like a furnace—clouds of smoke——"

"Draw it mild!" suggested Peter Todd.

"I saw him! You should have been there and seen the Beak's face! Scarlet with rage!" said Bunter impressively.

"Ha, ha, ha!"

"Crimson with fury!" said Bunter. "Practically foaming——"

"My hat! I'd like to see the old bean foam!" said Skinner. "Only Bunter ever sees these amusing things!"

"Foaming with rage, he gripped Smithy by the collar and dragged him away to the House!" said Bunter, who never could tell a plain, unvarnished tale. "I said,. Look out, sir; you'll throttle him!"

"You did!" shrieked Bob Cherry.

"I did!" said Bunter firmly. "I'm not so afraid of beaks as you fellows are! I felt bound to put in a word for poor old Smithy! The Head turned to me and said—— What are you grinning at, you beast?"

"The Head said that?" gasped Squiff.

"Ha, ha, ha!"

"No, you ass! I said that!" snapped Bunter. "The Head said—— Look here, you can jolly well cackle if you like, but——"

"The Head said you could jolly well cackle if you liked?"

"No!" howled Bunter. "I said that! The Head said, 'I'm going to make an example of this young blighter——'"

"The Head did?" howled Bob Cherry.

"His very words!" said Bunter.

"Yes, I think I can hear the Head saying that!" sobbed Bob. "Did he say some more things like that, old fat man?"

"Ha, ha, ha!"

"He said he was going to flog him!" roared Bunter. "I was only a few yards away. I thought I'd better keep behind a tree—you never know what the Beak may do when he starts, and a fellow's safer out of sight——"

"Ha, ha, ha!"

"And Smithy's getting it now!" said Bunter. "A fearful flogging! I can jolly well tell you the Head's laying it on! It sounds like beating a carpet outside his study window."

"What rot!" said Frank Nugent. "They don't flog a man for smoking! Touch your toes and take six——"

"The Head said——"

"Rats!"

"He said——" yelled Bunter.

"Rot!"

"Has anything happened at all?" inquired Skinner.

"You silly ass, I've told you it has!" yelled Bunter.

"Yes; that's why I think it hasn't!"

"Ha, ha, ha!"

"Hallo, hallo, hallo! Here comes Wharton!" said Bob, as the captain of the Remove came up the passage. "Heard the latest thrilling news, old bean? Bunter says that Smithy's copped and up for a flogging!"

"He's caught!" said Harry gravely. "The Head found him smoking in the quad and marched him off to his study!"

"Was he scarlet and crimson with rage and fury?" asked Bunter.

"Eh! Not that I noticed. He was in a wax!" said the captain of the Remove. "I'm afraid Smithy's for it this time."

"You didn't notice him foaming at the mouth?"

"No, ass!"

"Bunter did," said Skinner. "I told you fellows that only Bunter sees these things! Must be his specs that does it!"

"Ha, ha, ha!"

"Well, I can jolly well tell you that he was in a towering rage!" snapped Bunter. "Didn't you see him spring at Smithy, Wharton?"

"No!"

"Oh, you never see anything! He sprang at him like a tiger! Seizing him by the collar, he hissed——"

"Ha, ha, ha!"

"I say, you fellows, I can jolly well tell you that the Head was foaming with rage, and he seized Smithy by the collar and hissed—— Yarooooh! What beast is lugging at my ear!"

Billy Bunter spun round. It was Wingate of the Sixth who had taken a fat ear between a finger and thumb, having just arrived on the scene. He gave that fat-ear a twist, eliciting a fearful howl from Billy Bunter.

"That isn't the way to speak of your headmaster, Bunter!" the captain of Greyfriars pointed out.

"Yaroooooh!"

Wingate released the fat ear, which Bunter rubbed in deep anguish, and opened the Form-room door. The Remove went in and took their places, and Wingate ran his eye over the Form.

"Where's Vernon-Smith?" he rapped.

"I—I think he's with the Head, Wingate!" said Harry Wharton.

"Oh, all right!"

Books were sorted out for third lesson. Footsteps were heard in the passage, and all eyes turned on the door as the Bounder came in. His look was rather startling to the eyes of the Remove fellows. His face was almost as white as chalk, and his eyes seemed to burn like live coals. It was plain, at a glance, that the Bounder had been very severely through it.

Wingate gave him a glance, and started.

"What the dickens is the matter with you, Vernon-Smith?" he exclaimed.

"Nothing!" said the Bounder between his teeth.

"Have you been up before the Head?"

"Yes!" snarled the Bounder.

Wingate gave him a long look.

"Very well, you may go to your place!" he said quietly.

And the Bounder sullenly slouched to his place and slumped down.

Vernon-Smith sat silent through the lesson. He was in no state for class after his severe experience in the Head's study, and Wingate considerately left him alone. The Bounder was in a mood

for any reckless defiance or rebelliousness, and Redwing's eyes turned on him anxiously more than once. Third school was over at last, and the Remove were dismissed. A good many fellows gathered round Smithy in the passage.

"Was it a flogging, old bean?" asked Skinner.

"Yes!" snarled Smithy.

"Did it hurt?" squeaked Billy Bunter—which was exactly the fatuous question that Bunter would ask.

"Idiot!"

"Oh, really, Smithy——"

"Pretty thick, giving a man a flogging for smoking!" said Skinner. "Never heard of such a thing!"

Vernon-Smith gave a bitter, scoffing laugh.

"Oh, I'm specially favoured!" he said. "You'd get six if you were nailed, or perhaps only a hundred lines. I get a Head's whopping—and I can tell you the old bean laid it on! That's what they call justice here."

"Well, you're rather the man to ask for it, aren't you, old scout?" said Peter Todd. "You've got the Beak's back fairly up, you know."

"I'll make him sorry for it!" said the Bounder, between his teeth.

"Oh, don't be an ass!"

"Going to whop the Head?" asked Bolsover major, with a grin.

"Ha, ha, ha!"

"I'm going to make him sorry for it! I've said so, and I mean it!" snarled Smithy. "There's more ways than one!"

"Think it over first, old chap," said Newland. "Second thoughts are best when you're thinking of a stunt like that, Smithy."

"The bestfulness of the second thoughts is terrific, my esteemed and idiotic Smithy," declared the Nabob of Bhanipur.

Vernon-Smith gritted his teeth.

"You'll see! I've had a flogging for nothing—practically nothing—because I kicked over the traces last term really. I'll make the Beak sorry he laid it on."

Redwing caught his arm as Wingate of the Sixth came out of the Remove-room.

"Shut up, for the love of Mike!" breathed Redwing. "Wingate——"

Wingate had heard. He came down the corridor with a grim expression on his face. The Bounder faced him, a reckless and defiant glint in his eyes.

"Cut that out, Vernon-Smith!" said the Greyfriars captain quietly. "That sort of gas won't do! I'm making allowances for what you've had, or I'd give you six on the spot! But don't talk like that any more!"

Leaving it at that, the prefect went on his way. Herbert Vernon-Smith, scowling, slouched out into the quad.

THE FIFTH CHAPTER.
No Luck!

"I SAY, you fellows!"

"Hallo, hallo, hallo!"

"It's pretty thick, ain't it?" said Billy Bunter, blinking at the Famous Five, with annoyance and indignation in his face, as he came on them in the quadrangle after class.

"If you're speaking of your head——"

"Ha, ha, ha!"

"Oh, really, Cherry——"

"It's thick, but not pretty——"

"You silly ass!" hooted Bunter. "I say, I'm going out, you know, and I can't put on my tiepin after what the Head said. Pretty thick, ain't it, for a fellow not to be able to wear his tiepin?"

Harry Wharton & Co. grinned. Since

that little talk with the Head in the Remove-room, Bunter had not sported his celebrated tiepin. He felt it rather keenly. Bunter liked to be gorgeous.

"I was thinking I'd chance it," said Bunter. "But a fellow might walk right into the Head—and he's rather a beast! Fancy not letting a man wear his diamond pin! 'Tain't as if it was a paste pin, or anything like that."

"Why, you fat villain, you owned up to the Head that it was paste, and that you gave a man a bob for it!" exclaimed Harry Wharton.

Bunter gave a fat wink.

"Only pulling the old bean's leg," he explained. "He seemed to think that if it was real it couldn't be mine——"

"It jolly well couldn't be if it was real!" said Nugent.

"You see, my people are wealthy," said Bunter. "A hundred-pound pin is

nothing to wealthy people like us. I say, you fellows, can you lend me a tanner?"

"Ha, ha, ha!" yelled the Famous Five.

"Blessed if I see anything to cackle at!" grunted Bunter. "A tanner isn't much——"

"But a hundred pounds is!" chuckled Johnny Bull. "Can't the people who spring hundred-pound pins squeeze out sixpence as well?"

"Ha, ha, ha!"

"The fact is, I've been disappointed about a postal order——"

"We've heard that one," said Bob Cherry gravely.

"You're repeating yourself, old fat bean!" said Frank Nugent.

"Oh, really, Nugent! I say, you fellows, if you could afford to buy a valuable diamond pin—— I say, don't walk away while a fellow's talking to you!" roared Bunter.

But the Famous Five were gone.

The Owl of the Remove snorted and rolled out of gates. That diamond pin—valuable as it was, according to Bunter—was going begging in the Remove. Bunter had asked various prices, from twenty-five pounds down to five shillings, but the only offer he had received was of threepence, from Fisher T. Fish, the business man of Greyfriars. Bunter had refused that offer, which would have left him ninepence to the bad on his bargain.

It was rather rotten not to be able to sell his famous pin, and not to be allowed to wear it, either. Bunter was feeling very wrathy and indignant, and he hoped that Smithy would "get away" with his scheme for making the Beak "sit up." The Beak, in Bunter's opinion, deserved to be made to sit up most severely for refusing to allow a fellow to sport his gorgeous tiepin in public.

Billy Bunter was thinking of his wrongs as he rolled down Friardale Lane. Certainly he was not thinking of danger. If he was thinking of anything beside his wrongs and grievances, it was of Smithy, who had gone down to the village after class—as Bunter suspected, to the tuckshop there. Billy Bunter could think of no reason why a sensible fellow should walk down to Friardale on a cold and frosty day, except to drop in at Uncle Clegg's. Bunter also was going to drop in—by sheer chance, of course—in the hope of annexing some of the crumbs that fell from the rich man's table. Danger, certainly, he was not likely to be thinking of in the quiet country lane. But, as a matter of fact, that was exactly what was awaiting him.

Under the leafless trees, at a little distance from the school, a slightly built, shabby man, with sandy eyebrows and narrow, rat-like eyes, was loafing, with a half-smoked cigarette hanging loosely from a flabby lip. Had the Owl of the Remove seen him closely he would have recognised the sandy man who had sold him that famous diamond pin in a railway train in the holidays when he was departing from Wharton Lodge. But as he spotted Bunter coming along the lane the sandy man popped back quickly behind the trunk of a tree out of sight.

Standing there, unseen by the fat Owl, he glanced quickly up and down the lane. Nobody was in sight but Bunter.

"Crimes!" murmured Mr. Sniggerson. "Luck at last!"

Bunter rolled on, unsuspecting. As he came abreast of the tree the sandy man leaped out, and before Bunter even saw him he was down on his back, and a knee was planted on his chest.

"Ow!" gasped Bunter breathlessly. "Wow! Smithy, you beast——"

As Smithy was somewhere ahead of him the fat Owl supposed for a moment that it was the Bounder "larking." But the next moment he saw that it was not the Bounder. He blinked up in amazement at the narrow, rat-like face bending over him.

"You!" he stuttered. "What do you want?" He recognised the man who had sold him the diamond pin.

"I want that pin——" gasped Bunter.

"Look here——" gasped Bunter.

"Hand it over—sharp!" snarled the sandy man. "There ain't a crowd of schoolboys 'ere now, like there was the other day when I snatched it out of your tie. I got you, Mr. Bunter! Hand it over—sharp, afore I twist your fat ears off your fat 'ead!"

Bunter blinked up at him, alarmed, but more astonished than alarmed. A few days ago somebody, unrecognised by Bunter, had snatched his diamond
THE MAGNET LIBRARY.—No. 1,353.

pin and made off with it; and Harry Wharton & Co., having witnessed the transaction, had chased the rascal and got it back. Bunter had supposed that it was some pickpocket who had taken the diamond for a real one. Now he realised that it must have been this man—the man who had sold it to him for a shilling. Why he wanted it back was an utter mystery to Bunter. He had sold it of his own accord—for a shilling! Bunter wondered whether the sandy man was out of his senses.

He seemed savagely in earnest, at all events. It was rather a risky business, collaring a fellow like this in broad daylight, when anyone might have come along the lane. The sandy man had no time to waste. Kneeling on Bunter, he grasped a fat ear and twisted it.

There was a fearful yell from Bunter.

"Yarooooh!"

"Give me that pin, blow you!" hissed the sandy man.

"Ow! Oh crikey! Look here, what do you want it for?" gasped Bunter. "You sold it to me, didn't you, you beast? I never asked you for it—you fairly shoved it at me! It's mine."

"Give it to me!"

"Well, you'll jolly well give me my shilling back, if I do!" gasped Bunter.

"Eh? Oh! Yes, if you like—where's the pin?"

"I haven't got it——"

"What!" yelled the sandy man. "Don't tell me any lies, young shaver!" He twisted the fat ear again, and there was another fearful yell. "Hand it over, and sharp's the word!"

"Yarooh! I haven't got it on!" shrieked Bunter. "Can't you see I haven't got it on? The Head won't let fellows wear diamond pins, and I've had to leave it in my study! Ow!"

"Oh crimes!" muttered the sandy man. This was quite an unforeseen set-back. "Look here, blow you, is that the truth? I'll search you——"

"Yaroooh! Help!"

The sandy man removed his bony knee from Bunter's podgy chest and rose, still grasping the panting fat junior. Apparently his intention was to drag the junior through the hedge, where he could search him at his leisure out of view. But as he gave a quick, uneasy glance up and down the lane a figure came in sight, walking from the direction of the village. It was the Bounder coming back to the school.

Smithy sighted him at the same moment. He stared at the sight of Billy Bunter wriggling and gasping and panting in the grasp of the sandy man. Smithy, with all his faults, was the last fellow in the world to leave another fellow in the lurch. He had been sauntering along, swinging a parcel in his hand, when he sighted the scene in the lane. Instantly he leaped into speed, coming up the lane like a race-horse for the spot.

"Oh crimes!" gasped the sandy man.

He hesitated a moment! But he was no athlete; and the Bounder, school-boy as he was, was a strong and powerful fellow—and his look showed that he was keen for combat! After that brief hesitation the sandy man jumped away through the hedge and raced across the adjoining field—and he was out of sight when Smithy arrived at the spot.

THE SIXTH CHAPTER.
Halves!

"LEGGO!" yelled Bunter. His spectacles had slipped down his fat little nose. He yelled as the Bounder bent to grasp his arm and help him to his feet. THE MAGNET LIBRARY.—No. 1,353.

Blinking dizzily over his spectacles, the Owl of the Remove was unaware that the sandy man had departed, and that the Bounder had arrived.

"Leggo! Beast! Help!"

"You blithering, blethering, blathering booby——"

"Oh! Is that you, Smithy? I thought it was that other rotter——" gasped Bunter. "Ow! I say, lend a fellow a hand! Wow!"

He scrambled to his feet with the Bounder's aid. Setting his big spectacles straight on his fat little nose he blinked round.

"Where is he?" he gasped.

"That sandy-coloured merchant? Hooked it," answered the Bounder. "He cleared off as I came up! What the dickens was he handling you for?"

"After my tiepin——" gurgled Bunter.

"Ha, ha, ha!" roared the Bounder.

"Oh, really, Smithy——"

"Same chap who was after it the other day?" asked Vernon-Smith, laughing. "Why didn't you tell him it was a dud and save him the trouble?"

"Beast! That diamond is an heirloom—I mean, it cost my Uncle George thirty guineas——"

"And you can't sell it for five bob? Tell you what, send it back to Uncle George and say you'd rather have the money!" suggested the Bounder.

"Yah!"

"Well, did he get it off you?" asked Smithy, scanning Bunter's untidy tie. "You've not got it on!"

"The Head won't let me wear it, you know," said Bunter. "Luckily, it was left in my study. So he never got it."

"He's lost a bob's worth!" said the Bounder, and he swung on towards Greyfriars, swinging the parcel in his hand.

Billy Bunter's eyes were on that parcel. Smithy was back from Friardale sooner than the fat junior had expected. Bunter concluded that, instead of stopping for a feed at Uncle Clegg's, he had bought some tuck there, and was taking it in for tea. The parcel looked like it. As Smithy was on his return journey, Bunter had no desire to go on to the village, and he rolled after the Bounder towards the school.

With his interest concentrated on Smithy's parcel, he forgot all about the sandy man and the latter's mysterious desire to regain possession of the tiepin he had sold Bunter for a shilling. It was, perhaps, just as well for Bunter that that parcel drew him like a magnet in the track of the Bounder. For, at a distance, the sandy man was watching from behind a tree, and had he spotted the fat Owl alone again there was little doubt that Bunter's adventures would not have been over. As it was, the sandy man in the shabby overcoat shook a bony fist after the two juniors, from the distance, and slouched away to wait for another opportunity. Forgetful of his existence, Billy Bunter trotted after Herbert Vernon-Smith.

"I say, Smithy! I'm glad you came along," he panted. "Don't walk so fast, old chap! I say, it was awfully brave of you."

"What rot!" grunted the Bounder.

"It was, really—that fearful ruffian——"

"Any Greyfriars man could knock that weedy specimen out! You could, if you weren't so funky!"

Billy Bunter breathed hard. "Soft sawder" seemed no use to the practical, hard-headed Bounder. But the fat junior tried again.

"Well, I've always said that you were the pluckiest chap in the Remove, Smithy——"

"I've never heard you!"

"Well, I've always thought so——"

"What with?" grunted the Bounder.

"Oh, really, Smithy——"

"For the love of Mike, can it!" snapped the Bounder. "Do you think you can grease up to me and borrow a bob, or what? Go and eat coke!"

"Look here, you beast——" hooted Bunter.

"Oh rats!"

The Bounder had come to Bunter's help; but he had no desire whatever for his company, and he accelerated to shake him off. But Bunter was not to be shaken off. He accelerated, too, his fat little legs going like clockwork.

"I say, Smithy!" he gasped. "Shall I carry your parcel?"

Vernon-Smith stared round in surprise. That was a very unusual sort of offer from Billy Bunter! But the next moment the Bounder guessed what was in his mind, and burst into a laugh.

"What do you think's in it?" he asked.

"Well, you've been down to the village to buy something," said Bunter. "I suppose you've been to Uncle Clegg's—I say, I'd really like to carry the parcel! It looks rather heavy."

"It is rather heavy!" answered Smithy. "Carry it if you like." He laughed, and swung the parcel to Bunter.

"Is it a cake?" asked the fat junior, as he caught it. The parcel was not large, but undoubtedly it was rather heavy. "I say, Smithy, what about opening it here and taking a snack——"

"Oh, buck up, and don't jaw!"

"Well, look here, Smithy, if I'm going to carry your parcel for you, I think it's up to you to whack it out!" said Bunter argumentatively. "What about halves?"

"Halves!" repeated the Bounder. "I'm not going to open the parcel till I get it into my study, but if you like to scoff half of it there, you may."

Billy Bunter beamed.

"I say, Smithy, you always were a splendid chap!" he said. "Nothing mean about you, old fellow."

"Hear, hear!" agreed the Bounder. "Come on."

Bunter panted and puffed at the Bounder's heels, back to the school. He was tempted to drop behind and disappear with the parcel, but he was aware that the Bounder was too wary a fellow to be "done" like that! So he followed Smithy back to the school and rolled in at the gates after him.

Tom Redwing was in Study No. 4 in the Remove when Smithy came in, followed by Bunter with the parcel.

"Wharton's been asking after you, Smithy," he said.

"Kind of him!"

"I mean, for games practice—you cut it——"

"Yes, I had to go down to the village."

"Well, as it's the Redclyffe match to-morrow, old chap——"

"I've other things to think of."

Redwing made no answer to that. Billy Bunter landed the parcel on the table, and cut the string. The Bounder watched him, with a grin.

"You said halves, Smithy!" remarked Bunter, blinking round at him.

"Halves it is!" said Smithy. "In fact, you can have the lot, if you can eat it, Bunter, after carrying it for me. I don't mind."

"You're a real sport, Smithy!" gasped Bunter.

"One of the best!" agreed the Bounder.

Bunter's fat fingers hurriedly unrolled the brown-paper wrappings of the

Harry Wharton pushed open the door and was about to enter the Form-room when—— Plop! Something suddenly descended on his head from above—something sticky and smelly swamped all over him. "Urrrggh!" he gasped. He had got the full benefit of the booby-trap set for the Head!

parcel. Redwing was moving to the door.

"Don't go, Reddy!" said the Bounder. "Wouldn't you like to see Bunter feed?"

"Not specially!" answered Tom dryly.

"Perhaps he's going to offer you some!"

"No fear!" exclaimed Bunter hastily. "You said I could have it all, Smithy, and you're not backing out of it, see?"

"Only if you eat it," said Smithy.

"I'll eat it all right!" grinned Bunter.

He rolled off the paper and revealed Smithy's purchase. Then an extraordinary expression came over his fat face. It was not a cake!

It was a rather large tin can! But it did not contain preserved fruits, or anything of that kind. On the outside was an inscription.

"RED PAINT."

Billy Bunter could eat almost anything. In that line he could have beaten an ostrich. But even Bunter could not eat red paint!

He blinked at it with his eyes almost popping through his spectacles. Why a fellow should walk a mile to buy a can of red paint, for which no Greyfriars fellow could be imagined to have any use, was a deep mystery. Naturally, Bunter had not expected anything of the sort.

But there it was—red paint. Merely that and nothing more. The expression on Bunter's speaking countenance caused Redwing to burst into a laugh. The Bounder chuckled. Bunter blinked at the

can of paint, and then blinked at the Bounder. He had carried that heavy parcel in the belief that it contained tuck! And this was what it contained! This was why the Bounder had told him he could have it all—if he would eat it. Bunter was not going to eat it.

"Beast!" he roared.

"What's the row?" asked Smithy.

"Rotter!"

"Don't you want it?"

"Yah! Beast! Rotter! Cad! Yah!"

Bunter rolled out of the study, snorting, leaving the Bounder and Redwing roaring.

THE SEVENTH CHAPTER.
The Genuine Goods?

"YOU being a Jew——"

"Eh?" ejaculated Monty Newland.

"You being a Jew, old chap, I dare say you know all about diamonds and things," said Billy Bunter affably. "Jews do, don't they?"

Monty Newland gazed at Bunter. That fat and fatuous youth had rolled into Study No. 9 in the Remove, which belonged to Newland and Penfold. It was time for prep in the Remove, but Billy Bunter was too busy for prep, as he often was.

Bunter had been thinking.

This was unusual; but then the circumstances were unusual.

Even the obtuse Owl of the Remove realised that there was something extraordinary in the man who had sold him a dud diamond for a shilling, taking such lawless and violent measures to get it back again.

Everybody said that that diamond looked real. The Head himself had obviously been puzzled by so excellent an imitation. Now, it seemed, the man who had parted with it was desperately anxious to get hold of it again.

Obviously the sandy man could not possibly have wanted to get back a dud diamond worth only a few shillings. This was obvious, even to Billy Bunter's limited intellect.

What, then, did it all mean?

Was it possible, after all, that the stone was real; that that shabby merchant who had told Bunter that he was a dealer in artificial gems, had somehow got a real stone mixed with the duds?

If so, Bunter was bound, as an honest and honourable fellow, to let him have back the stone he had sold by mistake.

That, however, was not what Bunter was thinking of. He was thinking of what a wonderful stroke of luck it would be if it was so.

Hence his visit to Monty Newland. Newland belonged to the ancient race of Israel, and Bunter wanted expert advice. Of course, he had his own inimitable and wonderfully tactful way of putting it.

"You being a Jew, old chap," he said, "I dare say you've got a lot of relations who are pawnbrokers, and so on——"

"You blithering, fat idiot!" said Monty.

"Oh, really, Newland! I say, old chap, it wasn't me who called 'sheeney' through your keyhole yesterday," said Bunter anxiously. "Besides, you'd refused to cash a postal order for me, you know, and it was only a joke, too; and, as I've said, it wasn't me at all."

"Oh, my hat!" said Newland; while Dick Penfold grinned.

"But as I was saying," went on Bunter. "You being a Jew, you understand these things. I dare say you help your father at home in the popshop in the hols—what?" Bunter grinned agreeably. "He, he, he!"

"What way do you prefer to go out of a study, Bunter?" inquired Monty. "On your feet, or on your neck?"

"Oh, really, old chap! Look here, I want to know if this diamond is real," said Bunter. "Look at it and tell me."

"I don't know anything about diamonds, fathead!"

"Oh, rot! All Jews do," said Bunter. "You needn't mind a fellow knowing about the pawnshop—he, he, he! Look here, you tell me about my diamond pin, and if it turns out to be real, I'll stand you something when I sell it. See? I'm not asking you to do it for nothing."

"You want what you're asking for?" inquired Newland.

"Eh! Yes."

"Then I'll hand it out."

And Newland made a stride at Bunter, grasped him by his fat neck, and spun him round in the doorway. Then he planted a boot on the tightest trousers at Greyfriars.

"Can't!"

"Why not, you ass?"

"Too dazzlin'."

"Look at it, you fathead! Now look here, Mauly," said Bunter. "You're a silly idiot——"

"Eh?"

"And a howling fathead!"

"What?"

"And a blithering nincompoop!" said Bunter. "But you know a lot of things that other fellows don't. You know a diamond when you see one. You've got lots, though you never wear any. You could tell a real stone from a dud."

"Yaas."

"Well, look at this and tell me."

"But you know it's a dud, old fat bean," said Mauly. "You know you don't buy real diamonds at a bob each from men in railway trains."

"But suppose the man made a mistake?" said Bunter. "Suppose he got a real one mixed up with the duds?"

"Oh gad! Not jolly likely."

"Suppose he hung round the school, trying to snatch it back from me?" said Bunter. "Suppose he tried twice to get hold of it by snatching? Would he, if it was a dud?"

Lord Mauleverer stared.

"Nunno, unless he was potty," he answered. "If the man's done that, it

Lord Mauleverer handed the pin back.

"A fellow can't be certain," he said. "But that looks to me like a genuine stone. If it's a paste, it's a wonderful imitation."

"You'd take it as real in a jeweller's shop?" asked Bunter eagerly.

"Yaas."

"Oh, good!"

"Look here, Bunter," said his lordship seriously, "I may be mistaken, but I believe that's a real diamond. If it is, the man who sold it made a mistake. You can't keep it."

"Eh?"

"If you can find the man——"

"What man?" asked Bunter calmly.

"The man who sold you that pin for a shilling."

"Oh, really, Mauly! This diamond is an heirloom."

"What!" yelled Mauleverer.

"I mean, my Uncle Peter gave it to me for a birthday present."

"You frabjous ass——"

"I dare say you fancy you're the only fellow at Greyfriars who gets expensive birthday presents," sneered Bunter. "I can jolly well tell you that twenty pounds for a tiepin is nothing to my Uncle Rupert."

"You frabjous, foozlin' fathead——"

Thud!

"Yarooooop!"

Bump!

Bunter landed in the passage. The door of Study No. 9 closed on him with a slam.

"Ow! Wow! Beast!" gasped Bunter. "Oh, the rotter! What was he getting his rag out for, I wonder? Yow-ow-ow! Beast!"

The Owl of the Remove picked himself up and limped away. Monty Newland, for some reason utterly unknown to Bunter, had cut up rusty, and he was still in want of an expert opinion on precious stones.

He stopped at the door of Study No. 12 and looked in. Lord Mauleverer was extended on the study sofa there, thinking of prep. His study-mate, Sir Jimmy Vivian, was at the table, already at work.

"Busy, old chap?" asked Bunter, blinking at his lazy lordship.

"Yaas."

"You look it!" grunted Bunter, and he rolled in. "I say, Mauly——"

Lord Mauleverer sat up on the sofa.

"Prep, old fat man," he said. "Roll away!"

"You weren't doing prep when I came in, you ass!"

"Nunno! Prep's a bore," said Mauleverer. "But it's not such a bore as you are, old fat bean! Travel, there's a good porpoise."

Bunter took the diamond tiepin from his pocket.

"Look at that, Mauly!"

looks as if he must have handed you the real goods by mistake."

"Well, he's done it twice," said Bunter. "Now, you examine it, Mauly, and tell me what you think."

Greatly astonished, the schoolboy earl took the diamond pin. He had seen it often enough sparkling in Bunter's tie, but had never given it any attention; taking it for granted, like the other fellows and Bunter himself, that it was paste. But if the man who had sold it had made desperate attempts to get it back it could hardly be worthless. Even Bunter could see that; and it was clear to Mauleverer.

So he took the pin, and examined the stone in it with great keenness. Probably there was no other fellow in the Greyfriars Remove who could have given an opinion of any weight on the subject, except perhaps the Bounder. But Lord Mauleverer, though generally regarded as an ass in the Remove, had quite a lot of knowledge and wisdom tucked away somewhere in his lazy intellect. And certainly there were plenty of precious stones among the family jewels at Mauleverer Towers.

"It's a dud, Mauly," said Sir Jimmy Vivian, looking up from his prep. "It couldn't be anything else."

Mauly, intently examining the diamond, made no reply. Astonishment was dawning in his face.

"Gad!" he ejaculated.

Billy Bunter's eyes glistened behind his big spectacles.

"What about it, Mauly?" he gasped.

"Oh, cheese it!" said Bunter contemptuously. "I'm used to jealousy and envy, as a wealthy fellow, but, really, Mauly——"

"You blitherin' bandersnatch——"

"The actual fact is that my Uncle Arthur bought this tiepin for me specially as a New Year's gift."

"Look here, you howlin' ass——"

"Yah!"

Billy Bunter turned away scornfully, and rolled to the door. Lord Mauleverer, strongly tempted to help him through the doorway with a lunge of his boot, refrained; it was too much trouble to kick Bunter. But if it was too much trouble for Mauly, it was not too much trouble for his study-mate. Jimmy Vivian jumped up from the table, jumped after Bunter, and let out his foot as if he had been kicking for goal!

"Yaroooh!"

Bump!

For the second time that evening William George Bunter landed in the Remove passage with a heavy concussion. The door of Study No. 12 closed on him as he rolled and roared.

"Ow! Wow! Beast! Wow!"

Gwynne of the Sixth came up the passage. He was the prefect on duty that evening.

"What are you doing out of your study in prep, Bunter? Take fifty lines!"

"Oh lor'!" gasped Bunter. "Ow! Wow! Leggo my ear! Whoop!"

With a finger and thumb on Bunter's

fat ear, Gwynne led him to Study No. 7, and rolled him in. After which, Billy Bunter contrived to devote a little of his valuable time to prep.

THE EIGHTH CHAPTER.
Red Paint !

"HALLO, hallo, hallo! What the dickens is Smithy up to?"

"Looking for some more trouble!" grunted Johnny Bull.

It was in break the following morning. It was rather a misty morning, and visibility was not good in the Greyfriars quad. The Famous Five were discussing the weather, and the prospects of the football match that afternoon as they strolled in the quad. And they were quite near the Remove Form Room windows before they observed the Bounder. Vernon-Smith was in the act of clambering out of the window.

The chums of the Remove stopped and stared at him.

Why a fellow should enter the Form-room in break, and leave it by way of the window, was rather a mystery.

There was a hard, dogged expression on Smithy's face—a sufficient indication that he had been "up" to something. There was also a smear of red paint on his sleeve, and another on his hand, as the juniors observed. Catching sight of them in the quad below the windows, the Bounder gave a start, and scowled.

"Hallo, hallo, hallo! What's that game, Smithy?" roared Bob.

Smithy gave him a savage look.

"Don't yell, you fathead! Do you want to bring all Greyfriars here?" he snarled.

"Why not?" asked Bob.

"Oh, don't be a fool!"

"If a beak came along he might want to know what Smithy had been doing with red paint in the Form-room," remarked Johnny Bull dryly.

The Bounder started again.

"What do you mean, you ass?" he snapped. And he dropped from the broad, stone sill of the window to the ground. "Who's been doing anythin' with red paint?"

"You have, to judge by the smears on you."

"Oh gad!" Smithy noticed the smears for the first time. "Thanks for the tip! I shall have to get that cleaned off."

Harry Wharton looked hard at him.

"What have you been up to, Smithy?" he asked quietly.

"Nothin' that need worry you," sneered the Bounder.

And he walked quickly away, evidently anxious to get rid of the traces of red paint.

Wharton's brow darkened.

"Smithy's the man to ask for it, and no mistake!" remarked Nugent. "He had a flogging yesterday; but he's not satisfied. What the dickens has he been doing with red paint in the Form-room? The Head takes us in next lesson, and if there's a rag—"

"The howling ass!" muttered Wharton. "Skinner once put gum on Quelch's chair, and his gown stuck to it. Has that silly fathead been putting paint on the chair for the Head to sit in?"

"My hat! There'll be a row if he has," said Bob Cherry, with a whistle. "If the jolly old Beak sits in red paint he will be waxy. Smithy's an ass! It's rotten bad form to rag the Head!"

"Lot Smithy cares for that," growled the captain of the Remove. He stood looking up at the window. "I've a jolly good mind——"

"Look out! There's a jolly old prefect!" murmured Bob; and Wharton glanced round to see Wingate and Gwynne on the path by the Form-room windows. "Smithy only got clear in time," added Bob, with a grin.

It had been in Wharton's mind to climb in at the Form-room window, and ascertain what Smithy had been "up" to. That, however, was impossible, with prefects in the offing. He walked on with his friends; but his brow was clouded and dark.

"Ragging" the Head was quite outside the limit. Other masters were ragged sometimes, but nobody ever dreamed of ragging the chief. Smithy, it seemed, had thought of it. Causing Quelch to sit down in gum, or introducing rats into Monsieur Charpentier's desk, might be more or less funny, but rags on the Head were "taboo." It was one of the things that were "not done."

Moreover, the consequences were certain to be extremely serious. If the culprit was discovered, it might mean expulsion for him. If he was not discovered, it meant trouble for the whole Form, while a rigid investigation went on. Smithy cared nothing for that.

It was scarcely possible to doubt that Smithy's surreptitious visit to the Form-room had some connection with the fact that the Head was taking the Remove in third school which followed break.

Wharton turned his step towards the House door.

"Barging in?" asked Bob dubiously.

"I'm going to see what that reckless ass has been up to," said Harry. "If he's put paint for the Head to sit in, there's time to get it cleared off before the bell goes. Goodness knows what he's done; but whatever it is, it's better undone, I fancy!"

"Not much doubt about that," grinned Bob. "May save Smithy from the long jump. If he goes again he won't be allowed to come back as he was before. Let's look in, anyhow."

The Famous Five went into the House. Four of them waited at the corner of the Form-room passage, while Wharton went along to the door of the Remove-room to look in and ascertain what the Bounder's game had been there.

It was still five or six minutes to the end of break, so there was time to act. When the bell rang the Remove would collect at that door and wait for their headmaster, it being the rule that fellows waited to be let into their Form-room by the master taking them. Sometimes that rule was disregarded when the Form-room door was left unlocked, but in dealing with the Head all the juniors were extremely careful not to disregard rules. There was nobody, however, on the spot yet—nobody was likely to come in till the bell went.

The door of the Remove-room stood ajar a few inches. Harry Wharton pushed it open and stepped in.

What happened next came rather like an earthquake.

Plop! came something on the head of the captain of the Remove. Something sticky and smelly swamped all over him.

He staggered, with a suffocated yell.

"Urrrggh!"

He hardly knew what had happened for the moment. Then, as he wildly dabbed streaming red paint from his eyes and nose and mouth, he knew!

It was a booby-trap!

A large flat cardboard box had been perched on the top of the thick oak door, with one side resting on the lintel over the doorway. As soon as the door was pushed open it naturally fell—on the head of the person entering.

That even the reckless Bounder would have ventured to lay such a trap for the headmaster had never occurred to Wharton—he could never have dreamed of such a thing.

But evidently the Bounder had. And Wharton had got it!

There was no doubt that he had got it. He streamed with oozy red paint! Paint smothered him. It covered his head and his face and his ears, it streamed down his clothes, it oozed down his neck. Half-suffocated by streaming, oozing paint, Wharton staggered and gasped and gurgled wildly.

"Hallo, hallo, hallo!" yelled Bob Cherry, from the corner, as a crimson figure staggered out of the door. "What the thump——"

"Wharton——" yelled Nugent.

"Great pip!" gasped Johnny Bull.

"The g-great pipfulness is terrific!" stuttered the Nabob of Bhanipur.

The four raced up the passage. They stared at Wharton in amazement and dismay. He was hardly recognisable.

"Urrgh! Groogh! Oooch! Wooogh!" came in a wild splutter from under the thick coat of red paint. "Urrrrggh!"

On the floor lay a sticky cardboard box and a pool of red paint! Paint ran in sticky streams down the other side of the oak door. But Wharton had got most of it. He was of the paint, painty! And he tottered and gurgled and gasped, while his comrades gazed at him in dismay and horror.

<hr>

THE NINTH CHAPTER.
Rough on Wharton !

HARRY WHARTON dabbed wildly at paint. He clutched and grabbed at it. It smothered him. He could hardly breathe. The smell of so much paint at close quarters was quite overpowering. He rubbed it from his eyelids, he gouged it from his ears, he ejected it from his mouth, he sneezed it from his nose. He seemed to live and move and have his being in a universe of paint!

"Good gad!" gasped Johnny Bull. "And that idiot, that chump, that blithering fathead, meant that for the Head!"

There was no doubt about it! That was why the Bounder had been in the Form-room—why he had left by the window. After fixing-up the booby-trap he could not of course, leave by the door. The Famous Five had guessed that he had played some trick for the Head's behoof. But never had they dreamed of anything like this! What would have been the result had Dr. Locke received that swamping of paint was unnerving to think of.

Perhaps it was fortunate that Wharton had got it instead. At the moment, however, he was not feeling fortunate—he was feeling horrid!

(Continued on next page.)

"The dangerous lunatic!" gasped Bob Cherry. "Wharton, old man——"

"Urrrggh!"

"Rotten luck, old chap!" said Frank Nugent.

"Gurrrrggh!"

Wharton could hardly speak. He staggered away, still wildly clawing paint. What he wanted just then was steaming-hot water and soap—lots of both!

But it was not possible, of course, for a fellow streaming from head to foot with red paint to get away unobserved. Before Wharton was half-way to the much-needed bath-room, there was an amazed and buzzing crowd staring at him. Loder of the Sixth strode up to him.

"Who's that?" roared Loder. "What's all this! You young hooligan, you're leaving a trail of paint all through the House! You——"

"Urrrggh!"

"Who are you?" roared the prefect.

"Groogh! I'm Wharton! Oooooggh!"

"What have you done this for? Are you mad?"

"You silly ass!" spluttered Wharton, forgetting for the moment the respect due to a Sixth Form prefect. "Do you think I did it on purpose?"

"Look here——"

"What—what—what is this?" It was the Head's voice, and Loder of the Sixth stepped back as the headmaster rustled up. Dr. Locke gazed at the paint-smothered junior in amazement and wrath. "Who—who is it?"

"Wharton of the Remove, sir!" said Loder.

"Ha, ha, ha!" came from somewhere.

"Wharton! Is that you, Wharton?" gasped the Head.

"Grooogh! Yes, sir! Wurrggh!"

"What has happened? Some accident——"

"Yes, sir!" At that moment Wharton was feeling like giving the Bounder such a thrashing as would have turned him into a hospital case. But he did not think of giving him away to the Head. "Some—some paint fell on me, sir."

"You are in a shocking state! You are leaving a trail of paint on the floor. You——"

"I—I can't help it, sir! Urrrggh!"

"No doubt—no doubt!" said the Head kindly. "But this can scarcely have been an accident! It must have been intentional." Probably the Head, in the far-off days when he had been a school-boy, had heard of booby-traps! "Who did this, Wharton?"

"I—I didn't see him with the paint, sir," stammered Wharton—an answer which rather combined the wisdom of the serpent with the innocence of the dove. He could not give the Bounder away, and certainly he had not seen Smithy with the paint.

"Looks as if the kid had walked into a booby-trap sir!" said Loder, suppressing a grin. There were unsuppressed grins on all sides. Wharton's aspect struck many of the observers as funny!

"Yes, yes, no doubt! Where did this happen, Wharton?"

"At the door of the Form-room, sir."

There was no concealing that circumstance, as a pool of paint remained there in evidence.

"Bless my soul! Why were you going into the Form-room in break, Wharton?"

"I—I—I was—was going in, sir——"

"Is it possible," exclaimed the Head, "that this—this—'hem—booby-trap was adjusted at the door of your Form-room, Wharton?"

"Ye-e-es, sir!"

"Upon my word! I have never heard

of such an outrage! Why, it might have fallen upon me had you not chanced to enter the Form-room!" exclaimed Dr. Locke, aghast at the idea. Fortunately, it did not occur to the majestic Head that it had been intended to fall upon him.

"Urrrggh! C-a-a-can I go and—and wash, sir?"

"Yes, certainly! But investigation must be made into this! You are not aware who laid this dastardly trap, Wharton?"

"I didn't see him at it, sir."

"No, probably not—probably not—or you would never have fallen into the trap! But you are somewhat to blame, Wharton—you should not enter the Form-room in break without asking leave, and doubtless some mischievous boy knew of your intention—that must be it! This should be a warning to you, Wharton, not to neglect to observe even slight and apparently trivial rules. I trust you see that?"

"Oh! Ah! Yes! Quite, sir!" gasped Wharton.

The Head had no suspicion that it was on his majestic account that Wharton had entered the Form-room—and the junior was not likely to tell him.

"Go and clean off that—that paint as quickly as you can, Wharton! You are in a shocking state!"

"Urrgh! Yes, sir! Gurrrggh!"

Wharton trailed away, leaving red and sticky traces as he went. Trotter, the

page, was soon hard at work cleaning up those traces, and the pool at the Form-room door. Trotter had plenty to do. But Wharton's task was far harder than Trotter's. He turned on hot water and rubbed and scrubbed and scrubbed and rubbed till his skin was as red as the paint. The bell went for third school, unheeded so far as the captain of the Remove was concerned. He was still wearily rubbing and scrubbing.

The Head, sublimely unconscious of his narrow escape from a very startling experience, took the Remove in third school. But he was conscious of a good deal of suppressed excitement in the Form.

All the fellows knew now what had happened, and many eyes turned on the Bounder, who sat scowling.

Smithy's disappointment was keen, though there was little doubt that, later on, and after cooler reflection, he would be glad enough that he had failed to bring off his reckless scheme.

Third lesson was almost at an end when Harry Wharton came in.

A good many grinning looks were cast his way.

Fellows sympathised with his ill-luck, but they saw a comic aspect to the affair, as well. Billy Bunter grinned from one fat ear to the other. Bunter knew now why Smithy had fetched that can of red paint from Friardale the previous day, and he was greatly entertained by the fact that Wharton had "got" it.

The captain of the Remove was hardly clear of paint yet, after all his rubbing and scrubbing. There were still traces of it about his neck and ears, and

his hair was sticky. Such a coating of paint had to be given time to wear off. He gave Herbert Vernon-Smith one look as he went to his place. That look was expressive.

The Bounder shrugged his shoulders. If he had not feared the Head's wrath he was not likely to fear Wharton's. When the Head dismissed the Remove after third school the Bounder lounged away with his hands in his pockets, whistling carelessly.

THE TENTH CHAPTER.

Sold!

"I SAY, Fishy!"

"Mosey in!" said Fisher T. Fish, quite cordially.

Billy Bunter "moseyed" into Study No. 14.

Wednesday afternoon was a half-holiday, and though it was cold, and a little misty, most of the fellows were out of doors. The Remove had a foot-ball match booked for that afternoon with a junior team from Redclyffe School, though, for the moment, as it happened, Harry Wharton & Co. were thinking of matters other than football.

Fisher T. Fish, the business man of the Remove, was certainly not think-ing of Soccer. Soccer was not in his line. There was no money in Soccer. So far as Fishy could see, at Soccer a fellow simply wore out boot-leather, which cost money, and had nothing to show for it.

It is hardly necessary to mention that Fisher T. Fish was thinking about money that afternoon, for he thought about money every afternoon, and every morning, and dreamed of it at night!

Money being, from Fishy's point of view, the beginning and end of all things, Fishy regarded it as quite natural to think about it all the time.

So it was rather unusual for Fishy to extend the glad hand to Billy Bunter, a fellow who seldom or never had any money.

But he did. His bony face beamed with cordiality as the fat Owl of the Remove presented himself in the door-way of Study No. 14. It was not easy for Fishy's bony, sly, sharp features to assume an agreeable expression. But he did his best, and looked as agree-able as he could.

"Walk right in, old bean!" said Fisher T. Fish, with unaccustomed affability. "Squat down!"

Bunter rolled in, and squatted down.

Evidently, Fisher T. Fish was glad to see him. The fact was that, if Bunter hadn't looked for Fishy, Fishy had been going to look for Bunter.

Fishy, as usual, was on the make!

Only a few days ago he had refused to give Bunter five shillings for his diamond pin; and now he could have kicked himself for it.

Fishy was not only ready to give five shillings, but an increase on that sum, if he could get hold of the pin.

For Fishy knew more now than he had known then.

He had been struck, as many fellows had been, by the attention the Head had given to that diamond. That had not altered his belief that it was a "dud," but it had struck him, and made him think. Since then it had been talked of in the Remove that a pickpocket had tried to pinch the pin from Bunter. The fat Owl had told a dozen fellows how the man who had sold it to him had tried to get it back by snatching. That made Fishy think harder than ever. Then he had heard something still more startling. Jimmy

Many hands pinned Vernon-Smith, and the big can of green paint was upended over him. It streamed and swamped down him. It smothered him. Wild yells and howls and gurgles came from the Bounder. But he had to have it —and he had it! "Oh! Ow! Urrgh! Grooogh! Gruggggh!" he gurgled, struggling in vain.

Vivian had said in the Rag that Mauly believed the diamond to be a real one. Fisher T. Fish was driven to the same conclusion that Mauleverer and Bunter had come to—that the man who had sold the diamond as paste had made a mistake, and handed over a real stone.

Such a mistake was extraordinary, no doubt. But, certainly, it looked like it! Fishy had a supreme contempt for Mauly, as a dog-goned member of a played-out aristocracy. But he knew that Mauleverer understood these things, and was not the fellow to give an opinion without good reason. So Fishy wanted to kiek himself for missing his chance of "cinching" that diamond pin.

That was why he was glad to see Bunter. It was easy to guess why the Owl of the Remove had come; and it suited Fishy to let Bunter raise the subject. Had he looked too eager to get hold of the tiepin, Bunter would undoubtedly have put the price up.

Bunter sat down in Johnny Bull's armchair and blinked at Fishy through his big spectacles. Both Johnny Bull and Squiff were out of the study, and Bunter and Fishy had it to themselves.

"About that pin, Fishy——" began Bunter.

"Yep! I guess I don't mind looking at it, right hyer," said Fishy amiably. "The fact is, I guess I can sell a paste pin—man in the Fifth might buy one. Let's see it."

Bunter took the pin from his pocket. He generally kept it in his study, since the Head had forbidden him to wear it. Now he had rooted it out of his desk to try once more to make a sale. Fortified by Mauleverer's opinion on the subject, Bunter was thinking now, not of shillings, but of pounds! Pounds and pounds, in fact!

Fisher T. Fish extended an eager, bony hand, and almost grabbed the flashing, sparkling diamond.

He took it to the study window and examined it with great care.

Fishy was far from expert in such matters—or any matters, to come to that! Even in his money-making schemes he generally came a cropper. He wished now that he had a little more knowledge of precious stones.

Still, he could see that the stone looked genuine. He could see that the pin in which it was set looked like real gold. It was very different, for instance, from the kind of gold of which Bunter's watch was manufactured.

Was it the genuine goods?

It was borne in on Fishy's mind that it was. The Head had evidently thought so, and had been puzzled on learning that it was not so. Mauly thought so—and Mauly knew! And the man who had sold it—why was he so frantically eager to get it back again? Really, there was hardly room for a doubt in the matter.

But Fisher T. Fish was not the man to impart that opinion to the owner of the goods. With Fishy, business came first, and honesty afterwards—if honesty came in at all!

"Not a bad paste, Bunter, I guess!" he drawled.

"Oh, chuck it!" sneered Bunter. "That won't wash now, Fishy! Mauly knows real stones when he sees them, and he says it's real. The Head thought it was real, too. You jolly well know it is, too, Fishy!"

"I guess you don't buy real diamonds at a bob a time from galoots on railroads," said Fishy, shaking his bony head.

"My Uncle William——"

"Aw, can it!" interrupted Fisher T. Fish. "What's the use of giving me that guff, you gink?"

"Well, whether I got it for a bob or not, it's a real stone!" snapped Bunter. "The man must have had a real diamond among his paste, and made a mistake. But he sold it to me, all the same, and it's mine. Man who makes mistakes like that can stand the racket—see? It's mine! I shouldn't wonder if it was worth twenty pounds."

Fisher T. Fish's narrow eyes glistened. He knew that if that big diamond was genuine it was worth a great deal more than twenty pounds.

But again Fishy kept his opinion to himself. His game was to run down goods he was going to buy, to get them cheap.

"Twenty pink rats!" said Fisher T. Fish derisively. "If it's paste it's worth half-a-crown. If it's real, say a couple of pounds."

"Diamonds are awfully valuable," said Bunter.

"Not these days," contradicted Fisher T. Fish. "Why, they've found diamond-fields in South Africa where you can pick them up by the pocketful! They only keep up the price at all by cutting down production. I'll say that a guy who invests money in diamonds is running a big risk."

"I'm not selling that pin for two pounds," said Bunter. "I'd rather take it down to old Lazarus in Courtfield and give him a trial."

That was exactly what Fisher T. Fish intended to do, if he got hold of the diamond pin. But he gave a scoffing laugh.

"Fifteen bob would be about his limit," he remarked. "Second-hand dealers don't give much, even for the real goods. But the fact is, I fancy I could sell that pin to a man in the Fifth —a dressy man! I'll make it two-pounds-ten, and chance it!"

"Three pounds!" said Bunter.

If Fishy offered two-pounds-ten, it was clear that he believed the diamond to be

(*Continued on page* 16.)
THE MAGNET LIBRARY.—No. 1,353.

DON'T "BIRD" THE BEAK

New boys are warned that the penalty for passing the Head without "capping" him is simply frightful and the excuse that "you didn't know him" is never accepted. The Editor and Staff of the "Greyfriars Herald" therefore advise all new boys to raise their hats and make a deep bow to every male they meet within twenty miles of the school!

THE NEW Greyfria

No. 68 (New Series).

EDITED BY

GREAT NEWSPAPER HOAX

Skinner's Stern Condemnation

Greyfriars readers of the "London Morning Messenger" were rather surprised one day last week to read the following item on its front page:

"We are informed that, following the resignation of Dr. Locke from the headmastership of Greyfriars School, Dr. I. Smyte-Heverley has been appointed by the Governors to take charge of the school.

The new headmaster, who was educated at Borstal and Dartmoor, is a gentleman of striking appearance. Standing about five feet in height, he has a receding, ape-like forehead, beetling brows, heavy, drooping waxed moustache, protruding teeth, red hair, and a hawk-like nose in which he wears a gold ring.

Dr. Smyte-Heverley is well known for his somewhat eccentric style of dress. He is usually seen in public in a kilt, opera-cloak, black straw hat held to his hair with hatpins, and a fur muff. In his right eye he occasionally sticks a green eyeglass, which is tied round his neck with knotted shoelaces.

Greyfriars will be proud of its new headmaster!"

Having got over the first shock, Greyfriars readers of the "Morning Messenger" wondered what the thump it meant.

It was quickly discovered that the "Morning Messenger" had been the victim of a hoaxer who had somehow managed to introduce the bogus news item into the newspaper without its being detected. Naturally, the "Morning Messenger" was sorry, and a full and abject apology to Dr. Locke was printed in all issues on the following day.

But what a jape! What a hoax! While, as Greyfriars men, we had to frown at the idea of our school's name being lowered in the Press, we don't mind admitting that on the quiet most of us yelled!

By a curious coincidence, a Greyfriars man in the shape of Skinner of the Remove had been one of a conducted party which had visited the offices of the "Morning Messenger" the night before the affair. Hearing this, we sent a reporter along to find out what Skinner had to say about it. Skinner was in a mood of stern condemnation.

"It grieves me more than I can tell you to think that any self-styled practical joker could be so misguided as to perpetrate a hoax of this character," he said. "It is a lamentable business."

Our reporter asked Skinner how he thought the jape had been worked.

Skinner shrugged.

"From what I saw of the system at the 'Morning Messenger' offices, it could be done quite easily," he replied. "The hoaxer, I suppose, would slip a typewritten manuscript of the article into the pile of stuff waiting to be set up by one of the compositors. It is almost incredible that depravity could go so far as that—but it's the only possible way I can see."

"But wouldn't it be spotted by one of the sub-editors?"

"Oh, I managed that all right—that is to say, the japer could, in passing through the sub-editor's room, neatly transfer the proof to the checked pile going back to the machines without detection!"

"Great pip!" we ejaculated.

"Oh, there's no doubt it could be done quite easily once, anyway," Skinner said, with a shake of his head. "But what interests me about it is not so much the technical details of the method used as the degraded mentality of the hoaxer. What an utter rotter he must have been!"

And Skinner was still shaking his head sadly as he led our tottering reporter to the door!

MY WORST AND BEST EXPERIENCE

By Wun Lung

Poor little Chinee, likee handsome county, England; but sometime he have many bad expeliences, and the worst expelience is when he losee pigtail. Pigtail of Wun Lung, dear handsome leaders of the "Gleyfliars Helald," was one velly long pigtail. Wun

Lung's honoured and ancient father, he likee; Wun Lung's honoured and velly ancient glanfather, he likee, too; Wun Lung's honoured and old-as-the-hills ancestors, they likee much. Wun Lung velly ploud of long, thick pigtail!

Then one time, handsome 'Lonzy Todd makee big mistake. Velly bad man tellee Todd: "You cuttee off pigtail when Wun Lung asleep; Wun Lung likee you plenty much, then!"

Handsome 'Lonzy Todd, plenty big fool, he come along, bling big scissors, chopee off pigtail. Wun Lung wakee up; Wun Lung findee handsome pigtail gone; Wun Lung cly plenty much, play to ancestors "Sendee back pigtail!" But honoured and handsome ancestors no sendee! Now Wun Lung cly no

more; walkee all alound without pigtail all day long, but no cly; thinkee pigtail get in way plenty much, no wantee pigtail any more!

Allee samee, when handsome 'Lonzy Todd chopee off pigtail, that makee velly worst expelience ever!

Best expelience, dear leaders, is when big bad man Bolsover laidee Wun Lung's study for glub. Wun Lung come along, thinkee have tea, but no luck, big Bolsover he get there first. Allee glub gone!

Bolsover laughee; he say: "Me plenty hungly, eatee Wun Lung's glub, Wun Lung eatee tea in Hall!"

Then Wun Lung laughee. Wun Lung tell Bolsover:

"Plenty silly Bolsover; no eatee Wun Lung's glub, but glub for lats, got plenty poison inside!"

Bolsover no laughee then! Bolsover holdee tummy, yell: "Lat poison! Me die plenty quick! Sendee doctol, makee better!"

"Doctol no good!" Wun Lung reply. "Wun Lung put seclet Chinee poison in glub;

DICKY NUGENT'S WEEKLY WISDOM

They say Wingate is a noing kind of fellow, and I quite beleeve it.

I asked him for a late pass six times last term—and he didn't say "Yes" once!

CAN YOU UNDERSTAND IT?

Parents are impossible people!

After hearing a lecture from his pater on the need for aiming high in life, Kipps took out his airgun and shot a hole in a window in the attic.

And his pater, far from congratulating him for carrying out his advice so quickly, deducted the cost of a new window-pane from his pocket-money!

WOULD YOU BELIEVE IT?

Bunter makes a habit of travelling first-class on the railway. As he always intends to "stick" somebody for the fare at the other end, economy is no object!

Alonzo Todd is a small eater, and frequently refuses a second helping in Hall. Fortunately, he sits next to Bunter—who is always ready to help him out!

Dick Penfold's merry reflect his laughing attitu wards life. Penfold certainly l more than any other Rem excepting possibly Bob Ch

Herald

WHARTON. January 20th, 1934.

TOAST-BURNING CHAMPIONSHIP

Fags' Annual Toast-Burning Championship will be decided in the Second Form Room on the third Wednesday of the New Term. The Wingate Cup, suitably engraved, will be presented to the competitor turning out the blackest piece of toast. Time allowed: 25 sec. each side. For full partics., apply G. TUBB, c/o "GREYFRIARS HERALD."

doctol no under-
' Then Bolsover
l study, shoutee,
ie, no hopee!
!"
ung cheel him up.
ng say, "Never
r ol' Bolsy. You
t Chinee antidote;
u better, plenty
Bolsover cheel up,
Wun Lung velly
solly about glub.
Wun Lung's glub
w you givee seclet
tidote!"
Lung mixee plenty
ty ink, plenty soot,
mustard, makee
Chinee antidote."
linkee plenty much,
ll, lun away, never
Wun Lung again
ime.
un Lung tell evely-
h: NO POISON
B—WUN LUNG
APEE!
ood expelience that,
thinkee?
eek, in response to
tful and repeated
P. P. Prout, Esq.,
l contribute his
s. Don't miss this
eat, chums!—Ed.)

s Like It!

Angel, of the Upper
ho owed Paul Ken-
und all last term,
ttled the debt. He
cash from Peter
xchange for a col-
foreign stamps that
iciously like a col-
saw in a news-
op on sale for two-

tly there are
n even an "Angel"
end to "robbing
ay Paul"!

TO LEARN RILOQUISM?

in Coker's General
Classes! He'll
to talk out of the
r neck in no time!

WIBLEY'S WONDERFUL WATCH

Makes Greyfriars Envious, But——

Wibley has a simply wonderful watch.

It was given him at Christmas by a doting aunt, and every Greyfriars man who has met Wibley since has had to listen to a long and enthusiastic speech about it. Before we're very far into the term, every Greyfriars man will want to own a watch like Wibley's!

It's not much to look at, mind you. When Wib showed it to us, it reminded us more of an old sardine-can than anything else. But looks don't count with this particular timekeeper. It happens to be one of those ultra-modern watches that are built for hard wear, and the chief thing that interests the owner is the number of tests that have been applied to it.

The number of tests that have been applied to Wibley's watch will surprise you!

To begin with, it was placed in water for twenty-four hours.

When taken out again, it was still ticking merrily!

After that, it was thrown into a pot of boiling oil, left there for a week, taken out quickly and then transferred into the middle of a block of ice.

When melted out of this position, it was still going strong!

Then it was taken up in an aeroplane to a height of ten thousand feet and dropped on to a gasometer.

When picked up, it was ticking as furiously as ever!

So, you see it's a real up-to-date watch.

To a man who wants a watch for putting in water, Wibley's watch will prove eminently suitable.

To a man who uses watches only when immersed in boiling oil or frozen into a block of ice, Wibley's watch is just the thing.

To a man who is in the habit of hurling watches out of aeroplanes on to gasometers Wibley's watch will meet his requirements in full.

In fact, there's only one drawback we've discovered about Wibley's watch so far.

It's always wrong!

So much, then, for Wibley's watch!

BUNTER'S ICE-CHAIR A FROST

Safety First Skating a Failure

After the number of times Bunter has told us about his amazing agility and all-round ability on the ice, it came as rather a shock to us to see him gingerly venturing forth last week, holding a chair in front of him as a support if he started slipping. Bunter genially explained that he hadn't brought the chair for himself; with his usual generosity, he had been thinking of others less skilled than himself who might like to borrow it—meanwhile, he was holding on to it merely to show that it was his!

Strangely enough, Bunter didn't seem at all anxious to get rid of it, though he had several excellent chances while we were watching him.

For instance, an old gentleman who thought the chair was being held out for him and sat down in it with a grateful smile at the donor, had a rude awakening when Bunter seized his beard and jerked him away from it!

Then again, a crowd of merry skaters who imagined Bunter was offering it as a dumping place for their overcoats found, to their surprise, that their overcoats were tipped off and trampled on as quickly as Bunter could manage to do it!

One would at least have thought that when he heard an appeal for the loan of the chair from a charming young lady learner, Bunter would have regarded it as a heaven-sent chance to exercise that generosity that had made him bring it out. But he didn't; instead of parting up with the chair, he clung to it more tightly than ever!

Eventually, one of the lake attendants came along and told Bunter he would have to pay one shilling extra for bringing a chair on to the ice. We took it for granted for a moment that Bunter would leave it for some stray novice to pay for and go off skating on his own with his oft-described skill and speed. But he didn't even do that. He paid the bob instead!

We were reluctantly forced to the conclusion that Bunter was not such a genius on the ice as he has always made out. He had simply been waiting to be left alone so that he could learn skating by the "chair" method.

If that was his idea, he got the chance soon afterwards.

Bunter struck out boldly, pushing the chair before him.

He took two strides.

Then, somehow, his legs shot out behind him and the full weight of his body pressed down on the back of the chair.

The end was inevitable. The chair just collapsed and Bunter found himself lying face downwards on the ice, howling!

Dicky Nugent tells us he has ambitions to be a great film actor; but Franky Nugent, on the contrary, says he prefers a quiet life at home.

One wants to be a Picture Star—and the other to be a "Stick To Your Pa!"

GREYFRIARS FACTS WHILE YOU WAIT!

Russell, a keen naturalist, an expert tree climber. He s climbing to the highest s to view the surrounding countryside!

Tom Redwing, the sailorman's son, laments the passing of the old "windjammers," and would like to serve "before the mast" for the sake of the experience!

As a retort to his chum's "high-brow" efforts on the violin, James Hobson, of the Shell, has acquired a banjulele—and replies with vigorous jazz!

HE'LL SCARCELY NEED IT

Lord Mauleverer tells us that his uncle has asked him to keep a diary for 1934, making in it a note of everything he does during the year.

We've sent his languid lordship the back of a small envelope to enable him to do it!

TREVOR'S TONIC TOOTHBRUSH

The sensation of 1934! Stimulates as it scrubs! This amazing toothbrush, invented by Trevor, of the Remove, after years of patient research, gives you back the appetite you've lost through over-indulgence during the Christmas vac. Note the little feather on the end of the brush—just the thing to tickle the palate!

(Continued from page 13.)

real, and worth much more! Bunter could understand that!

"Guess again!" said Fishy. "I shan't get more than three pounds for it from that man in the Fifth Form, and I guess I've got to see a profit if I handle the thing at all."

"More likely you'll get five, you mean beast!" grunted Bunter. "Don't I know you?"

Fisher T. Fish suppressed a chuckle. He was not thinking of five, but at least fifty, for that diamond pin!

But even the prospect of an enormous profit could not make Fishy part with money if he could help it! He hated parting with money!

He tossed the diamond pin carelessly on the table.

"Take the thing and vamoose the ranch!" he said, with well-studied carelessness. "After you've moseyed along to see old Larazus, I guess you'll come back and yaup for two-pounds-ten!"

Bunter extended a fat hand to the pin—and Fishy trembled inwardly! He withdrew the fat hand—and Fishy breathed again!

"Well, I tried to sell my bike to old Lazarus once!" said Bunter. "He's a skinflint! He offered me five shillings for a bike, you know! And then he said he would be losing on it!"

Fisher T. Fish grinned. Certainly he would not have offered five shillings for the miserable wreck that Bunter called a bike!

"Look here, Fishy, make it three—"

"Nunk!"

"Three quids—"

"Nope!"

"Well, what about two-fifteen?" asked Bunter desperately.

Two pounds fifteen shillings represented an enormous amount of tuck—an amount that made Bunter's mouth water to think of it. That was much more attractive than a diamond tiepin, which was useless even for purposes of swank now that he was forbidden to wear it in public.

But Fishy shook his head. Feeling that he had "got" his man, Fishy was adamant.

"Two-pounds-ten—take it or leave it!" he yapped. "And I kinder guess my time's valuable, Bunter!"

"You're a mean beast, Fishy—"

"Shut the door after you!"

"But I'll take it—"

"Done!" said Fishy.

The American junior sorted out two pound notes and a ten-shilling note. His eyes followed them as they were transferred to Bunter's pocket. He hated to part with them. It gave him a pain. It made him feel as if he was at the dentist's. But when Billy Bunter rolled out of Study No. 14 with his cash Fishy's eyes turned on the diamond pin—and he found comfort! He picked it up, took it to the window again, examined it, pored over it, and gloated over it.

"Fifty quids!" breathed Fisher T. Fish. "Perhaps sixty—seventy! I

guess I ain't taking the first offer! Nope! Wake snakes and walk chalks, I guess that this is where I smile!"

And Fisher T. Fish smiled!

THE ELEVENTH CHAPTER.
Brought to Book!

"YOU utter ass, Smithy!"

"Thanks!"

"Thank goodness it never came off! Thank goodness for that, at least!" said Tom Redwing fervently.

The Bounder shrugged his shoulders.

"It would have come off all right if that fool Wharton hadn't barged in," he said. "He got it—and serve him right for meddlin'!"

"There will be trouble——"

"Rats!"

Redwing compressed his lips. He was in the quad with his chum after dinner—in an anxious and angry mood. There was hardly a man in the Remove who had not told the Bounder what he thought of him for his intended trick on the Head! Even Skinner said that it was outside the limit!

Had it succeeded, it was obvious that there would have been serious trouble for the Remove! Such an outrage would have shocked and excited all Greyfriars.

The Bounder might have escaped detection—fellows who knew would not have given him away. But that would have meant that the whole Form would have been under suspicion and under the Head's frown. It might have meant detentions for the whole Remove—in fact, there was no telling what the outcome might have been.

But, apart from that consideration, it was a rotten act in itself, and condemned by all the Removites. There was a limit—and it was outside the limit.

But the condemnation he read in the looks of his Form-fellows only made the Bounder sullen and resentful. Since dinner, not a fellow had spoken to him, but he could see them in groups, speaking to one another; and he knew very well that he was the topic. Not a fellow excepting his chum, Redwing—and Redwing was as disgusted and angry as the rest.

"Wharton's not the fellow to take it quietly, I think," said Tom.

"I wish I'd seen him!" said the Bounder, with a sour grin. "He must have looked a picture! But I was keeping clear."

"If the Head had got it——"

"I wish he had!"

"Well, every man in the Remove is glad that he didn't, and they're saying that you've got to learn not to play games like that on the chief. I'm afraid it means trouble."

The Bounder's lip curled.

"It's the Redclyffe match this afternoon," he said. "They won't rag a man they want to kick goals for them!"

"You may count too much on that!" said Tom.

"Oh rats!"

"It was a rotten thing, Smithy——"

"If that's all you've got to say, you might bestow your conversation on somebody else!" sneered the Bounder. "I've no use for pi-jaw!"

"Very well!" said Tom quietly, and he walked away to the House, leaving the Bounder alone.

Herbert Vernon-Smith drove his hands deep into his pockets, and tramped under the leafless elms. He was in a bitter, savage, resentful mood. At the bottom of his heart, perhaps, he was not sorry that his reckless jape had

failed. Even Smithy realised that it had been rather "thick." But as the matter stood he had scored a failure, and got the whole Form down on him—for no result!

And, headstrong and arrogant as he was, hard and unyielding, the Bounder liked to be popular. He liked to be admired, to be in the limelight. Half his reckless escapades were due to a desire to make fellows look at him in the quad and tell one another that Smithy was a devil of a fellow!

But he had gone too far this time, and nobody was likely to admire an act which even Skinner regarded as disgraceful.

He glanced round, and smiled a bitter, sneering smile as a number of Remove fellows came towards him under the elms. The Famous Five were there, but they were not alone. Squiff and Tom Brown, Peter Todd and Dutton, Hazeldene and Bolsover major and Dupont, Kipps and Monty Newland, Lord Mauleverer and Wibley, and six or seven other fellows were with them. It was, in fact, the principal part of the Form that came towards the mocking, sneering Bounder, with grim expressions on their faces.

He swung round and faced them, his hands in his pockets, his look cool and mocking! If it was going to be a ragging, the Bounder was not the fellow to cut and run! He had, at least, the courage of his misdeeds; and never lacked the nerve to face the music!

"Hardly time to change yet, is it?" drawled the Bounder, affecting to misunderstand. "The Redclyffe men won't be along yet awhile."

"Never mind the Redclyffe men!" said Harry Wharton. "We've got something else to see to before the football."

"You're goin' to settle up?" asked the Bounder.

"Settle up? What do you mean?"

"You owe me five bob."

"I owe you nothing that I know of!" snapped the captain of the Remove.

"For the paint——"

"The paint?" repeated Wharton.

"Yes; I had five bob's worth! You bagged it—I can see traces of it sticking in your hair now! If you bag a fellow's paint——"

Some of the grim faces melted into a grin.

"This is not an esteemed time to be funny, my worthy and execrable fat-headed Smithy!" remarked Hurree Jamset Ram Singh.

"Who's bein' funny?" yawned the Bounder. "I think Wharton ought to pay for my paint, after bagging it without my leave. I've got to get a fresh lot for the Head now!"

"So you're thinking of trying on that game again, are you, Vernon Smith?" asked the captain of the Remove very quietly.

The Bounder was not, as a matter of fact, thinking of anything of the kind, but not for worlds would the arrogant fellow have admitted it.

He nodded coolly.

"Why not?" he answered. "I don't see givin' up a jape because a meddlin' ass barges in and spoils it."

"Well, no Remove man is going to rag the Head, or try to, and get away with it!" said Harry. "There's a limit, though you don't seem to understand it. You're going to be made to understand, Vernon-Smith!"

"Yaas, that's the idea!" remarked Lord Mauleverer. "Sorry, an' all that, but you've got to have it, Smithy! There's a jolly old limit, you know!"

"Have you woke up specially to tell me so, Mauly?"

"Yaas."

"Now——" said Harry.

"Gloves on or off?" asked the Bounder. "If you're feelin' sore about the paint, I'm ready to make you feel more sore!"

"It's not going to be a fight."

"Why not? Cold feet?" asked Smithy.

Wharton's eyes gleamed.

"If you want a scrap, you can say so to-morrow!" he answered. "At present it's not a personal matter, but a Form matter. Because I got the paint, and feel sore about it, I'm standing down, and leaving the matter in Mauly's hands. I'm backing him up, that's all."

"Oh! That's why Mauly woke up, is it?" asked Smithy. "Well, if it's a

ragging, get on with it! I warn you that I shall hit out, and some of you will have fancy faces to show the Redclyffe men when they come over!"

"Are you going to whop the lot of us?" asked Bolsover major sarcastically.

"I'll try!" said the Bounder coolly.

"Oh, that's enough gas!" exclaimed Peter Todd. "You're leader, Mauly! Give the word!"

"Yaas. Get hold of him first!" said Lord Mauleverer. "I'm goin' to make the punishment fit the crime—see? Collar the rank outsider!"

Vernon-Smith's eyes gleamed, and his hands flew up, clenched and as hard as iron. He had said that he would hit out, and he kept his word. There was

a rush of the Removites, and the Bounder stood up to it, gamely and savagely, hitting hard and hitting often. But the rush overwhelmed him, all the same, and, struggling, panting, and with blazing eyes, the Bounder of Greyfriars was grasped on all sides and swept off his feet.

THE TWELFTH CHAPTER.
Making the Punishment Fit the Crime !

"**B**AG him!"

"Scrag him!"

"Got him!"

"Oh, my eye!"

"Ow! My nose!"

(*Continued on next page.*)

Strange things are always happening on the footer field—incidents which cause a great deal of comment when the game is over. "Linesman" is here to settle these arguments. Address your queries to him, c/o The MAGNET, The Fleetway House, Farringdon Street, London, E.C.4.

THE NATURAL GAME ALWAYS PAYS !

WHO will win the F.A. Cup? That is a question we always begin to discuss enthusiastically as soon as the early games have been worked off. Experience proves that we are very seldom right in our summing up of the teams with the best chances of coming through. The competition is such a gamble, really, that we are just as likely to name the winners by putting down the first club we think of than by any amount of logical reasoning concerning the strong and weak points of a side.

It cannot even be said that any particular style of play is the most likely to see a team through the Cup competition successfully. The trophy has been won, in the past by all sorts of teams; by teams which were better in defence than attack; by teams which relied almost entirely on their rearguard to pull them through; by teams playing hustle and bustle football; and by teams playing the scientific stuff really well. The way to win the Cup, really, is to play a natural game, play it well—and get the necessary bit of luck.

There are some teams, of course, who usually make a good show in the Cup competition, and others, equally good as footballers, who fail year after year. Aston Villa and Blackburn Rovers have each won the trophy six times. Yet there are other teams which have been struggling for years and years without a single success to their credit.

You may be surprised to learn, for instance, that such fine teams as Sunderland, Birmingham, Derby County, Liverpool, and Middlesbrough have not yet come through the knock-out competition successfully.

However, while there is life there is hope. Up to the season of 1923 Bolton Wanderers had no Cup Final success to their name. In fact, just prior to that date—when answering a correspondent who wanted to know if the Wanderers had ever won the Cup, I replied: "No, Bolton Wanderers have never won the Cup, and they never will!" That shows to what a state of despair I had arrived

so far as the Wanderers were concerned But, of course, time proved me to be hopelessly wrong. Between 1923 and 1929 this club without a previous Cup success carried off the trophy three times. So it may be the turn of one of the clubs which has not yet triumphed to do so this season.

A GREAT FIND !

I HAVE mentioned Sunderland—one-time dubbed as "the team of all the talents "—among the sides still looking for their first Cup success. This season Sunderland have shown wonderful form, and they have many fine players on their side. Their centre-forward, Bob Gurney, has been much in the football news during this season, and one of my northern readers asks me what I think of him. My view is that Gurney, properly supported, is one of the game's really good centre-forwards.

His entry into first-class football was really due to a tragedy. At Bishop Auckland, which is the birthplace of Gurney, two men were killed while doing an electrical job. With a view to something being done for the benefit of their dependents, a football match was played with the teams selected from local clubs.

One of the young fellows chosen to play in that charity match was Gurney, and he played so well that the Sunderland manager, who happened to witness the game, signed him on forthwith.

He has proved to be a great find. In playing for Sunderland, Gurney has realised an ambition which he and his father shared; that the boy should play for the club nearest his home.

I sometimes wonder if the young footballers who receive expert tuition from star men ever think how really lucky they are? This thought came to me the other day when I happened to be on the Preston North End ground during the week, and noticed some half-dozen lads being put through their paces by Bob Kelly. Everybody knows Kelly, of course—the player who has been in first-class football for twenty years, and who has been recognised as a star all that time.

Not long ago Kelly was given the job of coaching half a dozen of the younger members on the Preston North End staff, and I saw him at work. Before the coaching started one of the Preston directors emphasised to the young players how fortunate they were. He put a point of view which is often overlooked; reminded them that in most professions a boy—or his parents—had to pay for expert tuition, but the football clubs gave their young players the benefit of expert advice while paying them wages at the same time.

There was another point made by this director of Preston, too. He told the lads that while Kelly would do his best to bring them on in the game, Kelly himself, or any other expert, could not do everything himself; that it was up to the lads to make the most of their coaching. I pass on this idea to any of my young football friends who are lucky enough to get expert advice.

It is up to them to make a big effort to get the full value out of their coaching.

FAULTY PLACING OF THE FEET !

IN my postbag this week there are two letters from MAGNET readers touching on the same question.

They both happen to be forwards, and they are both worried because of the number of times they send the ball over the bar instead of underneath it. This is the sort of football blunder which is not confined to young and inexperienced players. Time after time, in every first-class match, the ball goes bang over the bar, and a scoring chance is thus lost. Some of the chances which are missed in this way are very easy ones, and the onlookers groan when the ball sails high through the air.

There are excuses for some of these failures, of course. Often a player has to shoot in a desperate hurry; to trust to luck, as it were. But I feel that much of the "over the bar" shooting is due to faulty placing of the feet, and I am now passing on a tip to my young forward friends which may come in useful.

It is to keep the other leg nearer to the ball.

Let me explain. Suppose a player is taking a shot with the right foot. If the left foot—that is, the one supporting the body of the "shooter"—is some distance behind, then the right foot must be fully extended. Hence the tendency for that foot to get under the ball. If, on the other hand, the left leg is only a few inches —not more than twelve—from the ball when the right foot is used for kicking, that right foot is much more likely to keep the ball low. Try it!

"LINESMAN."

"Got the rotter!"

The Bounder, still struggling savagely, was held in a dozen pairs of hands. Lord Mauleverer looked on, with placid calm. It was not easy to ruffle the serenity of his lazy lordship, and Mauly was quite unruffled now.

"Got him, Mauly!" grinned Bob Cherry. "Wow! My eye!" Holding the Bounder with one hand, Bob dabbed a damaged eye with the other. "Don't go to sleep yet, Mauly! Waiting for orders, you know!"

"Yaas! Carry him to Gosling's woodshed!"

"What on earth for?" asked Nugent.

"Because I say so, dear man! Ain't I givin' orders?"

"Oh, all right! Come on, you fellows!"

With the Bounder still struggling and resisting fiercely, the crowd of Removites surged away to the rather secluded spot where Gosling's woodshed stood. Why Lord Mauleverer selected that especial spot the juniors did not know; but it had been agreed that Mauly should take the lead, and he took it.

"Open the door, some of you!" said Lord Mauleverer, when they arrived at their destination.

"Why can't you open it, fathead?" demanded Wibley.

"Eh—I've got my hands in my pockets!" answered Lord Mauleverer innocently.

"You silly ass!"

Wibley opened the woodshed door.

"What next, O king?" asked Bob Cherry.

"Carry him in!"

The Bounder was carried in, fiercely resisting every step. But in he went, and the Removites crowded in with him, and the door was closed.

Lord Mauleverer glanced round the woodshed. On one side faggots were stacked; on another there were shelves where Gosling kept various things, such as tools and cans of paint. Mauly fixed his eyes on a large can marked "Green Paint."

He pointed to it with a slim forefinger.

"Take that down!" he said.

"Can't you lift it down?" asked Bolsover major.

"I'm givin' orders, old bean! You fellows are carryin' them out!" said Lord Mauleverer cheerfully. "Lift it down, and don't jaw!"

Bolsover lifted down the can of paint. It was large and heavy, and evidently nearly full.

"Get the lid off!" said Lord Mauleverer.

"I don't want paint on my fingers!" remarked Bolsover.

"Neither do I, dear man! Go it!"

"Rats!"

"Oh, I'll get it off!" said Bob Cherry. "I'm not afraid of soiling my lily-white fingers! Here you are, Mauly!"

Bob Cherry prised off the lid of the paint-can.

"Good!" said Lord Mauleverer. "Lots of paint! Mop it over Smithy!"

"Oh, my hat!"

"You dare!" yelled the Bounder.

"Ha, ha, ha!"

"I'm makin' the punishment fit the crime, dear man!" Lord Mauleverer explained patiently. "You fixed up a booby-trap crammed with paint for the Head! Wharton got it! It was rough luck on him! Well, the big idea is to make you tired of paint!"

"Ha, ha, ha!" roared the juniors.

"Good egg!" chortled Bob Cherry. "Couldn't be better! You've asked for this, Smithy!"

"Sauce for the goose is sauce for the giddy gander!" chuckled Johnny Bull. "Mauly, old man, you're a genius!"

"Yaas! Go it!"

"Let go, you rotters!" yelled Vernon-Smith, struggling frantically as Bob Cherry lifted the can of green paint.

"My esteemed and ridiculous Smithy, whoever is saucy to the goose must be saucy to the gander, as the English proverb remarks."

"Ha, ha, ha!"

"Stand steady, Smithy!" grinned Bob. "The stuff's for you—I don't want to get it over the other fellows!"

"Yaas! Keep still, Smithy, there's a good chap!" urged Mauleverer.

Herbert Vernon-Smith did not stand steady or keep still as requested. He struggled and fought like a madman to escape the paint.

But there was no escape for Smithy! Many hands pinned him, and the big can of green paint was upended over him. It streamed and swamped down him. It smothered him.

Harry Wharton had looked redder than a Red Indian after getting in the booby-trap, but the Bounder's state was worse. He was greener than grass.

Wild yells and howls and gurgles came from the Bounder. But he had to have it—and he had it!

Some of the other fellows got splashes and daubs. That could not be helped. But the Bounder got nearly all the paint—and there were three or four pounds of it!

"Oh! Ow! Urrgh! Grooogh! Gruggggh!" gurgled Smithy. If he had not been sorry before for dabbling in paint, there was no doubt that he was sorry now.

"My hat! It's a bit scented here!" gasped Wibley. "I'm leaving him to it!"

"The scentfulness of the esteemed paint is terrific!"

"Come on!"

The juniors crowded out of the woodshed. The Bounder sat there, drenched with paint, smothered with paint, reeking with paint. He was left to make the best of it.

Long after the Removites had departed, Smithy was still there, frantically scraping off paint. Under the green paint, his face was crimson. He was still busy, gasping, gurgling, scraping, when Tom Redwing looked into the woodshed.

Redwing stared blankly.

"Oh gum! Is that Smithy?" he gasped.

"You silly ass! Oooooogh! Yes!" panted Vernon-Smith. "Oh, I'll make them pay for this! I'll make them sit up! Grooogh! Look at me!"

"Ha, ha, ha!"

Redwing looked—and burst into a laugh! Really, a fellow who was green as grass was liable to cause laughter. But the Bounder did not feel like laughing. He gave Redwing a painty glare.

"You cackling dummy!" he roared.

"Sorry!" gasped Redwing. "But you—"

"You chortling chump!"

"Well, you look rather funny, old man—quite as funny as Wharton in the red paint——"

"You sniggering idiot!"

"Look here! You'd better get into the changing-room! You can get hot water and soap there!" grinned Redwing. "The sooner you get that off, the better. You've got to change, anyhow, for footer."

"I'm not goin' to play footer, you fool! They can play Redclyffe without me after this!" howled the Bounder.

"You'll be wanted——"

"Let them want!"

"Well, come and get cleaned, anyhow!"

The Bounder, breathing rage and paint, followed his chum from the woodshed. Fortunately, he was able to dodge into the changing-room unobserved, or his extraordinary state would certainly have drawn general attention. That, certainly, the Bounder did not want.

Wharton had had a troublesome task with paint that morning. Smithy had a much more troublesome one. He gasped with rage as he cleaned, and cleaned, and cleaned, at the clinging paint. It was likely to be a long time before Smithy planned another jape with paint in it! Undoubtedly, Mauly's idea was a good one, of making the punishment fit the crime!

" Hallo, what's this game ? " asked Skinner, entering the tuckshop with Snoop and Stott to see Bunter pressing the good things on the Famous Five. Bunter looked round. " My treat ! " he said. " Have some tarts. you men ! " Skinner blinked in amazement. " It's the genuine goods ! " chuckled Bob Cherry. " It seems that Bunter's postal order has come at last ! "

THE THIRTEENTH CHAPTER.

" Riches Take Unto Themselves Wings ! "

" I SAY, you fellows !"
"Bow-wow !"
"But, I say——"
"Scat !"

Harry Wharton & Co. were thinking about footer, and Bunter, as usual, was superfluous. The team from Redclyffe was shortly due, and it was a matter that required some thought. For, after the ragging in the woodshed, it was fairly certain that Vernon-Smith's back would be up, to a truly terrific extent. That ought to have made no difference in footer ; but in the Bounder's case it was very likely to make a big difference. In his rage and resentment, it was more likely than not that Smithy would turn the football match down, and the captain of the Remove would have to play another man.

There were plenty of men available and keen to play ; but the trouble was that Smithy was one of the best men in the eleven, and the best men were wanted to play Fane & Co. of Redclyffe. It was quite possible that if the Bounder stood out, it might make all the difference between victory and defeat. Which was a serious matter to the Remove footballers—though nobody regretted having given the scapegrace of Greyfriars a much-needed lesson.

Billy Bunter blinked at them loftily and reproachfully through his big spectacles. Bunter was not thinking of footer. He had, in fact, forgotten that there was a football match that afternoon. Bunter, with the dazzling sum of two pounds ten shillings in his pocket, was thinking of matters much more important than Soccer.

"I say, you fellows, look here !" persisted Bunter. "You men make out that

I barge in at other fellows' feeds, and never stand a feed !"

"Not much making out about it !" growled Johnny Bull. "You do !"

"Oh, really, Bull——"

"The bargefulness is generally terrific !"

"Well, it's my treat now !" said Bunter loftily. "Come along with me to the tuckshop, and ask for what you like !"

"Eh ?"

"What ?"

"I mean it !" said Bunter.

Harry Wharton laughed.

"We don't want a blow-out just before a football match, old fat man," he said, "and, anyhow, we can't afford your treats ! Money's tight."

"Ha, ha, ha !"

"Why, you silly ass !" roared Bunter. "Do you think I want you to pay ?"

"Eh ? Don't you ?"

"No !" roared Bunter.

"Don't say your postal order's come !" implored Bob Cherry. "Anything but that !"

"As a matter of fact it has !" said Bunter.

"Ye gods !"

"I told you fellows that I was expecting a postal order——"

"You did !" chuckled Nugent. "Lots of times !"

"Hundreds of times !" grinned Bob.

"Millions of times !" chuckled Johnny Bull.

"Well, it's come !" said Bunter.

"Gammon !"

"Look here !" Billy Bunter jerked three currency notes from his pocket, and held them up for inspection. "What about that ?"

The Famous Five gazed at that unwonted supply of cash ! There were two notes for a pound each, and one for ten shillings ! Seldom, in the history of

Greyfriars, had Billy Bunter been seen in such funds before.

"My only hat !" gasped Bob Cherry. "Do my aged eyes deceive me ?"

"Are things what they seem, or is visions about, as the johnny says in the poem !" chuckled Nugent.

"Are they real ?" asked Johnny Bull.

"Real ?" yelled Bunter.

"I mean, did you buy them for a bob in a train, like your jolly old diamond pin ?"

"Ha, ha, ha !"

"Beast !" roared Bunter. "Of course they're real !"

"Well, if they're real, whose are they ?"

"Mine !" shrieked Bunter.

"Mauly must be an ass, then, to lend you as much as that !"

"Mauly never lent them to me, you beast ! They're mine ! I told you I was expecting a postal order !" hooted Bunter. He gave the chums of the Remove a glare of scorn through his big spectacles. "You rotters ! Making out that a chap never stands a feed, and then when I ask you——"

"Well, this is so sudden, as Angelina said to George !" remarked Bob Cherry. "But if it's honest Injun——"

"Beast !" snorted Bunter.

"Couldn't help being surprised, old fat man——"

"Yah !"

"If you mean it, old fat bean, we'll come !" said Harry Wharton soothingly. It seemed that, for once, the Owl of the Remove did mean business, and the Famous Five felt a touch of compunction. Certainly it was the first time in their experience that Billy Bunter had offered to stand treat with the cash in hand to pay for the same. Still, this time it looked like "honest Injun." "We don't want a feed as we're going to play footer; but we'll join you in a lemonade and a bun."

"Come on, then!" said Bunter.

And the Famous Five came on.

They walked into the school shop with the Owl of the Remove, and Billy Bunter issued orders royally. But Mrs. Mimble gave him a far from grateful glance over her counter.

"Master Bunter, I have already told you, many times, that I cannot give you credit," she said.

Snort from Bunter!

"Who's asking for credit?" he demanded.

"Wha-a-at! I supposed——"

"Look there!"

Bunter slammed two pound notes and a ten-shilling note on the counter. Mrs. Mimble gazed at them as if they had been the ghosts of two pound notes and a ten-shilling note!

"Dear me!" she said.

"I told you yesterday that I was expecting a postal order!" said Bunter severely. "You refused to give me credit, Mrs. Mimble! Well, it's come!"

"Dear me!" said Mrs. Mimble again. She could not remember how many times she had refused Bunter credit on the strength of an expected postal order.

"Now, please serve me and my friends!" said Bunter, with dignity.

And, having seen the colour of his money, so to speak, the good dame lost no time in serving Bunter and his friends.

Bunter, in funds, was rather a new Bunter! He pressed the best, and plenty of it, on his friends—not forgetting himself, meanwhile!

But the Famous Five did not want to fill up with tarts and eclairs and other sticky and indigestible things just before playing Soccer. They accepted the treat out of consideration for Bunter's feelings; but they were very moderate. Bunter was far from moderate. In a very few minutes he was jammy and sticky and shiny—and still going strong.

"Hallo, what's this game?" asked Skinner, coming in with Snoop and Stott.

Bunter blinked round.

"My treat!" he said. "Have some tarts, you men?"

Skinner blinked at him.

"It's the genuine goods!" chuckled Bob Cherry. "It seems that Bunter's postal order has come at last!"

"Fan me!" ejaculated Skinner.

"Look here, Skinner, you cheeky beast, if you don't want any tarts——"

"I jolly well do!" said Skinner promptly. "Gratters, old bean! It's time that postal order came! Did it grow whiskers in the post?"

"Ha, ha, ha!"

Skinner & Co. joined in. Other fellows came into the tuckshop, and Bunter generously asked them to join in tarts and ginger-pop and other good things, meeting with few refusals. News was not long in spreading that there was a treat going in the school shop—with the much more amazing news that Billy Bunter was in funds and standing it.

"Bunter's postal order come!" ejaculated Peter Todd, as he came in with Dutton. "Who's japing?"

"Oh, really, Peter——"

"Honest Injun!" chuckled Bob. "Bunter's rolling in it!"

"Well, my hat!"

"You never believed that I was really expecting a postal order, Peter!" said Bunter accusingly.

"Admitted!" said Toddy cheerfully. "I never did!"

"Well, it's come!" said Bunter scornfully.

"Wonders will never cease!"

THE MAGNET LIBRARY.—No. 1,353.

"Beast—I mean, tuck in, old chap! Another time, perhaps, you'll be willing to lend a fellow half-a-crown when he tells you he's expecting a postal order! Pass over some more of those tarts, Mrs. Mimble, please—and some cakes—and ginger-pop—and those eclairs—and——"

"My hat! The fat old bean's going it!" said Skinner, who was eating as fast as he could. "Pile in, you men! Now's your chance—the chance of a lifetime!"

"Ha, ha, ha!"

Plenty of fellows were piling in. Good things were handed out galore. It was quite a novel and exhilarating experience to Billy Bunter to be standing a spread on this scale. Possibly he hoped that it would improve his credit in the Remove, and make it easier to extract little loans when he was short of cash again—as he was likely soon to be at this rate! Certainly he was very glad to demonstrate to unbelieving fellows that his celebrated postal order had come at last!

Mrs. Mimble, however, was keeping an account with a stump of pencil on a sheet of wrapping-paper. Suddenly she announced:

"That will be exactly two pounds ten shillings, Master Bunter!"

"Oh!" gasped Bunter.

"Many hands make light work." "Riches take unto themselves wings and fly away." Bunter's £2 10s. was gone!

"Thanks, old fat bean!" said Harry Wharton; and he left the tuckshop with the Co.

As they walked across the quad, the Famous Five came on Fisher T. Fish coming away from the House in coat and hat. Fishy, evidently, was going out, and, equally evidently, he was in high feather. His bony face was beaming.

"Hallo, hallo, hallo!" exclaimed Bob Cherry, giving him a smack on a bony shoulder. "Enjoying life, old bony bean?"

"Ow! Don't crack a man's back!" grunted Fisher T. Fish. "Yep! I guess I'm on to a good thing! Just a few!"

"Come into a fortune like Bunter?"

"Bunter!" Fishy grinned. "Yep! I guess two-pound-ten would be a fortune to that gink!"

"Did you know his postal order had come?" grinned Nugent.

"Postal order nothing! I gave him two-pound-ten for his diamond pin!" snorted Fisher T. Fish.

"Oh, my hat!"

"Ha, ha, ha!"

The Famous Five roared. They knew now the source of Billy Bunter's sudden

wealth. That celebrated postal order had not, after all, arrived! He had, at long last, sold his diamond pin!

"But you haven't really given Bunter two pounds ten for a paste pin he bought for a shilling?" exclaimed Harry Wharton.

Fisher T. Fish winked.

"I guess the guy that sold Bunter that pin made a mistake!" he said. "I guess it's the goods—the real goods! I surely guess that I'm going to get fifty pounds for that pin!"

"You bony, blithering, swindling worm!" gasped Bob Cherry. "You mean to say that you've diddled Bunter out of that pin because he didn't know its value?"

"Aw, come off!" said Fisher T. Fish. "Business is business, I reckon! I guess I got no time to worry any about lame ducks! Nope!"

And Fisher T. Fish walked down to the gates, leaving the Famous Five staring.

THE FOURTEENTH CHAPTER.
"Play Up!"

HERBERT VERNON-SMITH scowled as the Remove footballers came into the changing-room.

The paint was gone at last; the Bounder was no longer green as grass. To judge by his look, however, the Bounder's temper was not improved. His eyes glittered at the Famous Five.

Bob Cherry gave him a cheery grin.

"Getting ready, Smithy?" he asked amicably.

"No!" grunted the Bounder.

"The Redclyffe men may be here any minute——"

"What do I care?"

"The carefulness ought to be terrific, my esteemed Smithy!" murmured the Nabob of Bhanipur.

Wharton fixed his eyes on the Bounder with a grim look.

"You've had a ragging, Vernon-Smith!" he said. "You asked for it, and you got it! That's over. Now, you're down to play for the Remove. You're expected to play up when you're wanted."

"Blessed are those who don't expect!" said the Bounder sourly. "They don't get disappointed, you know!"

"Does that mean that you're standing out?"

"It means just that!"

Wharton compressed his lips.

"Very well!" he said. "It's no good telling you you're a rotter—you know that! Stand out, and be blowed!"

"Look here, we want Smithy!" said Bob uneasily.

"Nugent will take his place."

"Yes; but——"

"I can play Soccer, more or less, Bob!" remarked Frank, with a faint touch of sarcasm.

"Franky, old bean, you're my pal, but I'm not going to tell you that you can play Soccer like Smithy!" said Bob Cherry. "I'd like to, but I can't stretch it to that extent!"

"You silly ass!"

"H'm! Look here, Smithy——"

"Rats!" said Smithy, continuing to comb paint out of his hair. "You should have thought of all that before you played the goat in the woodshed!"

"That's got nothing to do with footer!"

"Hasn't it? I think it has!" sneered the Bounder.

"Then you're a rotter," roared Bob, red with anger, "and I've a jolly good mind to bung your head in that basin of water!"

"You can try it on, if you like!"

"By gum, I——"

Bob Cherry made a stride towards the Bounder. Wharton caught him by the shoulder.

"Chuck it, Bob! No time for ragging now!"

"That rotter——" breathed Bob.

"Oh, let him rip!" said the captain of the Remove contemptuously.

Bob Cherry grunted, but he assented. The Remove men changed for footer, some of them giving the Bounder dark looks. Frank Nugent changed with the rest, but with a rather clouded face. He was keen enough to play—keen as mustard; but, like a loyal man, he was thinking of the side more than of himself. He was quite a good man at the game, but he did not flatter himself that he was in the same street with Smithy. And though Wharton, as his chum, was glad to play him, he had a fairly clear idea of his chum's feelings on the subject as football captain.

When the other fellows went out of the changing-room, Frank Nugent lingered behind.

He looked at the Bounder.

Vernon-Smith was standing by the window, staring out at the fellows going down to Little Side, with a gloomy and glum expression on his face.

For a full minute Frank stood there, hesitating.

He wanted to play—he longed to figure in a fixture like that with Redclyffe School. He even nourished a hope that, with luck, he might bring off one of those brilliant shots that would make the fellows roar "Nugent! Nugent!" as they roared "Good old Bounder!" But——

"Smithy!" said Frank, very quietly.

The Bounder started and turned from the window. He was not aware till that moment that Nugent had stayed.

"Oh! You!" he said. He gave an ugly sneer. "You look a pretty figure in footer rig, Nugent—much prettier than I do! Let's hope that a pretty fellow will turn out useful as well as ornamental!"

Nugent flushed crimson.

"That's like you, Smithy!" he said.

"And it's like you to barge into a game you can't play!" sneered the Bounder. "What use will you be against those beefy men from Redclyffe?"

"A fellow can only do his best," said Frank. "And at least, I'm willing to do that!"

Smithy shrugged his shoulders. Then his expression changed.

"Sorry!" he said. "Go in and win, old man! It's a big chance for you; you may pull it off and keep the place in the team. Best of luck!"

Nugent laughed.

"You're a queer fish, Smithy," he said. "But I've stopped behind to speak to you. I'm keen to play, and you know it! But——"

"But what?"

"Look here, Smithy, be a sport!" said Nugent. "There's still time, and I'll stand down if you'll line up."

"Oh, my hat!"

"I mean it!" said Nugent. "Say the word, Smithy! You'll be sorry afterwards for doing a rotten thing; you always are in the long run!"

"You'll chuck up a chance like this?"

"Yes, yes! Say the word, old man."

Vernon-Smith looked at him long and hard, and stood silent. But the hard, sullen look was gone from his face. He spoke at last.

"If you mean it, Nugent——"

"I've said so."

"You're a better chap than I am," said the Bounder. "But that's no

news. Look here, I'm jolly glad that rotten trick on the Head never came off. I was sorry afterwards, though I wouldn't say so. I've heard that Quelch is coming back to-morrow, and I'm going to try to make a fresh start. I'll take you at your word."

"Good man!" said Frank; and if he felt a pang of disappointment he drove it away from him. "Get into your things! I'll change back."

Nugent changed back very quickly and ran out. He joined the Remove footballers on Little Side and received a general stare.

"What the thump does this mean?" asked Harry Wharton. "Why aren't you in footer rig, Frank?"

"Smithy's playing," said Nugent briefly.

"Oh!"

"Good man!" said Bob Cherry heartily. "The old Bounder's bark is always worse than his bite. He's not the fellow to let us down. Oh, good!"

Frank smiled—a rather wry smile.

"Sorry, old man," added Bob remorsefully. "But—but you know——"

"I know," said Nugent quietly.

The Bounder, in football rig, came speeding down to the field as the Redclyffe men arrived. He gave Wharton a rather doubtful and defiant look. But the captain of the Remove gave him a cheery nod.

"Good man!" he said.

The Bounder grinned.

"If you want me——"

"Of course we do!"

"The ragfulness has nothing to do with the esteemed and absurd Soccer, my estimable Smithy!" said Hurree Jamset Ram Singh. "The pleasure of beholding your ridiculous countenance on this ludicrous spot is terrific."

"Hear, hear!" chuckled Bob Cherry.

Redwing, in the crowd of Greyfriars fellows gathering round the ground, waved a hand to his chum as Smithy went into the field with the Remove. Tom's face was very bright. Nugent's, perhaps, was a little glum, as he watched the Bounder playing in the place he might have had.

But that glumness cleared off very soon. Smithy, always a good man, was playing the game of his life.

In the first half the Bounder beat the Redclyffe men twice, and the crowd roared applause. At half-time Bob Cherry gave him a thump on the back that made him stagger.

"Good old Bounder!" he chuckled.

And the Bounder chuckled, too, while he gasped. He liked popularity, and he liked the limelight. Now he was getting both in ample measure.

Redclyffe had equalised in the second half, when Wharton put the pill in and the Remove were one up again. It was towards the finish that Fane of Redclyffe dropped the ball neatly into the Greyfriars goal, beating Squiff all the way, and the score was level again.

With four minutes to go, and both sides panting after a gruelling game, it looked like a draw

But it was not a draw.

With the call of the whistle expected every second, the Bounder got through. The Redclyffe goalie clutched at the leather and missed it by an inch. There was a terrific roar.

"Goal!"

"Smithy!"

"Good old Bounder!" yelled Frank Nugent.

The whistle went.

"Smithy! Smithy!"

Grabbed up by his comrades, the Bounder was carried off the field. Only a few hours since the same fellows had been ragging him. It was a change. And the Bounder had to realise that it was a change for the better.

THE FIFTEENTH CHAPTER.

Too Late !

"I SAY, Fishy——"

"Scat!"

"But I say——"

"Git!"

"Beast!" roared Billy Bunter.

Fisher T. Fish accelerated. He was starting for Courtfield to dispose there of his wonderful bargain in diamond tiepins, and he had no use for Bunter. Bunter, whose riches had taken unto themselves wings and flown away, had a use for Fishy—if Fishy could be put to use.

He rolled after the transatlantic junior.

"I say, hold on a minute!" gasped Bunter. "I say, Fishy——"

Instead of holding on, Fisher T. Fish walked fast. Bunter trotted, his little fat legs going as fast as Fishy's long, thin ones. By the time Courtfield Common was in sight Bunter put on a desperate spurt and overtook Fishy. He clutched his arm.

"Look here!" he gurgled breathlessly.

"Leggo, you fat clam!" snorted Fisher T. Fish. "A bargain's a bargain, ain't it? I got no use for lame ducks. Scoot!"

"That's all right!" gasped Bunter. "I'm not asking you to call it off, you mean beast!"

"Oh! Not?" ejaculated Fisher T. Fish. "Wharrer you want, then, you gink?"

"Lend me——"

"Can it!"

"That pin was worth more than two-ten, and you jolly well know it!" snorted Bunter. "Well, lend me a quid——"

"Guess again!"

"What about ten bob, then?"

"Nunk!"

And Fisher T. Fish, jerking his bony arm loose, started again. Bunter, at the end of his wind, gasped "Beast!" and gave it up.

Fisher T. Fish disappeared in the direction of the town, and Billy Bunter

sank down, gasping, on a wayside seat. He was breathless. Bunter was no sprinter at the best of times, and still less so after packing away a large and varied assortment of foodstuffs. He sat and gurgled.

He had succeeded at long last in selling that diamond pin. Two pounds ten shillings for a tiepin that had cost him one bob really showed a handsome profit. But the two pounds ten shillings had gone. Cash never stayed long in Bunter's pocket when he had any. That handsome little sum was gone from his gaze like a beautiful dream.

"Beast!" murmured Bunter.

It was true that even Bunter was not hungry again yet. But there was tea to be thought of. And after that brief accession of wealth he was once more in his usual stony state. The least that mean beast Fishy could have done, in Bunter's opinion, was to lend him a pound. Evidently, however, the business-man of the Remove did not see eye to eye with Bunter on that subject.

Bunter had a long rest on the wayside seat. He did not observe a small man with sandy eyebrows, in a shabby overcoat, lounging along the road, till the sandy man was very close.

Then he gave a jump.

"Oh lor'!" gasped Bunter.

He recognised the man who had sold him the diamond tiepin and had later taken such lawless measures to get it back again. Bunter had forgotten him, but he had to remember him now. It was clear that the sandy man was still hanging about the vicinity of Greyfriars, looking for a chance at Bunter.

The fat Owl rose to his feet to cut. But the narrow, rat-like eyes were on him. The sandy man darted up.

"Hold on, sir!" said the sandy man very civilly. "No offence, sir. Just a word with you, Mr. Bunter!"

If Bunter could have won a foot-race he certainly would not have lingered for a word from the sandy man. After his previous experiences with that gentleman, the less he saw of him the better Bunter liked it. But as there was no escape for him the fat Owl was glad, at least, that the man was civil.

He blinked uneasily at Mr. Sniggerson.

"I—I say, I—I've got to get in to tea!" he stammered. "I—I say, I—I haven't got that pin on me, I really haven't."

The sandy man grinned faintly. If Bunter had been wearing the diamond pin the sandy man would not have wasted either words or civility on him; he would have snatched. It was because Bunter was not wearing the tiepin that the man with the sandy eyebrows was disposed to conversation.

"Well, sir, about that pin!" said the sandy man. "I dessay you're surprised at my wanting it back, but I'll own up it was more valuable than I s'posed when I sold it! You give me a bob for it, I'll go as far as a pound, if you'll let me have it back."

A couple of days ago Billy Bunter would have jumped at the offer. Now it was too late for Bunter to jump.

"Sorry——" he began, blinking very uneasily at the narrow face.

"I might make it thirty shillings, sir!"

"I've sold the pin!"

"Sold it!"

"Yes!" gasped Bunter. "I—I say, it—it's no good getting waxy—it was mine—I—I say—keep your temper, you know."

It was hard for Mr. Sniggerson to keep his temper. For a moment his bony hands clenched, and his rat-like eyes burned at Bunter. For that

moment the Owl of the Remove quaked with terror.

But the sandy man calmed himself! Hammering Bunter was a solace that could be postponed till he was quite sure that the diamond pin was out of his reach. He was not sure yet.

"Then you found out it was a real diamond?" he muttered.

"A—a fellow told me so——" stammered Bunter. "I—I got two-pound-ten for it! I've spent the money!" he added hastily, lest the sandy man should think of putting in a claim on the proceeds.

"Who'd you sell it to for that much?" The sandy man was quick on the up-take. "A dealer'd give more—if he'd give anything! You never sold it to no dealer!" The sandy man had good reasons for guessing that Bunter had not sold the diamond at a jeweller's. "A fellow at your school, p'r'aps?"

"Yes!" gasped Bunter.

"You could get it back?"

"Not for the same money! He's a beast who goes in for making profits," said Bunter. "I believe he'll get four or five pounds for it, from a man in the Fifth."

"Likely he'd be wearing it?"

Even the obtuse Owl saw the drift of that question. The sandy man was prepared to hang on, watching for a chance to snatch, if there was a chance. Bunter shook his head.

"No—he's bought it to sell," he answered. "Besides, the Head won't let us wear diamond pins. He was down on me for wearing it—that's why I hadn't got it on when—'hem! When I saw you look."

The sandy man compressed his thin lips. It was clear to him that the fat and fatuous fellow on the seat beside him had no knowledge of the real nature of that transaction in the holidays. He had found out that the diamond was a real stone, but not its real value, if he had sold it for so small a sum as he named, and obviously he had not guessed that it was a stolen stone. It had not even occurred to Bunter that the man in the train had pretended that the diamond was paste to have an excuse for selling it for what Bunter could give—in order to get rid of it for a time, because he feared a search by the police.

Bunter, evidently, suspected nothing of all that, but the sandy man wondered how far he could depend on the fat fellow's obtuseness. He had to take the risk; and the obtuseness in Bunter's fat face was, at least, reassuring.

"Well, this is how it is, sir," said the sandy man. "I made a mistake with that there tiepin, as you've found. I want it back, and I'd go to five pounds for it."

"Oh lor'!" gasped Bunter. "I wish I'd seen you yesterday."

The sandy man smiled quite genially.

"Well, sir, you get it back for me and I'll make it five pounds, and a pound over and above for your trouble," he said.

"That's all right," said Bunter. "I fancy Fishy will be glad to take five quid—that's twice what he gave! I'll try, anyhow. He's gone down to Courtfield now, but he will be back for tea, and I can see him. If you like to hand me the fiver now——" he said.

"When can you let me know?"

"After tea," said Bunter. "Wait near the school gates in a couple of hours, and I'll nip out and tell you. I fancy it will be all right. Have the fiver with you, though—Fishy wouldn't part with it without the money."

"I'll bring the fiver all right!" said the sandy man, "and a pound note along with it, sir! And you can bring a

" Let me thee it ! " said Mr. Lazarus, unable to take his eyes off the tie pin in Fisher T. Fish's hand.   The American junior handed it over. " You ain't saying it's not real ? " he demanded.   " It's value is not leth than a hundred pounds, sir," replied Mr. Lazarus.   " Wake snakes ! ".gasped Fisher T. Fish, his eyes gleaming with excitement.

friend with you to see fair play, if you like—no snatching !" He grinned. "It's on the square, sir !"

"Right-ho !" said Bunter.

The fat junior was feeling quite bucked as he walked back to Greyfriars. There was another pound in store for him, if he succeeded in getting the tiepin back from Fishy—and even Fishy, surely, would part with it for twice what he had given ! Bunter little dreamed what was happening to Fishy, in those very minutes ! He rolled in at the school gates—with only one cloud on his horizon, the pound, if it came, would not come in time for tea ! It was getting towards tea-time now, and Bunter was getting hungry.

The football match was over when he arrived; not that Bunter gave that trifling matter a thought. He rolled up to the Remove passage—and stopped at the door of Study No. 1. That study was crowded—not to say crammed. A little celebration was going on after the victory, and Study No. 1 was as full as it would hold ! To Bunter's astonishment the Bounder was there—evidently an honoured guest, with a cheery grin on his face.

"I say, you fellows——" squeaked Bunter.

"Hallo, hallo, hallo ! We won !" roared Bob Cherry.

"Eh ! You won what ?" asked Bunter.

"You fat, frabjous, foozling frump, have you forgotten that we played Redclyffe this afternoon ?" hooted Bob indignantly.

"Oh ! No ! Yes ! Gratters !" said Bunter. "I say, you fellows, I suppose you're asking me to tea after that splendid spread I stood you——"

"Oh, my hat !"

"What's Smithy doing here ?" asked Bunter. "You were ragging him, last I heard of him. Turn him out and make room for a fellow."

"You footling fathead !" said Harry Wharton. "Smithy kicked the winning goal for us this afternoon."

"Did he? Well, I would have, if you'd asked me to play ! You didn't !"

"Oh crumbs !"

"Ha, ha, ha !"

"I say, you fellows——"

"Roll in, Bunter !" said the captain of the Remove, laughing. "Make room for the porpoise, you men, somehow."

And Billy Bunter rolled in, and while the other fellows discussed the Bounder's last goal, Bunter discussed the cake ! Goals were all very well, to fellows keen on Soccer, but to William George Bunter, one cake was worth many goals !

———

THE SIXTEENTH CHAPTER.

Very Fierce for Fishy !

"MY cootness !" said Mr. Lazarus.

He stared at the diamond tiepin in the bony hand of Fisher T. Fish.

Mr. Lazarus seemed astonished.

Fisher T. Fish grinned serenely.

He had been sure—and now he was doubly sure ! He had not thrown away his two-pound-ten ! It was coming back with more added there unto ! Obviously that diamond was a real one ! Whether Lord Mauleverer knew or not, Mr. Lazarus, of Courtfield, knew.

"I'm selling this pin !" said Fisher T. Fish. "I ain't saying that I'm taking the first offer ! But I'm selling it, I guess ! You see, my headmaster won't let us wear gaudy things like this."

"My cootness !" repeated Mr. Lazarus.

"Well, what's the figure ?" asked Fishy.

Mr. Lazarus' black eyes were glued on the tiepin in Fishy's hand. He seemed unable to take them off it.

"Let me thee it !" he said at last.

Fisher T. Fish handed it over. Mr. Lazarus looked at it, turned it over and over, scanned it from the north, south, east, and west, so to speak. He looked at Fishy and looked at the diamond and looked at Fishy again.

"You ain't saying it's not real ?" demanded Fishy.

"No !" said Mr. Lazarus gently. "It is a real stone, sir."

"I guessed it was a cinch ! And what's the figure? You buy diamonds," said Fisher T. Fish.

"I buy diamonds!" assented Mr. Lazarus. "But——"

"Buy it or not, what would you call the value, Mr. Lazarus?" asked Fisher T. Fish eagerly.

"Not leth than a hundred pounds, sir."

"Wake snakes !" gasped Fisher T. Fish.

His eyes danced.

In his wildest anticipations he had hardly dared to dream of such a sum as that.

"Well, look here, what'll you give?" he asked, his voice trembling with eagerness.

"That," said Mr. Lazarus, "is another matter ! I shall have to consider ! Pleathe excuse me a moment."

"Any old time !" said the joyous Fish. "I guess I ain't pressed for time."

Mr. Lazarus turned to a desk and opened a bundle of papers, and appeared to give a certain paper there very particular attention. Every now and then he glanced from the paper to the diamond tiepin and back again. It was just as if he was comparing the tiepin with a written description—though that, naturally, did not occur to Fisher T. Fish.

"Pleathe excuse me while I go to the telephone !" said Mr. Lazarus.

"Take your time," said Fishy cheerfully.

Mr. Lazarus went into an adjoining room. Fisher T. Fish could hear the murmur of a voice on the telephone, but he could not make out what was said. Neither was he interested. He was walking about with quick, jerky steps, unable to keep still in his delight, dreaming golden dreams.

The old gentleman came back at last.

"Well, what about it?" asked Fisher T. Fish brightly.

Mr. Lazarus gave him a glance—a very peculiar glance.

"I want to show this diamond to a shentleman," he said "He will be here in five minutes, if you will wait."

"O.K!" said Fishy carelessly. "Phoned to a man to come and see it, what?"

"Just tho!" agreed Mr. Lazarus.

"I guess I'll wait, if you want."

And Fisher T. Fish waited, humming a tune; and Mr. Lazarus waited, with a very grave and very peculiar expression on his face.

The door opened.

Fisher T. Fish looked round, expecting to see the "shentleman" who was to see the diamond before Mr. Lazarus bought it. He found himself staring at Inspector Grimes, of Courtfield police station.

Mr. Grimes gave him a glance, and then looked at Mr. Lazarus.

"Is this the boy?" he asked.

"Yeth!"

"A Greyfriars boy, I think?"

"I guess so," said Fisher T. Fish, in wonder.

"And the diamond, Mr. Lazarus——"

"Here!"

The jeweller handed the diamond tiepin over to the inspector, who examined it with minute care.

All this was so surprising and so mysterious to Fisher T. Fish that he could only gaze on open-mouthed. He had "guessed" that it was some jeweller, expert in precious stones, to whom Mr. Lazarus had telephoned. Why he desired to show the diamond tiepin to a police inspector was a great mystery.

Mr. Grimes turned to Fishy at last. The grimness of his official countenance was almost unnerving. Fisher T. Fish began to feel an inward trepidation—he hardly knew why.

"Now, Master Fish—I think your name is Fish——"

"Sure!"

"Kindly explain at once how you came into possession of a stolen diamond tiepin!" rapped Mr. Grimes.

Fisher T Fish staggered.

"Stut-stut-stolen!" he gurgled.

"You did not know?"

The inspector eyed him suspiciously.

"Wake snakes! That dog-goned gink—— Done!" gasped Fisher T. Fish. "Me, a guy raised in Noo Yark, where they cut their eye-teeth airly! Done by a pie-faced, dog-goned clam! Jerusalem crickets!"

"Out of consideration for Dr. Locke I shall not, if it can be avoided, take you into custody," said Mr. Grimes. "But you must explain instantly how and where you obtained a stolen diamond!"

"Aw! You sure it's stolen?" groaned Fisher T. Fish. "You bank on it?"

"This diamond tiepin is the property of a Mr. Isaacs, a City gentleman, who was robbed of it in Surrey, on the road between Wimford and the village of Elmdale, two or three weeks ago," said Inspector Grimes. "The description has been circulated all over the country—every jeweller and pawnbroker——"

"Jumping Moses!"

"Where did you obtain it?" rapped Mr. Grimes. "It you can help us lay hands on the thief——"

"That gink Bunter!" yelled Fisher T. Fish. "That dog-goned, pie-faced clam has done me out of two-pound-ten!"

"Bunter! Another Greyfriars boy?"

"Yep! I guess I'll have that two-ten back if I have to scrape it off him with a small comb!" gasped Fisher T. Fish. "Yep! Some! Just a few!"

Mr. Grimes looked at him very hard.

"Very well," he said. "Provisionally, I take your word, Master Fish! You will accompany me to the school, where I can see Master Bunter and question him. I have a taxi outside! Come!"

Fisher T. Fish, his golden dreams shattered, groaned aloud as he sat in the taxicab with Inspector Grimes, whirling away to Greyfriars School.

———

THE SEVENTEENTH CHAPTER.
The Arm of the Law!

"BUNTER!"

Wingate of the Sixth looked in on the tea-party in Study No. 1 in the Remove. Bunter blinked round.

"It wasn't me, Wingate!" he said, in a hurry, as usual.

"You young ass! You're wanted in the Head's study."

"Oh lor'!"

Bunter rolled out after the prefect. Wingate led him to Dr. Locke's study and pushed him in.

"Here is Bunter, sir!"

Bunter blinked round the study in astonishment. He had expected to see the Head, but he had not expected to see Inspector Grimes, of Courtfield, or Fisher T. Fish. Both, however, were there, and Fishy, to his further surprise, gave him a look as if he could have bitten him.

"Bunter," said the Head, fixing his eyes on the amazed and alarmed Owl, "Fish states that you sold him a—er—a diamond tiepin——"

"Oh! Yes, sir!" said Bunter, relieved. "That's right, sir. You see, sir, you told me not to wear it, and being a dutiful and obedient chap, sir, I——"

"You do not deny possession of the pin?" asked Inspector Grimes.

Bunter blinked at him.

"Eh? No. Why should I?" he asked. "Everybody knows I had it."

The inspector smiled faintly.

"I have no doubt, sir, that this foolish boy, Bunter, is innocent in the matter, as I have said," he remarked. "He has been imposed upon in some extraordinary way. Master Bunter, where did you obtain the tiepin?"

Bunter paused a moment. He checked, in time, the desire to state that it was an heirloom in the Bunter family, or, alternatively, as the lawyers say, a Christmas present from his Uncle William. Even Bunter realised that it was not a paying proposition to tell fibs to a police officer!

"I bought it from a man in a railway train, in the hols," he answered. "He said it was paste, and sold it to me for a bob."

"A man with a sandy complexion and narrow eyes?" asked Mr. Grimes.

"Eh? Yes. H-how do you know?" stuttered Bunter.

This seemed like magic to the Owl of the Remove.

"That is the description, my boy, of the man who was arrested on suspicion of robbing Mr. Isaacs, and discharged

(Continued on page 23.)

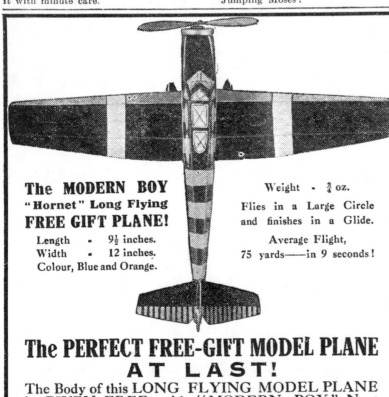

WHEN the GREAT APES CAME!
By STUART MARTIN.

HOW THE STORY STARTED.

GERRY LAMBERT and BILLY MURCHIE, two young airmen, are brought down in the African jungle by an army of apes —led by Big Ling, a giant ape-man—reared to crush civilisation by a renegade called Stein. Gerry escapes, but Billy is forced to lead an expedition to England which spreads devastation in all directions. After raiding the Tower of London and stripping the armoury of every available weapon, Big Ling and his "troops" make for the New Forest, where they ambush hundreds of British soldiers. Billy, who, in company with Gerry and Commander Walsh, of the R.A.F., is hard on the trail of the enemy. is hurrying off to warn reinforcements of Big Ling's next move. when he is captured. "We'll hand him over to the beasts as a sacrifice!" says Big Ling.

(Now read on.)

Bedlam Let Loose!

A SHOUT came from the door of the abode announcing that all was ready.

Ling rapped out an order for his captive to be watched and his companions to be taken prisoners, and then stamped out into the open.

Raising his voice he sent his howl through the forest, and the beasts replied once more, hurrying towards him as he marched on.

Gaining the road, he entered one of the lorries which had been captured, and studied the chart again, before looking up and giving a direction to the ape-man who had crushed his bulk into the driving-seat.

The cavalcade moved slowly at first, then gradually gathered speed. The gorillas followed in a long string behind the vehicles, loping like wolves, with tireless ape-men bringing up the rear.

Once on the main road at the edge of the forest the motor-lorries increased speed, leaving the army behind. The village of Ringwood was reached, and the vehicles stopped. Ling roared an order and the looting began.

Shops were wrecked, doors torn from their hinges, cottages were smashed at the hands of that mad mob of monsters. The inhabitants fled at their approach, but those who stayed, or could not escape quickly enough, were killed and thrown aside like broken dolls.

The main army arrived while the looting was going on, and completed the savagery. Motorists who attempted to pass through the village were hurled, with their cars, into the woods. It was Bedlam let loose!

So it was along the route—every village being sacked and left a ruin. Then followed a long run with minor incidents, until Salisbury was reached.

Ling raised himself in his lorry and scanned his army, several thousand strong, all dusty with the seventeen miles journey from Ringwood. To these creatures seventeen miles was no great distance, and their journey had been uninterrupted owing to the fact that the soldiers of Salisbury Plain had been drafted towards Southampton and the Great West Road, thus leaving the field clear for Ling.

"Forward!" he yelled. "Men of the forest, follow me!"

Down the hill that rises from the town the army plunged. Into the town they swept. It was a day when the markets were thronged with farmers and countrymen. A sheep fair was in progress. Pandemonium seized the people, and they fled before the gorillas.

Ling's club rose and fell, and his ape-men needed no encouraging. They cleared street after street, leaving a trail of dead and dying behind them.

Traffic jammed at corners, motor-cars were left stranded by their owners, the population trampled on each other in the wild scramble to escape. And after them went the gorillas with tooth and claw.

The cathedral was sought as a refuge by many; but Ling headed his forces towards it, bowed his shoulders, and charged into the sacred building.

But Big Ling's raid was not merely for the purpose of killing. Stein had taught him well how to gain means to carry on the campaign. The banks were looted, stores were gutted. Fire broke out, and was spreading without hindrance.

As Big Ling stood there in the cathedral, amid the wreckage he had wrought, the bells of the tower struck an hour. Ling stayed his hand, listening intently. He counted the strokes of the massive clock solemnly, and his face assumed a grave look.

Then he strode to the entrance of the cathedral, shouting to his followers to come out with him.

Turning to one of his lieutenants he issued an order:

"Collect the ruler of this city and his counsellors. Bring them here and put them into this large house. Thrust others with them—those you can drive in from the streets."

The ape-man nodded, but looked round bewilderedly at the houses on every side.

"King," he said obediently, "your word is law. But where shall I find the ruler of the town?"

Ling swung round and pointed to a trembling policeman, who was endeavouring to escape from the clutches of a gorilla.

"That is one of their order-makers. He will tell. Bring him to me!"

The ape-man leaped forward and threw the gorilla off the constable. who was fighting feebly with baton in hand. Dragging him forward, he presented the dishevelled figure to Ling.

At first the policeman did not understand what was wanted of him, but when he grasped the situation he pointed to a building.

"If it is the mayor you want, he is there——"

"Is that where he lives? Is that his hut?"

"It is the town hall!" gasped the policeman.

Turning to his ape-man, Big Ling made a sign and strode off. Across the square he went, throwing aside anything that opposed him. Lifting one car after another he piled them on the pavement. A cart laden with farm produce barred his way. He broke the cart shafts across his knee, and hurled the horse bodily among his gorillas, who dived for the prey. Then into the town hall he strode, bending low to enter, his ape-man follower at his heels.

A group of men fled at his approach, but Ling merely raised his finger and his ape-man hurled himself at the men, thrusting them into a wide room.

Ling listened for a moment to the orders his lieutenant gave, nodding with satisfaction. Then he strode into another room, tearing away part of the lintel to get through. Some clerks cowered behind a counter, but Big Ling heeded them not. His attention was drawn to a telephone on a desk. He lifted the receiver and placed it to his ear.

He was not used to telephoning, so he beckoned to a clerk, making no movement to hurt the man.

"There is a town called Marlborough," he said. "Show me how to speak into this magic."

"Marlborough, sir?" quavered the clerk. "It has been cut up. We were notified——"

"Help me to speak this magic!"

Ling's face glowered fiercely at the clerk, who lifted the receiver.

"Trunks," he quavered. "Marlborough—Marlborough, please——"

The man looked up fearfully, for Ling was watching his every movement.

"They say that they have been trying to get through from Marlborough. Here—here you are!"

Big Ling thrust the man aside hurriedly, lifted the receiver, and bellowed through the mouthpiece.

"Master! Master!"

Faintly over the line came Stein's voice.

"Is that you, Big Ling? You are up to time. What news?"

"I have conquered the city."

"And this town is in my hands," Stein assured him. "It is laid waste, and I am alone in the telephone exchange. This place, too, will be laid waste when I have spoken to you. Remember to do the same your end."

"I will remember, Master."

"Ling, break down every telegraph-wire, and then wreck the post office—I have told you all these things already. Obey, and you will be king indeed! Listen to me. Is the enemy in sight?"

"I have conquered, Master, as I told you."

"I do not mean the city you are in now. If one telephone fails, these people raise another. They have sent war planes to fight you. Planes are concentrating——"

The voice faded and was silent.

Ling shook the instrument, but there was no more conversation. Something had happened to the "magic," and it spoke no more.

It was the first time Ling had ever used the telephone, but he had been taught well by Stein in this and other things.

He flung the receiver down and seized another of the clerks by the collar.

"Take me to your office—post office—show me the hut."

Having no other alternative, the man obeyed.

The post office was reached, and into it Ling crushed his way, sending the staff scattering in all directions. He went through the building, floor after floor, wrecking, smashing, upturning.

He had completed his work when he heard a sound that made him stand erect. The droning of planes overhead made him gnash his teeth.

He tore a window-frame from its socket, threw it into the street, and then thrust his head and shoulders outward. He saw a squadron of planes flying in battle formation.

Squeezing himself through the window, Ling dropped to the ground. Then his hands went up to his mouth, and his cry broke out like a siren. Twice he issued that cry, then loped towards the cathedral, clearing debris and ruins in great jumps.

His orders had been carried out. The cathedral was packed with people, and

ape-men were still thrusting others inside the doors.

The gorillas came from every part in answer to his call. They and the ape-men pressed forward until the street was a mass of hairy, brawny beasts.

Ling towered above them majestically. "The ruler of the city!" he roared. "Bring him to me!"

He kept glancing upward, while a search was made inside the cathedral, and men shouted for the mayor.

More battle-planes had now appeared. They were over the city, and were circling, still keeping in formation.

The mayor was brought out at last, and he faced Ling.

The latter pointed upward to the planes.

"These are your fighting planes. Can you communicate with them?"

"There is a telephone to the air station——"

"I have destroyed your telephones."

A police-inspector who stood on the steps beside the door stepped forward.

"There is only one way," he said to the mayor. "We can semaphore them."

He turned towards Ling, whose eyes were upon him.

"I take it you mean to use us as hostages," he said coldly, but showing a calm that only a brave man could show. "Do you wish us to tell the air fleet not

---

STEP IN
and
WIN A WALLET

like: James Hill, of 15/77, Nelson Street, Parade, Birmingham, who sent in the following GREY-FRIARS LIMERICK:

Said Bunter: "They're beastly suspicious.
If you enter their studies they're vicious.
But Smithy's mince pies
Tempted my hungry eyes,
And Bob Cherry's tarts were delicious!"

You supply the limerick and I'll supply the wallet!

---

to drop bombs? If so, what are your terms?"

Big Ling thought for a moment before answering.

"Tell these aeroplanes," he said distinctly, "that if one bomb is dropped the town hall and all those inside it will be burned to cinders!"

He indicated the smouldering houses across the street with a wave of his hand. An ape-man was thrusting his way towards the cathedral holding high a length of blazing timber torn from a roof. Then Ling seized the inspector, flung him over his shoulder, and began to climb the walls of the cathedral with his burden.

Big Ling's Terms!

AN exclamation of horror burst from the people who saw the monster ape-man going up the face of the cathedral with lizard-like movements. A foot on a ledge here, a hand grasping a buttress there, and up the facade of Salisbury's marvellous cathedral Big Ling heaved himself. The police inspector he had lifted hung across his shoulders like a sack, his arms clutching at the garments

and the metal shirt-of-mail worn by Ling.

Right up to the tower above the entrance Big Ling swung, and there, beside the lightning-conductor, he set his victim on his feet. They had reached this dizzy height within a few minutes of leaving the ground.

The inspector steadied himself against the stonework, while Ling eyed the planes.

"Signal!" he commanded harshly.

The planes had dropped close enough for a view of the scene below, and now one of them circled lower still, almost on a level with the two figures.

The eager faces of the pilot and the gunner were plainly observed. The machine was one of Britain's newest aircraft, a flying wonder, and carried a gun capable of sending shells that could blow the entire town to bits in a few minutes.

The police inspector raised his arms and began to wave, signalling like a constable on point duty.

Ling watched him.

"I cannot make them understand," said the inspector, ceasing to wave after a while.

Ling's eyes gleamed as the plane approached. He saw the gunner sight his gun, and then a rattle of bullets burst out and peppered the spire.

The plane flew past, and then turned.

Ling unslung his club, which he had fastened by a thong to his harness. He stood up boldly, presenting a fine target to the gunner. As the plane came rushing to the attack again Ling's club left his hand like a boomerang.

Through the air it whistled, straight as any bullet. It crashed against the propeller of the machine, smashing the blades to fragments. The gunner let loose a stream of bullets, but the plane was out of control. Down it fell like a stone, past the spire on which Ling stood, to crash through the cathedral roof and lay, half-buried, in the ruin.

Ling watched it for a moment, then turned to the inspector.

"You lied!" he said. "You told them to shoot me, you told them that I was Big Ling!"

He gripped the inspector by the waist and hurled him through the air to fall amid the wreckage in the street below.

Swinging down from the spire, Big Ling sat astride the roof. Four airmen were in the fuselage of the plane, two of them dead, one injured severely, one almost unscathed. The latter was the pilot.

Groping in the wreckage, Big Ling found a bomb. Swinging it round his head, he hurled it with all his force. There was a blinding flash and a loud report as the missile found a billet on the roof of the railway station just as a train was puffing out.

Clutching another bomb, Big Ling climbed back to his spire and stood watching the other planes that circled above. He held the bomb at arm's length, threatening to drop it on the people below unless the planes moved off.

The pilots understood that grim threat. If they attacked Big Ling the cathedral and all it contained would be blown to smithereens.

In the street below, the crowds were watching the planes, anxiously wondering if the pilots would take heed of the giant ape-man's warning.

They did, apparently, for they rose higher until they were almost lost to view.

Lowering himself to the roof once more, Big Ling bent over the pilot, who was sitting up in a dazed way.

Printed and published every Saturday by the Proprietors, The Amalgamated Press, Ltd., The Fleetway House, Farringdon Street, London, E.C.4. Advertisement offices: The Fleetway House, Farringdon Street, London, E.C.4. Registered for transmission by Canadian Magazine Post. Subscription rates: Inland and Abroad, 11s. per annum; 5s. 6d. for six months. Sole Agents for Australia and New Zealand: Messrs. Gordon & Gotch, Ltd., and for South Africa: Central News Agency, Ltd.—Saturday, January 20th 1934.

"If you wish to live, if you wish to save those who otherwise will die, you will signal your planes to keep away," he said grimly. "There is an instrument in the wrecked plane by which you can speak."

He hauled the pilot across the tiles, dropped him gently enough into the cockpit of the wrecked plane, and repeated his terms.

The pilot fingered the knobs.

"I am in touch with them," he replied finally. "What am I to say?"

"Tell them to keep away," ordered Big Ling. "That is all."

The pilot's hands twirled the knobs again. A voice began to talk, but it was cut short.

"Hallo, hallo!" called the pilot. "I am captured by Big Ling. Plane wrecked on roof of Salisbury Cathedral.

Big Ling's terms are that you keep away——"

The ape-man bent his head and motioned the pilot to cease.

"Hallo!" bawled Ling into the instrument. "I am King Ling. Am I speaking to the king of Britain?"

"You are speaking to Croydon," came the voice. "Do not roar or you will deafen me. If you are Ling, what do you want?"

"I am King Ling. Call off your planes for twelve hours, or my army will grind the city to dust. Tell your king I have spoken."

For some time there was silence, and Ling waited. Then at last a voice came through, but not the same voice that had spoken previously.

"Hallo. Are you really Big Ling?"

"I am King Ling! The world will be mine!"

"Are you really Big Ling?"

"I am King Ling!"

Another silence; then the voice spoke again, and this time the message was curt and sharp.

"Very well, we will call off the planes for twelve hours."

"If you do not keep your word——"

"Our word will be kept. We are notifying the planes. We rely on you to keep your word and do no more damage."

Ling listened eagerly until the voice spoke again.

"Battle planes in Salisbury district. Hallo! Hallo! General call for all planes to leave Salisbury district. Orders to follow. Reply, please."

Faintly came other voices repeating the order, voices mingling with each other.

(*Continued on next page.*)

COME INTO THE OFFICE, BOYS!

Always glad to hear from you, chums, so drop me a line to the following address; The Editor, The "Magnet" Library, The Amalgamated Press, Ltd., The Fleetway House, Farringdon Street, London, E.C.4. A stamped, addressed envelope will ensure a reply.

YOUR Editor calling all "Magnetites"! By now you will have received the tenth and final sheet of free coloured pictures. Hope you are pleased with them.

Now get ready to cheer! You've only got one more week to wait—and then you'll receive the first of the next series of magnificent FREE GIFTS I have arranged for you. You know what they are, of course:

FOUR BARS OF WALTERS' DELICIOUS TOFFEE!

Something worth having, eh? And this next batch of splendid free gifts *starts next week.* Don't forget the date, chums, and don't forget to arrange with your newsagent to reserve you a copy of the MAGNET—particularly for the next four weeks, as there is going to be a record rush for the Old Paper!

The first bar of delicious toffee—Walters' "Palm Creemy"—will be given free with next Saturday's issue of the MAGNET. Then for the three weeks following there will be presented in this order: a bar of Walters' chocolate nougat, a bar of Walters' strawberry-flavoured toffee, and a bar of Walters' toffee (banana flavour). Now that I've done my part, I want you to pass on the good news to your pals. They'll thank you for the tip, and they'll thank you even more when they buy a copy of the MAGNET and sample Walters' "Palm Creemy" toffee! This is the opportunity to do two people a good turn at the same time—your chum and your Editor.

And now, turning to my post-bag, I really think I owe some of my readers an apology. Owing to the fact that my space has been rather limited of late, I have not been able to answer as many queries as I should have liked.

A large number of readers' queries have been answered by post, but in cases where my readers did not give their full addresses and names, I have been compelled to hold over their answers. However, I am going to do my best to deal with as many as I can this week.

I would like to point out, however, that it is not possible to answer queries in this chat for several weeks after I receive them. The reason, as most of my older readers will know, is that the MAGNET goes to press some weeks before you get it from your newsagent. As you can imagine, it takes a considerable time for your favourite paper to be written, illustrated, edited, printed, and distributed.

Now for the first query. A reader from Stoke-on-Trent, who signs himself "V. C. G.," asks me a question concerning

THE SINKING OF THE LUSITANIA.

This huge liner was torpedoed by a German submarine on May 7th, 1915, and, of nearly two thousand people aboard, no fewer than 1,195 lost their lives. The Germans were so pleased with this success that they struck a special medal to commemorate it. My Stoke reader possesses one of these medals, and he writes to ask if there is much value attached to it.

The actual value of the medal is not great, as it was an unofficial medal, and could be purchased by anyone in Germany at the time. A collector of War curios might be prepared to purchase it, but only for a few shillings at the most. The inscription on one side of the medal merely records the fact that the "Great steamer Lusitania was sunk by a good German boat," while the other side has the words "Geshaft Uber Alles," which means "Business above everything."

Now for a few

RAPID-FIRE REPLIES.

How Long has The MAGNET been Published? (Harry McRandall, of Montreal, Canada): Quite a considerable time—over 26 years, in fact! And it is still going strong!

The Earliest Greyfriars Stories (George Greaves, of Sheffield): Sorry, I cannot find space to publish the entire list of MAGNET stories up to date! There have been so many that it would take up my entire chat for some weeks to make a list of them all. Many of the earliest stories have appeared again in "The Schoolboys' Own Library," in response to requests from readers who wanted them republished.

Popular Fallacies (D. Page, of London, S.W.2): Sorry I have been unable to get a copy of the book you mention, but will certainly look it up, if I can. Many thanks for your letter.

Not a Motoring "Fan" (J. K., of Hammersmith): There has been no demand from my readers for such a series of articles, so, of course, I shall not be publishing them. But I am always pleased to receive suggestions—and criticism—from my readers. This reply is also for "W. G.," of West Dulwich.

HERE'S something that might be new to you. Harry Lees, of Gloucester, asks me if it is true that people in India who can't read, pay to have stories told to them? Yes, it is perfectly true—but you don't get very much for your money out there.

INDIAN STORY-TELLERS

take the place of your MAGNET to the Indian boys who aren't able to read. They sit in a circle on the ground, and the people who form the circle pay a penny each to listen. It doesn't take them long to finish a story—about five minutes. Then the circle either breaks up, or else everyone pays another penny and listens to another story. At that rate, any Indian story-teller who read out a whole issue of your favourite paper would make quite a good sum!

I don't think you fellows would care much for the native Indian yarns, though. They generally deal with animals who can speak, and, in fact, bear a remarkable resemblance to our old friend Æsop and his fables. Believe me, the MAGNET is a jolly sight better twopennyworth — especially when you get a bar of toffee with it!

And don't forget, the toffee is not the only good thing

IN STORE FOR YOU NEXT WEEK.

Not by a long chalk! Take Frank Richards' long complete school yarn, for instance. It is entitled:

"KIDNAPPED FROM THE AIR!"

and it's as full of good things as Walters' toffee is of sweetness—and that's saying something. You're in for a feast of fiction as well as a feast of toffee next week. In addition to the long complete Greyfriars yarn, there will also be a ripping, full-of-thrills instalment of our record-breaking serial: "When the Great Apes Came," and, of course, a side-splitting "Greyfriars Herald" supplement. Nor must I forget "Linesman's" first-rate Soccer article, and my usual "Come Into the Office" chat.

Cheerio until next week, chums! I know you'll be looking forward to that bumper Free Gift issue.

YOUR EDITOR

Ling lifted his head and looked up. The planes were now high in the heavens. It was their pilots who were speaking, and as they spoke the machines flew away in formation and were soon vanishing from sight.

The pilot who sat beside Ling moved his hand and jerked a wire loose, while Big Ling's eyes were glued on the disappearing planes.

"Twelve hours!" he muttered. "Twelve hours!"

Turning round, Big Ling lifted the pilot from the cockpit, hoisted him on to his shoulders, and bore him down to the street, where he set him at liberty. Then he gave an order to the ape-men who stood waiting.

"Food! Give the beasts food! Keep them from killing—for twelve hours! Set these people free. King Ling gives life to his subjects."

He paused and gazed at the mayor and the authorities who hung on his words.

"I will hold you to see that none leaves the town while I am here."

Having spoken thus, he sent groups of apes to tear up the railway lines at various points, and also to block the roads by means of fallen trees. Then he posted sentries on the hills in the vicinity.

It was long past midday when he had completed his designs, and thus isolated the town.

When he returned from his inspection, his gorillas were camped in the streets devouring the food they had foraged. The market-place was indeed a shambles.

Frightened faces peered from behind curtained windows as Big Ling walked through the ranks of his apes, bearing his club which he had retrieved.

He sat down at last on the steps of the cathedral, and began to feed with his army, his eyes watching the sun dropping slowly towards the western horizon.

(There will be another ripping, full-of-thrills instalment of this powerful adventure story in next week's Free Gift Number of the MAGNET *!)*

The PROFITEER of the REMOVE!

(*Continued from page 24.*)

for lack of evidence, as the stolen pin was not found on him," said the Courtfield inspector, with a faint smile.

"Oh lor'!"

"Evidently this foolish boy was made use of by the thief, sir!" said Mr. Grimes. "He acted in good faith, and was guilty of nothing but folly."

"Oh, really, sir——"

"If you have any idea where that man is now to be found——" added the inspector.

"I don't know where he is now," said Bunter. "But I know where he will be after tea."

"Wha-a-t?" ejaculated the inspector.

"He's offered me five pounds for the pin back, and I said I'd try to get it back from Fishy," explained Bunter. "He's going to wait to see me outside the gates after tea. In—in the circumstances, I—I'd rather not see him again."

"You certainly will not do so, Bunter!" said the Head.

"Yes, sir—I mean no, sir!"

"I have finished here, sir," said Mr. Grimes, with a cheery smile. "And if Mr. Sniggerson waits near the school gates for Master Bunter, somebody will keep the appointment—though certainly not Master Bunter!"

And Inspector Grimes, in a very cheery mood, took his leave. He was very keen to keep that appointment for Bunter with the sandy man!

"You have acted very foolishly, Bunter," said Dr. Locke, when the inspector was gone. "You should be more careful with your dealings with strangers."

"Oh, yes, sir; certainly!" said Bunter. "Ca-a-can I go now, sir? I'm afraid those fellows will have finished the cake——"

"What?"

"I—I mean, I—I've got some lines to do, sir."

"You may go, Bunter."

"Oh! Thank you, sir!" gasped Bunter.

"Hold on!" gasped Fisher T. Fish. "I say, sir, my two-pounds-ten! I say, I guess that fat clam—I—I mean Bunter, sir—I guess he's got to shell out. I mean——"

"In the circumstances, Bunter, you must return Fish the sum he paid you for the tiepin, as it turns out that it was not your property."

"Oh! Certainly, sir!" said Bunter, cheerfully. "I haven't the money at the moment, sir, but I'm expecting a postal order——"

"Very well, you may go!" said the Head.

And Bunter went—and after him went Fisher T. Fish. A bony hand clutched at a fat shoulder in the passage, and Bunter dodged and fled. There was a patter of feet on the Remove staircase. The tea-party were finishing the cake when Billy Bunter rushed into Study No. 1.

"I say, you fellows——" gasped Bunter.

"Hallo, hallo, hallo!"

"Keep that beast, Fishy, off!" gasped Bunter. "He makes out that I owe him two-pound-ten, because it turns out that that diamond pin was pinched——"

"Oh, my hat!"

"Great pip!"

"Old Grimes says it belongs to a man named Isaacs——"

"Oh, my hat!" roared Harry Wharton. "Mr. Isaacs' diamond pin! Then how the thump——"

There was a rush of pursuing feet in the Remove passage. Fisher T. Fish's wildly excited face glared in.

"Is that fat gink here? Bunter——"

Billy Bunter dodged behind the Bounder.

"Keep him off, Smithy!" he gasped.

"Ha, ha, ha!"

"You got to cough up two-pound-ten!" shrieked Fisher T. Fish.

"Your money's safe," said Bunter, behind the grinning Bounder. "I told you I was expecting a postal order——"

"Ha, ha, ha!"

"Lemme gerrat him!" gasped Fisher T. Fish.

But the excited Fishy was not allowed to get at Bunter. He rushed into the study, but a crowd of laughing juniors hurled him out again. The opinion of the Removites was that the profiteer of the Remove had got just about what he deserved. They hurled him forth, and a gasping Fishy limped away dismally, his only consolation being the possibility that Billy Bunter's celebrated postal order might arrive some day! To judge by his looks, Fishy did not derive much consolation from that possibility.

.   .   .   .   .   .

A sandy man who waited for Bunter as the shades of evening fell, by the gates of Greyfriars, never saw Bunter. He saw a portly gentleman, who did not part company with him again. And probably Mr. Sniggerson, as he sat beside Inspector Grimes in the taxi, reflected, too late, that honesty, after all, was the best policy.

Billy Bunter, on the whole, was fairly well satisfied with the outcome of the affair. He had, at least, bagged one tremendous feast. Fisher T. Fish was far from satisfied. Fortunately, Fisher T. Fish did not matter!

THE END.

(Billy Bunter and the chums of Greyfriars meet with further exciting school adventures in: "KIDNAPPED FROM THE AIR!" next week's grand yarn by Frank Richards. Gee, boys, you'll enjoy it ever so much, same as you will the bar of WALTERS' "CREEMY" TOFFEE which will be given FREE with every copy of next Saturday's MAGNET *!)*

"WHO WALLOPED WINGATE?" This week's sensational story of Harry Wharton & Co. of Greyfriars.

The MAGNET 2ᴰ

No. 1,359. Vol. XLV.   EVERY SATURDAY.   Week Ending March 3rd, 1934.

Who Walloped Wingate?

A Wonderful Long Complete School Story of HARRY WHARTON & CO., the Famous Chums of Greyfriars.

BY FRANK RICHARDS.

THE FIRST CHAPTER.

Black Ingratitude !

"MY treat !" said Billy Bunter.

Five fellows smiled all at once.

It was after class at Greyfriars School, and Harry Wharton & Co. had walked down to the tuckshop.

It happened—as it had happened before—that money was tight. Each member of the Famous Five, as it unluckily happened, was in the doleful, dismal state known as "stony." Each fellow, however, while only too painfully aware of his own stony state, was unaware of the stony state of his comrades. It was not till they arrived at the school shop and compared notes that the discovery was made. It was, as Bob Cherry mournfully remarked, a case of "I am stony, thou art stony, he is stony !"

Whereupon the Famous Five of the Remove left the tuckshop again without having sampled Mrs. Mimble's good things. Billy Bunter met them as they came out, blinked at them through his big spectacles, and stopped them with a wave of a fat hand.

Had any other Remove man stopped them and announced that it was "his treat," the chums of the Remove would have been interested. But such an announcement from Billy Bunter only made them smile. They knew Billy Bunter's treats of old ! It was not much use accepting a treat from Billy Bunter unless a fellow had money in his pocket to foot the bill. And the Famous Five had none !'

THE MAGNET LIBRARY.—No. 1,359.

"I mean it !" said Bunter impressively. "I say, you fellows, it's my treat—really !"

"Can't afford it !" said Johnny Bull, with a shake of the head.

"Oh, really, Bull——"

"Nothing doing !" said Frank Nugent. "You'll have to treat somebody else, Bunter ; we're all stony !"

"The stonifulness is terrific !" said Hurree Jamset Ram Singh.

That information, as a rule, would have caused Billy Bunter to roll away in search of fellows who were not stony. Now he did not roll away. He remained where he was, blinking indignantly at the chums of the Remove.

"I say, you fellows, I've said that I mean it ! It's my treat, I tell you ! You come along with me !"

"If you mean it——" said Harry Wharton, very doubtfully.

"I do, old chap ! Come on ! Fellows make out that I never stand a fellow anything !" said Bunter, more in sorrow than in anger. "They make out that I sponge on fellows, you know, and never stand my whack ! Well, I'll show you ! You come along with me, old beans !"

"Well, my hat !" ejaculated Bob Cherry.

Bunter seemed to be in earnest. The Famous Five exchanged glances. They were not very keen on a "treat" from Bunter, even if he was in earnest for once. Still, it would have been ungracious to decline.

"Let's !" said Harry.

And the stony quintet followed Billy Bunter. As he marched away from the tuckshop they expected him to head for the House. But he rolled in the direction of the Cloisters, and they followed

him in that direction. The treat, apparently, was to be handed out in that secluded spot. Why, was, so far, a mystery.

"Don't look round, you fellows !" murmured Bunter. "Wingate's got his eye on us, I believe."

"Eh ?"

Harry Wharton glanced round. Wingate of the Sixth, the captain of Greyfriars, was in the quad, talking to Hilton of the Fifth. He did not seem to be paying any attention to the party of juniors, and Wharton could not see that it mattered if he did. There was no law, written or unwritten, against a feed in the Cloisters.

"Don't get his eye on us, you ass !" whispered Bunter.

"Why not ?"

"Oh, really, Wharton——"

Bunter rolled on, and the juniors followed him under the old stone arches of the ancient Cloisters. Whether Wingate of the Sixth had his eye on them or not, they were out of his sight now.

"Here we are !" said Bunter, halting, and blinking through his big spectacles as if to make sure that the coast was clear.

"Yes, here we are !" agreed Bob. "But where's the feed ?"

"I didn't say it was a feed."

"Eh ? You said it was a treat !" said Bob, puzzled.

"So it is," said Bunter. "I'll explain if you'll listen for a moment instead of jawing, old chap ! It would have been a feed, and a jolly good one, but for that beast Coker of the Fifth ! He came along just when I was going into his study !"

"Wha-at ?"

"He's had a hamper!" explained Bunter.

The Famous Five gazed at Bunter. They knew all about the wonderful hampers that Coker of the Fifth received from his Aunt Judy, though they were not so interested in those hampers as Bunter was. On the subject of hampers Billy Bunter was a Bolshevik. Bunter's trouble was not whether the hamper belonged to him, but whether he could get at it!

"You fat worm!" growled Johnny Bull. "Mean to say, you've been grub-raiding in Coker's study——"

"Oh, really, Bull, I told you the beast came along just when I was going into his study! You know what Coker's like—he would have fancied at once that I was after his hamper if he'd seen me——"

"And weren't you?" asked Frank.

"Oh, really, Nugent! Look here, as soon as I saw Coker coming, I dodged into the next study for cover—Hilton's study; Hilton and Price. See?"

"Blessed if I see!" said Harry Wharton, staring. "If you'd bagged Coker's tuck, and asked us here to wolf it, we'd scrag you! But if you haven't——"

"Will you let a fellow speak—or won't you let a fellow speak?" demanded the fat Owl of the Remove warmly.

"Oh, get on with it!"

"Well, I had to stick in Hilton's study till the coast was clear. They weren't there, you know, and I squinted round the study——"

"You would!" snorted Johnny Bull.

"And in the table drawer——"

"You looked in the table drawer?" exclaimed Wharton.

"Yes, old chap!"

"You fat scoundrel, what did you do that for?"

"Eh? To see what was in it, of course!" said Bunter, blinking. "There might have been a box of chocs or something."

"Oh, my hat!"

"There wasn't!" said Bunter sadly. "Those Fifth Form rotters don't buy chocs—they buy cigarettes! Now, it's strictly against the rules for any fellow at Greyfriars to smoke or keep smokes in his study, ain't it?"

"Tell us something we don't know!"

"If a master or a prefect spotted those smokes in Hilton's study, they'd be confiscated, and Hilton and Price would get into a fearful row!" went on Bunter. "In the circumstances, I took away the smokes!"

"You've pinched that ass Hilton's fags?" exclaimed Johnny Bull.

"Oh, really, Bull——"

"Serve the silly ass right, if you come to that!" said Bob Cherry. "Have you chucked them away, or what?"

"Oh, don't be a silly ass!" said Bunter peevishly. "Catch me chucking away a half-crown box of cigarettes! That's the treat!"

"What?" gasped the Famous Five.

Billy Bunter groped under his jacket. He produced a cardboard box, adorned with gilt lettering Harry Wharton & Co. stared at it blankly Bunter opened the lid. The box was nearly full of cigarettes. The Famous Five gazed at them.

"They're jolly good!" said Bunter. "Better than the Bounder smokes—much better than Skinner's! Really good smokes, you fellows! We're safe enough here; nobody's likely to barge into the

Cloisters—see? Smokes all round, and as many as you like! Nothing mean about me, I hope! Help yourselves!"

Bunter selected a cigarette and inserted it into his large mouth. Stupefied, the Famous Five gazed at him. Billy Bunter certainly would never have spent his own money on smokes. Money was too valuable to be wasted like that. Still, Bunter rather fancied himself as a merry dog, and he would smoke a cigarette if he could get one for nothing. Now he had got quite a lot for nothing. Generously he was offering to stand treat to the Famous Five! This was Bunter's treat!

"Got a match, Wharton?" he asked.

"A—a—a match!" stuttered the captain of the Remove.

"Yes; give a fellow a light!"

"Couldn't you steal any matches while you were stealing the cigarettes?" hooted Johnny Bull.

"Oh, really, Bull! If that's the way you thank a fellow for standing you a treat—an expensive treat——"

"You fat rotter!" roared Johnny. "Do you think we want to smoke Hilton's filthy cigarettes?"

"They're not filthy—they're jolly good! And I believe they're Price's, not Hilton's! Gimme a match!"

?

There never was a head prefect and "skipper" of a school with fewer enemies than George Wingate. But, despite that popularity, there dwells within the age-old walls of Greyfriars a bitter, implacable enemy who will stop at nothing in his desire for revenge.

?

"Gentlemen, chaps, and sportsmen!" said Bob Cherry. "Bunter has offered us a treat! We decline without thanks! Now I vote that we treat Bunter—as he deserves!"

"Hear, hear!"

"I say, you fellows!" roared Bunter. "Leggo! Grrroooooogh! Gurrggh!" Five pairs of hands grasped Bunter all at once, and the cigarette slipped into his mouth as he roared. It was rather fortunate for Bunter that he had not yet lighted it. "Gurrrgh! Leggo! Urrggh! I'm chook-chook-choking—— Urrrggh!"

Johnny Bull grasped the box of cigarettes from the fat hand. He shoved it down Bunter's back. With one cigarette in his mouth and the rest down the back of his neck, the fat Owl of the Remove roared and wriggled and gurgled.

Bump!

Bunter sat on the hard, unsympathetic flagstones.

"If you want some more of the same, old fat bean," said Bob Cherry, "you've only to offer us another such treat!"

And the Famous Five walked back to the quad, leaving Billy Bunter gurgling wildly and making frantic efforts to extract a box of cigarettes from the back of his neck.

THE SECOND CHAPTER.
The Way of the Transgressor!

"OOOOO-ER!"

That peculiar sound proceeded from Study No. 7 in the Remove passage. Two or three fellows in the passage heard it, and glanced towards the door of Study No. 7.

"Ooooo-er! Woooo-er! Gurrrrg!"

It was tea-time, and Remove fellows were coming up to the studies to tea. Every fellow who passed the door of Study No. 7 heard that strange and horrid sound from within.

On a Channel steamer on a rough day that sound would not have been surprising. It was rather uncommon in the Remove passage at Greyfriars.

"I guess that fat clam Bunter sounds sort of sick!" remarked Fisher T. Fish, and he grinned and passed on his way.

"Grooogh-errr!"

Lord Mauleverer stopped and opened the door and glanced in. Mauly had a kind and sympathetic nature.

"Oh gad!" ejaculated his lordship at the sight of the interior of Study No. 7.

The atmosphere of that study was thick with smoke! On the table was a box of cigarettes. On the floor were several cigarette-stumps. In the armchair was Billy Bunter—leaning back, with a ghastly face.

Generally Bunter's complexion was rather like that of a ripe apple. Now it resembled wax.

His spectacles had slipped down his fat little nose. Over them he blinked dismally at Lord Mauleverer.

"You fat ass!" said Mauleverer. "Have you been smokin'?"

"Ooooo-er!"

"Anythin' a man can do for you?"

"Grooo-er!"

"Poor old bean!" said Mauly, and he ambled on. There was nothing he could do for Bunter! Bunter had to suffer for his sins.

The Owl of the Remove groaned dismally. Herbert Vernon-Smith, the Bounder of Greyfriars, looked in.

"Anybody killing a pig here?" he asked.

Groan!

The Bounder sniffed at the smoke, glanced at the box of cigarettes, and stared at Bunter. Then he burst into a roar.

"Ha, ha, ha!"

"Ooooer!" moaned Bunter. "Beast! Ow! Oooooh!"

"Ha, ha, ha!" yelled the Bounder, and he walked away, leaving Bunter to groan and gurgle and guggle.

Peter Todd and Tom Dutton, who had the pleasure—or otherwise—of sharing that study with Bunter, came in to tea, Peter with a parcel under his arm. They stared at the unhappy Owl.

"What the thump——" exclaimed Toddy.

"Oooo-er!"

"You've been smoking here!" roared Peter.

"Gurrrgh!"

"You fat villain! Where did you get those smokes?" demanded Peter. "You never bought them! You've pinched them!"

"Wurrggh! I—I wish I'd never seen them!" moaned Bunter. "I—I've only smoked six——"

"Oh, my hat! Only six! You blithering fat owl——"

"I—I think I'm dying!" said Bunter feebly. "I say, old fellow, call Quelch, will you, and ask him to send for the doctor! Ooooogh!"

"Yes, you'd better let Quelch know that you've been smoking!" grinned Peter. "You'll get six from Quelch!"

THE MAGNET LIBRARY.—No. 1,359.

"I—I—I'm fearfully ill!"

"You look it!" agreed Peter. "Look here, we've got sosses for tea——"

Bunter shuddered.

That news at any other time would have brought him out of the armchair with a bound. Now it seemed only to make him feel worse. For once in his fat career Bunter did not want to eat! The mere mention of food horrified him. His fat interior was in the state of Vesuvius just before an eruption. He had a feeling as if the inner Bunter had got loose from its moorings and was floating about! Really, it was awful!

"I—I—I say, d-d-d-don't you cook sosses here!" groaned Bunter. "I—I—I couldn't s-s-stand it! Oooo-er!"

"Shall I cook them in the passage?" asked Toddy sarcastically.

"Beast!"

"Get up and grease the frying-pan for me!"

"Urrrrggh!"

"Smoky little beast!" said Tom Dutton. "You're not keeping this muck here!"

Dutton picked up the box of cigarettes and tossed it through the open doorway into the passage. Cigarettes scattered far and wide.

Bunter was too far gone to raise any objection to that drastic method of dealing with his property. From the bottom of his fat heart he wished that he had never snaffled those cigarettes from a Fifth Form study. He never wanted to see a cigarette again as long as he lived—and, indeed, he did not expect to live long! He felt as if he was expiring!

Peter Todd threw open the study window and waved a book about to clear off the smoke. Then he started frying sausages for tea.

Generally the scent of frying sausages would have drawn Bunter like a magnet. He would have snuffed that delightful scent like a warhorse snuffing the battle from afar. Now it drew a horrible groan from him, and he staggered out of the armchair.

"Beast!" he moaned.

And he tottered to the doorway. He tottered into the passage. There he leaned on the wall and moaned.

"Hallo, hallo, hallo!" roared Bob Cherry.

The Famous Five came up the Remove staircase. They had come up to tea with Mauleverer; but they stopped at the sight of the suffering Owl.

"What on earth's the matter, Bunter?" exclaimed Harry Wharton.

"Wurrrrrgggh!"

"Ha, ha, ha!" yelled Johnny Bull. "He's been smoking those fags!"

"The smokefulness seems to have been terrific!"

"Poor old Bunter!" chuckled Frank Nugent.

"Urrrggh!" moaned Bunter. "I say, you fellows, I'm dying! I—I say, go and tut-tut-tut——"

"Which?" asked Bob.

"Tut-tut-ut-telephone for a dick-dock-doctor!" gurgled Bunter.

"Ha, ha, ha!"

A crowd of fellows gathered round Bunter His ghastly fat face might have moved a heart of stone. But there seemed to be a plentiful lack of sympathy among the Removites. The Bounder, standing in the doorway of Study No. 4, roared with laughter. Skinner and Snoop chortled. Every face wore a grin. Wibley of the Remove tapped Bunter on a fat shoulder.

"Brace up!" he said encouragingly. "I'll get you something for it, Bunter."

"Eh? What?" asked Bunter, with a gleam of hope

"A nice bit of fat bacon——"

"Grooooooogh!"

"Ha, ha, ha!"

"What about a chunk of lard?" asked Skinner.

"Wooooo—errr!"

"Or some cod-liver oil?" asked Kipps.

"Gurrrrggh!"

Those cheery suggestions did not seem helpful to Bunter! He leaned on the wall, shuddered, and moaned.

"Will you kik-kik-call a did-did-doctor?" he gurgled. "I say, you fellows, I'm awfully ill—awful. I'm dud-dud-dying! Gurrrgggh! Call Quelch——"

"You'll get over it, old fat man," said Harry Wharton. "Quelch will whop you for smoking! Better keep it dark."

"Beast!" moaned Bunter. "Grrggh!"

"Ha, ha, ha!"

Billy Bunter tottered along to the Remove landing. There he clung to the banisters in a state of collapse. He groaned and moaned. He gurgled, and he goggled! The sounds that came from Bunter were really heartrending. There was a step on the lower stairs, and Wingate of the Sixth came up. He stopped on the lower landing and stared at the ghastly face over the banisters above. Then he came up quite hurriedly.

"Bunter! What's the matter with you?" he exclaimed.

"Gurrggh!"

Wingate cast a glance round at a grinning crowd.

"It isn't a laughing matter, if this kid's ill!" he exclaimed angrily. "What's the matter with him?"

Then the prefect's eye spotted scattered cigarettes in the Remove passage.

"You young ass!" he exclaimed. "Have you been smoking?"

"Yurrrggggh!"

"Vernon-Smith!" rapped Wingate.

"Hallo!" drawled the Bounder.

"Are these cigarettes yours?"

"Not guilty, my lord!" grinned Smithy.

"Are they yours, Skinner?"

"Never seen them before, Wingate!" answered Skinner.

"Where did you get them, Bunter?"

"Grooogh!"

"Answer me!" snorted the captain of Greyfriars. "What have you got to say for yourself, you smoky little sweep?"

"Oooooogh!"

"Ha, ha, ha!"

"Well," said Wingate, "you're not in a state to be whopped now! I'll whop you presently. Come to my study when you feel better."

"Oh crikey! Grooogh! Oh lor'! Wooogh!"

Wingate, frowning, tramped away down the stairs, and the Removites, chuckling, dispersed to the studies to tea. Bunter was left clinging to the banisters, moaning and groaning. Probably for the first time on record Billy Bunter did not want any tea.

———

THE THIRD CHAPTER.

Between Good and Evil!

STEPHEN PRICE, of the Fifth Form, scowled.

Price of the Fifth was lounging in the window-seat in his study. Two other Fifth Form men were there—Hilton, his study-mate, and Blundell, the captain of the Form. Hilton and Blundell were talking football, and both of them seemed to have forgotten the existence of Price. Footballing fellows never took much account

of Price, who played no games, out of doors, at all events. Billiards was Price's game, which he could not play at Greyfriars. He listened to the talk between the other two, with a deepening scowl on his rather thin face.

"Well, look here, I'm jolly glad of this!" Blundell was saying. "Wingate asked me to come along and speak to you, Hilton, and I'm glad I did. You can play a good game if you like, and I'll put you down for the Form match with pleasure. You've got a jolly good chance of a place in the First Eleven if you show up well—which I fancy is a bit better than sneaking out of bounds and playing the giddy ox, what?"

"Oh quite!" said Cedric Hilton, in his soft, drawling tones. "Rely on me for Wednesday, old bean."

"It's a go!" agreed the captain of the Fifth.

"There's something you've forgotten," said Price, breaking into the talk at last.

Blundell glanced round. He gave the black sheep of the Fifth a far from pleasant look.

"What's that?" he snapped.

"Speakin' to Hilton!" answered Price. "You seem to be forgettin', Cedric, that you're booked already for Wednesday afternoon."

Blundell's brow contracted.

"If you're booked for Wednesday afternoon with Price, Hilton, you can wash it out!" he said.

"It's nothin' particular," said Hilton. "That's all right, Blundell. You can rely on me, as I've said."

Blundell nodded, and left the study. Price rose from the window-seat and kicked the door shut after him. Then he turned and faced his friend.

"We'd better have this out, Cedric," he said sourly. "This isn't the first time this term that you've let me down! Wingate's been givin' you pi-jaw all the term, and now Blundell and his crew have taken you up. Last term you never bothered your head about Soccer."

"Last term isn't this term!" said Hilton. "What's the good of going on playing the goat, Pricey? Both of us were heading for the sack, and we've had some narrow shaves. If you'll take my advice, you'll do exactly as I'm doing——"

"I'll watch it!" sneered Price.

"Well, then, let's agree to differ!" drawled Hilton. "No need to row about it, old bean!"

"If you're throwing me over——" snarled Price.

"Not exactly! But if I can get my colours, I rather think I'd prefer that to losing quids on the billiards-table at the Cross Keys!" Hilton laughed. "What's the good of playing the goat, Pricey? It's a mug's game! You fancy yourself at spotting winners—but you nearly always lose! And the Head——"

"Bother the Head!"

"Well, he has had an eye on us! And I really don't want to be turfed out of Greyfriars. I'd rather play Soccer."

"Gettin' funky?" sneered Price.

Hilton shrugged his shoulders.

"If there's a funk in this study, it isn't little me!" he answered.

Price gave him a savage look. The dandy of the Fifth had always been a reckless scapegrace—wanting many qualities, but not wanting courage. Price lacked that very quality, and the fact was well known to both of them.

This was not the first time that the handsome scapegrace of the Fifth had turned over a new leaf. He was easy going and easily influenced—almost as easily influenced by a good fellow as by a bad one.

Now he was under the influence of the games-men, Blundell and his friends had given him a warm welcome—Wingate of the Sixth had gone out of his way to give him encouragement. Price, who had always been his evil genius, saw his own influence fading away to vanishing point.

He did not expect it to last! He knew Hilton's vacillating character too well for that; but it looked like lasting the whole term—which did not suit Price's book at all. A wealthy and reckless friend was very useful to Price, who was poor and had expensive tastes.

"Hold on," he said, as Hilton made a move towards the door. "Where are you goin'?"

"No. I won't!"

"You've done so often enough before."

"I know that! And I was a fool for my pains!" snapped Hilton angrily. "A precious show I should put up on Wednesday if I got ready for the game by smoking cigarettes. I haven't smoked this term, and I'm certainly not going to begin now. Give a fellow a rest."

Price groped in the table drawer, and then bent his head to stare into it. The box of cigarettes was not there.

"Have you had the smokes?" he asked.

"Don't be an ass!"

"You're more than welcome, if you and the other pi-merchants! Do you think you can take me in?"

Hilton faced him, with a gleam in his eyes.

"I've told you that I know nothing about your rotten smokes," he said. "And you're calling me a liar! Well, now, I'll tell you this—I've put up with your filthy smoking in this study all this term, and I'll put up with it no longer. Bring any more smokes into this study, and I'll chuck them out of the room, see?"

"Will you?" said Price, between his teeth.

"Yes, and you after them, if you don't keep a civil tongue in your head!" snapped Hilton.

Billy Bunter groped under his jacket, produced a cardboard box, and opened the lid. "These are good smokes, you fellows," he said. "We're safe enough here—nobody's likely to barge into the Cloisters. See? Smokes all round, and as many as you like. Help yourselves!" "You fat rotter!" roared Bull. "Do you think we want to smoke Hilton's filthy cigarettes?"

"Staggerin' along to the games-study," answered Hilton. "I want to talk to some of the men there."

"About Soccer?" sneered Price.

"Why not?" demanded Hilton impatiently. "I'm playing for the Fifth on Wednesday. If you want to go to the Lantham races, you can easily find a fellow to go with—Loder of the Sixth, or Carne——"

"I don't want Loder or Carne," said Price sourly, "and I don't like bein' thrown over. I want my own pal."

Hilton hesitated, and did not leave the study. He sat on the edge of the table, swinging his elegant legs.

Price went to the table drawer and opened it. The fellow sitting on the table frowned. He knew what Price kept there.

"Look here, Pricey, if you're going to smoke, I'll get out," he said. "You don't want me here to watch you."

"You won't have a fag along with me?" sneered Price.

wanted them! I was only askin' you!" snapped Price. "They're gone!"

"What rot! How could they be gone?"

"Look for yourself."

Hilton slipped from the end of the table and impatiently came round to the end where the drawer was. Price had pulled it out to full length; and among the many articles it contained, nothing was to be seen of a box of cigarettes. Hilton stared into the drawer; and Price, standing back, gave him a bitter look.

"So that's it!" he sneered. "I fancied your pi-jaw was a bit thin! You make out that you've chucked smokin'——"

"You know I have!"

"Where are my smokes, then?" sneered Price. "I left a dozen at least in the box, and they're gone, box and all. For goodness' sake, chuck up trying to pull my leg, Cedric—you can keep all that for Wingate and Blundell,

"You cheeky cad!" yelled Price, his bitter temper breaking out. "You've had my smokes, and you want to make out——"

"I've told you I haven't had them!"

"Liar!"

"That's enough!" Hilton made a stride across to his weedy study-mate, his eyes blazing.

Stephen Price made a backward jump. He was feeling savagely angry enough to have knocked his erstwhile pal headlong across the study; but anger could not supply the place of courage; and the blaze in Cedric Hilton's eyes daunted him. The colour wavered in his face as he jumped away, and backed against the wall.

"Hands off!" he stammered.

Hilton burst into a contemptuous laugh.

"You'd better screw up a little more pluck from somewhere, Pricey, before you start calling a fellow fancy names!"

THE MAGNET LIBRARY.—No. 1,359.

he said, and he turned scornfully away and walked to the door.

Price's eyes followed him, glittering like a snake's. At that moment, the blackest sheep in Greyfriars hated his former friend more than any other fellow in the school. Hilton, taking no further notice of him, laid his hand on the door handle—and at the same moment there came a sharp rap on the door from without, and it opened.

THE FOURTH CHAPTER
Called on the Carpet !

"I SAY, you fellows !"

"Feeling better ?" grinned Bob Cherry.

"Nunno! Worse!" said Bunter.

Bunter looked better, at all events. It was after tea, and Harry Wharton & Co. were going down. Now that the days were drawing out, there was light enough to punt a footer about after tea. Billy Bunter met them on the Remove landing, with a rather worried expression on his fat face. He seemed to have recovered a good deal from the internal convulsions caused by the snaffled smokes; but he was worried. Wingate had told him to come to his study when he felt better. Bunter knew what to expect when he got there. He was not anxious to go.

"I say, you fellows, I'm feeling worse—frightfully worse!" said the fat Owl of the Remove. "If you're going down, will you drop in on Wingate, and tell him so. Tell him I'm suffering fearfully, will you ?"

"What are we to tell Wingate lies for ?" inquired Harry Wharton politely, and his comrades chuckled.

"Oh, really, Wharton——"

"Can't you run along and tell them yourself ?" asked the captain of the Remove. "You're a better hand at it than I am ! You've had more practice."

"Beast! I mean, look here, old chap, Wingate mightn't believe I am worse, if he saw me!" argued Bunter. "He's going to whop me for smoking, and I wasn't smoking, you know! Never touched a cigarette in my life."

"Oh, my hat !"

"But—but, Wingate mightn't believe that!" added Bunter.

"He mightn't!" chuckled Frank Nugent. "As he saw our giddy smokes all over the floor, and you as sick as a boiled owl, he mightn't!"

"Ha, ha, ha!"

"Well, if you tell him I'm fearfully ill, he may let the matter drop!" urged Bunter. "Tell him I'm practically lying at death's door! Tell him I'm lying——"

"No need to tell him that!" interrupted Johnny Bull. "He can guess that you are lying!"

"Ha, ha, ha!"

"You silly ass!" roared Bunter. "I mean——"

"Better go to Wingate and get it over," advised the captain of the Remove. "You're booked for six! What's the good of putting it off ?"

"You see, I don't want to be whopped!" explained Bunter. "It was bad enough to be made ill by Price's filthy cigarettes! Not that I smoked them, you know! I wouldn't! I took them away from his study just to give him a lesson—sort of joke on him, you know! But——"

Kipps of the Remove came up the stairs.

"Bunter here ?" he called out. "Here, Bunter, Wingate wants you! You're to go to his study at once !"

"Oh lor' !" groaned Bunter.

And he went ! He did not want to go; very much indeed he did not want to call on the captain of Greyfriars; but there was no choice in the matter when he received an order from the head-prefect, and he rolled away dismally to the Sixth.

Wingate was in his study talking to Gwynne and Sykes of the Sixth. The door was half-open, and Bunter heard the Greyfriars captain's voice as he rolled up.

"Blundell says that Hilton is playing on Wednesday! I'm jolly glad of it —he's a good man at Soccer when he chooses."

"When !" remarked Sykes dryly.

"Well, he's all right when that shady sweep Price isn't leading him by the nose!" said Wingate. "That fellow would have been turfed out of the school before now, if he hadn't been as deep as a well. He will go too far one of these days, and there will be a crash. I shouldn't like to see Hilton come a mucker along with him."

Billy Bunter, in other circumstances, would probably have lingered at the door to listen, and learn details to be reported up and down the passages later; but he was too worried now even to indulge in his favourite entertainment of eavesdropping. He tapped on the door, and rolled into the study. The three Sixth-Form prefects glanced at him, and Wingate reached out to an ashplant that lay on the table.

"Oh, here you are, you young rascal !" said Wingate. "I told you to come here as soon as you felt better——"

"I—I'm feeling worse, Wingate !" groaned Bunter.

"You soon will be, at any rate !" said Wingate genially, swishing the cane in the air. "Bend over that chair !"

"I—I say, Wingate——"

"Bend over !" rapped the Greyfriars captain.

"Oh lor' !" groaned Bunter. Dismally he bent over the chair. The way of the transgressor is hard ! Bunter had suffered internally for his sins ! Now he was going to suffer externally.

Whack ! Whack ! Whack !

"Yow-ow-ow !" howled the Owl of the Remove.

"You needn't get up yet, Bunter," remarked Wingate. "I want to know where you got those smokes! I'm going to whop you till you tell me."

"Oh crikey !" gasped Bunter. "I—I— I bought them, Wingate !"

"Where ?" rapped Wingate.

"I—I mean, I found them !"

"Exactly ! I want to know where."

"In—in the meadows——" stammered Bunter. "I—I was walking along by the river bank when I suddenly saw that box of cigarettes, and—yarooooh !"

Whack !

"Try again !" suggested Wingate, and Gwynne and Sykes grinned.

"Ow! Wow! I got them in a Fifth-Form study !" howled Bunter. "Wow! Ow! Oh scissors! Wow !"

"You mean to say that a senior gave smokes to a kid like you ?" demanded the Greyfriars captain angrily.

"H—he—he didn't exactly give them to me," groaned Bunter. "I—I happened to be in the study, and I—I happened to squint into the table drawer and—and I happened to see them, and —and I took them away because— because it's against the rules to have smokes in the studies, you know——"

"Whose study ?"

Billy Bunter blinked up at the captain of Greyfriars through his big spectacles. Bunter, with all his faults, was not a sneak, if he could help it. Wingate, as

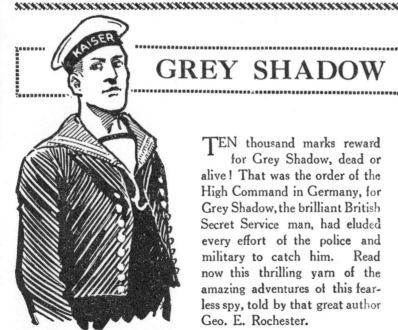

head prefect, was doing his bounden duty in investigating this matter. Bunter, on the other hand, was well aware that it was up to him not to inform against any fellow. But the ash-plant was swishing in the air, and it had an unnerving effect on the fat Owl of the Remove.

"I—I—I say, Wingate, I—I'd rather not tell you!" gasped Bunter, "I shouldn't mind Hilton so much, but that beast Price would take it out of me afterwards. He's got a rotten temper!"

Wingate looked at him long and hard. He laid the ashplant on the table.

"You can cut!" he said curtly.

"Oh! Good!" gasped Bunter. And fairly flew from the study. Gwynne and Sykes exchanged a rather peculiar glance, and Wingate rose to his feet, his face grim.

"I think I'd better go along to Hilton's study!" he remarked, and he picked up the ashplant again, slipped it under his arm, and walked out.

Gwynne gave a whistle.

"Is the old bean going to hand out whoppings in the Fifth?" he murmured.

"Why not?" said Sykes, shrugging his shoulders.

"Well, it isn't done, you know."

"Time it was—in that study!"

Wingate's brow wore a dark frown as he tramped up to the Fifth Form passage. He had done his best to win Cedric Hilton to better ways, and taken a great deal of trouble to that end. He thought that he had succeeded. But if the dandy of the Fifth was pulling his leg, and carrying on the same as usual in secret, Wingate was the fellow to come down with a heavy hand. In theory, Fifth Form seniors could be whopped by a prefect, like any other fellows at Greyfriars School. In practice, it was extremely uncommon for a senior to be whopped, unless specially called up at a Prefects' Meeting. Wingate, on this occasion, was going to make practice square with theory! He was taking his ashplant to the Fifth to be used there!

He rapped sharply on the door of Hilton's study, and opened it, just as the dandy of the Fifth was coming out. Hilton stepped back at the sight of him.

Wingate stepped in.

"Want anything, Wingate?" asked Hilton, in surprise.

"Yes!" said the Greyfriars captain tersely.

He shut the door behind him, put his back to it, and stood with his eyes fixed grimly on the two Fifth Formers.

THE FIFTH CHAPTER.
"Ben Over!"

GEORGE WINGATE slipped a hand into his pocket and drew out a cardboard box. It was a cigarette box, and Price started at the sight of it; Hilton glancing at it in careless surprise. Wingate tossed it on the study table.

"Is that yours, Hilton?" he asked.

"No!"

"Is it yours, Price?"

"No!"

"It belongs to this study!" said Wingate, "I picked it up in the Remove passage this afternoon; it had been taken there by Bunter of the Remove, who smoked some of the cigarettes it contained, and made himself sick."

"Silly little ass!" remarked Hilton.

He glanced at Price, with a grin. The missing box from the table-drawer was accounted for now.

"Bunter has let out that he got it from this study!" said Wingate quietly,

"I've whopped him for smoking! I'm going to whop the fellow who has been smoking here, too! There's not going to be two weights and two measures! I want to know whose cigarettes they were."

Hilton's handsome face darkened, and his eyes glinted. Price breathed hard.

"Very likely the young scoundrel was lyin', Wingate!" he suggested, "so far as I know, there have been no cigarettes in this study."

"We shall see! You've given me your word, Hilton, that you've chucked that dingy foolery!" said Wingate.

"I've kept it!" said Hilton curtly.

RHYMES OF THE REMOVE.
No. 5.

This week our clever Greyfriars Rhymester contributes a snappy poem entitled : GOOD LITTLE BUNTER.

Billy Bunter had a parcel
  As a special birthday treat ;
It was sent from Bunter Castle,
  Bunter's uncle's country seat,
(At any rate, he told us so,
And doubtless Bunter ought to know).

Bunter thought of tarts and sherbet,
  So he chirruped : " This is luck !
In the past my Uncle Herbert
  Always sent me gifts of tuck ! "
(" Never mind the past ! " we cried ;
" That's the present ; what's inside ? ")

Bunter said : " I'll have an orgy ! "
  But he had a shock instead :
'Twas a book : " Good Little Georgie,"
  Bound in leathered, coloured red.
(This sort of volume makes me grin :
It's " red " outside, but never in.)

The hero of this charming story,
  Georgie Green, a model youth,
With a view to fame and glory,
  Always, always told the truth.
(Especially, I have no doubt,
  When he was bowling others out.)

Every page saw Georgie stammer
  To his master, pleadingly,
Full of truth (if not of grammar) :
  " If you please, sir, it was me ! "
The master patted Georgie's head :
" Well done, my boy ! " the old ass said.

Though the book was rather " soppy "
  (As Bunter called it, with a grunt),
Billy thought he'd try to copy
  Georgie's frank confession stunt ;
Then Quelch would pat his head, and
      cough :
" Well done, my boy ! I'll let you off ! !!

Bunter tried it on next morning.
  Quelchy asked him to construe ;
Bunter answered, falsehood scorning :
  " Can't ! I did no prep ! That's true !"
(I thought old Quelchy would go mad ;
And Bunter shortly wished he had.)

Quelchy grabbed his cane up madly ;
  Bunter turned a trifle pale.
" Come out here ! " bawled Quelch, and
      sadly
  Bunter went. Let's draw the veil !
As for Georgie, he was dropped
In the dustbin—where he stopped !

"I hope so! But I've got to get to the bottom of this! If smoking is going on in this study, there's going to be a prefect's whopping in this study, too! Once more, Price, were those cigarettes yours?"

"Certainly not!" answered Price coolly.

"Bunter found them in this study, as I've said."

"Hardly! He was pulling your leg, old man."

"Very well!" said Wingate. "You deny it, and Hilton denies it! The matter will have to go before Dr. Locke then! It's between you two, and the Head will sift it out."

He turned to the door.

"I'm ready to go before the Head, as soon as you like!" said Hilton contemptuously.

"Hold on, Wingate!" muttered Price. His sallow face was pale. Price of the Fifth did not want to go before the Head. Price had too many shady secrets to keep, for that. Investigation once started might unearth other things more serious than smoking in the study! A fellow who continually, and with cynical indifference, broke all the rules of the school had to be careful.

Wingate looked round.

"Hold on?" he repeated. "What for?"

Price gasped a little.

"Look here, suppose a fellow had a box of cigarettes in his study?" he muttered. "No need to make a song and a dance about it. I daresay you could scare up a few in the Sixth, if you looked."

"Possibly!" said Wingate. "If I find any in the Sixth, there will be trouble, same as if I find them in the Fifth! I've got certain duties to do, as a prefect, and I'm going to get them done. Were the cigarettes yours—yes or no?"

"Yes!" muttered Price.

"That's enough then! I've whopped a junior for smoking—if I let a senior off, I should be a rotter! You'll bend over the table, Price."

Stephen Price stood facing him, his hands clenched. Price was a senior, a Fifth Form man, and it was almost unheard of for a senior to be told to bend over like a junior! He knew, too, that had Hilton received that order, he would have resisted with utter disregard of the consequences. The humiliation of it was almost more than Price could bear.

"You can't whop me, Wingate!" he muttered thickly. "You know you can't! A Fifth Form man——"

"Will you bend over the table?"

"You can call a Prefects' Meeting, and have me up!" muttered Price. "I'll stand for that! But——"

"You'll bend over that table, and take six, just as if you were a sneaking smoky little tick in the Second Form!" said Wingate coolly. "And if you don't do it, this instant, I'll take you to the Head, and leave it to him. If you'd rather be sacked, you've got the choice."

Price gave him a long look.

Then, white as a sheet with rage and humiliation, he bent over the table.

Hilton winced. Nothing would have induced him to do as Price was doing, if the penalty had been the sack on the spot !

"Wingate——" he muttered.

"Nothing for you to say!" interrupted the Greyfriars captain, and he swished the ashplant in the air. It came down with a loud whack on Stephen Price's trousers.

A gasp came from Price. Hilton, with a set face, left the study. He could not intervene, and he would not witness his whilom friend's humiliation. As he closed the door, the sound of the whacking ashplant followed him.

Six strokes fell; six of the best. Price remained motionless, bent over the table, his face colourless with fury. He tried his hardest to keep back a sound—it was too bitterly humiliating to yell like a fag under the cane! But hard as he was by nature, he was not tough physically, and he could not bear pain. In spite of himself, he gave a yell at the fourth swipe, and a ringing howl at the fifth.

The door opened, and Coker looked in.

"What's this howling row about?" asked Coker of the Fifth, staring. "Why—what—what——"

"Get out!" snapped Wingate.

"Oh, my only hat!" gasped Horace Coker, and he got out—and went back to his study in a state of dazed amazement, to tell Potter and Greene that Wingate was whopping a Fifth Form man.

Whack! The last swipe fell followed by a howl from Price. Wingate tucked the ashplant under his arm.

"That's a tip!" he said grimly. "I've had my eye on you a long time, Price—and I know whose fault it is that Hilton's played the goat so often. Now he's going straight, you're not going to get him playing the fool again if I can prevent it! You've got off with a whopping this time—next time you'll go before the Head, and you know what that means."

Wingate left the study without waiting for an answer.

Price stood and stared after him.

His face was drained of colour. He was hurt, and he wriggled painfully. But that was not the worst.

He had been "whopped" like a fag—he, a Fifth Form man, a senior! Coker—that ass, Coker—had actually beheld the whopping, and would be talking of it up and down the passages and studies. All Greyfriars would know about it under an hour.

Price clenched his hands with fury.

He had not dared to resist. The penalty for "punching a prefect" was the sack, short and sharp. Neither would it have helped him, for the stalwart captain of Greyfriars could have handled the weedy slacker of the Fifth almost like an infant. He dared not even think of standing up to Wingate in the gym with the gloves on; he could not have hoped to get the better in a scrap, and he hated getting hurt. There was nothing he could do—nothing—but swallow his rage and humiliation, and "mind his step" in the future.

When Hilton came back to the study an hour later it was dark. He turned on the light, and started at the sight of a white face looking at him from the armchair.

"Oh! You, Price!" he ejaculated.

He smiled faintly.

"No good nursing it, old man," he said. "Better chuck it right out of your mind. After all, you asked for it."

"Same as you did last term," muttered Price.

"Oh, let that drop!" said Hilton irritably.

"I'll make him sorry for it," muttered Price, between his teeth. "The rotten bully! He's always been down on me, and he's taken advantage of his position as a prefect!"

"That's rot!" said Hilton. "If those smokes had been mine, he would have told me to bend over, and you know it."

"Would you have done it?"

Hilton shrugged his shoulders.

"No; I'd rather be sacked! But you wouldn't, and you had your choice, Pricey. What's the good of brooding over it?"

"I'll get even with the brute, somehow!"

"Rot!"

"There are ways——"

"You'd better not tell me, then," interrupted Hilton. "And the sooner you forget all about it, the better. That's my advice."

"Keep it, you rotter!"

"Oh, all right! You're not agreeable company just now. I'll trot along and tea with Fitzgerald; he's asked me."

Cedric Hilton left the study again. Price was left alone with his bitter and revengeful reflections—rage and hatred and all uncharitableness running riot in his breast. He hardly knew just then whether he hated Hilton or Wingate more; his feelings towards both were black and bitter.

Gladly he would have revenged himself on both of them, but both seemed safely out of the reach of his vengeance. But it came into his bitter mind that there was one fellow, at least, upon whom his rage could be wreaked—the fat and fatuous Bunter, who had caused all the trouble by snaffling the cigarettes from the study. And having by that time recovered from the effects of the ashplant, Stephen Price left the study, and went to look for Billy Bunter.

THE SIXTH CHAPTER.
Painful for Bunter!

HERBERT VERNON-SMITH, the Bounder of Greyfriars, glanced over the balustrade of the Remove landing, and grinned.

What seemed to Smithy an amusing scene, met his gaze on the staircase below.

A fat figure was bounding up the stairs. After it came a much taller and rather thin and weedy figure.

The first was William George Bunter, the Owl of the Remove. The second was Stephen Price, the blackest sheep in the Fifth Form.

Bunter, as a rule, negotiated a staircase slowly and with care. He had a lot of weight to carry up with him. Now, however, he looked as if he had taken the hare instead of the tortoise as a model. He fairly flew.

His fat face was crimson. His little round eyes almost popped through his big, round spectacles. He puffed and he panted and he blew. But he did the stairs at wonderful speed. Price of the Fifth, grabbing after him as he flew, missed again and again, Bunter somehow miraculously keeping ahead. But it seemed unlikely that he would get so far as the Remove landing ungrabbed. Breath was fast failing Bunter.

Vernon-Smith grinned at the sight of the chase. But he was rather puzzled, too. If it had been Coker of the Fifth barging up to the Remove after a fleeing junior, it would not have been surprising. Horace Coker was born to trouble as the sparks fly upward. But Price of the Fifth was a quiet fellow, as a rule—quiet, sly, sharp as a needle, suspected of all sorts of "rotten" ways, but seldom, or never, losing his temper, in public, at least. It was quite a new thing for Stephen Price to be breaking out like this.

Smithy watched over the balustrade. Price evidently was on the trail of vengeance, and Smithy had little doubt that there was cause for it. Nevertheless, Fifth Form men were not allowed

to throw their weight about in the Remove quarters; and the Bounder was more than ready to chip in. Bunter came across the lower landing like a flash, and leaped up the Remove staircase. After him shot Price, and on the Remove staircase the Fifth Form sportsman grabbed a fat ankle.

Bump!

Bunter came down on the stairs in a heap with a fearful roar.

"Whooooop!"

That was enough for Smithy.

"Back up, you men!" he shouted, to some fellows in the Remove passage. "Fifth Form cads, back up!"

And the Bounder rushed down the stairs. After him ran Bob Cherry, Johnny Bull, Redwing, Ogilvy, Peter Todd, and two or three more of the Remove.

The Bounder was first on the scene. He arrived, fortunately for Bunter.

That fat youth was sprawling on the stairs, gurgling for breath, and Price's hand was rising and falling.

Smack, smack, smack!

"Yarooh! Yooop! Rescue! Help! Fire! I say, you fellows—— Yaroop!" roared Billy Bunter.

"You fat scoundrel!" panted Price. "Take that, and that ——"

"Yarooh!"

"And that——"

"Whooop!"

Then the Bounder jumped in. He grabbed Price by the collar, and rolled him over on the stairs. It was Price's turn to roar, and he did.

"Ow! Leggo!" yelled the Fifth Form man. "You cheeky young rotter—— Yoooh!"

"Back up!" yelled the Bounder.

"Coming!" roared Bob Cherry; and he came.

He did the last three stairs in one jump, landing on Price's sprawling legs. There was a fiendish howl from Price.

"I say, you fellows!" Bunter sat up, gasping. "I say, help! Collar him! Pitching into a chap for nothing, you know! Urrrggh! I say, wallop him!"

"Let go!" shrieked Price, struggling wildly.

But the Remove men did not let go. Price went over on his back on the middle landing, and the grinning Bounder sat on his chest.

"Got him!" remarked Smithy.

"Lemme gerrup!" gasped Price. "I tell you——"

"I say, you fellows——"

"Fifth Form men ain't allowed to barge up here!" said Bob Cherry cheerfully. "Roll him down, you men! First kick to me!"

"Ha, ha, ha!"

"Hold on a minute, you fellows!" Harry Wharton hurried down the Remove staircase. "Let's see what the man was after. If Bunter has been grub-raiding again——"

"I haven't!" yelled Bunter.

"Looks as if he has," remarked Toddy.

"I've told you I haven't!" roared Bunter.

"Yes; that's why it looks as if you have."

"Beast!"

"Give the fellow a chance to speak!" said the captain of the Remove. "What were you after Bunter for, Price?"

"Whatever it was, he's going through it!" declared the Bounder. "We're not taking swank from the Fifth!"

"Hear, hear!"

"Let him speak, all the same," said Harry. "If that fat burglar has got hold of a cake or anything——"

As Bunter leapt up the Remove staircase, Price, the sportsman of the Fifth, grabbed a fat ankle. Bump ! "Whooooop !" roared Bunter, as he came down in a heap. That was enough for Smithy. "Back up, you men !" he shouted, to some fellows in the Remove passage. "Fifth-Form cads ! Back up !" And the Bounder led the rush.

"He's been pilfering in my study !" gasped Price.

"Well, what has he bagged ?" demanded Wharton. "If he's got anything of yours, we'll jolly soon make him hand it over."

"Oh, really, Wharton——"

"Shut up, Bunter !"

"Beast !"

"Give it a name, Pricey !" grinned Bob Cherry. "I fancy I can guess what it is. Have you missed any smokes ?"

"Oh, my hat !" exclaimed Wharton. He remembered the "treat" offered by Billy Bunter that afternoon. "Is that it ?"

"I tell you he's been pilfering——" panted Price.

"What has he pilfered ?" grinned Bob. "Anything you can report to a prefect ?"

"Ha, ha, ha !"

Price did not answer that question. He would have been glad enough to report Bunter for pilfering, and get him a flogging or the "sack." But the loss of a box of cigarettes was not a matter that Price wished to bring to the notice of his headmaster.

"I say, you fellows !" gasped Bunter. "It's all gammon ! I haven't been near Price's study ! I never bagged his smokes ! You fellows can bear witness to that ! I offered you some——"

"Ha, ha, ha !"

"Let me go !" gasped Price. "I'll let the matter drop ! Get off my chest, Vernon-Smith, you young hooligan !"

"It was the smokes, of course," said Peter Todd. "Pricey won't report that to Prout or the Head ! Hardly ! He says he's willing to let the matter drop. Well, one good turn deserves another—let's let Price drop, too !"

"Good egg !"

"Ha, ha, ha !"

A dozen pairs of hands grasped Price of the Fifth, and hooked him up from the landing. Then he was dropped—on the lower stairs !

Bump !

As he picked himself up, panting with fury, the Bounder let out a foot. Price went down the lower stairs in a nose dive. A roar of laughter followed him—answered by a roar from Price as he landed.

"He, he, he !" gasped Billy Bunter. "Serve the beast right ! I say, you fellows——"

"Now give Bunter some !" said the captain of the Remove.

"Oh, really, Wharton——"

"All you fellows kick together ! Wait a tick, Bunter !"

Bunter did not wait a fraction of a tick ! He did the Remove staircase like lightning, and vanished.

THE SEVENTH CHAPTER.
Rubbing It In !

HORACE COKER snorted.

"Whopped !" he said contemptuously.

Potter and Greene grinned.

"Whopped !" repeated Coker. "A Fifth Form man ! Told to bend over, like a fag in the Remove ! What ?"

And Coker snorted again, in great scorn.

It was the following day, and Coker's remarks were called forth at the sight of Price of the Fifth in the quad.

Plenty of fellows were taking notice of Price.

His usual friend and companion, Hilton, was not with him. During that term they had been seen less and less together, and now it looked as if there was quite a break.

Price had other friends—fellows with whom nobody else was very keen to be friendly. There were black sheep in the flock at Greyfriars, as everywhere else, and Price's friends were of that shady variety. Hilton, reckless scapegrace, as he had been, was a fellow of a very different cut, and his friendship had meant a good deal to Price. It helped to keep his head above water, as it were, in the "swim" at Greyfriars. Price was a "rotter," and did not, in fact, want to be anything else ; but he did not like being barred by all the decent crowd.

What had happened the previous day had given the black sheep of the Fifth the finishing touch. A whopping from a prefect was almost unheard-of in the Fifth, and it caused great annoyance in that Form—all the men in the Fifth Form games study agreed that it was a disgrace to the Fifth. Yet they could not deny that it had been deserved ; that Wingate of the Sixth was not only acting within his rights, but doing his duty. So all their annoyance was concentrated on Price, who had let the Form down by incurring that whopping.

Every man in the Fifth told Price what he thought of him, not once, but over and over again. Had Price been a fighting man, he would have had a dozen scraps on his hands that day.

"Whopped !" said Coker, for the third time, raising his bull-voice so that the wretched Price had to hear it. "Disgraceful, I call it! I'd like to see a Sixth Form man whop me!"

Potter winked at Greene! As a matter of fact, they would have liked to see it, too!

"Letting the Form down!" went on Coker. "I'd have knocked the man across the study! But Price always was a funk!"

The unpleasant word reached Price's ears, as Coker intended that it should. He flushed crimson, and, affecting not to have heard it, walked on quickly. That was all he could do—unless he was going to punch Coker's head—which he longed to do, but dared not. A scornful snort from Horace Coker followed him.

"Bend over!" squeaked Tubb of the Third, passing near Price, and the unhappy senior again affected not to hear, and walked on.

He wondered how long it was going to be before he was allowed to forget that whopping.

Hilton of the Fifth came out of the House, and Price glanced at him. But Hilton did not seem to see him. He walked across to a group of games men—Wingate, Gwynne, Blundell, Bland—and joined them, without noticing his former friend.

Price drove his hands deep into his pockets, and slouched away.

His feelings were bitter beyond words. He was by no means sure that he had lost Hilton for good. This was not the first time that the dandy of the Fifth had yielded to better influences, but it had never lasted very long. Still, it looked like the genuine thing this time. And he knew that Hilton was ashamed of him—that he despised him for having bent over and taken a whopping like a fag! The alternative had been an interview with the Head, and probably the sack—which Price dared not face.

"I say, you fellows!" He caught Billy Bunter's fat voice. "I say, there's Price of the Fifth! He was whopped yesterday!"

But Billy Bunter was making that remark to five or six Remove fellows, and Price did not want a shindy with a crowd of juniors. They all looked at him and grinned. Coker of the Fifth, in Price's place, would have charged the whole bunch. Price walked on.

"He, he, he!" Bunter's fat cachinnation followed him. "I say, you fellows, I hear that Price was howling like a baby! Lots of fellows heard him. Blubbing, you know! A fellow told me he heard him begging Wingate not to lay it on so hard!"

"Ha, ha, ha!"

With a crimson face, the wretched Price slouched away to the House, and went in. He wanted to keep out of the public eye.

He went to his study.

There at tea-time he expected to see Hilton. But the dandy of the Fifth did not come.

Standing at his study doorway, Price kept an eye on the passage for him. Three or four Fifth Form men came along, Hilton among them.

"Comin' in to tea, Hilton?" called out Price, assuming the old friendly manner.

Hilton glanced at him.

"Teaing with Blundell!" he answered briefly.

"Been bending over lately?" called out Tomlinson of the Fifth, and there was a laugh from the seniors, as they went together into Blundell's study.

Price stood with a black brow. He was not feeling disposed for tea on his own, in a lonely study, and he went down to the quad again. There the first

object that met his view was the grinning, fat face of Billy Bunter.

Billy Bunter had not forgotten that smacking on the Remove staircase. Certainly he had deserved it; but the fat Owl of the Remove never liked getting what he deserved. Bunter's idea was to take it out of Price of the Fifth by "rubbing in" that whopping!

"I say, Price!" squeaked the Owl of the Remove. "Like me to lend you an exercise-book to stuff in your bags next time you see Wingate?"

Price made a stride towards him. But there were a dozen Remove men in sight, and he did not want another ragging from the Remove. He walked across the quad, unheeding the grinning Owl.

But there was a glint in his eyes. Even since that whopping he had been turning over in his mind schemes of revenge on Wingate, and on his former friend. Nothing practical had so far occurred to him. But Bunter, at least, could be dealt with—and Price knew how!

Thrashing Bunter would have been satisfactory, but it meant another shindy

---

BRAVO, BERKS!

The following Greyfriars limerick sent in by Philip Barnett, of Croft House Cottage, Pangbourne, Berks, has earned for its author one of this week's useful pocket wallets:

Said Fishy to Bunter: "I think
You're a great fat guy and a gink.
Where your brains should be
I guess you will see
An empty space or a kink!"

There's a chance for all of you to win these useful prizes. Get busy right away and address your attempts to: "Limericks and Jokes" Editor, c/o MAGNET, 5, Carmelite Street, London, E.C.4 (Comp.).

---

with the Remove, which was far from satisfactory. There were other ways—slyer ways, more in keeping with his character. It was almost too easy to lay a trap for the fat and fatuous Owl of the Remove to fall into. Bunter had "snaffled" cigarettes from Price's study—but it was not cigarettes that he had been looking for. Price gave the matter some little thought, and then went to the school shop.

Billy Bunter was there—blinking in at the window, like a fat Peri at the gate of paradise. Bunter, not for the first time, had been disappointed about a postal order, and the good things in Mrs. Mimbles' shop were beyond his reach. He was debating in his fat mind which man in the Remove was likeliest to be successfully "touched" for a little loan, when Price came along, and went into the shop.

A few minutes later Price came out with a parcel in his hand.

Bunter blinked at that parcel.

From its size, it looked as if Stephen Price had been doing some rather extensive shopping for tea.

Price glanced at him.

"Carry this to my study for me, will you, Bunter?" he asked.

Any other Remove man would have told the Fifth Former to go and eat coke! But not Bunter.

"Eh? Oh, certainly!" said Bunter at once.

Price handed over the parcel and

walked away. Billy Bunter blinked after him through his big spectacles thoughtfully. Then he went towards the House.

But he did not head for Price's study in the Fifth. He headed for Study No. 7 in the Remove.

THE EIGHTH CHAPTER.

Teaing with Bunter!

"I AM stony—thou art stony—he is stony!" said Bob Cherry mournfully. "We are stony, you are stony, they are stony!"

"The stonifulness," remarked Hurree Jamset Ram Singh, "is terrific!"

"Je suis stony!" went on Bob, putting it in French. "Tu es stony—il est stony! Nous sommes stony—vous etes stony—ils sont stony——"

"Oh, chuck it!" said Frank Nugent.

"What's going to be done?" asked Johnny Bull.

"Who's going to be done?" asked Bob.

"We can't stick Mauly again!" remarked Harry Wharton. "Mauly played up like a trump yesterday; but we're not sponging on Mauly."

"What about Smithy?" suggested Bob.

Wharton shook his head.

"Toddy——" said Nugent.

"Poor old Toddy!" Wharton laughed. "He can't stand a feed for five fellows, especially with Bunter in the study!"

"What about Wibley? Let's go and ask him to do some of his theatrical stunts, and ten to one he will ask us to tea!"

Harry Wharton laughed.

"Look here, it's got to be tea in Hall, and we may as well go down to it before it's too late."

The Famous Five, in a group outside Study No. 1, were discussing ways and means. The sad stony state was still prolonged; no remittances had arrived from kind relatives. Lord Mauleverer, certainly, would have welcomed them in his study, which was a land flowing with milk and honey. But they had a natural delicacy about sticking his openhearted lordship a second time. Stony as they were, they did not want to take Billy Bunter as a model. The Bounder, no doubt, would have played up, but they did not want to ask favours from the Bounder. It was tea in Hall or nothing, and they made up their minds to it.

"I say, you fellows!"

They were starting for the stairs when Billy Bunter came up, with a big parcel in his hand.

"Hallo, hallo, hallo! What have you got there, Bunty?" asked Bob Cherry.

"Oh, a few things for tea!" said the Owl of the Remove carelessly. "I say, you fellows, come and tea with me! I've got rather a lot."

The Famous Five stared at the parcel. Bunter, in possession of an unusual amount of tuck, was liable to the suspicion of having raided the same. But that parcel, it was obvious, had come direct from the school shop. It looked as if Bunter had been shopping on an unusual scale.

"Don't tell us your postal order has come, old fat bean!" ejaculated Bob.

"Oh, really, Cherry——"

"Wonders will never cease!" grinned Nugent.

"I say, you fellows, as a matter of fact, I've had a remittance," said Bunter airily. "I told you I was expecting a postal order. You cackled. Well, now you can jolly well see for yourselves! You make out that I never stand a spread! Just come along to my study and see!"

"No smokes this time!" grinned Bob.

"Look here, are you coming?" demanded Bunter warmly. "My spread won't go begging, I can jolly well tell you that! Lots of fellows I can ask! I'm asking you first, because we're old pals!"

"H'm!"

The Famous Five were quite unaware that they were Bunter's old pals. They did not yearn for that distinguished honour, either. They exchanged glances, and Harry Wharton shook his head.

"Thanks all the same, old fat bean——" he began.

Bunter sniffed.

"If that means that you're turning my spread down, Wharton——"

"Well, not exactly that; but——"

"But what?" demanded Bunter "Fellows make out that I never stand my whack. You've said so yourselves! Now, as soon as I get a postal order, I offer to stand a spread all round, and you turn it down! Yah!"

Bunter blinked reproachfully at the Famous Five.

They exchanged rather uncomfortable glances.

Put like that, it really did seem rather ungracious to refuse to accept the fat Owl's invitation.

It was not a case of smokes this time; it was tuck for tea, and, to judge by the size of the parcel, there was plenty of it. And Bunter, who might have been expected to "scoff" the lot without wasting a thought on any other fellow, was urging them to join him—making an urgent point of it. Really, it was scarcely possible for the chums of the Remove to refuse further.

"Well, if you'd really like us to come——" said Harry at last.

"Keen on it!" said Bunter. "You fellows are so jolly nice——"

"Eh?"

"Such sportsmen——"

"What?"

"The kind of fellows to stand by a fellow! Not the sort of fellows to let a fellow down! Just the sort of chaps I admire!" said Bunter.

The Famous Five gazed at Billy Bunter.

This sort of "soft sawder" was all very well and nothing new if Bunter was seeking to barge into a spread. But it was amazing when he was offering the spread!

"Do come on!" said Bunter. "I shouldn't enjoy the spread a bit without my pals! Do come!"

"Done, then!" said the captain of the Remove; and they followed the fat junior to Study No. 7.

Bunter's unexpected invitation came at the right moment, there was no doubt about that. It was welcome enough, in the stony circumstances.

Bunter plumped the parcel on the study table. The juniors glanced round Study No. 7. Nobody else was present.

"Toddy and Dutton are teaing out," explained Bunter. "I should have been fairly left if this hadn't turned up. Toddy's selfish, you know: when he's teaing out, he never cares whether there's anything in the study for me. You fellows get the fire going—what?"

The visitors in Study No 7 were prepared to make themselves useful While the fire was got going, and the kettle got ready, and crocks sorted out, Billy Bunter unwrapped the parcel.

He was rather curious himself to ascertain what it contained—though it did not, of course, occur to his guests that he did not yet know!

He grinned a happy grin at the sight

of ham and sausages, a box of tarts, a cake, and other good things.

Price, apparently, had intended to do himself well at tea in the Fifth! Possibly he had expected visitors! Bunter did not worry about that!

Bunter was by no means a dishonest fellow. He would not have touched a farthing that did not belong to him. But in matters of tuck, Bunter was a Bolshevik pure and simple. Tuck he simply could not resist. Somehow or other, he seemed to work it out in the depths of his fat and podgy brain that he had some sort of a right to tuck, wherever found.

In the Remove, no fellow's cake was safe from Bunter. Coker of the Fifth had kicked him times without number for grub-raiding in his study. Mr. Quelch had caned him, more times than he could remember, for surreptitious visits to the larder. Even at the school dining-table, under a sea of eyes, Bunter had been known to annex another fellow's pudding if the fellow was not looking. Annexing Price's parcel was a mere trifle to Bunter.

If he thought about the matter at all, it was only with a view to possible consequences. If he dodged the consequences, it was all right. There was, so far as Billy Bunter could see, nothing else to worry about.

Six fellows sat down to tea in Study No. 7.

Football practice in the keen air had made the Famous Five hungry. They were ready for a spread.

Bunter was always ready for one. He had done no footer practice, but he did not need that to give an edge to his appetite. His appetite was always in first-class working order.

"I say, you fellows, this is all right —what?" grinned Bunter. "Help yourselves, old beans!"

And Bunter helped himself liberally. There was quite a lot of tuck, though with half a dozen hungry fellows to punish it there was certainly not more than enough. And Bunter, in the gastronomic line, counted as two or three, if not four.

Bunter, as usual, handled the lion's share. Still, there was sufficient to go round, and the Famous Five were not exacting.

They made quite a good tea.

Every crumb, however, vanished under the combined attack.

Strange to relate, that seemed to please Bunter! He might have been expected to want to leave something over for supper. But he didn't! He seemed to want to get the whole of the supplies demolished at one sitting.

"Jolly good feed, what?" he asked cheerily when the Famous Five rose to their feet at last.

"Fine!" said Bob Cherry.

"Ripping!" agreed Nugent.

"The ripfulness is terrific!" said Hurree Jamset Ram Singh solemnly.

"I say, you fellows, don't be in a hurry to go!" said Bunter. "I—I say, hang on a bit, will you?"

"Oh! Yes! All right!"

"I—I'd rather like a bit of a chat!" said Bunter.

"Oh!"

As their host seemed to desire more of their company, the chums of the Remove could hardly rush off the moment the spread was over! Remove men at Greyfriars

were not Chesterfields; still, something was due to politeness. They lingered.

Bunter sat in the armchair and blinked at the door.

He was wondering whether Price of the Fifth would come up to the Remove to inquire after that parcel.

In fact, Bunter was rather surprised that Price had not been after it already.

If he had bought the stuff for tea he must have wanted his tea before this! Really, he seemed to be giving Bunter time on purpose to dispose of the tuck before inquiring after it.

Bunter did not want to be alone when Price came up.

Tap! The door opened.

"Hallo, hallo, hallo!" exclaimed Bob Cherry, as the sour face of Stephen Price looked in. "Come up for another ragging, Pricey?"

"This is Bunter's study, I think?" said Price.

"Eh! Yes! Here's Bunter if you want him!" said Wharton. "If you're on the warpath again, Price, you know what to expect."

"Nothing of the kind. Did you take my parcel to my study, Bunter?"

Price looked across at the fat junior in the armchair—noting, with the tail of his eye, as it were, the signs of a recent spread on the study table.

"Eh! Oh! Yes!" stammered Bunter. "You—you'll find it there, Price."

"I've looked, and it's not there," said Price casually. "If you put it there, all right! Sure you did?"

"Oh! Yes!" gasped Bunter.

"All serene!" said Price. "If you put it there, somebody's taken it away —I'd better report the matter at once. Whoever's got it will cough it up fast enough, I dare say, when the prefects get after him."

And with that, Price of the Fifth turned from the doorway of Study No. 7, and walked away down the passage. He left a dead—not to say deadly— silence behind him in Bunter's study.

THE NINTH CHAPTER.

After the Feast, the Reckoning!

HARRY WHARTON & CO. looked fixedly at Billy Bunter.

Bunter blinked at them.

The silence could almost have been cut with a knife! Price's footsteps died away down the Remove passage towards the stairs.

"You fat scoundrel!" Wharton broke the silence at last. "Have you been spoofing us again?"

"Oh, really, Wharton——"

"Did that parcel of tuck belong to that rotten outsider, Price of the Fifth?" breathed Bob Cherry.

"Oh, really, Cherry——"

"Spoofed!" said Johnny Bull. "Might have known it!"

"The mindfulness is terrific!"

"I—I say, you fellows!" stammered Bunter "It—it's all right! I—I told you I was expecting a postal order! If—if Price makes a fuss about it, I— I'll pay him for the tuck—when my postal order comes."

(Continued on next page.)

"So it was Price's?"

"Nunno! **Mine!**" said Bunter. "The fact is, I—I——"

"Cough up the truth, you fat freak!" hissed Johnny Bull. "Can't you see there's going to be a row about this? Price isn't a fellow like Coker, who would be satisfied with kicking you. He's going to make trouble."

"Well, he jolly well asked for it!" said Bunter. "Fagging a Remove man, you know! Like his cheek to ask me to carry his beastly parcel to his study!"

"You needn't have carried it."

"Well, I knew what it was, you know! And—and that beast Price pitched into me yesterday!" said Bunter. "He jolly well deserved to be punished, see? I say, you fellows, I suppose you're going to stand by a chap, after I've stood you a splendid feed?"

"You howling ass!" said Harry. "Is that why you asked us? I see now! But it's not a question of a fellow pitching into you, you blithering idiot. Though if Price wanted to thrash you for bagging his tuck, I certainly shouldn't interfere, for one. I wish he'd let it go at that!"

"Why, you beast——"

"He won't!" said Nugent.

"No fear!"

"I—I say, you fellows, what do you think Price will do?" exclaimed Billy Bunter, in alarm.

"You heard what he said! He's going to report to the prefects that a parcel has been taken from his study. That means an inquiry."

"Oh crikey!"

"It will come before Quelch—it may come before the Head!"

"Oh lor'!"

"You'd better cut after Price, and own up, before he goes to Wingate!" said Bob. "Once the prefects begin to——"

"Oh, scissors! The—the fact is, it—it wasn't Price's parcel!" stammered Bunter. "I—I lost his parcel—it—it's rather foggy in the quad, you know, and —and I dropped it, and—and couldn't find it again, and—and——"

"Are you going to tell the Head that?" inquired Johnny Bull sarcastically.

"Oh lor'!" gasped Bunter.

He blinked at the chums of the Remove in great alarm.

So far, Bunter had not given the matter much thought! At the worst, he had supposed that Price would be "after him," as in the matter of the snaffled cigarettes. Having shared the plunder with the Famous Five, Bunter considered that it was up to them to stand by him, and "put paid" to Price if he came up on the warpath.

Now he realised that the matter was much more serious than that! Price had not dared to report the pilfering of the cigarettes to the beaks. The pilfering of tuck was quite a different matter.

"I—I say, you fellows!" gasped Bunter. "I say, you've got to stand by me, you know! After all, you had as much as I did."

"You fat rascal!" roared Johnny Bull. "We never knew——"

"That's all very well!" argued Bunter. "But you had it, all the same! Look here, Wharton, you go after Price, and—and own up——"

"Own up!" gasped Wharton blankly.

"Yes, old chap! Own up that you snaffled the parcel," said Bunter, blinking at him. "Price won't dare lay a finger on you—everybody knows he's a funk! Look how he was whopped yesterday——"

"Scrag him!" growled Johnny Bull.

"I—I say, you fellows——"
THE MAGNET LIBRARY.—No. 1,359.

"I think I'll speak to Price!" said Harry, and he left the study, and ran down the Remove passage to the stairs.

Price of the Fifth was on the lower landing when he sighted him.

"Hold on a minute, Price!" called out the captain of the Remove.

The Fifth Former glanced round and stopped.

Wharton came down breathlessly.

There was a mocking gleam in Price's eyes. It had been easy enough to trap Bunter; but, rather unexpectedly, the cad of the Fifth had caught the Famous Five in the same trap! He had not forgotten that ragging on the Remove staircase; and he was going to make matters just as unpleasant as he possibly could for the chums of the Remove. That Bunter had stood a spread in his study with the tuck, and that Harry Wharton & Co. had shared it, was quite plain to Price, and it was his intention to make the very most of it.

"Well, what?" he asked.

"Look here, Price, there's no need to inquire what became of your parcel. You know Bunter pretty well, and you jolly well know what became of the tuck," said Harry impatiently.

"He's told me he put it in my study."

"Well, you jolly well know he didn't! You jolly well know he scoffed it!" said Wharton. "And the worst of it is that he asked us to the spread, without telling us what he'd done. If you'll let us know what it cost, we'll square, among us, as we had the stuff."

Price raised his eyebrows.

"Indeed!" he drawled. "So that's how the matter stands? Well, the stuff cost a pound, and it will certainly have to be paid for, every penny. If you shared the plunder with Bunter, I've no doubt that your Form-master will order you to pay your share of the amount."

"There's no need for the matter to go before Quelch."

"Isn't there?" smiled Price.

"No!" snapped Wharton. "You know how the matter stands now, and you'll be paid. What more do you want?"

"I'm afraid I can't let it drop at that!" said Price smoothly. "Stealing is rather too serious a matter for that, my young friend. As you state that Bunter stole my parcel, I shall go to Bunter's Form-master instead of to Wingate. I dare say he will send for you later."

"I didn't state anything of the kind," said Wharton, between his teeth. "Bunter's too big a fool to realise that bagging tuck is pilfering, and you jolly well knew——"

Price turned his back and went down the stairs.

"You're going to Quelch?" exclaimed Wharton.

"Certainly!" said Price, over his shoulder.

"You rotter!" shouted the captain of the Remove. "What did you trust the stuff in Bunter's hands at all for? It looks to me as if the whole thing's a put-up job."

"You'd better tell your Form-master so, if you think so," drawled Price, and he walked away to Masters' Studies.

Harry Wharton slowly went back to Study No. 7 in the Remove. A dismayed half-dozen waited there for the inevitable summons to Mr. Quelch's study. It was not long in coming.

THE TENTH CHAPTER.
The Heavy Hand.

MR. QUELCH was looking grim and stern when the juniors filed into his study.

The Remove master was not in his usual state of health, and it was rumoured in the Form that he was soon going away for a change without waiting for the Easter holidays. He was looking rather pale and worn, as well as grim and stern. His gimlet eyes gleamed under knitted brows.

Price stood by his table, with a serious and respectful manner, but with a lurking glimmer in his eyes which told that he was enjoying himself. Price was in hopes that these members of the Remove, at least, would soon have something to think about, other than his whopping from Wingate.

The Famous Five were red and uncomfortable. Their feelings towards the fat Owl, who had tricked them into this unenviable position, were deep. With flushed faces they stood in a dismal row before Mr. Quelch.

"I have heard a very extraordinary statement from this Fifth Form boy, Wharton," said Mr. Quelch coldly. "Am I to understand that a quantity of food, purchased by him at the school shop, has been purloined—I may almost say stolen—by members of my Form, including my head boy?"

"Certainly not, sir!" said Wharton quietly, his eyes flashing at Price for a second. "We had not the faintest idea that the things belonged to Price, when Bunter asked us to a spread in his study."

"Not the foggiest, sir!" said Bob Cherry.

"I—I say, you fellows——" stammered Bunter.

"Bunter!" rapped Mr. Quelch.

"Oh, yes, sir!" groaned Bunter.

"You were entrusted with a parcel to carry from the school shop to Price's study. You kept possession of it?"

"Oh, no, sir! I—I mean——"

"What did you do with it?"

"I—I—I——" Bunter gasped helplessly. "I—I—I——"

"Answer me immediately, Bunter!"

"I—I—I—we—we—we——" stuttered Bunter. "I—I whacked it out with these fellows, sir!"

"Do you mean to say that they were aware of the fact that it did not belong to you?" demanded Mr. Quelch.

"Oh lor'! No, sir! I—I didn't mention that!" groaned Bunter. "The—the fact is, sir, I—I never—I—I never——"

"You never what?"

"Oh, nothing, sir!" gasped Bunter. "I—I didn't know that beast—I mean, Price—was going to make a fuss like this about it, sir. I—I—I thought it would only be a row——"

"Price has very properly reported the matter to me, as your Form-master, Bunter. Wharton, I accept your assurance that you and your friends were unaware of the circumstances, and exonerate you, as far as that goes. You do not deny, however, that you helped Bunter to consume these—these comestibles?"

"No, sir."

"Very well, you will all be held equally responsible in indemnifying Price. Price states that the value was one pound, one shilling. That will be three shillings and sixpence each for the six of you."

"Very well, sir. We shall be glad to pay up, of course."

"You may lay your money on my table!" said Mr. Quelch.

The colour deepened in the cheeks of the unfortunate Co.

"We—we're stony—I—I mean, short of cash, sir!" stammered Harry. "We—we can't pay at the—the moment!"

Price's lip curved in a sneer. Only the presence of the Form-master saved him at that moment from being knocked along the study carpet.

"That is immaterial," said Mr. Quelch, taking compassion on the crimson confusion of the juniors. "I will

" Ooogh ! " gasped Bunter, as a running figure loomed out of the fog and crashed into him.   The fat junior rolled over backwards as if a cannon-shot had struck him.   There was a cracking sound as the ripe egg in Bunter's hand smashed, and the scent that spread around was thicker than the fog !

pay the amount and stop it out of your next allowances."

"Thank you, sir !   That will be all right."

"The rightfulness will be terrific, honoured sahib."

"Very well," said Mr. Quelch, "you may leave my study.   Not you, Bunter !"

"I—I say, sir, I—I——" stammered Bunter.

"You will remain, Bunter !" said Mr. Quelch grimly.

"Oh lor' !" groaned Bunter.

Harry Wharton & Co. left the study. Bunter, much against his will, remained.

"I scarcely know how to deal with you, Bunter !" said Mr. Quelch.   "I am accustor ed to making allowances for your obtuseness, for your unusual and extraordinary stupidity.   But this matter is very serious.   Price takes the view that you have committed what amounts to a theft."

"Oh crikey !" gasped Bunter.

"You have purloined what did not belong to you, Bunter."

"It—it was only tuck, sir !" groaned the Owl of the Remove.

"You must learn, Bunter, that pilfering is pilfering, whether the object pilfered is edible or otherwise," said Mr. Quelch.   "You fully deserve to be taken before your headmaster and expelled."

"Oh lor' !"

"I shall, however, make allowances, as I have done before, for your impenetrable stupidity, Bunter——"

"Oh, thank you, sir !   C-can I go !" gasped Bunter.

"You may not go, Bunter."

"Oh dear !"

Mr. Quelch rose to his feet and picked up a cane from his table.

"I shall not trouble the Head with this matter, serious as it is," he said.   "I

shall administer a punishment myself, Bunter, so severe that I have hopes that it will impress a much-needed lesson on your mind."

"Ow !"

"You will bend over that chair, Bunter !"

"I—I say, sir !"

"Bend over !"

"Oh crikey !"

With a dismal fat face, Billy Bunter bent over the chair.   The can rose and fell in a succession of swipes that sounded like pistol-shots.   Loud rang the cane—louder still rang the fearful yells of Billy Bunter.

It was not merely "six."   It was as thorough a licking as Mr. Quelch had ever administered; such a licking as Bunter had seldom or never experienced before !   Never in his fat career had his grub-raiding led to such disastrous results as this.

He yelled and he howled and he squirmed and he roared, and still the cane swiped and swiped.

Price looked on with a lurking grin. Billy Bunter had been the cause of his own humiliating whopping, and Billy Bunter had "rubbed it in."   Bunter was paying dearly for it now !

It had cost Price nothing.   He was fully indemnified for the loss of the raided tuck, as he had, of course, known that he would be when the matter came before authority.   It had cost him nothing but a little cunning scheming to revenge himself on the wretched Owl. He wished that it was as easy to revenge himself on Wingate and Hilton. In the meantime there was keen satisfaction in seeing Bunter squirm, and hearing him yell.

Mr. Quelch laid down the cane at last. He looked quite tired with his exertions. Bunter was more than tired.

"Go !" he snapped.

Bunter went.

He groaned his way down the passage. He groaned his way to the stairs.   He groaned his way up to the Remove.

On the Remove landing five fellows were waiting for him.   They waited with vengeful looks.

"Here he is !" roared Johnny Bull.

"Collar him !"

"Scrag him !"

"Burst him !"

"Ow !   Ow !   Ow !   Wow !" groaned Bunter.   "I say, you fellows——   Ow !"

They looked at him.

"He's had enough !" said Harry Wharton.   "Let him rip !"

"I'll kick him to-morrow !" said Johnny Bull.

"Yow-ow-ow-ow-ow !"

Bunter groaned his way onward !   He groaned into Study No. 7, and for a long, long time afterwards any fellow passing that study heard deep and horrid groans proceeding therefrom. Billy Bunter had often suffered for his sins; but never had he suffered so severely !   And he groaned and groaned and groaned as if he would never finish groaning.   Hours later, when prep came round, Bunter was still groaning—and did not cease to groan till Peter Todd hurled a Latin dictionary at him and threatened to follow it up with the ink-pot !   Then at last Billy Bunter ceased to groan, and the weary were at rest !

THE ELEVENTH CHAPTER.
A Bumping for Billy Bunter !

"THICK !" remarked Bob Cherry.   "The thickfulness is terrific."

"Doesn't look like footer !" said Harry Wharton.

(Continued on page 16.)

CAN MAN BECOME ANIMAL?

Is magic true after all? Can spells be cast? Is it possible for a man to be changed into an animal? All interested in these engrossing questions should turn up in the Rag next Wednesday evening at 8 p.m. when J. Bull, Esq., will lecture on "How Coker Made a Complete Ass of Himself"!

THE NEW Greyfria

No. 74 (New Series). EDITED BY

IS TREVOR ANOTHER CARUSO?

Surprising Song Recital

Trevor, who is not often in the limelight, has come into the full glare of publicity this week by announcing that he has a marvellous voice.

Bolsover, the celebrated leader of the phenomenally successful comb-and-paper band known as Bolsover and His Boys, was delighted to hear it.

"The only thing we lack is a good crooner," he told Trevor, with enthusiasm. "If you can croon jazz melodies to the throbbing rhythm of my band, fame, if not fortune, is yours!"

But Trevor, to Bolsover's surprise, only glared.

"Croon!" he said, contemptuously. "Why, I'd rather give up singing altogether. My singing, I'd like you to know, is of the operatic type. On the concert platform, of course, I condescend to sentimental ballads or sea-shanties—but crooning, never!"

On the strength of that little oration, many fellows felt impelled to turn up to Trevor's first song recital in the Rag a little later.

Their comments on "Prologue to Pagliacci" and "Un Peu d'Amour" were not altogether favourable, consisting mostly of yells of "Put a sock in it!" throughout both songs.

Their comments on "My Dreams," which followed, were even more unfavourable, as they consisted almost exclusively of tomatoes, hurled with unerring aim at Trevor's face, the result being somewhat on these lines:

"I dream of the day I met you—wooooosh!
I dream of the light divine—groooogh!
That shone—ow!—in your tender eyes,
love—grooosh!
When first—mmmm!—they looked in mine—woooogh!"

"My Dreams" concluded the show, and Trevor staggered off to the nearest bath-room, followed by the derisive howls of the audience.

"Do you think he really can sing?" we asked Hoskins afterwards—not knowing enough about singing to be able to express a personal opinion.

The eyes of Hoskins, musical genius of the Shell, were fairly gleaming as he made reply.

"Sing? My dear sir, I should think he CAN sing!" Hoskins said, rapturously. "Unfortunately, I didn't hear him owing to the noise, so I am unable to give a technical report on the quality of his voice. But about his ability to sing, there can be no question. Anyone who arouses the jeers of the un-initiated philistine mob that gets into the Rag to this extent MUST be good!"

So now you know!

WE COULDN'T RESIST THIS!

Somebody writes to tell us that to-day is the fiftieth anniversary of an occasion when the Sark overflowed its banks and a Greyfriars boatrace was rowed in Friardale Lane.

"Jubilee"-vit?

MY WORST AND BES EXPERIENCE

By Aubrey Angel

I'm a go-ahead kind of chap, with tastes considerably more advanced than those of the rest of the Fourth. Temple and his crowd find their diversion in football and similar puerile pastimes. I find mine in billiards, banker, betting and similar manly hobbies. ("Manly"! Ye gods!—Ed.)

This being so, it won't surprise you to know that I'm not averse to the consolation of an occasional cigarette. But it may surprise you quite a lot to know that my weakness for My Lady Nicotine brought me the worst experience I can remember, last Christmas.

My pater, Sir Philip Angel, caused it. He happens to possess a peculiar sense of humour, and when he discovered me smoking in my room, he didn't just read out a lecture as a normal pater would. He patted me on the back instead and said: "Well done, Aubrey! Glad to see you're becoming such a man!" Then he added: "Come downstairs and try something really worth smoking!"

I followed him. He went straight to his smoking cabinet and got out a box of enormous black cigars.

"Try one of these!" he said, cheerily. "I can recommend them!"

I told him I really wasn't very keen, and the old hunks glared.

"I trust, Aubrey, you are not insinuating that my cigars are not good enough——"

"Nunno, but——"

"Then smoke it to the end! Grown-up though you may be, I shall feel compelled to thrash you if you insult me to the extent of leaving so much as an inch of one of my cigars unsmoked!"

What could I do? I gingerly accepted one of his black kill-me-quicks and lit it. And the pater just watched over me and gloated as my face turned greener and greener!

I won't attempt to describe the extraordinary sensations I experienced as I smoked through that cigar. I know my limitations and no words of mine can adequately describe the fearful spasms that began to grip me!

I managed to get half-way through it. Then, with a strangled groan, I allowed it to drop from my lips, after which I tottered towards the nearest bath-room.

Cigar-smoking may be a manly kind of pursuit. But, so far as I'm concerned, it will be a long, long time before my teeth close on one of those torpedo-shaped products of Havana again!

The best experience I can bring to mind was an occasion when I had a "plunge" on a gee-gee. Ponsonby, of Highcliffe, told me he had a tip for a stone cert that was running in the Swindleton Stakes—Boneshaker was the nam[e] the animal, if I reme[mber] rightly.

I pawned my gold tick[et] a "tenner," enclosed the in an envelope, and addr[essed] it to Mr. Joseph I together with a letter a[sking] if he would kindly put m[e for] pounds on Boneshaker. I waited in eager anticip[ation] for the result.

When the evening came out, I don't mind [con]fessing I felt a bit s[hy] though, on the strengt[h of] what Pon had told m[e, I] thought I was on a really [good] thing.

I looked in the '[Press]' for the result—when I saw it, I a[lmost] swooned. Boneshaker failed me; he was in "Also Rans"!

I dropped the paper [and] went back to my study frightfully perturbed. And then I made the [dis]covery that turned de[feat] into really cheery opti[mism] once more.

I had forgotten to pos[t the] letter!

Believe me, the hap[piest] moment of my life was [when] I extracted that crisp, ru[stling] "tenner" from the unp[osted] letter and put it back in [my] pocket!

(Next week, as a contra[st to] the somewhat unsa[voury] reminiscences of the Bad [Boy] of the Fourth, we're goin[g to] have an article by Oliver K[irk] of the Remove. Look out [for it,] chaps!—Ed.)

STOP PRESS.

We have just stopped press to announce nothing unusual has turn[ed up] to stop it for.

WOULD YOU BELIEVE IT?

Horace Coker's unruly hair and untidy garb are frequent targets for Mr. Prout's wit in the Fifth Form-room. Coker told him that a fellow with personality needn't bother about trifles—and earned 500 lines!

Aubrey Angel, the cad of the Upper Fourth, says his Form-master, Mr. Capper, has taken to wearing a wig to supplement his thinning locks. Angel is careful to say this out of Capper's hearing, though!

Very little goes on amon[g the] Third Form fags that Sa[mmy] Bunter does not hear about [He] is a champion eavesdropper [and] is usually lurking behind the[m] if Dicky Nugent & Co. are b[rew]ing a scheme!

EMOVE FLYING SQUAD'S CAPTURE

Trapeze Expert Trapped

hy Bolsover should hold ving licence is a mystery. olds one, anyway. Last nesday he hired a car Courtfield and took ner and Stott and Trevor Treluce for a ride.

e laws of the land began perate, however, once y got his hired antique on road; and, having con- ned the law about dan- ıs driving by keeping to wrong side of the road as as possible, he soon d himself being chased by officers of the law—one ot and the other on a -bike!

inner and Stott and or and Treluce didn't like the look of things. Don't you think you'd r stop?" Skinner asked. would if I could!" was ver's succinct reply.

e fact was that he ln't! The particular l Bolsy had hired had n a rare lot of cranking nd a rare lot of starting; nce it did start, it didn't to want to leave off!

lsy doesn't know an l lot about driving cars, way, and what he did wasn't of much use to since this car had been ned some years before ver's birth! (Skinner us the garage people ht it from the Courtfield um!)

roared Bolsy and his ngers, leaving behind dense clouds of dust and l-fumes; and the farther went, the more they up the offences. They ted footpaths, brushed against lamp-posts, scattered pedestrians, s l a u g h t e r e d chickens and generally carried on alarming!

"Popper Court!" mur- mured Skinner, as they came in sight of Sir Hilton Popper's residence. "Old Popper's chairman of the magistrates, isn't he? Wonder how much he'll fine you, Bolsy?"

"Perhaps it'll be chokey without the option!" yelled Stott, from the back. Then he added: "Look out!"

Fortunately, Bolsover hap-

pened to be looking out—and just managed to avoid a collision with another car by driving through the open gates into the grounds of Popper Court!

We have always maintained that it's better to be born lucky than good-looking. Bol- sover, of course, lays no claim to good looks. But what happened next is positive proof that the gods of fortune are with him.

Just as it happened, · you see, at the very moment when Bolsy turned into the grounds of Popper Court, Sir Hilton was having a violent struggle with a housebreaker who was trying to escape out of one of the bed-room windows. The housebreaker had reached the top of the ladder that was reared against the wall out- side when Sir Hilton gave him a violent push that sent the ladder flying backwards.

But for Bolsover, the crook would have made a perfectly happy landing, for he hap- pened to be Slim Herbert, an unemployed trapeze expert who was never more at home than when balancing himself on the top rung of a ladder.

But Bolsover's hired car came rattling down the drive leading to Popper Court just as Slim Herbert arrived out of the blue—and Slim Herbert, to his surprise, found himself landing in the midst of a yelling crowd of Removites! A moment later, the car came to a stop—against the solid impediment of Sir Hilton Popper's ancestral home!

When the two perspiring policemen arrived on the scene a little later, they found a housebreaker to reward their efforts. They did think of arresting Bolsy, too. But after one look from Sir Hilton —they decided to rest content with one housebreaker!

Sir Hilton, you'll gather, was delighted. He christened Bolsy's outfit the "Greyfriars Flying Squad," and got the Head to give all the lucky bargees in the car an extra "halfer."

We'd rather have their luck than all our good looks!

SITUATION VACANT.

My doctor has ordered me to take a two-hour run every morning; but I fear it is too much fag. Who will offer to take the run in my place? Bob a day salary. Apply Lord Mauleverer, Study No. 12.

Doctor Vernon- Smith?

Bounder's Remarkable Cure

We really think Vernon-Smith should take up a medical career. Untrained as he is, he can already diagnose diseases with extra- ordinary accuracy—and cure them, too!

Take the case of Snoop, for instance. Snoop called on the Bounder one evening and complained that his face was too pale.

Smithy had a good look at it under the study light and promptly said "Anaemia!"

"You think that's what I've got?" Snoop bleated. "How do I cure it, then?"

Smithy pondered. Eventually, he looked up with a gleam in his eye.

"I think I know something that will put some colour into your cheeks," he said. "Come along with me."

He then took the patient along to Study No. 1, where an inquest was being held over the previous night's dorm. raid on the Fourth, which had failed lamentably owing to some person unknown betraying the Remove plans.

"Found out who sold the fort?" he asked the war council.

"Not yet!" growled Johnny Bull. "Wait till we do, though!"

"What are you going to do with him?" asked Smithy, carelessly.

Wharton replied that they were going to flay him alive.

Bob Cherry added that the victim would afterwards be hung, drawn, and quartered.

Tom Brown favoured something lingering, with boiling oil in it.

Bulstrode advocated making the culprit run the gauntlet at least a dozen times.

At this juncture, the Bounder turned round and examined his patient.

Snoop was cured already! His face, which had had a ghostly pallor only a minute before, was now as red as a peony!

Naturally, Smithy told the council of his wonderful success.

Snoop didn't wait to hear the end of the recital. For reasons best known to himself, he fled!

The war council are still hunting for him. Somehow, they seem to have an idea he may know something about the failure of that raid on the Fourth dorm.

But that's nothing to do with Smithy's success as a doctor, which is really the subject of this news item.

As to that, we think the way he brought the colour back to Snoop's face was really wonderful.

Don't you?

GREYFRIARS FACTS WHILE YOU WAIT!

Lung says the Chinese ate their ancestors ex- ly—which may account for espectful attitude towards uelch. Quelchy might not, knew, appreciate being ed as an "ancestor," though!

In the boxing ring George Wingate is invincible at his weight. In the final of an inter-schools contest he defeated Eric Kildare of St. Jim's on points—thus winning a hand- some challenge shield!

Mrs. Mimble makes a number of special sweetmeats which are un- obtainable elsewhere. Bunter offered her a testimonial if she would allow him unlimited "tick"—an offer Mrs. Mimble ungratefully turned down!

DICKY NUGENT'S WEEKLY WISDOM

On his way to the sannatorium this week, Dr. Pillbury slipped on a banana-skin I'd thrown out of the windoe and decided to postpone his vizzit for 24 hours.

So you see, it's not only an apple a day that keeps the doctor away. A banana does equally well!

(Continued from page 13.)

"Not quite !"

"I say, you fellows——"

"Kick him !"

Billy Bunter dodged.

It was Wednesday afternoon, which, being a half-holiday, should have been merry and bright.

Instead of which it was far from merry and far from bright !

February had been rather foggy, and it was winding up with the thickest fog ever !

There was fog on the land and fog on the sea, and the chums of the Remove, as they looked out into the dim mists, could hear the far-off, dismal hooting of sirens from unseen steamers on the shadowed waters.

Football, it was clear, was "off." That was clear, if the weather wasn't ! Even Bob Cherry did not think a game practicable that afternoon.

"May clear off !" he remarked hopefully.

But it did not look like it ! Fog on the land was thickened by rolling mist from the sea. The Greyfriars quad was a dim well of gloom. From the windows figures in the quad loomed like ghostly shadows as they passed—but very few fellows were out of doors. There was a light drizzle falling through the mists, which was discouraging.

"What about a walk ?" asked Bob.

"Um !" said his comrades.

"Wingate's gone out !" remarked Bob. "I saw him going into the quad ! He has a match on with the Fifth this afternoon."

"It will have to be scratched !" said Nugent.

"Could make a pun out of that !" remarked Bob Cherry thoughtfully. "Match scratched because there's no light——"

"Don't !" grunted Johnny Bull.

"I say, you fellows——"

"Waiting to be kicked, Bunter ?"

"Beast !"

Billy Bunter was waiting, though, apparently, not to be kicked ! Hilton of the Fifth came lounging along to the big window and stared out into the mist. His handsome face was rather clouded. This was the date of the senior match in which the reformed scapegrace of the Fifth was to have played in Blundell's team. It seemed unlikely that the match would be played.

"Nothing doing to-day, Hilton !" remarked Harry Wharton.

The dandy of the Fifth glanced at him.

"Doesn't look hopeful !" he agreed. "Seen Wingate anywhere ? He's not in his study."

"He went out a few minutes ago," said Bob Cherry. "Gone to see if it's a bit clearer on the football ground, I fancy."

Hilton nodded, and strolled away to the door. Perhaps he was keen on playing Soccer, or perhaps he was unwilling to waste the afternoon if

Soccer was not going to be played. Possibly he was remembering the excursion Price had planned for that day, which had been "washed out" owing to his new Soccer activities.

"I say, you fellows——"

"Oh, buzz off, Bunter !"

"That beast Price——"

"Bother Price !"

"He's gone out !" said Bunter.

"What about it, fathead ?" grunted Johnny Bull. "Does it matter two straws to anybody whether that worm has gone out or not ?"

"Well, look what a chance it is !" urged Bunter.

The Famous Five turned from the window and transferred their attention to William George Bunter. His remark was rather mystifying.

Billy Bunter had had a troublous time since the affair of the feed in Study No. 7. Quelch had given him a record licking, and since then he had accumulated an unusual number of kickings. All the Remove had chortled over the story of that spread, and over such great guns as the Famous Five being called up before a beak on the charge of grub-raiding. Bunter, of course, had taken them in—but fellows like Skinner & Co. affected to believe that the famous Co. had been "in" with Bunter in annexing Price's tuck. Which was annoying and ridiculous. Naturally, they handed out to Bunter what he deserved—much to his annoyance ; for often as the fat Owl had been kicked for his sins, he had never grown to like it.

"It's the chance of a life-time !" said Bunter, blinking at the surprised five through his big spectacles. "Look at what that beast did ! I know jolly well that he was pulling my leg the other day ! He meant me to scoff that tuck so that he could get me a beak's licking ! It was a plant !"

"Looks like it !" agreed Wharton. "And quite in Price's line ! He's a deep rotter !"

"It was a rotten trick he played on me, you know !" said Bunter.

"Nobody but you would have fallen for it !" growled Johnny Bull. "He couldn't have played it on anybody but a greedy, pilfering, dishonest young scoundrel !"

"Hear, hear !" grinned Bob Cherry.

"Beast ! Well, look here, I had a fearful licking from Quelch," said Bunter. "Price planned the whole thing, and got away with it. Just because Wingate whopped him over those smokes, you know ! Taking it out of me."

"Serve you right !"

"Yah ! Well, I'm jolly well going to make the cad sit up, I can tell you !" said Bunter darkly. "I'd thrash the brute, only—only I can't, you know !"

"Ha, ha, ha !"

"Blessed if I see anything to cackle at ! I want you fellows to back me up ! Price is out in the quad now—and it's so jolly thick that nobody can see anything. We go after him——"

"Eh ?"

"And bag him !" said Bunter.

"Bag him ?" repeated Wharton.

"Yes ; and you fellows hold while I wallop him !"

"Oh, my hat !"

"I'll give him what Quelch gave me, and some over !" said Bunter. "See ? All you fellows will have to do is to hold him so that he can't punch me. That's important."

"Ha, ha, ha !"

"Oh, don't cackle ! Can't you see what a chance it is ?" urged Bunter. "We don't get a fog like this every day ! Chance of a life-time."

"You blithering owl !" exclaimed

Bob. "Think Pricey would take it smiling ? He would go straight to the Head if a crowd of Remove men set on him and walloped him."

"I've thought that out !" said Bunter astutely. "You see, in this fog nobody will see us ! Who's going to believe Price if we deny it ?"

"Wha-a-at ?"

"We all tell the same tale when we come before the Beak !" explained Bunter. "We swear that we never saw Price—never went out of the House at all, in fact—and the Head's bound to believe us if we all stick together."

Harry Wharton & Co. gazed at the Owl of the Remove dumbfounded. Bunter, evidently, had thought it out !

"See the idea ?" asked Bunter brightly. "Safe as houses ! Come on !"

"We—we—we're to set on Price in the fog, and—and tell the Head a bushel of lies about it afterwards !" gasped Bob Cherry. "Is that the idea ?"

"That's it, old chap ! Come on !"

"Oh, my only summer bonnet !"

"I don't suppose the Head would take Price's word, anyhow," added Bunter. "He's untruthful ! All the fellows know that he tells lies ! He deserves a jolly good whopping for that alone ! If there's anything I despise in a fellow it's untruthfulness !"

"Ye gods !" gasped Nugent.

"Come on !" said Bunter. "I don't know what he's wandering about in the fog for, but he may come in any minute. No time to lose !"

The Famous Five lost no time. Certainly they were not likely to fall in with Bunter's remarkable scheme for making Stephen Price of the Fifth suffer for his sins ! They were not bothering about Price ! But they lost no time in dealing with the happy Bunter !

They grabbed him all at once.

Bump !

Billy Bunter sat down suddenly and unexpectedly. He roared as he sat.

"Yarooh ! I say, you fellows—— Yarooooop !"

"Bump him !" said Harry Wharton.

"I say, you fellows—leggo—whooop !" yelled Bunter frantically as he was swept up—and swept down.

Bump !

"Beasts ! I say, old chaps—— Yaroooh !" shrieked Bunter. "I say—Whooop ! Look here, you old chaps—I mean, you beasts—— Yooooop !"

Bump !

"Ow ! Wow ! Leggo ! Help !"

Bump !

"Yoo—hoo—hoooooooop !"

Why the chums of the Remove were bumping him, Bunter did not know. But he knew that they were bumping him, hard ! On that point there was no doubt—not a possible, probable shadow of doubt !

Bump ! Bump !

"Yow-ow-ow-ow-ow-wow-whooop !"

Harry Wharton & Co. sauntered away, leaving Bunter roaring. The fat Owl's mental efforts in thinking out that astute scheme of vengeance on Price of the Fifth had been a sheer waste. It was plain that he was getting no backing from the Famous Five. He had got a bumping—merely that and nothing more !

THE TWELFTH CHAPTER.

Blow for Blow !

STEPHEN PRICE breathed hard and deep.

In the dimness of the fog in the quadrangle of Greyfriars he could see hardly a yard before his nose. Only by groping his way could he be sure that he was on the path.

But he could hear! The thick mists made no difference to that! And from the fog voices came to his ears. He stopped silently, and listened, his sly, cunning eyes glinting under his knitted brows.

There was a stick under Price's arm. It was a walking-cane which he had picked up in the study before going out.

Black and bitter thoughts had been in his mind when he went out into the fog with that stick under his arm. He had seen Wingate of the Sixth leave the House, and guessed that he had gone down to look at the football field. Half formed, vague plans had been in his mind when he followed. He had slipped quietly out of the House, unaware of the fact that Billy Bunter's eyes—and spectacles—had been on him. He was not thinking of Bunter—he was done

with Bunter, and had almost forgotten his existence.

He was thinking of his enemy—the prefect who had made him an object of scorn and ridicule in the Fifth Form by whopping him like a fag!

Billy Bunter was not the only fellow who had thought, that afternoon, that the blanket of fog over the school gave a fellow a chance!

From day to day, since that prefect's whopping, Price's bitterness had intensified, till the thought of vengeance on the captain of Greyfriars occupied almost the whole of his thoughts.

But the thing seemed impossible! There was nothing he could do—he was helpless! Even had he dared to tackle Wingate it was the sack for attacking a Sixth Form prefect—and anyhow, he dared not! But when he saw Wingate leave the House in that blanket of fog, other ideas came.

He had not made up his mind—he was still thinking it out, calculating the risks, counting up the pros and cons, when the sound of voices came to his ears and he listened. The speakers were Wingate of the Sixth and his former friend, Hilton—and they were not three yards from him, though obviously quite unaware of his presence.

"No good wastin' the afternoon, Wingate——"

"I fancy it is going to clear off!" came Wingate's voice. "Anyhow, the game's not due for an hour yet. If the wind rises it will clear."

"It doesn't look like it."

"Well, we'll hope for the best, Hilton! The men will be ready, if we get a chance to play."

"Well, yes, but——"

"But what?" There was a rather sharp note in Wingate's voice.

(*Continued on next page.*)

Linesman Calling

If you're in doubt over any Soccer problem, don't scratch your hat till your hair comes through, but write to "Linesman," c/o The MAGNET, The Fleetway House, Farringdon Street, London, E.C.4. He will be only too pleased to give you his expert opinion.

WHO SCORED THAT ONE?

I GET a very real kick from the knowledge that when I talk to readers of the MAGNET they listen. This week I got an additional kick from the knowledge that my "listeners" not only hear at the particular moment, but they remember what I have told them. That's fine! But, of course, it also means that I have to be careful what I say; be wary lest I should contradict myself.

The letter which reminds me of these things comes from a Sheffield reader. I may as well quote it: "You have always insisted in your broadcast," he says, "that it does not matter who scores the goals in football so long as the goals are scored. But there are evidently some people even connected with the big clubs who don't agree. The other week I went to the Sheffield Wednesday ground and noticed that they have put up a big board, for all the spectators to see, and on this board there is posted, during the match, not only the position in which the game stands, but also the scorers of the goals. Numbers are put up when a goal is scored, and those numbers can be identified by a reference to the official programme. It seems that the Sheffield officials think it matters who scores."

Now it is quite true that this innovation has recently been installed on the Sheffield Wednesday ground, as my correspondent says. When a goal is scored by either side a number is put up. The number refers to a player, and he can then be identified because the players are numbered on the programme.

This is one of several new ideas initiated by Mr. William Walker—the former Aston Villa player we used to call Billy—who took over the managership not long ago.

I do not think, however, that it is quite correct to say that this new idea proves that there are football officials who think it matters who scores the goals. It doesn't matter to the club concerned. But the

Wednesday manager thinks it matters to the spectators who attend the games; that the name of the player who puts the ball into the net interests them. I quite agree. I believe the same idea would be appreciated on other football grounds. As to the view that this will encourage selfishness among the players I don't believe for a moment.

A GREAT RESPONSIBILITY!

BETWEEN the members of real football teams there is usually a spirit of comradeship, and without it no team can hope to succeed. I saw not long ago an interesting case of the players of a football team trying all they knew to enable a particular player to score. Arsenal were playing Crystal Palace in a Cup-tie. The Arsenal score had run up to half a dozen, and, of course, they were certain of victory. All the forwards except Bowden had scored at least one goal. So the rest of the players tried their utmost to make openings for Bowden to score, even sacrificing their own chances. That's the spirit!

In reply to another correspondent, the referee is definitely instructed not to stop the game for a free kick or even for a penalty-kick if he thinks that by so doing he will benefit the offending side.

This power to refrain from blowing the whistle puts a great responsibility on the shoulders of the referee, of course, as he may think a player who has been fouled is going to score, and then that player may fail to do so.

The recent Cup-tie between Tottenham Hotspur and Aston Villa reminded me of one of the strangest incidents I have ever heard of in football, and in a way it concerns this power to refrain rule. Many years ago Aston Villa and Tottenham were playing a Cup-tie on the Villa ground. One of the Tottenham players was fouled as he was making for goal and the referee was about to blow his whistle to stop the

game and give a free-kick to the Spurs. There was some dirt in the whistle, however, and it refused to function. While the referee was struggling with the whistle, the player who had been fouled recovered, and went on to score. A goal was duly awarded, which was quite right. But if that whistle had been in good working order Tottenham would have had a free-kick, not a goal, and they might not have won the match!

FIRST LEAGUE FOOTBALL IN FOUR DAYS!

CAN you tell me the name of the player who has made the quickest rise from obscurity to first-class football? This is another question which has reached me, and I am not sure that I can give a definite answer. But I can tell of a player with a record in this connection which would be difficult to beat. This is Harry Race, the inside-right of Notts Forest. Some seven or eight years ago Race, who lived in Durham, could not get a job in his native county, either at his ordinary work in a coalmine or with a football club. He tried to get a show with several first-class teams, but they would not have him. Eventually he wended his way. bit by bit, to Liverpool, and there so impressed the officials with his earnestness that they agreed to give him a trial in a Central League match. The game was duly played; Race did very well indeed, and as Liverpool had a mid-week match on their programme four days later and were in a dilemma for a forward, Race was put into the first team. What is more, he played very well with the first team, and scored a goal!

From obscurity to first-league football in four days! As I say this may not be a record rise, but we can certainly say that the player "raced" to the fore-front.

Now I'll turn to a technical point. A young full-back says that playing against a certain particularly clever player he is "given the slip" every time, and he asks for a tip which will save him this experience. I can certainly give him one tip which may come in useful, and that is not to go in to tackle at all, but to play what is called the stand-off game. There is one thing the very clever "diddling" wingers love and that is for full-backs to make flying tackles. The thing they do not love, is for full-backs to stand off, and wait for them. I know several clever wingers who are always held up by defenders who keep within a few yards of them. The winger cannot then slip the back, and is reduced to swinging the ball into the middle. Try this stand-off tactical idea.

"LINESMAN."

"Well, I don't see hangin' about! Blundell doesn't think there's much chance of a game to-day."

"He will be glad enough if a chance turns up! Look here, Hilton, don't be an ass! Blundell's got you down to play, and if you're thinking of going out of gates, wash it out."

"Well, I was thinkin'——"

"Wash it out!" said Wingate tersely.

"I don't see it!" There was a sulky sound in Cedric Hilton's voice. "What's the good of hangin' about wastin' time?"

"Any special attraction out of gates?"

"Well, the pictures at Courtfield would be better than loafin' about the House."

"A lot you care for the pictures at Courtfield!" said Wingate gruffly. "Don't be an ass!"

"Well, the pictures at Courtfield would be better than loafin' about the House."

"A lot you care for the pictures at Courtfield!" said Wingate gruffly. "Don't be an ass!"

"Well, I'm goin' out."

"You're not!"

"Who says I'm not?" Hilton's voice was angry now.

"I do!" said Wingate. "You're in the Fifth Form team; and ought to be glad of it! You're not letting Blundell down if there's a chance to play the match to-day; and I think there's a chance. You'll be on hand if you're wanted, like the other men."

"I shall suit myself about that!"

"You won't! I happen to be captain of the school and head of the games. You'll stay where you're wanted, Hilton! Has that cur Price been getting at you again?" added Wingate scornfully.

"I've had nothing to say to Price—and don't want to! But——"

"Well, that's that! You're staying in."

There was an angry mutter from Hilton that the listener did not catch. Then there was a sound of a fellow tramping away in the fog.

One of the two speakers had gone! The other was still standing not three yards from Price—which? Price guessed that it was the captain of Greyfriars, but he could not be sure. The stick slipped down from under his arm into his hand, and he grasped it hard.

"The silly ass!" he started a little as Wingate's voice came to his ears. "The silly owl!"

Having expressed his irritation in that exclamation, the Greyfriars captain moved away. Price heard his footsteps grinding on the gravel of the path.

His heart beat as he stole after him on tiptoe.

This was his chance!

Silent as the snake which in other respects he resembled, the cad of the Fifth tiptoed after the fellow he regarded as his enemy.

Wingate's burly figure loomed up in the mist in front of him. Price could have touched him by stretching out his hand.

His eyes burned.

The fog wrapped him like a blanket, there were no eyes to see! This was the fellow who had thrashed him like a fag! For a second more he hesitated, his coward heart quaking at the fear that Wingate might look round. But the Greyfriars captain had no suspicion that anyone was behind him in the fog —he had heard no sound of the stealthy feet. Price made up his mind at a jump. It was a chance of vengeance that would never recur—and it was safe—safe!

He leaped forward, and a violent shove in the back sent Wingate crashing on his face, taken utterly by surprise.

The next instant Price's knee was jammed in the small of his back. And the stick rose and fell, once, twice, thrice, with terrific force.

Lash! Lash! Lash!

Wingate, utterly amazed and astounded, was helpless for the moment. Then, as he heaved under his assailant, Price leaped away and vanished in the fog. Wingate scrambled to his knees, dizzy and dazed.

"Who—what——" he panted.

A vague sound came to him from the fog. That was all! His assailant was gone. The Greyfriars captain got on his feet. He had received only three swipes from the stick, but they had been dealt with terrific force, and he ached with pain.

"Who was that?" roared Wingate. "Who——"

His voice echoed through the fog. But he realised at once that his unknown assailant was not likely to

answer or to show up, and a chase in the blinding fog was futile. With a set face and glinting eyes, the Greyfriars captain tramped up the path towards the House.

THE THIRTEENTH CHAPTER.
Not According to Plan!

"**B**EAST!" murmured Billy Bunter.

Bunter was lost!

He blinked to and fro in thick fog, and took the spectacles from his fat little nose, rubbed the mist from them, replaced them, and blinked again.

But it was useless to blink.

Even with the aid of his spectacles the Owl of the Remove could not see two or three feet from his fat nose.

He was lost—in the Greyfriars quad —and where he was, and which way to turn, were mysteries to William George Bunter.

Bunter had not foreseen that when he left the House. Bunter never did foresee anything! He had calculated on the fog to hide him from all eyes! He had not calculated on it to hide everything from his own eyes! Once having missed the paths, Bunter was done!

"Beast!" he breathed.

He was referring to Price of the Fifth.

It was, of course, all Price's fault! But for that beast Price, Bunter would not have ventured out into the fog at all.

Having failed to receive any backing from Harry Wharton & Co., Bunter had resolved to "try it on" on his own! We was almost as keen for vengeance on Price as Price was for vengeance on Wingate! Like the cad of the Fifth, the Owl of the Remove realised that this was a chance that would not recur.

Not that he was thinking of whopping the Fifth-Form man all on his lonely own! Bunter was armed with a ripe egg, which he intended for his enemy! That egg had been overlooked in the study cupboard in Study No. 7 for some time, and when Bunter had spotted it there even he had been doubtful about disposing of it in the usual way. Now, however, he had found a use for it! He would have preferred to "wallop" Price, with the Famous Five holding him for the purpose; but the Famous Five had let him down—and wallopings were off! Still, if he landed that over-ripe egg full on Price's ill-favoured features, Bunter considered that he would have got a little of his own back!

"Bunging" a bad egg into a Fifth Form senior's face was, of course, a frightfully risky proceeding, in ordinary circumstances. It would have led to a fearful thrashing from the Fifth Former concerned, and perhaps from the "beak" as well; but in the fog, as Bunter astutely calculated, it was all right!

Bunter had it all cut and dried!

All he had to do was to run down Price, who was somewhere out of the House in the fog, "bung" the egg into his face, and vanish in the fog without being spotted!

It seemed simple enough when Bunter had planned it!

It was not so simple when he came to carry it out! In a few minutes, Bunter missed the path he was on, and found himself wandering—lost to the world!

So far from finding Price, Bunter was now in need of being found himself!

This was rather a "facer" for a vengeful fellow on the trail of vengeance!

"Beast!" groaned Bunter.

He groped about in the clinging mists,

"A fellow who would attack a man from behind is a rotter," said Price. "And it looks to me as if you did it, Hilton!"
Smack! Hilton's open palm struck Price across the mouth, and he went down with a crash on his back, and lay panting.
"You lying worm!" roared Hilton. "Get up, and I'll knock your words back down your throat!"

seeking a path. Thoughts of vengeance were abandoned—all Bunter wanted was to get back to the House.

Where was he?

Somewhere within the wide walls of the school, that was all he knew. He might be only a couple of yards from the House steps—he might be in the middle of the quad—really, he might be anywhere—there was no telling!

He groped on! His eyes and his spectacles were of little use to him; but he listened intently with his fat ears, hoping to hear some sound that would guide him. The bang of a door, the slam of a window, or a calling voice, would have been enough.

Suddenly he heard a sound in the fog. It was at a little distance, but the sound of a heavy fall came to his ears. Someone, apparently, was out in the fog, and had fallen over!

To Bunter's surprise, that sound was followed by another—three sharp cracks in swift succession, like pistol shots! It sounded like three terrific whacks with a stick! Who was whacking with a stick, and what he was whacking, and why, were mysteries to Bunter. He blinked through the thick mist in the direction of the startling sound in sheer wonder.

There was a sudden rush of footsteps. Before the fat Owl realised that the footsteps were coming in his direction, a running figure loomed out of the fog, right upon him and there was a crash.

"Ooogh!" gasped Bunter.

He went over backwards as if a cannon-shot had struck him. And the fellow who had run into him, taken as much by surprise as Bunter was, sprawled headlong over him, panting.

"Urrrrggh!" gasped Bunter.

There was a cracking sound! Bunter had forgotten the ripe egg in his fat

hand. He was reminded of it now! That egg was jammed between Bunter and the fellow who had fallen on him. Naturally, it broke; and the scent that spread around was thicker than the fog!

"Ow! Ooogh! Who—urrrggh——" gurgled Bunter. He grabbed wildly at the sprawling figure over him. "Ow! Knocking a fellow over—ow! Who are you, you beast—yow-wow! Oooh!"

The face that was only a few inches from Bunter's was the face of Stephen Price of the Fifth! At a distance of only a few inches, even Bunter could see it clearly enough; and even at that startling moment, Bunter could not help noting the white, stricken terror in it.

But it was only for a moment that he saw it. Almost in a moment the other fellow leaped away and vanished.

Bunter sat up dizzily.

"Urrrggh!" he gasped. "That was that beast Price—gurrrggh!"

He set his spectacles straight on his fat little nose, and blinked round him. Price was gone! Not even a sound of his running feet came back.

"Ow! Beast!" gasped Bunter. "Grooogh!"

He had to remember the egg!

Price, no doubt, had got some of it; but most of it was smeared over Bunter! And the scent of it was horrid.

Sitting on the cold, unsympathetic earth, Billy Bunter jerked out his handkerchief and dabbed at that horrid egg. From a distance he heard a shout, which he recognised as Wingate's voice. But it was not repeated. He dabbed at the egg. He dabbed and dabbed and dabbed. Some was on his waistcoat, some had gone down his neck. From the bottom of his fat heart, Bunter wished that he had never brought out that egg for Price of the Fifth!

He staggered to his feet at last.

He had found Price in the fog—or, rather, Price had found him! He had got most of the ripe egg himself! And he was still lost!

"Oh lor'!" groaned Bunter.

Haunted by the clinging aroma of the egg, the fat Owl groped and stumbled and fumbled on. Suddenly his feet caught in something, and he went headlong

Bump!

"Yarooooh!" roared Bunter.

He sprawled in damp grass! Sitting up, he groped about him, and made the discovery that he had fallen over a low chain, stretched between two low posts! But he knew where he was now—he had stumbled over the chains of the Sixth-Form green Picking himself up, he groped to the path beside the green, and groped and fumbled away towards the House, feeling every inch of the way, in terror of getting lost again.

He gasped with relief at the sight of an arched doorway at last. A gleam of light came to his eyes—the electric light was on in the House. He gurgled, and stumbled in.

"Hallo, hallo, hallo!"

Bob Cherry had come along to look out at the weather. He forgot the weather, and stared at Billy Bunter.

Bunter was damp and muddy and eggy. There was an eggy aroma hanging round him. Bob sniffed.

"What the thump——" he ejaculated.

"Oh dear!" gasped Bunter. "Thank goodness I've got in. Oh lor'! All your fault, you beast! If you'd come out with me this wouldn't have happened!"

"What the dickens did you go out in the fog for, you fat duffer?" demanded Bob.

"I was going after that beast Price!"

groaned Bunter. "I had an egg for him—— I was going to bung it at him, you know——"

"You howling ass!"

"Beast! And he ran into me in the fog, and burst the egg all over me——".

"Ha, ha, ha!" roared Bob Cherry.

"And I'm all eggy——"

"Ha, ha, ha!"

"And sticky——"

"Ha, ha, ha!"

"Beast!" roared Bunter, and he rolled on in search of a wash—even Bunter, who had a rooted objection to washing, as a rule, realising that he was in need of a wash now. He left Bob roaring with laughter. Bunter on the trail of vengeance struck Bob Cherry as comic. And Bob's merry roar followed the eggy Owl as he went.

———

THE FOURTEENTH CHAPTER.

Startling!

"HEARD?" asked the Bounder, with a grin.

"Which and what?" yawned Peter Todd.

"About Wingate——"

"What about Wingate?" asked two or three voices.

"He's been whopped!"

There was a buzz in the Rag. A crowd of fellows had gathered there, chiefly occupied in making uncomplimentary remarks about the weather. But they forgot the weather as Smithy announced the startling news.

"Wingate—whopped!" gasped Harry Wharton.

"Gammon!"

"Rot!"

"The rotfulness is terrific."

"Tell us another, Smithy! An easier one."

"Honest Injun!" grinned the Bounder. "It's going the rounds already. Frightfully important matter, you know! Any of us men can be whopped, any old time; and who cares a brass farthing? But when one of the high and mighty Sixth gets a few on his bags——"

"Well, it's a jolly serious thing, if the head prefect of the school has been whopped!" said Harry Wharton, staring at the Bounder "But is it true?"

"It's the sack for somebody!" said Frank Nugent. "What silly idiot has been pitching into Wingate?"

"Nobody knows," grinned Smithy. "A rather deep card, whoever he was. From what I hear, Wingate had gone down to the football field to have a squint at it—they've got a match on in the Upper School, you know. Coming back to the House, he was barged over in the fog——"

"Oh, my hat!"

"Some person or persons unknown, as they say in the police reports," chuckled the Bounder "Whoever it was, barged Wingate over from behind, and laid into him with a cane, or a stick—three of the best!"

"Great pip!"

"The pipfulness is preposterous!"

"And Wingate never saw him?" asked Harry.

"So they say. The jolly old fog gave him a chance—he whopped Wingate, and hooked it before he could be spotted. Never thought of leavin' his card, it seems."

"Ha, ha, ha!"

"But who——" gasped Bob Cherry.

"Echo answers who," said Smithy. "Whoever it was, he will keep it fearfully dark if he can—it's the sack for pitching into a prefect. Aren't the prefects the jolly old Palladium of a

public school?" And the Bounder chortled, evidently much amused.

"Some frightfully reckless ass, I should say!" remarked Squiff. "But who the deuce could want to whop old Wingate? He's got hardly an enemy in the school."

"He's got a few," said Johnny Bull dryly. "Fellows he's called to order. You know anything about it, Skinner?"

"I!" ejaculated Skinner. "What do you mean, you silly ass?"

"Well, Wingate's whopped you twice this week——"

"You silly chump!" howled Skinner. "Think I'm idiot enough to lay into a prefect? I'm glad he got it, if you come to that; but——"

"Catch Skinner taking the risk!" grinned the Bounder. "I fancy it was one of the seniors—most likely a Sixth Form man. Or——" The Bounder broke off with a whistle.

"Or what?" asked Wharton.

"Might have been a Fifth Form man!" grinned Smithy. "There's a Fifth Form man who's been feelin' jolly ratty with Wingate lately."

"If you mean Price——"

"Better name no names!" chuckled Smithy. "'Tain't safe. But if I were Wingate, I'd ask Pricey where he was at the time."

"Price hasn't the nerve, I imagine," said Wharton. "It wants a lot of nerve to handle the captain of the school."

"Not from behind. And Pricey is the man for that. But if it was Pricey, you can bet that he's covered up his tracks, safe and sound. He's deep."

There was a buzz of excited discussion in the Rag. It was interrupted by the arrival of Billy Bunter, fresh from his recent wash—looking newly swept and garnished, so to speak.

"I say, you fellows," squeaked Bunter, his little round eyes gleaming with excitement behind his big, round spectacles.

"Hallo, hallo, hallo! What's the latest, Bunter?"

"I say, you fellows, have you heard?" howled Bunter. "Wingate's been whopped——"

"We've had that from Smithy!" said Harry Wharton, laughing.

"Oh!" said Bunter, disappointed, Bunter liked to be first with the news. "Well, I'll bet I know more than Smithy does. I say, all the Sixth are jabbering about it, like a lot of old hens. They say that the Head is going to hold an inquiry. I say, Wingate was knocked down from behind, and stunned——"

"Stunned!" yelled the juniors.

"Yes, stunned! And as he lay senseless, he was beaten to a jelly. Most of his bones broken——"

"Go it!"

"It's a fact, you fellows! He tottered into the House groaning horribly, covered with blood——"

"While he was senseless?" asked Skinner.

"Ha, ha ha!"

"No you ass—after he recovered his senses. Of course, he recovered his senses before he tottered into the House. I hear that he's going into sanny, and the doctor's sent for."

"Not the undertaker?" asked Skinner

"Oh, really, Skinner! He's an absolute wreck!" said Bunter impressively. "Can't walk or talk, you know. He was unable to utter a word when he got in. He told the Head——"

"Oh my hat!"

"Ha, ha, ha!"

"He's lying in his study now——" went on Bunter.

"While you're lying here?"

"Beast! He's lying in his study

groaning fearfully. If you go along to the Sixth, you'll hear him groaning. Awful!" said Bunter. "It's rather heartless to cackle when poor old Wingate is lying on his back, unable to utter a sound, and groaning horribly, and——"

"Ha, ha, ha!"

"Of course, it rather serves him right," went on Bunter. "He's a beast; he whopped me the other day for smoking—I mean, he made out that I'd been smoking, and whopped me. I say, you fellows, nobody seems to know who pitched into him, or just when it happened. But there's no doubt that he's fearfully injured—crippled for life, I believe—he may never be able to walk again——"

Wingate of the Sixth at that moment walked into the Rag. All eyes turned on him at once.

Evidently Bunter's account was exaggerated.

Not only could Wingate walk, but there were no signs whatever of injuries, fearful or otherwise. He looked his usual self, except that his face was set and grim, and that there was a gleam in his eyes. He glanced sharply over the crowd of juniors, at face after face.

"Any fellow here been out in the quad since dinner?" he rapped out.

There was no answer. The fog had not tempted the juniors out of doors. But Bob Cherry glanced at Bunter.

Bunter looked alarmed.

"Better answer, you fat ass!" whispered Bob.

"Oh, really, Cherry——"

"I want to know if any fellow has been out of the House?" said the Greyfriars captain. "Sharp's the word!"

"Not guilty, my lord!" said the Bounder.

Wingate gave him a look. If the unknown fellow who had attacked him was a Removite, the reckless, mutinous Smithy was the most likely.

"I don't think any Remove man has been out, Wingate," said Harry Wharton. "It's too jolly thick in the quad——"

"Speak up, you blithering fat idiot!" whispered Bob to Bunter. "You've nothing to be afraid of, you ass!"

"I haven't been out!" hissed Bunter.

"You fat chump, I saw you come in."

"I mean—I—I mean, I—I—shut up, you beast! Think I'm going to have it put on me?" hissed Bunter.

"You howling ass——"

"Beast!"

Wingate gave another sharp glance over the fellows in the Rag, and then went out. He left a buzz of excited discussion behind him. Billy Bunter's fat voice did not join in it. He rolled out of the Rag; for once having nothing to say, which was unusual; and for once, doing some thinking, which was still more unusual.

That afternoon, fog-bound in the House, the Greyfriars fellows had dismally expected the dullest of dull times. Instead of which they had been unexpectedly provided with the sensation of the term. The "whopping" of a prefect, who was also captain of the school, was an utterly unheard-of and unprecedented occurrence. It was a matter that the Head was bound to take up. It was a matter that could hardly end in anything but the expulsion of the offender, if and when detected. It was a thrilling excitement, for all the fellows in all the Forms, from the Sixth to the Second. All over Greyfriars, that afternoon, fellows were asking themselves, and one another, the question to which, so far, there was no answer—who whopped Wingate?

THE FIFTEENTH CHAPTER.
Coming to Blows!

"WAS it you?"

Cedric Hilton asked that question as he came into his study in the Fifth.

Price raised his eyebrows.

He was seated at the study table with books before him. Not a studious youth, as a rule, Price seemed to be spending that foggy afternoon "swotting."

"Was what me?" he asked.

"You know what I mean?" snapped Hilton.

"Not the foggiest!" said Price easily. "Has anything happened?"

"Wasn't Wingate here?"

"Wingate! He looked in about a quarter of an hour ago, and asked me if I'd been out of the House since dinner. I told him I hadn't."

"You told him you hadn't," repeated Hilton.

"Naturally, as I've been swotting at this stuff for Prout ever since dinner. He didn't even say why he wanted to know," yawned Price. "If the fog clears off, I'm going out when I'm through. You comin'? I fancy your footer's off for to-day."

Hilton looked long and hard at his study-mate. The Bounder was not the only fellow who had thought of Price, when the news came out that Wingate had been attacked in the fog in the quadrangle.

But Price's face was unconcerned.

He was, so far as he could see, perfectly safe. He was absolutely certain that Wingate had not even seen him, let alone recognised him. He had lost no time in getting back to the House; and he got in by a back window, to make assurance doubly sure. He was back in his study, sitting at his books, before the row started.

There was only one dubious point—he had run into Billy Bunter and knocked him over, in the fog, in his flight. He had glimpsed the fat face and spectacles, and knew that the fellow he had knocked over was the Owl of the Remove.

But he did not believe that Bunter had recognised him. The fog was thick, the fat Owl was short-sighted, and he had been winded, and gasping for breath; and Price had vanished again almost instantly. It was an unfortunate happening, in the circumstances; but Price did not believe that it spelled danger. He was, of course, quite unaware that it was specially on his account that Bunter had been out in the quad—that he had been in the fat Owl's mind all the time. Still less was he aware that Bunter had, in point of fact, recognised him, and already mentioned the meeting to another Remove fellow. Had Stephen Price been aware of all that, he would hardly have looked so cool and unconcerned.

He yawned, as if tired from his work, and laid down his pen. Through the open doorway came a buzz of voices from the passage. Several of the Fifth were discussing the matter there, and Coker's bull voice could be heard.

"Has anythin' happened?" he asked again. "Wingate looked as grim as a gorgon when he looked in here. He's got his jolly old back up about somethin'. You been rowing with him!"

"I had a few words with him in the quad," said Hilton. "So far as I can make out, he was attacked a few minutes afterwards."

"Attacked!" repeated Price.

"Yes. Some fellow knocked him over and laid into him with a stick."

Price whistled.

"Sure you've got it right?" he asked. "That sounds pretty steep to me."

"The whole House is buzzing with it," said Hilton curtly. "It's up before the Head."

"Yes, I suppose they'd make a fuss about it," drawled Price. "Common mortals mustn't lay their hands on the great panjandrum. You must have been a fool to do it, Cedric."

Hilton jumped.

"I!" he ejaculated.

"Wasn't it you?"

"What do you mean?" shouted Hilton furiously. "Do you dare?" He made a stride towards the fellow at the table.

"Keep cool!" said Price calmly. "You asked me if it was I, before I knew that anythin' had happened at all. I don't see why I shouldn't return the compliment, and ask you whether it was you—was it?"

"You know it wasn't!"

"I don't know anything of the sort," said Price deliberately. "You've admitted that you were practically on the spot at the time, at all events. Has it come out that anyone else was?"

"Nobody knows, so far. The prefects are going up and down the House asking fellows questions. I hear that the Head has given orders that all fellows who were out of the House are to be reported to him so that he can question them."

"That includes you."

"Of course it does!" said Hilton angrily. "But nobody, I suppose, is going to suspect me of attacking a fellow from behind. If I hit Wingate, I should hit him facing him."

(Continued on next page.)

"I'm going to speak to Price." It was Coker's bull voice in the passage. "I'm going to ask him where he was."

Hilton's lip curled.

"I'm not the only man in the Fifth who thought of you, Pricey," he remarked.

"I may not be the only man in the Fifth who's thought of you," said Price venomously. "If you did it, you won't find it easy to land it on me."

"You rotter——"

"Easy enough to call a fellow names," said Price, raising his voice a little as Coker's heavy footsteps came tramping towards the half-open door. "But a fellow who would attack a man from behind is a rotter, if you like, and it looks to me as if you did it, Hilton. I shan't say so outside this study, but if you did it——"

Coker of the Fifth stared in. He had heard every word uttered by Price as he came to the door.

He stared blankly at Hilton.

"You!" he ejaculated. "Was it you, Hilton? My hat, if it turns out to be you, you rotter——"

"You silly fool!" yelled Hilton. "I know no more about it than you do."

"Well, I came here to speak to Price," said Coker. "I was going to ask you, Price, where you were when Wingate was whopped. We all jolly well know what you feel like about Wingate whopping you in this very study——"

"My dear man, I haven't been out of the House," drawled Price. "If you want to ask questions in this study, you'd better ask a fellow who was. Hilton may be able to tell you somethin'."

Horace Coker stared at Hilton again.

"Have you been out of the House?" he asked.

"Find out!" snapped Hilton.

He had no mind to be questioned by the egregious Coker.

"That's not an answer," said Coker.

"It's all you'll get from me."

"Look here——"

"Oh, don't barge into my study, fathead! Run away and play."

"That won't do," said Coker quietly. "If you can't answer a plain question plainly, Hilton, it looks to me——"

"Get out!"

Hilton slammed the door. Coker got out in rather a hurry, his nose having a narrow escape from the slamming door.

Price laughed.

"That sort of thing won't wash," he remarked. "If you want to keep it dark, old man, that's not the way."

Hilton's eyes glittered at him. His suspicion was strong that Price was the guilty party, though he had no doubt that the wary rascal had covered up his tracks too carefully to be in much danger of detection.

"I can see your game, you rotter!" he said, between his teeth. "Nobody will ever know who whopped Wingate; and you'd like to put a spoke in my wheel by putting it about that I did it. That fool Coker's got it into his thick head already."

"Looks like it," agreed Price. "And I fancy Wingate will remember that you were on the spot, and nobody else was. Look here! What's the good of gammoning? You know you did it!"

Hilton's eyes blazed, and he fairly jumped at his whilom friend.

Smack!

His open hand came across Price's sallow cheek with a crack like that of a pistol.

Price leaped up from the table, his eyes burning, his chair flying backwards with a crash.

THE MAGNET LIBRARY.—No. 1,359.

"You rotter!" he yelled. "You dare——"

"Now put up your hands!" said Hilton, between his teeth, and he came at Price, hitting out as he came.

Price had no choice about putting up his hands. He was no fighting-man. But there was no help for it, and he put his hands up, and in a moment there was a fierce scrap going on in the study.

"Hallo! Is that a fight?" came Potter's voice from the passage. The door was thrown open, and half a dozen Fifth Form men stared in.

Crash!

Price went down on his back, and lay panting. Hilton stood over him with clenched fists and blazing eyes.

"Get up, you cad!" he shouted. "Get up and have some more!"

"You rotter!" panted Price. "You bully! Keep off, you hound!"

"What's the row about?" asked Greene of the Fifth.

"What's it about?" snarled Price. "It's about what's happened to Wingate. Hilton's pitching into me because I told him I knew he had done it—that's what the row's about!"

"You lying worm!" roared Hilton. "Get up, and I'll knock that back down your throat!"

Price did not get up. He lay on his elbow, panting and snarling. The Fifth Form men in the doorway exchanged glances.

With a glare of scorn at the sprawling senior, Hilton stalked out of the study. The fellows made room for him to pass, and he went down the passage. Then Price slowly picked himself up.

"You think it was Hilton?" asked Potter.

"I know it was!" snarled Price. "And I fancy you'll find that Wingate knows it, too!" He wiped a trickle of crimson from his nose. "He's admitted that he was there, right on the spot—and Wingate knows that! You can ask Wingate if you want it from him!"

"I'll jolly well ask Wingate!" said Coker, and he marched off.

Price shut the study door.

He dabbed his nose, which persisted in trickling red. That nose was rather damaged. But Price was not dissatisfied. Nobody would ever know for certain who had whopped Wingate—but a good many fellows would suspect Hilton—very possibly, Wingate himself!

The schemer of the Fifth had killed two birds with one stone—not only had he returned Wingate's whopping, but he had put the suspicion of that cowardly act on the fellow who had dropped him.

Wingate was whopped—Hilton was under suspicion—and the cad of the Fifth was secure—doubly secure! Fortunately, perhaps, for his satisfaction and peace of mind, Price had forgotten the insignificant and unimportant existence of Billy Bunter of the Remove!

THE SIXTEENTH CHAPTER.
Bunter's Secret!

"WHO whopped Wingate?"

"Ask us another!"

It was the one topic of Greyfriars. It was discussed in all the studies. After prep, a crowd of juniors in the Rag were discussing it again. Nothing had come to light. It looked as if the matter was going to remain a mystery—with all sorts of doubts and suspicions abroad.

The name of Hilton of the Fifth was bandied up and down the passages. Owing to the thick fog that afternoon the assailant had escaped unrecognised—but, owing to that same fog, hardly any fellows had been out of the House. That boiled it down, so to speak, to a very few possible "suspects."

"I'd have bet a pony to a peanut that it was Price!" the Bounder remarked. "But it seems that Pricey was in his study, swotting for Prout. I hear that he's said out plain that it was Hilton."

"Blessed if it doesn't look like it!" said Harry Wharton. "It's come out now who was out of the House at the time. Gwynne of the Sixth—but he's a pal of Wingate, and that washes him out. Hobby of the Shell had groped over to the tuckshop, but Hoskins and Stewart were with him—and they're witnesses for one another. Tubb of the Third was out of doors somewhere—but Tubby——"

There was a laugh. A Third Form fag was not a likely object of suspicion in such a case.

"And Hilton!" added Wharton. "It seems that Hilton was not only out of the House, but had been speaking to Wingate, in the fog, only a minute or two before he was attacked. So he was right on the spot."

"But why should he?" asked Nugent. "They've been friendly enough this term. Hilton's taken up Soccer, and Wingate has been backing him up. Have they had a row?"

"Must have had, if it was Hilton that pitched into him," said Peter Todd. "Likely enough, too. But——"

Harry Wharton shook his head.

"I fancy there was somebody else out of the House who hasn't owned up to it," he said. "He wouldn't, of course, if he had whopped Wingate! If it comes out that another fellow was out, and hasn't admitted it, they won't have far to look for the fellow who whopped Wingate."

"Oh lor'!" murmured Billy Bunter.

Bunter was not taking part in the discussion. He was listening to it with both his fat ears, in a very worried frame of mind.

He blinked uneasily at Bob Cherry.

Bob was the only fellow who knew that Bunter had been out at that critical time. Bob had not forgotten seeing Bunter come in, and had not forgotten what the fat Owl had told him when he came in. From that, Bob had drawn his own conclusions; but he had not stated them in public. It was not his business to catch the offender, or to mention Bunter's name. But he felt very uncomfortable at keeping his knowledge to himself.

"Might have been anybody!" said the Bounder thoughtfully. "Even a fag like Tubb could have done it, if he'd wanted to. You see, Wingate was barged over suddenly from behind, and whopped before he knew what was happening. Then the fellow bolted in the fog. If it comes out that any chap was out of the House, and has denied it——"

"That will settle it!" said Johnny Bull.

"But, who the dickens——" said Squiff.

"It's a jolly old mystery!"

"Bunter——" began Harry Wharton.

Billy Bunter jumped up.

"You beast!" he yelled.

The captain of the Remove glanced round at him.

"You there, fathead? I was going to say——"

"Beast! It wasn't me!"

Wharton stared at him, and burst into a laugh.

"You blithering Owl——"

"It wasn't!" roared Bunter. "I wouldn't have touched him! As if I'd whop Wingate! I'd like to, of course, but——"

"Ha, ha, ha!"

" You're a pretty complete rotter, Price," said Wingate, scornfully. " But I'm not keen on getting a Greyfriars man sacked on a personal matter. I'll deal with you myself. Trot out the boxing-gloves, Hilton !" Hilton obliged, and the Greyfriars captain tossed a pair across to Price. " Ready ?" he asked.

- "But I didn't ! You make out that it was me, Wharton——"

"You howling ass !" roared Wharton. "I was going to say——"

"Beast !"

"I was going to say——"

"Rotter !"

"Will you let a fellow speak ?" hooted Wharton. "I was going to say that you told us that Price of the Fifth had gone out, some time before it happened, when you wanted us to go after him with you, and——"

"I didn't !" gasped Bunter.

"You didn't ?" yelled Wharton.

"No, I jolly well didn't ! I never even thought of going after Price, and I never asked you fellows to back me up, and hadn't the faintest idea of bagging him and walloping him. I never even dreamed of going out. It was too foggy for me. I never spoke to you fellows at all——"

"Oh, my hat !"

"And after I spoke to you, I went to my study——"

"Ha, ha, ha !"

"And stayed there !" asserted Bunter. "As for going out after Price, it never even crossed my mind. If that old egg is gone from the study, I expect Toddy chucked it away. I never took it out to bung at Price."

"Well, my hat !" said the captain of the Remove, staring blankly at the fat Owl. All eyes in the Rag were turned on Bunter now. Bob Cherry grinned. He had felt bound not to mention what he knew of Bunter's proceedings that eventful afternoon ; but Billy Bunter had his own inimitable way of keeping a secret !

"I never stepped outside the House !" went on Bunter firmly. "Why, you beast, if they knew I was out at the time, they'd make out that I whopped Wingate ! You jolly well know that ! You're trying to put it on me, you

rotter. Bob Cherry jolly well knows that I wasn't out ! He saw me come in !"

"Ha, ha, ha !" shrieked the Removites.

"You can cackle !" howled Bunter. "But I think it's pretty sickening to make out that I did it ! Beasts !"

"So you were out of the House, Bunter ?" yelled Skinner.

"I wasn't !" roared Bunter.

"Bunter all the time !" chortled Skinner. "Fancy Bunter having the nerve to pitch into old Wingate ! No wonder he tackled him from behind !"

"I didn't !" shrieked Bunter.

"Bunter, you awful ass !" gasped Wharton. "Surely you weren't idiot enough——"

"Isn't he idiot enough for anything ?" chuckled Skinner. "Wingate whopped him for smoking the other day, and Bunter got his own back in the fog this afternoon ! What a nerve !"

"Was it you, Bunter ?"

"Fancy Bunter——"

"I say, you fellows," howled Billy Bunter, in great alarm, "it wasn't me ! I tell you I wasn't out of the House !"

"We jolly well know you were !" grinned Skinner. "Did Bob Cherry see you come in when you hadn't been out ?"

"Yes, exactly—I—I mean——"

"Ha, ha, ha !"

"I mean, he didn't see me come in ! He never saw me at all ! I wasn't out of the House ! I was in the Rag all the time, sitting over the fire——"

"You've just told us you were in your study !" chortled the Bounder.

"I—I mean, I was in my study, sitting over the fire——"

"Try again !" grinned Peter Todd. "I was in the study, old fat bean, and didn't come down till I heard the row on. If you were there, I never saw you."

"I—I—I mean, I—I was in Quelch's study ! He—he—he sent for me about some lines——"

"Will Quelch say so if they ask him ?" chuckled Skinner.

"Oh lor' ! I—I mean, I—I was in Hall——"

"So was I," said Bolsover major, "and you jolly well weren't there, you fat fibber !"

"I—I mean——"

Billy Bunter paused, blinking dismally at the grinning Removites. Generally Bunter was not at a loss for a fib. But he was at a loss now. It was not an easy matter to prove an "alibi." The fog had kept nearly all the fellows in the House, and there was somebody or other to prove that Bunter hadn't been anywhere where he claimed to have been.

"Give him time !" chortled the Bounder. "He will make up a good one if he's given time ! Weren't you in the library, Bunter ?"

"Oh, yes ! Exactly !" gasped Bunter, catching at a straw like a drowning man. "That—that's just where I was, Smithy !"

"Then you're all right !" said Smithy. "I happen to know that the Head was in the library, so he will be a witness for you !"

"Oh lor' !"

"Ha, ha, ha !"

"I—I mean, I wasn't in the library, you beast, Smithy !"

"Ha, ha, ha !"

"You blithering bandersnatch !" roared Bob Cherry. "Why can't you tell the truth for once ? If you owned up when Wingate asked us whether any of us were out of the House——"

"I'll watch it !" gasped Bunter. "The beast jolly well knows that I'd like to whop him, and he would have believed that——"

"We'd better keep this dark, you men!" grinned Skinner. "It's the sack for Bunter if it comes out!"

"I never did it!" wailed Bunter. "You beast, Skinner——"

"We jolly well know you did!" said Skinner. "What beats me is where you got the nerve from! Whopping the captain of the school——"

"I didn't!" shrieked Bunter. "I never went into the quad at all, and I jolly well saw another fellow there, too, at the time——"

"Ha, ha, ha!"

"Whom did you see there?" demanded Wharton.

"Oh, nobody! I wasn't out of the House, you know!"

"Did you see Price?"

"How could I when I wasn't there? He never barged into me and burst that egg all over my waistcoat! I never told Bob Cherry that he did—did I, Bob, old chap?"

"You did!" answered Bob.

"Beast!" roared Bunter.

"Ha, ha, ha!"

"I say, you fellows, don't you get saying that I was out of the House!" implored Bunter. "They'll all think it was me! That beast Price would say so, too! He's making out that it was Hilton now, but he'd just as soon make out that it was me! And Wingate knows I'd like to whop him——"

"Thank you, Bunter!" said a quiet voice.

"Oh lor'!"

Billy Bunter spun round like a fat humming-top, and his eyes almost popped through his spectacles at the sight of Wingate of the Sixth, standing in the doorway of the Rag.

"Dorm!" said Wingate in the same quiet tone. "Gwynne, old man"—he called to another Sixth Form man in the passage—"will you see lights out for these young sweeps? I've got to talk to Bunter for a few minutes!"

"Oh crikey!" groaned Bunter.

And the Removites marched off to their dormitory, leaving Billy Bunter with the captain of Greyfriars!

THE SEVENTEENTH CHAPTER.
Brought to Book!

PRICE of the Fifth smiled. Prep was over in the Fifth, and in that study not a word had passed between the two former friends during prep. Cedric Hilton rose, and pushed his books away, and, still without a word, turned to the door.

There was a dark cloud on his handsome face. Price passed his hand over his nose, which still felt rather painful. But he was solaced by the cloud on Hilton's face, and he smiled. The fellow who had turned him down was under suspicion, and he, after his revenge on the captain of the school, was perfectly safe. He felt that he had reason to be satisfied.

If he had had any uneasiness on the score of that unlucky meeting with Bunter in the quad, it had evaporated now. Nothing had come to light; it was not even known that the fat Owl had been out of doors. Obviously—to Price—Bunter had not known, in the fog, who it was that had barged him over; on that side he was quite secure. And he had put a very effective spoke in Hilton's wheel—the one-time scapegrace would hardly keep on pally terms with the games men when he was suspected of a miserable, cowardly attack on the head of the games.

Price's satisfaction was keen—but it THE MAGNET LIBRARY.—No. 1,359.

was destined to be short-lived. There was a tap at the door, and Wingate came in.

Hilton gave him a sullen look.

"Want me?" he asked, with a half-sneer.

And Price smiled again. His impression, for the moment, was that the suspected Fifth Form man was to be called up before the prefects.

But the smile faded from his face at Wingate's reply.

"No; I want Price."

The Greyfriars captain came to the table and stood looking across it at the cad of the Fifth. Stephen Price felt his heart beating rather unpleasantly. He told himself that nothing could possibly have been discovered—that nothing could have come out; but Wingate's steady gaze disconcerted him.

"You've told me, Price, that you were not out of the House this afternoon," said Wingate quietly.

"That's so!" assented Price.

"I found you in this study when I came in——"

"I'd been here over an hour, then, swotting for old Prout! What about it?" drawled Price. But there was a slight tremble in his drawl.

"You did not barge me over from behind in the fog—and whop me before I could make a move?"

"Hardly!"

"You did not bolt in the fog?"

"I've said not."

"You did not run into a junior who happened to be out of the House?"

Price's heart gave a jump.

"No!" he muttered.

"A Remove junior who, as I've just learned, had a grudge against you, and had gone out with some fatheaded intention of biffing an egg at you and dodging away in the fog."

"Oh, my hat!" ejaculated Hilton, and he smiled. It was his turn to smile now! Certainly there was no trace of smiling about Price!

Wingate glanced round at him.

"I'm sorry, Hilton, if I let the idea come into my head for a moment that it was you that did that rotten, cowardly thing," he said. "I know now that it was Price."

"It was not!" said Price between his teeth. "And I defy you to prove it!"

"You mean that you did not know that Bunter of the Remove had recognised you?" said Wingate contemptuously. "As it happens, he did. The young ass was keeping it dark because he was afraid he might be suspected of having done the trick himself."

"If he was on the spot probably he did!"

"I think not! I've questioned the young ass, and I think I've got the truth out of him. But if you deny it——"

"Every word!" hissed Price.

"Very well," said Wingate grimly. "I've sent Bunter to his dormitory now, but it will come before the Head in the morning. I dare say Dr. Locke will be able to settle where the truth is in the matter. If it comes before the Head you know what to expect. That's all!"

Price's face was like chalk. The bare thought of standing before the Head and desperately denying what was obviously true made his heart sink. It was the "sack" for whopping a prefect! But from one of Wingate's words the wretched, detected schemer drew a gleam of hope. If it came before the Head! If!

"Stop!" breathed Price. The Greyfriars captain's hand was on the door.

Wingate turned.

"Well?"

"Give a fellow a chance!" muttered Price huskily. "You said if—if it comes before the Head! It needn't!"

"The Head has left it to me to deal with, or report to him, as I think fit! If I tell him I've dealt with the matter that will be sufficient. If you choose to tell the truth——"

"You'll deal with the matter?"

"Yes."

"Oh!" gasped Price.

"You're a pretty complete rotter, Price!" said the Greyfriars captain scornfully. "But I'm not keen on getting a Greyfriars man sacked on a personal matter. But—the truth!"

Price licked his dry lips.

"I—I own up!" he muttered. "It was because—well, you know why it was. You made me look a fool to all the Fifth, and—and——"

Wingate nodded.

"Quite! I've said that I'll deal with the matter myself—and I will! Got any gloves here, Hilton?"

"Eh? Yes!"

"Trot them out!"

Hilton grinned and sorted out the boxing-gloves. Wingate tossed a pair across the table to Price.

"Ready?" he asked.

Price rose slowly to his feet. It was better than going up before the Head to be sacked! He realised that! But during the next ten minutes he rather doubted it!

*   *   *   *   *

"I say, you fellows, seen Price?"

And Billy Bunter chortled.

Bunter was feeling merry and bright that morning!

Who whopped Wingate was no longer a mystery!

There had been no official statement on the subject. But there was talk in the Fifth and Sixth which reached the ears of the juniors. And if anyone had doubted it, the condition of Stephen Price that day would have banished all doubts.

He had not gone up to the Head to be sacked, he had not had a "prefects' beating," but that he had been severely "through it" was only too clear from his aspect. Wingate, evidently, had settled the affair, more in accordance with the customs of the Remove than with those of the Sixth Form! And it was days before Price recovered from that terrific thrashing. And—though he was not much given to repentance—it was probable that he repented very deeply and sincerely of having "whopped" Wingate!

THE END.

(Look out for another grand long story of your old favourites—Harry Wharton & Co. in next week's MAGNET, entitled: "THE MYSTERY OF THE HEAD'S HAT!" You'll vote it one of Frank Richard's extra-specials, chums!)

The MAN BEHIND the SCENES!

BY HEDLEY SCOTT

Starring FERRERS LOCKE, DETECTIVE, and his clever boy assistant, JACK DRAKE.

HOW THE STORY STARTED.

CHRISTOPHER DEAN is attempting a double Atlantic flight when his machine is wrecked by a bomb which has been cunningly hidden in the fuselage. Clinging to the wreckage, Christopher encloses his log-book and a piece of the bomb in a vacuum flask which he tosses into the sea. The flask is picked up by some Greyfriars boys with whom FERRERS LOCKE, the famous detective, has been spending the day. Locke suspects MERVYN VILLIERS and sets JACK DRAKE to watch the house. Meanwhile, he discovers that a big insurance was effected on Dean's life by JULIUS TANKERHEAD—an old jail-bird friend of Villiers. Villiers, however, denies all knowledge of the man, yet within a few moments of that denial, Jack Drake phones through to his chief with the information that Tankerhead has just called on Villiers and was greeted like an old friend.

(Now read on.)

" Bert Entwistle ! "

"COME back at once, my lad—as quickly as you can !"

With that sharp command to his assistant, Ferrers Locke replaced the telephone receiver, and began to walk up and down the thick pile carpet, his head sunk upon his chest, his brow furrowed in deep concentration.

He had made up his mind to a certain course of action when Jack Drake arrived.

"Here we are, guv'nor !" exclaimed the youngster boisterously. "Took a taxi !"

"Good lad !" smiled the great detective. "Now listen to what I've got to say ! Listen carefully !"

"O.K., guv'nor !"

"To-morrow, my lad, you will be Bert Entwistle, of Pegg Bay, Kent."

Jack's interest was betrayed by the slight elevation of his eyebrows, but he asked no questions.

"To-morrow," resumed Locke, "you will call upon Mr Mervyn Villiers, of Malplaquet Crescent, and tell him——"

For quite fifteen minutes the detective outlined his instructions, and finally asked his young assistant to repeat them in every particular. Parrot-wise, Drake voiced them almost word for word.

Locke flashed him a rare smile.

"Good, young 'un ! There are not many boys of your age who could so faithfully repeat what had been said to them. Your powers of concentration are improving. Now, let's get busy !"

For something like two hours Ferrers Locke and Drake were busy in the laboratory before the former announced that it was high time they snatched a few hours' sleep.

Shortly after breakfast the next morning Jack Drake, clad in baggy, blue trousers of a coarse material, thick woollen jersey, and reefer jacket which smelled strongly of the sea, allowed Ferrers Locke to practise his skill as a make-up specialist upon him.

In something under half an hour a complete transformation had taken place. Jack's face now possessed that leathery, weather-beaten appearance of one who follows the sea as a profession; his hands and forearms were similarly treated, suggesting that their owner was one accustomed to much manual outdoor work

Locke surveyed his handiwork with a critical eye, added a few deft touches with a lining pencil, and pronounced himself satisfied.

"You look a sailorman, wearing his Sunday best, to the life, my boy !" he remarked. "Now, don't forget to walk with a slight roll !"

"How's this, guv'nor ?" asked Drake, moving across the room as if it were the heaving deck of a ship.

"Good enough, Jack ! Good-bye—and good luck !"

Touching the bulging pocket of his reefer jacket, Drake winked at his chief, and let himself out of the detective's chambers—by the back door. Soon he was rolling along the busy streets of London, a young sailorman on a visit to London to the life !

He blinked at the imposing residence of Mr. Mervyn Villiers, in Malplaquet Crescent, undecidedly, and then, as if having made up his mind, he rolled to the door and rang the bell

A superior-looking manservant opened the door, sniffed at him disapprovingly, and was about to slam the door in the youngster's face when he realised that the caller had forestalled that move by jamming his foot over the threshold.

"No hawkers allowed here, young man !" rasped the superior manservant.

"Ho, messmate !" came the boisterous return. "I'm not a hawker ! You slip along to the bridge an' tell the skipper —lemme see, his name's Villiers—tell him that I want to see him on important business !"

The manservant was not impressed. He sniffed audibly.

"I'm sure my master would not desire to see you !" he answered, recoiling from the somewhat overwhelming aroma of tar and brine which enveloped his young visitor.

"Ho, messmate !" returned the young sailorman. "Tell him that Bert Entwistle—that's me—has picked up something in the sea concerning his pal, Christopher Dean——"

At mention of the name the manservant's face expressed a sudden alarm. Now, no longer eager to speed the young sailorman on his way, he invited him inside with a greasy smile, and departed hot-foot to find his master.

Humming a sea-chanty to himself, Drake waited, and was at length invited into a sumptuous apartment, wherein sat Mr. Mervyn Villiers, enjoying a fragrant cigar.

A meaning nod passed between the manservant and his master, what time Jack Drake toyed nervously with his peaked cap and rolled slightly from one foot to another.

"Take a seat, my young friend !" smiled Mr. Villiers.

Awkwardly Drake complied, and sat on the edge of the armchair with about as much outward show of comfort as if it were the edge of a volcano.

"Well "—Villiers' rather closely set eyes smiled at his young caller invitingly—"what can I do for you, young man ?"

Drake coughed, and then fished from his reefer jacket a leather-covered vacuum-flask.

"Well, skipper—begging your pardon, Mr. Villiers," he began—"I was out in Pegg Bay with the smack yesterday when I caught sight of this flask a-bobbin' up and down, so I fished it up." He unscrewed the cap of the flask. "An' this, skipper, is what I found inside."

His blue eyes never left the florid
THE MAGNET LIBRARY.—No. 1,359.

features of Villiers. They noted the sudden interest, not unmixed with a measure of alarm, that sprang into being in the big man's eyes.

"How interesting, my lad! Let me see that flask!"

Drake could have sworn that the man's hands trembled slightly as he took the flask and examined the log-book and the piece of bomb casing it contained. Followed a few moments' heavy silence, then Villiers looked up, with a smile.

"How very interesting!" he remarked. "But what a pity that some misguided person should perpetrate such a wicked thing in the name of one of the finest sportsmen who ever lived!"

Bert Entwistle, alias Jack Drake, looked perplexed—according to plan.

"Skipper," he made answer, "I'm afraid I don't follow you. As I read it, that vacuum-flask and the two things it contained tells me that your pal, Mr. Dean, met with foul play when he tried to fly the Atlantic a few months ago."

"My dear fellow," replied Villiers, "I appreciate your sentiments, but I am afraid you have been the victim of a wicked hoax. In short, these things are not genuine. I am sorry," he added, as his caller's face fell, "I'm sorry, Mr. Entwistle, that you have had your journey to London for nothing."

"Oh, that's all right, skipper!" answered Drake. "Somehow, at the back of my mind, I had a feelin' that perhaps some dirty rotter fixed this up for a joke; that's why I didn't mention finding the flask to a soul——"

"Good!" exclaimed Villiers involuntarily, and his eyes glinted curiously. "I mean, in the circumstances—ahem—that was very wise. No one likes to be made a fool of." He seemed to consider awhile, then he forced a smile. "Look here, Mr. Entwistle, please allow me to recompense you for all the trouble and expense you have been put to."

Drake demurred, but Villiers would have none of it.

"Here, take this, young fellow!" he insisted, handing the young sailorman a five-pound note. "No, really, I insist! And, if you will accept a spot of advice from me, don't say anything about this affair to a soul! Why"—he laughed breezily—"you'd be the laughing-stock of Pegg—what?"

"Bert Entwistle" grinned awkwardly and agreed. Pocketing the five-pound note, he lurched to his feet and announced that he would not take up any more of Mr. Villiers' valuable time.

A few seconds later he was being shown out by the manservant. But the moment the door closed behind him, Drake dodged round to the window and cautiously peered in. What he saw brought a glimmer to his eyes, for there was Mr. Villiers pointing furiously at the flask, the log-book, and the piece of bomb casing, during which his manservant peered at them with unbelieving gaze.

Drake, of course, could not hear the words that passed. It would have been better for him had such a thing been possible.

"By thunder, Morris!" Villiers was saying hoarsely. "To think that little things like these would put us all in prison! Don't you understand that we've had a narrow escape?"

"Gosh, boss!" gasped Morris. "Those things of Dean's fair give me the creeps! They're genuine, all right!"

"Of course they are!" snapped Villiers impatiently. "It's his, his writing that——"

"Gee! If those articles had fallen into some hands, instead of a stupid, ignorant sailorman," grated Villiers' servant, fingering his throat significantly, "I shouldn't feel mighty comfortable now! But, boss, supposing that kid talks——"

The same thought was obviously passing through Mervyn Villiers' mind.

"That's the trouble," he muttered thickly; and an evil, murderous look crossed his florid face. "He might talk. He might talk unless—unless——"

He leered up at Morris wickedly.

"We can't afford to take chances, Morris. That dolt of a sailorman must be silenced somehow."

A reflected evil now blazed across the once superior-looking features of Morris, the manservant. Then he pursed his lips and snapped his fingers in a horrible fashion.

"Leave that guy to me, boss. I'll soon settle him—nice and proper! I've done it before."

Mervyn Villiers tapped a bejewelled set of fingers on the small lacquered table by his side, and nodded.

"You're right, Morris. Get busy!"

The exchange of views, hurried and yet determined, had taken barely two minutes. Well inside five minutes Morris, seated at the wheel of his master's streamlined sports car, was trailing the rolling figure of Mervyn Villiers' late caller.

Still whistling, Jack Drake sauntered along in a leisurely style, feeling somewhat elated with the way things had gone. Obviously Mervyn Villiers, professional sportsman and patron of sport, was a double-dyed scoundrel. He had told Drake without a blush that the flask and its contents were the work of a practical joker. Yet his actions, seen through the window, suggested that he believed them to be genuine.

| Gazetteer Token | 6 |

Printed and published every Saturday by the Proprietors The Amalgamated Press, Ltd., The Fleetway House, Farringdon Street, London E.C.4. Advertisement offices: The Fleetway House, Farringdon Street, London, E.C.4. Registered for transmission by Canadian Magazine Post. Subscription rates: Inland and Abroad: 11s. per annum; 5s. 6d. for six months. Sole Agents for Australia and New Zealand: Messrs. Gordon & Gotch, Ltd., and for South Africa: Central News Agency, Ltd.—Saturday, March 3rd, 1934.

Little did the cunning Mervyn Villiers appreciate, just then, that Ferrers Locke had anticipated his reactions to Bert Entwistle's call, and it said much for the detective's powers as "an amateur forger" that the exercise book which contained a log of Dean's attempted Transatlantic flight was accepted as genuine.

The real log-book, flask, and incriminating piece of shell casing were actually, at that moment, reposing behind the closed door of Locke's secret safe. Those in Villiers possession now were clever fakes!

Drake, mindful of these things, felt quite pleased with the way he had carried off the imposture. Then happened one of those things which are almost inexplicable. He looked into the large "traffic mirror" of a stationary touring car, which gave a view of the traffic speeding behind his back. And in that quick, fleeting glimpse Drake saw a fast two-seater sports car, apparently out of control, thunder towards him, its near-side wheels already encroaching on the pavement.

With an ejaculation of alarm Drake wheeled, felt something hit him, and then collapsed in a motionless heap. Yet before his senses left him he was sure that the face of the driver at the wheel of the out-of-control sports car was the face of Mervyn Villiers' superior-looking manservant.

Shrieks arose on all sides as various people witnessed the tragedy, for tragedy it appeared to be. On the edge of the pavement, with blood streaming down his face, lay the young sailorman. Bending over him, a victim of horror and anxiety, apparently, was Morris. Striding towards the gathering crowd now came a policeman.

He bent over Drake, felt the youngster's heart, and informed the agitated driver that so far he had cause to thank himself that the boy still lived.

The driver explained, nervously, haltingly, that his steering column had suddenly refused to function; that he could not have avoided that terrible accident. Inwardly, however, the villain was censuring himself for not having made a better job of that "accident."

He was still telling himself so when the ambulance arrived, and Drake, now shifted to a stretcher, was gently lodged within the ambulance.

Followed the usual formula of taking the driver's name, inspecting his licence, and so on. Then Mr. Morris, abandoning his car to the care of a breakdown gang, entered a taxi, and asked to be driven to the hospital where the victim of the accident had already been taken.

Amazing things were taking place in that hospital, for Drake, in the privacy of the emergency ward where such street accidents were taken, "came to" with horrifying effect.

"I'm all right, sir," he grinned, at a bewildered group of nurses and doctors. "This is only a slight cut in my napper. No bones broken. But, doctor"—he beckoned the surgeon to his side, whispered who he was, and added—"if that guy who knocked me down comes nosing round here, keep him waiting for news of me until I have phoned my chief."

Drake had to repeat this more than once before the doctor was convinced that the youngster was not quite mad.

The surgeon dismissed the nurses, and personally got into communication with Ferrers Locke. He heard quickly enough then, by reason of Locke's description

of his assistant's disguise, that the young sailorman was actually Jack Drake.

"Is he hurt?" snapped the detective into the telephone, and breathed his relief when he received a negative answer. "Oh, splendid! Put him on the telephone, doctor—there's a good chap. This is a highly important case."

In a few moments Drake was through to his beloved chief, and, adding his own assurances that he was not hurt, except for a slight flesh wound, asked for instructions.

"The chap who knocked me down was Villiers' manservant," he added. "I'll swear I'm not mistaken! Deliberate attempt to put me out for keeps, guv'nor, if you want my opinion."

Ferrers Locke's instructions were not long in coming over the wires.

"Just lie doggo for a bit, young 'un, until I come round. But put me on to the doctor again."

The much amazed surgeon once again conversed with the celebrated detective.

He was more astonished than ever at what he was asked to do.

"I'm afraid, Mr. Locke, that is impossible," he stuttered. "It's—it's—well, irregular and inhuman, to say the least."

Ferrers Locke snorted his impatience.

"I tell you it is necessary," he replied, "and, as a governor of the hospital, I will take full responsibility for any consequences."

"Very well, sir," replied the surgeon. "I will do what you ask on that understanding."

He carried out his instructions very creditably when, in an adjoining room, he encountered a harassed-looking

(Continued on next page.)

individual, who stated that he was the driver of the car which had knocked down the young sailorman.

"Calm yourself, Mr. Morris," said the doctor gently. "I have bad news for you."

The crafty Morris jumped eagerly at the bait.

"You mean the poor fellow is——"

He did not finish the sentence, but the inference was that the young sailorman was dead. The surgeon was not put to the unhappy position of having to tell a lie. He merely shrugged his shoulders, and Morris jumped to the conclusion that the worst indeed had happened.

His mean soul, thereafter, cunningly prompted words of deep regret and remorse; his face and general tearful expressions seemingly backed up his sorrow.

Knowing something of the true nature of things, the surgeon was sorely tempted to grab this hypocritical scoundrel by the scruff of the neck and pitch him out, neck and crop, from the hospital. Instead, he held himself in check and bowed the conscience-stricken driver off the premises.

A few moments later Ferrers Locke arrived, carrying a suitcase. Inside it was a change of clothes for Jack Drake, now happily little the worse for the fall he had taken. A strip of plaster at the back of his head, and a few minor bruises, were all that showed of his narrow escape from death.

Locke shook him warmly by the hand.

"Young 'un," he said enthusiastically, "we've struck one of the biggest cases of our career. And we're not letting up until we've put Mr. clever Mervyn Villiers in his proper place. Now, how do you feel? Ready to go home? Good! Change into your own togs. For the time being Bert Entwistle is dead. You follow?"

Drake grinned, removed his sailorman make-up in the privacy of the surgeon's own room, and donned his ordinary everyday clothes.

"Mr. Locke," remarked the surgeon, when the transformation was made. "I'm holding you to your word over this strange business. The authorities —the police——"

Ferrers Locke stayed him with a gesture.

"Leave everything to me, doctor," he replied confidently. "I'll square all this business. Later on, when things have developed, you will be able to tell your colleagues how you helped to unmask one of the greatest swindlers the world has ever known! Good-day to you, and many thanks!"

.   .   .   .   .   .

"Well?"

Mervyn Villiers' hands were twitching with nervous excitement. On the little table was a half-filled decanter and a tray of glasses.

Before him, smiling in triumph, was his trusted servant Morris.

"Well?" demanded Villiers for the second time. "Why don't you tell me what's happened?"

Morris paused another second, the better to enjoy his triumph, then he winked knowingly and calmly helped himself to a measure of refreshment from the decanter.

"It was plumb easy, boss. Never done a neater job in my life!"

"Well?" shrieked Villiers. "What the devil does that mean exactly? Speak up, you grinning idiot!"

"It means, boss, that your clever sailorman will never speak again. He's through with the sea," he added callously. "Reckon he's through with everything! The surgeon at the hospital said so."

Which wasn't quite accurate, of course, but it served the purpose of restoring the colour to Mervyn Villiers' flabby face.

"Phew!" he breathed. "I've been on tenterhooks all the time you've been gone!" He grinned. "But I'll say you're a specialist at 'accident' cases, Morris. I'll give you a testimonial any time, what? Ha, ha!"

His eyes dwelt on the vacuum flask, the log-book, and the piece of shell casing.

"We'll get rid of these things at once. I don't like the idea of them hanging about the place."

"You're right, boss. They remind me, too, of an unhappy past. Here" —he picked up the flask and the log-book and stalked towards the brightly glowing fire—"I'll burn these for a start."

He thrust the exercise-book into the heart of the flames, and watched it burn to ashes. Next, he crushed the vacuum flask between his strong hands and watched the flames play havoc with that. Finally, he picked up the jagged piece of shell casing and fingered it reflectively.

"This, boss, is the most dangerous titbit of the lot," he remarked, turning it over and over in his hand.

"How so, Morris?"

"Why, boss, Tankerhead's Steel Works manufacture their steel to a secret formula. A clever analyst could trace this piece of steel back to him. But we'll soon put the kybosh on anything like that, because your humble will dump this in the river before the morning's out!"

He laughed, helped himself to another glass of liquor, and then aggressively held out an open palm.

"Guess Tankerhead got paid out his insurance money yesterday. Forgotten, boss, that a share of it was promised to me?"

He made no attempt to hide the threat in his voice.

Villiers glared back at him sourly, grinned in half-hearted fashion, and withdrew a bundle of notes from his wallet.

"Here you are, Morris. You earned them, anyway."

Morris counted the notes and pocketed them.

"You've forgotten something, boss. My price for putting a guy on the spot is ten guineas."

Reluctantly Mervyn Villiers parted company with an additional ten-pound note.

"That's O.K., boss!" smiled Morris greasily. "Now, what's the next lay?"

Villiers drummed his fingers on the lacquer table.

"Tankerhead is framing the Athletic's big match with Malpen Villa. He reckons it's money for jam!"

"Good!" grunted Morris.

And in that self-same moment, a couple of miles away, Ferrers Locke was addressing Jack Drake.

"Jack, my lad," he said, "we're up against a big organisation of crime, operating behind the world of sport. I'm sure of it. Villiers is in it—so is that gaolbird friend of his, Julius Tankerhead. It will pay us to keep a watchful eye on Mr. Julius—he's had a long run of freedom——"

"Twenty years since he came out of Dartmoor!" interrupted Drake. "I've been hunting up the records."

"You're quite correct," smiled Locke. "But it won't be twenty years before he is back behind prison bars—mark my words!"

(Mervyn Villiers and Julius Tankerhead will need to go very warily with Ferrers Locke dogging their footsteps! Look out for a heap more thrills in next week's gripping instalment, chums!)